The Thirteen Ravens

A TALE OF TWO BROTHERS

H. W. Zadow

ISBN-10: 0-578-40132-0
ISBN-13: 978-0-578-40132-4

To my readers – I welcome you to delve into my story.

Thank you!

Table of Contents

Preface 1
One: Thirteen Ravens 3
Two: The Riverside Village 9
Three: David and Liana 14
Four: First Love 28
Five: Liana's Dream 38
Six: Birth of Kosta 49
Seven: "Little Lord Thomas" 55
Eight: Gentle Heart 66
Nine: Rapid River 86
Ten: The Search 96
Eleven: Lord Thomas' Recollections 107
Twelve: Loneliness 126
Thirteen: Innocence of Youth 134
Fourteen: Calculated Risk 162
Fifteen: Cybilia Prozatti Weds Thomas Komarod 183
Sixteen: Kosta 199
Seventeen: Michael and Rabinna Hartigard 212
Eighteen: Predetermined Death 225
Nineteen: Kosta and Kathryn Wed 237
Twenty: Together 248
Twenty-One: Angel 256
Twenty-Two: Kosta's First Visit to His Brother 262
Twenty-Three: The Guilt 280
Twenty-Four: Joseph 283
Twenty-Five: Cybilia 295
Twenty-Six: Mark and Sabrina (Shara) 301

Twenty-Seven: The Ravens 306
Twenty-Eight: The Murder 312
Twenty-Nine: The Castle 323
Thirty: Fire 334
Thirty-One: Lord Thomas -Waiting 340
Thirty-Two: Work at the Castle 345
Thirty-Three: The Harvest 358
Thirty-Four: The Migration 365
Thirty-Five: Inferno 368
Thirty-Six: The Hunt 374
Thirty-Seven: The Spider isWaiting 377
Thirty-Eight: Escape 384
Thirty-Nine: Decision 386
Forty: Lasting Love 391
Forty-One: The Change 397
Forty-Two: Patrick and Olivia 399
Forty-Three: Breakdown 405
Forty-Four: The Surrender 409
Forty-Five: The Waiting 419
Forty-Six: Darkness 421
Forty-Seven: Strange Omens 425
Forty-Eight: Despair and Panic 428
Forty-Nine: The Third Night - Solutions 431
Fifty: Morning After 439
Fifty-One: Kingdom of Magda 443
Fifty-Two: Suspicion - Retribution 451
Fifty-Three: Journey Home - Town of Roses 458
Fifty-Four: Lady Kora Swirtz 468
Fifty-Five: The Old Man 476
Fifty-Six: The Plot 488
Fifty-Seven: The Courier 503

Fifty-Eight: Unexpected Stranger 511
Fifty-Nine: The Unnerving News 521
Sixty: The Horseman 527
Sixty-One: Kidnapping 533
Sixty-Two: The Extreme 537
Sixty-Three: The Kidnapping Solved 539
Sixty-Four: Going Home...547
Sixty-Five: Lost Love Reclaimed 555
Sixty-Six: The Will... 563
Sixty-Seven: The Ravens..571
Sixty-Eight: Tarnished Pride 573
Sixty-Nine: The Visit..580
Seventy: Midnight Stroll 589
Seventy-One: The Last Dinner 594
Seventy-Two: The Bloody Bed...600
Seventy-Three: The Move 603
Seventy-Four: The Second Dinner 609
Seventy-Five: The True Story 616
Seventy-Six: Agnostic Thomas 625
Seventy-Seven: The Spring Blizzard 629
Seventy-Eight: Long-Awaited Spring.. 635
Seventy-Nine: Ravens Returned 642
Eighty: Sudden Strike 649
Eighty-One: The Beginning and the End 655

Preface

In the invisible spiritual paradise unseen to the human eye, Thirteen Spirits listened intently to the Elders, Gleryk, Olymar and Smeto, as they spoke of the inescapable unique situation relating to the twisted Fate and doom brought out by greed, lies and jealously to certain individuals.

Thirteen handsome young men with eyes black as coal, a bit slanted, but alert. Long ebony plaited hair tied with a black silk ribbon, a white pearl dangling at the end. Garbed in white silk robes, black and gold waistbands with their names and numbers embroidered in red. A black silk cape draped over each shoulder, red sandals on their feet.

Chosen by the Elders, these thirteen privileged spirits were to inform, influence and have the last word in resolving the life-long struggle for survival of one brother and curtail the other brother's evil actions, bringing justice. These young Spirits accepted this earthly mission of great responsibility, constant surveillance and to inscribe into each individual's book of life every incidence of importance.

In the world below, in a village, in a certain home, troubles were brewing. Now the time has come for the scale of justice to weigh their merits and deal accordingly. Only these chosen ones have knowledge of the outcome of this situation.

The Thirteen Spirits, for their lengthy journey and constant vigilance, were empowered by their Elders with endurance, courage, and patience. With their heads bowed, eyes closed, arms crossed on their chests, they stood in wait.

"It is a privilege to be chosen. We pledge not to fail," Mamut, the leader, spoke for all.

Smeto called out the Spirits names as they stood at attention, "*Mamut, Abimust Benokai, Denos, Erisott, Fujiron, Hatuii, Insemir, Jemolai, Kirree, Kotur, Kruegg and Lournven.*"

The Elders stood. Olymar extended his arms as if embracing them all and said, "Farewell...good luck and light speed."

Gleryk, the third Elder said, "You may depart."

All thirteen, with their arms crossed on their chests replied in unison, "We are honored to serve, till we meet again!"

Mamut spoke his last words as he alone bowed low to the elders. "May the light shine upon you, oh wise ones!"

Transforming into Ravens, they descended to Earth.

Therefore, as all this happened a long time ago, let the tale unfold...

One: Thirteen Ravens

Once upon a time, a time of the past, hundreds of years ago, during the Medieval era strange things happened. Only those who had lived during that time knew the true story. Over time, the story was embellished, changed or portions omitted. In spite of that though, it happened.

Although the exact region has since been forgotten, it was most likely somewhere in Europe. Perhaps in a valley surrounded by mountains or in the flat lands where it blends with the horizon. Land lush with green prairies or tall trees or rivers running through with willows standing along the banks, their long branches touching the water. It could have been in a dark dense forest where wild and ferocious animals roamed.

From the beginning of time people relocated from place to place, as did the nomads, migrants and wanderers. Everyone had stories to tell, as well as the Gypsies. These Gypsies roamed across the countries from north to south, and east to west. As people traded with these wandering gypsies, they listened to their memorable tales and then passed them on to others.

People settled in small villages and towns, they always had a need to travel. Those with ambitions relocated from quaint villages to small towns, then moved on to larger cities searching for wealth, others searched for adventure. Foreigners mingled at markets, speaking unfamiliar languages and garbed in unfamiliar fashion, fabrics and styles. A great hubbub of chatter, laughter, shouting, and yet, amazingly they found ways to communicate in this progressive and explorative wide world.

Those who resided in one place since birth were unaware of such worldly changes. They found the colorful apparel of the newest vogue intriguing. When resettling into new surroundings and new people, they had to adapt quickly or they were lost. Whatever allegories parents and grandparents heard of and how they narrated these to their children and grandchildren, one can only imagine. Grandparents were the best storytellers.

One story in particular *must* be told and remembered and *must* continue to live.

This happened in a faraway land, in villages surrounded by mountains. In the dark dense and eerie forests where old hags and young witches lived in small shacks, brewed potions and chanted curses. Their piercing laughter reverberated through the trees, shattering the peace of the wild inhabitants. Wolves, protectors of these witches and their shacks, ran in packs and howled. At night, the spying owls hunted small rodents. On silent wings, they would swoop down to grip anything and all with their strong talons, flying through open windows of the shacks, circling over huge caldrons, dropping these little creatures into boiling water as ingredients for magical stews along with the magical plants.

At twilight, these witches moved like ghosts through the forest in search of certain night blooming delicately fragrant flowers; Jimson weed was one of them, and Nightshade the other, along with certain mushrooms, plus, a slew of other ingredients. Plants such as these were fundamental for magical potions, weather lethal or curative, or love; as these old witches were experts.

When the new moon walked across the sky, all the witches, warlocks, conjurers of voodoo, magicians and wizards convened on the highest mountaintop for their usual rituals. Witches on brooms swooped acrobatically across the sky, along with the owls, ravens and common crows flew in from different parts of the country. Many bonfires burned brightly, their singing and laughter resonated. Entranced, they danced to the strange rhythm of the drums, its constant throb echoed down to the valley across mountaintops and beyond. Those who stayed awake through the night and listened to a woman's powerful and beautiful high soprano joined by voices alto and baritones, creating a choir by low hum, with the rhythm of drums throbbing, one never could forget. At first light of dawn, the group harmoniously sang a ritualistic song in homage to a new day, and then went on their way.

This was the time when daytime was welcomed, but the darkness of the night most frightening. This was the time of the dark ERA, when ghosts levitated over swamps at midnight and drifted on the wind to the villages, peering into windows. Bats swooped across the dark sky, and goblins roamed the land.

Those believing in witchcraft and witches remained indoors, but for the unbelievers there is a warning!

"GUARD YOUR SOUL—BEWARE—EVIL IS LURKING—EVERY WHERE!"

The villagers completed their chores before dusk. What with the scary stories, unexplained sightings, they feared the darkness.

Early mornings found these people gaping at the outside walls of their homes covered with footprints. They whitewashed their homes many times over, but footprints returned, causing aggravation.

Villagers, unable to cope, consulted their religious leaders for advice. They were assured, that, "No ghosts or evil spirits will harm you, you are good people. Light candles pray for the departed souls. With perseverance and faith, peace shall return." Unfortunately, peace did not return...goblins returned!

A severe thunderstorm rumbled through leaving behind damage. Once they cleared the debris and made repairs, villagers noticed the footprints were gone. Perhaps now they could relax a bit.

Months later at night, every house, barn, stable and chicken coop glowed with dots, even trees, wagons and animals. This was most annoying since the villagers had no idea what or why they were there. Many a time at dinnertime candle flames fluttered, and then winked out. Families sat in darkness, children screamed. Dogs growled, backed off into corners or leaned against a human leg for assurance from harm. Cat's backs bristled, tails stiffened, puffed out like brushes. They hissed, staring into space; their yellow eyes followed something invisible.

The parents relit the candles. "Hush, hush, children it is just the breeze, do not be afraid," they said softly.

The children glared at them in fear. "Breeze? What breeze? The windows are closed, Father!" the children exclaimed.

The villagers apprehensively retired for the night, expecting upon awakening new pranks in the morning. To their surprise, abruptly all had stopped; tensions released like taught violin strings. Now much needed rest and sleep for which they longed for is theirs again. All was well. Life was good. Children played, swam in creeks and slept soundly.

One day, one of the constables nailed an announcement on the side door of the Village Hall. Passers-by heard the banging, stopped, craned their necks asking what was happening. The constable read aloud to these curious Villagers:

Attention All Citizens:
By the order of our Honorable Hollin Smolts the Mayor of Riverside Village, has declared, that, all the people of Riverside Village shall gather in the Village Hall to celebrate long awaited "Peace" which has at last returned, on

first Saturday, the month of August 13. Women of the village are to prepare food and the men to provide refreshments. Come all, eat drink and dance, but keep an eye on your children!
Mayor, Hollin Smolts

The news quickly spread and everyone eagerly waited for that Saturday morning. Villagers then congregated at the Village Hall. Tables filled with prepared dishes by village women, and many kegs of wine stacked along the wall. When Mayor Hollin Smolts began tasting dishes of interest, everyone followed. When the music began, young and old grabbed a partner; hand in hand, they stepped lively to the rhythm. Their children played outside in the dirt, but at dusk, all children accounted for were inside the hall. The festivities ended late in the evening. Parents gathered their sleepy children and quickly headed home. Those who overindulged in wine slept soundly.

Life would be boring if all went so well, things must happen. Who is to know what the future holds. What is permanent in life? Nothing ever is!

Strange how the elderly women, gifted with extra sensory perceptions and analyzers of dreams, foresaw ill tidings to come. Dreams discussed only among themselves. To reveal their concerns aloud meant dangerous accusations of being witches. Secrecy and silence meant a long ripe age, their experience their teacher. For those determined awaits fortune. For the weak and humble, misfortune which follows like a shadow. Improving or disrupting lives of those involved in this tale, perhaps will become, as they say... *notorious few*.

The gypsy caravans headed south to warmer climates and arrived in the village at the end of summer. As always, they set up camp near the forest for privacy. Several bonfires burned brightly. Their wares hung on wagons and from trees. Large caldrons sat on hot stones with soups over boiling. On iron spits whole pigs roasted, turned by youths, and potatoes baked in the ashes.

Those who welcomed the gypsies listened to the world news. Skeptics had their own opinions; to them, all seemed a bit farfetched, still, learning something new is more exciting than the sameness out of their own windows. Far beyond the mountains and forests beckoned great new world. After several weeks, the gypsies moved on, and with them young men went along, to experience a winter in a warm climate of which the gypsies bragged so much. Believing or disbelieving in all those disturbing news the gypsies had brought, many had ignored them.

These villagers faced their own pressing problem right in their backyards, having to deal with wild boars at harvest time. After many seasons enduring enormous losses of crops, the villagers had enough so they constructed lookout blinds up in the trees, snares of ropes, and dug deep pits covered with branches and camouflaged with grass and leaves. Men up in the trees waited and an owl hoot was their signal to each other, bows and arrows ready to slaughter. Always after sunset, the boars numbered at least a hundred. Cautiously sniffed the air for men's presence at the edge of the forest before moving towards the fields. Boars charged to trample, with tusks uprooting and devouring fields of potatoes, beets, cabbage, carrots, beans, peas and turnips plus many other vegetables. A volley of arrows hit true, some boars fell into the pits as they ran, and others fell where they stood; it was a blood bath. Others that survived ran off squealing and continued to forage. Several nights of easy hunting brought down dozens of wild boars but also much work for all the villagers. Quartered portions of meat were distributed to everyone. Cooking, curing and smoking the loins, ribs and shanks, the villagers wasted nothing. Many boar heads hung as trophies on walls. At those times, the aroma permeated out the chimneys into the wind. The wolves and foxes hung around, sniffing, hoping to snatch a meal. Their catch consisted mostly of chickens out of the coops, if they were lucky. Hides tanned for use as windbreakers in their homes or barns as protection from bitter cold and wind. Sheep hides used as blankets on beds for children, wool spun for stockings, slippers, booties, coats and jackets, sweaters and all sorts of apparel.

Spring is beautiful when Mother Natures' seasonal inner clock awakens; it always came with changes. Storks returned to roost on rooftops. The never-ending harmonizing chatter of nocturnal creatures echoed. The sleeping soil awakened to bring forth color, fragrance, and essentials for life to all living creatures and humans. Flowers bobbed their heads. Verde pastures emerged with perennial profusion of flowers. Trees adorned in emerald corona welcomed by all for their shade. Each day budding shrubs burst into bloom, their sweet fragrance drifted in the air. Yes, spring...a wonderful season...but only in beauty. However, by far, not at all generous with necessary staples for the table, for which, one must plant, and wait to reap. The outdoors beckoned to hard work. No matter what, life must go on. Yet none foresaw what was to transpire in the years to come.

In late spring, again, the gypsies rattled in with wagons loaded for trade. They talked about world events, horrible wars, assassinations of kings and disagreements among people. Fear and unrest intensified in countries. People perished by the hundreds as enemies savagely massacred entire populations of small towns and villages; looting everything in sight, livestock and food confiscated, burning entire villages.

Curious villagers put one question to them, "How did *you* escape from such onslaught?"

"Our friends fleeing from the massacre came upon us on a road through the forest," they said.

"As a large group, to be safe, we turned off the road changing direction moved through the dense forest. We reloaded our belongings onto the horses, leaving behind our wagons camouflaged well with forest dead trees and many branches. In addition, we gathered a heap of leaves around the base. When we were done, it blended well and looked natural. We know our beaten paths and forests. On foot, we moved up the ravine, where we often rested when traveling. We followed the ravine, settled in first mountain cave, often used in winter many a time," Hatma, the gypsy leader replied.

"These barbarians, are they heading in our direction, do you know?" villagers asked.

"No, we do not know. We left the caves because we were running out of supplies - a risky but necessary move. Thank the Lord above each village we came to was peaceful and untouched. We hesitate to ask, should we leave or stay here in this forest, of course with your permission?" Hatma asked.

"It is up to you, we cannot decide for you," the villagers replied.

After trading, specifically needing sheep hides and down quilts, the gypsies moved on and the villagers shrugged off such news.

Two: The Riverside Village

The Riverside Village was situated in a serene valley with green prairies and seemingly fertile fields. Vegetable gardens in back yards and flower gardens in every front yard. Mountain peaks jutting up all around. The pine trees grew half way up the slopes and waterfalls cascaded down noisily from high peaks, glistening in the summer sun. However, one must keep in mind in winter the waterfalls froze into icicles, clinging one atop the other. Overall, the other three seasons, overload of toil, fair, but for the wild life and shrill cries of many birds echoed.

Picture-perfect, as perfect a scene as it could ever be for its Medieval Era. It seemed as if this valley rested in the palm of Mother Earths' hands. Perhaps this picture-perfect valley portraying this image conceals deep secrets?

Through the center of the village meandered a deep wide river, Rapid River it was named so for a reason. In springtime, it flowed rapidly and in summer, it flowed unruffled. Large willows along the banks shaded its depths; water deep and dark seemed to stand still. Now and again whirlpools swirled eerily; forbidding, well known for their danger. Years ago, the first settlers of this village constructed a bridge on the river's narrowest span for crossing out of necessity and convenience to settle on both sides, for travelers, to reach neighboring villages and trade markets and other parts of the world.

This sheltered village over the years grew into a strongly united peaceful community. Here everyone knew everyone. Whenever, someone had a need of something help was there, through all seasons, keeping busy improving lives any way possible. Village council members during wintertime were in charge of making all sorts of plans. However, yearly functions, including bazaars and merriment for all citizens had been the responsibility of women. After heavy winters, snowmelt cascaded off the cliffs, rushed down to the valley below overfilling streams and rivers rapidly. Fields in low areas glistened as shallow lakes. For weeks, water sat evaporating, seeping slowly into the soil, until was firm enough to plow.

Oh, on those merry weekends villagers gathered. Girls, women and their children dressed in their finest apparel, cottons and silks, skirts of many colors and floral blouses with ribbons and sashes all purchased from the passing gypsies. Braided or curled hair topped their heads with ribbons, flowers, and sparkling combs; also from the gypsies. The women baked honey cakes, prepared meats and vegetables for the tables to share. The young mingled, sang, whirling on the dance floor, carefree and happy. Yes, for some love bloomed, but for others love withered.

Often young men and women from neighboring settlements joined in as well in these festivities. Many kegs of wine sat empty, those who overindulged in the wine habit, soon were in a stupor until following morning, ah, the headaches that followed, imagine. Nothing mattered. Evaporated and forgotten were the rumors of terrible sightings and frightening war scenarios, which rubbed against their ears now and then.

However, strange things *began* to happen in this peaceful valley, as it had in other parts of the world.

Those in deep sleep heard nothing. Insomniacs walked the floor, plastered faces to the windowpane, peering into the night, and saw darkness -- nothing else. Severe storms rolled in with blinding lightning and crashing thunder. Howling wind uprooted trees. Houses creaked and groaned. Thatched roofs blown off and objects flew far across the land. Those were natural occurrences, nothing to be frightened about, storms come and go, seasons come and go and everyone lives on.

Those who traveled late in the night out of necessity observed unusual glowing misty shapes or thin ribbons winding through the trees, levitating across prairies. Such things never appeared here before, those seeing with their own eyes, wondered, "What on earth is going on, since when?" Others having absolutely no interest in hearing about these sightings simply muttered, "Such is life, pay no mind." However, to others this was unnatural... these rumors, were they only rumors?

Since the spring planting was complete, frequent rains came, they waited for wind to dry up the fields, seedlings overtaken by weeds, required weeding from sunrise to sunset. Hungry and fatigued, villager's reserves dwindling with each passing day, they awaited anxiously for early vegetables. As the long summer dragged, now with only occasional rain meant fewer crops, changes in the weather, decreased harvest. Those who had full pantries had small worries. Their satiated children slept peacefully. Others with less acreage and large families suffered hunger and empty sacks in their pantries. However, these people strongly believed in unity. Therefore, compassionate farmers shared their provisions with those in need.

Looking at this beautiful valley and the quaint homes in this village nothing appeared out of the ordinary, it appeared peaceful, as it should be, after all this was an unusual village. Moreover, unusual villages had endured unusual phenomenon.

While awaiting harvest, projects were completed. The daily chores involved children as well to learn responsibility, even the little tykes fed the fowl, ran excitedly to tell mothers that the chicks packed away all the seeds. They were together and had each other. Regardless of the twists in weather or hunger, or those rumors, it was as it should be. On hot and humid days, children splashed in shallow creeks, while parents watched with pride. On cool evenings, everyone relaxed. Taking into consideration all those ghostly stories and disturbances they heard of but as yet nothing tragic occurred in this village, just an occasional bloody nose, fistfights over something trivial.

However, as days and weeks slipped by people experienced something strange, especially at dusk for some unexplained reason, something eerie hung in the air. People stayed indoors, noiselessly shuffled about, straining for any unusual noises, candles lit in dark corners to brighten the rooms. Some strange fear hung over this peaceful valley, a heavy cloud about to burst and a deluge of havoc drop from the sky. They all felt it. What was out there? No one dared to venture outside alone. On extremely hot evenings, it was impossible to leave the small windows open, spiders, there were too many spiders; everyone killed them by the hundreds. Villagers of all ages were bitten, sick with fever, eventually died. For these villagers this was a terrible tragedy. People cleared away anything and everything from around their homes and barns to burn. Domestic animals, found completely drained of blood on the outskirts of the forests where they grazed, also burned. The villagers assumed that the cause of uneasiness at night were the bats. Others disagreed, bats suck blood but never drain it all out of a large animal like a horse or a cow, *be realistic*, they argued. Their opinions were that something other than bats roamed out there. With it all, anger erupted, tensions and tempers flared, shoving and punching each other; but law controlled these outbursts. Besides, other important issues waited.

In this beautiful well-kept valley, things will happen. When it will occur, no one knew, what will occur, no one knew or expected, but these events will happen and nothing will ever be the same. This event will live through many generations and will never die.

People in this village had not yet experienced anything heart stopping. Lately, something caught their attention, but mostly at night, as never before made them uncomfortable, a feeling of foreboding, heavy atmosphere a dark invisible force felt but not seen hung over them. People whispered in softer tones as if in fear of speaking aloud to each other. Not an inkling of what is and why they felt this way.

Yes... these people were unable to foresee any impending tragedy, but for these eerie feelings. Who will be involved, no one knew. Could it happen? Yes. It is inevitable! When... soon, very soon! This uneasy eeriness lasted months, until that summer night.

From early morning on that particular day, oppressive heat and excessive moisture hung in the air, moisture beads slid like tears, from trees and all plants as if it had just drizzled. Complete stillness, a most uncanny, unusual day. People from early dawn perspired profusely while working dropped their tools, sat down in the shade to drink tea or water and rest awhile, unable to continue their usual daily tasks. Hours dragged, the scorching noon sun overhead forced everyone indoors. The sun began to set over the mountains and the long shadows fell over the village. Children at suppertime complained to parents it was too hot, and they do not like this heat. Adults expecting the evening to cool off a bit, however, as the hours slipped by the stifling air lingered, it was still and quiet. As if that was not enough, a dense fog moved slowly over the prairies. It obscured homes and trees as it passed through the village and moved into the forest. Villagers peered out the windows, walked out into the darkness speaking low, others called aloud to check if anyone else was outside, replies echoed just as perplexed. A scene such as this seldom occurred creating an eerie and unusual deathly silence, as if; the nocturnal creatures were suddenly extinct.

Nothing else to do but go back indoors, bolt the doors, sit and sweat, or go to bed try to sleep and sweat, but within their stifling homes without open windows and fresh air, sleep was impossible. The hours dragged. Midnight, past three, just a few more hours dawn will come. Usually dawn came in a bit cooler with a light breeze, but not this morning, most likely, it will be a hot day, but in daylight, the eeriness should dissipate. This morning is a mirror of yesterday's morning. Hot. Humidity hung low, again moisture dripped and slipped off the leaves and everything around. Very unhealthy, breathing became difficult. When the breeze drifted in from the marshes, the air smelled of strange miasma. Drifting from all directions, irritating noses, and throats burned, suffocating feeling. Everyone, wondered what in the world could this odor be?

When the gypsy caravan rolled into the village several days later to their usual camping spot was at the edge of the woods, within minutes villagers came with handkerchiefs over their mouths. Bartering began and ended in a hurry on certain purchases only. What the gypsies needed bought or exchanged from the villagers often for other items. The villagers and gypsies held cloths over the mouths, the air too acrid to breath. Gypsies knew of the eerie fog, which, rolls in early evening out of the forest and disappears when the sun rises. The villagers talked about the unfortunate demise of Varka a young man; gypsies were shocked, they knew Varka since he was a little boy. Gypsies visited Varka's parents to find out how he had died. Shocked and frightened, realized that the "*Dark Shadow*" took his soul. An old gypsy woman said to Varka's parents, "He should have never passed alone by the cemetery about midnight." Later they visited Varka's grave. This time their stay was short. They always told these villagers of many adventurous encounters in the big world beyond. This time they had to move on. With them went a sad story about Varka. Which they will tell whomever they meet and who will listen of a young man and the *Dark Shadow*. Clever were these gypsies, they came and went leaving behind stories of fear and restlessness, but joy as well.

Three: David and Liana

On the outskirts of Riverside Village on a rise stood a small thatched-roof dwelling with one dirt streaked window, half-hidden by the overhang. The house stood neglected for too long, grey from rain, its exterior needing badly a fresh whitewash. On a summer day, David and Liana a young newly married couple pulled up in a one horse drawn wagon, full of bundles, three chairs but no table. Cooking pots wrapped in a feather quilt, two pillows and bed sheets from Liana's sister. David's mother gave them four mugs for coffee, tea or milk, utensils, and a calf named Blaza. Those were their possessions. Having inherited this home after her grandmother, now this residence will be theirs. The rusty hinges rasped when David pushed to open the front door. They stepped over the high threshold into the dark interior; musty smell and dampness chilled their noses. Interior dingy, grey and water leaks streaked its walls, a number one priority of whitewashing. Roomy but empty abandoned of life.

They walked into the kitchen. There was a huge hearth built of stone, black from soot, in need of scrubbing. In the corner behind a torn drape sat a large dirty tub, perfect for bathing and privacy. This was to be their home, but they felt its gloom. Liana and David stood inside for a long moment taking in all work and cleaning time.

"David, with a lot of cleaning, we will make this house our little domain," Liana said, smiling up at him.

"But, we have no bed to sleep on; not even a straw mat. We came here with just what we could carry in bundles and load the wagon," David said with a concerned look on his face.

"Well, in this case we are going to visit Aunt Olivia. She will put us up for the time. You make the bed, and... the table," Liana said.

"You are right, this is early summer and much could be done," David said.

They settled in after all the work was finished with the help of Aunt Olivia's friends and neighbors; their small house looked fresh, clean and cheery. Their marriage began with just the few essentials received from parents, Aunts and friends such as; grain for planting, few pots, a teapot, pillows and blankets. A horse and, while still a calf, Liana named her Blaza, were the most important for their lives. David fenced off part of grassy area for the horse and little calf Blaza to graze on not far from the house. Liana each time she glanced at them, she thought of her mother; she missed her mother.

It took several days of cutting down trees, loading the wagon full of saplings and small branches then unloading by the house for a few days to dry. They harnessed the horse to drag large tree trunks, which gave them most trouble. David and Arkushin his neighbor were exhausted at the end of each day. Between chores and going off to work, he chopped and stacked it all against the side of the house. Liana with her kitchen all set up now could cook and bake bread.

"David, we should invite Aunt Olivia to our home, it is only proper, after all, she helped us so much and now that all is complete. I want to bake and cook dinner too. And look even the curtains are finished, which I had sewn by hand," Liana said.

"Liana, how did you manage to do all this sewing? And, I must say you did a nice job," David said, as he inspected her work.

Aunt Olivia arrived with field flowers and a present. One look at the home and she was impressed by its complete transformation into a fresh, clean look. Aunt Olivia entered into a now-cheery home, full of aroma where months before it smelled of mildew and neglect. Liana and David greeted her warmly. David took Aunt Olivias arm and walked her into the parlor. The parlor's large window faced south, now sparkled clean, a pleasant view, and now had curtains. Months before its glass was obscured by dirt and streaked with rain. Table covered with white linen tablecloth and three chairs, and an oil lamp, mugs, plates with cakes, bread and butter and utensils waited. Nothing else was in the room. Liana pointed out all the improvements around the kitchen and the pantry.

Liana led her into their bedroom. "Aunt Olivia, David and the neighbors knocked out that wall and added ten feet more out to the north, and installed new windows," Liana explained.

"Well, I see they have done a good job, now it is very bright and large," Aunt Olivia said.

Their bed stood on the north wall, two windows one on the west and one on the east wall. A small chest stood in the corner on it an oil lamp, and an extra chair made by David leaned against the wall. Aunt Olivia, Liana and David sat at the table having dinner their subject in conversation the renovation of the house.

"Well, how did you manage to extend the roof?" Aunt Olivia asked. David explained how the neighbors pitched in enough material for the whole addition.

"You know this dingy house had only this large living room and the kitchen. Two small bedrooms and a very small window on the north side of the house. This oversized doorway without an actual door for privacy. We felt exposed sleeping practically in the parlor, which I surely did not feel comfortable with at all. Imagine how embarrassing, if someone came over unannounced and your bed is not made...or you are still in it," Liana said.

"But I see you do have a door now, David had made it quick enough," Aunt Olivia said. They had a good laugh at Liana's remark. Time ticked away as the three of them enjoyed tea and sweet cakes. Aunt Olivia congratulated both on a remarkable job they had done on making their home so cheery. Liana had baked for this occasion an extra-large loaf of bread and one cake for her to take home, just a small "thank you" for helping them.

Aunt Olivia liked Liana from the moment they met months ago. Glad to have at least one family member close to her, she had to express her feelings while visiting Liana and David. Liana was a little girl when Aunt Olivia last saw her, now she is a young beautiful married woman.

Liana loved her husband and her simple way of life. She never minded all the chores, cleaning and cooking. She washed laundry in the creek and then carried back the heavy load to the side of the house where she hung it on the line. The small windows sparkled. Although with the interior whitewashed for a fresh clean look, still on cloudy days the interior seemed a bit dim.

One thing that concerned her was the dirt floor. They were not the only ones in the village with a dirt floor; most of the villagers had them. Young and newly married, they had not realized that without money installing a hardwood floor would be impossible. While sweeping the floor, which she did several times a day, Liana thought... *with a forest full of oak trees, why should we not have a nice hardwood floor? It would be so much warmer and cleaner especially for little children just beginning to walk. I must talk with David about that.* Because she disliked the floor so much, she decided to lay down rugs made of sheepskin, bear, goat and one cowhide. Every time she looked at the cowhide, she felt sorry for that cow. However, her feet had not touched the dirt and she enjoyed its warmth.

They lived in a simple square shaped home. Liana kept in mind that they would need to add more rooms once children came. She loved the pantry-storage area, which they also used as their closet for coats. She kept all the kitchen items in there...flour sacks and small jugs with lard and oils, along with hats hanging on pegs and boots on straw mats.

The kitchen table always had a white linen tablecloth and an oil lamp. To conserve oil, Liana lit candles on cloudy days. For a change, she set out two glass globes with candlesticks given to David by a customer as a wedding gift. The wild flowers she gathered stood on the table in a stone pitcher, making their home pleasant and cheery for David's return. David had built a long narrow counter with two shelves underneath for storing pots. It stood beneath the kitchen window where Liana would prepare meals while enjoying the view of the mountains. A drape concealed a tub for bathing in a roomy alcove between the pantry and the large hearth.

Being that their home was small, when Liana cooked or baked, the inside of the home would get hot.

"You know in the wintertime this hearth will heat up the entire house, which is fine, but now it is summer and the heat is oppressive. I feel like collapsing sometimes. When you are away, I run to the creek and jump in to cool off. David, can you find out if there is something else out there other than this huge oven?" Liana asked.

David looked at her. "Would you have time to jump into the creek with me right now?"

Liana wasted no time. She was first to run out the door as David followed. Laughing, she threw off her skirt and blouse she ran into the shallow water and sat down in her shift. David stood for a moment. Glancing around to see if anyone was watching, he dropped his pants and his shirt, both landing on the grass. He jumped into the cool water and they splashed at each other, laughing and kissing. Meanwhile, up in the trees, across the creek, thirteen pairs of eyes watched as the couple enjoyed their time together.

"Liana you are tempting and irresistible. I need to feel you close to me, no one will see us here," he whispered and held her close.

David kissed her and reached for her shift, pulling the strap as it gently slid off. She responded and this time together was their time. They were young and happy, in secluded privacy, clinging to each other, forgetting about the rest of the world. Warm days of summer kept them busy but not busy enough to not sit and soak in the creek.

Summer slipped into autumn, and now harvest time began. After the harvest, gathering and storing did not stop. The men went into the forest to cut down many trees for firewood, supplying each house in the village for the winter. David stacked all the firewood and turf just outside the back door near the kitchen. A north side lean-to built of branches, straw mixed with mud to keep wood and turf dry. The original outhouse, being a bit too far for safety became an unpleasant discussion but remained in its original place all through winter.

David was known for his carving and excellent workmanship and Liana was so proud of him. He was so busy with work that it was piling up, causing him to work late into the night. David's profession as carpenter, furniture designer and excellent carver, took him away from home many days, sometimes weeks at a time. Liana understood that and did not mind being alone. Of course, she missed him, but Aunt Olivia was close by. Besides, she had plenty of her own work to do.

One particular afternoon, as Liana gathered wild flowers and grasses, she glanced across the creek and noticed big black birds perched on the willow branches. At first, she thought nothing of them; her mind was on David's return. The black birds flew away and later she forgot about them.

She had mixed feelings when she realized she was expecting a child, not that she did not want a child, but perhaps it was a bit too soon. With David away, having a newborn, being alone during the day and sleeping alone at night would be a hardship facing her. Besides lacking necessities for daily living, now they will need much more for a child. Nine months is a long time, but enough time to learn what to do with a newborn and to prepare for the birth.

David was excited when Liana told him she is expecting his child. David embraced her and kissed her lips and her neck, which made her giggle. He was so happy he made a crib for their child. One pleasant evening Liana, Aunt Olivia and David strolled along the mountainside, when suddenly Liana noticed the black birds perched on an oak tree.

"David! David look! They are back, the black birds!" Liana pointed at the oak tree.

"Those are ravens. My, they are huge!" Aunt Olivia replied.

David observed the birds for a while.

"Strange, I counted thirteen of them. I wonder why they are here. We have lived here several years now, and I have never seen ravens in this valley. In fact, as I travel, I have not seen one, not one," David said puzzled.

In the middle of September, with the assistance of the midwife, their first-born child came into the world. A son, having strong lungs, he screamed loud and clear. Liana, though weak and tired from labor, laughed. Her newborn quieted down eventually, greedily he started suckling at her breast and all was well. His name, Thomas, but Liana added a title to his name, little *"Lord" Thomas Komarod."*

Thanks to Aunt Olivia's help and care, Liana was back to her duties in a short time. She was young and healed quickly. Her days not only filled with work, but also a demanding child, at times overwhelming. Her time of rest was during his naptime, on her bed, holding her son close to her bosom.

Liana and David also heard from Aunt Olivia about trouble with the gypsies, the girl and the cross, and of the young husband and his teenage son, lured away by the gypsies. Liana feared the gypsies and being alone with their newborn son brought concerns for their safety so Aunt Olivia spent many nights with her until David returned.

David's passion was carving. He carved in his spare time, if he had any. While the crops germinated and grew, he traveled to other villages and towns to work and at the same time sold his carvings. On the way home, from his last trip David purchased grain, a horse and oil. Since his reputation brought him more work. His luck was with him when he purchased a bull of fine breed, for a minimal price. Liana in her spare time mended and sewed for villagers to save her share. Being creative, she made trinkets, selling them or trading for things she needed. Liana was a down to earth person and liked by many, and being young she had many friends with children.

The weather was changing, winter would be upon them any day and it kept her indoors. Short gloomy days dragged, and the nights seemed endless. Drifts of snow and freezing temperatures held. Firewood used sparingly. Aunt Olivia moved in with them for the entire winter, not only helping Liana with the child, but she was safer with them.

At the first sign of spring, Aunt Olivia returned to her home to find it in good condition. Spring planting kept them busy, little Lord Thomas now seven months old, weighing a bit too much. Liana carried him around whenever he fussed, interrupting her work. At the end of the day, she was exhausted.

The time came to stop breastfeeding her son, but he threw fits, kicking and screaming to high heaven. David at home while between jobs was amazed at his toddler's temper.

"Liana is he this angry when I am away?" David inquired.

"Is he ever - almost every day, I am stressed, tired, and you know I have chores. David, I am at a loss of what to do," Liana replied.

"Is he like this when Aunt Olivia is over?" David asked.

"Oh yes he is. He only wants his way, and he gets it too." Liana paused. "David, for heaven's sake, he is old enough to eat our food and drink from the cup, but he insists on breastfeeding. I am tired, it has been a year and a half, and it has to stop," Liana spoke, almost in tears.

David agreed with Liana, it was time to wean the boy from the "*ninny*" as little Thomas called his mother's breast. From now on, he is to be strictly on solid food and drink milk from a cup. Whenever little Lord Thomas had his fit, David picked him up and said sternly, "Thomas, no more Mama's 'ninny' you are old enough to eat what we eat. That is final."

Thomas fussed a bit but obeyed his father. From then on Liana slept and felt better, had energy to spare. David noticed how fast his son grew, displaying clearly inborn intelligence. His certain way of looking at them and that twinkle in his eyes, fascinated both parents.

Months passed by quickly. Little Lord Thomas was now two and a half, he ran around the yard chasing chickens or geese. Liana noticed he does not speak as well as other children his age. Every day as she worked about, her eye was on her son. He followed her and played, sometimes prattling inaudibly to himself and sometimes he swung his stick as if chasing something away from him, frowning. Liana wondered if he was seeing things or chasing flies. Her son kept busy swiping grass, twigs and stomped on ants, swung at bees, until the day one stung him on the leg. In other words, anything that moved or not he had to swing at it. His preoccupation surely made her life easier not having to carry him on her hip as before.

When alone, the nights were unbearable, more than not of being overtired, restless, sleep evaded her and as the silent dark hours dragged, with every little noise her heart skipped a beat and stirred fear. Liana anxiously awaited David's return, having his arms around her, then and only then, she felt safe.

However, being together, they were happy. She glowed, her heart bursting from happiness and love for David. The chores seemed to disappear quickly each day. Having David at her side, she never minded the hard work. The child was happy too. Little Lord Thomas followed David everywhere. David talked to him and sometimes little Lord Thomas actually talked back, enjoying his father's lap and attention. Dinnertime was the most precious time for the three of them. Little Thomas ate greedily whatever David put on the plate. After all, his father was home and Little Lord Thomas was *three* years old now. When David asked him if he liked his dinner, the boy replied, *"Mmm...is good."* Liana and David exchanged meaningful glances.

However, when David was away little Lord Thomas fussed; he disliked some of the vegetables, or soups. He disobeyed constantly. His temper tantrums tried her patience. It was clear their child was controlling her when David was away. She decided to ignore him for a while and just observe. Little Lord Thomas seemed to be content on being ignored. Her feelings grew uneasy, eerie misgivings about her own son.

While kneading dough for bread, her hands sticky, he chose to scream and fuss, trying to have his own way. To pacify him, she gave him a chunk of dough to play with. For a while, he played with it, but when it became too sticky, he did not like it anymore. Demanding to wash the dough of his hands, *now*, Liana told him he has to wait a minute, but he refused to wait. He then walked about touching everything; he even smeared the sticky dough on the windowpane. Liana suppressed her anger but her son saw she was upset. She had too much to do as it was, and now, clean up after him. That was the last time she would give him dough to play with.

While he napped, she rested, thinking, *what was the problem? Why was this child so unruly and so disobedient when David was away? Moreover, it is not just once or twice, but all those times David is away.*

She promised herself that she would make mental notes of her son's behavior daily then share all details with David upon his return. At last, when David returned safely home, she told him what went on while he was away. He agreed to observe the boy.

David accredited for his quality work, now was in demand, and their life style slowly improved. Life was better and brighter. The boy grew stronger and stronger. He ran around getting into everything. She noticed whenever he tripped or fell, he did not cry, he just righted himself and kept going. It was as if he felt no pain and never ran to her for comfort or pity. She thought that was odd. Nevertheless, she loved her son. He was learning, eager to hand things to her, but only in his happy mood. Otherwise, he gave her looks of defiance. Liana at those moments felt tested, he was feeling her weak points. She began resenting her son's behavior. There were nights when her eyes refused to close, she stared into the darkness, thinking...thinking...*he is just a child. Her son is twisting her around his little finger, which should be the other way.*

Occasionally she noticed something different about him. Little Lord Thomas now at *five and a half,* had questions, which at times she could not give him a correct answer. Little Lord Thomas visibly became angry. She told David about his son's questions and his reaction when she does not give him an answer. They wondered, why he questioned her.

At suppertime, he ate little but poked at his food on the dish.

"Next time he refuses to eat, tell him you will tell me," David said.

One afternoon David had gone to the market, she washed dishes in a small tub, Little Lord Thomas asked, "Mother what is heaven?"

Liana was surprised, she collected her thoughts and explained.

"Look up at the blue space above us the sky, seems far and endless, I believe that is heaven."

After several days, Liana noticed her son sitting on a chopping block looking up at the sky.

"Mother, my eyes hurt when I look at the sun, why?" Little Lord Thomas said as he chewed slowly on small pieces of meat.

"You should not look directly at the sun. It is too bright it will make you blind," Liana said.

"Mother, blind...what is blind?" he looked at her squinting. Liana walked up to him unexpectedly from behind and quickly covered his eyes tight.

"Do you see anything, now? This is what the word 'blind' means," she said, holding his temples. Little Thomas pulled her hands from his face, jumped away and screamed at her.

"I will not be blind! I will tell Father you covered my eyes! I do not like you Mother!" Liana gasped from shock.

She stared at him thinking; *what is wrong with him, what temper, with such rebellion towards me, I cannot believe this*! No matter what outburst of reaction he displayed to her at any moment, she spoke to him tenderly.

"But Little Lord, you wanted to know what it was like to be blind, that is the only way, I could explain to you. I am sorry if I frightened you, I did not mean to. I should explain your questions in a different way. Oh, will you come and give me a hug? I love you, you know that."

Little Lord Thomas stared at her then turned away.

"Well, if you are behaving this way to me, then I must tell your father about your meals and how you waste food," Liana said.

Little Lord Thomas dropped his jaw and glared at her, a glare she could not imagine a child would be capable of. He slowly rose from the chair and slowly walked across the living room. Without a word, his eyes never leaving hers, he went outdoors. Liana was speechless. Several days later Little Lord Thomas came to her with another question while she was kneading dough for bread.

"Mother, how do birds fly?" he asked her as if nothing had happened.

Liana kept on kneading and answered his question not looking at him.

"My son I really do not know, perhaps father will explain to you better than I."

Little Lord Thomas lowered his head and after a minute or so asked her again.

"Mother...I want to fly! But I cannot, why?" he whined with a sour face.

"My son, because you are not a bird, birds have feathers, and their wing feathers are important for flight, I am sure you have observed them, do you observe the birds Thomas?" Liana smiled.

"Yes I do! Must I have feathers to fly?" he asked.

"Yes, you do," Liana simply answered.

The boy went outside and sat on a stump. He was observing the birds flying down from the trees to the ground where they were pecking at something. Holding a stick in his hand ready at every chance, he aimed to hit the birds, but the birds flew away. After a while, he came back in and sat down at the table. Liana noticed that he seemed to be in deep thought. What went through that little brain of his she could only imagine. Liana often wondered what sort of questions he would ask her at the age of ten.

One morning little Lord Thomas sat on a stool across from Liana while she milked Blaza the cow.

"Mother...how does a cow make milk?" he had a small stick in his hand, with which he swiped at flies, disturbing the cow.

"Cows graze on grass and I believe they somehow convert the grass into milk. Now, stop swiping that stick, you are irritating Blaza, go out and play." Little Lord Thomas satisfied with that answer traipsed out of the barn.

When David came home, he asked his father, "Father, what is water?"

"Son, when you are a little older I will explain everything to you, you will understand better," David said and ruffled his hair. Little Lord Thomas jerked his head away.

One particular Sunday morning David took him fishing to the river. Waiting for a bite, Little Lord Thomas said, "Father, I want to swim in the water like the fish."

David looked at his son and after a minute, he explained, "Son...you are a boy. A thinking and speaking human being. Humans were created to breathe air. There are many creatures, besides fish, that live in the water. We humans could not, and we would drown. Do not come near the water by yourself, you might fall in and your lungs will fill up with water, unable to take a breath, you will drown." The boy contemplated his father's reply, but said nothing more.

They sat and fished for a while. Suddenly, the line jerked on the tip of the bamboo pole and dipped into the water. David, with both hands, held onto it then slacked the line and pulled back. He walked the line back and forth to tire the fish, and suddenly, it bellied up. David hooked a good size pike, his son screamed with excitement. Little Lord Thomas ran home to tell mother they caught a big one, and to their surprise they noticed their son big-eyed watched David gut it and chop off the fishes head.

David was away again, on a promising big job, never failed to say he loves them, and always hugged his son. Several weeks went by, Liana prayed every night for his safe return. After hearing all those rumors and mysterious things happening, no one was safe these days, especially on the road in the middle of nowhere.

Liana realized she had missed her menstrual period, which means... she is expecting a second child. David has his son to carry his family name, so she wished for a daughter.

Liana experienced strange feelings, which over time stole into her heart and mind. Dreams, horrible dreams, recurring and lingering for days; were they a premonition? She was sure of one thing: her son would become a notorious individual. She tried to suppress those feelings, keep her mind occupied with daily chores. Nevertheless, each approaching evening, recurrent waves of the same feelings returned, an awful sense of emptiness bothered her. She wept. Somehow, she felt that she would never see her son grown, to be as strong as David. She felt she would never grow old with David, share all the joys or tribulations throughout their lifetime together, to share their dreams was not to be. That *ache, why, why is it constant, why it lingers in my heart*, she could not understand. When a sudden rush of tears blurred her vision, she always turned away from her son.

There were times her son's calm demeanor puzzled her, he looked at her and smiled. Such a strange smile, a slight curve of his mouth, slow turn and tilt of his head, eyes in deep shadow their expression could not be read, she pondered, pondered why, why is he so, she could not dismiss these observations from her mind.

She hated to be alone so much and sleep in an empty bed, when they first were married and began their life in this little home...she did not mind, but now, she missed David terribly. The one and only man she knew or ever loved. She loved him so much she would die for him, without him she could never survive, wither away, she felt that he loved her as much, they were meant for each other, are as one.

They were blessed with a son, their son, and life to her had meaning, she lived for them, worked for them, will die for them if she must.

She bent over and tucked her son to bed it was the only time he touched her face. She sat on the edge of his bed held his hand, gently stroked his hair until he fell asleep.

Storms raged through usually at night. Little Thomas feared storms, throwing back the bed covers ran across the room, whimpering jumped in under his mothers covers. She held him tight, and prayed that lightning does not strike the house. Cleaning up after such storms took some time, little Lord Thomas dragged small branches, Liana stacked them in bundles against the house, but the thick trunks left for David to chop.

Lonc trccs hit by lightning burst into balls of fire. By morning, nothing stood but a small charred stump. Mighty is the power of the elements.

Some nights unable to sleep, she envisioned that evening at the festival. That evening she had met David. She first noticed him leaning against the wall, close to the doorway, talking with a younger man. How he swept her off her feet with that first dance. She was attracted to him. They danced all evening. As at the evening drew nearer to a close, she introduced David to her parents. She knew that they were destined to be together.

The memory of those days made her smile, she loved him. Soon he will be home, soon.

Liana decided to tell David later, much later about all of the strange feelings she struggled with alone, unable to understand their meaning. She must sleep, her son will wake up soon and he is so demanding, plus all the other work, sometimes it was just overwhelming, but Liana strong willed, determined kept up with it until David came home.

In those times, everyone seemed to be cautious expressing feelings of friendship. Over time though, one or two would become good neighbors or good friends. Whenever Aunt Olivia visited, between Liana and Aunt Olivia it was an immediate bond, rightfully so, because they are related. They chatted several hours, enjoying tea with honey, preparing lunch or dinner depending on time of day. Liana desperately needed to mention her sons' behavior and her strange feelings.

"Aunt Olivia, please, listen...I hope you...I am not imagining things about ah... little Thomas, but I have observed. I need your opinion." Liana blundered, she stuttered, embarrassed to talk about such things.

"Liana he is your first child so it is normal to be so observant, analytical and cautious. If you could describe some of those things he does, perhaps I could help, but remember I never had children. Although, I, in my lifetime cared for many, I will try to help." Aunt Olivia said in a low voice, for Little Thomas not to hear.

However, after a time together sipping tea, Liana relaxed and told Aunt Olivia everything about her son.

"Perhaps I expect too much of a five-year-old boy," Liana concluded.

"He will outgrow his questions, his looks, try to overlook all of it, give him time to grow up and learn, but what bothers me...rather puzzles me the most is, his refusal to show affection to you...after a moment Aunt Olivia continued..., one reason...it could be David. David is not home to spend time with the boy. On the other hand, little Thomas has to grow and learn about you and David, all the work here, and the hardship of life. Then he will realize at an older age it is normal to return his love to both of you."

Liana understood Aunt Olivia's answer. She decided to drop the subject. She was unsure what benefit or affect this *overlooking* would be to the boy or her. Aunt Olivia's visits though lately infrequent always lifted her spirit and made her day brighter.

Afterwards for several days Liana pondered her son's character, *how much has Aunt Olivia noticed, and what will she say when she comes again. Aunt Olivia may not grasp my true feelings or understand because she has never been married or had children. Besides, she does not spend time with other children, now, much less with little Lord Thomas. Only time will tell.*

However, this mystery must remain as it is. Time must pass. Years must pass. Not all will be as clear as pure water. Destiny will reveal the truth and bring justice.

Several weeks later unexpectedly Aunt Olivia rode in on her horse, bringing with her cookies for little Lord Thomas. After hugs, she handed the cookies to little Thomas, he took the cookies sat at the table and ate a few, gently rewrapped the cookies and went to play on the blanket spread on the floor.

"I will stay only for a short while, Liana I thought about our last conversation, I came to ask you a few questions, if you do not mind." Aunt Olivia said.

"Aunt Olivia, I do not mind, what is wrong?" Liana asked, glancing at her son.

"Liana you seem to have a lot on your mind lately, do you want to share it with me?"

"I do have things to tell you," Liana replied.

"I see a bit of sadness in your eyes, but please do not be angry for my honesty, I know you too well," Aunt Olivia said softly. Liana caught off guard, after a moment replied. "Aunt Olivia...I do want to share and must tell you, but I cannot tell you today, please, forgive me." Aunt Olivia, older and wiser, understood.

"Next time I visit, promise me you will tell me the story how you and David met, I would love to hear it again."

"Oh yes, I will repeat my story to you anytime, you know that." Liana smiled and nodded.

"You know it is late in the day, I must be going, my sweet girl take care, I will see you soon." Aunt Olivia patted Liana's shoulder and left. Liana and little Lord Thomas watched from the doorway as Aunt Olivia mounted the horse, waved to them, they waved back at her.

Four: First Love

"It is so vivid in my mind, seems like yesterday, it was during the spring festival at the town hall. All my friends were there, some boys a bit older then I, all evening I danced with all of them, and I mean all of them. However, you know they were just friends. Then, I saw a young man come through the open door to the hall. I noticed he was glancing around as if looking for someone. Then, he looked in my direction. At that moment, the musicians had a brake and many people sat relaxing, drinking beer or lemonade. Only the small children ran around the dance floor. I was sitting with my parents, I was quite sure he was a stranger.

"Mother you see that young man standing by the door...he is a stranger," I said.

"Yes, I see, seems to be alone," Mother whispered to me. "You know in a small village everybody knows everybody, and everybody knows what everyone is doing. You did not live here then, where did you live Aunt Olivia?"

"Well yes, I spent a number of years in several foreign countries. However, I have my reasons. I would rather not talk about that part of my life. I decided to return here to my inherited little home, you two were married and arrived here without a bed to sleep on. I met David that day. Remember you stayed with me while your home was in repair. Later I brought you a crystal vase a belated wedding present," Aunt Olivia said and smiled...but do continue, please!"

"Yes...yes I felt his eyes follow me every now and then, as my partner and I danced by, he looked at me. Most of the evening he stayed by the entry door. He was having a conversation with someone. I guess his friend. I never asked David after we were married who the other fellow was. Anyway, I glanced his way. He pointed to the door and said something, the fellow walked out. He stood alone and I felt his eyes on me, then. Aunt Olivia I was so nervous. I know I blushed. Liana paused for a while...I felt scrutinized and awkward, my knees were almost knocking, and I almost lost my composure. As I danced with a charming friend, we whirled again right by the door, just then my friend let go of me and I found myself in this stranger's arms, he whirled me around the dance floor. He looked into my eyes, not once looked aside at the other dancers, our eyes locked, he held my hand tight, I fell in step, oh, Aunt Olivia he is a good dancer. Neither one of us dared to speak. Suddenly I was a bit irritated. I thought as we whirled. 'What nerve of this fellow, who is he...I have never seen him here before. I will say to him, when the music stops, what nerve, to barge in like that, not a well-mannered gentleman at all.' Nevertheless, I was lost in the eyes of this handsome fellow. My heart thumped, I knew I was blushing. My cheeks were on fire and our palms damp of sweat, I felt his warmth radiating through me, merging us into one. Incredible as it may seem some powerful magnetism held us. We both felt its power. Abruptly the music stopped. He still held me. His charming voice soft and gentle disarmed me as he spoke. "May I know your name, my pretty young lady?' We stood oblivious to everyone around us. We held hands. 'Liana,' I said. 'A very becoming name, Liana... for a beautiful young woman. I am David, David Komarod, I am at your service, now, and always.' Aunt Olivia...he kissed my hand and I was so nervous I curtsied. I stared at him without a word. I felt a shock surge through me, from head to toes."

"Tell me Liana, what is the first thing you noticed about David while you were dancing?" interrupted Aunt Olivia.

"Oh, I will tell you. His eyes; his eyes disarmed me. Even today, his eyes disarm me!" Liana laughed, and continued, "I detected a slight accent, but embarrassed to ask of his nationality or country's origin. He followed as I inched my way to my parents where they sat on a bench. When we walked up, my Mother smiled. I guess I seemed to be entranced. My parents glanced at each other knowingly. My Father said they observed us on the floor. Yes, they knew. It made no difference that he was a stranger, or that he came from another country, town or village. His nationality not important or weather he was poor or rich. What mattered was two people fell in love, and love conquers all."

Aunt Olivia looked away for a moment, her hand on her chin, she said softly.

"I fell in love once, but our love was not to be, but you know Liana, it lives in my heart, I will love him till I die." She had that faraway look in her eyes.

"Aunt Olivia how sad, tell me about..."

Aunt Olivia clasped her hands and cried out. "NO. Some other time, please continue."

"Well, where was I... Aha, I fell in love with David because my heart told me so. I felt a sincere goodness radiating from within his heart, kindness radiating from his eyes. Fate had given me this sense to know, I guess. I felt it. Socializing with other boys at certain functions quite often, that is true, but I never felt anything towards any on them, they were just friends. I never experienced such overpowering feelings. Yes, in minutes I was attracted to David whom I just met. I wanted to be with him...that was my deep positive feeling, a desire of spending the rest of my life with this young man. I.. remember he stayed at my side for the rest of the evening. He told me how smitten he was by me. He told me he had attended festivals in other villages. No other girl has ever captivated him as I, here this night he finely found his love and his heart was mine. He found *me*. He wanted me now and for always."

Liana had tears in her eyes every time she recalled their first meeting.

Aunt Olivia smiled when Liana retold the story. She, when young had found true love at one time, but never spoke of it, whatever had happened, she remained alone all these years. After Aunt Olivia left, Liana put her son to bed, undressed, slipped into her nightgown, and slid under the covers. Reminiscing again about David, drifted off to sleep. The little house stood dark and quiet until dawn.

Ever since she could remember, Liana dreamt almost every night. Now being a wife and mother still had strange dreams, but thank goodness less frequently. Some nights were dreamless, but whenever she had a dream, upon awakening many of them she could not remember. Then, when her dreams were frightening, startled out of her sleep she panicked, she knew these were not just dreams, but were nightmares, her body clammy of perspiration. Her strength drained because of these terrible dreams, her day seemed long, unusually fatigued, unable to concentrate, could not liberate her mind of these terrible dreams, and kept thinking; *these dreams, what do they mean. Could someone have cursed me, why?* Sometimes she stayed awake staring into the darkness, thinking of her life until sleep closed her eyes.

Her thoughts were about David from the moment she slipped out of bed before her son had awakened. Prepared breakfast for him and brewed coffee; she waited for her son to finish his breakfast. She sat thinking about her dream, and the chores. This bothered her, should she tell him about those strange dreams, or not. What if...he would not understand...and, laugh at her for worrying about some silly dreams, she decided never to mention any of them to David.

David worked away from home having Liana and their son on his mind. How Fate had brought them together. He wondered is Fate and God one and the same? If not, then perhaps the Will of Nature. There must be an explanation, a way to understand and grasp the magic of love. Before he ever met Liana, he earnestly prayed for a good-hearted, woman to share her life with him. He never asked for riches, but enough to provide for his family and a bit of spare change for a rainy day. The Good Lord or Fate heard his prayer and the path of life led him straight to her. The most important was to respect one another, live in peace, love, show compassion and understanding for one another, and a healthy long life. Now he is sharing a life with her, strongly united they were as one. Love grew stronger with time. The Good Lord blessed them with a healthy son and he loves them both, all he needs now is work to provide for them.

He disliked being away, and he knew Liana felt the same, but he never passed up an opportunity to work. Excellent workmanship created reputation, a secure future. With each job completed well, now he was in demand, compensated well plus offered food and lodging for which he was grateful. Thankful for the talent he was born with. However, he missed Liana's closeness, her beautiful brown eyes, her smiling face, her long thick brown hair, her slender lean body. Oh! He loved her so much, he lived for her alone, she had his heart and, her heart was his forever.

The fields at harvest time stood ready, neighbors as busy as they were, often came to help them; otherwise, David and Liana struggled and finish on their own. At times when unexpected conditions occurred everyone had considerable losses, harvests were meager, barely enough to hold them through the long winter. Part of the grain set aside for next spring planting, which was necessary. Those families less fortunate never forgotten, if the harvest had been bountiful, storage bins overflowed, everyone pitched in to help those people. Aunt Olivia sometimes too ran short. David and Liana shared their bounty with her.

Autumn's visible change of color all around was an unmistakable sign of winters coming, when the trees shed their leaves, morning air seemed a bit cool, and crispy. Birds flew south, except for a flock of Ravens perched on trees here and there. Steel grey clouds rolled across the sky, cold, gloomy and rainy days now shorter. On one such day, David caught by a sudden storm on his way home, the wind whipped at him at his back with icy rain, without any shelter in sight but bare trees and a bucket, which he used to protect his head. Chilled to the bone, drenched, came home shivering.

"Here my sweet girl, this bucket, given to me as part of my pay." David handed it to Liana.

"David, that is good, we need extra buckets for water, especially in the winter. When do you think the men will dig our well? It is so hard to carry water in buckets from the creek while you are away," Liana said and put her arms around his waist.

"I talked with neighbors, come spring we will dig ours, then dig Arkushin's down the road," he said.

"Oh that will be wonderful to have it so close to home, David I love you, now go wrap yourself in a blanket I will heat water for the tub," she said and kissed him.

She kept the fire burning in the hearth to warm the home on chilly days, pot of water sat in the hearth for tea. She poured the steaming tea in a cup and handed to him, David sat on the bed bundled up in the down coverlet and drank it slowly. Thomas sat next to him on the bed. She came back to refill his cup but David took her hand and kissed it. Liana kissed his forehead and went to fill the round tub with hot water, which, stood in an alcove of the kitchen behind a drape.

"Thomas did you bathe today," David asked.

"No," little Lord Thomas replied flatly.

"And why not Thomas?" questioned David.

"Father I... just did not feel like it," little lord Thomas replied.

"Well, I am...I am chilled to the bone. A hot bath will do me good, for sure," David said as Little Lord Thomas slid off his father's bed and went to sit on his own bed without a reply.

David put one foot into the hot water than the other; sat on the edge for a bit; then lowered himself into the tub up to his chin and closed his eyes, waiting for shivers to stop, after scrubbing roughly, washed his hair, rinsed it towel dried; quickly dressed in nightclothes; ran and slipped into bed. Liana in the meantime at the stable filled the bin with oats; rubbed down the horse and threw a blanket on him. This horse was the only one they had. Plowing made easier for David and faster travel to his jobs. They cannot afford to lose this horse. This was their way of life. David traveled to work. Here in the village work for David was minimal, and he refused none. He worked the land, relieved Liana of daily chores while at home. Liana had some time to catch up to her personal agenda. At those times, they were happy being together. However, each time he went away Liana dreaded those days, evenings dragged, and though she had more time to make her crafts, and little Lord Thomas played alone. Time moved on.

Liana thought about her family, her mother and father, she missed them so terribly and wanted to see them, but now her only dearest friend was Aunt Olivia.

While David was away, she was alone in this dim house with her son who seldom spoke to her. She had a thought; *perhaps we should get a puppy for little Thomas to grow up with, and we do need a watchdog, I would feel more secure while David was away. When David comes home, I will wrap my arms around him and he will tell me he loves me, as he always does; he is a good provider and a husband. I know he will agree with me.* She whispered and smiled. While her son slept, those were moments she wished for David to be near and hold her in his arms.

One late afternoon as Liana sat at the table, little Lord Thomas played on the cowhide blanket on the floor. She heard a knock at the front door, her heart skipped a beat; someone is coming.

Thomas ran to the door. “Father?” he shouted.

Liana ran after him, grabbed his arm and held him back. She opened the door, and there stood Aunt Olivia. Liana turned up the lamp to brighten the room. Aunt Olivia noticed a distressed expression on Liana’s face.

“It is only I, why the look dear...is something wrong, anything happened?” she asked.

“David is not back yet and I am concerned,” Liana replied.

“Oh my dear I came to see how the two of you are getting along. When were you expecting him back?” Aunt Olivia asked calmly.

“Ah two days ago, I am worried. Oh, I am so glad you are here. Are you feeling well?” Liana asked.

“Well yes, I have been a bit under the weather, but do not worry, I am fine now. The weather is horrible. Perhaps David’s project took longer to finish, he will come home I assure you. Ah...besides the days are shorter now. I thought I would spend a little time with you,” Aunt Olivia said, lightly patting Liana’s shoulder. Liana embraced her. Thomas stood at her side not making a move to hug her. He had a nickname for Aunt Olivia, since he learned to speak, “Antee O.”

“What did you bring me?” he asked, interrupting their conversation.

Aunt Olivia had brought something for him, as always. He especially loved her cookies. She handed him the cookies wrapped in a cotton towel, he took them, ran and sat down on the cowhide blanket and slowly one by one ate them.

"Now Thomas, are you going to eat all those cookies yourself?" Aunt Olivia asked.

"Yes, I will eat them all, they are *mine*." Thomas stressed the word '*mine*' loudly.

"You will not share with your mother, or leave at least one for your father?" she asked again.

"No," little Lord Thomas replied coolly.

Liana was embarrassed by her son's behavior.

"When I heard the knock, I feared of someone coming with bad news, but thank God it is you, I am so glad to see you!" she said.

They sat at the table, Liana turned up the lamp a bit more and Aunt Olivia updated her on all the gossip, frightful news as well as good.

Little Lord Thomas, as Liana named her son, sat nearby playing with a toy horse, which of course David had carved, and a few rocks. Liana filled two cups with aromatic tea and added a teaspoon of honey.

"Thank you, on such a day, the aroma alone is as relaxing as it is healthy, hmm...tastes good!" Aunt Olivia exclaimed.

"David's present from a client. It is very tasty tea. The clay pot is full enough to share with you to take home," Liana said, as she walked over to Little Lord Thomas handed him a cup of tea. Aunt Olivia said she liked the nickname.

"I love that boy of yours. I care for you and David. I am very glad we are living this close. We are family," Aunt Olivia said.

"I love you too. Aunt Olivia you do know why I chose this nickname for him," Liana replied.

"Yes...I do. I remember David telling us about the large bustling city and the castle on the other side of the mountains, where a handsome king lived, unfortunately, leading a sad and solitary life," Aunt Olivia remarked.

"Very unfortunate, perhaps that is why I nicknamed my son Lord Thomas, not because of the king who lived alone, but because he was rich and handsome. I am sure my son will find someone to love when he grows up; he is only a child now," Liana smiled.

"Little Thomas has grown taller, you take good care of him," Olivia complimented.

Liana leaned closer and whispered to Aunt Olivia. "I have something very puzzling to share with you. If you cannot stay today, please come in a few days. It is bothering me. Aside from this, I have good news and you are the first to know. David does not know yet, but he will when he comes home." Aunt Olivia studied Liana's face and knew it was important.

"Well, first tell me the good news or perhaps I should guess," she smiled as she took Liana's hand in hers, squeezing it gently... "You are going to have a baby, am I right?"

"How in the world did you guess?" Liana exclaimed.

"Well my dear, it is easy, your face is glowing. I am so happy for both of you," Aunt Olivia patted Liana's hand.

"Yes, I am pregnant. I may be wrong but I should deliver sometime in May. Aunt Olivia that is what I wanted to talk to you about, little Thomas..."

Aunt Olivia interrupted her, "What is he doing that disturbs you so much?"

Liana caught her breath, exhaled and continued.

"Well, he is acting very distant lately. He never wants to hug me, or let me kiss him, as before. He comes to me whenever *he* wants something, and asking so many questions, for which sometimes I have no answers."

"Well then, he was born an independent child. Have you mentioned this to David?" Oliva asked.

"Yes I have but David does not see the change. Little Thomas behaves very differently with him. But the minute David is off to work, he reverts to his odd behavior," Liana said in a low voice.

"In what way is he different?"

"Well, when I feed him, he fusses; he picks at his food and pushes it off the plate. It happens so many times it just infuriates me." Liana replied and made a tight fist, and tapped the table.

"And how does he act when David is home?"

"Oh well, when David is home he is an angel. He obeys, pays attention and eats everything on his plate. At other time, he licks the plate. I am truly at a loss, what to do or say anymore. Remember the cookies, did you notice? He did not share!" Liana said with a bit of frustration.

"Does he know you are going to have a baby?"

"No not yet...I am unsure of his reaction, I think I should wait," Liana replied.

"He might ask questions when you begin to show, than you can try to explain but for now say nothing. May the Good Lord bless you, your son and of course David. I wish you an easy term. I am thrilled for both of you. You said the due date is in May?" Aunt Olivia asked.

"Yes, if I calculated correctly, in the middle of May," Liana replied.

"Ah...the wonderful month of May, I cannot wait! What a blessed event!" she cheerfully exclaimed. Rising up to leave, she embraced

Liana, and kissed her cheeks. "Please forgive me, but I have to be going, it is getting late, I do not want to be caught by those ah...you know who!" Aunt Olivia whispered.

Neither woman noticed that Thomas observed them while they were whispering. She walked over to the blanket where Thomas was playing, he stood up to give her a hug, he always patted her face and kissed her on the cheek. Oh, that made her day and she laughed aloud. Little Thomas asked would she bring more cookies for him next time she comes, and sat back down on the floor. Walking out the door, her hand on Liana's shoulder,

"Now you take care of yourself and the boy." she said. Liana reached out for Aunt Olivia's hands, held them in hers.

"Thank you so much for coming, you are my inspiration and support, I value your friendship. Yes, yes, you must hurry home. God keep you safe, and thank you for a wonderful visit...Aunt Olivia interrupted... "Before I forget I must tell you the gypsies are coming."

"Oh! No! Not gypsies!" Liana gasped, wide eyed.

Aunt Olivia laughed seeing Liana so distraught said reassuringly to her niece, "My dear, I was told the gypsies were several days or perhaps weeks of travel before they reach our village, someone was wrong, do not worry, they are camping on the other side of the village." Liana backed up and sat down at the table. Aunt Olivia followed. "What is wrong Liana?"

"I am sorry but I felt faint when you said they are here, I am afraid of those people. Aunt Olivia, I welcome your visits you always make me feel so much better, but tonight...oh...I felt suddenly so strange. Will you come soon, please, come during the day. No! Perhaps not during the day; come stay the night, please, I am afraid!" Liana said seemingly frustrated.

"Liana do not worry David will come home soon. Just relax, you know you must not excite yourself so much, you are in delicate condition," Aunt Olivia whispered.

Aunt Olivia headed for the door with Liana and Thomas right behind her. She climbed onto the wagon sat on a blanket, her wrap over her shoulders, jerked the reins and said to the horse, go on home, and the horse pulled away.

The afternoon turned chilly and windy. Liana bolted the door and straightened around the house. Prepared supper, they ate together, Thomas was not talkative at all, for once, he took his empty plate carried it into the kitchen where he gently set it into a tin dishpan. Liana could not believe it, this was a first time ever he had done this. Something has changed in him. He came to her and said, "Momma I want to go to bed. I am tired."

Liana embraced him, kissed his cheek, this time he did not resist.

"You do look sleepy, go, you helped me so much today, good-night my son."

Little Lord Thomas having his own bed now liked the feeling of being wrapped up in goose down quilts. The minute his head touched the pillow, he was sound asleep.

However, this night, Liana lay dismayed recalling this evenings conversation with Aunt Olivia...*the gypsies are here already, oh no, they are trouble, kidnapping children and stealing whatever they can, I must tell David. I hope they stay where they are. Why so late in the season I wonder. Rumors are these gypsy women entice men with some kind of tea spiked with potions to confuse them to forget their wives, abandon their children. Men are comatose when at dawn the gypsies move on. Oh...not the gypsies, not here*...and she drifted off to sleep.

The gypsy caravan rolled in rattling and banging their cooking pots, which hung on the outside of the covered wagons. As usual, they set up camp at the edge of the forest far away from Liana's house. The wagons loaded with many beautiful worldly wares such as, fine silk fabrics, lace, threads of colors imaginable, and wool carpets, these items the villagers greedily traded and bartered for whatever the gypsies wished.

The gypsies drove away with plenty of food. The one vital item the gypsies bartered for were goose feather quilts, as winters are unpredictable and quilts were a necessity. Although they traveled south to a warmer climate, during their long journey weather had unpredictable changes.

Liana and David could not afford such luxuries but content with a bountiful harvest and good health. David's earnings supplied only the most important staples. When Liana's neighbor showed her gold chains and earrings, a string of pearls and silks, she felt sad but not envious, being young, she wished for such luxuries. Someday things will change, only time will tell. She appreciated all they had. She knew David would surprise her with a gift someday. The gold wedding bands were gifts from their parents. David planned to save and surprise Liana on their anniversary. He knew her wish.

Time marches on, seasons change, months become years; time does not stand still for anyone, rich or poor, and time cannot be bought, either diamonds silver or gold, not at any price.

Five: Liana's Dream

Dawn came too soon. Liana woke up with a start from a very disturbing dream. Unable to rid the vivid scene out of her mind, she tried to focus on the dim room, but it hung over her as a very real nightmare. Feeling exhausted, she sat on her bed, focusing, eyes darting over grey shadows in the room. Breathing shallow, as minutes passed she felt fully alert. She looked around the room. She had not noticed, in the darkness that her son's bed was empty. She fell back on the pillows thinking of that dream. Little Lord Thomas alone sat on the chair watching and waiting for his mother to awake. As he approached her bed, his eyes glued on her face, he began to scream. "*Momma, Momma*!"

"Why are you screaming?" Liana sat up, alarmed, and looked at her son.

Tears leaked down his face, he stammered, "Momma you did n-not hear me screaming! I...I am sss...scared!"

Liana embraced her son. "Little Thomas I...I am not feeling well, you must be hungry. I will make something for you. After you eat, I will rest." she said while wiping away his tears.

She slipped off the bed, dressed and went into the kitchen to make scrambled eggs and bacon, along with a warmed a glass of milk. Suddenly, feeling queasy from the smell of food, Liana made coffee and forced herself to drink it. Once she felt a bit better, she went out to do her usual chores. She scattered seeds and refilled the water pans for the chickens and geese. After milking the cow, she led her out of the barn to graze in the fenced pasture with the horses.

When she came home with the bucket of milk Little Lord Thomas still munched his breakfast. She ate a slice of bread with butter and had another cup of coffee, wishing Aunt Olivia would come to help her. This day began badly. She cleaned up as much as she had to. Feeling queasy, she sat on her bed. The sun streaked through the window but she did not care, she had to lie down again, at least for an hour.

"Thomas, please stay close to me and play, do not go outside alone. I must rest, if I should fall asleep after a while wake me, would you do that for me, son?"

"Momma, are-are you sick? You wake me up, screaming at night," he said.

"Do I scream? Oh, I am so sorry! Sometimes I have a bad dream. Now let me rest."

Liana fell onto the bed and closed her eyes. The house was quiet. She slipped into a deep dreamless sleep, and then awakened by her son's voice.

"Mama it is dark, please wake up. I am hungry!"

He did not like her sleeping, leaving him alone. Little Lord Thomas nudged her shoulder, hard. Liana opened her eyes and blinked, it was dark and her son stood by the bed.

"Why Thomas, why did you wait so long to wake me? I must make dinner and feed the animals. Oh, I am sorry I slept so long. Did you nap too?" she asked.

"No Momma, I did not, I was afraid to sleep," he said.

As quickly as she could get her mind together, she took a deep breath, she traipsed to the kitchen and prepared their dinner, wishing Aunt Olivia at this moment were with her. While Thomas ate, she walked out to feed the animals. Liana thought, *"Well at least he worries about me, is it really worry? That little slave driver, he will not even let me rest."*

As weeks passed still Liana's dream lingered. Many a night she desperately needed to sleep and when she did fall asleep, it came back vividly...as the first time...

She heard the sound of thunder, yet this thunder was not sporadic, it was continuous in its rumbling, crashing sound, approaching faster, louder and closer. Liana intently listened, stricken with fear; suddenly she realized that the thunder was the sound of hoofs of many horses. The sound seemed to encircle her, as if horses were approaching from every direction. In darkness, she stood barefoot in the snow. The thin shawl wrapped tightly around her shoulders, still the cold pierced through her, and all this seemed very real. She turned, strained to see from which direction the horses were to come at her, but the sound surrounded her, unable to scream, her voice suppressed within.

Out of the darkness emerged four pairs of black horses charging directly for her, growing in size, hoofs inches above her head, suddenly ascended high up. The deafening beat of the hoofs as if on cobblestones echoed infinitely and sparks of lightning shot from their hoofs. Fear stricken, she stood motionless.

Now four white horses appeared in a single file, bells on reins dragged on the snow, as they neared her, the white horses ascended above her and disappeared, but the bells did not jingle, in fear she dropped to her knees, the cold snow bit her legs and hands. As she quickly rose up to her bare feet, now, surrounded by high drifts, clad only in her nightshirt, her shawl had also disappeared.

Bewildered and frightened she tried to run but instead felt sinking what seemed to be a snow pit; in a blink, she was in the middle of a frozen river in total darkness. She heard horses returning, bells jingled louder, louder, she heard cracks of a whip, she, realized it was not the whip, but ice cracking. She ran towards shore barefoot over the crusty ice and drifts, she looked at her feet and saw blood, yet, she felt no pain. She looked back to see a trail of bloody footprints in the snow, her own.

The four pairs of black horses raced over her, disappearing into the darkness, then returned, again. Horrified, she fell to her knees.

The horses circled much higher above her several times, she trembled, fearing so many hoofs. She covered her ears to muffle the piercing jingle of the bells, but the intense noise came in waves.

The white horses returned closer and lower this time, she saw their hoofs coming down seemingly to trample her; yet they did not. As they passed over, their misty shapes dissipated.

Suddenly she stood in total silence. The snow around her began to vanish. Liana turned a full circle in total darkness. She staggered, and a sudden weightlessness seized her, and spun her into a dark oblivion.

She tried to scream for help but her voice stilled in her chest, her arms grasping empty space. Nothing was around her, only darkness total darkness. Seized by despair trembled, she was falling into an empty void. Feeling limp, weightless, lethargic, drifted, and no one was there to rescue her. Her last thought, *"David...where is David? Why did he leave me?"*

Liana awoke and caught her breath; her breathing shallow. She realized and recognized that this dream was the most horrifying of all the dreams she had ever experienced. She groped around the bed for the covers. She must have thrown them off. She was cold. Confused, trembling, what time it was she could not tell. The drapes on the window pulled together. She pulled the covers up to her chin and closed her eyes. Fear gripped her as this terrible vivid dream lingered. She sat straight up on the bed still dazed. She felt her heart pulsating in her neck. Her trembling hands clutched the covers.

She was not quite awake, seemed to be still in it. *It was just too real, too real!* She whispered, and felt a chilled weakness wash over her. She fell back on the pillow and cried into it. Washed of energy, she remained motionless, thinking...*this dream I shall not forget. It will follow me like my own shadow. Torment my mind every waking minute. Why...what does it mean? I must tell Aunt Olivia, perhaps she would know, she is good at analyzing dreams.* Liana turned over laboriously when she heard a scraping noise. Thomas sat on the chair at the table, waiting. She wondered how long has he been sitting there. She closed her eyes again. He came up to her and touched her shoulder lightly.

"Momma wake up, I am hungry, Momma!*" he* practically shouted in her ear.

Liana jumped hearing his call.

"Oh my son...is it that late? Why I did not mean to sleep so long? I hear you... so dark...you are hungry?" she asked.

"Yes I am. Momma, I fed the chickens." His smile stretched from ear to ear.

"Really? You did that all by yourself?" Liana asked.

"Yes." Little Lord Thomas leaned on her and she cuddled him close.

Liana warmed a bowl of soup for her son, and then went out to the barn to do her usual chores. The sun sat low, half way beyond the horizon, while she struggled with her lingering dream. She pushed the memory of it away hard, thinking of things around her and began to feel a bit better. The fear she felt before left her. Several days had gone by, in the early evening, as she sat at the table, she heard the gate open with a grind. She jumped and ran to meet him.

"Ah! My David is back!" she called out.

Into David's open arms, she ran and he crushed her to him, kissed her long and hard.

"Thank God you are home. David I missed you so," Liana said catching her breath. They walked slowly arms around each other into the house. Little lord Thomas was not at the table, where *she had left him.*

"Where is my son?" David asked.

"I guess he did not hear the gate grind. He was drawing pictures, here, look at them." Liana said pointing to the table.

"He may be in the bedroom," David said.

David peeked in and Little Lord Thomas did not look up. Liana and David glanced at each other, "He must be in his nasty mood," Liana whispered.

"Thomas I am home!" David opened his arms to his son. Thomas laid down the pencil. His face expressionless, no sparks in his eyes, just a slow walk to his waiting father with open arms.

David embraced him. Little Lord Thomas with his arms dangling at his side said, "I missed you Father." He took a step back, turned, and went back to his bed to resume drawing, not looking back.

"Well now, that was some welcome," David said to Liana, and hung his cape on a hook.

During suppertime, David asked his son, "What have you been doing all the while I was away?" Little Lord Thomas stuttered and replied that he did not do much, but he did feed the chickens. For that, David ruffled his hair, but not a word spoken about his mother's screaming in her sleep and he glanced at Liana.

When she washed the dishes and stored them in the cupboard, Liana set the teakettle on to boil for tea. The three sat and talked, sipping tea and eating cookies. Liana updated him with all sorts of trivial news. Little Lord Thomas listened and when Liana mentioned the gypsies he asked excitedly, "Mother where are the gypsies? I want to...could we go and see them?"

"No...I think not. It is too cold, most likely they've packed up to head south," David said.

"But Auntie O said they sell things!" his expression showed a bit of anger.

"Thomas, you must wait until spring," David said.

Little Lord Thomas walked away, sulking. In his room, he sat on his bed until it was bedtime.

David and Liana talked quietly half through of the night. "We have to keep an eye on our son. I was told they kidnap children, you know!" Liana said. David laughed and reassured her that that will not happen.

"Aunt Olivia told me so, David, they are not very good people!" she said a bit alarmed. "However..." she whispered, "I have a surprise for you...I am pregnant."

David was very excited. "Oh really...how wonderful! How far along are you now, my love?" he asked.

"Oh not too far along and I do hope it is a girl," Liana pressed closer to him.

"I have a son. Now, you need a daughter for you," David said and kissed her.

"Oh, David our family would be complete, I will be so happy. I do hope my wish comes true. Our baby should be born sometime in May...this is the end of September. I know it will be rough during the cold winter, but I hope for the best. David, as long as you will be home with us I will be all right."

"Liana, did you tell Thomas about the baby, that he will have a brother or a sister?" David asked.

"No, I did not tell him, not yet. Aunt Olivia suggested I should wait to see if he notices and asks questions," Liana explained, cuddling closer.

"Well, that is fine, we will wait. Aunt Olivia is a wise woman," David said. Liana said nothing more. With her head on his chest and arm across his waist, David felt her arm go limp, he knew she was asleep. Still awake listened to her even breathing. The house stood silent. Soon he too slept.

Little Lord Thomas seemed happy to see his father, but did not show it and was less talkative, shying away a bit. Observing his parents on the sly, he listened, paying more attention to what they were saying. David wondered, *why does the boy shies away lately,* but being preoccupied, did not question Liana about it.

The month of November turned out to be quite dry. Before the snow and hard freeze blows in; as winters were unpredictable, the more reason to prepare for it.

"Ah! Liana I must leave one more time to finish my project before winter sets in." David told her and said he needs a bundle of warm clothes, just in case of freeze or snow, and the horse needs a blanket. Liana helped prepare him for his trip.

"Oh David it is so difficult for us while you are away. I...I...oh David ...how long this time?" They clung to each other on that day he was leaving, little Lord Thomas walked from the table to David and gave him a weak hug then returned to the table and sat back on the chair, his eyes cast down ignored David and Liana kissing.

"David, when will you return? I will miss you so much!" Liana wrapped her arms around his neck, tears rushed to her eyes.

"My love, I will be back as soon as possible. Remember I love you and Thomas very much." David crushed her to him.

This small village could not provide for anyone steady income for a good living, much less to prosper. Therefore, one must seek any sort of work elsewhere. One must provide for many hungry mouths. Life went on and life ended. Liana felt life stirring within her.

They were lucky this year. Winter arrived less harsh compared to the previous ones. Weeks before the holidays many young people were busy hand creating, tiny gifts wrapped in fabric tied with ribbons. Children decorated live spruce trees cut down from the forest with candy, cookies, nuts and ribbons, snowman made of cotton hung on threads. On interior doors, wreaths hung of lace and ribbons, and pinecone stars hung on windows. Pine branches with bows sat on tables as centerpieces. It was that time of year to exchange recipes and bake sweet cakes and breads. Villagers went around collecting clothing, shoes, small gifts and food for the needy families who lived on the outskirts of the village.

Christmas will be simple for Liana, David, little Lord Thomas and Aunt Olivia. While Aunt Olivia visited, shortly before the holiday, one of the neighbors came knocking on the door for donations, collecting for the poor children, especially quilts and warm clothing. Anything anyone could spare, especially boots. Liana asked little Thomas would he give up one of his toys. He sternly replied, "No," Liana gave away her warm sweater. Liana, in the spur of the moment, said to the woman, "Wait right here." She walked into her son's bedroom pulled his pillow off his bed and gave it away as a gift for a needy child. Everyone felt an obligation to help those in such great need. Especially now during the holiday and the cold winter. In return, for the generosity of these villagers these men and women always were ready to help with spring planting, during harvest season and in many other ways. Liana did not say a word to her son, but noticed little Lord Thomas gave her a sly look and smirked at her.

Liana gave him a cold glare and in a low cool voice, she said. "Now Thomas, do not think that I gave away my pillow, unfortunately for you...it was your pillow."

She turned and sat at the table, her back to him, she pressed her lips tight, her fists on her cheeks, waiting for him to explode, and, explode he did. Little Lord Thomas walked into his bedroom, stood by the bed and yes his pillow was gone. He screamed at the top of his lungs, running straight at her. Liana did not look back. Little Lord Thomas, with raised fists charged from behind and hit her hard on the back. When Liana turned he was ready to hit her again, but she grabbed his wrists and began shaking him while he screamed, "I hate you! I will tell father you gave away my pillow, I hate you!"

At that point, Aunt Olivia's heart jumped, this, she did not expect from the boy. Thomas was greedy and mean, disrespectful. Disappointed, she began to pick up dishes from the table, keeping a peripheral eye on Little Lord Thomas.

Liana was enraged at her son "How dare you hit me? Just wait and see you'll be sorry!" she grabbed him by the collar and shoved him on the chair.

"You sit right here and do not move an inch, because if you do I will show you anger that you will never forget. Aunt Olivia is my witness, how mean you are to me." Aunt Olivia did not even look at Thomas as he sat and whimpered. With his forehead resting on his folded arms on the table, he snuck a quick glance at her.

Liana walked outside, heading for the barn; her body trembling as she wept from anger. She never thought her son would erupt with such violence and such pent up hostility towards her. In a few months the baby will come. What will happen then? She just could not imagine. More concerned as ever before, more so than the fear of gypsies, she had a fear of her own son she must talk with David.

Aunt Olivia spent the night with them. Thomas pouted all evening refused to eat dinner Liana took his plate away and sent him to bed.

Morning came and he attempted to hug Liana but she pushed him away; ignoring him completely.

David arrived home around noon and noticed it was too quiet. "Something is going on," he thought. Aunt Olivia gave him a meaningful glance and told him she needs to go home. Not waiting a minute longer, she walked out, climbed onto her wagon and drove away.

It wasn't till late in the evening, while in bed, that David would learn what took place. He too, was shocked that his son had the nerve to hit his own mother. With Christmas was just a few days away, nothing more was said.

On Christmas Eve, only two small presents lay under the Christmas tree. To be exchanged between the two women. Thomas eyed the little box made of wood tied with a ribbon, and wondered if it was for him. Dinner menu no differed then any day of the year. While dinner cooked, David dressed warm called for his son to come to the kitchen, when Thomas came, David held in his hands the coat and gloves and a hat.

"Where are we going Father?" he asked.

"We are going to have a big fight outside with the snowballs, just the two of us," David said. At first, Thomas gaped at his father but then smiled from ear to ear.

"All right we are going to have a big war! I am the Black King and you are the White Knight!" Thomas shouted and ran out. The two women looked at each other puzzled...king and a knight...where in the world that came from? David and his son fought with snowballs until they were exhausted. The boy's cheeks flushed with color and he was sweaty, but in his eyes, she saw a happy spark. Aunt Olivia set two big mugs of hot milk on the table along with some cookies; which disappeared in no time. After dinner, Little Lord Thomas surprised to see the box still under the tree, but dared not ask whose present it was and why only one. Little Lord Thomas slept soundly until morning. The first thing he noticed, the box under the tree, gone. He was still a child but his mind sharp and devious.

At the table, late in the afternoon next day while conversation topics were of spring planting, their neighbor Arkushin and his wife Rieza, rapped on their door carrying a present of Christmas bread, and a bottle of wine. Half an hour later, four more couples were knocking on the door bringing cakes and a roast as gifts. Welcomed in, all sat and chatted for they all were friends. Aunt Olivia was there, offered to make fresh tea and help with whatever Liana needed. However, Thomas, frowned disliking these grownups talking loudly, laughing and smoking pipes, walked away from them and in the bedroom sat on his bed and seemed to be somewhere other than the room.

The excitement of Christmas was over, children played with their toys and grownups patiently waited for spring.

David and Liana were so grateful they could rely on Aunt Olivia. For Liana, morning sickness prevented her food to stay down a bit too much. Thomas noticed this, but never asked why she was sick.

Concerned with Liana's condition Aunt Olivia's visits were more frequent now. Liana had not gained much weight and still not showing.

"Liana my dear, have you been resting enough? I know how anxious you are to work outside in the garden."

"Yes, I am resting frequently. With Thomas keeping busy to himself, I have time to do so much more," Liana replied.

"Where is little Thomas?" Aunt Olivia asked.

"Ah, he is with David in the stables. David is teaching him how to repair a few things." Liana responded.

"That is good. Start him off at early age. Is he eager to learn?" Aunt Olivia asked.

"No, not always. He is rebellious at times, more with me then with David," Liana replied.

"You will have your hands full when the baby comes. I just wonder how he will react having a newborn screaming in the middle of the night. Did you discuss that incident with David? Has he decided what to do?" Aunt Olivia asked.

"Well, he will have to get used to that, or sleep in the barn. In a few more months we will find out about that attitude of his." Liana replied.

"Is your baby active? Olivia asked.

"Oh yes, he or she is kicking hard. I know I am not showing much but perhaps that is good for the baby's sake, otherwise Thomas would already feel hatred toward this child," Liana replied thoughtfully.

David and little Thomas walked into the house while Liana and Aunt Olivia sat at the table sipping tea.

"Mother, Father and I worked hard with...on...ah...those things, we are hungry, and you *must* make lunch for us right now*!*" Thomas said arrogantly.

Aunt Olivia's eyes grew wide and she burst out at him.

"Why Thomas, how dare you speak to your mother with such demands!" Then she caught herself and apologized to Liana and David for her rudeness.

"No need to apologize, do not worry, Thomas had no right to speak to his mother in that tone of voice anyway, and *he* must apologize," David said.

Thomas' brows creased as he stared at the three adults at the table. He clearly displayed a grimace on his boyish face; icy rage glowed in his eyes. He turned and walked briskly to his room and sat on his bed until David called him to come and eat lunch. During lunch, no one spoke. Liana was embarrassed and did not look at her son. She started to become very concerned what his reaction will be when the baby comes.

David broke the silence with the subject of the spring planting and the weather. Aunt Olivia was relieved with the distraction; her tears were about to spill. She pushed them back not wanting the boy to see. Thomas finished his lunch and without a word, he walked away from the table.

David called him back. "Apologize to your mother and Aunt Olivia."

Thomas squirmed, those words he clearly could not say, but mumbled a mere, "sorry" *and walked away.*

Aunt Olivia cleared the table and washed dishes.

"Aunt Olivia, you have been so helpful, thank you. Now Liana, about the delivery time, will it be in May?" David asked in a low voice.

"I miscalculated. I think early June," Liana replied. Olivia expressed her concern about her minimal weight gain. Little Lord Thomas paid no attention to their conversation since he was upset at Aunt Olivia after how she spoke to him, and about his fathers reprimanding. David and Aunt Olivia agreed to keep Thomas at her home when Liana goes into labor. The boy should not hear his mother's screams.

Six: Birth of Kosta

David went off to work for three weeks. Surprisingly, for Liana, these three weeks flew by quickly. Many days the weather was too hot and steamy which made breathing difficult for Liana. Her weight gain seemed to come on suddenly and almost excessive. She was forced to rest in bed more often and would prop up her swollen legs on pillows.

David now at home, tried to ease her discomfort. Pressing chores kept him busy. However, the last week of April became worse than ever. The north wind blew in and stirred the air a bit but not forceful enough to move the humidity out of the valley.

Thomas sat on his small bed but it was too hot and he was sweating. Feeling miserable, he walked outside and sat in the shade. He noticed ravens perched on the willow across the creek, again. Thomas came in and told Liana. Aunt Olivia looked out the window. "Yes. They are there on the willow. Why I wonder, I have seen them here before. Perhaps just a coincidence, or perhaps for fish; fishing is good in this creek, for sure." she thought and smiled.

Later, in the middle of the night, they awakened to a severe storm. Lightning streaked the sky and thunder rumbled, the house shook and the earth trembled. Never in their lives had they experienced such an angry storm.

Liana disliked storms. She was glad that David was near her. Thomas shrieked when the blinding lightning flashed and lit up the room. He slipped out of his bed and ran to them whimpering from fear. Liana moved over to let her son slip between them. Every time the lighting struck and the thunder roared Liana cringed and put her arm around the boy and David put his arm over them. Finally, when the storm passed they were able to sleep. The storm had flooded fields and roads. The hot sun at high noon turned the air dense, which was unbearable.

Liana felt irritable. Her large abdomen caused back pain and she felt awkward, restless. She wept for no reason and scolded Thomas for no reason at all. She blamed all misery for her and those around her on the weather.

"I apologize my son. I am really sorry. I am very uncomfortable, please forgive me!" She hugged him and kissed his cheeks. But

Thomas did not reply when she asked him to forgive her, he just walked away without looking back. Aunt Olivia pretended not to see his behavior. She could not understand why he refused to speak to her, or his mother. Even David was somewhat perplexed at his attitude, never expected his son to have such insensitive feelings.

David reminded Liana several times that the boy must have realized she is going to have a baby. As many times as they talked about her delivery, making plans where to put the crib, and why David made fewer trips, he must have figured it out. They talked about all these plans with Aunt Olivia, notifying the mid-wife, to be ready.

Little Lord Thomas did not ask questions, he came to understand his mother was expecting a baby and he was angry and hurt. David promised Liana he would have a talk with his son soon but with so much to do each day, he did not have time to talk with his son as promised. Weeks passed and soon Liana would go into labor. David's anxiety surfaced and both had lost their patience. Liana, with constant back-pain, had difficulty walking; much less to work around the house or outdoors. David insisted she should stay in bed and let him do all the work. After all, with Aunt Olivia helping, Liana had really nothing to do but rest.

During one windy night, silent rain fell while they all slept. Upon awakening, Liana, with a cup of tea in hand, walked outside for fresh air. She took a deep breath and smiled, immediately feeling better. The wind had moved out the moisture leaving the air feeling cool, clean, and dry. She breathed deeply as she hobbled around. Suddenly, she experienced pain which took her breath away. She clenched her teeth, held her belly and waited. Aunt Olivia had gone home for a few days and Liana was alone outside. Contractions at first were bearable and far in between, but feeling more uncomfortable as time went on. As contractions gripped, the pain became worse, even sitting down on a chair was uncomfortable.

"David! It is time!" Liana cried out.

David rode to the nearest neighbor and began pounding on the door. Their teenage daughter opened it, and stood gaping at him.

"Come! Stay with Liana. I must go for the midwife Mrs. Katelyn O'Klardy. Liana is in labor!" David exclaimed.

"David, take Deena now. I will walk and stay with Liana until you come back!" Rieza called to him.

David lifted Deena up; she swung her legs behind him. He turned the horse and headed back home. She jumped off the horse and skipped into the house. Thomas, confused and a bit frightened, sat with big eyes watching.

David came to him took by the hand. “Come Thomas, you are going to Aunt Olivia’s now.”

He lifted his son up onto the saddle and mounted behind him and rode away. Thomas had no questions. Arriving at Aunt Olivia’s, Thomas slid off the saddle into his father’s arms. She saw them and opened the door to welcome them in, knowing the time has come for the childbirth.

“Thomas, you stay here with Aunt Olivia for a few days and behave,” David said.

After a few moments of small talk, David mounted his horse and rushed back home. Midwife Katelyn O’Klardy was already at the house with her assistant. Both waited for many hours keeping Liana as comfortable as possible.

“Liana, try to relax your whole body, it will help. Do not tense up when the contractions begin,” midwife Katelyn O’Klardy said holding Liana’s hand.

Liana said with teary eyes, “I will try, I will try!” She travailed long and her contractions were unbearable, her labor this time much worse than with the first child.

At last, with the final push their child entered this world. The midwife delivered the child and immediately handed the newborn to her helper. When they wrapped the child in a blanket, Katelyn called for David. He had hoped for a girl, but it was a son, tiny, but healthy.

David held his son in his arms, looked him over and his heart melted from emotion. He walked over to the bed and laid the boy into Liana arms. She looked at the newborn with tired eyes, she kissed the child’s forehead but did not even ask if it was a boy or a girl.

“Please let me sleep now, I am so tired” is the only thing she said to David as she closed her eyes and fell asleep.

David sat at her bedside watching her sleep while Katelyn cuddled the infant in her arms walking around the room. Soon enough the newborn began to whimper; he was hungry.

Katelyn rocked the child in her arms but he wailed louder. Liana woke up after only having a short nap and the midwife laid her newborn son into her arms.

“Is it a girl?” Liana asked.

Katelyn uncovered the infant, the child began to wail loudly and flailing his little arms.

“Liana you have a healthy, beautiful tiny son!” she exclaimed.

Liana's heart sank with disappointment; her wish not granted.

She could not hold back her tears. "Oh... how I hoped for a daughter, but now, I have two sons," she whispered. Her newborn boy was strong and healthy for that she is thankful. She will not love him less. The child lay close to her breast; suckled greedily for he was hungry.

Aunt Olivia came back with little Lord Thomas several days thereafter. David took him by the hand and led him to the crib.

"Thomas meet your little brother, you were this tiny *six* years ago." David whispered.

Thomas did not like what he was looking at, tiny head with black hair, pinkish wrinkled skin, eyes closed, and cheeks twitching. When the baby began to squirm and cry little Lord Thomas stared at his toothless gaping little mouth. He looked up at his father and then at his mother in bed, he did not speak to them, had no questions, just backed away, ran and sat on his bed.

Aunt Olivia hugged and kissed Liana on the forehead. "Rest my dear, David and I will take care of everything."

David and Aunt Olivia walked outside so mother and baby could rest.

"Aunt Olivia, how did Thomas behave with you, had he any questions?" David asked.

"David, your son has an attitude problem. Moreover, he feels resentment toward both of you. Watch him closely with the baby." Aunt Olivia warned. "On the way home, I asked him, if he liked visiting with me?"

"What did he say to that?" David asked.

"He flatly said NO to me," Olivia replied.

Not sure what to say or how to react they both went back inside. Their lives are going to be stressful for several years from now on, until the second son walks and talks.

They named their newborn son after David's great-great-grandfather of Greek ancestry, Kosta. Liana remembered David telling her about his great-great-grandfather, and what a wonderful person he was; kind, sensitive, loving, and that everyone loved him.

The attending midwife came for a visit a few days later to check on Liana, she did not like what she discovered, Aunt Olivia noticed her worried look and she understood even though she had never had children.

Katelyn nodded motioned to David to follow her outside.

"What is wrong?" David asked.

"David... Liana's physical frailty forbids her to have any more children."

Seing his expression of disappointment and fear she continued. "Do not expect me to perform miracles, David...please you must understand. If she should become pregnant once again...both of you will pay the consequences dearly. I know, I have seen much of this before."

David realized the importance of this moment. Being that this was detrimental to Liana's health, she must know her life will be in danger if she should become pregnant again. Unable to tell her himself, David asked the midwife to explain it all to Liana. She listened and later she thought it through and realized she could never have a daughter. This was hard to accept and she cried for days. David was speechless, he could not bring himself to speak to her or console her. The sadness in her eyes tore at his heart; feeling helpless, and guilty. However, *over time, all wounds heal.*

Weeks went by, and with rest, her strength gradually returned. Aunt Olivia was of great assistance to them. She tried to involve little Thomas in small things, but Thomas had excuses. As to the newborn, there were no sleepless nights because he was such a good baby. He cried very little and only kicked when hungry; a patient baby. When Liana nursed him, his little fingers dug into her breast and she smiled; feeling proud, her pain eased and worries dissipated. God gave her a good son, for all the pain she endured. Several months slipped by, both mother and baby were doing very well.

David expressed his concern for her health, but she assured David not to worry all would be well. However, not all was well at all.

Little Lord Thomas sat at the crib and stared at the tiny baby. What was he thinking? He had no questions. Liana was busy with the baby and David with chores. He seemed to be just a shadow in the house, now. Little Lord Thomas became annoyed when his baby brother cried. Many times, he just walked away from the crib, not once did he call his mother to tell her the baby is crying. When Liana picked up the baby to breastfeed, she sat on the sofa in the parlor Little Lord Thomas gave her sly looks. Liana noticed his behavior so she made sure she turned away from him.

Other times, when he sat at the table watching her, she called him over.

"Come here my son...look at your little baby brother. Not long ago I held you like this. Come look at him. He is so tiny and helpless he depends on me and you too."

Little Lord Thomas just shook his head, *no,* and watched his little brother nurse from across the room. Liana thought it was rather odd that her son refused to come near her and the baby. She will have to talk to David about his strange behavior.

"Perhaps he is envious, or resentful? Maybe he thinks all the attention you give is for the baby and he feels abandoned?" David asked.

"But how else am I to care for the baby? David, he is six and a half years old already. He is old enough...old enough to understand!" Liana replied. Annoyed, she continued, "you know how much Aunt Olivia cares for little Thomas and gives him a lot of attention. He is rude to her and refuses to mind her. He will not let her touch him. When I call him to come closer to the baby, he runs outside. I just do not understand." Liana expressed concern.

The next day, David took Little Lord Thomas by the hand and led him to the crib, and told him to touch the baby. Little Lord Thomas reluctantly took the tiny hand in his and held it, but quickly pulled away.

Several days later, he said, "Father, I want to touch him again, he is so soft."

"Yes of course my son," David replied surprised.

Little Lord Thomas took the baby's hand gently in his and held it for a minute, then squeezed hard. The baby began to wail, his little face red from pain and shock. Liana and David never expected this act of cruelty to a tiny baby. In anger, David jerked him away by his arm and scolded him loudly.

"Thomas how could you inflict such pain on the baby? Why did you hurt him? He is an infant, a helpless baby, your brother. Do not ever hurt him, ever, do you understand?" David said as he grabbed his first-born son by the shoulders and shook him hard. His voice boomed, "Go sit on the bed and think about what you have done." David turned away to hide his tears.

"Liana, watch Thomas carefully," he said and walked out of the house.

Lianna nodded, watching him go. She was not sure if he had seen her nod as she held infant Kosta in her arms, rocking, kissing his tiny hand. She could not stop crying. Little Lord Thomas. In truth, he had equal attention, more so when David was home. Working at home and waiting between jobs, David found time to talk to his son. Encouraging him to be helpful but his first-born son felt ignored and loved less. Now that the baby entered their lives, his resentment was aimed at his baby brother and his parents.

Seven: "Little Lord Thomas"

One year later Little Lord Thomas was seven and a half. Aunt Olivia as well as his parents felt he understood their daily routine. David and Liana tried to include him in every chore or project done in a day. Little Lord Thomas helped with certain requests by either parent, still felt rejection.

While playing outside, he always carried a stick. He walked by the vegetable garden and noticed flowers blooming among the green vegetables. Suddenly he sliced at the flower heads watched them fling off and petals scatter, he kept on and on destroying all of them, as long as no one noticed, but Liana noticed, she ran out and screamed at him.

"Come inside immediately! Why did you destroy the flowers?" Her temper now short, she continued to scream, as he hung his head low. "Well, I want an answer, now!" she demanded. She heard the baby cry. She grabbed his shoulder and dragged him inside the house.

"You will not answer me? So you will sit on this chair right here, and do not move a muscle until your father comes home! That means two days! Do you understand?" Little Lord Thomas said nothing just glanced at her as she walked over to the crib and lifted baby Kosta. Liana began to cry from anger.

Seven-and-a-half-year-old Little Lord Thomas sat and did not move for hours. Evening came. Aunt Olivia entered the house and noticed something amiss.

At one point he said, "Mother I need to go to the outhouse now!"

Liana said to go, and when he ran outside Aunt Olivia followed him and waited for him to come back home. Liana reminded him to sit on the chair and not to move. Late into the evening he sat, Liana did not speak to him at dinnertime. She could not allow him to go to bed hungry, after all, she loved her son. Little Lord Thomas nibbled and pushed his food around the plate, trying to get attention, no one said a word so he ate far too little to last until breakfast.

During the night, Liana felt a nudge on her shoulder. Startled sat up seeing her son standing near the bed.

"What is it Thomas?" she asked.

"Mother...I am sorry. I will not do that again. Mother...I am hungry. May I have a slice of bread and milk, please?"

"Yes. Go help yourself." Liana fell back on the pillow.

Liana waited for him to eat and watched him lie back into his bed. She was terribly upset, among the flowers were a variety of certain vegetables growing for seed collection for the next year's planting, but this time her son destroyed all of them. He did terribly unthinkable things for his age. He squeezed the chick's necks until it stopped kicking, limp, and dead; ran with it to the hog pen dropped it for the pigs; watched as it was trampled in the mud. He hit the sleeping pup; this puppy was to be his dog, his companion, he did not care, he ignored his puppy. The poor thing yelped and ran away. Liana heard the puppy's cries but at that moment, she was busy feeding baby Kosta. Chasing after the chickens was a challenge; but when he managed to capture one, plucked the tail feathers, and laughed as the chicken ran off rear naked. Little Lord Thomas dug shallow holes in the ground and buried a little chick alive, he stumped on the ground a few times and stood on it for a while and waited, then he dug out the chick to see if it was dead or alive.

Where were his parents? Well, David was away on a job; and Liana busy with the baby plus chores; she had not noticed at first why there were fewer chicks.

Little Lord Thomas was bored. This was summer, children his age played in groups, but he was not invited to join them, not at all. Three boys watched Little Lord Thomas beat a frog to a pulp, or simply pull them apart. The boys ran home told their parents of what they saw. The boys mother said, *stay away from him and do not tell anyone what he is doing*.

The roosters chased and pecked at his legs. He was angry but left them alone. Geese chased and nipped at his legs when he cracked their eggs, then he chased and beat them with a long stick. For a boy of his age he was wise, but cruel. When Liana had done the evening milking and she was not looking, he ran back into the barn climbed to the top of the stall, looped the rope over her head, pulled it closer, first he patted and scratched her neck and rubbed her ears. Then, with a stick, jabbed it into the cow's nostrils to see it bleed. The cow balked, the rope slipped out of his hand, the cow ran to the back of the stall, bellowed, and gored the stall's planks in pain. He liked to see them mad. Of course, he knew they could not hurt him, locked up in stalls. Then he would sneak closer to other cows with a long stick, poked their udders, which on Blaza made a good size scratch. Liana noticed all three cows had bruises, all three! She wondered where and how that happened, from then on she took time to inspect each area where the animals grazed, the fenced off lot was clean of any shrubs which could scrape their udders. She had not seen any protruding nails or splinters in the stalls. However, what puzzled her drops of blood on the straw, in each stall. She felt eerie and suddenly had her suspicion. This was something she had to discuss with David and Aunt Olivia. Liana, afraid to approach the bull, she left his inspection to David. Soon in their priority plans was to purchase a second horse. Liana wondered if little Lord Thomas would also hurt the horse. On other days, Little Lord Thomas to relieve his hostilities and anger beat on the fruit tree trunks, with all the strength pounded hard and long to exhaustion. Then he dropped to the ground and cried because the fallen un-ripe fruit was small and inedible. He was young in years, but his display of aggression was from a demented brain. These cruelties went unnoticed for a time.

Then Little Lord Thomas stepped carefully, noiselessly to the pigpen, and with a pitchfork jabbed at the napping pigs in a corner. The startled pigs squealed in pain, ran around the enclosure and the rest of the hogs spooked, creating a commotion. Little Lord Thomas's eyes sparkled from excitement and he grinned. He loved to inflict pain.

David had just come home from his trip. Liana made fresh coffee, they sat at the table and she was telling him what she saw in the stalls; suddenly they heard loud squeals, Liana jumped to her feet. "What, what is happening?"

David ran out quickly in the direction of the pigpen, he stopped short, he noticed the barn door barred from outside. He ran to the north side of the barn pushed the wide door open and caught his son jabbing the pigs with a pitchfork.

David never imagined such insensitivity their son, at age eight possessed towards the living creatures. David ran and grabbed the pitchfork. Little Lord Thomas had no time to run or react, and fell to the ground. David grabbed his arm and dragged him into the house, forced him down to sit on the chair and shouted, "Do not think of running off, I will catch you faster than you think!" David faced his son and after a short silence questioned him.

"Why in heavens name did you do that for? I am glad I caught you. I would never have believed if anyone had told me that you had done this. Did you break the eggs? I saw them broken. We need geese for down, and you go around destroying living things? Mother and I work hard to provide for you, and you hate what we do for you? Answer me!" David said sternly. Little Lord Thomas did not reply. He stared ahead, his eyes blank. Liana asked him, "Did you hurt Blaza and the other cows?" Little Lord Thomas glanced at her and clamped his mouth. It was clear he had blocked it all out. Liana sat at the table with the baby on her lap, observing Thomas. He did not avert his eyes; he stared at them, yet clearly beyond them, without a bit of fear, or remorse.

From that day on, Thomas was to go wherever David went and be in his father's sight at all times.

David handed him a shovel one morning. "Now start shoveling out the manure and be quick about it, we have much to do today," he said roughly. Little Lord Thomas disliked that idea but carried out the task without any protest. He realized his mistake. He was caught red-handed, now he must work, at least the switch had not come off the hook. At the end of the day, his whole body ached. His arm muscles hurt so much he could not cut a slice of bread for himself for dinner. Furthermore, when he tried to stand his legs wobbled. He was completely exhausted and he slept fitfully. He hated to wake before dawn each morning, and to follow his father every minute. Shoveling manure was not for him, he knew, though still a child, he knew he must behave, or he will be his father's shadow for the rest of his life. David tried to explain all about the animals.

"We need them in our life, and they depend on us, did you know that animals have been here on earth from the beginning of time?" Little Lord Thomas shut his ears and would not listen. Little Lord Thomas had no choice but to follow his father and mind him, and do each job well. Moreover, no matter how much tenderness and affection they displayed or pleasing manner, psychological approach and reverse psychology in some instances to reason with their boy, they could not find a way to penetrate his stubbornness, his cold heart or twisted mind.

Endless explanation how wrong it was to torture and inflict pain to innocent animals was futile and unforgivable. In the end, they gave up, hoping and believing their son will outgrow this shocking behavior. They relieved him of his punishment. He was free to do what he wanted. However, David warned him never to hurt any animals. Liana in her heart felt a deep emptiness and a sense of loss.

At his age possessing such a rebellious behavior and violence is beyond one's comprehension. This horrible realization hit them: if he is cruel to animals, helpless animals, what about them as parents, should they fear for their life, while they are asleep...and what of the baby?

Aunt Olivia felt helpless. She advised David and Liana that no one should know of his behavior. They loved their first-born son without a doubt, but this discovery about his character, as parents they found themselves at a loss. Their feelings crushed and attitude changed.

Several years passed by during which their son's expressionless face became harder to read. What was he thinking? He spoke only out of absolute necessity to them or Aunt Olivia. Nevertheless, his mind continued to lean towards sadism and malice, but now most of it was towards his little brother.

At age ten and a half Lord Thomas as usual sat stiffly at the table during dinner. He chewed his food slowly, keeping his eyes on the plate. His hair now combed back and tied in a ponytail, like his father's. He broke the silence in a cool tone of voice, keeping his eyes down,

"Father...Mother...please...I do not wish to be called, 'Little' anymore... 'Lord Thomas' will suit me well."

Taken aback by such a request, Liana held her spoon in mid-air and asked,

"Why Little Lord Thomas what on earth...have you...grown up already? You are still a ten-year-old boy and that is an affectionate nickname I gave you when you were born."

At that, he repeated firmly again, "Lord Thomas, Mother, please!"

David observed his first-born son's face had not a twitch of nerve, as if his face was a mere form of clay.

"Thomas if you feel you are grown up that much not to be called 'little' in that case you are grown up enough to do your share of work," David said to his son. No one spoke. David broke the silence saying.

"Ah, yes, by the way, *Lord Thomas*, as of tomorrow, you will clean out the chicken coop. Thereafter, each day feed them and bring fresh water from the creek for all the animals." David stressed "all," observing his son for a reaction. Liana did not interfere.

Lord Thomas, not expecting conditions, jerked his head up and, eyes wide with shock, glared at both of them. Lost for words, he dropped his head after minutes of contemplating pros and cons.

"I shall do whatever you wish father," Lord Thomas said.

For the following weeks, Lord Thomas followed his father and did all the work as was instructed to do. At the end of a long day, he was exhausted, his muscles ached as he sat at the table not speaking or looking at his parents, but kept his eyes on the plate.

David noticed how determined his son could be, and eased off on the work for a while. He slept a bit longer each morning from that time on. Kosta was *four* and a *half*. Kosta a child, too trusting and innocent to recognize his brother's intentions, went along with whatever his older brother said, and followed him everywhere. While David was out on a job for two weeks, Lord Thomas took Kosta out of earshot and vision of his mother and said.

"Come Kosta, I will take you someplace and show you something. This is something beautiful and wonderful, you have never seen before." Kosta looked up at his big brother.

"Thomas...what is ...something...where? Thomas, tell me where Thomas! Tell me, tell me, where!" excitedly little Kosta pleaded, jumping up and pulling on his arm. He too had a small ponytail, whenever time came for a haircut he screamed not to cut it off, he wanted to be like his brother and father.

"All right I will tell you, but you must not tell mother that I took you where the swans are nesting, you must promise," Lord Thomas demanded.

"I promise. What is promise, Thomas?" Kosta asked.

"Promise means, you will not tell mother, understand now?"

"Yes..., I aha...understand now."

"Kosta, now *you* tell me what it means." Thomas asked.

"I will not tell mother. What are swans, Thomas?" Kosta asked.

"Swans are big beautiful graceful birds in flight or swimming on water, in the springtime nesting in swamps or marshes. Oh my God, how many questions do you want me to answer you, Kosta!" Lord Thomas shouted.

Kosta as little as he was knew he could not ask anymore.

Liana busy in the house had not noticed they strayed away and headed directly for the small lake surrounded by marshes and peat fields, which were quite a distance away. Liana just happened to step out of the house to throw some crumbs for the chicks. Their home sat on a rise, she could see her sons in the distance walking along the creek away from home, a feeling of apprehension filled her and goose bumps ran down her whole body. Liana sped after them. Soon the distance shortened between them; surely, they would hear her now. Liana called them on top of her voice

"Thomas! Kosta come back! Come back Kosta! Thomas come back home!" Liana ran again trying to catch up, but halted for a minute to catch her breath. She inhaled deeply then cupped her hands to her mouth and hollered. Lord Thomas pretended not to hear her calling, but little Kosta turned around and ran towards her. Lord Thomas irritated had no choice but to turn back.

"Momma, why you call us back, I want to see the...the swans!" Kosta ran shouting.

"What? Swans, what swans!" She looked at Lord Thomas angrily.

"Ah...the swans are nesting in the marshes close to the peat fields. I wanted Kosta to see them... that is all Mother," Lord Thomas replied.

"Momma what are marshes and peats?" Kosta asked her, not knowing what that meant. Liana glared at him. She inhaled, checked her anger, otherwise, she would beat him.

"Why were you going there? That is a dangerous place, and it is very far! You know better than going without permission! It is not for little children, how did you know about the marshes and the peat fields?" Liana's hands squeezed the towel in her hands from anger.

"Err...ah...Father told me, and the swans are nesting there now. They are the most beautiful birds I have ever seen, and I love to observe them through the reeds, so I wanted Kosta to see them, that is all Mother," Lord Thomas explained.

Liana had an uneasy feeling her son had lied. She ordered them to go into the house. "Come Sunday we will walk over there and see those swans, do you agree? And I will discuss this with your Father; you should never go to a place so dangerous, by the way, when was the last time you had gone there and with whom?" she asked sharply.

"Oh...I do not remember...really, I think Father took me," Thomas stuttered.

"Aha, my son, you are lying to my face. We will know the truth when your backsides on fire for lying." Liana pointed her finger at him. Lord Thomas disliked the idea of mother discussing this incident with father. What is he to say on Sunday when they walk to the peat fields and the swans are not there, that was not what he intended, his plan been foiled again. Remembering sometime ago his father's words; one day all the men will go to cut peat, you will go with us, but never go *alone*. Now he felt angry, very angry with his little brother for telling on him. Kosta had promised not to tell.

When the boys sat on the stumps alone outside, Lord Thomas slapped Kosta on the back very hard and said, "Why did you have to tell Mother? You broke your promise! I told you not to tell!" Kosta fell forward onto his knees, frightened cried out.

"Why you hit me... Thomas, you hurt me...I...I forgot." Kosta's tears ran down his little face. Lord Thomas realized that that was a wrong thing to do. His quick eye glanced around to be sure mother had not seen that slap. Lifted Kosta off the ground and sat him back on the stump.

"I will never take you anywhere with me anymore, ever! You hear, never!" Lord Thomas said angrily. That night he thought about how badly the day had turned out, *every time I have a plan, my plan is ruined by someone or something unexpected, such as my little brother, but then he is little...I should not expect much from him."*

Upon David's return from his job, Liana told him all about the marshes and the peat fields, the boys were going there without asking or telling her.

"David, did you ever show him or take him to that place?" she asked.

"No absolutely not. I did tell him one day we will go with the men from the village to cut peat and what it was used for, but, I stressed to him how very dangerous the marshes were and, he should never go there alone. Why that little schemer, what is wrong with him...he is becoming a little liar!" David's anger flared.

Lord Thomas again clamped up. Again, he was lectured about dangers, and by disobeying, he will be punished. The willow switch came off the hook and Lord Thomas received a few swats across his legs. He did not cry out, and he had no intention of apologizing. Out of the house he ran to the barn and there he cried real tears, rubbing his legs, he was very angry. His teeth clenched with tight fists beat his thighs and then his forehead.

It was evident after that incident Lord Thomas had changed. Therefore, chores replaced punishment. In the years that followed, these two boys were under constant watch by the Thirteen Ravens. Lord Thomas was twelve and a half. At this age his attitude, character and behavior changed considerably. Outwardly, he smiled, accepted and tolerated his brother, but inwardly no one knew his true feelings. Kosta was six years old.

David and Liana loved their sons and were good to them. They rarely reprimanded either one of them, instead they lectured. It had to be something really drastic and unforgivable, only then the willow switch came off the hook. The punishment, more work in the barn or fields. All through summers and winters in their home things changed as well, the somberness, the silence, each had something to do, purposely avoid conversations of planning next spring's planting. The boys kept to themselves. Kosta expressed his desire to learn to carve. Lord Thomas had desires to grow up and be out of this dingy small home, nothing else to do but work. Work is a way of life, without work to sustain your life...you perish.

Liana, now a mother of two, at times felt a certain pain in her heart which made her weep, observing the boys working hard in the fields. Nothing else could they think of but work, which was good discipline, important for their upbringing, respect for what nature offers, endurance and molding of their character, but her first-born son's character she could not foresee.

Once on a Friday, David took his son to the market. Lord Thomas impressed by the crowds of merchants and people could not believe his eyes. Excitedly inspecting the stands, eyes darting in all directions looking at all and everything there, this day he noticed shabby men hobbling among people, without thinking he pointed at them and said to David.

"Look Father, those men are twisted like old weathered trees, they are comical, anyway what are they doing here?" he laughed aloud. David pulled him by the arm roughly.

"Do not ever laugh at anyone crippled, men, women or children, never!" David said angrily. They learned from little to always be honest and truthful, have compassion for unfortunate crippled children or adults and be kind. It was so from the time the boys were able to speak.

Since David was away from home more than not, Liana observed the changes in their sons...while attending school for a few months because of his obnoxious behavior, interrupting the teacher whenever he felt like it, taken by the scruff of his collar was thrown out of school. When Lord Thomas walked into the house much too early in the day from school, Liana asked why is he home, he told her everyone went home early, that is all. Two days later, a teacher from his school rode in on a horse. Liana invited the teacher in and served tea and cakes. The teacher, explained the true situation with her son, and real reason, the decision was to expel him from school. Lord Thomas refused to go back to school and apologize to his teacher. Great embarrassment for his parents, of his schooling no one mentioned again, besides, Lord Thomas did not care. David never said a word to Lord Thomas about the school incident. David wanted to test his son's honesty. David's heart sank when several weeks passed and his son Thomas had avoided the reason he is not in class, or, the cause of not being in school altogether. With the lapse of time, it had fallen into the background, forgotten.

David eagerly accepted odd jobs, anywhere, sometimes, but more frequently than not, very far away from home. Lord Thomas on his birthday received a present from his father, a carving of a swan family of four. Lord Thomas studied it very carefully and said.

"This is *us*...our family, four of *us*...together! Father this to me will be a reminder for the rest of my life, what families *should* do...stay close *together!* Thank you, I do love it!"

David felt happy that Lord Thomas appreciated his special work of art. That day, Lord Thomas placed it on a shelf above his bed, and never touched it or mentioned it ever again. Time passed, birthdays came and went. David went off to work. Liana and Kosta tended to everything around the house and barn. Kosta was young but with constant lifting and carrying heavy loads of hay or buckets of feed, working right along with her, had strengthened his muscles. Right after breakfast, instead of going to the stable Lord Thomas wore his brown leather vest, run his fingers through his hair tied it into a ponytail and off he went. Many mornings Liana was not aware he was gone until breakfast. She began to watch how many days in a week he slipped out early and how many days he stayed home. "*He is going out again*," she thought watching as he stepped up onto the chair and slipped out the window, closing it behind him. Liana never said a word. Kosta was close to his mother, he loved her very much, and anything she needed done if he could do it he would. She recognized the difference between her boys, and she wondered. Lord Thomas was tough, rough and loud, when away from home. He loved attention, which he had, from his so-called palls, but at times, they teased him about reading and writing.

"You are a peasant, and will always be a peasant if you cannot read or write," Midge the shortest boy said.

Lord Thomas hissed back at Midge,

"Stop with that peasant business, or I will make you shorter than you are." However, their comments cut him deep, easily aggravated, and being short tempered. For the boys he was easy picking for a fight. Mostly they wrestled so as not to have bloody noses and black eyes. Most of the time he was the winner, he laughed his irritable guttural laugh. His pals always stared at him seemingly in sheer fear.

"Where in the world did you learn to laugh like that?" one of them asked.

"He was born with it, as soon as he opened his mouth he did not cry, he laughed, scared his mama and papa to poop...I mean to death," Jacoby added. Lord Thomas was offended and punched him in the nose. The rest of the boys from that moment on avoided any action or comments, which would trigger his temper. All games and bets involved money, or anything of interest to him. At home, he was composed, quiet and obedient. No matter how much his little brother irritated him, he controlled his temper well, and avoided laughing. Lord Thomas liked to stay out after dark. Liana worried, asked Kosta to go look for him. Often times Kosta refused.

"Mother it is dark, I have no idea where to look, I am afraid to wander in the darkness. He will be home soon." Kosta once waited outside at the corner of the house, just to please his mother.

"Why do you wait here for me? You, for once could tell mother that you are afraid of the dark. Now the truth, you are afraid of the dark! You are!" Lord Thomas said, and he laughed. Kosta had chills run through him.

"Please do not laugh like that, you scare me!" Kosta whined. Lord Thomas laughed repeatedly just to be a nuisance. Liana had a strange premonition her son would grow up to be a heartless and ruthless individual.

Eight: Gentle Heart

It was very clear from observation that Kosta was sensitive, gentle, polite, and kind. Liana heard comments that Kosta had "a heart of gold," but as with all children his age, he was naïve. No matter, life will teach him, he is still very young.

Everything living on this earth interested him. He picked wildflowers, filled the tin cup with water and sat it on the table. David had carved a large cup with a boy and dog on it, which he gave to Kosta on his birthday. Kosta was overjoyed. At his young age, he appreciated and cherished every little thing. Kosta loved his Mother as no other boy ever had. Mother was his friend; he talked to her about his feelings, ideas, plans; she listened, but in her heart felt sadness, for she knew, this son of hers is too trusting, in his lifetime would be abused in many ways. She tried to tell him to be strong, stand on his own feet steadfastly, not to be pushed around by anyone.

"Life oftentimes is not fair, as we know, but one thing you must remember, that God is watching all people and everything they do," she told him. "But whatever you do, be fair." Kosta, unlike his brother, was more of a homebody.

Lord Thomas often left his share of chores incomplete, having no concern at all knowing either his mother or Kosta will finish for him.

However, when David was at home, Lord Thomas said, "Father would you please tell us about those places far from home." David gladly described in detail the places and people at the markets with different customs, apparel, foods, and language. Lord Thomas absorbed it all like a sponge. One thing was impressed on his mind more than anything else those mansions many stories high. Lord Thomas, intrigued an expression of disbelief at one moment interrupted his father.

"Father how many days is it to the city where you worked and had seen all this you are talking about?" David lost his train of thought and was quiet for a moment.

"Why Thomas, are you thinking of going there to see for yourself?" Lord Thomas without hesitation said.

"Yes of course Father, I am interested very much, I would love to go, see for myself. I must know." Liana was not surprised at all with all those times her son wandered off for hours. These were medieval times, when witches, gypsies and magicians roamed and easily could lure an eager boy his age from home, promising much.

David was a hard working quiet man, rarely erupted into anger without just cause. Although he was quiet, the boys learned to recognize his sharp icy stare whenever he was angry. He was tall, brawny, black hair tied in a ponytail. His eyes soft and kind, and mysteriously blue overshadowed by long black lashes. However, only worry and anger shadowed his eagle eye, his character and faith unyielding. His pleasant disposition dimmed and the hand of steel hardened, to them he was a shield protecting his family from harm. Liana loved those blue eyes, and loved everything about her husband. Whenever he returned home, after supper, he went to the barn to do the chores.

During the summer David worked on commissioned projects for many clients. The fact was, while absent from home Lord Thomas was responsible for the barn and stable shoveling out the manure. The smell always turned his stomach. Each morning in that barn he cursed and muttered how he hated the job, he swore that when he grew up he would never do this kind of work ever again! The smell on his hands irritated him. He washed them repeatedly to get rid of the stink.

Kosta with still-weak muscles tried to lift a heavy fork full of hay, huffing, puffing, and sweating, forced to take breaks. Liana watched as he struggled. He was a young David, her David. She admired her son who was an exact image of David. Those big blue eyes and black hair and those eyebrows, just like David, to her he was a precious gift, she was thankful for a good son.

She loved her first-born son without a doubt whom she nicknamed "*Lord*" but concerned and unsure of his wayward character. His interests were not of home and family in time she understood he belonged to the outside world.

Kosta struggled with buckets of water. When Liana prepared to bake the bread, her son seemed to be a step ahead of her needs. Kosta chopped wood, stacked it against the house. One particular morning, while concentrating on chopping small branches, Lord Thomas approached and stood off to the side, watched.

"Hey there, be careful, that ax will slip and chop off your leg!" he shouted to Kosta. Kosta startled dropped the ax, shaken, about to cry. At night, had a nightmare where he did split his knee, woke up screaming in the middle of the night. Lord Thomas smirked when father consoled his younger son.

"Leave the chopping to me, and do simpler chores, feed the chickens, or collect the eggs." However, Kosta did not find eggs every day. *What is wrong, why so few eggs? Perhaps the chickens had too little scratch.* Liana thought. She decided to search for the chickens nesting places. She walked in on her son crouching with a sack at his side gently placing eggs into it. Cautiously she moved out of sight, observed her son for a minute then backed away, went home, she waited for him to bring in the eggs, but after waiting an hour or so went to look for him, he was gone. Liana surmised that her son sold the eggs. On those mornings when Kosta found several dozen eggs ran with the basket shouting. "Look mother I found eggs today, look!" They enjoyed a good breakfast together.

Lord Thomas older by six and a half years, had visions of ways to attain and accumulate possessions for himself. Working in the stinky barn was too offensive and without profit. He respected his mother, but he thought that his father should have a bit more ambition, because of these feelings there were days he felt rebellious and dissatisfied in all obligations.

Lord Thomas told Kosta scary stories, determined to weaken his eagerness and make a wimp out of him. One morning when Kosta carried a basket of eggs, Lord Thomas hid behind the barn, tripped him with a broom, many eggs cracked. "Ah, that was a funny prank I pulled on him." Lord Thomas smirked, and ran off. Kosta upset at his clumsiness apologized to his mother. Lord Thomas enraged to no end, every time he thought he had succeeded in discouraging Kosta to do good, Kosta excelled.

Many mornings, Lord Thomas had slipped out at sunrise. Confronted later in the day or evening by his mother about his share of work, he repeatedly promised to do his share later. He repeatedly questioned Kosta when father would be home not knowing exactly when all chores were done together to prove he kept his word, and is a good son. Liana, never complained about the boy, yet David recognized that something was amiss seeing her to the point of exhaustion.

Lord Thomas often asked Kosta, "when is father coming home," cautious not to stay out late. Kosta never snitched. Besides, no one really knew the exact hour father would come home. Father had no schedule. Depending how intricate the carving of the project was or how far he traveled. Kosta as a toddler loved to watch David carve beautiful things. With time, Kosta's interest became carving. Whenever time allowed, both sat and carved and Kosta had asked many questions. David always had answers. Liana knitted or sewed in her spare time, if she had the energy. Lord Thomas sat around watching, a pang of envy cringed his heart, he suppressed it, *do not dwell on it,* he thought. Having little patience, at chipping and chiseling pieces of wood and making shapes. His mind churned other ideas.

Matured at sixteen and a half, Lord Thomas understood their meager life style. Desperate to run away in search of comfort, money, land and servants, just like those his father talked about in the distant places. His way of life was far from comfortable...it was merely a miserable existence. As for himself, he could not imagine toiling like this without future advancement towards prosperity.

He shuddered to think that his future would be cleaning and inhaling the foul smell of manure in the barn and stables. The smell of chicken poop in coops made him feel ill, many a time he vomited. Lord Thomas could not stand that either. Every time he helped Kosta shovel the manure into piles, piles grew into mounds for fertilizer, his stomach churned and any moment vomit its contents, especially on sweltering days, drenched with perspiration, his clothes absorbed the stink. Those times, he ran to the creek and in his under-clothes, dove into cool water, scrubbed his body with soap many times over, and then ran home changed into clean clothes. He would feel mortified if his friends detected that smell. He felt a strong aversion of living in this small and dingy house, unfortunately at his age he had no choice after all, he was born in this dingy house and in this house, he will sleep for the next several years.

One day early in the morning, Jacoby and Midge came riding in. Lord Thomas wasted no time to slip his foot in the stirrup and swing his right leg up behind his pal. The three of them rode off to experience the thrill of speed and freedom to ride the countryside not caring how many hours or direction they rode. Riding double, they happened to come upon an enormous estate surrounded by trees, what looked like an orchard. On both sides of the lane leading to the estate poplars grew tall and straight like sentinels, a slight breeze rustled a warning, intruders not welcomed. He asked his pals who lived there, but neither knew. Enchanted, his aspirations high, visualized himself living in a place of such elegance, someday.

Lord Thomas many an evening rode with his pal Midge to that residence on a prominent rise. Hidden well in the brush, they watched from afar. He forced Midge to swear to secrecy about these outings. Since this property was far, Lord Thomas decided to bend a little pride and plead with his father for a horse -- yes *plead.* This was not going to be easy. Lord Thomas never had the courage before, but this time he would swallow his pride. *After all, I am their first-born and I should have a horse, yes, my birthday has passed and I did not receive a present, hmm...a horse that is a good idea,* he thought.

Lord Thomas was not aware that his father knew of many such huge houses. David traveled to many areas and visited many homes. They had a reason why they never even mentioned such places to the boys. So not to give false hope, such a place they never in their life could afford.

Into the lives of the boys entered a different kind of concern, rarely talked about. Then, as time went by Kosta noticed a change in his mother, a change coming on slowly. Liana had slowed down much due to an unmistakable lack of energy, her cheerful disposition no longer evident on her tired pale face. Her need to rest became frequent in the afternoons. Kosta many a day found his mother sitting on a bench leaning against the wall of the house. Spells of coughing weakened her, some days she was unable to cook supper. Kosta questioned, but she dismissed his questions, with just a simple, "hard times, my son, just hard times, and she added, and I am getting old, you know."

"Where is my brother, the "Lord" Thomas? Why...he never helps, he is never around to lend a hand to mother, he does not care...he must not love them. He is out, off to see the world. That is all he thinks about, ha... but comes home to eat and sleep! Mother does everything for him! I must talk to him, he must see," Kosta thought. Many times his mother wept. He could not ask her why, he knew she would cry the more, just like before when he questioned her about life, so he just eyed her from afar. He felt heavy-hearted seeing her cry. He stared out the window feeling restless as his mother was, waiting for father to come home. *"All these years working at home, mother has never been anywhere outside this village,* Kosta thought, *that is not fair."*

Days and hours dragged on. David finally arrived, tired, but glad to be home. He had earned more than enough this time to buy essential things for his family. That particular Friday afternoon David came home unexpectedly. Lord Thomas was out, as usual. Liana slept on the sofa. Kosta covered her with a blanket when she fell asleep. He sat at the table looking out the window, waiting. The moment he saw his father, Kosta ran out and dragged the gate open. The wagon rolled in, Kosta ran up to greet him smiling and then, his smile vanished.

"Father what happened to you!" Kosta cried out. David slowly stepped down off the wagon and hugged Kosta.

"Oh Father! Who did this to you, but thank God you are *alive*!" Kosta clung to him. David patted his back.

"Yes, I am back, come help me unhitch the horses." Together they led the pair into the stable to feed and give fresh water. Kosta rubbed down both of the horses.

"Son, jump up on the wagon and hand me those packages and sacks. How is your mother?" David asked.

"Mother is resting, Father what is wrong, lately Mother looks so tired!" David looked at his son's face.

"Oh yes son, she is tired, with all this work to be done, and I am away so much, and you...are not strong, I know you help Mother as much as you are able. Where is your brother? Is he home?" Kosta, holding a small sack, looked away, and David knew.

Kosta cried when he saw his father's face, the cuts and the bruises, his shirt torn, and on the right side of the head a bleeding bump.

On the stove in the kettle, the water was still warm, warm enough to wash his father's face, his right hand had a black bruise, and Kosta brought out a clean shirt. This they did quietly as not to wake Liana. Kosta boiled some more water and made tea. David sat at the table, slowly sipping it.

"Father, tell me who did this to you, where, how far from home," he whispered. "Son, I will, but my jaw hurts, later when we are all together. It is surprisingly interesting," David said.

Before dusk, Lord Thomas walked in to adjust his eyes to the dimness he stood in the doorway, wondering why it was so dark, and quiet. Then he saw Kosta and father at the table, he froze. He knew, tonight he was caught and tonight would get the tongue-lashing, if not worse. David did not bother to look up, his fist supporting his head, eyes cast onto the bare table, in the other hand holding a cup.

Lord Thomas suddenly shuddered, a dread he had never felt before, something was terribly wrong, too quiet. David did not look at him. Lord Thomas thought, *ah... no scolding... Father knew all along that I skipped out of the house neglecting my share of responsibilities.* He stood in the doorway, waiting, hesitating. David turned up the oil lamp, to brighten the room. Lord Thomas noticed his mother on the sofa reclined on pillows her eyes closed, sleeping or resting. She looked very pale, in all these years he never noticed, really. *Tonight is the very first time I see her like this, is she ill, has she been ill?* he thought. He had never bothered to ask how she felt each day. No aroma of dinner cooking, the stove stood cold. Lord Thomas felt very uneasy. He could no longer stand there in the doorway, so he mustered up his courage and muttered.

"Father, how wonderful to see you home again!"

David lowered his arm, stood up, and slowly walked toward his son. As he approached Lord Thomas, he realized how tall he had become. David grasped his arm, led him to the table and shoved him hard onto the chair. He was caught red-handed this time, feeling his heart flapping around like fish out of water. Lord Thomas stole a glimpse of the bruises and cuts but did not comment.

Suddenly Liana opened her eyes and sat up, seeing David and her sons at the table rose and shuffled to the table. "David," she whispered. David sprang to his feet, put his arms around her and kissed her cheek.

"Are you feeling better, my dear?" David asked.

"Oh, well, yes, I rested today," she replied. David helped her sit down at the table.

"I am sorry I overslept. I will prepare dinner now; it will not take long, I precooked it all earlier."

"No!" David's voice boomed and his fist came down hard onto the table. Kosta jumped. Lord Thomas stiffened.

"No, you will not do any such thing! Thomas will finish cooking tonight! Prepare the supper Thomas!" David shouted. Lord Thomas's brain screamed out in fear, *"Oh! Thomas you do not know how to cook. Oh! Thomas you never looked into a cooking pot before! How and what to cook*; *If I mess this up I will be cooked!"* Father's strong voice penetrated his ears like lightning.

"Thomas, go to the kitchen and cook dinner, enough for all of us!" he shouted.

"But, father... I...." Lord Thomas muttered.

"Nonsense, you will learn as of now, and from now on every day, until you will learn to respect your mother and brother, what you have, and where you live! Do you understand?" David's voice boomed. Kosta jumped to his feet to get the plates, as it was his daily duty. David in a loud voice asked, "Where are you going Kosta?" Kosta stopped in his tracks.

"Father, I set the table, every day, we need utensils and plates, and I could reach them from the shelf with no problem, now!" he explained.

"All right Kosta, but first brew some tea," David said.

"Yes father, I will," Kosta muttered. Liana noticed David's face as he turned up the lamp to full brightness.

"David what happened to you, oh my God, how bad is it, do you need a doctor?" she cried out and tears glistened in her eyes.

Lord Thomas' brain worked overtime, looking for things he needed, but in embarrassment he dared not ask. He did not hear, or wanted to hear that something had happened to his father, he did not even turn to glance at him.

No one spoke, but waited patiently for the late dinner. At last, dinner came to the table on steaming plates. Not daring to sit down, Lord Thomas stood behind his chair. David pointed to sit and eat. A plate of smoked pork thickly sliced and lumpy mashed potatoes with a pat of butter, slightly burned carrots with butter and dill, and four glasses of milk. Without looking at his son, David broke the silence.

"Not bad. You were lucky it was all precooked. Tonight, you will wash the dishes too," David said.

"Thank you father," Lord Thomas said, but thought; *this night I will remember, because of my carelessness, an oversight not knowing when father was coming home.* His obedience saved him embarrassment and his silence a punishment.

"Father, tell us what happened to you on the way home, please," Kosta said.

"Well, I finished my project sooner than expected, and drove down to the market to buy a few things, when I reached the Creek Bend Crossing I was ambushed by a group of youths. I think they were youths. They demanded money, I gave them the change from my pocket, but they wanted more, I told them that I had no more. They were enraged, so they jumped me and beat me up." David breathed hard.

"Father did you beat them up good too?" Kosta asked.

"Oh, yes they will remember today for sure... for a long time," David said. Lord Thomas sat and listened.

"Father did you get a good look at them, or did they wear masks?" Lord Thomas asked.

"Oh yes I did. During the scuttle I knocked a few unconscious the rest of them ran off holding their noses." David forced a grin.

"Did you really?" Kosta exclaimed with a big smile.

"I hope they will not try to attack you again, they might come with weapons, seriously," Lord Thomas said.

"I doubt very much there will be a next time," David said.

"David, are you sure, perhaps they will ambush you, with a much larger group?" Liana asked.

"Well, you might be right, but I will prepare myself, you see there is no other way home, but the Creek Bend Crossing, unless someday people will build a bridge over the shallow section of the river," David replied thoughtfully.

"Is the creek that deep that you cannot cross it with the wagon, Father?" Lord Thomas asked.

"No, it is the same creek as the one here by our house. However, over time from erosion it has deepened; dips down as it flows rapidly, one day we will go fishing and you will see the big fish and the bottom is nothing but big boulders. Too deep for a wagon, besides the banks are too steep, but still everyone calls it Creek Bend Crossing. At that point it veers to the South sharply no other way, Thomas."

The hours slipped by and it was late. Time for a good night's sleep, David's ribs ached and his knee, he had a trying day.

When everyone was in bed, Lord Thomas thought back... *years ago, Father used the switch on my legs, but only a few times. Ah... yes, I was cruel to those little animals, and I beheaded the flowers and beat the fruit trees, but I did not get the switch for the fruit trees. I know I did not.* He justified his actions thinking...*but I was young, I was angry and my punishment, follow my father everywhere, now that, I will not forget... ever. I have been sneaking out so long, thinking no one noticed. How stupid and naïve I have been! Ah... I felt free, and got away with it, until tonight. My pals had planned the ambush. However, they never had met Father, they did not know it was him, but one. I must tell them to be very cautious. Father returned early, unexpectedly. Mother well... why she had not uttered a word on my behalf. I am her first-born son. Then, why would she? She has Kosta now. However, I should respect them, but tonight I will not forget, ever. Kosta the sissy...he does not count. Holding on to Mother's aprons, always following her like a little toddler, talking about things, which do not interest me at all.*

The following day David thought about a second ambush. To be safe he should prepared for it.

"These youths want my gold," David was saying to Liana, "Well I think I know what to give them in place of my gold, after which, they will never ambush anyone again." David smiled at her.

"What are you thinking of David, what are you planning, tell me," Liana pleaded.

"Liana it is almost summer, where could I find an anthill? I need many ants, the red ones; and a sack. Also I need bees, many bees," David said.

"Are you serious... ants and bees?" Liana looked at him then laughed.

“Yes ants, and bees. Do not tell the boys. Later if it happens I will tell them,” David said. The mounds of red ants and a beehive were found in the woods. The small sacks lay on the wagon floor ready for the moment. In the meantime, David found a new road leading home, much out of the way. Since the first ambush, David rode through the forest, to the south, the lumberjacks told him to follow a path cut out for that purpose, no matter if it meanders this way or that way, not to worry, coming to a fork, there, turn left onto the main road and into the village. Although it took too much time the long way home, David came home safe. The boys had waited in ambush, it mattered not who came along. Riders on horseback were not bothered, a horse could ride off fast, besides, none of them wanted to be trampled and hurt. Each wagon rolled along was the wrong one, four horses or two, kept rolling. This group had waited an entire week for that particular wagon with a logo written on both sides, which never came. Frustrated they went home empty handed.

The ants and the bees were well cared for, David was prepared well. Then the summer turned up its heat, and David forced to take the shorter way home. After avoiding the old road for many weeks, he felt those thugs had given up waiting in this heat, covered up in sheets. He was not expecting an ambush until that one day, David noticed someone run across the road a good distance away, at the big oak tree. He knew they were there, seeing one of them run and hide behind the tree. David reined the horses to a stop a good distance from the tree. He reached for the sacks, laid them next to him on the seat, and waited. The group of youths (about a dozen) walked out from their hiding spot and stood in the middle of the road waiting. David was undecided; should he run them over or take the chance to fight, or hand them the sacks. His choice, hand over the sacks. To fight such a large group alone outnumbered, he would lose. David poked the horse’s backside with the whips tip they ambled forward. At a safe distance he halted, David shouted, “Which one of you is the leader? Come forward, I have sacks of gold for you, if you let me pass unharmed.” The group turned to a tall fellow the one who stood in the back of the group, discussing what to do. The tall boy waved his arm, and from behind the huge oak came forward their leader. Clad in a long robe, which looked more like a sheet, his face covered as well, but two slits for the eyes to see, he motioned to the others and all of them walked off the road, hid behind the oak tree. The leader walked briskly toward David, his arm outstretched, motioning for the sacks. David said nothing but reached into his pocket, opened his palm and said, "a few more for your trouble," dropped two gold pieces into the sack and untied the little sack with the ants, retied the outer one and handed it to the boy. He did the same with the bees.

"When I pass unharmed you will share the gold with your friends, agreed?" David said. The boy nodded and took the heavy sacks and ran to the others waiting in the shade of the oak. David cracked the whip, horses galloped at full speed, passed the boys, around the bend of the Creek Bend Crossing, galloped across the bridge then being out of their sight stopped and listened. For a moment he heard nothing, then, screams came from the group. *It worked,* David thought and laughed all the way home. Liana was working in the garden when David drove up. She saw him and wondered why he was grinning. David jumped off the wagon and ran to embrace her tight.

"Liana, they were waiting for me at the bend in the center of the road. I said to them, 'which of you is the leader? Come forward, I have the gold for you if you let me pass unharmed.' The leader came up all covered from head to toe with a sheet, to take the sacks, but he did not speak, just nodded. Then I drove away fast. When I crossed the bridge, I heard a lot of yelling," David told her grinning.

"But David will they try again and this time really harm you," Liana said.

"Ah my sweet woman, let us wait and see, then worry. Where are the boys?" David asked kissing her lips. They walked to the wagon for the packages.

"Thomas left early this morning, he wanted to see his friend and I allowed him to go after his share of the chores were done," she said.

"Did he really finish the chores?"

"Yes, quickly, he must have been in a great hurry," Liana said.

"And where is Kosta?

"Kosta is fishing at the creek. He hopes to catch fish for dinner," Liana replied.

To be alone like this, a rare moment indeed, the boys were growing up and out of the house. David opened his arms and she ran to him, he held her, just feeling; breathing; hearts beating; longing for love; a moment in time to be close in feelings and body, a wonderful feeling, what they had in mind could not happen, the boys may be home any moment. An hour later, Kosta came in with three small catfish in the bucket.

"Oh Father you are home! Look, I sat waiting for the big one, but all I have are these for supper," Kosta said. David wondered when Thomas would show up, but Thomas did not come home until dusk. At dinner David not looking up in the dim light.

"Well Thomas did you enjoy your visit with your friends?" David asked, turning up the lamp on the table.

"Yes, I had a great visit, thank you Father," he replied.

Kosta told Thomas about the three small fish he caught – not enough for dinner, a bad fishing day.

"You want big fish. I know a spot where you will catch a huge pike or some other," Lord Thomas said laughing.

"And where is that spot, Thomas?" David asked, wondering why Thomas kept his left hand in the pants pocket, since he had come home.

"Ah...my friend told me...where the creek runs deep, on our side, far from the house. he said to look for a huge tree, but he did not know what kind it was," Lord Thomas said and took a gulp of tea. David and Liana had not pressed for detail but David's mind raced, scenes from the encounter earlier in the day, recalling how tall these youths were and how they walked, strange none of them spoke a word, he did all the talking. One thing to him became clear; having covered faces, no one could later identify any of them by voice alone. At breakfast next day, Liana noticed a red swollen bump on the left side of his neck.

"Thomas have you been bitten by a mosquito? Here let me rub a bit of ash, it will stop the itch."

"No, Mother no, it is not itching at all, now!" Lord Thomas moved away from the table quickly and was out the door. Several days later, the two brothers walked to the creek, Kosta carried the blanket and Lord Thomas the small basket of snacks and a jar of water. They fished until noon, the distance between the boys somewhat narrowed, they were blood brothers for a moment.

David and Liana strolled down the bank of the creek, looking for their sons. It must have been half an hour still no sign of either one.

"We must have gone too far, but how could we have missed them, if they sat on this side of the creek?" David wondered.

Suddenly, just ahead, they saw their sons in a skirmish, but what they saw was disturbing. David sprinted toward them, Lord Thomas' back to him not aware his father was upon him. David grabbed Thomas by the collar from behind and jerked him away from Kosta. Losing balance he fell backwards, shocked, to see father standing over him, glaring.

"What is going on here?" David shouted. Liana ran up to Kosta as he was coughing and gasping for breath sitting on the grass.

"What happened? Kosta why was he strangling you, what is going on between you two?" Liana questioned, shaken.

"Ah...nothing...really...it was nothing. I do not know...ah...I am fine, Mother," Kosta stuttered.

David proffered his hand to Thomas to help him up, and noticed his top left hand red and swollen. *Why?* However, for the moment he said nothing, as if not noticing.

"Now gather up, march on home, I want to know what the problem is with you two. Thomas you are much older, you should be wiser, seems you have some growing up to do," David said. Lord Thomas lagged behind them with his hands in his pockets.

His heart pounded, visualizing a beating with the switch...*no he will not do that, I am too old for beating. Work, he will put me to work, all of the work*, he was thinking.

At home, chore time, and yes Lord Thomas was to do it all. Kosta offered to help. David said, *no*. Family discussion during dinner was all about planting, rotation of seeds, oil and profits, which was not what the boys expected. After dinner, the boys cleared the dishes and washed them placing everything into their usual places. David sat and selected a few sketches for his carvings, set them aside and then went to bed. The atmosphere in the house hung heavy, the usual chatter was missing, not only his parents but Kosta's too.

Lord Thomas lay awake, thinking, *Father omitted the scuffle incident during discussion on purpose. Does he know, but how would he know, Father talked about the fields, crops, and that we should build a storage room, out of stone. In addition, father saving money to add stalls for additional horses. Work, more work. Stone...where in the world did Father get that idea! Stone, from where... the creek, oh, it will take a ton of stone, I do not like that at all."*

Kosta also wondered, *Father omitted the incident, I guess he had a reason, but I cannot tell Father what Thomas had done. If I do, Thomas will do something terrible to me, he promised me that I will not see the light of day, and I believe him. I must ask Mother what it means, "light of day."* Kosta fell asleep.

Within the weeks of working away and at home, David had not found one stone at the chicken coop, not one. David was disappointed and angry. Had he not distinctly said to the boys, *start collecting large rocks*? They had time. He needed this done before the foxes carry off all the chickens. The foundation and the whole structure must be finished before winter.

"Liana where are the boys?" David asked, wiping the sweat off his face.

"They are fishing again. I told them to collect the rocks. Thomas said he will, when you are home with them," Liana said.

"What...why those wise imps, this time they will not get away with it, they are trying my patience!" David shouted angrily.

"David dear, do not upset yourself so much, they love to fish, and it is summer, they should be home any minute," Liana softly spoke, wrapping her arms around his neck.

David walked out, scanning the area for the boys. He went behind the house to the chicken coop and came face to face with a fox, a chicken in its mouth. Once it saw David, it ran off. David was furious, he ran into the house.

"Liana, Liana a fox just ran off with a chicken!" David shouted.

"Well David, go and find Arkushin and his son to help us, I am going out myself right now," Liana said nodding her head.

David did just that, after a while returned with five men, not wasting any time they went up the hill and down to the creek to begin the tedious work loading the stones into wagons. They chopped down straight saplings for markers. The time it took for them to measure off so many feet in each direction, each man hammered in the saplings waist high.

The boys came into the kitchen barely able to carry large fish, enough for everyone's supper.

"Thomas, Kosta, Father wants to see you both right away by the chicken coop," Liana said.

"Mother we are tired, this fish is heavy, and I dragged it all the way home! Mother I am so thirsty," exclaimed Kosta and collapsed into the chair. Lord Thomas walked out quickly to see his father.

Liana took a second look at her son, his face, neck, arms and legs, red, too much sun. "*They must have sat all day under the sun; he is sunburned, and feverish.*"

Liana handed him a large cup of water. Kosta drank it all at once, and put his head down on the table. Liana nudged Kosta gently, no response, she shook him, no response, Liana panicked, ran out to David. He dropped whatever was in his hand and ran into the house. Lord Thomas and the men trailed behind them. Kosta was asleep at the table. David lifted him and gently laid him on the bed.

"Liana bring a wet cloth for him, he is burning up, sun fever. I will go to Reiza, she will know what to do for sunstroke," David said.

After a while, David came home with Reiza with Arkushin trailing behind. Arkushin glanced at Lord Thomas.

"Hey Thom how is your hand? Brodin said you got it bad, you know the ants. Konrad said he will never do that again." Arkushin laughed. What David heard confirmed his suspicion, but he did not flinch. David sat on Kosta's bed thinking, *Let him sweat, in time he will come clean, I will deal with him then.*

"Ah yes, oh it is fine, that was my fault I did not see the ant hill and sat right on it," Lord Thomas replied quickly but in a lowered tone. Arkushin caught on, and dropped the subject, nodding to the boy to come outside. Out of earshot of the others, Lord Thomas's face turned crimson as he said,

"I wish you had not mentioned that in front of my father...I do not think he knows, please do not tell him...please. Besides we were just having fun, no harm done to anyone." One thing Arkushin had not known that it was David on the road that day.

Kosta suffered a mild sunstroke, but pulled through. From then on, he wasn't allowed to fish with his brother, and had to stay close to his parents, learning to build a new style of chicken coop and the stable foundation.

The new stone structure encompassed the original chicken coop. To collect the stones at the bottom of the mountain they used horse and wagon to load and unload at the site. It took weeks, digging deep to set the pilings in first followed by the stones for the wall, the mixing of mud and straw was difficult. The men worked early in the morning setting several layers of straw and rock to dry during the day, then tending to their own daily chores. They built a wall higher than their chest.

With oak limbs as thick as men's arms set in between the rocks, close together, the foxes could not penetrate. The pitched roof of oak timbers topped with thatch to prevent any animal jumping inside. The door to the chicken coop was made of wood and strips of steel with two latches on the outside for safety. Nesting boxes stood on stilts and small ladders for the chickens to climb. When it was finished, the men gaped, amazed what a modern and safe structure stood before them. Now they began to talk all at once each wanting the same structure for their animals. David told them while working in a large settlement all the buildings even homes had such foundations. The roofs covered with what looked like flat squares of thin stones. What materials were used he did not know, but it is less dangerous in case of fire than straw thatch. If they want to see for themselves, they are welcome to come along on his next trip. It is time for all of them to modernize not only their community, but for safety as well. At the council meeting, David described to the villagers the things he had seen in other parts of the country.

"You all must see the new chicken coop at David's home," Arkushin said.

After the meeting, they all came admiring a stone, mud and straw structure.

Later David recalled that Thomas, out of shame had worked right along with us. Not once complained about how exhausting it was. I observed, forced effort, not one ounce of gusto as seen in the other men.

At the end of the day after the meeting and dinner, Lord Thomas retired to bed, exhausted.

At dusk the thirteen ravens perched silently on trees across the creek, no one noticed.

Liana noticed her first-born son's mood swings, but did not reprove or question his behavior. Just let it be. After all, he was a teenager. He needed space, time to grow up. When Lord Thomas's mood changed, he disregarded his younger brother completely. On observing her younger son, his moods were steady. He cared much for all that encircled him. Kosta learned from his neighbors, from observation and his parents.

Lord Thomas learned the way of life from strangers, who led him to believe that priority in life was to care for only himself. They stressed this strongly to him and he absorbed it all like a sponge, believing them, his friends, and strangers. Time slipped by.

David had the hardwood floors and a room added on, which made their home larger, but its gloominess and stuffiness had not changed Lord Thomas' feelings. His friends (at least most of them) lived in larger homes, with large windows, which made the homes bright and cheery, and were nicely furnished. There were times he felt that if he was able to leave and never come back home, he would. However, circumstances did not allow him such freedom. Spring and summer, he loved the most; however, he disliked the dreary fall. Still he ventured out to visit his pals.

Unfortunately, summer was ending, and because of the construction of the stable, he was unable to venture off to his friends frequently. It irked him, as he had a score to settle with one of them. He has not forgotten. Autumn colors were noticeable a bit more each day in the trees, in the fields, the green grasses ever changing yellow to ochre and browns, and at dawn the frost in the crispy air touched noses. Harvest time again, it seems never ending work, men gathered, but the trashing of the grain was left up to the women and girls. However, young men were in charge of storing it in bins, barrels and sacks, before winter.

Lord Thomas felt down deep in his heart that he had no excuses reasonable enough not to help his parents. Else, he could not look into their tired eyes from shame. Though he detested hard work, still he had some feelings of responsibility to them; after all, he is their son and still living under their roof and shared meals with them ninety-nine percent of the time.

Kosta's muscles were developing as he, too, helped with the workload. They worked from sunrise to sundown and left nothing undone.

As weeks passed, David stayed home for some reason. Winter was almost knocking at their door, but that could not be a reason to be this somber and quiet. The usual discussion on future or current problems were omitted. Lord Thomas dared not ask why. One thing he had courage to ask: could he go visit his friends. Of course, Father had no objections. After several years, the horse he begged for came right on his birthday, the best present ever. Many times while riding his horse he thought, *sometimes it is good to humble ones pride a bit; to get what one wants,* and he laughed. Lord Thomas felt awkward now, as if his father cared less about his friends or his whereabouts.

Many, many nights the boys heard their parents whisper, but unable to discern what they whispered about, ears strained and concentration intense, they fell asleep.

Most nights when Lord Thomas heard whispers, he assumed their main topic must be about him, which brought out an uneasy feeling of guilt. He wondered if they were criticizing him, or were they praising his brother. It bothered him so much that some nights he tossed and turned until dawn without once falling asleep. His head on his arm, he strained to listen as his parents whispered. His brother fell asleep after a while and his labored breathing and snoring prevented Lord Thomas from hearing, which irritated him. Obsessed, uncertain, his suspicious mind gnawed at him. He imagined all sorts of ways to discover what it was all about. At one point he considered crawling under their bed, but changed his mind, not only of being discovered, besides the floor is hard and cold. Moreover, he would be mortified if they caught him eavesdropping that way, an idea not practical and shameful. Besides such behavior would mar his character image.

During such days, returning home from visiting with friends, he took a nap.

With the light of dawn, David and Liana got up and dressed. Kosta woke few minutes later and went along to begin morning routine in the barn. Lord Thomas still slept. Liana prepared breakfast.

Lord Thomas slept soundly until the aroma of bacon permeated throughout the house and tickled his nose. Drained by sleepless nights, many mornings he slept in longer to recharge. Fully awake, he dressed hurriedly, noticing his mother alone in the kitchen. He figured Kosta and his father were in the barn already. Greeting a "Good morning mother!" he hurriedly walked out to help with the chores in the barn. David and Kosta were just closing the barn door; the chores were all finished. The three of them walked back through the back door just in time for breakfast. They removed their boots and set them outside on the mat, the slipped into warm woolen slippers. It was cold out. Liana had set the small pot of tea and coffee carafe and cups on the table, Lord Thomas and Kosta gave a hand with the rest of the food. They ate breakfast in silence. Their eyes were on breakfast but their facial expression somber. The hot coffee tasted good; now and then, a slurp echoed, and David or Liana coughed. Kosta glanced at them. He too slurped the hot tea, which burned his lips a bit. David looked at Kosta and smiled, Kosta gave a side-glance at Lord Thomas. His eyes were on the swirling tea as he stirred it and seemed to be in deep thought. Though he was aware of what went on at the table, did not speak; sensing something was wrong but had not the nerve to ask. He thought, *what happened here, why this gloom all of a sudden? Is it sudden...or had I not noticed it before. Will this gloom hang here all winter long? I shall go stark crazy!*

Kosta enjoyed watching the sunrise no matter what season. Dressed accordingly and ready to go with his father outdoors to observe the changes, clouds fascinated him, dark grey or greenish, blue, or pure white, billowing ever changing shapes, here darker, there yellowish then pinkish, the clouds kept moving up, way up and away, no bird could ever dare to fly that high. He stared at the sky of early dawn in amazement, pondering, his world was so mysterious. On mornings when the temperature dropped low and the air, calm, the haunting, fascinating mist stood still. Other times it drifted ever so slowly twisted into strange forms then dissipated. The whole world intrigued him. The world around him was awesome, a painting. Father and son talked of this enchanting overcomplicated mystery.

Not far in the dense pines perched the thirteen ravens, watching.

On Sundays after lunch, Liana and Aunt Olivia reminisced of their families and friends, but not many still kept in contact. They were the last two remaining in the family, although it was not a large family. All others over time had passed on. The boys from day one and into their teens knew Aunt Olivia and considered her a kind and loving person. Being an unmarried woman, she always referred to them as "her children."

Liana and Aunt Olivia were quite close. Liana discussed openly of all her private feelings, fears, especially dreams, this special bond, feelings of closeness, expression of thoughts, cherished moments of importance captured and understood. Though Aunt Olivia was older, Liana trusted and respected her opinion. They talked about her son's differences in characters, and her life with David.

Aunt Olivia did not bring up the dream. She waited.

"I still feel that dreadful fear, as if it was yesterday. I fear it becoming a reality," Liana said not waiting to talk about it.

"Years ago I promised to keep it a secret throughout our lifetime," Aunt Olivia said. "Yes, I made you promise not to tell David about that nightmare, please keep this promise." Liana smiled. Aunt Olivia concerned tried to comfort Liana by minimizing the enormity of this dream and its meaning, which had such an effect on her niece.

"Liana, forgive me for being frank, perhaps you dwell on dreams too much. Do not fear dreams. Some are meaningless and never come true, with daily responsibilities on one's mind they fade from memory. Of course, after years some may come true." She raised her hand to stop Liana from interrupting, "I know... yes, you have those odd feelings. In addition to dreams, you fear gypsies. Do not let this one or any other dream control your life, my dear girl." Aunt Olivia tried to ease Liana's fears. Liana promised not to dwell on that horrible dream, but keep busy with chores instead, concentrate on the present day just as Aunt Olivia had suggested. As years passed undisturbed, but for natures grimaces. Aunt Olivia kept her promise.

David stayed at home more frequently, which puzzled Lord Thomas.

Aunt Olivia regretted not telling David of Liana's dream. She should have told him after Liana confided in her. She should have broken that promise. He should have never let on that he knew. If he had remembered, they could have lived. As it was eons ago, *one cannot escape one's destiny.* Fate, predestined Fate led their lives.

As it is... *Fate measures the weight of burden for each individual, knowing his or her strength of endurance.* However, as they say also...that, *we choose our destiny.* A wish for our one lifetime is to have an uncomplicated, happy life from day one to the final day, and want for naught. Why then lives are so complicated, we stagger, fall, must rise again to keep on, why such burdens, grief, despair, loss, and struggles. Living each day as it comes, never knowing our final day weather it is peaceful or tragic; we shall never know.

Nine: Rapid River

At the time when Lord Thomas was about nineteen and Kosta only thirteen, the boys faced and endured a tragic loss, which drastically changed their lives. This loss held their path of life as one for a very short time. Destiny, after time, led each in a different direction, for the road of life is long but without clues to where it leads. Whichever road these two brothers were on, or wherever life's road leads, for them and everyone the future is unknown but written in the book of life, and, precisely lived.

This year, the beauty of autumn's rich palette of color never came. This year was different. Autumn charged in with freezing rain. Miserable gloomy days became short, and the nights were long. Day after day clouds hung low, pouring down cold rain. As the temperatures plunged, rain changed into light granulated snow. It swirled, danced in the wind across the countryside through the woods and through the village streets. Children, having to stay indoors, looked out the windows, mesmerized by the show of the snow until dark of evening. During the windless night, granules changed into large, heavy, wet flakes; it fell for many days and nights. Time dragged. Temperatures dropped. The sudden wind whined and whistled day and night. Drifts rose high all across the valley. In such weather, villagers stayed in the warmth and safety of their homes. The icy paths from home to barn crunched under boots, soon covered up by fresh falling snow. Temperatures held well below freezing and high snowdrifts covered the entire countryside.

The boys were aware of their mother's illness. It became apparent right after harvest, but lately had a persistent hold on her.

Kosta worried about his mother and expressed his concern to his brother Thomas.

"Sounds like bronchitis since the beginning of fall, and now winter has a grip on the world around us, making Mother's condition worse, she needs to stay in," Thomas said.

Kosta approached his father with a worried look on his youthful face, asking, "Father we should go for a doctor, Mother needs help." David wrapped his arm around his shoulder and said, "I will go for help, when the blizzard passes somewhat."

Liana slowly shuffled about, coughing violently. Over the years, she had had many bouts with bronchitis. Dry summers gave her a bit of relief. However, depending on the winter's severity, she suffered, her lungs weakened considerably. Now the unrelenting cough tore her lungs, not allowing her any rest despite being propped up on pillows in bed. David feared her condition could turn into pneumonia.

All her young life she worked hard, and frequent bouts of illness had weakened her immune system. Her system's low resistance exposed her to all sorts of ailments. This year's winter contributed a great deal of misery. None of the herbal concoctions suppressed the rasping in her chest for long, when the herbs wore off the coughing returned. David was beside himself. The snow fell wet and heavy. He tended to all her needs non-stop. He sat on the bed and held her in his arms while she shivered from fever. This went on for days and nights without relief. Restlessness and helplessness overtook him. A strong feeling of urgency prodded him to act now.

It happened mid-winter late one night. The high fever ravaged within her, consuming her. She was delirious, murmuring only few words at a time in broken sentences.

Sleep, she needed sleep. But her sleep interrupted by constant coughing and hacking. David knew she needed help now, he felt an extreme urgency. *NOW*. But it was very late at night. Her fever was high, face flushed, hands hot and her eyes glassy. Her rasping voice was weak, breathing shallow. She was barely able to force her voice out from her congested lungs, asking for David.

"David...where...are you...David, David!"

David took her hand in his and reassured her, "I am here beside you my love. I will get help as soon as the blizzard eases a bit, hang on, I will get you some tea." He kissed her hand.

"The boys...where are...my boys?" she whispered.

Then she turned her head and lie still. Suddenly she would say something about a dream... "Oh my baby, our little girl..." she was saying, "David... she...was...so...cold, so... cold...why...she had to...why...did she die...my...baby girl...David." She laid still. The cold compresses on her forehead had little effect on the high fever.

David, in a panic, feared for her life. She needed a doctor; the only doctor in the area lived across the river. To ride out this late wake the doctor and have him brought to the house would take several hours. The reality...in this deep snow it would be slow going. He had a sickening feeling that if he waits, by morning she would surely expire.

Lord I cannot lose her; how could I live without her; although the years I was away we never drifted apart. Our strong love melded us into one being; we cannot be apart now; she cannot die, not now... I need her; the boys are almost grown; soon they will be on their own, live their own lives. I need her to be with me to grow old together. I love her more than life itself." He prayed. David listened to her broken sentences. *Dream, what dream? What baby girl...we...she could not have been pregnant...was she? Did she lose a baby...a girl...she wanted a girl, a daughter...oh God! She never told me...she suffered so! Oh Liana...you carried such pain and loss all these years...you did not share with me...I would have helped you ease the pain...he tried to understand what she had said. It is not important now. I cannot... I cannot imagine when she was pregnant.* He tried to recall, think..., *was it summer or spring, perhaps winter?* For the life of him, he could not remember when. *She never had any signs of the condition, did she strain herself. Perhaps it happened when I was away. I will ask her later when she recovers. No need to dwell on this now, she is in dire need of help...now*! Tears leaked down his face. He was not ashamed of his tears, not at this moment, tears for his beloved Liana.

Lord Thomas watched his father sitting at her bedside weeping. His heart cringed. Strange feelings tugged at his heart. This ill woman was his mother; he began to realize how little he knew her. He knew down deep in his heart she lived her life caring for him, never complaining, never cross with him. How selfish he has been all these years. Always thinking of himself, years passed, he stayed away. yet she never reprimanded his behavior. At this moment, he knew this sick woman pale and thin woman on the threshold of death was his mother, and he had broken her heart.

Yes. She is his mother. She is gravely ill. Now he is soberly aware that he is losing her. She might die tonight. Yet, his feelings are chilled and his mouth is clamped shut. Unable to tell her, he loves her...perhaps he does in his own way. That might or might not be true. Otherwise, he would have been a different son. He should have cared more for her, and he should have been more open with her, told her of the wonderful new things from around the world he has seen while he was absent from home for several days at a time. He withdrew from them. Having had few forced conversations with his father, brother and, his mother. Nevertheless, they accepted him, and loved him without discrimination or regrets. His mother's obvious love was always in her eyes, her display of affection towards him in her actions, but every time she looked at him, he averted his eyes. For all the love she held within her heart; he ignored; now he sees, now he realizes he had caused her pain. Now, of course, is too late. What was lost between them, for that, he felt shame, sorrow and regret. Surely, at this moment, he feels the need of her forgiveness. Only one way to have a clear conscience is to ask her forgiveness and, tell her he loves her, she needed to know now! These might be his last words to her; spill them! Shout it out to her that he loves her and is sorry for his disrespect.

Instead, he sat on his bed; every emotion escaped him, his heart a brick of ice, unmoved. At one moment, he heard a tender voice whisper in his mind a question, *"What happened to you...what happened to your emotions? Are you in darkness...you...a wicked son? Did you sell your soul to the devil?"* Lord Thomas startled feeling oddly, he heard these words clearly, glancing around expecting to see someone but no one was near him. Whoever whispered these words stirred within him uneasiness and quilt.

Liana called for her sons, she needed her sons. She needs help right now. Lord Thomas walked over to David.

"Father I will ride over and bring the doctor," he said in a low quivering voice.

"It is risky. You do not know where the doctor lives," David said. That is the truth; Lord Thomas never took interest about such important things. Kosta's face was streaked with tears. "Father I know where Doctor Triest lives!" he said as he wiped his face with the sleeve.

"No, you are too young," David protested.

"But Father, Thomas and I will ride together, we will be safe," Kosta pleaded.

"I truly feel I should take Mother to the doctor. We will dress her warm, wrap her in a down quilt, lay her on the bearskins and the down quilts and do not forget a few pillows inside the sleigh and ride over to the doctor's home, it would save time and the doctor would not refuse to help her. Then we will spend the night at the doctor's home where he could care and watch over her closely..." David said to his sons.

"Father we all should go...Thomas and I will keep Mother covered," Kosta interrupted.

"If I have to go alone for the doctor he might refuse to come here, due to the late hour and the weather. I cannot risk that, especially if whatever is needed would be there at hand." David ordered them to get things ready, as the snow has stopped falling.

David had to weigh the pros-and-cons to go by sleigh or go alone. He had no reservations taking her, on the contrary he felt positive it is the right thing to do.

"We will dress her warm and cover well, it is not that far, really, but what worries me is not the bitter cold, but the snow, the horses will have a hard time in some areas, the high drifts, you know, that is the problem." The boys listened and it seemed to them quite reasonable, they seemed to agree. Father's decision was final.

David asked Thomas to hitch the team to the sleigh and lead them up front. Kosta brought out the bearskins and spread them on the seat, then laid the goose-down quilts on top for warmth.

Unable to stand, knees buckled from weakness, she sat on the edge of the bed. Lord Thomas, kneeling behind her on the bed, held her shoulders. She trembled. David dressed Liana in a long warm wool skirt, a cotton long sleeve blouse; Kosta wanted to slip on the warm sweater from Aunt Olivia, it was her favorite, she waved it away. Kosta threw it aside on the bed. On her feet, they pulled up the wool leggings and sheep skin boots. David wrapped a quilt around her frail body, lifted her in his arms and carried her out to the sleigh.

She did not ask what they were doing or where he was taking her. Instead, Liana weakly, feverishly, whispered their names. When the cold air hit her, she moaned and her eyes opened wide, with every breath the frigid air ripped her lungs, rasping, suffocating cough at full force cut off her breath, her frail hands grasped the quilt to cover her mouth. She sat propped with pillows on sides and her back, at one moment she laid down her face hid from the wind. David asked her if it was better for her that way. She nodded. Bearskins shielded her well from the freeze and cold. Kosta wept, leaned into the sleigh, lifted the bearskin reached for her hand and kissed it. Tears streamed from his eyes and his voice broken, called to her.

"I love you Mother, I love you! Please get better! Do not leave me...MOTHER!" he wanted her to hear him; he needed her to come back.

Liana's feverish eyes met his, she squeezed his hand and he knew she loved him. She closed her eyes and buried her face in the quilt.

Lord Thomas walked over to the other side of the sleigh leaned down to kiss his mother's hand, but even if he wanted to say what he should out of respect, he could not. He was lost for words. His teeth clenched. His fists shoved deep in pockets.

David was extremely nervous and feverish himself, almost in a state of panic, he did not notice the difference in their son's behavior, as he hugged his boys, he said to them,

"Pray we make it there and back, pray that mother recovers. Remember we love you. Be good to each other, take care of each other, and remember, you are blood brothers forever." The wind moaned across the countryside and whipped at the dark leafless trees.

David jumped up onto the sled and snapped the whip, the horses turned slowly onto the road, bells jingled as they disappeared into the darkness.

The boys stood for a little while watching, listening as their parents rode away.

The wind howled strangely, mournfully. The sleigh tracks swept over by the drifting snow were gone. The night was dark and eerie, and the whole village stood silent, no sign of life or light anywhere. The boys went back into the house. They were alone. The oil lamp turned up, making shadows dance on the walls, and silence prevailed. The room was warm, but for some reason they felt a strange chill. The only thing they heard was the wind outside whistling and whining. They sat on their beds not speaking. Neither knew what the other was thinking. That night, Father's last words spoken to them before he rode away into the darkness with mother, echoed in their ears.

Out in that darkness the village slept. The snow had stopped falling. All around nothing but darkness and endless snow and only two people were out, two desperate people in search of help, heading in a direction where they knew a helping hand waited. David snapped the whip repeatedly above the horses. The bridge was far. Now and then, the moon peeked through the clouds, illuminating the way somewhat. The icy air pierced through David's lungs. David knew the snow was deep. However, he did not anticipate the snow to be *this* deep, and the horses were unable to trot freely. The sleigh sank in the drifts as they struggled to make headway; the horses steaming breath dissipated in the cold air and frost formed around their nostrils.

David should have turned back home. That should have been the right decision. Bitter cold and wind whipped at his face. In desperation, he lost his sense of reality and rationality. Disregarding danger to her or himself, he focused on the distance to the doctor's home. He wanted her to live, her life was on his mind, not danger of freezing in the middle of the road, and no one was out to hear them, or help them.

The doctor resided on the other side of the river. That meant the long stretch of road led away from the river, then curved to the bridge and over to the other side of the village; precious time would be lost going the long way. The village road any other time would be compacted by use, during the day, now, over the new snow the sled could not glide. Unfortunately, David did not consider this fact. He impulsively headed directly to the Rapid River where the old willows stood dark against the white snow on the opposite bank, which shortens the distance by at least an hour. Cross the open field where it meets the sharp turn and just pass a few houses to the doctor's residence. David had shortened distance and time.

He knew where to turn onto the narrow lane between homes, which, then opened to an open field. The horses strained, the snow was deep but the frozen river just a short distance away. They were almost there. David cracked the whip it echoed in the quiet night.

They reached the river and the sled slid over the drifts and onto the snow covered frozen Rapid River. The horses stepped cautiously on this hard and crusty surface. The light of the full moon peeked through the clouds just for a moment, and the wind had calmed, for which David was thankful. As the sled neared the center of the river the clouds parted, like heavy drapes, and the bright light of the moon shone on the ice it glistened. A sudden loud crack and a snap echoed across the frozen countryside and beyond. Suddenly the horses reared up in fear, feeling ice-giving way. David tugged the reins to the left, away from the sudden imminent danger of which he had never imagined could face them.

The center of the river had but a thin layer of ice, which for an unknown reason, never solidified completely. Who knew? Only from a bird's eye view, one could see for what it was, but not from its bank or the bridge.

The ice gave way; four terror-stricken horses thrashed the icy water. Screams echoed in the night. The sled teetered precariously against the edge of the thick ice, but the fast-moving water tugged. David knew they had no chance, they were about to sink.

"Liana, Liana! Oh my God, this is not real!" David reached out for Liana in those few seconds, leaned over and grabbed her hand and pulled her quickly out and managed to jump onto the edge of the ice, as he fell, Liana fell into the icy water. David still held on to her. "David!" Liana screamed.

The weight of the horses and the sled sank quickly and so did the pillows and bearskins under the ice. Liana tangled in a quilt hooked onto the sharp ice, and bobbed. David sprawled on his cape on the ice held her left hand. With his free hand tried to reach her right arm, now limp in the icy water. The fast flowing water tugged at her body; that river wanted to swallow her. The quilt was slipping from around her body, any second she too would disappear beneath the layer of ice. David desperately struggled to pull her out. Half of her was out of the water, if only he could hold on and save her. However, the rushing river was no match for David. He tried, deliriously tried. He gripped the ice with his left hand for support to pull her out, but David's fingers were numb. She was slipping away from him...Liana's half-frozen upper body was pinned against the ice. The water tugged at her, but David held on to her. She felt nothing; heard nothing; her eyes wide open stared into his. All around her was silence, pulled by the frigid current to struggle and hold on was futile... Liana with her last breath screamed David's name. David never heard. He concentrated on saving her. Her frozen fingers wrapped about his, but could no longer hold. David grabbed her wrist with his other hand. He could not let her go alone, and, that split second, hand in hand, slipped off the ice and together went under. David's cape lay frozen to the ice.

The Rapid River had won.

Horses and sled were on the bottom of the Rapid River. David and Liana together flowed with the swift, icy, dark and deep water somewhere far to an unknown place of rest.

The waters, disturbed by the weight of the sled and horses, splashed over the surface then quickly leveled off... as if nothing had ever happened. Silent was the night. Only the broken ice could tell the story. The Rapid River swallowed two innocent souls forever into its icy grave.

When the clouds parted, moonbeams shimmered and danced on the ripples of the gaping hole. The Rapid River flowed on and on, it had a destination and was in a hurry.

David and Liana began their life dancing together. With their two sons together, they faced and overcame life's hardships. That winter night they died, together.

It is normal for anyone to plan and hope to grow old together. Enjoy life unfolding for their sons. Someday watch grandchildren at play laughing in the sunshine, run through the fields of golden wheat, or play in the snow. Together they were now, without a second chance to happiness and a long life. Their spirits are now together somewhere in the space of time and eternal peace.

Liana's secret dream, which David never knew of, died with her.

At home, their two sons waited.

They sat on the beds not speaking, waiting, anticipating, should their parents return late to be ready for them. Waiting to hear the familiar jingle of the bells, but all around was silence, only the wind moaned and whistled through the cracks in the windows frosted over obscuring the dark world.

Long into the night they waited, the fire died out in the hearth. The glow of the flame shrank. The oil lamp burned down low; soon it will draw at the last drops of oil and extinguish itself. Kosta sat on the bed and stared at the lamp. He was too tired and too cold to refill it, but he will in the morning. The cold crept into the house made him shiver, his knees and fingertips were numb. Kosta slipped under the covers with his clothes on, wrapped himself up to his chin and covered his ears. He muttered to himself; *I will not fall asleep...I will wait for them...I must...the wind is whistling so. God...please keep them safe, bring them back...I need my mother and father...please.* Kosta closed his eyes and listened to the moan of the wind.

Lord Thomas also waited, staring at the oil lamp, but made no effort to refill it either. His thoughts were similar, *No sense refilling it now, it is late, and no sense waiting all night. Father said he would return in the morning. Mother will not die. She has had such episodes before and she pulled through. Anyway, the doctor will help her, having all sorts of medications, and if they do not return... Kosta and I will go to the doctor's home. Might as well get under the covers too, it is too cold.* He threw back the covers and slipped under the quilt. He soon felt warm and relaxed. The two brothers slept without dreams. These two brothers will never understand the horror of death lasting but a moment, a moment such as that, their parents never deserved, for they lived for love, and they were *pure* love; that night; for love, they died together.

The village slept. Only the wind softly whistled and moaned now and then. The river flowed on and on silently. No one should have been out there, not in that weather or at that hour.

That night, Findan, a bachelor, rode home on his horse from card games. Approaching the bend to the open prairie, he thought he heard screams, though his fur hat pulled over his ears, nose covered with a wool shawl was not mistaken, for it was not the wind but screams coming from the river. He pulled off his hat and listened, screams...the river! He turned and galloped across the field to the river. The man reined up at the willows. He scanned the whole area as far as he could see in the darkness and saw nothing. But when the moon peeked through the clouds, he noticed a dark patch in the center of the river, a reflection of moonlight glistened where the ice broke. He could not see more than that. He galloped back to the nearest house banged on the door to alert someone, anyone. A couple of men opened the door. The man said he heard screams and saw a black patch on the ice.

"Anyone out tonight in the middle of that Rapid River had no chance, no chance at all," said the senior man sadly.

"Besides, by the time we get dressed and run out... whoever was out there crossing must have gone under, it is too late my friend, may they rest in peace, poor souls," said the younger man. While they were talking the rest of the family awakened hearing voices stood by listened. "It is too late," repeated the family.

The witness Findan was invited to sleep over since it was bitter cold, and he accepted, quickly boarding the horse in the stable. In the morning, the two men went to the river's edge; from the distance, they saw something dark on the ice, but nothing else.

Villagers gathered in silence, prayed for the soul, or souls, who had perished beneath the dark waters. They asked Findan if he had seen how many were there, he said, "No, it was too quick, then silence." Very unnerving and eerie. They stood on the snow bank, eyes riveted on the grey area like a giant mouth, gaping, waiting for more victims to swallow.

"Am I seeing things or is that grey area not frozen solid yet?" a woman asked.

"Very possible, winters are unpredictable, that is why one should not risk crossing it," an old man said. Their eyes riveted on something black on the ice, but none dared to go out there to retrieve it. They felt sorry for the horses when that man told them he heard their terrifying shricks, how it echoed. No one could helped them, no one! What a waste of life, very tragic.

"You saw horses? How many horses were there?" a young man asked.

"Well I do not know how many, it was too quick, I know I heard their screams," Finden said somewhat embarrassed.

Ten: The Search

The following morning, without speaking to each other, the brothers still waited.

The boys assumed that their parents had stayed overnight at the Doctor Triest's home. Negative thoughts never crossed their minds that something tragic had occurred.

Lord Thomas dressed quickly, donning a wool sweater. He lit the turf, and when its glow burned hot, sat the kettle on for tea, and then sat down at the table. Kosta had his coat on and walked outside, the rising sun through the broken slow-moving clouds shone brightly; it appeared the day would be fair. The drifts created a strange scene, a white sea of snow, high waves of foam crashed into the air and suspended, now smooth resting frozen against homes and trees. The earth slept beneath winter's blanket of snow. Nothing was out there for him to see, no birds, no foxes, no wildlife at all, only stillness. He stood and eyed the world around him. His empty stomach growled. The cold forced him back into the house. Lord Thomas sat at the table sipping tea. Kosta poured a cup for himself and dropped onto the chair. The room felt much warmer. Kosta gulped the tea quickly, sat the cup on the table and walked over to the stove to prepare breakfast for the two of them, bacon and eggs and day-old bread. The aroma of bacon made their mouths salivate.

Kosta was an all-around handy boy, eagerly learned from his parents. His favorite meal was breakfast. There were many mornings years ago, while Lord Thomas slipped out of the house, whenever father was out on a job, Kosta prepared breakfast for Mother and himself. Rarely did Lord Thomas stay to share breakfast and bond as a family.

This morning Lord Thomas noticed how efficiently and skillfully his little brother prepared their meal. Neither of them had anything to say. The brothers waited as hour after hour passed, but still there was no sign of their parents. They had a strange, odd and foreboding feeling, exchanged glances, their expressions displayed concern.

Lord Thomas stepped outdoors, ignoring the cries of the hungry animals and cows ready for milking.

Kosta stuffed food quickly into his mouth and drank tea in gulps. He jumped away from the table and ran to the barn. The chores awaited and he was not going to sit around and listen to the animal's bellows.

Time kept on passing.

Lord Thomas cleared off the table and washed the dishes, at least he could do that. Barn chores were not for him. By the time he forced himself to go help, Kosta rushed around the barn perspiring, throwing feed here and there trying to satisfy the demands of the hungry animals. Lord Thomas stood in the doorway and watched. Kosta had it all under control. He dared not ask how he managed to clean up so fast. Kosta sat down on the three-legged stool to milk the cow. Lord Thomas walked up and asked, "You must have a system at this, and did Father teach you?" Kosta startled upon hearing his brother's voice, almost spilling the milk out of the bucket. Luckily he grabbed it in a split second before he could grasp what was said. He opened his mouth to reply but Lord Thomas walked through the doorway back to the house not looking back.

Kosta, now near total exhaustion, continued to milk the cow, when suddenly he heard his name called. He glanced over his shoulder, expecting to see his brother, but no one was there.

He set the bucket aside, dashed to the barn door, swung it open hoping to see his mother, but no one was there. Kosta backed into the barn and sat on the stool to finish milking. It seemed minutes later when he heard the voice again, and this time he was sure it was his father's. His heart palpitating, he froze, but turned his head slowly over his shoulder.

He saw them. They stood in the doorway, together. They were real and they were smiling. They were back! He saw them! Kosta slowly rose from the stool and was about to run to them, but they vanished. Dumbfounded he stood staring at the barn door. Out of the barn and into the house he ran screaming, wide-eyed, and breathless. The bucket was half full with milk, which he roughly dropped to the floor, spilling some, pale and trembling. Lord Thomas, startled, jumped at the sudden noise. Seeing Kosta in such a state, he ran up, grabbed his shoulders, and shook him, shouting, "Kosta what is wrong with you, what happened? What are you screaming about?"

"I saw them! Are they home? Where are they? I saw them! Did you see them?" Kosta pulled away rambling on, running into the bedroom looking for his parents.

"Who, what are you talking about? Who are THEY?" Lord Thomas blocked Kosta's way, grabbed his shoulders again shook him.

"Kosta stop, slow down, what are you babbling about?" Kosta blinked and snapped back to reality. He glanced about. They stood alone. No one else was there, only the two of them. Lord Thomas walked him to the table. Kosta slumped into the chair and began to sob and tremble.

"Something happened to them... I saw them... they were in the barn... something is wrong! Oh my God, something is wrong...! Something happened!" Kosta blubbered.

Lord Thomas listened and chills ran down his spine. *Perhaps they did appear to him,* he thought, *perhaps something did happen...they should have been back hours ago. I need to saddle up and go to the doctor's house and find our parents.* He immediately went into action on this instinct.

Lord Thomas always laughed at his friends when they talked about ghosts. He never believed in ghosts, period. However, as he saddled up his horse, something strange took hold of him. This was different, he felt a presence beside him, a slight touch on the shoulder. Though he refused to admit it, he felt it, this was real. Hackles rose on his neck, but to shrug off these feelings he could not.

The thought of losing his parents disturbed him. He had wronged his parents and the guilt tugged at his conscience. He knew he had failed to ask his mother for forgiveness when they were leaving. *But Kosta said he saw both parents in the barn, he must have been hallucinating, he is so worried about them... but... how could this be possible? That cannot be, not both... not now! Unbelievable,* he thought and for a split second, his knees buckled, at that moment he took control of himself. A strong feeling urged him to hurry. *What if they are not at the doctor's home, then something did happen, where are they? What could I possibly say to Kosta if...?* Thoughts whirled, he felt shaky, his stomach ready to empty what little food he had eaten which was nothing. He had to search for them right this minute.

In the house, thirteen-year-old Kosta sat at the table sobbing.

The horse saddled, Lord Thomas went into the house and said to Kosta, "Stay home and wait for me, I will go find the doctor's house and find out what happened. You stay here. Are you positive they appeared to you in the barn?"

"Yes! Yes!" Kosta shouted.

He dismounted at a house along the main street, ran up to the door and knocked. A woman peered through the crack of the door.

"I need directions to the doctor's house, please I am..."

"Yes, just down the road on the left, the sign... look for the sign!" she said and closed the door. Riding up he saw the sign and Doctor Triest's house. He glanced around the yard but didn't see a sled anywhere. Last night was bitter cold, the horses must be in the stable. He walked up to the door and knocked. The door opened, the doctor was surprised to see such an early visitor.

"Yes? May I help you?"

"I apologize for calling this early in the morning, but I am looking for my parents."

"And who are your parents? Who are you?" Doctor Triest eyed Lord Thomas.

"Doctor Triest... my name is Thomas Komarod. I am looking for my mother and father, David and Liana Komarod. Late last night they were on the way to you, Mother is ill," Lord Thomas explained.

"Young man, not a soul arrived here last night, and you said...they were coming to me last night in this weather?" Doctor Triest asked, surprised.

"Yes, my parents, the Komarods. Mother has been ill for some time, but during the last several days she became gravely ill, Father was coming to you for help," Lord Thomas explained again.

The doctor said to Lord Thomas that he knew the Komarods. "But I am telling you, no one arrived here last night, they would be here right now. I have known your parents for a long time. From the looks of you, you have grown up a fine-looking man, but over the years I have seen very little of you. And I know your mother was ill for a long time... but... they are not here."

Suddenly Lord Thomas realized what father had done to save time. He had taken a short cut, across the river.

"Doctor... I fear the worst at this moment. Father did not mention anything of taking a short cut across the Rapid River... to save time... Doctor... something must have happened to them, oh my God, where are they! Thank you Doctor Triest," he said and stepped away from the house, quickly leaped into the saddle and rode away. Fear tore at his heart. What happened? Where are they?

The doctor stood in the doorway, watching him ride away. On his face appeared grave concern and fear. He had this dreadful feeling that they went down...down to the bottom... "God have mercy on their souls...oh...the poor boys," the doctor whispered.

On his way back home, Lord Thomas, in panic, began to question everyone he met along the road.

"Were you out last night? Have seen four white horses a man and a woman in a sled?" Everyone replied, "No... we were not out in that bitter cold last night."

Lord Thomas rode on, needing to ask someone, anyone, if had they seen anything. He came to the tee in the road, to the open field, which led to the river, there he saw a group of people huddled close and a man stood on the edge with a horse. Lord Thomas rode up to ask them the same question.

"Yes, I was here last night. I witnessed the unfortunate accident. I heard screams. I... oh it must have been quick... as they plunged into the Rapid River..." the witness replied.

"How far off the shore did you say they were?" Lord Thomas interrupted.

"As I was saying...I was on my way home and I happened to be here just past the field, perhaps four houses down, it was not far, but you could never mistake such screams. Clearly I did see... you see the clouds parted and the moon shone on the water, I saw the broken ice...I did. You look, come and look at the broken ice, it might have frozen overnight a bit," the witness said.

The others stood and glared at the ice. From high on his saddle Lord Thomas could see the broken ice, a thin opaque crust visibly forming at the edges, but the irregular hard edged center gaped dark and forbidding and the cape no longer visible. Lord Thomas sat motionless. Chills shot through him...pain constricted his chest and sorrow screamed in his head. That was just too much. Even though he did not show affection openly as he should have, because of his certain issues, nevertheless he did respect and love them in his own way. Tears burned his eyes. It was hard to suppress them. He turned his head away from the stranger. Speechless, teeth clenched, his jaw hurt. His eyes closed, he fought back waves of emotions, waiting for these waves to subside. The stranger had noticed the pain on this young face but said nothing.

Suddenly Lord Thomas noticed a rider approaching at full gallop. It was his brother Kosta across on the other side of the river. Lord Thomas screamed, "Oh my God it is my brother, I must stop him!"

Findan followed. Lord Thomas galloped past several houses, over the bridge and back toward home. He turned off towards the river to head off Kosta and get there first. However, Kosta reached it minutes before him. He sat on the horse staring at the frozen river.

"What made you come here? I told you to stay home!" Lord Thomas yelled, hands trembling.

"I...had a...a...feeling to come *here*... I had to see...for myself!" Kosta stuttered, out of breath.

Findan realized they were brothers and repeated what he had heard the night before again to Kosta. The shock was just too much for the boy. The emotional fury burst out of control. He jerked the reins, jabbed the horse's belly and galloped along the Rapid River. To Kosta, this was too painful to accept. Turning the horse around and forcing the animal to gallop to the bridge and back along the river's edge, wild with emotion, screaming. "NOT TRUE! NOT TRUE!"

The horse suddenly halted.

Kosta leaned on the horse's neck, his arms wrapped around it tight. He hid his face in the coat sleeve to muffle his screams. Suddenly he sat up, turned the horse toward the river, jabbed horse's belly, and stirred him over the snowdrifts. The horse leaped but suddenly a terrible thing happened: his front legs slid and split, hind legs went under, the horse toppled over on its rump, and Kosta screamed as he was thrown. The horse kicked, slid and tried to rise on the slippery ice, but to no avail. It kept him down, sprawling and sliding. Kosta fell onto the crusty snow. The fall knocked him hard on his back, leaving him gasping, frightened and stunned. He sat on the snow for a several minutes then rose slowly. Cautiously approaching the horse, he patted his neck and took hold of the reins. Lord Thomas ran up to help. The horse attempted to rise. His every muscle twitched, legs slid, unable to secure a foothold. Kosta himself felt unsteady and frightened. The two of them managed to turn the horse a full circle back to the snowdrift. Frozen clumps could give him balance to rise and back onto solid ground. At last, it was over. The horse grunted shook his head, then nudged Kosta's side, as if to say, "Thanks that was a close call; I am fine now. Just do not try it again." The man stared perplexed.

"Did he just try to gallop to the center of the river? That would have been foolish! How stupid! Both would have drowned! Did he want to join his parents?" Finden the witness cried out facing Lord Thomas. An unbelievably tragic scene unfolded before Lord Thomas's eyes as Kosta's tears rolled down his face as he pulled his hair repeatedly with both hands.

Finden the witness continued shouting, visibly distressed. "Thank goodness the horse fell... young fool and his horse would have drowned. I cannot believe what I had just witnessed!"

Lord Thomas grabbed Kosta's sleeve and pulled him away from the horse as he tried to mount it. Being taller by a head, he embraced him and held him tight. Kosta's body went limp as he sobbed uncontrollably and shivered. Lord Thomas said through clamped teeth, "Go home now, I will be home shortly," and swallowed emotions. He helped Kosta mount the horse again. Kosta did not need to reply. He knew he must go home. A slap on the rump and the horse lopped toward home while Kosta leaned forward on his horse's neck. Neither noticed drops of blood from horse's bleeding legs.

This day and this scene would remain in Lord Thomas's mind for years to come. His brother lost control of his raging emotions. A moment of grief, an open wound in his heart; feelings of turmoil; a moment he could not stop Kosta from expressing, at such a time as it was.

Lord Thomas searched both sides of this wide river for any signs of evidence but found only deep ruts in the crusty snow still visible in some places from the sled, nothing else. Findan, the only witness, mounted his horse as well and rode away. He understood the young man needed to be alone. Lord Thomas at his young age unexpectedly faced with this tragic loss, now felt emptiness. It was impossible for him to fathom what their last moments of life were like; truly, such a horrible death they did not deserve.

Lord Thomas heeled the horse and rode away from the Rapid River to the main road. He tried to stay calm, control his rage and sorrow at least for Kosta's sake. When he entered the house, he found his younger brother at the table resting his head on his arms, sobbing. At thirteen Kosta's life crumbled, pain ripped his heart. He loved his parents. Now, they are gone forever!

Lord Thomas sat down at the table unable to speak. Seeing his brother exhausted from emotional upheaval, the house quiet but for Kosta's sobs, he laid his hand on Kosta's arm. Kosta had never heard such tenderness and gentleness in his brother's voice before, or manner of approach; it stopped Kosta from sobbing.

"Kosta... please stop crying, we must not break down. I hurt too. I feel the pain as you do. The loss is ours and ours alone. We must go on and live our own lives from now on. That is what Mother and Father would have wanted us to do. Remember Father's words...think what he always said." Hearing his own words of the reality of loss, emotion gripped his throat. He too was on the verge of losing control but held it all back for Kosta's sake.

"I know what Father used to say to us, 'be strong, embrace and endure the worst times, bravely, love each other, you are blood brothers!' Thomas...why THEM, Thomas, why did they die NOW!" Kosta's voice quivered, he screamed with rage.

Lord Thomas stared at the frost-covered window, trying to answer why. He had no answers, not this day, not this day, or ever. They needed this day to mourn and expel the fury that shook their mind and heart. Neither one could not stand up to embrace or endure this day bravely. Not today, not tomorrow, or the next day, only time will heal the sorrow and slowly diminish the ache, but as of today...deep in their memory...this day will live.

Lord Thomas rose from the chair. As he walked out of the house, he said, "I stopped by at Aunt Olivia's on the way home and told her to come over. she said she will be over this afternoon."

In the barn alone with his feelings, to think of a way to change this meager way of existence, to reach the goal he was aiming for, he glanced around and began pacing. *So much undone, so much to do. How did they do all this work, how will he manage with Kosta. Kosta learned and worked beside them all the time, he knows what to do, but I, I am not like Kosta and never could I be. This way of life, surely I will not live, to spend the rest of my days shoveling manure out of this barn, no, never. That is a promise I had made to myself a long time ago and I must keep it, at any cost*, he thought.

Though he seldom wept in his life, today his tears streamed down his cheeks. They slid into his mouth and he tasted their saltiness. Today he let them flow. He dropped onto an old stump on which his father chopped wood. His head hung low between his shoulders. Elbows on his knees, his head rested on his clenched fists. Knuckles white. He remained in that position waiting until the churning fury, which came in waves crashing and ebbing, subsided. Composed somewhat, he dried his eyes and wiped his face with the sleeves. In his determined strong voice, he promised himself aloud he would never cry again, ever.

To overcome this grief it will take time, especially for young Kosta. He needs moral and spiritual support to adjust. *I know I must help him, but for how long, how long must I be Kosta's big brother, how long? Aunt Olivia will help. She will reason with him, he will mind her*, Lord Thomas thought.

Their parents were gone together forever, an unexpected unthinkable, unfortunate tragedy for the boys to live with. There would be no funeral, no caskets, no remains for viewing for family and friends to pay their last respect. Come every spring, they will throw wreaths into the Rapid River in their memory.

That morning Aunt Olivia had been surprised to see Lord Thomas when he came in; his somber expression told her immediately something happened.

"Thomas...what is it...why...you are here so early...you look as if you have lost your friend..."

"No... Aunt Olivia, not my friend...my parents" Lord Thomas replied and tears welled in his eyes, his vision but a blur.

"Thomas what are you saying, how, when, oh my God!" Aunt Olivia swayed weak in the knees, about to fall. Thomas caught her just in time. She collapsed in his arms. Lord Thomas held her under her arms and slowly walked over to the table and sat her down on the chair. Her face was ashen she was unable to speak. Lord Thomas filled a cup with water from the kettle on the stove and held it up for her to drink. Aunt Olivia, with trembling hands, took the cup and sipped a little. She sat staring into the cup. At this moment, her mind was blank. After a while, she asked looking up at him.

"What happened, tell me now, I want to know, how it happened," Aunt Olivia said.

"As you know Mother has been sick. While this blizzard raged, Father could not go for the doctor, so he waited. Then he decided to ride in the sleigh with Mother over to the doctor's house, ah...it was late... he crossed the river... and the ice broke and... they...went under...and the horses..." Lord Thomas could not look at her, tears streamed down his cheeks.

"Oh my God, oh no... No! No! No!" Aunt Olivia cried aloud in shock, reeling. Lord Thomas stepped over to her chair picked her up and carried her to bed, covered her with a quilt. He found a kitchen dishcloth, dipped it in water, and placed it on her forehead. She remained unmoving or speaking for a long time. Lord Thomas sat and watched her, not knowing what else to do. Then he stood up and walked out of the house, walked over to the neighbor which, was down the road, and asked for their help. The couple came over quickly, questioning him. He told them what had happened to his parents. "She is in shock," the neighbor said.

Aunt Olivia opened her eyes. The neighbors said to Lord Thomas, "We shall gladly stay with Aunt Olivia, if you have to go home." Lord Thomas thanked them, kissed Aunt Olivia's cheek and left.

About suppertime, Aunt Olivia arrived by sleigh. The boys were surprised she came at all. Kosta ran to her screaming.

"Why... Aunt Olivia, why!" She wrapped her arms around him. His head on her chest, he mumbled inaudibly. Aunt Olivia whispered, "Let it go my boy...let the pain go. I will hold you. Cry until you cannot cry anymore." Kosta wept for as long as he had to. Lord Thomas went out to unhitch her horse and led it to the stable. He threw a blanket on its back and returned to the house. She prepared supper and they ate together. She stayed with the boys for several days. Kosta wept and stared out the window, talking to her a bit now and then. The house was silent otherwise. However, just being together offered them a little bit of support, at least spiritually. Her physical presence only filled the empty space. Lord Thomas each day rode over to her home and took care of all she instructed him to do. This is still a long winter. He could not venture out too far for visits with his friends, to tell them of the tragic accident. As time passed, Aunt Olivia was able to think more clearly, working with the boys hand in hand.

She thought about Liana's dream and her promise of years ago. She kept her promise never to tell David. Now, she realized, how terribly wrong it was to keep that secret from David. If she had told him, would he have understood? Would he have remembered that dream at that most crucial moment when faced with imminent life-threatening danger?

At this time of her life, she undertook the responsibility of two fragile lives that needed her love and care. She felt obligated to give them what little attention she could. They were old enough to clean and cook, reap the harvest, care for the entire property; but they were alone; they needed someone to be there at those moments when sorrow ripped at their hearts and about to burst, to spill tears; especially Kosta. She, as their aunt, could never take the place of their parents. She had to stand by them for as long as it takes, to help accept their new way of life. Her own sorrow and loss of years ago, locked deep within her heart, alone. Her care, love of the boys shone through her actions. She knew Kosta needed her much more. As for Lord Thomas, in time he will learn when and how to overcome grief. Lord Thomas suppressed his emotions when they came in waves. His heart grew colder knowing well he must adjust to the loss of his parents. One day he will. He was, he is, and will be, strong. From the first day thereafter, a life of hardship began for these two brothers. Lord Thomas was responsible for the farm. Kosta, in his web of sorrow, refused to help him.

"You go and find out for yourself now!" Kosta snapped back bitterly.

Kosta picked at his food and his sleep was disturbed by horrible dreams, which lingered in daytime. He stood at the frost-covered window scraping at it with a chip of kindling and wept. With swollen eyelids and bloodshot eyes, his vision limited, eyelids mere slits. His head ached and his young heart, broken forever. He felt alone and lost. Aunt Olivia consoled him. It was not the same. She was not his mother or father; she could not ever take THEIR place; she was not THEM; and he wanted THEM; he needed his PARENTS!

"Why! Why did they have to die, why?" Kosta whispered and cried bitter tears. At those moments when Aunt Olivia embraced him, she too wept. Aunt Olivia applied compresses to his head and a warm cloth soaked in tea to his eyes, which relieved the swelling somewhat. At one point, she summoned the doctor for advice, but even the doctor himself could do little for Kosta's depression.

The only consolation was time...time and work would heal. At any age, such a loss was difficult to bear. His mother's sewing basket sat in the corner on the floor, Father's tools and carvings lay on shelves; all reminders of them. Mother's sweater, a gift from Aunt Olivia, which she wore and walked about the house, now was so cold.

Aunt Olivia's presence intensified the reality. Still, she, in her best ability, helped them deal with the future.

Eleven:

Lord Thomas' Recollections

Lord Thomas's heart chilled. Feelings cooled seeing his brother in such mourning. He refused to cry or grieve as his brother, but he should, after all. They were his parents too and died so tragically.

He wept only those few times. He remembered his promise to himself; he would not weep again, ever. He kept that promise. While they were alive, he planned his future. After they were gone he continued with his planning, facing an enormous undertaking. He was determined to be accepted by the elite society of its time. He realized he must throw himself into the world, mingle and learn; see what it takes to be one of them, the high and rich society. He planned ambitiously. His cunning approach and his gift of gab should open doors for him and propel onward with the help of his friends. As for his brother, he worried none. Did he miss his parents? Yes, at times felt somewhat hollow. Did he hate his father for the rash decision that caused their death? Yes he did. Father's mistake of crossing the Rapid River was never mentioned. Besides, who knew the ice was that thin? Why blame him? He was in great hurry and panicked out of sheer distress.

Why, in his recollection of years past he saw himself distant and indifferent. Many nights he watched Father and Kosta carve, which annoyed him. Was he jealous? Yes! He confessed to that. Enraged fury drove him mad. In that state of mind, he ran to calm his nerves. When fury passed, then, he walked home. Since they had perished, he considered how much grief he had caused them over the years. Presently, Thomas could not avoid seeing the sadness in Kosta's eyes. His memory brought back those cruel tricks he played on his little brother. He felt sure they knew it all. Had they forgiven him? Had they? He was inconsiderate then. Anger often became his weakness; it seemed to overtake his thoughts and feelings. He told himself he had to be strong and go on living his own life. As much as he tried to live his life while they lived, ignoring all responsibility to them and his brother, thinking he was wise, well, now he must get his life together. Kosta, with Aunt Olivia's help, will overcome his grief.

Lord Thomas longed for summer. When it comes he will escape, becoming free from the repugnant smells. He wondered, *on that day while fishing, my friend found us, we argued, he slipped about the ambush. I gripped Kosta's throat to force a promise out of him, never to tell father. Suddenly Father, came from behind threw me to the ground hard my back, it ached for days. He reached out to help me rise, I gave him the wrong hand, he saw, but never mentioned it, what was he waiting for, now both are dead, I will never know.*

Time and life will be the best teacher to these two brothers under the watchful eyes of the Thirteen Ravens, concealed among the greenery in the summer, blending with the ever-changing colors of fall. When winter trees stood bare, nevertheless these phantom ravens were watching, resistant to the winter's freeze. These two brothers will not evade their destiny as it is written. Life must be lived accordingly. At the end of each day, we know what was, but who is to know what will be tomorrow or in the future.

Lord Thomas adjusted, somewhat, after a time of frustration with himself. He felt that things were looking up, so he kept reminding himself to plan for a better future. The brothers did not mind Aunt Olivia staying with them from day one. Snowstorms moved in dumping more heavy snow. Kosta was thoughtful at times, his gaze in oblivion; other times he approached Aunt Olivia with questions. Aunt Olivia, perplexed by these sudden questions, explained simply why his parents had to die now.

"Are they in heaven? Can they see me? Where are they? Do they know how much I miss them? Are they happy?" Every few days he asked these same questions, tears flowing. She could only give him simple answers, for she did not know. No one knew. Then one early morning as the three of them breakfasted, Kosta said, "Aunt Olivia I had a dream about Mother

"Tell me of your dream, how did she come to you? Did she speak to you?" she asked, observing his face.

"She was close, as close as you are, right here. She was smiling, her lips moved but I did not hear her voice; it was so real, I woke up crying... Aunt Olivia, I cannot hear my mother's voice, why?" he asked.

Aunt Olivia asked for specific details in his dreams. Kosta described looking up at the ceiling.

"Mother wore her hair atop of her head in that usual bun. Her dress was different, none I have seen before, at least I do not remember it, her face glowed, and she smiled. On her finger, she wore a gold band. I remember that gold band. But I cannot hear her voice."

He repeated to her of the morning in the barn while he was milking the cow. They appeared to him together, he was positive they stood in the doorway, smiling at him.

"I remember that morning, Kosta stormed into the house looking for Mother and Father, he saw them in the barn and thought they had returned," Lord Thomas interjected. Aunt Olivia understood and believed in their spiritual apparition to Kosta, because of his innocence, goodness of heart, like none other.

Their spirits perhaps appeared to him for the last time, before they traveled into eternity, perhaps not. Perhaps that is why he is still dreaming of her, in life he was very close to her. He loved his father too, but his mother was special.

When Kosta poured his heart out to Aunt Olivia, tears flowed, which he could not stop. She comforted him explaining, "She loves you, her love will live in your heart all your life, she is watching over you, be glad she comes in your dreams... I do not dream of her as often, you know I am very tired at the end of the day. I sleep like a rock. Oh, I meant to ask you, do I snore very loud?" Kosta looked at her and a faint smile appeared in the corner of his mouth.

"Yes, sometimes," he said.

"Sometimes my snoring wakes me in the middle of the night. Perhaps that is why I do not dream of anything much, especially of your parents. If I do, I do not remember a thing upon awakening," she said and laughed.

Her remark about her snoring made Kosta smile for the first time in weeks. She was glad of that. With time, Kosta began to be more mindful of things needed done for Aunt Olivia. One morning he slipped out of bed, quickly dressed and came into the kitchen. Aunt Olivia had most of the breakfast ready. He put his arms around her, she embraced him and held him close a moment.

"I will have a cup of coffee and go to the barn to care for my menagerie, then I will have breakfast," Kosta said and was about to leave.

"But Kosta the breakfast is ready, it will be cold by the time you finish in the barn, please eat, I am hungry too. Besides, Thomas is taking care of all the chores this morning." Kosta was surprised but agreed. They sat down and Kosta woofed his breakfast down. He stood up and stepped over to Aunt Olivia and lightly kissed her on the cheek. Then he ran out to the barn to help Thomas with the chores. Aunt Olivia stared after Kosta and thought, *the morning has come he is back to the daily routine, as he had when David and Liana were alive.*

"I will finish, you go have some breakfast and coffee, Aunt Olivia is waiting for you," Kosta said to his brother.

Lord Thomas was just about finished. Relieved, he dropped the pitchfork and stalked past Kosta without a word. He entered the house, disrupting Aunt Olivia's thoughts. She poured a cup of coffee for him and cooked his breakfast. He cleared dishes off the table and placed them in a dishpan.

"Thank you, Aunt Olivia, for a delicious breakfast. I need to rest a bit, if you do not mind."

"Oh goodness, you are very welcome, thank you for your help, yes, do go and rest," Aunt Olivia said.

Kosta from then on took charge of the heavy household chores. Work never belittled him, his unselfish nature was to do things for others. Aunt Olivia had only light tasks. She encouraged Kosta in a roundabout way to carve small objects. Perhaps he would, to give those needy children as presents, a good distraction to his mind.

"Thomas, do you dream of your parents often?" Aunt Olivia asked during dinnertime many evenings.

"No. Once in a while I do dream of my mother, but, when I wake up, I do not remember details at all." His answer was always brief, and evasive of the subject. He paced from window to window, or in his bedroom, where he would secretly lie down on the bed and read a book.

Kosta one evening needed to ask his brother something but halted in the doorway of the bedroom. Thomas was reading a book with his back to the door. Kosta backed away, discovering Thomas' secret. Kosta sat at the table and stared into space. Aunt Olivia noticed something was amiss and asked him in a low voice, "Kosta what is the matter with you?"

Kosta's finger on his lips signaled, to hush. "I will tell you later," he whispered and walked over to the shelf, picked up his carving project and began nervously gouging at it. She observed and thought, *what has agitated Kosta to a point he left the table, why is he so irritable*?

Kosta and Aunt Olivia listened to the wind whistling as it whipped at the windowpane. Kosta thought, *my brother never told Mother or Father that he learned to read. Now Thomas is reading books openly, not then; why not teach me too?* He could not tell Aunt Olivia, the bitter cold prevented Thomas for days, to venture out to visit his friends.

Kosta never questioned Lord Thomas why this big secret reading and hiding the books. On a fairly warmer day, Lord Thomas had decided on visiting his nearest friend. Kosta took the opportunity to mention discovering by accident Thomas reading a book.

"Aunt Olivia, about that night, I was shocked to see him read a book. I was wondering lately and wondering who taught him to read?" Kosta said.

"Someone must have tutored him," she said looking surprised, "but, where and when?"

"It must have been his friends. I wonder who they are," Kosta replied.

"You or your parents have never met any of them or, had they ever been invited, here?" Aunt Olivia asked again.

"No! I never met any of them. He must have been ashamed of this house... now I know! His friends are educated aristocrats! He must have pretended to be rich... how else he got away with it... they would not accept him, otherwise. I hope I am right, or I will eat straw like the cow!" Kosta exclaimed, frowning. Although he was young, he surmised it quite well. Aunt Olivia laughed at that comment, surprised at such words. She had to think of questions and answers quickly.

"Kosta, you mean Thomas not once opened a book in front of your parents?"

"No...not once. I would have been delighted and very interested in learning about the world and all people in it. Father told us so many stories about people and places, and I loved to listen. I visualized myself visiting foreign countries, mingling among foreigners," Kosta said sadly.

"Perhaps whoever was instructing him never allowed the books to leave the premises, did you ever think of that?"

"Why are the books here, now? Why keep it such a secret, why not tell ME, I am his brother!" Kosta's brows pulled together, raised a tight fist hit the table so hard the spoon flipped up and clattered to the floor. Aunt Olivia did not flinch, but reached down for the spoon continuing the conversation.

"Let us assume that Thomas thought you might not be allowed to go with him, but then why not, that is a puzzle you know. You might be right. It is strange for him to act this way, but do not fret about that. You too will learn soon enough; you are far behind learning, you should have been in school. I will help you accomplish that!"

Kosta heard the gate grind, glanced out the window and hastily waved his arm at her.

"Aunt Olivia Thomas is coming!" they ran into the kitchen, on the cutting board, Kosta began to slice freshly baked bread.

"Ah...this delicious aroma makes me salivate. May I have a slice, please, wonderful aroma. I am famished." Lord Thomas asked politely as he entered. Kosta handed a slice to him, his eyes downcast.

"That is a first. You mean your friend did not feed you lunch?" Kosta muttered. Lord Thomas heard the remark and noticed his capricious expression, but ignored it. His brother was still *grieving* and *dreaming. Yes, he is still dreaming.* Lord Thomas thought. However seldom in conversation had mentioned dreams of his father, if he did talk about them, said very little because those dreams made him feel apprehensive, some sort of omen, or given a warning, which he could not shake or understand. Determinately blocked every word in his mind and dismissed them as foolishness. Many times, he listened while Kosta described in detail his dreams to Aunt Olivia.

"Ha! Little fool... let him dream. Let him talk about his dreams. Perhaps he will talk himself out of his depression. And be his normal self soon, and I will be released from this drudgery," he muttered. "I have no time for such nonsense. I have realistic dreams, dreams of comfort and wealth. I will sell my SOUL to be RICH." Forced, not by his choice but forced to this unpleasantness, each morning as quickly as possible he worked about the barn and stables, forgetting every person who constantly cared for him, but himself.

Lord Thomas overcame the loss of his parents faster than Kosta. He was of tough constitution, determined not to waste time because he had a life to live. He remembered his parents constant harping on and on about being tough and strong. So now, he is taking all of their harping to heart. Therefore, he swore to himself, *no matter what it takes or how long....I must do just that...go on...and live my life.*

Aunt Olivia after a time was aware of Lord Thomas's inner strength. However, she had reservations about his icy glare at times, a faraway look and constantly engrossed in thought, or perhaps, detaching himself from them, and the claustrophobic house.

Fact was he never divulged his future goals to Kosta, or, Aunt Olivia. Even though, she was his last living relative. Did he consider her as his Aunt, or just a temporary *Nanny*? He outgrew his nickname for her, "*Antee O,*" it seemed out of place now, embarrassing. Aunt Olivia's care of them had more concern for Kosta, but not Lord Thomas. Now, they managed quite well.

Living with the boys was to her advantage as well, convenience, conversations, fulfillment of nurturing these boys in their sorrow, she loved them. Whenever feeling out of sorts, Kosta was there for her, whereas, Lord Thomas exhibited a small bit of concern as well, yet frowning sourly. Deep in his eyes hid dark indifference and irritation.

Lord Thomas was antsy cooped up indoors for so long. He needed to get away. On any fair day, he rode over for a visit to his friends for several hours. Returning home, smiled broadly.

"Did you enjoy your visit?" Aunt Olivia would ask.

"Oh, yes indeed. It is wonderful to socialize. It is quite energizing."

"Kosta you too need to visit your friends, it would do you good." Aunt Olivia glanced at Kosta trying to catch his eye.

"I would if I could finish all my work, besides now the days are short, and I am tired, perhaps in the summer." Aunt Olivia did not reply nor did Lord Thomas.

There were moments Lord Thomas wanted to be alone. It was time for Aunt Olivia to go home. He preferred to be with his brother, to be free of her watchful eyes. She seemed to be slyly scrutinizing his every move, which he disliked, but patience had to be controlled. When the boys stayed indoors, Kosta carved beautiful little things.

"Let me try my hand at this so-called carving, perhaps I will be as good as you," Lord Thomas said stretching the word *carving*.

"Carve that one, use the blade next to it. Father told me to observe or imagine closely the item you want to carve, and carve it exactly," Kosta said pointing to a piece of wood.

Lord Thomas held his father's carved dog, turned it over in his hand several times, made his observation, sat it down and began to shape its image. His hands were too rigid, unsteady. After a quarter hour passed, he nicked his finger and bled a bit. Abruptly he laid the wood and the blade on the table and walked away. Surprised at his action Kosta asked, "Are you finished already?"

Lord Thomas just glared at him. He was angry at himself, knowing he was not born with such talent or patience. Kosta picked up the small piece of wood, examined it, and walked over to the window where Lord Thomas stood, staring out.

"Thomas this is quite good...why did you stop? Why not finish it... you should never give up, Thomas... Father..."

"Leave me alone, I do not want to finish it... this is scrap, a waste of time!" Thomas gruffly shouted at Kosta.

Aunt Olivia controlled her temper and emotion. She did not reprimand Lord Thomas for his outburst. She traipsed into the bedroom and went to bed. Kosta sat down at the table and continued carving. Thomas' outburst hurt Kosta's feelings. Thomas stood at the window and seemed to be in deep thought. Kosta cleaned up the shavings off the table, placed his work on the shelf and without a goodnight went to bed. It was quite late and quiet. Now and then, the sporadic wind whistled through the many cracks breaking the silence. Suddenly Lord Thomas realized he was alone and felt odd. He sat down at the table turned down the lamp and thought about that little piece of wood. He lacked the gift and imagination to quickly complete a piece the way his father and Kosta were able to. He was not born with patience for animals or people. To earn a degree in any field was out of the question anyway. He, as a poor boy would never reach such status. He knew nothing of his ancestors, or of his parent's origin. Were they members of a high society circle? He had no knowledge of such documentation. In which case his future is in jeopardy, he will, and, he must find a new direction and begin his first step of his goal, which is, education. Whirl his way into a rich high society circle. Then with time marry into riches.

Lord Thomas will never know if Aunt Olivia had pertinent information or documents, but too embarrassed to be so inquisitive, at least not now, perhaps he should at least ask her one question, which when inquiring at the courthouse will direct him to such evidence. Well, he will think about asking her, later. Presently his only concern was how to change his way of life. This village so detached from the rest of the world one could never prosper, much less live easy. Recalling his father's tall tales of large cities, two- and three-story high mansions, stores, churches with high spires and the architecture most ingenious. Huge markets the likes none had seen... one must go there and see it all with their own eyes. That was his desire, but to venture into such a world one must have money, which he had none. He turned down the lamp until the flame flickered, stretched and died. Lord Thomas sat for a while in the dark then tiptoed to bed.

Winter months dragged. Skies turned the color of lead, days were short and nights long; it seemed like warmer days would never come, but now and then, the sun peeked through thinning clouds, its warm rays melted away some of the snow, blue sky and warm sun renewed one's energy. At last, after bleak winter months passed, spring rains washed away the dreariness; winter was gone. The countryside came to life to that familiar scene, surely taking on a new meaning for all.

For Lord Thomas, one thought stayed constant on his mind: *advanced education. I must complete my education. If I do travel to those bustling cities I heard so much about, I must. It excites me just to think about it, but to travel I must have money. This is my dilemma. I have none. Perhaps I will convince Kosta to sell half of his carvings, which clutter up the house. That would solve my problem. Anyway, my plan is to marry a rich girl. However, one way or another, I must acquire wealth to attract wealth. At present, I have nothing, nothing. I am penniless. A rich girl would never marry a pauper. My aspirations are high, and I know I am of exceptional character. I do have intelligence and common sense. Aha, most important, the girl must turn my head. She must be beautiful to be tolerated the rest of my life. I will not marry a.... why...that is a foolish thought. What a way to think of my future,* he laughed his rasping laugh. *Yes...yes I will ponder on this later.*

Springtime planting is backbreaking. Since the tragic deaths of his parents, each spring memories flashed back, it has been three years since, and his life has not moved forward fast enough. Three years he had a burden on his shoulder: Kosta's recovery. Aunt Olivia had the larger part, soothing his sorrow. Lord Thomas hated winters, winters slowed things for him. However, not much to do through summer either, that is, for some individuals, others now busy with pending projects, which, should have been worked on during winter. Others spent many hours in merry making or dancing and lolling around waiting for the summer months to pass, and, they do pass quicker than fall and winter, of course depending on the weather too. The young, did not want to talk about the upcoming backbreaking work of harvest, however much it is staring at them. Well then in order to have enough food for families to live on, one must do their share.

Lord Thomas stayed away from home most of the summer. Hours spent with his friend, Jacoby Stimmes, a trusted friend devoted to educating Lord Thomas. At times Jacoby Stimmes asked about his brother and Aunt Olivia. Lord Thomas's reply was always the same.

"They are managing well. It is summer, now less work for both of them. I do go to the market each Friday, though, for business, that is my share of work. Whenever they do need help our neighbor is always there for him."

His friends were more important. Disregarding his brother and the chores, he felt he had done his share during winter. He waited anxiously for springtime to be free to roam with his friends, now he was. He cared less that his brother was all alone, lonely, not having anyone to talk to, Aunt Olivia after a hard day's work, retired early to bed, after all she was older, she lost muscle and weight, tired easily, needing much rest.

Kosta was alone but for his only friend Rex an old sheep dog, and Lucifer the old black cat. Kosta put up shelves anywhere there was space, which quickly filled with figurines, creating a houseful of mute companions. Finding time after chores, he persistently worked on carving from loneliness.

Kosta had a plan of his own. All of his figurines he will sell, somewhere, some day, he recalled his mother's words, "*one day you will be famous*," so he carved with dedication and perfection. Keeping in mind, he has his father's talent and he will not waste it. He checked his carvings, feeling joy and pride knowing that he was true to them.

He was alone, too young to have so much hard work and such responsibility, but he learned through mistakes. Losses he had, but those are behind him now. Those meager harvests were just a test of his strength and stubbornness, with constant encouragement from Aunt Olivia had proven for the good, every year at harvest time he hoped for an abundant crop, not only for them, but also for others who had less.

The little property, which these brothers inherited, had given them nearly enough to thrive on for a year. Kosta was proud and happy to provide for Aunt Olivia as well, and he truly learned to love her. She was the only one who stood by him in his sorrow of losing his parents.

Lord Thomas had no interest in this little property. He perceived his life in a different light, to be *in* with the high society became an obsession, he observed and learned the ways of the wealthy quickly, that is where he wanted to be, with his mannerism and quick wit no doubt will get him there. Quite often, he ponders amazed, that this far he has been in the circle with his rich friends; and this far no one questioned. He looked far toward the horizon, leaving all the hard tasks for his brother and Aunt Olivia. In the last three years, Kosta and Aunt Olivia had done quite well, and with her encouragement he believed he would overcome adversities in the future, she said so, no matter where destiny will lead him.

During her stay, on warmer days Aunt Olivia and Kosta would ride to check on her home. Her neighbors knew she lived with the boy's, still she just wanted to chat with the families next door and give those children a small gift of her favorite cookies.

She and Kosta cooked together, he learned much since she had lived in different countries she showed him how to prepare different dishes and use different spices. He enjoyed cooking and learned quickly, besides knowing only what his mother had taught him. Since she had died, he completely forgot to use spices. At dinner, one evening Aunt Olivia announced her decision. She is going back home.

"I feel that we are old enough to live on our own," Lord Thomas voiced his opinion. Kosta disregarding his comment begged her to stay with an outburst.

"But you cannot leave us now! I like you to be with me! I want you here! Who will I talk to when you leave?"

"My dear Kosta I feel I need time to rest and think. My dear boy, I will come see you. I am not that far. Do not think I will not. I will miss you, my dear boys," she said.

"Kosta be reasonable. Aunt Olivia has fulfilled her responsibility to us. Now we have to manage..." Lord Thomas said sternly.

"Yes...now you say '*WE*' have to manage? You mean *I ALONE* have to manage, *ALONE!* You are hardly ever home!" Kosta shouted and hit the table with his fist. Aunt Olivia jumped and stood up abruptly from her chair, with a voice of authority, which the boys had never heard before she shouted, "Now listen here you two. It is time each of you accept your responsibilities. After all, you are now adults, yes adults! You, Thomas, must help your brother much more, do not think that I have been blind to your pretentious air of style and distinction. You, young man, do not fool me a bit. Come down off that cloud of yours and roll up your sleeves! Get some dirt under your nails, like everyone else, you hear?"

Lord Thomas sat fuming, feeling stripped of his secret, and his face turned crimson, he glared but dared not raise his voice or his hand at her. Kosta sat trembling, never expecting Aunt Olivia to have such a booming voice.

Aunt Olivia stood for a moment then said, "I am leaving in two days. One of you must take me home. Thank you for your hospitality." She shuffled off to the bedroom not waiting for further conversation or objections from either one of the boys. Neither spoke, or looked at each other, both felt tension. Kosta felt a sense of loss, again. However, Lord Thomas felt a spark of relief.

What were they thinking... a separation, their relationships between themselves and Aunt Olivia? Two days later, Kosta drove Aunt Olivia home and promised to come and help with the chores.

"Oh, but I will miss you terribly," he said as he kissed her hands before leaving in gratitude for her tireless dedication to them. Thereafter, Lord Thomas rarely paid her a visit. To save face he asked about her, as if to show his concern, and to keep Kosta from asking too many questions and being blameworthy giving him guilty feelings. After all, she had cared so much for them, disregarding her own life's comfort.

Several times Lord Thomas surprised Aunt Olivia with a short visit and bringing a small bottle of lamp oil or a small sack of coffee. Strange thing, whenever he had planned to visit his Aunt Olivia he dressed in his old work clothes, but going out to see his friends he wore his "*special*" attire. Kosta often wondered, *who had given him that special attire*?

These brothers, strong handsome young men, now, with daily chores built a striking physique and strength. Lord Thomas disregarded Aunt Olivia's outburst, his indifference proved it. Though muscular with quite handsome features, genes from both parents, piercing blue eyes, but when angered, darkened. Anger always flamed his face crimson, that he could not change. Even his friend Jacoby Stimmes recognizing this became cautious in conversation. However, glancing at Kosta, he was a spitting image of father. Truly, spitting image of his father, gentle blue eyes, raven black hair tied in a ponytail, father's features, and just as tall.

However, whenever the brothers faced each other at the table, most conversations were somewhat short and often blunt. Lord Thomas was not seeing Kosta sitting before him but, his *FATHER*; each time he had to look at his younger brother made him irritable and very uneasy, averting his eyes staring at objects in pretext of interest around the room. Kosta noticed, but never mentioned or questioned the reason.

They matured. Minds and bodies changed. Outlook on life changed. So did their brotherly feelings. They had nothing more in common. Their brotherly bond no longer held; they drifted apart.

Lord Thomas' stiff, standoffish, and cool attitude made Kosta feel distant and small. Glances averted, the reason known by both. Life led them in different directions. Kosta labored in the fields and carved. Lord Thomas watched with clenched fists, thinking, *why...why is Kosta refusing to sell his carvings... as many times I have mentioned before...why is Kosta so upset....* Lord Thomas was thinking.

Because with time Kosta learned how manipulative his older brother had become, having been questioned many times why not let go of some of the carvings. Kosta felt he would never see all of the profit. His brother, indeed, is in great need of money, and selling his carvings would fill his brother's pockets. As for the produce going off to the market, well Kosta had calculated each sack before loading onto the wagon. Kosta was not a fool, after all.

That particular evening when Lord Thomas approached Kosta with the proposition of selling the statues, Kosta said he would think about it, but next morning his answer was, "NO, I will not sell. Not now, I am not ready to part with them."

Lord Thomas gritted his teeth, lips pressed tight. Fists in his pockets, he sat tensely, not replying but thinking, then he said, "I must tell you on few occasions I have casually mentioned to my friends of your carvings, and, they seemed very much interested. Actually, wanted to come to the house and see your collection, but I came up with a good excuse. You know this house is not very presentable. Dingy, dark and old, musty air... stale. You need to open the windows and air it out—"

Kosta interrupted him in mid-sentence. "Oh, really... are your fingers broken? You cannot open one window! Do you ever clean up? No, *I* do! And I have to clean after you!"

"Of course, I did not say it this bluntly..." Lord Thomas did not flinch at Kosta's remark but continued, "I myself would be embarrassed to describe it in such a way...so they asked me to bring a few pieces for show, and they will pay well if they like your work...think about it." Lord Thomas's eyes twinkled beneath his eyelids, thinking of a small commission of gold for him and for Kosta the rest.

Kosta thought about his brother's rudeness and felt insulted and deeply hurt. *How could my own brother deride our home to those spoiled, snobbish aristocrats with hankies up their sleeves, inhaling the ever-present perfume, always on the heels of beautiful ladies panting like salivating hound dog puppies waiting for a crumb.* Kosta bluntly replied, "*NO!*" and that was final. They did not speak for several days. When Lord Thomas was at home, he observed Kosta carve, looking eerie in the lamplight. *He truly is the image of father, carving as he used to when he was alive and he himself was just a boy. Why not me? I should be the exact image of Father, I am the first-born son,* he thought. After all, carving required patience, he had none. Lord Thomas seemed disgusted with such a meager craft.

Kosta sat thinking, *Thomas used to say, a waste of time, start something more profitable. Drop these worthless fire logs, which are only good for kindling in the winter... that rasping laugh. I hate that laugh.* Hearing that laugh, chills ran through Kosta, always. Those words were like daggers his feelings were hurt.

"You said my work will be used as kindling by someone, now you want to sell them? I know you need money."

Lord Thomas, taken aback by his brother's tartness, replied, "Yes, I did put it that way, now I see why you refuse to sell." Lord Thomas seeing Kosta upset realized the time to smooth this up is now, or Kosta will never sell. "Kosta, I do want to apologize, I realize what I had said before was hurtful, but, do not get me wrong, it is frustrating to be in this situation, as we are, I wish to make you realize how much better it would be for both of us, you must believe me. And you must think about it thoroughly."

Kosta did not look up or reply. He reflected on the words his Mother used to say as she kissed his forehead, *"Kosta, some day you and your sculptures will be famous, you will see, your work will be known throughout the country, and I visualize you creating timeless statues. You will be famous. I feel it."* When he was a boy learned to carve with father. Father pointed out the flaws in the cuts, or proportions, Kosta appreciated his instructions. Precision and perfection is the key. The two carvings on the shelf covered with a cloth were busts of his parents, which his brother never seemed to notice. Kosta felt resentment for those hurtful words and had no intention exposing them to his brother.

Lord Thomas's plans to achieve his dream were different. Whatever were his plans, his desires and secret feelings he kept hidden within. He looked around the little homely house shared with his brother including all the clutter. Kosta had no time to clean up after carving, the wood chips on the floor, his tools on the table, next to his cup, small wonder, having much to do all day long. Aunt Olivia cooked dinner just about every day. She helped clean up the place and then she would return home. Kosta sat alone and carved until exhaustion overtook him, literally shuffled into bed, like an old man. Each day for him, it was the same routine, really, not much time to clean his house or go out and socialize.

Lord Thomas began feeling claustrophobic while at home, like a caged animal with no way out. Oh, but he had an out, all he had to do is go out the front door, and he was free. What about his brother, was he free... free of responsibilities? No. A revolting fury came over him.

"Kosta, do you ever think of improving your way of life?" Lord Thomas asked.

"Yes often... very often, especially at night... but only when sleep... evades me," Kosta replied slowly.

"You seem not to have any interest in what the world is like, how vast it is, do you?" Thomas asked.

"Oh but you are wrong. I am not an imbecile. I am interested, in fact very much. But, what good is it just to be interested or wonder what it is like, I cannot read about it and I cannot ever leave this place, I am harnessed, a yoke around my neck and, a ring in my nose. Like that ox. You know this to be a fact, Thomas," Kosta replied sharply.

Lord Thomas restlessly walked around the small room, thinking, *Kosta is right, daily work is up to him.*

He started to say, "Kosta somehow you need to have time for yourself..." but immediately clamped his mouth realizing that that would have been adding fire to fire. He never bothered to tell Kosta where he was off to, since he was not obligated to do so. Usually coming home late, there were times Kosta was fast asleep, and the oil lamp still burned dimmed low. However, being out with his friends he always mentioned his brother's carvings. That he truly did. His friends began teasing him that he is jesting, not believing that his brother truly is a gifted carver.

The need to convince Kosta to give in, and sell his carvings made him anxious. He needed money and time was running short.

Lord Thomas had at times risen early to do his share of chores, but he detested the smell of manure, cleanup, milking, the strewing of heavy straw for bedding and, fodder for the horses. The old dog barely able to move around now, always stayed out of the barn and out of sight, the old dog obviously sensed something negative, keeping his one good eye on *him.*

There were times his subconscious voice whispered, *how unfair of you evading responsibilities. Your brother needs more help.* Lord Thomas hated that little voice, tried to ignore it. Yet at other times felt guilty. In this dingy home, he was born, and grew up but now he is feeling claustrophobic as if the walls were closing in on him, he needed to be free of it; he preferred mornings for his bit of chores, quickly cleaning up and, just as quickly wash away the foul smell from his face and arms. On those days, Kosta prepared breakfast. They ate together not engaging in deep or lengthy conversation. Plans for spring planting or harvesting somehow never entered into discussions. Kosta acquired advice many a time from neighbors, which was good enough for him, besides, Lord Thomas, had no interest in any of it.

"Aunt Olivia is not feeling well, you need to visit her," Kosta said.

"Oh, she is not well? What is wrong with her? Is it contagious? I will visit in a few days, she should be well by then, you think?" Lord Thomas asked.

Kosta's anger choked him up, he could not reply, but he coughed, as if food stuck in his throat.

"She does not have a contagious disease. Do not be afraid, you will not catch it," Kosta said wiping his face and mouth with a napkin.

Lord Thomas did not repeat the question. After breakfast, leaving the cup and dish on the table, without a mere, '*thank you for the breakfast,*' with just a few steps was out of that house felling free, on clear and sunny mornings. Rainy days forced him to stay in the house, in his room sprawled on the bed read books, perfect escape, absorbed in the unfolding story he was oblivious to his surroundings at least for a while. Kosta in his free time sat and carved.

On clear days, Lord Thomas changed into his good brown breeches and a fancy tan shirt and went out for the entire day. His love of nightlife, full of mysterious intrigue and suspense by which he felt empowered, expecting respect wherever his foot crossed a threshold, as a master would. He was not involved in any criminal undertakings, not any more. Surrounded by his pals his cunning approach gradually ruled them.

Lord Thomas now and then thought about his parents. The unfairness of it made anger simmer within him. One particular morning, he said to Kosta while both were cleaning up the barn.

"Ah my naïve brother, someday others will do this sort of work for me, I am no fool. You will see. I refuse to spend the rest of my life with a yoke around my neck such as this," being careful not to use *dirty work*, he caught himself using the word *yoke*. To cover his slip of tongue, he laughed, his strange raspy laugh. As always, it chilled Kosta's bones.

After a moment Kosta replied, "Thomas, you are right, it is not a pleasant life, but do we have a choice right now? This is our property and this is all we have. This is all our parents possessed, it was not their fault they were poor. We are very fortunate having this much, a small parcel of land and a roof over our heads, I believe in time it should get better."

At these words, Lord Thomas spun around, fists clenched stared at Kosta, rage evident on his scarlet face, he shouted, "You are weak! You have no backbone! You will always be a meek fool, a grimy peasant! As to our parents, I spent years thinking about them. Father made an unforgivable mistake crossing that river! He should have known it was risky! He was in a hurry! He should have gone to the bridge, the long way, and they would have been safe! That mistake cost them their lives! That was foolish! He killed her... he killed my Mother!" Lord Thomas shouted.

Kosta's temper flared as he listened, but when he heard these words, *"he killed my mother"* anger hit him like a bolt of lightning. He dropped the pitchfork. In just two strides he had Thomas by the shirt collar in a choke and raised him up on his toes. Thomas was caught off guard, but dared not react. Kosta was taller, though younger, strength of a bull. Kosta glared eye to eye and shouted.

"How dare you, you high class manure scraper! Mother named you little Lord Thomas and that *title* stuck to you! You grew up believing you were special! You looked down on us. What did you know! You were out! You did not care to know how ill mother was! She was pale and feeble! Did you notice dark circles under her eyes? No, you did not care, you never really looked at her did you, and you dare say, *he killed my mother*? Did you help them, no! You were out with the *BOYS!* You never wanted to dirty your delicate hands and smell of manure! Oh but you shared food with me...with them! She was weak but each day she asked about you when you were out! Wondering where you were. Did you hear father whisper to her at night?"

Lord Thomas tried to free Kosta's grip from his throat, amazed at his strength, Kosta towered over him, shook Thomas and squeezed tighter his face reddened more, Thomas from tiptoes, slowly buckled his knees, to wrestle free would have been a mistake. Barely breathing unable to interject one word while Kosta yelled... "Father tried to comfort Mother, but comfort was not enough, words were not enough, she needed medication, and she needed you and me by her side! Where were *YOU!* Kosta shook him again...Perhaps bowing and kissing those *aristocratic ladies' fingertips*! You are an ignorant, selfish and egotistic fool! They loved you! They were decent! They tried their best. Father was best. You proved to them time after time you were better. You hurt them! You broke mother's heart! Everything they did was for *US*. Father out of despair made that mistake. I do not hate him! Do not ever say it again, that Father killed her, you are a blind idiot! He died with her! He loved her more than life itself! You are a selfish and greedy fool!"

Kosta stared into Thomas's eyes, his anger peaked, his breathing rapid, his nostrils flared breathing fire, still squeezing, tears welled up in his eyes. Kosta let go and shoved his brother, his foot slid lost his balance and was about to fall back on his backside, a quick drop to his knee and his hand for support, which landed in manure. He realized he was a step away from falling into a pile of manure. He froze, breathing hard, clearing his head thinking what took place just now, slowly rose from crouching took several steps back and bend down, his eyes on Kosta, picked up a pitchfork. Kosta his back to his brother fought tears, ground his teeth, consumed by anger.

Lord Thomas seething raised his arm moved it back ready to strike, but then dropped his arm and the pitchfork. He stood staring at his brother's back. He turned and went out the door. He walked in a daze until he stepped into the gurgling creek. The cold rushing water snapped him back to reality. For a minute he wondered why was he in the water and why did he come here? He stepped out of it and sat down on a stump.

He stared into the rushing water but in his mind, Kosta's razor sharp words spewed out at him echoing in his ears, loud and clear. It took some time for him to absorb and get over Kosta's outburst, such strength, Kosta's words shocked him. Lord Thomas began to think back to his younger years.

I never considered myself selfish, or egotistic, but I see...now I was, still am, Kosta is right. I was seldom home, I chose to be blind to the situation. So many sleepless nights I heard whispers I wondered is it about me. I helped little with planting and the harvest. I purposely avoided conversations with them...especially mother. Father...distant...seemed cold, now I know why, they tried to talk to me...but I just ran to my friends. I took them for granted, assuming they would live forever. I would have control of my life, I would show them that I would accomplish something more than they ever have had in all those years, how childish. I hate my brother for slapping me with the truth, all these years he shied away with good reason. No matter...too late...it is over, I must go on. My life waits, it is urgent to reach my goal. For a moment, his mind went blank. His head hung low on his chest, and then he raised his head and looked about the surroundings. He sat on a stump on which his father chopped wood many a time... *Now, I do feel a void, emptiness; I cannot shed a tear, I cannot. Kosta was close to them, but how could they have; why would they have favored him; I was their first-born son. It is his fault. I hate him. He knew what went on, never told me. Avoiding me, no...I avoided him. He kept it from me. He thinks he is wise. Well I am wiser. I will show him. I will reach my goal, wait and see. He should have said something to open my eyes. A good brother would, seeing I was ignorant to the fact. I was ashamed of being poor. I must admit now, I was ashamed of them. My brother, ha, I could never be like him and...I never will work like him, and I will not live like him! I must tell him what I think now...* He walked back to the barn to confront his brother. He never heard the rustling and whispers across the creek in the trees concealed among the leaves; the thirteen Ravens were there. Thirteen pairs of eyes watching. Kosta was in the barn finishing up. Lord Thomas angrily shouted, "Why did you keep it all from me? What kind of brother are you?"

Kosta replied sharply, not looking up at Thomas, "Are you still blind as before? By the way Father knew of your ambush!"

Lord Thomas's jaw fell, stunned. He was about to say something to that, but closed his mouth tight, realizing at that moment that all this time Kosta carried the pain in his heart alone.

"Oh by the way, buy a cow, Blaza's days are numbered," Kosta said, not looking at his brother. Lord Thomas, at the close of market day, found the corral for cattle and chose a year-old heifer, paid for her from the profits, and brought her home. Within a few months, old Blaza showed signs of her end. Kosta and his neighbor stood by as Blaza took her last breath. His brother was not home to help him. Kosta trusted their neighbor and paid attention, learned quickly what to do in cases like this and to be observant to everything around him. As weeks and months went by, these two blood brothers were drifting further and further apart, as if two mute strangers lived together in a small dwelling, leading separate lives. Lord Thomas stayed out frequently from anger and ruminating on the past. At times, Lord Thomas had been gone for four or five days and nights. Where he slept, or with whom, only he would know. Kosta never asked. Though young, he realized that the distance between them has widened and will more so in time, and so he must adjust to his solitary life. While alone in early evenings, Kosta walked along the creek, his dog trailing along. However, on the branches of the trees across the creek thirteen pair of eyes watched him, now, and will watch him for the rest of his life.

Twelve: Loneliness

Kosta took charge of Aunt Olivia's major chores. Besides all his work, he began his education as Aunt Olivia promised. *It would save precious time for all of us if Aunt Olivia lived with us again. I should ask her,* Kosta thought.

Although he was lonely and tired, every chance he had before sunset he sat on an old stump near his favorite old willow and listened to the brooks gurgle and the chirp of life around him, enjoying the tranquil spot and moment. Without fail his two four-legged friends always tagged along. This was the hour of meditation and recollection of the years with his parents. He remembered mornings with his father, happy conversations with his mother. He missed them so much his chest hurt and his throat tightened. But he did not weep. His life was now a struggle as as theirs was, but regardless of how great their stress was, they never complained.

His beautiful mother's words he will not forget. At times, it seemed he heard their voices in the gentle breeze. Felt his mother's touch, and father's hand on his shoulder. They were here with him, he believed, in their spiritual existence. His sorrow subsided, feeling peace and renewed emotional strength, a reason to go on living. Always his outing uplifted his spirit, leaving him clear-headed and a bit happier, appreciating his surroundings and loving Aunt Olivia. His brother definitely did not want to have anything to do with him; he swore that no matter what the future brought, he would survive. He is and will keep busy. There were moments of contrite feelings not for himself but his brother.

Visiting Aunt Olivia one early morning, they sipped coffee and chatted away trivialities and important decisions. Kosta could relate with Aunt Olivia. No matter how small or silly an observation or fear was on his mind, she never ridiculed his feelings. Aunt Olivia wondered each time the black birds were in their conversation, why these birds fly in frequently so close to Kosta's home.

"Kosta, I suggest you plug up all those scratched out holes around the door; the chickens found out how to scratch big enough dips underneath the door. I know these tiny chicks do follow the hens, I have seen them myself," she said.

"I declare, you are right, I have seen them too, I had a hard time catching all of them and slip them back into the cages, but I did lay large stones to keep them in, yes that is the first thing I will do, secure it well, when I get home. Thank you. You are so observant. I will pound oak branches all along the enclosure. Surely they will not get out," Kosta said and smiled.

"I will come help you, it is still early in the day. Then I will cook supper. We will spend a cheery and eventful day," Aunt Olivia said. She rose from the table, picked up her shawl and in just a few minutes, they were on their way to Kosta's home. After several hours of pounding in the small spikes into the spaces scratched out by the chickens, all holes were secured. After dinner she cleared off the table and washed the dishes. Kosta dried and put them up on the shelves in the cupboard. With hot tea and sweet cakes for dessert, Aunt Olivia and Kosta studied for a while. When Lord Thomas showed up at home, Kosta drove Aunt Olivia home. In the several months, Kosta learned to recite the alphabet and scribble letters, spell and read three letter words. He stumbled at times a bit, but with concentration was doing quite well. He was on cloud nine. The mention of his brother very seldom entered into their conversation. "When is the tutor arriving?" Kosta asked. Aunt Olivia assured him at one time that the tutor should arrive directly to his house. She kept asking what time Thomas comes home every night.

"Hard for me to say, he comes at different hours," Kosta replied.

"Kosta have you met a nice girl yet?" she blurted out, startling him.

"No not yet, I am not ready... ah... Thomas usually is in before midnight, but on weekends he is not home at all. It should be safe for the teacher to come over. That is if he will not be offended, you know my home, one big pile of clutter. Aunt Olivia I am so curious, I cannot wait to learn to write and read books. I feel that if you stayed with me and the teacher was over Thomas would not think anything of it, no need to tell him who the man is, but if I visit you often, he might just get suspicious. What is your opinion on this?" Kosta asked.

"But Kosta, if Thomas is out all day what does it matter? I will sleep on it. It does make sense though. When the teacher arrives we will decide," Aunt Olivia replied.

"Good let us leave it at that then. Once I learn to read, I hope to find a girl just like mother, or someone like you, you and Mother were close in character," Kosta said, blushing a bit. Aunt Olivia smiled and assured him all will be fine.

"Just do not wait too long, you know I am getting very old, I want to be at your wedding, it would be the greatest day of my life... so hurry up and find a girl, you are old enough, you know!" She winked and smiled. While galloping home Kosta thought about what she had said. The neighbors waved and the girls smiled. Whenever he worked outside, children ran to him. *Children, my parents will not see my children, if I ever marry, how sad. But one consolation I have in my heart, they will see them from heaven,* Kosta thought.

He smiled at the girls and waved back at the neighbors. Many invited him over for lunch or dinner, but he declined politely. Kosta was wary of their intentions. Their daughters were of marrying age. He had no interest in these girls. Those were his feelings at this moment. His concern at present was improving his living conditions, he would be mortified and embarrassed to have a girl see such a dingy and cluttered house. Months dragged by. Kosta's heavy yoke on his shoulders bent him to the ground. Toiling from sunrise to sunset, his hands were dirty and he always had dirt under his nails. His neighbors commented and marveled at his perseverance and endurance. Last several year's loses were minimal, and everyone breathed a sigh of relief. Whenever the fury of elements created havoc, the pantries were empty and survival crucial during winter.

Time did not permit Kosta to take the produce to the market. Thomas 'agreed' to go since he mingled among people, having a gift of gab and easily sold all produce each market day, bringing home gold for other necessities.

Thomas never mentioned to Kosta of the trip to the far countries, but he must do so, now, or, at least within a few days or weeks before going away. Not wanting Kosta to think that just because he stays out all night something tragic befalls him; a spark of thoughtful consideration for his younger brother.

"I suggest you think about selling your carvings, having extra money will give you security, help you purchase supplies for yourself and feed for the animals, if you have a heavy winter, while I am away..." Lord Thomas trailed off.

"What? You are going away! When, why... where are you going?" Kosta threw all these questions at his brother, brows furrowed, visibly upset.

"Let me finish... you did not let me finish! Now Kosta listen, consider the benefits. You will have no need to plant as much in the spring, in fact, you will have more time to carve, and it would give you an opportunity to clean up the house a bit more. I see you have put things in order rather well, so far, now get it whitewashed inside and out, organize, to be more comfortable, and you will feel better too, and proud of yourself." Lord Thomas talked loud almost to the point of screaming. Kosta hung his head and did not reply. Lord Thomas let Kosta dwell for several days and consider the benefit of his suggestion.

"I agree to sell half of my collection. You do have a point there. I would breathe a little, it would be a relief, and rest. I am so exhausted. And I would have time to see Aunt Olivia more often, but Thomas please be fair, do not overcharge, it should benefit us both." Kosta eyed Thomas.

"Kosta have no fear," Lord Thomas laughed at that remark, "I visit different markets. I perfectly know what to charge, worry not... we will come out good." *Now things will roll, I will gain by this; my plans are on the right track*, Thomas thought, bursting with excitement, but squelching it.

Lord Thomas roamed like a gypsy, restlessly from one town to another, from village to village. He was searching; clueless to what was he searching? The relentless urge to search would not let him rest. Nevertheless, his wandering always led him back to his dingy and dark house in which he slept and planned. Whenever he was at home, observing his brother's precise moves as he carved amazed him.

"How is it possible for you to work so quickly? Truly, you are a master, a gifted artist. How do you do it?" Lord Thomas asked with true interest.

"Sometimes I wonder myself, somehow it comes easy to me," Kosta replied.

"How do you whittle the shape and the proportion so quickly?" Lord Thomas asked his brother.

"I... I guess I inherited this talent from Father, he taught me to concentrate, to hold the image in my mind, which I am to work on," Kosta explained, not looking up at his brother and he was thinking, *it has been a very long time since Thomas approached me in such a friendly way, perhaps he has a plan.* Kosta's intuition was correct. Lord Thomas did have a plan. Lord Thomas's new way of life and destiny was about to turn, he was on the right path of his own life, but the plan and what was still to be was unknown to him. Surely, it will take a lifetime to live it. Much less to for-see and understand its entirety is rare. His constant planning at last took hold, he saw bits and pieces coming together, and these results made him happy.

Mingling among the crowds of strangers Lord Thomas Komarod acquired an education in many ways. Because of it, now a great void stood between him and Kosta.

It was apparent he was above the meager life surrounding him. Yes. He resided in it only temporarily, only sleeping in that small dismal house out of necessity, in that small bed, feeling the confinement, as if the walls were closing in. The smallness of this house compelled him to leave, he did not understand why, but at the first sign of wondering 'why' he suppressed it. Even though the house situated near the mountain and the river had a wonderful view, green summers, autumn's artists palette swept across the countryside into a fiery panorama. Winter scenes serene, cold and lifeless, captivated one's eye to its wonderland of a certain charm.

Lord Thomas had little appreciation for these natural wonders; to him they were misery. Soon this miserable life must change, that is, if he does not deviate from plans already in motion. Of course, everything in his plan will and must be to his benefit. It had crossed his mind though if he does succeed would he share a bit of his fortune with his brother. Forgetting that no matter how much time must pass and how much effort it will take to succeed, never hesitating, but instinctively returned to this dingy house and his brother. Whatever thoughts went through his mind, however much he disliked all those chores, he came to help Kosta more often than not lately. Kosta appreciated his help and always thanked him for it.

I do not worry... if my brother is satisfied with his way of life, it is his choice, he thought. However, of himself, he was proud. His will and determination has driven him to reach the desired lifestyle and rise above the rest. "My plans must work, my plans must work," he repeated. Lord Thomas Komarod, rising before dawn, quietly lit the stove and made fresh coffee. The special coffee he had brought from a large city some time ago. The aroma had always awakened Kosta; he too enjoyed a fresh cup before starting his grueling day. Kosta as always prepared breakfast and they ate together but did not tarry around, as work waited. While cleaning and feeding the animals, from the corner of his eye Lord Thomas caught a glimpse of a black cape. He froze. Hands trembling, he stared at it, recognizing it to be his father's.

"Kosta, come here!" Lord Thomas shouted.

"Why are you shouting, what is it?" Kosta asked.

"When and who gave you this... cape; from where... and when?" Lord Thomas said eyes wide and pointing at the cape on the peg.

"It is Father's cape. A fisherman delivered it to Aunt Olivia," Kosta said.

"You never mentioned it, why not?" Lord Thomas asked, his hands shaking in his pockets.

"Thomas it slipped my mind, anyway I knew how you felt about them, and I did not think you would want to see it... that is all."

"What do you mean how I felt about them... do you mind explaining yourself?" Lord Thomas shouted.

"What am I to explain, it is Father's that is all," Kosta replied.

"We shall discuss this when I come back from the market, I have to go now," Lord Thomas grumbled under his nose. He packed the carvings in a large sack and was about to leave, he turned to Kosta and said, "By the way, I have been meaning to tell you, our horse is too old to do heavy hauling, he should retire." Without waiting for a reply climbed up the wagon step and sat on the bare seat, he swung the small basket with lunch into the back behind him. Loaded wagon with sacks was about to ride out when Kosta ran up, "Thomas, buy a good horse with the profits, the carvings I mean, or two horses if possible." Lord Thomas nodded and rode off to the market. He enjoyed mingling among the hubbub created by crowds of people. When interested individuals admired the carvings and eagerly purchased several pieces, he felt elated. By mid-morning, the sack was light and he carried it over his shoulder with ease, in his satchel-jingled gold, and he realized that over summer he would fulfill his dream, having saved enough for travel. Adventurous travels should empower him in achieving his goal, besides education.

He mingled. He should have gone home and not wasted time, but for an unexplained reason, he felt agitated and anxious. Impulsively, he decided to head home, but the next minute he found himself among crowds wandering around observing. Life is the best teacher, and life here such as it is one could build on, but once returning from his travels, this market place could prove to be profitable, very profitable. This was not the time for him to realize this, not yet.

Children ran among the crowds shouting, laughter resounded. When someone screamed all heads and eyes swung in that direction. Being part of this human beehive was exciting. He meandered through the crowds. At a corral, he spent a good hour looking over workhorses, evaluated their worth... *on second thought not today, perhaps next week...* he considered himself to be clever. Next week he might just buy a couple of these horses at a much lower price. As hours ticked away, still he hung around the market. Then his stomach growled, time to get a good sandwich. Savoring his lunch, he sat on a barrel inside his kiosk away from the crowds for a little while observing, for some reason feeling impatient and restless.

His annoyance dissipated the moment he happened to glance at a girl. She stood out among the crowd. He chewed each bite slowly, glanced at her again, and slowly he rose to his full height. The barrel was empty, which he easily moved closer to a covered stand and jumped onto it. Something happened to him; he watched the group as they strolled through the crowds. He jumped down, wiped his mouth with a handkerchief and disappeared among the crowds keeping her in sight. He was near enough to scrutinize her more closely, without realizing his interest intensified. She seemed different. She was. The way she carried herself; radiant, elegant and refined. He liked what he saw. Dressed in finery, her dress shimmered in the strong sunlight and seemed to be soft. What fabric was it? Curiously, he followed, she strolled arm in arm with someone older, assuming to be her father, followed by several men.

How strange, all those plans of visiting other cities and countries flew like pigeons out of his mind. He intended to be at the market every Friday from this day. Could it be possible that the reason he hung around all day was for this? Sudden feelings stirred within him. Such feelings had not awakened before or ever experienced until now. He has been in the company of many girls, poor and rich. Rich women differed from the peasant women. Thanks to his friends, he learned to classify and judge such differences in the lives of people. However, whenever among a group of higher means, Lord Thomas was a perfect "gentleman." Today a pretty girl caught his eye and he was smitten. What came over him? It was not like him to feel such a strong attraction, especially to this girl, for the first time. He was sure she has never been here before, certainly not selling, buying yes, and just looking, yes. He followed the group keeping his eyes on her, bumping into stands and people.

The sudden urge to walk up and present his simple persona to her was fierce. He realized it was best not to, it would be foolish, laughable, so he kept his distance but his eyes followed her group. A commotion caught him off guard and he lost his attention of the girl, headed for the argument yards away. When nothing bloody happened, he glanced back but the girl with her father and friends were gone out of his sight.

Will she come again? he thought... *what if today... wait do not panic. I must not approach her, why, my attire is of a peasant, they would turn me away. I shall wait for another Friday. Meet her I will, I must, I must meet her. She must be a part of my plan surely, it had to be so; is it meant to be? Why else I am so interested in her. Is this why I hung around at the market all day? Was today a predestined coincidence for us to be here?* Suddenly he frowned, *that girl never looked back, anyway, why would she, to her, he does not exist, not yet*. Gloom seized him but only for a moment. There they were strolling back towards him. Quickly he disappeared behind a large stand; bent over as if interested in something there. When the group had passed him, he followed them.

I must admit I am a bit childish, she is not looking for anyone, but I will make sure she will notice me next time... she will long for me, and I will charm her off her feet. Lord Thomas lost track of time, the market was less noisy now; more than half of the crowds were gone. After all, it was the end of the day. The girl and her father were long gone. Still he wandered passing empty stands feeling enthusiastic and lighthearted. Until he reached his wagon, time to head home. Lord Thomas relived each moment of the day, on the way home he remembered *those girls with that girl. They must have been her friends, surely! I paid no attention to the girls at all, she, and her father I focused on, on them only*, he thought.

Thirteen:

Innocence of Youth

Cybilia, as a little girl always clean and pampered, was never permitted to play in the dirt like other children. This spoiled little girl, now an attractive young woman, came to the market.

Cybilia, young inexperienced, sheltered, was always with family and her best friends, Julietta, Clara and Dora.

This Friday was her first time with her friends to come to this market. Her father had described what went on at the market. She observed people and their wares for sale. She and her friends passed one stand after another followed by her father and his men. They strolled toward the aroma of freshly baked bread and pastry. Smoked meats and baked goods stirred their appetites. Cybilia and her friends sat on barrels, enjoying sandwiches for lunch. Then they strolled by stands of fruit baskets, pyramids of eggs, variety of vegetables, grains, livestock for sale or trade. Horses, goats, sheep, and sows with litters. Geese, ducks and pigeons, birds and, chickens, and crafts for all seasons. People milling and shouting — the noise was deafening.

She and her friends Julietta, Clara and Dora found something of interest. They walked quickly back to her father chatting excitedly all at once.

"Oh Father this is wonderful, everything you need is here and I have seen fabric I like. I cannot believe all these people! They must come from all over the country. This is so exciting! This has been such an experience for us; Father, thank you for all of us to come here today!" she exclaimed. Her father told her they could come again whenever they wished, but never alone. He put his arm around her shoulders and whispered into her ear. Cybilia and her friends walked away, her father resumed his discussion with his men.

Abruptly someone was shouting. The girls stopped, craning their necks over the shoulders of the crowds where the shouts were coming from. The voices were hushed now, but she noticed a fellow with his back toward them crouching next to a dairy cow.

She saw an elderly man under the belly of his cow waving his arm and shouting. At first she dismissed the incident, but her attention and interest fell on that young man. He must have caused this commotion over there. She studied him, and when he straightened up, she found him interesting.

"Look there Julietta, that fellow, he is arguing with that old man, you see?" Cybilia said, hiding a smile.

"I think that old man's cow is worth the price or whatever he asked, she surely gives a lot of milk, look at her udder," Dora said.

"What! What are you talking about, the cow?" Julietta snorted at her.

"Look, the old man is walking away with his cow." Dora pointed.

"I guess a sale lost for that old man," Cybilia said. Lord Thomas turned toward the girls and stared.

"Oh! Look at him! Good looking, is he not? Broad shouldered and look at those muscles!" Julietta and Clara giggled behaving like silly little girls.

"Oh... I would not mind at all if he kissed my fingertips," Dora exclaimed.

The girls walked on until they came to a crate of chickens. Cybilia noticed quite a few were different from the rest. These had feathers on their legs, sort of pantaloons, the girls laughed hysterically. Cybilia's father approached.

"Father we definitely need to buy these chickens wearing pantaloons! I think Mother would be hysterically interested in those." Cybilia pointed. The girls giggled.

"Yes, I see... her father nodded...they are sort of funny," and proceeded to purchase all the funny chickens. The girls walked on to other stands.

"Where is that fellow, do you see him anywhere?" Cybilia asked the girls. "Oh... Cybilia look he is right there by the baskets of eggs!" Julietta pointed in Thomas's direction.

"We should stroll by like sophisticated ladies. Pretend we do not see him," Cybilia said to her friends. They walked by, looking straight ahead. Lord Thomas watched with squinty eyes. He knew at which one of the girls he was squinting. He wanted to meet her, and soon. His heart drummed and his knees buckled... *I dare not come near her now. Today is not the time, but I will see her again. I must.* After all, he was twenty-four now. Nature is stirring strange desires in him. *I must find a way to meet her. Get to know her. Who she is and where she lives. I must know if she is wealthy! Ah, she must be rich! It is evident by her apparel, very fine fabric indeed, newest of vogue, very fine indeed. I must plan this well. It must work*, he thought. Inconspicuously, he followed them, as close as possible as the girls meandered through the crowds back to her father.

Lord Thomas squirmed away quickly, his back to them he heard her say, "Oh Father those funny chickens you bought for Mother. She will love them. They are so different, thank you Father!" Cybilia kissed his cheek.

"All is taken care of, chickens are in a crate, now run along, remember we must be heading home, soon!" her father replied.

Cybilia excitedly chatting with her friends about the fun they were having, glad her father allowed them to come today, especially today...she turned full circle but the one she looked for was lost in the crowds. They were moving towards the carriage. The wagons waited ready to depart. Lord Thomas observed from afar, half-hidden behind a horse. He was sure... *aha... she is looking for me. I feel she will be back without a doubt.* From his summation he liked what he observed, his gut feelings told him that even though he knew nothing about her... *he must have her... well, so this was her father*, their manner definitely of aristocratic upbringing. Lord Thomas noticed.

But being poor, surely he did not differ that much from all the rest of the milling merchants. Most were shabby, some well-dressed, he was in his work clothes; but confident of his manner; he was educated to a degree; nevertheless, he definitely felt he belonged to the upper class. Lord Thomas riding back home burned within, aware of the class of people he belonged to, though the truth stared him in the face; he was a poor man, and the fact is his parents left no legacy. Now he will never know. They are dead. He felt angry. Had he the nerve even to think that he could squirm into and belong to the high society circles. He felt a sudden letdown, and almost backed off, almost lost his determination to fulfill his plan, now that he saw that young woman.

He breathed deeply to untangle his twisted nerves and promised himself that according to his plan he cannot falter. It was not right to introduce himself now, he will bide his time. His courage back in his spine he rehashed the events of the day; *It did not look easy to step into that circle to be acquainted with her father, it was evident he had his men around, it was clear when they strolled, the crowds sidestepped out of their way. No doubt they are rich, his curiosity tore at him... peasants never have guards! Perhaps they were visitors or friends, but their apparel not elegant enough for his rich friends, those were his guards for sure.* He kept thinking. Lord Thomas was not aware whom he tried to capture for his own.

The events of the day in his mind, anticipation to see her next Friday made him tense. His heart palpitated. *Patience... patience... patience wins!*

In the distance down the road he saw a man leading a frisky horse. He kept his eye on him, when they were about yards from each other Lord Thomas reined in and halted the wagon, jumped off and approached the man.

"Good day to you sir! You have a fine stallion there! He tipped his hat.

"What? Oh yes, yes! Young fellow I am... I had little to eat today...I feel I am about to faint," the man replied holding his cupped hand to his ear.

"You did not eat? Wait up... I have a loaf of bread, here take a chunk." Lord Thomas shouted, because the man was hard of hearing.

"I have no more money at all, now..." said the man as he chewed the bread "...this stallion is eating it all up. He is too much for me to handle. I am too feeble. Say... young man would you consider buying him? Save me the trip to the market. I must eat... no family to help me." Lord Thomas waited just for that moment.

"But the market is about to close, you have a long way still. What is your price? By the way, what is your name?" Thomas asked.

"Well... ah... my name is Tuman, ah... young fellow just a handful of gold coins will do... say enough for a year, perhaps." Tuman tilted his head sideways, squinting.

"So you are Tuman... you say, sir?" Lord Thomas going around the stallion inspecting thoroughly also glancing at the man.

"No objection, my taking a closer inspection of your stallion?" Lord Thomas asked.

"No objection young man, you might just as well look at his teeth, too," Tuman said. Lord Thomas walked around and the stallion stomped and danced with his front hooves. Lord Thomas, satisfied with the looks of the stallion, walked up to the man. He was about to undo the satchel, to count off the coins into Tuman's palm, when suddenly the stallion nudged him hard. Lord Thomas almost lost his footing and dropped the coins to the ground. The man fell to his knees with trembling hands and picked as many as he could. Lord Thomas picked up several for himself, or else he would have none to show Kosta. He muttered swear words, had no intention giving all away, surely that man heard many foul words in his lifetime but had ignored or perhaps had not heard, being hard of hearing. Lord Thomas's spill of all his coins surely displeased him, but Tuman was glad of it, he will have enough for a year, just what he had asked for.

"Thank you, thank you!" The reins he handed to Lord Thomas and said, "Now, I am going your way, please let me ride back with you." Without waiting for an answer, he scrambled up onto the empty wagon and sat down. At the crossroads the man climbed off the wagon, tipped his crumpled hat, holding the loaf of bread close to his chest said, "Fate will reward you, remember this day." From that point on he walked home. Lord Thomas rode up to the barn, holding the reins to his newly acquired prize. Kosta, busy in the stable, his back to the door, was startled when Lord Thomas shouted, "Kosta take a look at my prize stallion!" Kosta, surprised, goggled at the stallion. "Where... where, Thomas where on earth; how... did you...?" Kosta stuttered, in disbelief.

"A real beauty, huh, I just bought him on the way home from an old buffoon...what do you think?" Lord Thomas laughed his rasping way.

Kosta, speechless, cautiously approached the horse and the stallion's muscles quivered, his eyes a bit too wild. He jerked his head nervously, grunting. Kosta raised his hand to pat the stallion's neck.

"How much did you pay, Thomas we need a work horse not a stallion. How much did you pay?" Kosta asked.

"I paid from today's profits. That old fool wanted enough gold for a year... and I think he got it..." Lord Thomas pulled the satchel from his belt and handed it to Kosta.

"What do you mean, enough for a year?" Kosta asked, studying his brother.

"Well, I dropped the satchel with the gold coins when the stallion spooked from the jingle..." Lord Thomas failed to say that the stallion nudged him hard, he still felt it too. "That old fool was no fool, and grabbed it all of the ground. I was lucky to get what is in the satchel." There was nothing else for Kosta to say about this incident.

Later that evening, while having a bite to eat, Lord Thomas described freely in detail all about a rich girl at the market. Kosta listened, clearing the dishes off the table, washing, drying and putting them up into the cupboard. He sat down in his usual place, whittling his imagined creatures as his brother prattled on and on, gesturing with his arms. Kosta occasionally glanced at Lord Thomas, listening attentively. Questions circled in his mind.

"Hey brother you have fallen for this girl, have you not?" Kosta asked.

"Ooh yes I have! She is a Lady..." Lord Thomas said, grinning.

"Your eyes twinkle like two stars at night, and it is only the first time you have seen her?" Kosta kept on.

"Love at first sight, as they say," Lord Thomas replied grinning.

"Easy... easy brother, take your time, what is your hurry?" Kosta said.

"Why waste time? Why... I must move fast or she might marry someone rich. She is a gem, and a precious gem at that!" Lord Thomas interjected.

"If she is meant to be yours then she will be. I truly am glad for you though. I hope you will tell me more, come next time." Kosta observed his brother and noticed a sudden change of expression. Lord Thomas glared strangely for a moment then angrily blurted out, "Who are you to tell me to take it easy? What do you know of love! Your love is cleaning out the manure and feeding those stinky animals! The barn is your second home...your love...aha ha, ha!" he laughed. I am disappointed in you. Perhaps I should not tell you about her at all!" he shrieked.

Kosta slowly rose, walked up to Lord Thomas, looked into his eyes, and calmly said, "Now listen here, I am very glad that you... found someone, truly I am. You were always the lucky one... you get what you want. I did not mean to upset you. There is no comparison, your life and mine. I wish you the best... truly. As for me, I... ah... never mind... it does not matter." Kosta walked away, not giving Lord Thomas a chance to respond.

Lord Thomas sat for a while mulling over what Kosta had said, finally he spoke.

"I am sorry, please ignore my outburst. It is just that I am so excited, I know it is foolish...to feel this way... but nothing ever occurred to me like this before. I am sure you know I met many girls, none... I tell you none had ever captured my eye... pulled my heartstrings as this girl... I hope you do understand. And I will tell you in detail... no more outbursts from me, I promise... truce?"

Kosta smiled and said, "Yes truce."

Come Friday with a loaded wagon, Lord Thomas was off to the market. Each week gained profit, which he would share with Kosta, counting off a small commission into his pocket; after all, he did the selling. Why, to his surprise Kosta's carvings sold. Profits for the carvings he gave to Kosta; somehow could not pinch off any as his share, after all Kosta slaved over them, not he. Kosta overjoyed that all his carvings had sold. "*My work sold, someone appreciated my talent, how wonderful!"* recalling his mother's words *"You will be famous someday."* Kosta worked on. "*We need a workhorse, I must remind Thomas."*

Lord Thomas planned his future.... imagining in the evening while in bed what it would be like to be with *that girl* in a huge home with her parents, brothers and sisters (if she had any), pretty maids, and horses. All these thoughts ran through his mind as he drifted off to asleep.

After many Fridays spent at the market mingling, cleverly approaching people to ask a question here or there about the girl and her father, met with little success. His patience flared into a fury. However, at the times when he acquired a tiny bit of information, he smiled. By being overly courteous and respectful to the elderly he surely had turned many heads and gained attention. His brother's carvings sold well, and he impressed upon the crowds that these were his own work. Not once did he consider that he was committing fraud and this would reflect on his character whenever the truth surfaces. He continued watching and waiting each Friday for *that girl* to appear. She had not. As each uneventful Friday passed and the girl or her father had not arrived, he became more infuriated, which caused severe headaches. The waiting and wondering if she will come drove him insane. *What if...she never comes, but she must come! I must find her. I must find her at all cost. Perseverance will prevail,* he muttered as he paced.

Headache or no headache, he cannot miss Friday. Some of the merchants, especially those who knew his father, whispered, "Look at Thomas Komarod, what a sophisticated and elegant young man he has become." Others coming from other areas agreed with the locals, overlooking his work clothes each Friday. One outsider pointed at his boots and said, "Look at his boots! The toes curled gaping at the sky," the man roared. The other man laughed and said, "Yes, soon his toes will peek out at the world too." The group of men stood and laughed and then one raised his hand and said, "Hey... look down at our boots, we are laughing at ourselves as well. Besides, all of us wear work clothes on market day."

"We could hardly come here in our Sunday high heels with polished buckles, could we?" the other added. They laughed hysterically.

"We cannot be criticized by anyone of not being in style!" More laughter resounded and a few more men gathered to join in the noonday fun.

"Hush now, here he comes, hush." All of them stood with just thin-lipped smiles. When they questioned Lord Thomas about his family in conversation, Lord Thomas cleverly evaded these questions, making up fictitious scenarios for those too inquisitive. His flirtatious character turned many heads, especially girls. Children ran to him as he always had some funny tales to tell them. All the credit should go to his trusted friend Jacoby. Jacoby's tutoring had not gone to the wind, but absorbed like a sponge by Lord Thomas. Unfortunately, Jacoby moved away.

Noontime. The hot sun stood at its apex. Lord Thomas sat on a barrel in the shade of his kiosk, observing people, and suddenly his eyes followed a short fellow waddling as a duck brought memories of Midge, the shortest in his group of friends. Hard to forget that grin from ear to ear. Those funny and witty stories... he had a way with the girls too... poor fellow, fell off his horse in such a peculiar way, and died. Lord Thomas liked Midge, and he missed him now.

Although Lord Thomas far from being rich, but his earnings, pinching off the profit on the side, and saving for months afforded a fine tailored outfit. Lord Thomas strolled around like a peacock just to impress his higher-class group of friends.

Cybilia's father seldom came to the market. The servants alternated on market days. Lord Thomas, not knowing any of them, just happened to acquaint several by chance in conversation. His charm disarmed these women, besides, what he needed to know cleverly pulled their tongues, and they naively complied. These young girls, with rosy cheeks and flapping long lashes wide-eyed, swinging hips and large bosoms to catch one's eye -- he knocked them off their feet. Thomas became known as the Komarod "gentleman" at the market. The servants talked about him back at the estate in the kitchen, and the men at the estate added their opinions as well. Cybilia listened with great curiosity, *"Komarod, Komarod gentleman," she must remember his name, but what is his first name?* she thought and smiled. She would find out from these girls in the kitchen and servants, better today, than another time.

"Who are you talking about here? Must be someone special that you have him constantly on your tongues?" she questioned.

"Oh Miss Cybilia, what a fine gentleman he is and handsome at that," the young servant girl said, folding her hands in a praying fashion and shyly twisting her shoulders and her eyes looking up to the ceiling. Cybilia smiled at this comical young girl.

"If he is so handsome, perhaps I should have a look at him and give you *my* opinion, before I lose my senses, as you girls have." Cybilia laughed and walked out of the kitchen.

Cybilia waited for Friday to go to the market again, just to get a glimpse of this elegant young man. Several weeks passed. She arrived before noon with the servants, a bit late to sell and purchase items on their list. That morning her father had driven out to a city to negotiate business and would not return for several days. Mother had not once interfered at Father's objections of Cybilia's visits to the market. However, her mother encouraged Cybilia when they were alone to mingle with people but warned her to be careful, for there were unscrupulous people out there. She herself had experienced such in her past. Regardless what or who is out there it is important for Cybilia to be educated in *that* department. Therefore, that day she was free to go to the market again.

On that day, arriving just at sunrise, Lord Thomas had a head start. People in carts and wagons had been waiting to have the best picking at whatever their need. As the other merchants arrived and set up, his wagon was nearly empty of produce but for the carvings, which by a miracle all sold later in the day to complete strangers speaking an unfamiliar language. Lord Thomas through the years had never seen these individuals before, but then, the market is huge. One must stand and keep one's eyes on shoplifters, not wandering around looking for strangers. They must have been passing through and happened to stumble on this huge market. No surprise at all, people travel constantly from far south or perhaps west, those from the north or east are easily recognizable, having many similarities overall judging their language and apparel. Lord Thomas noticed these people were wealthy they had gold, much gold, and were not miserly with it. By now, high noon, the sun overhead a bit too warm and bright, he pulled his hat down to shield his eyes. Now his stomach growled. It was time for lunch. He reached under the seat for his lunch, but it was not there. He had forgotten it at home. Now he had no choice but to buy his lunch at the kiosks. He walked over to the adjoining kiosk and asked the man if his son was free to go and buy a loaf of bread, a chunk of cheese and a pickle. The teenager, glad to earn a few pennies, ran off to buy the items for Lord Thomas. Slicing the bread, he gave two to the boy with some cheese, and a few pennies. He sat in the shade on the barrel, leaning his back against the side of the wagon. He cut a thick slice of bread, a slice of cheese, and cut the large pickle in half, then ate it quickly and washed it down with water. He wrapped up everything in a flour sack, climbed into the wagon, stretched out his body, and rested his head on a sack, arms crossed over his closed eyes. Those arriving predawn always rested during noontime. It seemed the din of the whole market subsided a bit at that hour.

Unnoticed on the horizon, a sudden storm moved in with strong gusting wind. Out of the dark heavy clouds rain came down in a torrent and everyone ran for cover. Lord Thomas sprinted out of the wagon and dashed for shelter, now crowded with people. He was very drenched. He stood barely under its roof, waiting for the rain to pass. Puddles everywhere, he stood in one of them up to his ankles. The water seeped into his boots. He turned his head when someone said, “oh no!” He eyed the crowd, craning his neck to see who it was and caught a glimpse of a familiar profile. Her hair drooped and her wet dress clung to her shapely body. People grimaced at him as he inched his way motioning to them and pointing at her, they understood and allowed him to squeeze through, and he stood behind her.

Cybilia was not concerned that someone stood a bit too close behind her yet instinctively turned her head. At eye level, she faced an unlaced shirt exposing a man’s hairy chest. Slowly she lifted her head and met a handsome face with a pair of blue eyes looking into hers, and for a few seconds Lord Thomas froze. They stared, eyes locked for a moment. She felt her blood rushing to her face. She blinked and looked away. He felt good being near her. His heart drummed and fluttered.

“What a downpour. It came upon us so suddenly. Hope it passes quickly,” he said, leaning closer to her ear to break the silence and smiled. Cybilia, caught off guard, blushed even more and stiffened. Then she dropped her eyes, embarrassed. She did not turn to look at him or reply. She remembered him, that first time when she was with her father and friends. It was he, squinting, and he looked her way. Her heart beat fast and she was flustered. Now he stood near her. He was tall to her because she was slim and at least a head shorter, but just the right height for a woman. She felt her face turn crimson. When someone pushed him against her back, he whispered an apology into her ear. No one was talking inside the huge shelter, but here and there whispers rubbed against one’s ear. Everyone was anxious for the rain cloud to move on and drop a flood elsewhere, and finally the wind blew away the soft drizzle. Then the bright sunrays glistened in the puddles. People ran over to their wagons, small stands and kiosks. Here much work waited for everyone, such as emptying rainwater, gathering overturned baskets scattered by the wind and cleaning up. Again the hubbub returned.

They were alone, just the two of them in the shelter, a thatched roof on poles, there were two walls on the south and west side of it, protection from the harsh sun in the summer. Still she could not walk away. Lord Thomas stepped in front of her to face her. Cybilia did not look at him but stared straight ahead.

He did not press her for conversation but waited a bit.

"Are you here with your father?" he asked, breaking the silence again.

"I came along with the servants," she replied not looking at him. Abruptly her eyes were on him and with an angry voice asked him curtly, "My father... You know my father. Who are you?"

Her outburst took him aback. He knew that was a wrong question. Not knowing how to explain his face flushed from embarrassment and eyes cast down blurted out.

"May I introduce myself, Miss... Miss... I am Lord Thomas Komarod." He bowed and reached out for her hand. Cybilia slowly, hesitantly extended hers, as he kissed her fingertips, he looked into her eyes, eyes the color of violets. He held his breath. He could not look away. *Captivating eyes, but right now icy,* he thought. He swam in those eyes and would not let go of her hand. She was confused. Flustered... Lost for words, but pulling herself together she knew what to say to his introduction, in a low, cold, mocking voice, she said, "So... you are the famous 'Lord Komarod, the 'gentleman,' I heard about you from our servants, but, to me you do not appear a 'Lord.'"

What she had said struck him like a dagger, rattled his nerves, he raised his eyebrows. He inhaled deeply, then said politely, "And...what makes me appear not to be a Lord?"

Cybilia eyed him from head to boots, her head high peering at him through her lashes, she replied, "Well, first of all, a *Lord* never brings wares to the market in person to sell... servants do." Cybilia held her head high and continued peering at him.

"Ah yes, you are correct. My pretty Miss, my appearance is indeed an absolute deception, a mere disguise, nothing to do with who I am. Not at all competitive, but on the contrary I am equal among all *these merchants,* is that wrong? Or perhaps... is it offending my... or should I say degrading my class?" He came back at her in a low well-controlled voice.

Cybilia seemed to be lost for words, again. After a moment of silence not looking directly at him, she spoke as if she was speaking to herself, "I am confused by your words, Lord Komarod, deceptive disguise, an illusion, a false image of oneself?"

Lord Thomas stabbed again by her words, looked at her for a very long moment, smiled and whispered. "Life in itself is a deceptive illusion, and disguised promises. As for me... oh I, I love mystery. Fate is a mystery, our meeting today was not by chance, but you and I... by the hand of Fate were meant to be here, now, that is a mystery. But I assure you I am not an illusion."

Cybilia flushed with heat all over her body, defensively tried to explain, "But I came today purely out of necessity. I had no inkling you would be here as well, our meeting was purely coincidental."

"Ah...but my Lady, my feelings tell me that today you came to find *me,* to find out for yourself who I really am. Mystery always intrigues me. As you mentioned, your servants gossiped about me. I apologize for my appearance. Overlook my arrogance for I found the nerve to speak to you. Perhaps I do not meet your standards. You take me for a peasant the way you look at me, that I am surely. In my disguise I present myself at this market as you see me, forgive my insolence. And I might add... I never miss market days, if you ever need me I am at your service, though I do not have the pleasure to know your name." He grinned at her broadly, but within him his blood boiled.

Cybilia completely disarmed, stiffened, "Forgive me for speaking so harshly to you. I... but I have introduced myself. You have forgotten, my name is Cybilia...short Vie." She smiled ignoring all he had said.

"Cybilia, Cybilia, very unusual name, though I do not recall your introduction. However, I prefer to call you Cybilia may I... if it pleases you my Lady?" Lord Thomas asked.

"Yes, you may. I apologize for my oversight," she replied.

The rain had stopped long ago. People had cleaned rainwater out of everything. The two of them stood in that large shelter. Neither spoke. Their eyes were on each other, oblivious to what went on. Abruptly she looked away, her eyes searched the crowd for servants.

"It is time for me to go now." She took a step forward. He blocked her way. His heart fluttered. His throat tight, but he blurted out, "Must you? Will I see you again, my Lady Cybilia?"

She gave him a long look, as if studying his face again, to remember. Lord Thomas felt his blood surging and he blushed. She smiled at that, which gave her a feeling of satisfaction.

"Yes, I will be here, three Fridays from today," she said.

Lord Thomas could not show disappointment; again, he bowed, not reaching for her hand.

"Today the pleasure is mine. I assure you I will wait patiently to see you again, my Lady Cybilia," he spoke softly.

Leaving him staring ahead, she walked away, disappearing among the crowds. She rode away into the distance with her servants. He felt a spark in his heart, a spark of happiness and a pang of longing. "This was a good day, you will be back, and I will be here... waiting," he whispered.

On the way home, Cybilia was on his mind. He saw her face and the way she looked at him, eyed him up and down, he glanced down and saw his boots muddy soggy and the tips turned up, he did not miss the last look she had given him. "I will be waiting like a spider to snare a moth. And I need a new pair of boots," Lord Thomas said aloud. All the way home he smiled, a faraway look on his face.

During dinner, Lord Thomas described to Kosta those people who had purchased his carvings and handed the small purse to him. Kosta stuffed it in his pocket. Kosta learned counting with Aunt Olivia. Now he walks and counts everything he sees. Lord Thomas never had an inkling that his younger brother is able to count and read now. Kosta will never tell him, but eagerly will later compare and hide his profit. He listened as his brother described in detail his meeting with Cybilia, their conversation and that she will be back. Kosta observed his brother's face.

Thomas acted like a courting peacock. He seemed to be on a cloud. Though touched by love, he had not lost his sight on his plan to succeed, but for now has sidestepped off his path a bit. He was young and clever. To everyone he seemed honest and always courteous as a fine *Gentleman*. However, his dark side unseen, continued to lay low.

On the fourth Friday, Cybilia arrived along with her friends and servants. Lord Thomas found himself at her side, being attentive as a perfect "gentleman." Her friends and servants went on their way to make their purchases from their lists. At the end of the day, they shall meet at the carriage, with loaded wagons will be on their way home.

"I am here with my friends. My father was not able to come today," Cybilia said when they met. Lord Thomas took a step closer to her. She did not back away. When she raised her head, he was much taller than she was, of course, but today he noticed much more than the first several times. How perfect her hair was and her soft lips had a bit of color; her eyebrows were perfect arches and her lashes long... Their eyes locked and he fell into them as if into pools of clear water. It was evident she had an interest in him as well because she did not move. They stood and stared at each other, oblivious to the throngs of people around. He had a strong urge just to touch her hand, but he stopped himself instinctively. Instead he stepped back and bowed low. Cybilia laughed.

Lord Thomas smiled at her and said, "My young lady must think I am a clown."

"Yes in your attire and your comical bow, yes a bit awkward," Cybilia replied still smiling.

"Well then, I shall be your clown... forever... if you like." Cybilia did not reply at that but turned and began walking towards a bread kiosk. He followed, thinking, *I must be discreet; time must pass, after all, I am sure servants are watching. She is young but I dare not ask her age, not yet, and inexperienced. She is flirting with me; calls me a clown; I will prove much to her later.* Cybilia bought a sandwich and Lord Thomas as well, and they walked to his stand and sat on barrels and ate, sipping tea from tin cups.

Oh but the young have strong feelings as well. Lord Thomas glanced at her often. To him, she was a fragrant flower in full bloom ready to be picked, held close to his lips and kissed, then thrown away like petals being plucked and tossed away. After all, he is older (exactly how much older he did not know, yet), and has seen much and gained experience.

Hmm... today's conversation flows quite easily, not butting heads, or arrogance, surely not on my side at least, he thought, *she had acted that way out of fear, being so young. Perhaps my approach seemed overbearing; I had tripped her off balance. I must take a step back. Make sure she is relaxed when with me. Perhaps, I will learn where she lives.*

They walked, later along many kiosks on which displayed all sorts of merchandise. Those men who knew her father bowed, with a greeting, "Good day Miss Prozatti." She nodded to them.

"Ah, a very good and prosperous day to you as well," she replied. Cybilia recalled mother's warning... *remember your reputation is important you are a young woman. To be alone with him means trouble you know the servants do talk.*

Lord Thomas made mental notes on those merchants. He must keep an eye on these men and remember their stands. Cybilia walked beside him listening as he talked of other markets elsewhere where he has been and what merchandise sold at what prices. She relaxed, aware of her strange feelings. She considered this as a pleasant encounter. He was her very first man who had spoken to her in a romantic way. She felt at ease with him, now seeing him many weeks, but she must step lightly, not muddy her reputation.

Lord Thomas, after weeks of observing her, was right. She had feelings for him. He sensed desperation in her behavior... or was it plain curiosity? His mannerism had changed from a stiff aristocrat to actions of a precarious rooster around her and he wanted to make her laugh and relax. Forgetting all else, she kept her eyes on him, on him only. Yes, he was finally on his way to accomplish his goal. He will have Cybilia, but with patience. Beside her, with time, he will be in her circle of high society. His chest burst with happiness and anticipation. His next step was her family. Cybilia was young but wise and observant, and acted her part at moments while strolling with Lord Thomas back to her friends, waiting at the carriage.

"Forgive me but I must hurry, my friends are waiting for me, I must go now," Cybilia said.

"How far of a—"

Cybilia cut him off in mid-sentence. "Not that far, it is rather a pleasant ride, less than two hours. But it is time to part, by chance to meet again," Cybilia replied and brushed past him quickly, leaving a breath of unrecognizable fragrance. No chance to kiss her hand. For a minute he thought that was odd. Then dismissed it... she was in a hurry. Lord Thomas waited until they rode out of sight. He strolled over to his old wagon and jumped on it to head home. He imagined her home to be cheerful and bright with many windows, elegantly furnished, and many servants... *Should I have offered to take her home in this old wagon? Heavens... no...no... I did the right thing... it would be too soon... patience wins especially with careful calculations surely it will be to my advantage*, he thought. He dreaded their gloomy stuffy house, where Kosta always sits and carves his asinine figurines. The sun now dipped closer to the horizon, and soon darkness will shroud the countryside. He should be home by then. Lord Thomas never took the time to look at the countryside, or listen to bird's singing, or which flowers are in bloom.

But as his wagon rolled along someone was watching, soaring high above him, thirteen pairs of eyes were watching.

Cybilia's mother suddenly became ill. Therefore, Cybilia refused to leave her side. No persuasion changed her mind by anyone not by Jullietta or Dora not even for an hour to venture out to the market. Her place was with her mother. Four long weeks, she kept vigil at her bedside, until mother's crisis passed. Feeling well enough for Truda, first housekeeper and Cybilia's nanny, she now cared for Lady Marianna of illness known only to them. Cybilia and her friends Dora and Jullietta would spend a little time at the market come next Friday. Cybilia was anxious to see Lord Thomas but, as always, remained poised and her demeanor stable, not a twitch of anxiety on her face, at least not when in the company of her friends. Most frequently, Lord Thomas had been on her mind. Some nights she was unable to sleep she was thinking... *is he as nice and gallant as everyone says he is? My eyes met his eyes I could not look away. I felt magnetism, drawn to him. I believe he felt it too. We have met quite a few times and had short conversations. He is a "gentleman" with such good manners, but still I had better be cautious. Definitely, I must mention these meetings to my father. However, he might forbid me to go to the market. Though I know Mother will pacify him, she always does.*

As weeks slipped by, Lord Thomas looked forward to seeing Cybilia again. He wondered why she failed to send an explanation of her absence. He got upset to the point that he behaved rudely to an elderly woman when she got in his way. The curious crowds watched and heard the woman scream at him, creating an ugly scene. Lord Thomas quickly disappeared into the crowd.

On the way home, he was furious with himself for being such a fool losing his temper.

At last, after four weeks, Cybilia saw him as he ran to hide behind a wagon stacked with baskets as she was stepping down from her carriage. He was near enough to observe her and her company. His heart raced, over several minutes he watched.

At her side stood a young man pointing at something. She shielded her eyes with her hand then turned to him and nodded in agreement. The young man walked away, disappearing into the crowd. Cybilia walked by the wagon, aware of him watching through the spaces of the baskets. Lord Thomas followed her. He admired her casual dress, appropriate for the market, not overly dressed, a dark blue simple skirt, a white blouse with wide kimono sleeves, and a shawl on her shoulders. When she stopped to wave at a servant she turned, and she was face to face with him. Lord Thomas stepped back raised his arms with surrendered expression on his face.

"He missed her lovely face, her beautiful eyes; he looked for her every market day, why she stayed away so many weeks, perhaps he had offended her in some way; if so he apologized." He was speaking very fast yet in a soothing voice.

When he first met her he found her attractive, but after seeing her all these months, he realized she also had charm, personality and intelligence, those captivating eyes gave her that certain beauty.

Cybilia, speechless, took in the scene and listened, his actions impressed her that he worried and missed her. Definitely, it was clear what he wanted: to be with her. Finally, when he stopped talking, she explained her reason for not coming to the market.

"Mother has taken very ill and I stayed at her side. It had nothing to do with you. You had not offended me at all. It just happened, but I am here and I would like to make it up to you, will you give me a ride home today? That is, if you have time." She looked into his eyes and waited. Lord Thomas heard her say, "Today, take her home, if he has time and is willing."

Lord Thomas opened his mouth but then clamped it shut. He could not believe what he heard and needed to absorb it.

"With pleasure, of course I will take my Lady Cybilia home, if you do not mind the old wagon and the old horses," he answered quickly, forgetting about the young man with her earlier in the day.

"Just follow the carriage. They will go slowly ahead of us, just for us, oh... by the way my cousin is with us today and he will ride along, that is, if you do not mind." Cybilia said.

"Absolutely... I do not mind at all, it will be a pleasure to meet your cousin," he replied, grinning.

When her young cousin appeared, he seemed to be Cybilia's age, perhaps a bit older. Cybilia said he should sit in the wagon, to keep them company. He objected with disgust, of course, quickly ran and slipped into the carriage, and it rolled away. Cybilia laughed. Lord Thomas did not push the horses too hard, but rather allow the horses to saunter at their pace. As they rode along, he apologized for the slow pace.

"Why, this is just perfect, a good chance to be together and talk." She began to shower him with many questions. "Where do you live exactly? I know you told me it was quite far, but I would like to know, where."

Lord Thomas described a town over the mountains, which happened to be miles from his village home, which was true; he had visited once with Jacoby years ago. His description was so exact and picturesque Cybilia became very excited, and she smiled broadly. She studied his face.

"I would like to go visit that town someday, it sounds pleasant. I wish to travel the world, but my father forbids me... my father told me I was too young. Do you have brothers and sisters?" she asked.

"I have one brother, no sisters. We do have reunions with our cousins every so often, but it takes time to organize everyone to one sitting," he replied turning his head away from her, pretending to see something of interest in the distance.

She contemplated his reply then asked him, "You must have servants to work the land, as we do. Your family must own a large parcel of land?"

"Oh... well... yes we had many acres, but had sold almost a half of the property, now we own just enough for my brother and myself, back-breaking work, as you know." Lord Thomas smiled at her. "This is really slow going. I do hope your friends are not bored. I am glad the sky is clear. Ah... so you have not been anywhere yet, did you say, too young? What about your friends, have they traveled to large cities?" he said, changing the subject.

Cybilia felt a bit awkward, and for a moment sat silent. She did not want him to know about being away at school and living with her Aunt Elizabeth, her mother's twin sister.

Lord Thomas to break the silence said, "I would like to ask if it would not offend you, Miss Cybilia... about your cousin, where does he live."

"Marcell, my cousin, he lives in London, England. But Marcell was born in France," she replied, hoping he would not ask if she had been to London.

Lord Thomas mulled that over for a while then said, "I promise you sweet Lady Cybilia, someday, you and I will visit many grand places, but first I must attain my life's goal."

That statement perplexed Cybilia, but she did not question him, she felt it was too rude and personal, after all, this was the first time they were alone together. Both looked at the countryside, not speaking, keeping their thoughts to themselves.

"And if I may ask, what school had you attended and where? Lord Thomas?" Cybilia looked at him waited for an answer.

He did not immediately reply to her question, he had to think... where did he go to school?

"Well, my young Miss, my school happened to be in the largest town, south of our village. I had the privilege to be under the instruction of a retired professor. Unfortunately, my schooling was cut short because of the accident..." he stopped, looked away. Cybilia did not question further, she was intelligent enough to realize something painful touched his memory. She was positive he would tell her later.

Lord Thomas hoped what he had told her was enough. He will make her wait for the full explanation one day, but not now. Rather, with great eagerness, he waited to arrive at her home. Thinking of meeting her parents made him feel uncomfortable for some reason, perhaps it would not be proper today. Perhaps by stretching the time, her parents would be in greater anticipation of meeting *him*... perhaps... Cybilia broke his train of thought.

"My friends will turn off the road shortly but we will continue on, coming up, you will see on the right a long lane with tall poplars, turn off there," she said, pointing ahead.

Before the poplars came into view, Lord Thomas halted the horses. He stared ahead. Cybilia spoke not a word, sat stiffly and waited. Lord Thomas turned to face her, scooted closer to her. Immersed deep into each other's eyes he reached over gently and took her face in his hands. She closed her eyes, and he kissed her lips tenderly, then hard. Cybilia did not resist. When he pulled away, her head remained tilted up, he kissed her again. Her lips were hot. "Cybilia...Cybilia," he whispered. Before she opened her eyes, she said, "Thomas...Thomas please, kiss me again..." He kissed her again. Feeling wilted, she smiled, rested her head on his chest. His heart beat fast. Hers drummed from excitement. He held her close to him. With Cybilia's arm around his waist, they rode in silence, until the poplars came into view. Cybilia moved away from him. They turned into the lane; on each side, poplars grew close together like sentinels. On a rise, an impressive home came into view, with emerald green lawns, evergreens and oaks strategically planted around the home. Lord Thomas looked both ways and asked Cybilia, "Those trees, are they... they are apple trees?" He did not wait for her reply, "What an orchard, huge mature trees."

"Yes they are apple trees, Father makes apple wine.," she said. As they entered through the gate, he was dumbfounded. He clenched his teeth. *This is huge, huge*, he thought. He smiled to conceal his surprise. Cybilia had not noticed. He helped her step down off the wagon and walked her to the front door. She invited him in, but politely he declined, explaining, "Urgent matters are waiting at home, forgive me and, it is rather late, I do have a long way home. But I will be delighted to... next time, if you wish to meet again." He bowed sensing eyes watching him, he kissed her hand, and she blushed slightly.

"Yes of course, I would love to see you again without a doubt," she replied. When she walked through the front door, the butler gave him a demeaning look, closing the door behind her. Lord Thomas smiled, turned the wagon around, and rode away. When he was far enough out of sight, he whipped the horses and they galloped as fast as their old bones could take it.

Lord Thomas felt he had accomplished at least a small part of his plan.

Whatever his future holds is up to Fate, he worried none. Nothing concerned him from that day on, no need to imagine or think about. They say, *love is blind* and it must be so, because Lord Thomas was blind to everything around him but Cybilia. He realized he was madly in love with this young miss, but he loved her more when the enormity of the estate hit him between the eyes. *Soon, I will be above poverty soon, it must happen very soon*, he thought.

Lord Thomas omitted the fact that he drove Cybilia home. He felt he was not obligated to do so, perhaps next time, as months pass and his plans are shaping up he will tell Kosta later, much later. The profits of the day's sale he handed to Kosta, then ate the meal, which Kosta had prepared. Then he muttered in a low voice that it has been a tiring day and went to stretch out on his bed, Cybilia on his mind. Kosta washed the dishes after doing the evening chores.

The next several market days for Lord Thomas turned out to be disappointing and discouraging. He came home spent and angry. Kosta noticed his changed demeanor and figured something went awry but waited for his brother to tell him what happened. Lord Thomas after dinner while sipping tea quietly said, "She did not show for the last five weeks, I do not understand why... this is driving me insane! No one would tell me why. Her servants did not speak to me in friendly manner, I do not understand why or what have I done? I did not offend her in any way. I know I did not!" Lord Thomas in an outburst of anger banged the table with his fist. The teacup rattled but did not break. Kosta taken aback by his outburst, decided not to question, just sat and waited.

Lord Thomas, irritated and dispirited, stood up quickly and began to pace the floor, not speaking to Kosta. When the dog got in his way, Thomas kicked him. Kosta jumped up in two strides faced Thomas. Kosta's cold, angry stare was like a knife ready to kill.

"You do not kick an innocent animal, especially a dog, *our* dog!" Kosta walked over to the dog and patted him gently. Thomas stood eyeing Kosta but not a word of apology, not to a dog. Friday came and Lord Thomas refused to go to the market.

Kosta took the opportunity to be away from the daily grind. Up before sunrise, he boiled coffee and ate a thick slice of bread with butter and honey. Then he cut a thick slice of smoked bacon and a thick slice of bread for lunch, loaded everything onto the wagon and rode away feeling a certain pleasure and freedom. The market is such a different world; he recalled being there with his father a long, long time ago. People milling, shouting, each voice louder than the other to sell their wares, and the choice of merchandise, all displayed, arranged attractively, it was breathtaking, exciting, children, old people, young women and girls scurrying to and fro. He never realized what the market represented, not only an opportunity for gain, but also this was a world in itself, to search, find, and be discovered.

Kosta was not sure which stand belonged to him, when asked an old man, he pointed to an empty one.

"If you work for Lord Thomas Komarod, drive your wagon behind that empty one. Fill that stand with whatever you have."

Within minutes Kosta quickly arranged all the produce in the front and the eggs in a round basket on the side of the table. The carvings were last out of the wagon, and cookies Aunt Olivia had baked, arranged high in a pyramid on a clean cloth. She told him, *sell them*, she would bake more, and of course why not? When several well-dressed men approached Kosta's stand, inspecting the carvings on display, they pointed and discussed each one, ignoring Kosta. To his dismay, Kosta tending other customers overheard these men talking about his brother, referring his *brother* as the talented carver. Another man joined the trio with a woman at his arm as they were inspecting the carvings, praising Lord Thomas and *his* work as, "*excellent, outstanding, perfection, what perfection!*" Kosta paid attention to what these people said.

"Young man, why is Lord Thomas absent, is he ill?" a redheaded balding man asked.

"Sir my *master* is out attending an important engagement this morning." Kosta simply replied. These customers assumed Kosta to be but a servant. The more Kosta thought about what people said the more enraged he became, but he checked his anger well nodding to men purchasing his wares and smiled at children and bowed to women buying Aunt Olivia's cookies; children ate and demanded more, until they sold out. Just before he was to leave, a young girl ran up and called to him, "Hey there, you work for Lord Thomas?"

"Yes I do. Can I help you?" Kosta replied. The girl handed him a sealed note addressed to his brother.

"Make sure you give him this note, and do not lose it, you hear!"

Kosta took the note and said, "Oh you bet I will not lose it. I will keep it close to my heart." He shoved the note into the inside pocket of his coat.

All the way home Kosta contemplated the events of the day. His decision was not to mention anything, wait and observe what happened. Arriving home in the late afternoon, Kosta found his brother relaxing at the table reading a book and sipping tea. Kosta handed him the note. His negative feelings stirred, he walked out to take care of the horses and the rest of the animals. Seeing Kosta they all began to moo and cluck and the pigs squealed for food. Kosta was infuriated at the brother's insensitivity in ignoring these poor creatures.

Lord Thomas unfolded the note carefully and read.

"Since you were absent today, your presence is requested by my parents at the residence of the Prozattis. Dine with us tomorrow, Saturday, and do arrive before sunset.

Because I arranged it, please do not disappoint me."

Cybilia Prozatti

"Ha...lucky me, an invitation...lucky me, I am going to Prozattis home! Yes! *THE* Prozattis and Cybilia arranged it, how clever of her!" he said, excitedly talking and pacing the floor. When Kosta returned from the barn, he got busy cooking supper. Thomas came up to him and shook the note in front of Kosta's face.

"And what do you think of this? Ha! She arranged it, an invitation to dinner tomorrow at Cybilia's home. Tomorrow, imagine that!"

"How do you know where she lives? It is for tomorrow?" Kosta asked.

"Oh yes, I know where she lives from the servants, and I must say... they were eager to give me the directions, and, of course I am going! I would not miss this opportunity for a bag of gold! This is my chance of a lifetime! Brother, my foot is in the door!" Lord Thomas replied, grinning.

"What about your travels, did you abandon those plans?" Kosta asked again.

"No... I have not changed my plans, yet, but, after tomorrow, perhaps...I will venture off once, but...tomorrow will be the deciding day." Lord Thomas said calmly. As they sat at the table someone drove up, Kosta stood up and walked to the door, it was Aunt Olivia.

"Ah... Aunt Olivia please come in, sorry you just missed dinner. I have cooked more than enough, if you like, have you eaten yet?" Kosta asked walking her to the table. "Hello Kosta, ah, yes I have had my dinner. Oh! Thomas you are home!" she exclaimed.

"Well Aunt Olivia, how nice to see you again." Thomas's reply barely heard, rather muttered.

"But may I share a cup of tea, if it is no problem, if you do not mind my visit and a chat with you both," Aunt Olivia said.

"You do not have to wait, it is ready," Kosta said.

Aunt Olivia sat and observed Thomas while Kosta filled three cups and sat one in front of her. Lord Thomas joined them in discussing health, weather and the market buzz, but his invitation to dinner was omitted. Aunt Olivia drove home after several hours spent with the brothers. Lord Thomas plopped on his bed, closed his eyes, anxiously awaited sunrise, sleeping fitfully. At first light, he lit the stove with small dry turf blocks as he watched them burst into flame quickly. Suddenly he recalled that day when he took Kosta for a walk to the marshes, but mother saw us and called us back. Kosta being so young and naïve tattled on me. He shrugged that thought and filled the kettle with water to boil. The aroma of fresh brewed coffee permeated throughout the house. Awakened from a deep sleep Kosta inhaled the aroma. Suddenly remembering yesterday, he felt his blood boil. He sipped the sweet brew, recalling comments made by those people about his brother. Tight-lipped keeping his tongue behind his teeth he sipped coffee quicker then he should have. Lord Thomas noticed that Kosta was in a hurry but said nothing, knowing well that morning chores waited. This morning he would not mess with manure and get all smelly and sweaty. Just before Kosta left the table, Lord Thomas took his cup and walked into the bedroom. Kosta sat for a while alone, stood up slowly not scraping his chair, took his cup sat it in the wash pan and went out to the barn. There he thought... "*He pretends like nothing is going on, keeping it from me, well I found out, I always had that feeling that he is not honest with me. But I will not let him know that I know.*" Kosta released his anger cleaning out the manure not realizing how quickly.

That Saturday early afternoon Lord Thomas dressed in his best attire, mounted the horse without a word to Kosta, and rode off. On the way he visualized all sorts of scenarios, facing Cybilia's parents for the first time, he shuddered an untimely doubt seized his nerves, what *'if'* to ward off such negative *'ifs'* he talked aloud.

All along the way, many eyes watched him ride; eyes of the thirteen ravens. He turned off the main road onto the lane.

Screened among the rustling leaves of the poplars they watched. Riding along the lane, he scanned the area. He knew he was on time, the sun was low in the sky and the sunrays cast a gold shimmer on the countryside. His heart skipped a beat. Such a pleasant scene, his heart beat faster, as he neared halfway down the lane to the huge house. However, at one moment, his stallion Star suddenly reared up, came down hard, stumped nervously, danced sideways and turned a full circle; he was about to rear up again, refusing to go any further. Lord Thomas, caught off guard, held on for his dear life, annoyed, and swore at the animal and heeled hard at the stallion's belly. The stallion felt the stab of pain, and galloped onward his head lowered sideways agitated tried to bite his rider. When dismounting at the gate, Star was still nervous, but by his master's soothing words had calmed down a bit. Unexpectedly a groom appeared, and took the reins and led the stallion away. The front door opened before Lord Thomas reached for the knocker.

"Welcome to the Estate of Lordship and Lady Prozatti, whom should I announce?" the butler grumbled sourly. Lord Thomas stepped into the foyer; the butler closed the door behind him and stepped ahead stiffly into the parlor. The aroma of food permeated throughout the home. Thomas was famished. His mouth salivated. He swallowed hard. His eyes darted, overwhelmed, impressed by what he saw, he tried to remember not to look a fool. He inched forward not hearing the sourly butler say to follow him, when the butler tugged his sleeve for lagging behind, he awkwardly apologized to the butler, but did not give his name, the butler disappeared into the interior of the house. As he entered the dining room, Cybilia and her parents sat at an elaborately set and beautifully arranged table with fruit on two plates; cakes on two plates and steaming tea in a silver carafe. There were four crystal glasses filled with white wine. Crystal candelabra with three candles stood in the center of the breakfront and another crystal candelabra with five candles in the center of the table all lit up gave off a pleasing ambiance. The window coverings in the dining room were drawn, only the candle light lit up the room. For a minute he wondered why, the day was not over yet; he stood just at the threshold of the dining room waiting to enter.

Cybilia's father Sir Prozatti made no move to rise. His arms folded across his belly but he welcomed him with a slight nod of his head. Cybilia's mother Lady Marianna gave Lord Thomas a weak tread-like smile, and arched her left eyebrow, which remained arched; she eyed him from head to his boots slowly as he stood in their full view, then she looked over at her husband, eye to eye contact, their facial expression unreadable yet seemed unprejudiced. Clearly, a bit reserved and a slight aloofness on their part was evident. Lord Thomas felt stripped and exposed down to his underclothes, his left arm behind his back concealing a tight fist, he strained to control his nerves, to leave a lasting impression. He stood confidently. Bowing low in a voice clear and strong, he spoke. "Permit me to introduce myself...my name is Thomas..."

Cybilia, jumped to her feet and seemed to glide over to Thomas, she took his hand.

"Forgive me Father...Mother...Thomas Komarod, Lord Thomas Komarod, the gentleman I told you about..." she looked up at Thomas. "Please join us for dinner," she spoke quickly. Her parents glanced at each other meaningfully.

Cybilia holding his hand led him to the table, at which time her father said with a heavy accent, "Welcome, to our humble home. I am Paulo Prozatti, and my wife Lady Marianna. Please do sit, enjoy a glass of wine." Thomas' nerves abated somewhat, but then as time dragged in conversation, rather it was an interrogation; their way of scrutinizing his character; lay it as if on a plate; and pick it apart bit by bit at this moment by mostly questions. However, he was not a fool. Absolutely he presented to them his best side, elegance and intelligence, thanks to Jacoby, his friend. With a bit of humor, tension had loosened somewhat between the four of them. Now he felt warmed by wine; the candles smoked stifling the air in this dining room. A small hint of unbuttoning his vest; run his finger inside his shirt color, his neck a bit damp, neither seemed to notice as he did so, not even Cybilia. Perhaps they wanted him to sweat that is why they pretended not to notice. They dined and conversed on particular subjects, but the subject on heritage, wealth or education was not mentioned. If at any moment confronted with such a question Lord Thomas would have been in hot water. He also realized that sweat glands from nerves erupted; sweat ran from his armpits down his sides. He was flustered a bit of what to do, but did not flinch. Instead he continued to be self-confident, keeping in mind not to raise his arm too often, as he had been used to with his friends.

The servants catered to him, as if he truly was a *Lord,* this appealed to him, and he absorbed it all like a sponge. Lord Thomas did not intend to over stay, he was about to leave and was about to say so; but at that moment, Sir Prozatti said, "Marianna...Cybilia, this is a moment we must toast our guest with a glass of our own apple wine." Lord Thomas felt it was not the time to leave although it was late. On the contrary, he must stay and learn more. He did notice the endless orchard as he rode up.

"Thank you, but I could not overindulge. I appreciate your hospitality and kindness," Thomas politely replied, his arms close to his sides.

"Nonsense, I insist on a toast in your honor...a fine gentleman as you are, Lord Komarod. You must give us your opinion of our wine."

Lady Marianna Prozatti raised her glass. To insult the hosts surely would be rude, and unforgivable. His arm slowly moved forward, but not too high. The three glasses lowered to his and clicked a toast to all present.

"Lord Thomas, do try, you will like it. It surely will surprise you!" Cybilia smiled and said. Therefore, he did taste the wine, which was exceptionally velvety rich and smooth, so smooth he could have downed a whole bottle right then, except he was not alone. They smiled at him.

"Sir Prozatti, indeed it is of the best quality and taste," he agreed. *Ha*...as if he had tasted the world-renowned wines in his short life.

Sir Prozatti nodded, his arms crossed on his belly smiled. Cybilia and her mother looked at each other and laughed and conversation continued. He was not sure if they laughed at him or was it the effect of the wine. It was time to leave, Sir Prozatti's eyelids drooped, and his head rested on his chest, Lady Prozatti yawned several times. Lord Thomas, feeling fuzzy, stood up holding on to the table, and apologized for over staying. As steadily as he could, he walked over to Lady Prozatti and reached for her hand, which she extended limply. Bowing, he kissed her fingertips, and bowed again.

"Lady Prozatti...excellent dinner, scrumptious, your warm hospitality will not be easily forgotten to be sure," Lord Thomas said. He gave a firm handgrip to Sir Prozatti, but the father's handshake was limp. Lord Thomas for a second thought, "*Italian's handshake is firm, not like a wet noodle,*" and then kissed Cybilia's hand. He felt Prozattis eyes were on him. Sir Prozatti walked around the table and led him to the front door.

Lord Thomas repeated again, "Sir, thank you for your warm welcome and allowing me to dine with you, I appreciate your hospitality." Cybilia's father murmured something inaudible and stepped back closing the door behind him. The cool air hit him, it was very dark all around, suddenly a lamplight appeared from the corner of the house, Thomas, recognized the young stable groom leading Star to him. He stuck his boot into the stirrup swung his right leg over the saddle with the gate being open rode away into the darkness. On the way home, the cool air sobered him quite enough and the scenario at the table came to his mind, he visualized the entire evening, puzzling, the initial welcome, rather stiff, but during dinner, relaxed. Later on overzealous with hospitality, this seemed a bit overwhelming, confusing, one could lose balance, and trip ones tongue. What were they trying to do...observing my every move and eyeing me like a pair of vultures, waiting for a slip in my articulation, or behavior, and they would have ejected me out through the window. However, I kept my composure until I drank too much wine. My conversations with the old man ah...yes...Sir Prozatti...flowed smoothly I think..., though I am proud of myself. They were impressed the moment I walked in, my boots spit polished, and my new suit, fit me to a tee, my physic, slim but strong. Oh...but that damn sweat ran down my sides, I could feel it. Damn armpit odor crept up to my nose; when they were evaluating me, my nerves unraveled. If they had detected the odor, would have classified me a stinky peasant. I wonder why Cybilia and her mother laughed at my comment, the wine. I must find a solution for that problem. How I wish, Jacoby were here. He would have helped me with it. Lord Thomas talked aloud to himself all the way home, it was dark and late no one out there to hear him. He must tell his brother all about it. Lord Thomas booted Stars belly to a faster gallop. At last, he arrived home, relieved that he had not encountered any wild animals. He led Star into the stall, dropped the saddle to the ground and stormed into the house. Kosta startled jumped to his feet. *Thomas with a grin on his face, surely news must be good,* he thought.

"God, you scared me! Why are you making a racket?" Kosta shouted at his brother.

Lord Thomas stood in the middle of the room and said to his brother.

"I finally have done it, finally it happened! I, LORD THOMAS am at the threshold of my goal!" Kosta was speechless. His brother dressed so aristocratically whirled around the room several times. Kosta later recalled that discussion of goals or plans for their future, never was, *why, we hardly talk to each other, now he is telling me about some wealthy people. What an unbelievable change*! Kosta thought.

Lord Thomas kept the lie to himself that he lived in the next town. Regretfully he told Cybilia their visits must be occasional. Besides that, he decided to curtail visits with his friends. Lord

Thomas returning home in a wagon one day from a nearby village from the corner of his eye in the copse caught a movement. He wasted no time to flee if this is an ambush or wild animals. Horses galloped, wagon rattled, crossed a bumpy meadow, to reach the main road. He reined the horses to a slow amble now on the road. The old horse showed exhaustion. Any moment he could drop dead. He let the horses amble on slowly. The old horse foamed from his mouth and coat glistened. He needed water, but in this area none; none he knew about, he is too old. At home, unhitched and led the horses into stable filled buckets with fresh water.

"The old horse is not good for long runs and heavy loads anymore, keep him on the farm," he said to Kosta.

Fourteen: Calculated Risk

The day Cybilia entered his life a chapter of it had changed. He was determined to win her for his own. He, by shear chance, now owned a fine stallion named him Star, with a richly ornate expensive saddle. He rode to Cybilia not just to impress her, but for her to name his solid black stallion, but for the star on his forehead. If she could not guess the name for his beauty, he will tell her. Cybilia had not seen his horse the first time he was invited; it was too dark. The groom led him away and she was indoors. He imagined Cyblia to be excited and impressed. To face Cybilia's parents again, he had strong reservations, answers to their questions might throw him off guard. However, for as many times as he had the pleasure of visiting her, he could not help but think of, time of engagement will come soon, followed by marriage. That is, if it happens at all. The reality of not being wealthy gnawed at his stomach; *should they demand a disclosure of my wealth? I have nothing, and I do not know of any one of importance whom I could trust to vouch of my worthiness to marry their daughter. Profession presently, none per se. Any means of providing for their daughter and our future family, if they ask, I have none. Out of the question, the home I live in is unsuitable for a girl of her class.* Now I have described a true picture of myself, I own nothing, and am nobody, and usually my pockets are empty. Such thoughts occupied his mind, whenever he found himself on the road to Cybilia.

His visits in general were relaxed, however, returning home time after time, thoughts of insecurity crowded his mind...*I am at the mercy of my brother, so to speak, regardless if my name being on the property documents or not, besides I am never there, I do not deserve even a tenth of it. However, I will continue to reap the profits, until I wed Cybilia.* Lord Thomas laughed...*I am as naked as a jaybird! If her parents object, consider me unsuitable and forbid her even to meet with me... Why they may ask her what she sees in me, if she agrees with them, my plans will fail. I must take that risk...if my foot crosses their threshold and I step in, through the door of wealth by marriage...indeed...I am taking a calculated risk... indeed.*

He was nervous, sweaty palms and sleepless nights. He must find a solution to this dilemma. Loving her, he does. *It is crucial to search for my family tree. My father's birth certificate, documents of ancestry, and mothers birth certificate I had never asked them about such documents, never entered my mind also their marriage certificate, which will be proof of my genealogy. To falsify the truth; and then discovered I had lied and fail to prove authenticity I will pay for such fraud with my head.* He shivered at that thought. This drove him to confusion. One moment swayed to falsify his lineage; then leaned towards an honest confession; *primarily I must prepare a very convincing emotional speech if confronted by Cybilia's parents on that subject, or I will go insane!*

The summer was ending; he could not believe another fall was ahead; yearly laborious harvest waits. Lord Thomas hated that season. Shame, shame would not allow him to evade his part of the responsibility, after all he dined and slept in that home. When the morning air felt crisp, a clear sign, dreary fall days are coming. On a fair day, he decided to visit Cybilia, as long as the weather held. However, while riding along he imagined having a discussion on a particular subject, which meant, '*him*' with her parents. Old Prozatti a master of making wine but...*I know nothing of making wine, though I am quick in learning, and I do have a gift of gab...Jacoby said so. I will win if I stand my ground.* The more he thought about this idea, the more he was convinced that..., *that is precisely what I must do. I should have a talk with old Prozatti, man to man. Give him time to consider daughters future. If they reject me, I will humble myself, kneel, emotionally...oh I am good at acting the part...appeal to them in the name of love. I will say, I cannot forsake her, our hearts will be broken, if Cybilia discovers they caused their separation she will be devastated, and so will I...hmm... sounds like blackmail...hmm. Blame Fate for that. To forbid them to marry would shame her yes...no, I cannot say that..., or she would be disgraced..., oh but I did not disgrace her in any way...I just kissed her... no, I cannot say that either. I will say...*another thought frightened him...*that her father will feel insulted and threatened, feel guilty and retaliate by calling me names...probably in Italian...then throw me out. If Cybilia throws a tantrum, if she will... well I do not know if she will..., ah that...is a calculated risk. If I am lucky, they may retract their refusal. I wonder. What about Cybilia, what if they describe me as a trickster. I charmed her, and she fell in love. I withheld the truth from the start! What if old Prozatti is very* *perceptive and sees through me. Hmm... she might be mad as a badger and be first to reject me. I must take that chance. This game is like catching a raw egg, if you do not catch it, tricky business caching a raw egg it lands on your forehead it will crack and your face has raw egg dripping and sliding down to your mouth. Oh God that happened to me several times when I played with my pals, they gave me a nickname, Egg Face, of course, but not for long, I beat that out of the skinny Andreas, I did not like him from the start when he joined our group. Never knew what happened to him, one time at the meeting he did not show, I asked Jacoby about him, he said nobody knew. His parents moved from the small hut on the outskirts of the village just a few weeks ago. Well enough of that no more details, that is long gone and buried. I have before me an urgent situation right now capturing Cybilia. I must charm her so that she falls for me blindly, insanely, completely.*

With each visit, Lord Thomas came with his planned speech in the back of his mind. Prepared to tell the truth, if all else fails, throw his miserable self at their mercy, and let *love* conquer.

Cybilia's parents politely conversed but discretely observed. It seemed the atmosphere had become more at ease, and the butler smiled when opening the front door, why even gave a quick bow. Things had changed and now he felt being on a fence, not knowing which way he will have to jump. Nerves were on edge again, his palms moist, and his armpits leaked.

In the weeks that followed, their relationship grew more electrifying, when alone, their arms tangled in embraces and burning kisses. Although his visits were infrequent, at times Lord Thomas visited for days. Those nights he slept in the guesthouse. One of the manservants slept there also, early in the morning awakened by the manservant walked to the main house for breakfast. Thereafter, each day they spent together Cybilia as instructed by her father went around the grounds and walked through the distillery. Lord Thomas absorbed it all, eager to be part of her life and part of the riches. Besides, now accepted as one '*who belongs*.' He recalled his first initial introduction and all following visits, seemed well taken. His sophisticated manner left an impression on Cybilia's parents. Sr. Paulo Prozatti of Italian winemaker's family for generations, and Lady Marianna Sandeweig, and her twin sister Elizabeth. Marianna became promiscuous at an early age disowned by parents and Elizabeth devoted to her parents lived at home. Prozatti's only daughter was Cybilia. Lord Thomas wanted *her*. He surmised that she prepared them well beforehand, because the questions he so dreaded most were never asked. His emotional pressure relieved he even slept much better and seemed less abrasive to Kosta.

Lord Thomas impressed upon her parents his considerate and thoughtful self. His conversations with her father were interesting. Lord Thomas cleverly paid attention to loosen her father's tongue interjected carefully his opinions, and questions. Lady Marianna sat fanning just a bit under her chin; her arm moved slowly with a bit of rhythm. While her eyes moved from him to Cybilia than to her husband, and back to him. He noticed; to boost her ego directly complimented her at opportune moments. Cybilia starry eyed tiptoed around her parents.

Lord Thomas gave of himself in bits and pieces to be recognized as worthy by her parents, but also the staff. Compliments to the cook, for his own assurance remembered to bring small momentous to each one, next time. What information he needed servants offered freely of the daily routine around the estate. Among each other, they whispered...*from the looks of it, he is going to be the new master of this estate soon.* Whenever he came into the kitchen, young shy girls turned heads to hide their curious eyes and smiles. Except one young woman, ah that one, her cool glances and aloofness caught his attention. Lord Thomas wondered, *she seems suspicions of me, as if she knows who I am. In time I will take care of her, in the meantime I will charm her and the others with some little complements for their services.*

When cold wintery days arrived, Lord Thomas dared not risk illness by taking long trips. With nothing to do but the chores, was antsy unable to sleep, but to get out of the dingy house he visited Aunt Olivia, who lived close enough, which surprised her. Lord Thomas held back all the information of his upcoming marriage to Cybilia. However, Aunt Olivia knew it all from Kosta. She avoided asking his help with chores. She knew how much he disliked dirty work. Lord Thomas after several hours returned home refreshed, more talkative, grinning silly. Time dragged, winter kept him from Cybilia, his impatience piqued. High winds and drifts swept through, dumping wet and heavy snow, which fell day and night. Travel was impossible and dangerous.

The thought that Cybilia could change her mind unnerved him; *winters are long, she is young easily could be swayed. Her parents could plant little seeds of doubt now and then. In addition, of course, he considered that girl in the kitchen...hmm... I wonder. True... Cybilia loves me, but a rich new suitor in my absence could sweep her off her feet. Would anyone venture out in this weather to see her? I doubt it.*

Pacing from window to window scraping at the frosted glass with his fingernail to look out, but as far as he could see, the world lay dormant beneath the snow. When frustration chafed, he felt like a caged lion plucked from his tropical domain and dropped into the desolate frozen North Pole. He could not sit still. Everything irked him. Kosta noticed his brother's nervousness seldom spoke to him. Lord Thomas walked back and forth from house to barn for fresh air, but the air in the barn was much too stifling and foul, he walked over to the horses stable, but it was just as bad, and just as cold, so he came back to the house. On some days, he gathered eggs, while carrying the basket, he recalled when Kosta was a teen, ran in a hurry with a basket of eggs, tripped on the broom handle put there by him. He smiled, it was rather funny then, but now, if Kosta had done the same to him, he would be very angry. *Well... that was a long time ago, no need to dwell on that, now we are adults,* he thought.

Lord Thomas yearned to be with Cybilia during the holidays. His plan was to drop in unannounced for Christmas. Having a pair of leather gloves for her over which he haggled with a stubborn merchant. Kosta's large carved horse for her parents, for which he had to beg.

Kosta recalling that day at the market, when those men thought he was a *servant;* never mentioned to his brother what those men said to him. He would not dare, besides Christmas is just a few more weeks away. Another time, at the right time, he will discuss all of it with his brother the "aristocrat."

On a spur of the moment one morning, four days before Christmas, Lord Thomas decided to make the trip, since it was still early morning. The sun shone through clouds promising a fair day. Lord Thomas hurriedly prepared for his visit. Within several hours, while on the road wind whipped at him now and then. On the horizon, dark clouds, seemed slow moving, but the sun still peeked through clouds quite high above him. He rode on, cape collar up, sheepskin hat pulled over his ears, and shawl wrapped around his face from the wind; then the clouds obscured the sun; it became dark and large snowflakes swirled becoming thicker as he rode on. Where trees and shadows had been before, now the grey countryside and horizon merged. Anticipating a long and difficult trip, his horse covered with a wool blanket, another wool blanket shielding Stars chest with straps secured to the saddle. Lord Thomas urged Star to gallop faster to head off the storm wherever the going was light. He reached the halfway point to Cybilia's home, now the snow came down thick wet and heavy, visibility nil. Horse and rider barely visible in the blizzard, he felt the temperature plummeting and the snow now formed a crust on the now invisible road. The sheepskin hat pulled down covering his forehead and the shawl wrapped around his nose and face, the chill penetrated his heavy wool suit and cape. His feet were numb, his ears burned from frost, hands inside the cape wrapped close around his body. He was the only human on the road. Snowstorm blanketed the countryside. Hard to follow the road, and here and there, he passed by a grey shadow of a farmhouse. Remembering previously, he knew he was on the right track. Snow kept falling.

At last, he reached the long lane. The poplar trees stood bare, whipped by freezing gusts of wind. He reached the gate, slid off Star, shivering, rang the bell on the fence. The servant laboriously opened the gate pushing aside the snow. The fence encircled half of the house all the way to the stable. Lord Thomas entered through the back door of the kitchen. The girls startled, suppressed a cry. The pretty one with the long black hair skipped to him tugged off his cape, clumps of snow on his shoulders dropped to the floor. The sheepskin hat was one crusted chunk of ice. He was trembling from the cold. He dropped onto a chair. She called for a man to come and pull off his boots. The corpulent cook's helper fetched sheepskin slippers into which he slipped his frozen feet. He could not control shivers that shook him. Nose and hands were numb. The cook told the girl to bring a blanket, and hot tea with honey. He walked into the empty parlor, dragging the blanket on him surprised no one was there to greet him. Lord Thomas reached for the carafe of wine from the silver tray. He filled a glass and drank it quickly, filled another; walked over and sat in a high back chair close to the fireplace. Legs stretched towards the heat. He felt the wine rush through him quickly warming him.

The servants brought tea, a dish of hot soup to replenish spent energy and to warm him. Lord Thomas slurped greedily, drank tea and devoured the sweet-cakes. Then drank too much wine. He sat and stared at the flames dancing in the hearth. His head buzzed. That girl with the black hair came in and asked if he wished a cup of fresh coffee. He nodded, *yes thank you*. She left. The shivering stopped. He dosed off for a little while, feeling completely satiated and comfortable.

Suddenly awakened by voices, he jumped to his feet. Sir Prozatti stood near him, next to him stood a man who seemed to be a bit younger, smiling. Lord Thomas embarrassed, explained what had happened to him, they both dismissed him with pleasantries. Cybilia was not with them. Disappointed wondering where she was, asked of her whereabouts, and was assured not to worry she will reappear soon.

His blood boiled when through the front door came in a very distinguished man, taller than Sir Prozatti. Cybilia and her mother at his side, she did not expect to see Lord Thomas, now her face took on a stone expression. She placed a large sack on the sofa and excused herself leaving the parlor followed by Lady Marianna. No one spoke. Lord Thomas kept his eyes on that fellow standing at the window looking out at the placid scene, hands behind his back; Lord Thomas noticed large gold rings on both hands, which instantly made him nervous for some reason. The butler carried in a silver tray with glasses of wine. Sir Paulo Prozatti reached for the glass, motioned to Lord Thomas, "come one glass is for you," he said.

"Yes, well, Madran come join us for a toast and introduction." Sir Paulo waved him over. Madran walked slowly away from the large window and joined them.

"Lord Thomas, meet Madran our new distributor from Italia, and this is my dear brother, Lorenzo. Now Gentlemen, may I introduce to you Lord Thomas Komarod, our frequent guest. This holiday he found himself *unexpectedly* in our humble home. Cheers, cheers, salute!"

They sipped and smacked, eyebrows danced on Madran's forehead, impressed, a big smile stretched on his face.

"Ah, hmm... perfect, easy on the palate, very marketable!" Madran said.

The butler stuck his head into the parlor to announce, "Sir, dinner is served in minutes." At that moment, mother and daughter entered the parlor, both attractively dressed and Lord Thomas glued his eyes on Cybilia.

Lord Thomas by now felt revived from being half frozen, and was his usual self again. Throughout the home festive decorations and arrangements were not only handmade, but also purchased from other towns, and Italy as well, he had earlier found out from the dark-haired serving girl, she seemed impressed by him. Servants were passing each other bringing in many platters of meat and vegetables for the main course. Spiced cakes, fruit compote and bottles of wine sat on the sideboard. Aroma permeated throughout, inviting the hungry. Sir Prozatti called out to the girl with the raven hair. "Attenna, bring us appetizers, please!" Lord Thomas thought, *Aha...her name is Attenna...good to know.*

A live nine-foot tall fir tree decorated with hand-made ornaments stood in front of the window. Packages of different size wrapped in silks tied with ribbons and some wrapped in white cotton cloth each had a different color ribbon, stacked high on a round table in the corner of the parlor. Everyone dressed in fine Holiday attire, but it was not the Christmas day yet, it was still several days to come.

Cybilia looked wonderfully attractive, she glowed like sunshine, and he loved her. Lady Marianna, her hair pulled back off her face, ringlets atop her head held with pearl combs. Dressed in a silvery silk gown, white lace adorned her bare shoulders and laced cuffs on sleeves. On a long gold chain, long enough to reach her cleavage hung a large pearl cupped in a gold shell; one's eye could not miss but take in such a lasting image a perfect subject to be immortalized on canvas. Large pearl earrings, bracelets on both wrists complemented the set.

Madran was first to approach her, eager to pay her a compliment, bowed, holding a wine glass in his left hand, reached for her hand, which she extended rather quickly Madran, spoke softly.

"Lady Marianna you look ravishing, a pleasure to be with your family, especially for Christmas." He lifted her hand to his lips and lightly kissed it.

She smiled and replied, "Why thank you Madran. You are welcome at any time of the year, not only at Christmas time." She noted that Lord Thomas now stood several steps behind their guest, watching her. He liked what he saw, she gathered. However, this was an important moment and she should store it in her memory for future analysis.

Lord Thomas felt she seemed to approve his being with them. Lord Thomas also greeted her with compliments and kissed both her hands, noticing rings on her fingers. However, did not comment out of respect. Later discovering by overhearing conversation in the kitchen, that he "annoyed" Lady Marianna with his overly attention. Sir Paulo also mentioned having him underfoot as a "nuisance." His blood boiled. He was sure his face was crimson, as usual, but of course held his tongue as he mingled sipping wine. At every chance, stood by Lady Marianna just off to her side as she conversed with both men.

Cybilia entered the parlor wearing a green gown, covering her completely up to her chin, long snug sleeves defining her slim arms. Hair as gold as the sun brushed back off the forehead, thin braids neatly tied at the back with green narrow ribbon, swayed loose down to her waist as she stepped lightly in her holiday slippers. He was at her side in just a few strides with her arm on his they strolled over to Uncle Lorenzo and Madran the wine vendor. Lord Thomas relaxed, somewhat. However, those words spoken by Sir Prozatti...*he found himself in our humble home...* echoed in his mind. *I will analyze that statement later, no reason to be jealous of her Uncle. He is not a threat. As for the statements made about him in the kitchen, well...I will rehash that too, later.* He was thinking. That evening, dinner served with time lapse in between which lasted close to midnight. Lord Thomas had not thought about sleeping arrangements, felt uneasy; hoping not to sleep in the men's quarters. As it turned out, Uncle Lorenzo, their guest Madran and Lord Thomas slept in the guesthouse. To reach the guesthouse they had to ride horses, at one thirty in the morning. Horses led into the stable for the night. Snowdrifts high against the stable walls and house, going was quite rough with just a lantern in freezing temperature. Morning came a bit too soon, but the fresh coffee tasted good. The three men returned on horseback to the main house, before lunch.

The young lovers were inseparable forgetting all others present as they sat on the sofa and talked. Sir Prozatti conducted business with Madran. His brother Lorenzo listened, following them around the winery; in winter employees are always busy with necessary repairs. The clouds moved on. The sun broke through raising the temperature slightly and held for several days. Cybilia insisted on sleigh rides and horseback riding, since the days were warmer, which turned out to be miserable the horses were unable to walk through the deep snow, they abandoned that outing. The young couple enjoyed each other's company, occupied with activities each day. Several hours in the day they spent their time at the guesthouse, of course someone was present at all times to serve whatever their needs.

Lord Thomas really experienced love, ease, and comfort that week with Cybilia. One day, though dark clouds drifted across the sky, Cybilia insisted on a sleigh ride, which would give them time alone, alone. Cybilia dressed in a sheep hide coat and hat and a muff, she wore wool stockings and knee high boots of sheepskin on her feet. Wrapped in sheep wraps, Lord Thomas held her in his arms. Her head on his chest, he kissed her hair. She lifted her face to him and impulsively their lips locked in a kiss, she pulled away after a moment, neither spoke but studied each other's faces. Lord

Thomas leaned to touch her ear with his lips and whispered, "Cybilia... will you be my wife."

Cybilia entirely taken aback by his sudden proposal, she lowered her head to think. Lord Thomas watched her, waiting for her to reply. She hesitated a moment; but to him seemed very long, of course she whispered, "Yes."

He held her tight, Cybilia's head on his chest. The sled slid over the newly fallen snow, fairly compacted now by use but still the road a bit bumpy. Horses unhurriedly trotted. The bells jingled. Feeling happy holding her close, and assured that soon he will have her for his own. As the winter wonderland scene sped by, he, for the first time noticed this beauty around them. He closed his eyes and suddenly a scene flashed vividly of the night his parents perished in the frozen river. He shuddered and shouted to the driver.

"Turn back, turn back." The driver heard the shout and halted, turned the sled around and headed back home. Cybilia puzzled, closely observed her future husband as his face flushed and perspiration appeared on his forehead.

"What is wrong, are you feeling ill? You look distraught. Thomas, Thomas what is wrong?" she asked, handing him her handkerchief to wipe perspiration off his face.

Thomas unable to speak, emotions raged like a furious storm within him. Anger and sorrow comingled. He wanted to scream and run. However, having Cybilia near him, with difficulty quelled his emotions and clamped a vice to control his nerves. He sat, stared ahead waiting to calm down and wishing they were home. He needed a stiff drink. Cybilia was somewhat confused to see him in such a state, though hesitated to ask questions. Lord Thomas shifted in the seat and leaned to rest his head on her shoulder. Her arm around him gently caressed his face. She kissed his lips, cheeks and eyes. Her doting calmed his nerves.

"Cybilia... I absolutely must speak to your parents this evening," he whispered.

She just smiled. All the way home neither spoke. The driver pulled up close to the back of the kitchen, Lord Thomas helped Cybilia out of the sled and held her arm to keep her from falling on the slippery ice. They entered the kitchen and the aroma of dinner cooking made them hungry.

During dinner, Uncle Lorenzo and Madran conversed with a language unfamiliar to Lord Thomas but he gathered their conversation is about the business, he thought, "*that is good, as soon as I marry Cybilia I expect to take control of the business.*

That Madran is an asset..." and stored it in his memory. Cybilia, her mother and Lord Thomas sat and listened as they talked about weather, coats and dresses of the latest fashion, which excited the women, but Lord Thomas had little interest in that department. Of course, not ignoring Lady Marianna but certainly with one ear, just pretending to be interested. Having several glasses of wine felt at ease, when at dinner, everyone gorged themselves on delicacies, washed it down with wine. Thereafter, Sir Prozatti, and Lady Marianna led his brother Lorenzo and Madran their guest to the parlor with wine glasses in hand. The butler will surely call them to the sweet desserts and hot-spiced tea. The girls will clear the dishes. Set the porcalain tea set and fresh napkins, as always the best for the last.

Thomas sat next to Cybilia on the sofa. He gripped his courage, his hands in his pockets, feeling any moment sweat will pour out of his pores, which would be embarrassing. Preparing his little speech in his mind, words he must choose carefully to ask Cybilia's parents for her hand in marriage; *my stomachs cramping, my throat dry, I fear rejection. I am not a rich man. They know little of me. Because she fell in love with me, well...that might not be enough.* These dubious thoughts reeled in his mind. He felt that, surely, he would break out in sweat, if he does not calm his nerves with a drink. No, he needs fresh air, cold air to chill his tension.

It was the right moment. Lord Thomas abruptly stood up bowed to Lady Marianna. A nod of his head to the other men muttered an excuse, marched through the kitchen ignoring women's comments bounded out for a breath of fresh air. The door slammed behind him. The chill shocked him. The only pale light illuminating the snow came from the candlelight through the tall windows. Though the hour not as late, as back then, on that night, when their parents perished in the river, he shivered remembering. Attenna the black hair girl, abruptly opened the back door and called him back in, said Miss Cybilia is looking for him. She is waiting at the dining table. Attenna gave him a big smile.

He walked into the dining room for the sweets, slices of cake and a cup of hot-spiced tea. He kissed her cheek and asked Cybilia if she would like a cup too, to which she said, "No thank you." Lord Thomas smiled at her.

"Why were you out there, it is dreadfully cold? Thomas you are grinning?" Cybilia asked.

"My sweet girl, I just needed a moment to cool my nerves." Now I am observing *them*. They are very professional on the subject of wine. She sat down and filled her cup with tea. Lord Thomas raised an eyebrow, “Why Cybilia...I offered you tea and you refused, now you filled your cup yourself...what is the meaning...” Cybilia raised her hand to forestall him.

“Why Thomas...how childish of you, I changed my mind, no reason for you to cater to me!” Lord Thomas felt embarrassed; his face turned crimson. He held his tongue, said nothing more to her remark.

“Yes they are. It seems,” she continued, “discussions go smoother in their own language.” Cybilia laughed. She turned her head towards the three men, listening but not understanding any of it. Lord Thomas sat down on the chair next to her thinking, “*Tonight must be the night; I want an answer tonight.*” Wishing these two foreign guests would retire to bed already; but from the looks of it their heated discussion at times will drag past midnight. As if reading Thomas’s mind Madran eased out of the chair laboriously, stretched a bit and said, “Gentlemen, Marianna if you excuse me, I shall retire; the trip was long. Last night we stayed up late. We shall continue this conversation tomorrow.”

Lady Marianna and Sir Paulo absolutely did not mind, in fact they were tired as well. Madran bowed and kissed Lady Mariannas hand, bid them good night and walked out of the parlor, following old butler through the kitchen and out into the dark night, where a sled waited to take Madran to the guesthouse. A sleepy eyed young girl led him to his bedroom. Madran did not pay attention what the room looked like, stripped of his suit and donned the nightshirt, which the girl laid on the bed slipped under the covers, in just a moment fell into deep sleep.

Uncle Lorenzo as if on cue jumped up and walked to the sideboard where all the wines stood, began to refill all the glasses with red wine. Cybilia’s parents sat by the fireplace and held empty glasses. This was the opportune moment for Lord Thomas, though his heart drummed, his face hard as stone, his stomach cramped fiercely; his knees refused to bend as he walked; no one would detect the turmoil in him, not at this moment. In just a few steps, he stood stiffly before Cybilia’s parents. He bowed low, his left fist tight behind his back. His face hid uncertainty; rather stiffly, awkwardly bowed leaning a bit too forward but quickly caught his balance. His left ankle bent as he caught his stumble in front both parents. In a controlled, calm voice, he dared to ask for their blessing and permission to marry their daughter, Cybilia.

Cybilias parents observed his awkwardness and quelled a giggle; taken aback a bit surprised, Lady Marianna’s eyes grew large though she was tired and Sir Paulo’s lips took a downward turn.

Cybilia did not mention anything about her feelings for Lord Thomas. They looked at each other knowingly and Lady Marianna said, "Please excuse us Lord Thomas, we need a moment alone with our daughter."

"Yes of course," Lord Thomas replied, without hesitating took a few steps back and walked out of the parlor. Knees weakening as he passed by Cybilia and Uncle Lorenzo in conversation, he did not dare interrupt.

Standing in the kitchen alone, his clenched fists in the pockets, felt inferior. Fear of rejection almost strangled him, but with difficulty forced to wait patiently. On the table stood a bottle of wine, he poured a large cup of it and sipped, waiting. It seemed longer than a moment, it seemed like hours, but he waited. He thought; *if not now, I will have her later. They will see that I am good for her, and they will accept me, wait and see, I will prove this to them. I shall wait until they both die, and they are getting old. Then, no one will object, ha, then all of this will be mine and she will be mine without question. Now, I must wait.*

Attenna walked in through the back door startled him. She kept an eye on Lord Thomas, seeing him in the kitchen nervously pacing, dared not speak, but Lord Thomas peripherally saw her and thought; *something about her bothers me, she is always around, she must know something, the way she acts, soon I will clear this up, soon.* The door to the kitchen creaked and opened with a bang, Uncle Lorenzo walked in. Lord Thomas's knees weakened. However, the ever-smiling face of this Italian Uncle Lorenzo popped his bubble of fear, refilled his cup, "Drink it," he said.

"I am extremely nervous. My stomach is cramping," Lord Thomas confessed.

"No need to worry, your luck is with you. You have charmed them and they approve, you lucky dog... you passed by a hair," Uncle Lorenzo was saying.

Lord Thomas had no time to absorb what Uncle Lorenzo had said, just then Cybilia flung the door open, aglow, smiling, she reached for Thomas's hand and said, "Come, my parents wish to speak with you." She led him into the parlor. He was so nervous he never noticed the glow of happiness on her face. Her father motioned him to sit down on the side chair. The way both of them looked at him made him shiver.

"Frunn..." Sir Prozatti called to the butler, "bring us the strong spirit for this occasion."

Lord Thomas did not grasp the meaning of the stronger spirit, but sat and waited. Frunn returned with a bottle of rum. After having downed quite a few thimbles, Lord Thomas felt fire surging through his veins, a concoction of wine and rum burned in his brain. *Oh...so that is the trick..., now... I... will be..., interrogated...* thought Lord Thomas.

His heart raced in his chest and he felt warm under his collar. Lady Prozatti observed him, a thin thread-like smile on her face, continually fanning, though it was cool in the parlor. Cybilia sat next to her mother.

"Lord Thomas Komarod until today, we, Lady Marianna and I knew very little about you. We are aware you do not have the ability and means to support our daughter or having a profession, but from observation, we regard you as well-bred and quite well educated. Therefore, you must know, Cybilia strongly expressed her wish to have you as her husband...or else. We must permit this to happen. At present, we only agree to an engagement, which will last one full year. Following arrangements and preparations, marriage will take place next fall. In the meantime you and I, we have much to discuss. That is all we ask of you," Sir Prozatti said.

"I must add one more thing, we request that sometime in the early spring we shall arrange an engagement celebration, young man be prepared," Lady Marianna said.

Lord Thomas's head buzzed, hearing the words "one full year."

Lord Thomas was stunned, but held his posture erect, if at this moment he had to rise his knees would not allow him, they turned to jell. He had nothing to say, gladly agreed with a "*yes of course*" to everything her father said. His head spun, he heard but half who said what to him, nothing mattered, all he knew she was *his*! Slowly he rose from the chair holding onto the armrests. Graciously bowing, then stepped up to kiss Lady Marianna's hands, gripped her father's hand hard, and bowed again. Embracing Cybilia completely lost in excitement kissed her forehead, her eyes, her cheeks, her hands and he kissed her lips. The young displayed love for one another and her parents applauded, at that moment the young lovers were embarrassed and apologized, Cybilia ran to embrace her parents. They toasted several times to a happy marriage and a long life. Lord Thomas felt the need to leave or he would scream from excitement. Uncle Lorenzo applauded. Embraced Cybilia and slapped Thomas' back wishing both *prosperous future and happiness, and many children*, at the same time inviting the family for a summer vacation.

"Thank you, you are so gracious, surely we will not miss it in the world," Lord Thomas heard himself saying. However, during that evening, temperature dropped dangerously. The whole household was discussing the weather and the bitter cold. How dangerous to be out. Cybilia and Lord Thomas were alone in the parlor. Uncle Lorenzo left and so did her parents tired after a long and exciting evening. Then he said to Cybilia he needed to leave.

"Stay a few more days, it is late and too dangerous, perhaps the weather will warm up tomorrow," she begged. He stayed. A very wise decision as he learned later, while the dangerous freeze swept the country, several people and horses found in the spring on the road frozen to death beneath the high drifts. Lord Thomas understood that Fate had kept him alive. Several days had past and he was ready to go home.

"Sweetheart I hate to leave you, but I must, it is important for me and it is a long way home. I cannot delay, today is quite warm. I must leave now, evening approaching, I fear the temperature might drop again. Cybilia I thank you...your insistence saved my life," he said as he held her in his arms. Cybilia in tears kissed him tenderly.

"Well then go... but I miss you already, come back soon," Cybilia said.

"I will be back, that is a promise, I will miss you too and my heart will miss you," Lord Thomas replied.

Christmas was a joy for the neighboring children. Kosta watched them as they dressed the snowman in old clothes and a woman's summer hat. For Kosta himself it was difficult, his mind clouded with memories, he preferred to stay in and be alone. Unexpectedly Aunt Olivia arrived to spend the holiday with the boys.

"Kosta, where is Thomas?" she glanced around.

"Thomas..., he..., gone off to spend the holidays with that rich family," replied Kosta. Aunt Olivia detected bitterness in his voice. She was glad she decided to come. Kosta should not be alone.

"When is he coming back, did he say?"

"I do not know he did not speak to me when he left." Kosta said dryly.

"Well, no matter we will dine together," she said and began to scurry around warming dinner, which she had cooked at home. Though the weather was nasty, they heard a knock on the front door, Kosta opened it and there stood Orzak, bundled up in a wool shawl, only his eyes were visible. Kosta's neighbor's son three houses down the road.

"Well come in, it is cold out there." Kosta said and pulled him in by the arm. The boy slipped into the warm kitchen. Kosta unwrapped, the shawl from Orzaks face and asked.

"What brings you here in this nasty weather?"

"My parents sent me here to invite both of you for lunch tomorrow," Orzak said.

"Yes of course, thank you we will come," Kosta said.

Aunt Olivia handed the boy a cup of hot tea, he drank it and said he had better head back home.

"Wait right here I will get the horse and give you a ride home," Kosta said.

While Kosta was out Aunt Olivia had asked, "How many sisters and brothers are in your family Orzak"

"I have two older sisters, about Uncle Kosta's age, we call him Uncle you know; and my brother is younger," Orzak told her.

"How old are you my boy?" she asked.

"Today is my birthday I am eleven and my name is Orzak." He smiled.

"Orzak, yes I know, what an unusual name...oh Kosta is waiting for you, quickly wrapped the boys head with the shawl and said, "Go now see you tomorrow, Orzak. Oh one moment, what time tomorrow?" she called after he was out the door. The boy ran up to the horse. Kosta lifted him up and sat him in front of him, quickly trotted away. Orzak told Kosta to come at noon next day. Christmas day at noon, bundled up they walked to lunch with Orzaks family. Kosta sat next to Orzak and his younger brother at a large table. Aunt Olivia sat across the table from Kosta. The daughters sat with Aunt Olivia and parents at each end. He seemed lost in such a large family, the girls blushed and giggled at Kosta's small talk with them. The older girls catered to Aunt Olivia and Kosta with tea, cakes and fruit compote. Upon leaving, Kosta out of gratitude kissed their mother's hands and expressed appreciation, for her thoughtfulness and wonderful Holiday hospitality.

During that week, they dined with other neighbors. New Years Eve they spent alone. Kosta was young in years but had matured quickly being on his own. He and Aunt Olivia together cheered each other up, loneliness dissipated. As far as he was concerned she could stay with him all winter, he would have less concern for her safety.

Morning talks always brought out the past of those happy moments and funny episodes to laugh at.

Lord Thomas returning home on New Year's Day was so excited he could not wait to tell Kosta all about his visit. Their official engagement is far off, in the spring, he knew that many of Prozattis social friends will attend, and he will be at his best.

Uncle Lorenzo invited everyone for an extended stay during the summer at the Villa, wherever that might be. Lord Thomas eyed the white winter countryside, his chest swelled with pride, as he thought; *yes! I wonder what my father would say to me now!*

Suddenly, remembering that night and their tragic death. He recalled that that afternoon with Cybilia on that sleigh ride..., they too used sheep hides. Chills ran through him and a sudden unsavory nausea cramped his stomach, and was about to vomit. No, I will not vomit I need...I need to shout, release the tension pent up for so long; *Yes! Fate is on my side now! Yes, my life is truly turning around, for the better*! Lord Thomas thought and sudden tears trickled down his cheeks. When his emotions subsided, he cried out, "No Father...it is not the same, nothing will be the same. My life will be different. *I will* make it different. I already have! I do not need to cook, or, learn a real trade, or shovel manure! Toil in that black soil from sunrise to sunset, waiting and watching for the result to reap a meager harvest. Suffer winter cold! Endure scorching summer heat! Plowing and planting, straining my back and tasting salty sweat. Sweat stings the eyes! Oh No-No, that kind of life is not for *ME*! Others will do the dirty work. I will be the *MASTER!* I will give the orders to the servants. No one will rule *ME* from the day I marry Cybilia...*NO ONE!*"

His words echoed across the terrain as he shouted. For a moment, he stopped shouting and wondered of Kosta's reaction to his news. He had passed the village, now was on his street and home. Dismounted led the horse inside the stable, threw some hay and walked through the heaps of snow. He turned back into the stable, he forgot to remove the saddle and rub down Star his prize stallion, and fill the bucket with water. While going through the motion, unable to clear his mind of his brother. Melancholia took hold of him, he felt a bit sorry for Kosta. "But why must I be sorry for my brother? Ah must be all that wine and rum combination, I should not care. I do not care what happens to him. He must live on his own and think of his future, I will not be a tutor or a nanny to him. Unfortunately, all responsibilities and toil fall on my brother's shoulders. Ah, he will survive. He has so far. Kosta does have a good head on his shoulders I see it clearly. While I will rise above poverty, I will leave behind this peasantry life. Working in the fields, I hate it. Anyway, it is just too bad I will not help Kosta, but others will. He cannot object, and absolutely has no right to stop me! As far as I am concerned, I must acquire more education, one can never have enough education and there is so much to learn. At the next discussion of the wine process, I will hint to my future father-in-law that I should be more involved, that is if he so wishes. The sooner I have the knowledge, the sooner my father-in-law will be able to rest. As for me, I must be ready for the high society friends with Cybilia. He muttered on and on to himself.

Lord Thomas imagined a leisurely life with Cybilia. He laughed, that eerie laugh echoed, and he laughed again just to hear it reverberate through the stable, his laughter spooked the horses. This night he felt no fear and his confidence unyielding. He fell on the hay dizzy, closed his eyes and felt falling, falling, spinning and fell asleep. He woke up freezing but somewhat sober not knowing how long he had been asleep.

Lord Thomas at late hour walked into the house, after eleven days. Aunt Olivia and Kosta were still up and working on a project. Surprised to see his Aunt Olivia seated at the table with Kosta, smiled.

"Happy New Year to you, I wish you both a prosperous, healthy New Year."

Aunt Olivia glad to see him hugged him, planting a kiss on his cheek said, "Thomas you are half frozen! Kosta we need to heat up the house a bit, it is ratter chilly in here," she said. Kosta threw a small log on the fire. Thinking... *it is too late in the night for a large log. Soon we will go to bed.* She noticed a sparkle in Thomas's eyes, something good had happened and she was ready to hear it.

Out of his heavy cape appeared a bottle of wine, he sat it on the table with a bang.

"Aunt Olivia, I fell asleep on the hay in the stable. I had a few too many but this is from the Prozatti family...to my family; let us have a toast to our New Year. And I have news for both of you."

Lord Thomas uncorked the bottle and filled three tin mugs.

Aunt Olivia and Kosta sipped wine as they sat at the table. She admired his new suit. Indeed, he looked elegant. Lord Thomas eagerly told them of the incredible visit with the Prozattis over the Holidays and described a pretty picture of all that happened in those eleven days. Aunt Olivia and Kosta listened but neither made comments or questioned, after they heard the story Kosta congratulated his brother. Aunt Olivia gave him a hug. The hour was very late. The three of them retired to their beds.

After winter follows spring, the months flew by as always, villagers loaded up with work hurried to complete it all.

Through spring and summer, Lord Thomas made only four visits to Aunt Olivia and his brother. Lord Thomas wanted to be away, to get his feet wet in a new way of life with the rich. Aunt Olivia and Kosta combined their effort and managed not only plow the fields but seed the fields, of course with the help of neighbors, Ahnut and his son seeing Aunt Olivia working right along with Kosta so hard, felt sorry and told his wife to call on the others, of course all came to help. Kosta and Aunt Olivia took turns going to the market. Not once, had they met up with Lord Thomas there, if he had been there and had seen either of them, he evaded them well among the crowds.

The time slipped by quickly. The engagement announcements sent out far in advance to family and friends. On the day of the engagement, Lord Thomas had arrived several days ahead of the guests. The women scrubbed and cleaned the whole house; cooks were busy with menu preparation. He wondered about these relatives. When would they arrive? How far must they travel? Since the Prozattis or Cybilia had not mentioned relatives before. The only relative he had met was Uncle Lorenzo., none other. Uncle Lorenzo not once had spoken of his wife during his stay. He wondered, perhaps they had arrived and are staying elsewhere, but where? He also wondered, at the market, had they been to the market. To ask too many questions was not wise at all, he must bite his tongue and hide his anxiety.

On the engagement day, his face turned to stone when a small group of guests arrived, plus a dozen or so of the family. He had never met any of them before, for all he knew they could have been at the market. They could have known of him. As for him knowing them, never had he seem any of these faces before. He felt let down and though his face showed no disappointment he smiled, bowed and kissed every women's fingertips. They noticed and their tongues chattered in their own language, which he could not understand, but in his eyes, the icy glare he could not hide. His curiosity got the best of him, he had forced himself to ask Cybilia what they were chattering about, and why were these people so loud, unfortunately, she did not understand them either, both had to ask Sir Prozatti. Her father laughed and translated it all to them, "They have great praise for you both, and, charmed by you, Thomas Elemina said you two are beautiful people." Sir Prozatti winked.

The chattering family from Italy strolled around the orchard; Sir Prozatti led them through the winery. Wine bottles were in every room of the house and kitchen, all the while their loud voices echoed, disregarding others, and it appeared that this family had taken over the house. They were in every room. For Lord Thomas and Cybilia being the center of their attention a bit overbearing dragging Cybilia from room to room her father at her side interpreting. Lord Thomas now had to be on the sideline and could not wait for these Italian peasants to leave. Four days later the whole crowd drove away singing and laughing, in two carriages. Sudden silence now prevailed. Everyone relaxed. Sir Prozatti one day before the other guests were to arrive said to Cybilia and Thomas,

"You will meet my close neighbors and friends; it will be quiet, no loud talks and excitement. You must excuse my Italian family it is natural for them to be gesticulating with their hands and voices to express happiness."

Expecting guests to be near Cybilia's parent's age, or older, instead he met middle-aged and younger. Lord Thomas observed but failed to note wives of these guests, which belonged to which men. The reason being all these women dressed elegantly came into the house together. The men were in a debate about something as they walked leisurely into the house. Several of the younger men were near his age. He presumed them to be sons, but whose sons he could not ask, not at the moment. They were crowding around Cybilia, which upset him; he hid his displeasure well; asked particular questions of these younger landowners, owners of orchards incomparable in size to Prozattis. Lord Thomas surmised well these guests invited for a purpose.

Lady Marianna urged Cybilia and Lord Thomas to speak to all those present and pay attention; and take part in discussions. Dinner conversation always involved wineries, productivity and distribution as far as they could deliver. After elaborate display of sweet table and spiced tea. Next day, the men walked through the distillery and, were gone for several hours. In the meantime attention given by the women to the bride to be, but Lord Thomas played his part, overseeing the menu for the next day, his were mostly questions, not directives. After all, this was only their engagement. He had to curb his strong desire to order them around, *not yet, I must wait*...he thought.

Lady Marianna discretely eyed Lord Thomas from time to time, wherever he seemed to appear or stand and listen to conversations. The women were discussing the upcoming wedding and each having an opinion of the style of dress for Cybilia, since the wedding will be shortly after harvest. For a short time, none could come to an agreement on the color for the dresses, since it would be fall. Cybilia agitated expressed her opinion, she told them she will decide on the color and not them, and walked away. In her bedroom, she sat and stared into space, her mind blank.

Fifteen: Cybilia Prozatti Weds Thomas Komarod

Lady Prozatti engaged the services of Zita, a young woman from a large city who's experienced in current fabrics, fashion, design, and outstanding handiwork. Lady Marianna conveniently had settled Zita in the guesthouse. The three of them traveled to Berlan a large city to purchase silk fabrics, threads, laces and gloves, having it all at hand. Cybilia and her mother being on premises for all the fittings, for Zita, this was the best opportunity to earn a huge sum of gold. It did not matter how long it will take to complete the dresses. Cybilias wedding gown and her mother's dress became Zitas top priority. All her customer orders were given to other girls to complete. Ah..., what power shiny gold pieces do possess! The wedding dress fashioned of the best silk fabric and intricately designed. Cybilia surely will be a beautiful bride. Lord Thomas engaged his friend tailor Turkin Woolden at the "Needle and Spool Shop," to sew his suit for the big day, knowing well his reputation and quality work. No need to travel far his shop is conveniently close just at the near-by town. Small world, Lord Thomas not aware that his tailor's daughter is working on his fiancés dress, her mothers, and the bridesmaids dresses; that was a surprise to him. Cybilia one day told him when he mentioned his tailor, "Zita had moved and began to work for a large dress shop in France, where the elite circles had bought the best silks and wore the most expensive and modern of their time and styles." The subject of sons and daughters never entered in their conversations between visits. Lord Thomas wide eyed replied, "I tell you my sweet, as many times as I have done business with him I never had seen children or a wife, and I assumed Turk was a bachelor. Besides, we discussed business."

Weeks and months flew by. Lord Thomas convinced by many who told him the proverb, *"Those who marry in the early autumn, held fortune in hand."* Ah, he liked a prediction such as that.

Lady Marianna busy with the menu contemplated on the guest list, making sure no one with an obnoxious character is invited, and she knew of several. Such were her husband's so called friends. Then her thoughts drifted to her daughter, would she be loved and happy. Lady Marianna thought of Lord Thomas, back when the very first time arrived for dinner had impressed her. She was not concerned his visits then were however frequent. She felt her daughter found a plaything or perhaps a companion at first. Cybilia to her was still young and naïve several years back. *Perhaps, an infatuation, perhaps...a dashing handsome "Lord" captured her with sweet talk. A spider weaves a silky web to captures flies, or some other. "Lord" Thomas cleverly has spun a web around Cybilia, now she is a prisoner of his charm."* She thought.

Lady Marianna sat staring into nothing. Then said aloud, "Nor did I foresee this union. They will wed soon, I am losing my daughter."

As to his heritage did it matter, no, never was mentioned in all their conversations, discovering through the grapevine he is in reality poor, but then being poor is not a disgrace or a crime, depending on the circumstance. On the subject of his parents, when she learned of the tragedy, informed her husband; therefore never touched on it in his presence. She imagined herself when young and what situations she had fallen into in her life, until she met Paulo by chance while working as a barmaid. He, a well to do merchant of high social standing, in with the English Society had rescued her from the slum of a bar.

Paulo, her Italian husband, how fortunate she has been since then. She is now a Lady of leisure. Life has been and is good. It matters more what the person does with one's life. Ambition to succeed drives one individual more than another in pursuit for wealth and accomplishment. Since, he proved to be respectful and sincere means more than an air of confidence, and a gift of gab. Seems of steadfast character, and his constant attentiveness to her had not been overlooked, and the result does not matter. Now what matters our daughter's wedding. As a mother, I will stand by if she needs me. She thought. For Lady Marianna this was a trying time, though the newlyweds would be close, residing in the guesthouse. Now and then she had a disturbing thought; *Lord Thomas...had he charmed Cybilia to the point of her falling blindly in love in him?*

"I do count on his keen interest in the whole operation of the estate in the near future. His input and contacts of importance without any doubt will lead them to a greater success and wealth for Cybilia." Paulo said to Marianna as they strolled through the orchard out of earshot.

"But Paulo dear, remember what we have discussed, the legality of it all, and her rights as heir." Marianna said.

"I do remember, *cara mea*, all is in order." Paulo replied.

The villages buzzed with surprise, excitement and gossip. Wealthy farmers invited by Prozzati to their daughter's wedding, everyone graciously accepted. The whispers among closer friends expressed pity for the bride, others pity for the groom's younger brother. With time, gossip slips off the tongues and travels at lightning speed.

People loved to attend weddings, especially to taste Prozattis renowned apple wine. Surely as the sun rises each morning, all eyes glued on the bride and groom with a little buzz from the wine comments will silently spread. Days slipped by quickly, but on that big day...

Men and women were out dressing two pairs of white horses. The black carriage gilded with gold, best of its time adorned with red and white roses. Red and gold ribbons fluttered in the breeze, fresh fern and other greenery for interest. Red meant love, white roses, it is said, purity, peace, and gold, what else but riches.

Lord Thomas the morning of the wedding day at home was one bundle of nerves. No matter what Kosta said to him seemed wrong. Aunt Olivia noticed Thomas' outbursts, in private had a talk with him, Lord Thomas cooled down somewhat, he stared down at her. She could not tell what he was thinking as she stared back at him. His eyes were cold. She walked out and sat on the sofa. When he dressed, he walked out through the pantry door, mounted his stallion Star and rode off to Prozattis to marry Cybilia. Aunt Olivia and Kosta watched as he rode away, they looked at each other and felt the others pain.

"Not a word to us." Aunt Olivia said.

"Nor did he tell us where it would take place." Kosta said as he stood on the doorstep outside, his eyes followed his brother riding away down the dirt road. The fact is Thomas never mentioned to either of them where Cybilia lived or how far. Aunt Olivia stood by his side and studied Kosta, his face expressionless and his eyes dark and cold. She felt a slap in the face and knew he felt it too.

"Kosta all this shall pass, time heals as always." Aunt Olivia whispered. She pulled his sleeve and they stepped inside, she closed the door.

Aunt Olivia stood at the window thinking and suddenly she knew a way to find out where the wedding would take place. Quickly she marched over to the neighbor asked politely if her son Orzak would hail down anyone, anyone at all and ask for directions to the wedding of the Prozattis the wine maker. Gladly the boy obliged. Aunt Olivia promised a reward, and after several hours, Orzak came with directions...yes..., she had the directions!

"We are going*!*" she said.

At first Kosta refused, but after a while agreed, saddled two horses and Aunt Olivia mounted the older horse. Kosta surprised to see how gracefully his Aunt still rode. She smiled at him seeing his surprised look.

"Kosta do not be shocked. I do ride on occasion whenever I am asked, I do love to ride fast not crawl." Aunt Olivia jabbed the horse and sped away, Kosta followed. They rode with the rest of the uninvited along the way. When they reached the turnoff to the estate they stared at the white ribbons on every tree stirred in the soft breeze. Their eyes followed to the end of the lane where stood an enormous home. They looked at each other and held their breath.

"This is where my brother is going to live? Kosta asked.

"Is this real? Kosta pinch me!" Aunt Olivia said.

Kosta did not reply just kept on riding. Villagers gathered in groups, stood along the road waiting to cheer the bridal party when they come rolling along to the church.

Two people leaned close to the corner of the church; the huge church door opened wide. Kosta pushed it away from the wall just enough to hide behind it with Aunt Olivia having a crowd of onlookers to shield them had a good view to watch. Their horses' tied to a tree with a group of other horses.

"Aunt Olivia, look up," Kosta whispered.

"Oh my, Church of Miraculous Tears!" Aunt Olivia whispered back.

Three equestrians rode up. The onlookers cheered and waved handkerchiefs. Children held wild flowers in their hands waving. Between the two equestrians, Lord Thomas sat stiffly on Star his black stallion, his attire of light wool breeches knee length, stockings and shoes with buckles of the newest vogue, collar wrapped around his neck, lace ruffles dangled from this collar down to his belt. Cuffs of lace ruffles peeked from his shimmering coat sleeves, Lord Thomas changed his wool coat to silk for this special day.

Not once did he glance or acknowledge the cheering crowds, but ratter sat straight in a pompous pose. In the distance, the carriage with the bride drove up. The onlookers cheered and gaped at the black carriage, adorned with red and white roses, and ribbons of red, white and gold. Greenery and ferns hung in massive sprays tied with green ribbons. On the horse's necks wreaths of ribbons fluttered in red, gold and white. At the Church of Miraculous Tears, Cybilia's parents seated in the front pew, waited. The two bridesmaids wore dresses of rusty shimmering fabric with beads on the hams, around their necklines; sleeves dotted with beads all around the wrist and beads defining their cleavage. In their loose flowing hair...rusty fall flowers. When the church bell tolled once, silence fell. The ceremony began. Among the whispering crowd inched forward Aunt Olivia and Kosta. The bride's parents and three quarter of the pews occupied by guests, the others pressed in tightly to get a glimpse of the bride and groom and hear the ceremonial nuptials.

Lord Thomas stood at the altar faced Cybilia. When a sudden surge of emotion gripped his chest and cramped his stomach, a strange and intense pang of regret and sorrow tugged at his heart. At this moment, memory of his parents flashed in his mind. He wished they were alive and here to witness, give them their blessing. He missed them now, but they were gone. It has been years since that night, the ice never completely had frozen over the center, unaware not expecting this to happen in mid-winter. Horses, sled, plunged into that frozen river, together they died so long ago. Now, true feeling and longing for their presence comes years too late. Throat muscles tightened, tears blurred his vision; he gritted his teeth; this wave of emotion by force of will he crushed. *No, not now I am not going to break, not now!* He told himself. *The ceremony must go on. I adjusted well to life without them all these years. I grew up without them and as of today, I will begin my new life with Cybilia. I will not regret my choice of a woman as my wife.* Lord Thomas looked at Cybilia and smiled faintly.

At the far back of the Church of Miraculous Tears, stood Aunt Olivia and Kosta. He wiped away tears, his thoughts were the same, same heartache, loss of his parents, now he is losing his biological brother, as of this moment their brotherly ties severed permanently, and he felt it. Nevertheless, he was glad for Thomas. Unbeknownst to all up in the trees thirteen pairs of eyes watched.

Ceremony over, the bride and groom strolled out of the little church and passed by the cheering people, Cybilia nodded to them and took bunches of wild flowers from the children. Aunt Olivia and Kosta had a glimpse of her full dress made of silk and lace, a string of genuine pearls on the bride's neck, given to her by her parents, of course, surely not given to her by Lord Thomas.

"*The Komarods*" were a stunning couple.

The newlyweds regally walked followed by Jullieta the bride's maid of honor and Doreena their ring bearer. The newlyweds settled into the carriage, followed by a second carriage with their parents and the brides-maids. Cybilia overheard a woman say, "why a black carriage, it is bad luck!" The other poked her ribs, "hush, they might hear you!" she said. Cybilia heard but ignored that remark. Kosta and Aunt Olivia backed away into the crowd. They came uninvited, and would not think of embarrassing his brother by their presence, they slipped out of sight.

At the estate, the celebration lasted for two whole days, thereafter until the last of the guests departed. The band played on, platters of food and drink overflowed.

The guesthouse in the rear of the main house stood in a park like setting readied for the newlyweds. All presents received taken by Attenna and Truda to the guesthouse, for safekeeping.

Lord Thomas felt lucky, power of control surged through him. Best wishes and complements from the guests and invitations to come visit, if time allows, he took it all in, eyes darting all around with awe, wealthy single young women eyed Cybilia; could be envious. Lord Thomas smiled at all of them and kissed their fingertips, at which Cybilia criticized him. He should never display such an interest in them when his wife stood next to him. He innocently asked her,

"Well, what should I do then?" Cybilia looked at him with pulled eyebrows and said.

"Wait right here, I will be back in a minute," she lifted her dress and ran to mother, Cybilia found her in the kitchen of all places with a couple of women. Cybilia grabbed her mother's arm and whispered into her ear. Both ran off without a word to the women left standing in the kitchen. Cybilia whispered to her new husband something, Lord Thomas's cheeks turned crimson. Sideways he glanced at his mother-in-law, who was staring at him.

"Now, I learned my lesson, this surely will not happen again." he whispered back and then kissed her cheeks. The guests applauded, but he thought, *I should not offend my wealthy wife*. His excuse was simple; he is ecstatic and having too much wine. He loves her and is fortunate that she loves him. Lord Thomas pacified Cybilia and kissed her lips lightly with guests watching. A comment said loud enough for all to hear,

"My, my..., that *is* true love, I see." Someone snickered, women giggled, and, someone else said, "*eager*." At that moment, Lord Thomas stiffened. His eyes searched the room for a face to match the voice, he found a short stout man, onion nose red from overconsumption of spirits. The room fell silent, out of nowhere Lady Marianna stood by him; she clamped her hand on Lord Thomas's arm and squeezed. Lord Thomas had enough sense not to make a scene, placed his right hand on hers and leaned towards her planting a kiss on her forehead. Lady Marianna pulled his arm to leave the room taking hold of Cybilias arm as well and they walked out of the parlor. Sir Paulo slowly walked over to the stout man and whispered something, and together they left without a word to the guests. A moment of tension lasting at least fifteen minutes dissipated. The murmurs and laughter of men and women voices echoed. This took place on the last night of the celebration. Guests began to form groups and many expressions of hospitality spoken began to depart. The large parlor soon became empty of guests. Lady Marianna had lectured Lord Thomas a bit, but never showed anger or disappointment, she was too wise for that. Sir Paulo and the stout onion nosed man sat in the kitchen having a heated arm waving talk. However, not one word said for all to hear. Hours later, the man escorted to the guestroom to sleep it off. At last, the exhausted newlyweds having a bite to eat before retiring to the guesthouse. They found themselves completely alone in their bedroom. Cybilia apprehensive stood in the middle of the room still in her wedding dress. Not knowing what to do or envision she had never experienced lovemaking. Her now husband, knew she is a virgin. Therefore he should have been romantic, caressing, kissing, slowly ignite her passion, gently arouse her desire to be as one with him, after all he was older and had acquired experience long ago. Lord Thomas also stood still dressed. He looked around the room, candlelight flickered and shadows danced on the walls, but neither had said a word. He walked about extinguishing each candle, leaving just two. The room became dim and private. He removed his coat and shoes, pulled off his knee-high stockings, barefooted he walked over to her placed his hands on her shoulders pulled her to him and kissed her gently. He looked at her and kissed her again hard as he had done the first time taking her home. Cybilia responded to the second kiss, and she kissed him back. Lord Thomas knew he had awakened her feelings. He stepped behind her and began to unbutton her dress. She stood unmoving. Her dress fell to the floor instinctively her arms went up to her bosom. He stepped in front of her and fumbled with her corset, had no idea where to begin, Cybilia amused by his clumsiness helped him to remove the corset. Now, she stood only in her petticoat her breasts exposed, he loved them, kissed her nipples and Cybilia shivered. Lord Thomas walked her to the bed, turned the covers and she slipped beneath the covers. Cybilia watched as her new husband dropped his breeches and only clad in his underwear came to bed. In the dim light to him, she was beautiful he reached for her under the covers and fumbled with her petticoat, she complied and dropped them to the floor, and he too removed his underwear. He inched towards her, as she had not moved; he knew she was wary not knowing what this was like, because her mother never spoke on this subject. He raised himself on his arm leaned to her and whispered,

"Cybilia my love come to me."

"Thomas I...I am sorry I had never..."

"I know my love, relax, allow me to love you, I will be gentle," he whispered.

Not knowing what to expect yet curious she allowed him to do whatever he wished to her. Cybilia was rather surprised, and began to like those jolting feelings occurring here and there. Unexpectedly, she stirred turned to him and the ignited passion and her need of him blazed like never before. She allowed him to enter ever so gently into her private paradise; and when he had done so; she cried out; tried to push him away he caused her pain; which is a natural moment. Thomas held her tight and his hot lips pressed hard against hers. Locked in a long kiss he had not moved but kissed her passionately, until she relaxed enough for him to enter deeper and continue slow rhythm. His sweat ran down his back, armpits dripped, rivulets of sweat ran down his face; but he held back, he had to hold back. Cybilia entranced by the waves of ecstasy ready to explode like a volcano. Thomas knew and Cybilia knew reaching the height of lust that moment, together wrapped in each other's arms as one consumed by fiery passion and desire for each other, their love burst. Lord Thomas smiled both breathing hard. He slid half way off her to let her breath. He was a heavy and strong man. They clung together, legs tangled in sheets. He whispered and she listened to his sweet cooing; how much he loves her, and she is his world, she made him her man, and she is now his. He kissed her hair lifted her chin and kissed her lips; she was tired and sleepy; completely spent fell into deep sleep. He felt exhausted. One candle burned down, the other still flickered soon its flame will die. However, he lay on his side admiring her nudity and flawless soft skin. He ran his hand over her curves, she did not stir, for a moment his want of her again stirred, instead he let her sleep. He thought how strong and long was his performance, and was proud of his act. Because from the day he saw her at the market his aim was to play a game; she was his victim per say; to sink his claws into unsuspecting prey and at last, after such a long wait; he conquered his quarry. She was his Cybilia, nude, exposed now he controlled. He fell asleep not knowing when. Next morning Lord Thomas awakened by the rooster's shrill crow, sat up in bed, but the bedroom was still in a grey shroud of morning. Cybilia was not in bed. He jumped out of it barefoot walked and peeked into every room. He found her standing on the veranda in her night shift, a wool shawl wrapped around her shoulders. She was thinking, so that is lovemaking. I need to ask mother why the pain and why my legs are so weak. I do love him and his gentleness. I should ask Thomas why his brother had not come to the wedding. He has not mentioned a word about him. I feel there is more to this..." her thoughts interrupted.

"Why sweetheart, why are you up so early?" he wrapped his arms around her hips touched her lightly her pleasure island; she spread her legs just a bit, he cupped his hand there and she shivered. He kissed her passionately. Cybilia relaxed responded in same need. He led her to bed and the moments they had this time awakened much more pleasure than last night. She this time desired him and said, "Thomas I want your little soldier to be on guard always." He laughed and promised, "My soldier, for you, will stand at attention always."

"I rise early every day before sunrise, I love sunrise," she said. Thomas as he kissed her nipples said, "He will also rise before sunrise for you." Cybilia smiled broadly. They were quiet for a while then she said.

"I gather you do not wake this early, do you?" he did not reply but was thinking; *everything we need from the start is right here, and nothing lacking, nothing! Here we will reside. Until the old man will...* Cybilia poked him hard,

"Thomas did you hear what I asked you?" she frowned at him.

"Oh yes, of course rising early...no, not always." His eyes were on the scenery before them, it was a beautiful morning, indeed. The newlyweds enjoyed each other's attention doting on each other's whim; bonded as husband and wife should. However, on pleasant mornings breakfasts waited on the veranda at their home, on the east side of the house. After breakfast for several days, they laid in bed exploring, each other's feelings. Napping snuggled tight. Their life began frequently loving fiercely. Honeymoon within weeks was over and Thomas had to start working. From their deep sleep, noises woke them; workers erecting a shop a bit too close to their home, irked him. Cybilia to get his mind off the noise began asking all sorts of questions, mostly about his life, and Lord Thomas replied as best to calm her down. Changing subjects and hoping she swallowed all he said. No one invaded their private moments, everyone understood, that newlyweds needs must be in the privacy of their home. Although for noon meals and dinners, butler Frunn delivered messages one-hour prior lunch in the kitchen, then the sleepy-eyed girl slipped a note under their bedroom door. They laughed at that but seriously minding Cybilias parents who insisted to dine at the main home. At the table, Lord Thomas and Cybilia felt uncomfortable, all eyes were upon them, conversation light and casual, excluded business. After the honeymoon was over, Sir Prozatti and Thomas, now his son-in-law strolled around the grounds, not each day but once a week. To his son-in-law's eager questions, he explained briefly pertaining to how many kegs or bottles of wine produced and distributed, but avoiding pertinent details, sudden change of subject averted to point out other incidentals leading to just what he wanted Lord Thomas to know. Sir Prozatti was not an old fool, after all. To become wealthy one must work hard. His son-in-law will work hard and long hours, and sweat will run down his back from head to his crotch and toes.

During harvest time, Sir Paulo Prozatti as always hired extra help out of their district. Lord Thomas did not show eagerness to exert himself physically. His aim was purely observing on the sideline, following workers, asking questions, finding new faults, which took Sir Prozatti by surprise; he did not have time to explain, work had to move with speed. A bit annoyed, but with a smile placed a hand on shoulder politely asked his son-in-law to help carry kegs of wine to storage as not to waste time. Lord Thomas dared not show his dislike, rather apologized and walked off feeling as one of the employees. Work was not for him, as he promised himself long ago, "others will work for him" and this is his new life. Therefore, he tried to manipulate everyone including his father-in-law, out of strenuous lifting and sweating a bit too often.

Sir Prozatti observed but said nothing.

The picture was very clear to Cybilias father. Many evenings he sat alone thinking deeply. Now and then, he found good reasons not to work every day at all. He and Lady Marianna early morning rode away returning before supper. Lord Thomas out of embarrassment forced to oversee the workload. Without realizing, all employees were mindful of him. At the same time they were enjoying themselves, laughing taking frequent breaks and joking with their new manager as he worked with the crew. He had no time to dwell why his father-in-law had not been teaching him or being at the winery at all. Whole operation of the orchard and farming Lord Thomas though stumbled learned with a bit of difficulty. *Strange...*he thought..., *it is not that difficult at all, I am glad he stays away, these men here tell me what I want to know. Old Prozatti is clever, he knows exactly how to make me work hard, and I am working hard...well we shall see for how long he will keep me toiling like this. He must have a plan of some sort; I must wait.* Now he realized how much he enjoyed it all. He had a free hand in all of this: one morning Sir Prozatti marched into the winery; and at that, moment things had changed. The whole place became quiet and work went on smoothly. Not as before many hours wasted on trivialities, mishaps, and they were careless feeling free. Even the head-manager joined them in this relaxed environment, since the owner was absent. Sir Prozatti began his inspection early mornings before any of the employees began their work. Daily activities and production registered in the journal of which known only to Sir Prozatti to discuss and his manager. Lord Thomas dared not ask why the absence, has it been illness, long deserved rest or perhaps teach his son-in-law a lesson. Business records Prozattis head-manager delivered at the end of each month. Those were mornings all differences then and now compared under his own management and presently his son-in-law clearly turned out very questionable, considering and evaluating each man and their trustworthiness.

When Sir Prozatti returned to work, he held a new schedule not only for one but all employees. Lord Thomas's responsibility the orchards. Relieved of the pressure and scrutiny working with his father-in-law, however not knowing what to do there among the apple trees, questioned the senior employees what is he to do; they said there is much to look for. Lord Thomas had no idea what to look for, became agitated, and swore feeling like a cretin. Old Prozatti allowed his son-in-law several months of free reign among the apple trees. His records had sufficient proof, his mistake, trusting his son-in-law, much too soon, now he backed off.

Lord Thomas realized after some time that the old man spun a clever lesson on his character. Secrets to the business had not been an open book...but with time, they would be, the more reason to work hand in hand, and gain experience in its process. Being young but clever to appease his wealthy father-in-law had to show great interest for which Sir Prozatti overlooked. So he thought. His future for eventual control of the whole operation and management depended on trust and his willingness to learn. Lord Thomas had patience now, and he had a plan. People were coming and going from surrounding areas at certain times, either, as extra help, or purchasing casks of wine. There were moments of uneasiness, Lord Thomas, feared recognition by someone, exposing his past.

Lord Thomas relaxed, with time none of his fears of past ghosts had faced him. He was relieved when all the hired help returned to their own homes and work.

Lord Thomas enjoyed his position and all his possessions.

Sir Prozatti gradually began to trust him; evaluating Thomas as he learned the winery operation from observation. Lord Thomas experienced the feeling of power and control, which soon he knew would be in his grasp. Clever he was, questioned everyone endlessly to familiarize himself to the smallest detail of it all.

Lord Thomas as months slipped by realized he was free to do what he wished. Cybilia of course had no objections, when many an evening he went out to come home late, drunk, had fallen into bed fully clothed, but for his shoes. Cybilia could not sleep in the same bed. His snoring forced her to sleep in the other bedroom. She needed rest and quiet. In the morning, Cybilia was not in bed, she was up early, and was not on the veranda, which irked him. Lord Thomas took his time to dress and then peek into other rooms. Not finding her, walked down stairs to the dining room where Cybilia sat sipping tea or coffee, alone, greeting her with a cheery good morning, a quick kiss on her cheek, acting as if nothing happened. Avoiding the reason why he was out so late, or why she failed to wake him. Besides, she never asked. Cybilia never mentioned to her parents of his late outings.

The road curved away from the guest home sheltered by large trees, her parents seldom had visited them in the evenings, daytime only. The servants retired to their separate quarters close to the main house.

The honeymoon was long over. Cybilia was expecting his child, but had withheld the news from him. She watched as he worked right along with her father on hot and humid days. Complaining the heat got to him and that her father is a slave driver, physically wearing him out completely. Prozatti was not a fool.

Lord Thomas was about to leave one evening, after a day of lifting many wine barrels.

"Why do you have to go out so frequently?" curiously Cybilia asked.

"Well my dear...I do have new clients to do business with, I will tell you in detail later, I *must* go now, or I will be late and as you know a good client shall not wait." Lord Thomas told her.

Left alone keeping busy, but thinking of where her husband could be and with whom. Feeling dejected, in the two years since they married; he spent little time with her, had been always somewhere or other out of her sight. She on the other hand, young and naive had not minded at first, being a good wife. With time passing, she had learned much. Now, he is aware she is expecting his child. Lord Thomas smiled broadly when she told him she was expecting a baby; but deep within he wondered why Cybilia waited four months to tell him she is pregnant.

Cybilia thinking that would keep him home with her; it had not. Disappointed she wept from anger. In addition, disturbing thoughts ran through her mind and many times, she asked him.

"What sort of business are you transacting especially at night, again? As I recall...my father hardly ever had done business at night. Besides clients came to him."

"Tonight my dear I am off to see the owner of an Inn." Lord Thomas covered her with kisses and hugs and patted her abdomen.

"Aha...the owner of the Inn happens to be a woman?" Cybilia remarked and smiled.

"Now make sure you and my boy rest." Lord Thomas did not reply to her question instead said. "Before I met you, my dear, I had visited many Inns, I do not recall, or know of any woman owning a business, yet." Cybilia wide eyed did not blink but glared into his eyes, lost for words. Lord Thomas held her shoulders and patted her abdomen again, kissed her lightly on the neck and barely touched her lips. Strange...each time he cooed her in such a way disarming her and she loved him. "How can you be so sure it is a boy Thomas?" Cybilia asked.

"My dear, I know, period," he replied laughing. She observed that his "I love you sweetheart," no longer spoken as frequently as before, replaced by, "my dear" she never expected to be alone so many nights, especially in her condition. Cybilia had time on her hands to observe and think. Wondering why her best friends had visited her so seldom. Cybilia became a bit depressed, had forgotten the fact, that they were single women, free of responsibilities, besides they were not pregnant. The distillery she visited on her good days quite often, chatting with her father, lately he seemed a bit peeked, and before long, she noticed quite a bit of indifference and tension between him and Thomas.

One afternoon, Cybilia sat with her father on the side of the warehouse in the shade, it was rather a hot day; when she heard Lord Thomas calling for his father-in-law, loud and arrogantly, she jumped to her feet, motioned her father to sit and do not answer, she ran around the corner of the building, waited, listened and watched.

"Hey, there you are old Poppa Prozatti, what taking a break? I need you to stack kegs. You are not doing your job. You say to me, *do your share*! Well I do my share. Now you do your share!" he shouted and walked away. Cybilia shocked pressed her hand on her mouth. She waited and then turned the corner made sure her husband had gone back to the distillery.

"Father is he like this to you often?" she asked. He did not reply, seemed to be in a daze. She shook his shoulder; when he looked up at her; his eyes were teary.

"Come Father, we need to talk." Cybilia led him into the house and sat him at the table in the kitchen, sat the kettle on for tea, they were alone. Her father glanced at her and said.

"He changed. He is a bull, rude bastard. I will take care of him, wait and see. Do not say a word, you know nothing, you hear*!*" her father was angry.

"Father this is between us. Yes, I will not say a word from now on. But father, why?"

Sir Prozatti said to her lowering his voice.

"I have been watching from the corner of my eye, my daughter. He is greedy. I know what he wants, before and now..., you..., you must watch him." His hands trembled holding the teacup.

Her heart sank thinking of what father said, *I know what he wants, before and now*...She *will* watch him like a hawk. She will play her part. Cybilia from then on spent a lot of time with her mother they talked for hours.

"Father must reduce his work days. It is taking a toll on him. We need to hire a few strong men." Cybilia said to her mother. Her mother frowned at her daughter.

"But he should not be working at all. Lately comes home exhausted. I truly believe his health is declining; he does not slpeep well and barely crawls out of bed. He is weak; and now has dark circles under his eyes; you know we eat well, we never lack for anything; I do not like this at all."

Cybilia sat thoughtful for a while, then said. "Thomas is pushing him too hard, I heard him force father to carry kegs, imagine kegs at his age?"

They sat not speaking but thinking. Lady Marianna said.

"We had a steady production over the years and good profit, now it has doubled. I do not understand whatever for!"Cybilia noticed a bit of fear in mother's eyes.

"Mother perhaps it is his age; as well as yours; I have grown into a woman now, and am pregnant, I am sure you have made that observation." Cybilia cracked a smile and her mother for a moment kept her eyes on her daughter, then she said, "Yes I thought about you and us, you are right, still, since he began working with father things changed, especially your father's health." They sat not speaking for a long while. From that moment on, they decided not to mention this subject in their conversations at dinnertime or at any other time when Thomas was present.

Cybilia's preparations for the newborn were slow in progress, four months until delivery. She sent messages for her friends to come; it is urgent, her friends came and spent the whole day with her to cheer her up. When Cybilias friends left that early evening, she began feeling restless and nauseous. Thinking she had overdone with her friends, she had not rested all day. Had she overeaten? She could not remember what they ate. Why is she feeling this way, could it be nothing at all? Perhaps all women feel put of sorts. Cybilia was about to call her maid and have the coach take her to her mother, when she felt a sharp pain in her abdomen, she doubled over on her bed. When the pain stopped, she stood up but did not move; something warm ran down her leg. She lifted her skirt and screamed. In the adjoining room, her maid heard the screams and came running.

"Go quickly fetch my mother," Cybilia said through her clenched teeth holding back her scream of pain.

That evening mother sat with Cybilia, not knowing what to expect. However, pains increased, and on that night, Cybilia lost their first child. On that dark night among the branches in the nearby trees, thirteen pairs of shiny black eyes watched.

Cybilia could not believe she had miscarried; she wept and rested in bed. Silence and gloom hung in their bedroom. Lord Thomas crushed completely had not spoken to her for several days. He was angry with her. Had not asked her if it was a girl or a boy, he would not dare. That evening he had been out drinking with his pals, besides she would not have told him. Cybilia stayed in bed to recover and overcome her lost daughter. Her tears flowed from sorrow every day. She had time to analyze the situation, when she recovered Cybilia spent most of her time with her parents. As they had decided how she should act. Keeping her head clear, eyes open. In his presence, as of then she was sweet and bubbly; she asked him to visit his brother. His excuse was always not enough time, and too much work. However, he will never know what secrets her happy face concealed or how she felt. He will not know her disappointment in him. His feelings about the lost child when mentioned; he had said only once, "We shall surely have another." Cybilias tears welled up and she cursed him silently. However, from that day on nothing changed, she played her role. He will never know how much her heart had chilled. Her desire and love waned into uncertainty. Each time he left her alone at home, doubt filled her heart. Cybilia decided to tell her parents everything that is going on in her life. They agreed to pretend all is fine, praise him for his effort and hard work...and smile. Unaware of the evil entering their home, everyone went about their business. However, as the weather changed so did their health. By sheer chance, Lord Thomas discovered something although skeptical, began to shrewdly scheme. He would bide his time, being still young, hardworking, and respectful, his attitude changed toward his father-in-law; ever so slightly, but deep in his mind he knew what to do.

Sixteen: Kosta

The younger brother Kosta still lived his unchanging way of life and never varied responsibilities, a quiet young individual leading a quiet life. Never begrudged anyone, never spiteful or harmed anyone. Never sought power to amass worldly possessions or control others. That never was his character, unlike his brother.

Yet, out of necessity, improvements had brought a bit more comfort to his life and pride of ownership. His solitude and coming to maturity came to him naturally. Wishing to have little bit more than what he had now certainly would not be wrong. To work this hard alone, did he not deserve a better life?

Girls entered his thoughts. One thing was sure, he had no intention to spend the rest of his life alone, he needed someone to love and have love in return. He began to feel restless, realizing solitary life was misery, *but I have absolutely nothing to offer to the girl of my dreams...perhaps someday, but what girl would come into such a meager lifestyle as this? I must improve myself somehow, not just enough to be comfortable and secure, but much more. Full pantry without ever having shortages or worries, I could not look into the eyes of my loved one, if I had so little to offer her*. Kosta thought.

So he rolled up his sleeves and worked extra hard on all his crafts, he carved different and unusual items hoping that these would attract people who had interest in that sort of art. His bust of a young girl was his prize possession and he enjoyed looking at her face. There were moments he wondered why he was inspired by a vision in his mind to carve this beautiful face in one evening to perfection. This one was special. He will never sell it, unless he was starving. He often inspected her face for faults. She was beautiful with a soft smile, never realizing he had carved a girl of his dreams, however remote; not ever expecting to meet her in person.

Kosta thought; *it must be the guidance of the Lord and my father, that I should do such fine work.*

From the day, Kosta's brother married Cybilia, he and Aunt Olivia not once had an invitation to visit that estate. Kosta often wondered; *how did he do it... by what means? My brother married into a wealthy family, and, such wealth...very puzzling, indeed.*

Kosta's possessions were meager a plot of nine and a half acres, a large portion of it not fertile. A good size creek flowed through all the way to the Rapid River. In addition, the other part of it the forest inched closer ever so slowly to the house. Lord Thomas gave up his inheritance of half ownership, to Kosta. Married into wealth, Lord Thomas had no need of this bit of property. Kosta could not imagine giving up this place.

Most of his best carvings stood on the large piece of furniture, over which he designed and labored many nights. This piece held his mother's dishes, jugs, jars, and one drawer held utensils and his tools. This cabinet, he had seen a long time ago at the market a useful piece of furniture, which impressed him for its usefulness, a piece of furniture to be proud to display. He made it a point to make one, perhaps redesign it carve it his own style. From the sale of his carvings, he saved enough profits to purchase raw material to make a similar cabinet. At the mill, he purchased the planks, paid extra for cutting the boards to size and at the same time bought the necessary varnish for a fine finish. Kosta came away with all he needed, those men were helpful with information he had not had before.

Many nights he carved by the fireplace, engrossed in his thoughts, overlooked his shabby life. Embarrassed at times when someone came over to borrow his fine tools. Some women sometimes teased him about girls and marriage. His answer always was short and simple; *when I am ready.*

Kosta often wondered, when and how could he reach such height of success, as the gossip circled about his brother. Kosta overheard at the market one day, "Cybilia will inherit three hundred fifty acres of land. The winery will be hers too. They live in a huge guest home on seven acres Cybilia owns at least one hundred chickens, a small orchard, the home will be hers, four slick horses and many servants." *inherit all...,* Kosta's ears burned..., *now that is what I consider luck, a good life, and, a good rich woman at that,*" he thought and laughed.

One market day, Kosta was busy stacking baskets full of potatoes, beets, carrots and cabbages pyramid style, making neat piles of the remaining vegetables on shelves, for better viewing for customers. Kosta's back was turned he did not see a teenage girl in front of his kiosk, staring at him. He walked over to the table and asked her if she needed something; to his surprise, she handed him a small note, turned on her heel and walked away. Kosta was about to thank her but she disappeared among the crowd. He unfolded the small piece of paper carefully, read the greeting, refolded it just as carefully and shoved it into his pocket. At home, he grabbed a bite to eat, went out to do the evening chores. Saddling his horse rode over to Aunt Olivia. Irritated, disappointed, that the short tutoring was not enough to read such fine handwriting. Aunt Olivia greeted him as always with a smile and a pat on his shoulder.

"Well, what brings you here, my boy?" she asked.

"Aunt Olivia, today I received a note, I cannot read this...such scribbling, please read it. I know it is from Thomas."

"But of course I shall read it to you."

Greetings Brother

Please honor us with your presence on the second Sunday of this month. You should arrive early afternoon for a festive family gathering. An occasion you should not miss."

Lord Thomas Komarod

P.S. bring along Aunt Olivia.

Direction is simple, take the main road from home follow for one hour and a half turn left onto a lane of poplars, you will see the orchard and the estate of the Prozattis.

Kosta listened to what she had just read. Kosta's eyes grew big. Aunt Olivia saw anger on Kosta's face, she handed the note back to him.

"My brother, what nerve, with this note had to insult us!" Kosta took the note tore it to pieces.

"We are not going, besides I do not own a time piece, an hour...how do you tell an hour by the sun?" Kosta shouted dropping onto a chair. Aunt Olivia smiled being wiser.

"Oh but Kosta, you would miss out on so much...not the food or company, just to observe...will give you an incentive, ideas of what life has to offer, and this is just a small part of the world, of which you have not seen yet, as had your brother," she replied.

"Yes, I believe you are right, we will go and we will not embarrass ourselves or them," Kosta said, nodding his head.

"Now mind you, he also included the directions, imagine that." Aunt Olivia grinned.

"Like we would not find him on our own? We just ask someone, that is all." Kosta laughed.

"That proves he has no inkling we were there at his wedding, hah!"

"And, he never will," Kosta added.

At the family gathering, all went as expected. Prozatti family welcomed Kosta and Aunt Olivia graciously. The conversations were pleasant and no one looked down on Kosta or Aunt Olivia.

Lord Thomas scurried around being a good host, conscious of his in-law's comfort, and ordered servants to have everything perfect Cybilia observed, exchanged meaningful glances with her mother. Aunt Olivia seated next to Lady Marianna and Kosta sat near Cybilia. Aunt Olivia was right about observing the ways of the rich. That day Kosta learned quite a bit, but what he had seen in his brother eyes, he could never understand. Trying to analyze the attitude and his quick orders to the servants, seemed unrealistic, to Kosta, his brother was one of the servants. Not the relaxed sophisticated son-in-law married into a rich, reputable family.

"Why was Thomas running around like that all through dinner, Aunt Olivia?" Kosta asked.

"Perhaps trying to prove something to us, but what? I cannot tell you that, even Cybilia glanced at him too many times, annoyed," Aunt Olivia replied flatly.

"I noticed the servants were nervous. Sir Prozatti talked over all that commotion did you notice?" Kosta said, "and Cybilia...well...we will talk about her later."

"What about Cybilia, Kosta, what do you want to say," Aunt Olivia asked.

"Ah, it is nothing really Aunt Olivia, not now, really not now," Kosta replied and looked around as if sensing something or someone watching or following them. A chill ran through him and, shook him. All the way home, they rode in silence from the last sentence spoken. Still Kosta was thinking, "*I had an opportunity to meet Cybilia in person today. Last several years, not once were we invited, as if I, and Aunt Olivia did not exist. Cybilia is very nice and beautiful. I feel, I could relate to her, something in her eyes, a strange link of feelings, as a friend, of course.*"

It was quite late when they arrived home, horses led to the stall for the night. Arkushin's son Orzak, that day cared for Kosta's farm animals. Aunt Olivia's animals her neighbor tended to. She spent the night at Kosta's little home. In the morning she wanted to have a talk with Kosta, but he refused and said perhaps tomorrow. Following morning their discussion turned into a depressing picture, each felt that the invitation to that dinner was strictly a show; and that the two brothers could never be close again. Their life styles were unmistakably opposite. It only means one thing, leave things as they are and live your life. Kosta now determined, distributed and sold his carvings all over the area.

Time permitting, early evening especially in the summer took a walk along the creek, sat on his favorite willow stump. Peace and serenity around him energized his mind and spirit.

During bad weather, he carved or cleaned things around the house and thought about all those girls he had met in other villages, but somehow none suited him. Kosta grew tall, strong and handsome, though a bit shy. His thick black hair pushed back and tied into a ponytail, his father's style. Strong chin, high cheekbones, full lips and straight nose after his Mother, and Father's sharp blue eyes. Never intentionally drew attention to himself, he was quiet and simple, but at the market there were many attractive girls giving him second looks.

On one particular day, as he rode his horse down a well-beaten path through the woods to the nearby village, in deep thought, he noticed far in the distance someone approaching. As that someone came closer, it was a young woman. His heart skipped; and suddenly beat rapidly. *This has never happened to me before. Something is wrong with my heart; I must talk to Aunt Olivia about it*, he thought. The young woman came closer and closer. Kosta stared ahead, what seemed to be a mirage emerging from an undistinguishable form into an unmistakable image of a beautiful woman, he stared breathless, his hand on his chest, captivated.

As she came up a little closer she noticed a man on a horse, he seemed to be waiting at the tree. She too kept her eyes on him; *why is he waiting there by the tree... on a horse*? She was concerned a bit for her safety, not exactly knowing why. At a crossroad quickly walked off the path, for a moment she ran and soon was out of his sight. She slowed down and bent over her hands on her knees to catch her breath. She sidetracked, but then turned back in the direction of the path, leaving him far behind. The thought never crossed her mind that he could easily give chase after her with the horse, if he had wrong intentions.

As many times as she had passed through this familiar strip of woods, she had never been frightened of any animals. She had met families, couples; crossing paths with senior women or men; but had never felt danger, ever; *but, today that man on a horse, waiting,* she wondered. She must be more alert from now on. *I am sure he is harmless. Still, one cannot ever be sure of someone else's intentions, perhaps he is a gypsy*?" she thought to herself.

Kosta realized waiting here at this tree had frightened the girl enough for her to run. *I should explain*, he thought, *perhaps I will see her again someday.* He reached the village, headed to the shop, where his crafts were on display, hoping profits would allow him to purchase urgent items. Paul the shopkeeper was glad to see him.

"Hey Kosta, my friend, good news, everything sold!" Paul shouted.

"Seriously Paul, each piece sold?" Kosta asked, smiling.

"Yes really. Here is your gold." Paul clapped his hands. They chatted for a while and Kosta returned home.

Since that day, the girl's image crossed his mind quite often, seeing as she fled from him bothered him fiercely. He became jittery and irritable. He had no one to talk to, but his dog. *Aunt Olivia, I must go and talk to her,* he thought. After cutting his finger while carving, which he never, ever had done before, surely Aunt Olivia could explain it. Aunt Olivia to him was as his stepmother from the time his parents perished in that river. From the time, she returned to her own little home, he always managed to help her with much needed chores. He loved her as a son loves his mother, feeling obligated and responsible for her. She was his strength at every crucial moment in his life. Riding as fast as his horse could, quickly dismounting at her front door. Rapped sharply, when the door opened slowly, her face lit up with a big smile seeing him.

"Who is this handsome fellow at my door? Come in, but what brings you here, Kosta are you all right?" Aunt Olivia spoke in her soft voice.

"Yes, I am all right, thank you, good evening Aunt Olivia. I apologize for this late visit. I hope you were not retiring to bed. I had to see you. I must talk to you," Kosta rattled on. Aunt Olivia walked him into the kitchen by the arm. She noticed the bandaged finger as he sat down. He seemed to be frustrated about something. She sat across the table and reached over for his hand.

"Kosta, slow down, what happened? How did you get hurt? Kosta stared at her a while, collecting his thoughts. Kosta sat quiet, seemed his mind was wandering elsewhere, not with her. "Aunt Olivia I have to tell you of the incident in the woods... with that girl."

"Well, I am listening, what happened and what girl?"

"I went to see Paul, I rode my horse, I stopped at a huge tree, I do not recall why I stood there, but suddenly I saw in the distance someone approaching, it was a girl...a woman...a young woman. She was like a mirage."

"Well...did you see her close enough to see her face, hair, was she tall and slim or short and fat; how close?" Aunt Olivia asked.

"No...Yes...I did see her vaguely...I was on my horse, when I saw her coming I waited, but Aunt Olivia I could not understand why my heart beat erratically. I guess I frightened her, she ran away!" he talked quickly without taking a breath.

"Yes...you frightened her, being that you and she were alone, I am not surprised at all that she ran, did you see her face, will you be able to recognize her again?" she asked him.

"Ah yes! Aunt Olivia I see her vaguely in my mind, I cannot forget her. She is my constant thought! It bothers me. I see many girls in villages and the market as you well know. No, nothing ever happened like this before, it is just that, she took me by surprise; I walked and rode my horse that same path so many times, I have passed people there. I think... she was smiling as she ran off. I stared after her until she was out of sight. Aunt Olivia although she was quite far something happened to me. I do not understand this at all..." He stopped and covered his face with his hands.

Aunt Olivia understood immediately, her little boy has grown up and was in love with a fleeting image of a girl in the woods. He was fragile, she knew and any adverse comment would hurt his feelings. She must speak to him kindly.

"My dear Kosta, you may see her again, be patient. If she was on the same path as you, then go that way again. Perhaps in a weak or two, go to the same place again, wait for a while, perhaps she will come your way as before. Remember what is meant to be, will be. I always tell you, your destiny is in your book of life, and you will live it. You will always be strong to endure hardships and remember that laughter and joy will be there also. Now remember, next time walk," she smiled at him.

He listened to her soothing voice. She calmed his frazzled nerves, he felt much lighter in spirit, and he stayed and talked. She served special tea and cookies. They enjoyed each other's conversations.

Kosta riding home more relaxed, but his mind focused of Aunt Olivia and could not stop thinking, she looked *tired and old, very thin,* fear of losing her too soon gnawed at his mind. *"I want her to be with me for a long time, I need her. If I get married I want her to be there, I want her to care for my children."* A voice deep within whispered, *"Worry not, she will be with you, time of her eternal rest is not yet known."* That voice chilled him. Suddenly Kosta found himself at his front door. He looked around, *my God I am already home?* He led the horse to the stall for a rub down and feed.

Days turned into weeks and again he walked the same beaten path. It was time to make an exchange at Paul's shop, pick up his profits, if any. Then he thought of Aunt Olivia, she told him what he must do. Now he was near the same tree, he sat down and leaned against its trunk; stretched his legs and closed his eyes. It was peaceful but for the birds chirping and a distant yelp of a dog or some other animal.

Suddenly he heard twigs snapping, he opened his eyes glanced around but saw no one coming. His heart began to flutter again, but remained in the same position on the ground. "*What is going on with me?"* he thought.

The young woman stepped cautiously when she noticed him, she stopped, waited, he was alone, no horse, just him sitting on the ground, his back against the tree, this time, she asked without hesitation or fear, "Sir, are you feeling ill?

Kosta startled, he only nodded, unable to speak. Her concern was real. Kosta stared at her*, is it really the same girl? Yes it is! What should I do?* Kosta stood up too quickly, weak in the knees leaned against the tree and slid down to the ground.

"Sir...What is the matter with you? You look very pale! Why...you do need help!"

He sat and stared at her, and suddenly he knew, she was the one, her hair, her face, her eyes, and that smile, he has seen this girl before, but where? Kosta relaxed a bit, but still felt weak. He nodded and whispered, "Thank you, you are very kind."

She sat down on the knurled large tree root, her skirt pulled over her knees, with fingers plaited hands on her lap, studied his face closely. She noticed at his side a sack. She recalled seeing same color sack on his knees, the first time; and he wore the same coat.

"You feel like this often? Perhaps you need to see a doctor."

Kosta did not reply, just gazed at her. Suddenly she realized at that moment,

"Were you here before on a horse? About two weeks ago; I saw you... and I ran away." Her eyes now met his. They were blue, very blue.

Kosta recovered his shyness a bit.

"No...I mean yes, I am fine, this...it...just happened now. Suddenly I felt so weak. I do not understand what happened to me just now. Yes... I was the one...before, now I remember! You were running away from me, were you frightened of me?"

"Yes somewhat I was afraid, never before had I met a man on a horse." She raised her hand to shield her eyes as she kept looking at his face.

"I meant you no harm," he said staring at her, still sitting on the ground.

She remembered that day, when she saw him, her first reaction was caution, unsure of what to do, who he was, and why he waited by the tree, on a horse. Feeling uneasy, she ran.

"I do come this way ah...but I...my... my sister is expecting a child; she asked me to come for a few days to help with certain things," she said feeling more at ease.

Kosta still looking at her said. "I am so sorry... I... please forgive me I did not mean to stare. I did not mean to be rude...it is rather strange. We are talking as if we knew each other a long time. I failed to introduce myself."

"Oh my...I am sorry too! My name is Kathryn." Bursting into laughter, showing sparkling white teeth.

"My...ah...I am... Kosta. I live at the outskirts of Riverside Village to the east." He pointed.

"Oh how coincidental, my sister lives in Riverside Village also. I live beyond these woods, a bit to the south. Our village is small. To walk it is rather far, but, it still is early in the day," Kathryn said. They looked at each other, and Kathryn asked, "So it was you here by this tree; waiting on a horse?"

Kosta a bit surprised that she had remembered and now recognized him.

"I am a carver and I was on my way to a shop where my articles are on display."

"Is that why you carry this sack with you?"

"Yes, I always restock the shelves," Kosta replied.

"Oh... that must be tedious work," Kathryn said.

"Yes it is, but I love it, carving is my passion," Kosta replied.

"And do you have some in your sack now?" she asked.

"Oh yes I do, would you like to see them?" Kosta said.

"Oh I better not, not now. It is rather late, ah... no thank you," Kathryn said and rose from the tree root, straightened her skirt and turned to go.

"It was nice seeing you again...though this time without fear. Take care of yourself. I must go now." Kathryn quickly walked off without looking back.

Kosta called after her., "It was my pleasure indeed...and I do hope we will meet again...." His voice trailed off. He tipped his hat, saying softly *goodbye,* he watched her as she walked out of sight. Leaning against the tree thinking, *she is beautiful; will I ever meet her again?* All the way to the village, her image lingered in his mind, and her sweet smile. He became curious about her married sister, who is her sister? Where does she live?

Perhaps the next time they meet he will not forget to ask Kathryn her married sister's name, is she the same one of which Aunt Olivia had mentioned, the bride was pretty.

Kosta walked, but did not feel the ground beneath his feet, he felt light in spirit and body without realizing it. His heart sang. He imagined embracing Kathryn, loving her, and in return loved by her forever; *but that would be impossible, I am just dreaming. I have nothing to offer her.* His heart sank realizing at this moment his life was extremely meager, he was not as lucky and successful as his brother. He is a gifted carver, which is true, he could fashion anything out of wood having excellent imagination, he was an excellent furniture maker, he has made many beds, his little house was crammed with all sorts of projects and he never refused or overcharged. Yet life's improvement was slow coming somehow, he often wondered, why.

On that day, he walked into a small cobbler's shop, where their lifelong friend had agreed to display Kosta's carvings.

As he entered the little shop, Paul stood by a table working on something.

"Good day Paul, how is your business these days?" Kosta greeted his friend. Paul's face had a somber expression he muttered a weak "hello." Kosta knew immediately that something had occurred here, he has never had such a cool reception by his friend. Paul without waiting for a lengthy conversation reached into a box for a pouch with a few gold coins from previous sales and handed it to him. Kosta emptied them into his palm and counted. Paul saw the disappointment on his young friend's face.

"Kosta you are my friend and I do want to help you, but I was told that you are overcharging!" Paul said.

"What—I...am overcharging? That is absurd!" Kosta could not believe such an asinine lie. "Why...you know I practically give the stuff away, who told you that, tell me!" Kosta exclaimed in shock, visibly upset dropped into a chair.

"Kosta I am very sorry. I am only repeating to you what the man said to me; he came to my shop one day looked around picked up one of your pieces and said: "these prices are too high; the shop in the other village has better prices. And he walked out, I have never seen the man before, believe me!" Paul said.

"Paul which village, did he say?" Kosta asked.

"I do not know...I had no chance to ask...he walked out quickly. Weeks had passed I...that incident slipped my mind. Then one day another man came in with a massage for me...If you continue to sell these carvings, these worthless kindling's; you shall regret it," Paul said.

"Did he actually say he knew these were mine, did he mention my name?" Kosta thoughtfully asked.

"No...your...your name was not mentioned at all, come to think of it...but if he should come around again, I will ask him...and I regretfully must tell you that I must stop selling your carvings. Kosta, this man threatened me, he will physically hurt me. I could read it in his wild eyes. He meant it," Paul said with a worried look in his face.

"But...why...please, do not reject my work. You know I am not under cutting anyone; or am I in anyone's way, as far as I know and you know I am the only carver in this area; just me Paul. Moreover, my work is of the finest quality. Paul you are my only hope, I...this helps me...to survive. You always helped my parents, and you knew them well. They often came to you, Paul." Kosta was shocked.

"Yes I knew your father was a good man, but you must understand...I was threatened, look at me...I am old and alone! This is all I have, what if they harm me, or if I lose my shop, if you know what I mean, I am so sorry, Kosta, please understand and forgive me but I cannot help you anymore," Paul said with downcast eyes.

Kosta packed his carvings into his sack and without a grudge towards Paul gave him a strong handshake.

"I will come to visit once in a while, and do not worry, no one will harm you."

On the way home, he could not fathom the sense of what happened, *well what now...what another obstacle? I have had many of them in my life already. Where is this other village with better prices?*" Kosta thought. His shoulders slumped, as if suddenly a millstone weighing a ton hung around his neck. His spirit sunk so low he felt it in his feet. Who is this someone...downgrading my fine work. Worthless kindling... worthless kindling...wait a minute... I know who said that to me once. My brother said it. Could he have been here and said this? How would he know where I sell my work? I should have asked Paul to describe this individual to me. Perhaps I would recognize him at the market. I am suspicious of my brother; why should I be; he is rich and would not bother with my worthless carvings, besides, people use that expression about something or other," Kosta spoke aloud.

Then the image of Kathryn interrupted his thoughts, *Kathryn...Ah, what a girl. My heart tells me that Kathryn will never leave my heart or my mind. Perhaps, perhaps we will meet again. She would brighten my life. What if she is not interested in me, she was polite to me, nothing else. That is all. Regardless of feelings, I need to talk to her.* As he was wishing with a sad heart, an inner voice whispered, *all will be fine, do not worry.*

When Kathryn walked into her sister Rabinna's home, grinning, her eyes sparkled. Rabinna surprised to see her so excited.

"Kathryn whatever happened to you...you are aglow...tell me," Rabinna asked.

"Is Michael in the house?" Kathryn asked breathless.

"No, he is out in the field, why?" Rabinna replied.

"Let us have some tea before I tell you the story," Kathryn said. When the tea steeped long enough Rabinna filled two cups, added a teaspoon of clover honey and stirred. Then she went to the pantry brought a plate of cookies and set it in the center of the table. She sat across from Kathryn sipped the tea and said.

"Well, tell me all about it."

Kathryn took a sip of tea and began,

"Oh Rabinna, "Kathryn began, "he was so nice. His hair is very black, and eyes as blue as the sky... handsome, and looks muscular...from what I could see!"

"Kathryn! You noticed *that?*" Rabinna asked laughing.

"What? Oh... yes! He sat leaning against the tree with his shirt unbuttoned. Yes! Rabinna he made my heart sing."

Rabinna, the first time, I saw a man on a horse waiting by this huge tree, I became frightened so I ran away, I had no idea what he had in mind, or where he came from. Today, I saw a young man sitting on the ground leaning against the tree. You know the same tree...for some reason; I was not afraid today. Well I stopped and we talked. However, you know, he made no effort to stand up or say much, and when he spoke, he spoke softly, very shy... and then I noticed a sack next to him, I asked what it was for, and he said he was a carver. Oh Rabinna, he was so nice. His hair was midnight black; his eyes were blue like the sky; his skin tanned, and he is so tall and so very strong. I tried not to giggle and act silly you know; I kept my composure, after all, we just met, but Rabinna, I want to meet him again, somehow I must."

"Kathryn, you are repeating yourself and you are stretching the story. You told me the story twice over. He made a strong impression on you. And, it looks like he just had stolen your heart." She mimicked Kathryn with her hands folded in a praying fashion.

"Oh Rabinna, he was so nice," they both laughed. Rabinna could see how exited Kathryn was just talking about this man.

"*Very* well, we will try to find out about this young man, who he is, and where he lives, by the way, what is his name? Oh...never mind I will tell Michael, he will find him," Rabinna said which calmed Kathryn's excitement.

"Do you really think that Michael could find him?" Kathryn asked beaming.

"Well, if he is a good carver then he is known by many people, so, why not!"

When Michael came home, Rabinna explained what had taken place today, and it is important to find this young man for Kathryn. After a long thought, Michael said, "Rabinna I have no clue who this man could be, but I will inquire, with luck perhaps we will find him." Kathryn must have shown much disappointment from her expression. Micheal winked at Rabinna. While having supper Kathryn said but a few words. Michael observed Kathryn and agreed that she looked and acted different. After a while, he broke the silence.

"I have been thinking that it would be impossible for me to find him, I am quite busy, but I will question the neighbors, perhaps they know of or heard of someone of that description. There are ways to find out. Who knows... it is a slim possibility, but I will try." Michael shot a glance at Kathryn. She was looking down, disappointed. Michael added not looking up from his plate.

"This fellow in question might live in this area, perhaps." Then Kathryn remembered the sack.

"Rabinna, Michael, he is a carver. I saw a sack on the ground next to him." She almost jumped off her chair.

"Michael, ask the neighbors," Rabinna suggested. After several days, still Michael had no news.

"Rabinna, I will be gone for several hours, or longer, I think we found him. Say nothing to Kathryn, until I return," Michael whispered.

Seventeen: Michael and Rabinna Hartigard

Kosta devastated by Paul's news each day fell deeper into depression. For weeks, he woke up late to do his chores. He moved lethargically and ate little. Sat and stared out at the sunset, elbows on the table supported his chin in his palms. In the darkness, Kosta sat for so long his body became numb and rigid. His visits to Aunt Olivia were few, his excuse, too much work. She offered to come and help, he objected. She left it at that, wondering why he tried to hide gloom.

When one evening, a loud knock on the door snapped him out of his daze. He jumped up startled, his body rigid, but walking to the door had somewhat loosened his limbs; he flung the door open, there stood a man.

"Are you the carver?" Michael asked.

"Yes I am," Kosta replied.

"My name is Michael. I would like to ask you a favor," the man asked sharply extending his hand for a handshake.

"I am Kosta, I am the carver. Please come in and have a seat, here...at the table." Kosta hesitated for a second, not expecting anyone. Michael entered, walked to the table on which a small lamp flickered dimly. Kosta quickly turned up the flame to brighten up the room. At Michael's first glance, this was a lonely, solitary little home. The shelves with figurines meant one thing; spare time is not wasted. Kosta sat across the table and waited for this stranger to speak, curious why he came. They sat just for a minute looking at each other before Michael spoke.

"I live across the bridge on the outskirts of the village...," Michael's hands in action as he talked... "My good man, I heard that you take on all kinds of work. You see, we need a crib for our baby. That is my wife is expecting a baby, soon. I will supply all the material and whatever you need, if you would take on the job, I will pay well." Michael smiled and his hands rested on the table.

Kosta surprised. Observing this fellow sitting across from him, not sure, if this is real. Is he that someone who threatened Paul? He withheld his excitement.

"How did you find me?" Kosta asked.

"Well, I... in conversation with friends and neighbors, I asked if any of them knew of someone who was good in that sort of profession. You, my good fellow, came highly recommended.

"Hmm...but who was it? Do you know his name? Kosta asked, still being cautious "His name I do not know, sorry, I failed to ask. I did not ask. I had too much ale that night. Lucky me, I took with me the slip of paper with directions to your home." Michael told a little fib and felt a bit abashed. Kosta's spirit somewhat lifted, but he still not smiled.

"Glad to be of service, of course I will make the crib. How soon do you need it? Do you have an idea, style or a sketch for the crib?" Kosta asked.

"I do have a sketch at home. My first objective was to find *THE* carver and come to an agreement for the project," Michael replied.

Their conversation broached different subjects, which stretched out for several hours.

Michael was older by at least five years; nevertheless felt quite at ease conversing with Kosta, feeling that out of this meeting, a lasting friendship is in the making not only between them, but Rabinna as well. Kosta certainly is handsome and Kathryn is very attractive, well then, their meeting in the woods by chance surely meant one thing, they were destined for each other.

They agreed on a handshake, Michaels grip was very strong. Michael gave directions to his home, detailed directions and description of the home, to be sure Kosta did not get lost.

"Do you sell your work, or display with business proprietors, or the market?" Michael asked. To that question, Kosta replied, "Yes I have, our family friend a cobbler displayed my crafts, but for some peculiar reason he refuses to continue..."

"Oh that is awful, did he give you a reason, why?" Michael interrupted.

"Well yes, he claims someone had threatened him if he continues to sell my crafts," Kosta replied.

"Did you find out who the man was?" Michael asked.

"Ah, no, that warning came from a messenger," Kosta answered.

Michael walked over to the shelves to inspect all those carvings, and a moment later enthusiastically exclaimed, "Kosta, these are beautiful! It will take no time at all for you to become famous. Well, I must go, now. I apologize taking up much of your time tonight, see you soon!" Michael headed for the door. Kosta followed Michael outside, watched him mount his horse and ride away. He turned and went back in sat down at the table and thought; *how strange, mother said the same thing long ago.*

After several weeks working on neglected projects, he had finished it all and was glad, all scraps and tools were stored away in the chest drawer. He swept the floor, glanced around the room, as if expecting company and agreed it looked neat. He boiled buckets of water for a hot bath; sat in the tub longer than usual; scrubbed his body until the bath water turned cold. Shaved his three-day old beard; dressed in his best pants and a shirt, cleaned his fingernails, checked himself in a mirror and was about to leave but realized he forgot to clean his ears and shine his shoes; using the tip of his washcloth wiggled it cleaning his ears; and then walked outside and shined his shoes. Now he was on his way to find Michaels home. He had crossed the bridge, rode through the village, and at the outskirts on the far side of the village came upon the white house, a white fence in front, and a wide gate, which stood open. He dismounted and led the horse to the post inside the front yard. Kosta looked up at the big oak tree, which practically covered not only the front yard, half of its canopy sprawled over the house as if to protect it from all elements. Kosta liked what he saw. His heart thumped, he swallowed hard. He walked up to the door, hesitated for a moment then knocked. When the door opened, Michael stood grinning.

"Welcome! You found our home, so good of you to come. Wonderful, wonderful, please come in, have a seat. Permit me to tell my wife Rabinna you have arrived. She will bring us some coffee, if you like coffee, I will be right with you."

Kosta followed Michael, sat down at the table.

"Yes! Thank you, I love coffee," Kosta replied rather timidly

Kosta's eyes took in an impressive little home, simply furnished, pleasant and clean, uncluttered, unlike his own. Michael not his wife came back from the kitchen carrying a tray with two cups, matching coffee pot, from which the aroma permeated the room. Michael smiled, gently set it on the table.

"Enjoy the coffee. Feel at home, ah, pour a cup for me. I will be right back with the sketch," he said.

"Thank you kindly, I will," Kosta replied. Kosta sipped the coffee and waited. Michael returned with a rolled up paper in hand; sat down, took a sip of coffee and unrolled the paper. Kosta studied the rough sketch, when he heard someone come into the room he glanced up and there stood a pretty woman. Kosta stood up quickly and bowed.

"My wife Rabinna, we are expecting our first child in about six months. Rabinna this is Kosta, he is *the* carver and furniture maker, and I engaged him to make the crib for our baby," Michael said.

"Ah, are you the carver?" surprised Rabinna asked.

"Yes, I am the carver and carpenter, my pleasure to meet you Lady Rabinna." Kosta kissed her extended hand. Kosta's handsomeness struck Rabinna and suddenly she knew this is the fellow Kathryn had described meeting in the woods. She excused herself and left the room. Kosta sat down to discuss the making of the crib, completely unaware of whom he was about to meet. After about ten minutes two women entered the room, when Kosta looked up, he froze; before him; stood the girl he had met in the woods. He glanced at the three people smiling at him. He stood up too quickly his chair toppled backwards; it fell with a racket; too late; he was not quick enough to grab it, embarrassed, his face flushed, stuttered an apology. Rabinna looked at Kathryn and saw her cheeks flushed. Michael laughed.

"Kosta please sit down...it is all right, Rabinna please introduce Kathryn."

Kosta bowed, unexpectedly but pleasantly surprised, his vocal chords constricted unable to utter a word, at last, clearing his throat several times, managed to say.

"Miss Kathryn—I... what a coincidence...it is a surprise...my pleasure meeting you again." Kathryn blushed, palms sweaty, responded in a low whisper.

"Thank you...it really is a strange coincidence."

Rabinna realized Michael found this young man for Kathryn. She leaned on him. "Michael how did you find him?" she whispered.

Kathryn and Kosta stood staring at each other. Michael reached over and tugged at his sleeve.

"Kosta please sit down we have to perfect this sketch!" Kosta glanced around the room.

"My God, I thought I was dreaming. Forgive me but I am pleasantly surprised, I did not know. This to me is a great pleasure. Believe me. I never thought I would see Kathryn again. Michael this puzzles me, how did you ever find me?" Kosta exclaimed, side-glanced at the women retreating to the kitchen.

Michael confessed to the fib and his drinking.

"I do not drink much, occasionally we all do. Kosta, the real truth is Kathryn was the one who insisted on finding you."

"Never in my life I imagined this happening to me, Michael, she really asked you to find me?" Kosta felt giddy.

"Now Kosta, we must finish our business deal, relax and have some more coffee," Michael said, laughing at this young man's expression. After a long visit and many cups of coffee, interrupted only twice when Rabinna and Kathryn brought in plates of hot food. The women left them alone. It was evident to them the bonding of friendship between the men. Kathryn peeked, but Rabinna pulled her back.

"If he sees you peeking he will shy away... well, he might." Kathryn's eyes grew wide from fear of losing him. Rabinna smiled at her sister. The sun dipped beyond the mountains when Kosta rode home, feeling as if drifting on a cloud not sitting on a horse. Perhaps this was his day, the beginning of happiness, a new life. He never felt like this before; it had never occurred to him that he was as of this day; in love, was it love... or a mere infatuation, they were both young, it just turned out that way. Infatuation or not, Kosta daily thought about Kathryn, though she never came to visit. Kosta would protest fiercely if she would want to. Besides, surely Michael told her what condition his house is when they first met. She did not press it.

Embarrassed of his simple cluttered home, he could not allow it, not now, but someday surely, he will invite her and show her all his carvings. He promised himself to reorganize and clean it up. He worked extra hard, because now he had a goal, a future, of which he was sure. They met whenever time permitted at Michael and Rabinna's home. Michael always came up with some work for him. Kosta, besides working his farm, often helped Aunt Olivia and told her all about Kathryn and how they met, and how nice her sister Rabinna and her husband Michael were, and soon she will meet them.

Summer passed quickly, it was harvest time again, work, hard work stared at him, but he would face it, he could do it all himself, as he had done so many seasons before, and as always someone came along to help when he could do no more. Day after day, he worked in the fields. He wiped his face with a handkerchief already damp of sweat. Hungry and thirsty still he pushed on. The crops had to be gathered and stored. He worked and smiled, because now he had a reason to.

He felt energized. Weariness and loneliness no longer weighed him down. Especially that day while working in the fields, he saw them coming to help him, Michael, Kathryn and Rabinna. He found no words but gripped Michaels hand in gratitude. Kathryn had brought a big jug of coffee, she handed him a filled cup, he drank it greedily, refreshed, thirst quenched. He watched as she worked right along Rabinna. Kosta glanced at Rabinna and wondered why she is working this hard when she is so close to delivering her child. Michael was ahead of him.

"Perhaps Rabinna should rest a while. She might hurt herself and the baby," Kosta caught up to him and said. Michael looked over his shoulder at his wife and Kathryn. Truly, she was rushing to keep up with the men. He looked ahead but the strip seemed too long to get it all done in a day.

"Rabinna rest a while and please bring us water!" Michael shouted. She raised her head and turned to Kathryn. Rabinna pointed behind her, the jug; Kathryn understood, rose up from her knees and ran to fetch the water jug. Kosta watched her as she came toward them. Soon after, they all had to stop for Rabinna had enough. She was bending over for too long; her back ached. She gave Michael meaningful glances. He understood and told Kosta it was time for them to go home; time to do chores. Michael held Rabinnas arm as they walked to the wagon. Kathryn stayed with Kosta.

"*I am grateful Lord for these wonderful people,"* Kosta thought as together they worked an hour or so longer before sun would set, neither spoke. Kosta drove up with the wagon closer to load all the heavy baskets with onions. Kathryn offered to help but he said she had done enough for today.

The sun dipped towards the horizon, another day was over. "*Rabinna and Michael must be at home by now*," Kathryn thought. Kosta drove into the back yard unloaded all the baskets setting them against the ground cellar. They held hands as they walked to the stable to unhitch the horse from the wagon. Kosta saddled his horse to take Kathryn back home to Rabinna. Kosta spontaneously pulled her to him embraced her. She did not pull away. He tightened his arms and crushed her to him. Kathryn did not resist when he kissed her, she eagerly responded, when their lips parted they looked at each other, Kosta surprised at himself began to apologize, "Forgive me Kathryn, I do know what came over me, I should not have been so..." Kathryn interrupted taking his face into her palms, she kissed him.

"Kosta it is all right do not fret, I wanted you to kiss me, and really I did."

"But Kathryn I have never kissed a girl in my life, you are my first girl..." Again she stopped him.

"I have never kissed a boy either, you are my first. Before you take me home I want you to kiss me many times, and on the road too." She stood on tiptoes and kissed him. Again, he crushed her to him and both trembled. He knew they could not be apart for much longer, their passion afire. Arms tightly wrapped about each other they stood not wanting to let go. However, Kosta would never disgrace or shame her. He respected her too much. For the moment they could only embrace, steal a kiss and wait. Their passionate moment subsided Kosta helped Kathryn mount the horse; he swung his leg over the saddle, keeping her in front of him. They rode back and all the while his arms wrapped close around her, he felt her leaning back, he kissed her neck and she turned to kiss him back. At her sister's home, Michael and Rabinna met them at the front door to invite him in for supper. However, he declined.

"Perhaps another time, besides I need to stop by Aunt Olivia's for a little while. Thank you from the bottom of my heart for your help, thank you." He mounted his horse and rode away. Kosta from that day on had changed. When he walked, he walked surefooted, straight, strong and tall, confident in himself.

All the villages were ready for winter, the weather changed to rain, mud and cold; days became shorter. Harvest supplies stored away. Supply of lamp oil and firewood measured to last all winter, and far into spring. Due to winter's severe weather, Kosta's visits to his friend Michael were only out of necessity. The crib stood ready for delivery. Kosta visited Aunt Olivia quite often though, as he promised. Expressing to her his frustration, his concern not knowing how Kathryn and her mother fared, of whom the two of them had many discussions.

Kosta on a first fair day, decided to deliver the finished baby's crib, in the sleigh, he covered it with a blanked and rode on to Michael and Rabinnas home; Kosta and Michael carried the crib inside the parlor; Kosta glanced toward the kitchen as if expecting Kathryn to charge at him hearing his voice, but she was not there. Michael touched Rabinnas arm and nodded his head, she quickly got his attention by loudly saying how impressed she is with all perfected details on the crib.

"Kosta such excellent work and you carved ribbons on the headboard too." Rabinna smiled when Kosta bowed slightly and said, "It was my pleasure Rabinna, blessings for you and your baby."

Michael thanked him for such a fine job.

"It was an exciting project. Rabinna have you news of Kathryn and mother, are they doing well?"

"Oh they are fine, the winter cold bothers mother but soon you will see them," Rabinna assured him.

"We would like to invite both you and Aunt Olivia for Christmas dinner, although it is a month away," Michael said.

"I will tell her about Christmas dinner, she will be excited to meet you and Kathryn" Michael handed Kosta a small leather pouch, his pay for the crib.

Aunt Olivia accepted the invitation, when Kosta told her stopping for a short visit on the way home. She smiled broadly and said, "I am excited and eager to meet your girl and her family of which you constantly talked about."

Weeks slipped by and it was Christmas. Kosta dressed in his best, wore a warm cape on the way picked up Aunt Olivia. She sat in the sled, Kosta made sure she was dressed in warm clothing plus, blankets, even though it was not a great distance, best not to take chances, winters are dangerous. Disregarding the weather, they ventured out to celebrate the Holiday. When Kosta and Aunt Olivia arrived, Kathryn blushed when she opened the door for them. Aunt Olivia with outstretched arms came forward and embraced Kathryn it was a moment Kosta would not forget, he observed the sincerity on both faces as their eyes held and sparkled a certain bond right there and then. Kathryn turned to Kosta and said.

"Kosta she is a beautiful woman I am so glad to meet her and she wrapped her arms around Kosta's neck, and kissed him on the cheek. She hung their cloaks on hooks in a small closet. They followed her into the parlor. Kathryn introduced Aunt Olivia to Rabinna her sister. The two women embraced, according to custom. Rabinna beamed at Aunt Olivia, instantly liked the older woman.

"We welcome you, Aunt Olivia to our humble home. Please excuse me, I will go and fetch my husband and my in-laws, they are in the kitchen," Rabinna said, turned and walked off.

"Come I want you to meet mother," Kathryn said. Aunt Olivia and Kosta approached the sofa on which Lady Grazine a widow, crippled by arthritis unable to move freely sat waiting.

"Mother I want you to meet Aunt Olivia and Kosta Komarod." Lady Grazine barely lifted her hands to both of them. Aunt Olivia gently took her gnarled hand leaning down to kiss her cheek. Kosta kissed her other hand. She smiled.

"Young man it is a pleasure at last to meet you, Kathryn talks about you continuously. Welcome, please sit down here beside me."

Kosta blushed glanced at Kathryn then at Aunt Olivia. Kathryn seemed embarrassed her eyes downcast. Aunt Olivia put her arm around her.

"My dear, there is nothing to be shy about." she said and smiled.

Kathryn returned her smile. "Mother I will introduce Aunt Olivia to Michael's parents and his brother Bartlow. Just then, Rabinna, Michael and his parents came through the door. Michael grasped Kosta's hand tightly and grinned from ear to ear.

"Ah good fellow, glad you were able to make it. This bitter cold is holding now for the last week; anyway, meet my father Edwin Hartigard, my mother Beatrice and my brother Bartlow."

Kosta smiled wide, bowed to Lady Beatrice, kissed her hand. She smiled and said in a high pitch voice,

"Very nice to meet Kathryn's *boy*, as usual she has good taste...as in everything," Rabinna said a little perturbed. "Now mother Beatrice, do not be prickly!"

Sir Edwin glared at her and told her to go and sit with Grazine, and she did, waddling away like a duck. Sir Edwin grumbled something, turned to his son Bartlow,

"Well boy do not stand there, we need a drink for this occasion." Michael laughed. Bartlow moved quickly over to the sideboard and poured the wine. They were polite and Kosta felt at ease. He noticed everyone were most gracious to Aunt Olivia. Kosta felt he belonged here with these strangers, more so, then with his own blood brother. It was crowded but no one complained. They were together as one big family; it was a joyful Christmas. The wine flowed, fresh vegetables from the cold cellar, a scrumptious fat goose and wild game enough for everyone. Afterwards, Rabinna and Kathryn gathered the dinner plates from the table and washed them quickly. While the rest sat in the parlor talking of all things, spring planting. Rabina and Kathryn prepared the table for holiday cakes and spiced tea. Everyone sat at the table but for Grazine and Aunt Olivia. Corpulent Beatrice carried a tray with cakes and three cups of tea to join them. Kosta glanced at Aunt Olivia, she was talking with the other two women; her expression relaxed; she was happy. The hours had quickly passed. Winter days are short. It was dark out though still early. Small gifts exchanged between them, were little treasures a time to give more from the heart, than to receive. Kathryn knitted gloves for Kosta. A beautiful embroidered tablecloth Rabinna gave to Kathryn. Michael did not exchange gifts with Kosta. Rabinna received from Kosta a carved figurine of a child sleeping on its stomach, knees curled under; its cherubic pudgy face on its hands. Aunt Olivia came with a basket full of her special cookies wrapped in embroidered napkins; tied with a red ribbon, for everyone. For Kathryn in his pocket Kosta had something very small, but special. Aunt Olivia received a large jar of honey and lamp oil, a gift from all her new friends.

At the time Kosta's mother Liana was ill, she removed the gold band from her finger and handed it to Aunt Olivia asking her to, "Promise...promise me this...you will give my wedding band to Kosta at the proper time...when it comes." Olivia felt that Liana had made a good decision. Kosta now was more deserving than his brother Thomas ever was.

Aunt Olivia years later being critically ill, she explained to Kosta why she happened to have his mother's gold wedding band. Now he is a grown man, a very handsome good-hearted man to understand it all.

Earlier, when Kosta came to take her to dinner, she asked, "Kosta do you have a carving as a present for Kathryn?"

"This Christmas I have in my pocket, something small and shinny and I intend to propose to Kathryn," he replied. Aunt Olivia approved his decision, indeed.

Hesitantly he looked at Kathryn, those gathered around the table were her family, and he thought, "*would she accept this simple gold band*?" His heart skipped a beat. Chills ran through him. He wished his parents were alive and with him for this occasion. They would be proud. However should Kathryn reject him... he will be mortified. She was his first love, and he knew she would be the only love in his life. Rejection frightened him. He had to have a word with Michael for reassurance. Kosta quickly approached Michael, tugged at his sleeve for attention while he was discussing something with his father-in-law. Michael turned to see Kosta wearing a frightened face, excused himself and they walked out of the house. Briskly they walked into the barn.

"Kosta what is wrong? Why are you so upset, have you seen a ghost? Did someone say something to you?" Kosta tongue-tied tried to express his feelings but the words were stuck in his throat. After a moment, Kosta blurted.

"No no, nothing of the sort... I am unsure...I mean, Michael...I fear she might..."

Micheal interrupted Kosta in mid-sentence,

"I know what you are trying to say. Kosta you fear rejection. Kosta listen, I understand, Kathryn will not reject you. I am positive a hundred percent. Come, it is too cold out here. I cannot wait. Propose to her, the whole family is here, it is Christmas a perfect occasion and timing, Kosta, do not hesitate. I know she wants you! She loves you."

They came back into the house and Kosta sat down next to Kathryn. Aunt Olivia surmised that these two men had some sort of a plan. Michael filled all the glasses with red wine.

"Let us have a toast for an important moment here and now." Michael announced to all. Rabinna glanced at him.

"Yes let us have a toast to *us!* Today we are all together *family* and best *friends*. Yes to us!" She raised her glass. Michael corrected her politely. "Rabinna my dear, this important toast is to Kosta and Kathryn, we drink to them." Aunt Olivia understood and smiled when she caught Kathryn's eye.

Kathryn eyed both of them questioningly, but they said nothing more.

Kosta and Kathryn raised their glasses took a sip and with a gracious, "*thank you*" the room fell silent for a moment, all eyes were on the couple. Kosta rose slowly, handed Michael his wine glass and knelt on one knee facing Kathryn, no one spoke just stared anticipating his next move. Kosta reached into his pocket and produced an embroidered handkerchief tied with a purple ribbon, an insignificant little bundle in the palm of his hand. Kosta took her wine glass and handed it to Michael. Kathryn for a second stared then slowly untied the ribbon. She gasped seeing the gold band and was pleasantly surprised. She was not expecting this at all. Holding it in her open palm, her eyes filled with tears. She glanced around everyone's eyes were glued on them. She wrapped her arms around his neck, and cried from happiness, Kosta spilled his feelings to her.

"Kathryn, I love you very much, from the moment I saw you in the woods, I knew then my heart is yours and I will love you forever. However, all I have to give you is what is in my heart. I do not possess riches, as you know very well, but I will love you... for as long as I am to live on this earth...you will make me the happiest man. I will endure all the labor without complaint...work for you and our children to improve our life the best I can...please...say..." He could say no more. Everyone held his or her breath waiting for Kathryn's reply.

"Kosta, yes, I do love you. You know I do. Yes I will be your wife as long as I am allowed to live on this earth also, and I will work hard to make our life comfortable and happy, I will not complain for shortages, beyond our control," Kathryn whispered.

Kosta slipped the ring on her finger and kissed it. Taking Kathryn's hand turned to Aunt Olivia, she rose to face them moved to tears, took their hands gave her blessing and kissed their cheeks.

Then they approached Kathryn's mother to receive her blessing. Rabinna and Michael watched as the two vowed to each other a lifetime commitment. The whole family moved to tears.

Rabinna, tears streaming down her cheeks ran up to Kathryn embraced her with joy she said, "Kathryn, I give my blessing to both of you, I am overjoyed that my sister found love, I wish you well." The two sisters looked at each other and were of the same thoughts. *This moment, we will remember and cherish.* Michael shook hands and embraced Kosta like a brother, slapping his back hard. Michael's brother, Bartlow congratulated the engaged couple as well. Aunt Olivia moved deeply by those words of promise, wept. Then Michael raised his glass,

"We all are witnesses to their engagement and upcoming wedding," everyone shouted.

"Cheers, cheers! We are all witnesses and we give them our blessing to marry." Lady Hartigan added, "And many children." They peeled with laughter and toasted again and the conversation led to the wedding date, which would not take place until sometime in the spring. Trees and shrubs will bloom permeating the air with fragrance; flowers will burst out in profusion. Thereafter each day marked off meant a day closer to springtime.

Kosta felt calm at the end of a long day, on the way home Kosta saw Aunt Olivia to her home and made sure she would be warm and safe. It turned out to be a good day, a very happy holiday. He missed Kathryn terribly. When he arrived home, it was dark and silent inside without that holiday cheer. Kosta had good neighbors they had done chores for him this day. Nevertheless, he went to check on his animals; made sure stable and barn doors latched for the night. He fell into his small bed and relived events of this day. Happiness; he felt such happiness. All those wonderful people made him feel good. He envisioned every face feeling calm and relaxed. Thinking of holding Kathryn in his arms, and was about to fall asleep, when his brother's face appeared and burst his happy thoughts. Kosta opened his eyes in the darkness seeing before him a smiling face, which he tried to shake off. The room was cold but Kosta threw the covers off, wearing his gown and socks he walked over to the table and turned up the lamp, he took a good look around his home. He sat down hard on the chair. Hands covered his face, one wish swirled on his mind for his life to be different. "*All will be good when you and Kathryn marry. She will help you. Make you happy,*" an inner voice spoke softly. These words took away all his fears and frustrations and anxiety left him.

Suddenly he felt chilled to the bone. Turning off the lamp quickly walked to his bed and slipped under the cold covers. He shivered for a while waiting for sleep to come. The warmth of the feather quilt relaxed him. Heavy eyelids closed. As he slept, he found himself in a dream with Kathryn hand in hand walking knee high across a field of rye. In his dream, he was happy and Kathryn smiled, as she always does when he is with her. Kosta awoke to a fiercely barking dog, his dog. Remembering his dream, he wished it had not ended. Before dressing, he opened the door to let the dog out then dressed warmly.

Eighteen: Predetermined Death

Lord Thomas worked hand in hand with the rest of the employees around the property. Besides overseeing every detail and organizing from a list given him by his mother-in-law, regarding accommodations and comfort for the Prozattis Italian family must be ready who are arriving two days after Christmas. Cybilia mentioning her "*family*" Lord Thomas's nerves tweaked sharply realizing that it has been years not months since he thought about Kosta, much less inviting him. Now being part of her family, Cybilia having her share of work and all arrangements complete, the rest fell upon him to receive guests and entertain them. When "*the family*" arrived, they were a bit shy spoke a foreign language, the entire staff stood lined up ready to greet the guests. For a few moments when they all marched in through the front door, everyone was silent. Sir Prozatti introduced his family, and that is the moment erupted chaos, hugs and kisses ahs and oohs admiring Cybilia and Lord Thomas. Cybilia wanted to know what they were saying. Her father translated exactly word by word: "You Cybilia, are a beautiful woman, but a little thin," said grandma Prozatti.

"Papa must make you eat a bit more, put some meat on your bones," Aunt Alfia said. Both glanced at each other, Cybilia a bit embarrassed laughed heartily, but Lord Thomas just smiled at the group crowding around them. Sir Paulo raised his voice above the din and waved them over to the dining room. After downing several bottles of wine they all relaxed, Frunnz filled glass after glass, no sooner he finished the last empty glass, started over again. The girls carried in platters of meats and vegetables, sat it all on the table, in a few minutes, everything disappeared off the large platters. Women chattered in Italian and the men in their baritone voices spoke loudly. Women fully satiated, walked away from the table and sat on the sofas discussing something, gesticulating, arms in motion among themselves. No one knew what they were discussing, then all of them rose at once and nodding their heads to the men in the dining room followed by Lady Marianna and Cybilia disappeared. The dining room now somewhat quieted down, the group of men stayed up late smoking drinking and talking low. Next morning were up before sunrise, ate big breakfasts leaving crumbs on each plate; children roamed and climbed onto everything laughing and screaming. Sir Paulo and all the kin folk mostly men hollered at each other, arms flailing, each day overindulged in the bubbly until their brains swam. Sir Paulo told them to dress warm to come with him to see the winery, they were happy for Paulo, business is good they said to him, but winters he takes it easy, they said. Yes, that is true, he told them, lately, he slowed down, not feeling well, he told them. Then you must stop working altogether, you have a good son-in-law now, take it easy. Sir Paulo nodded agreement, he held back telling any of them what sort of man his son-in-law is, he knew his family well. Back at the house dining, conversation and drinking continued. "These people did not need to be entertained; they entertained themselves, Lord Thomas thought... and they snored like an off-key orchestra playing an Italian serenade, in my house." Early in the morning of the third day, with a big breakfast and much strong coffee they gathered themselves and their presents from Sir Paulo and Lady Marianna and drove away in covered wagons like the gypsies disregarding the weather. Suddenly the large home was in complete silence; everyone breathed a sigh of relief. Sir Paulo gathered everyone in the dining room and said.

"All of you have done well...now let us have a toast and go rest for several hours; our quiet guests are not arriving today, we have time to clean up." Everyone cheered and applauded, sat down to a good lunch than retired for a nap.

To entertain the distinguished guests from the immediate area Lady Marianna and Sir Paulo were in charge. Lord Thomas relieved of this duty felt more reserved, yet observed; they were Paulo Prozatti's longtime business partners. Therefore, his gain depended on his presentation of self.

Lord Thomas having connections through his father-in-law realized a promising future.

Winter still dragged on, and more snow fell, and temperatures plunged often. When spring arrives, the force of employees will do the work. Sir Prozatti did not partake in many tasks, therefore, decided now to place all responsibility on the shoulders of his son-in-law. Lord Thomas beamed, now being the head of all operation. Living in seclusion, the guesthouse far from the main home, he had not noticed that a prominent physician summoned to examine

Sir Paulo visited quite often. Doctors concluding advice; exhaustion; too much on his mind to deal with; Sir Paulo retired to idle time and relaxation, without activity whatsoever, with much rest Paulo Prozattis spirit and health bounced back. Unfortunately, after several weeks of working he began to feel frail of body, loss of initiative for not only the business, but daily trivialities as well, the consequence, mind fading and body wasting away; his time of toil was over. Lady Marianna had much to consider, *why, what is the cause his illness, her husband now was like night and day; but several years ago, he was strong like a horse, perhaps that did him in; but he had plenty of rest during wintertime also in the last months...hmmm. Besides, I do not like his glassy staring eyes...and he is not that old...*

Lord Thomas quickly discovered that with careful manipulations, little twists here and there could and did contribute to his prosperity. Cybilia had no objections to the increase of wealth for her own needs. She had much to her disposal. Cybilia had spoken with her mother about their trip, mother agreed without a moment's hesitation. The truth of it was Marianna deep down wanted them to go.

"Do not fret about father, the doctor is nearby, take the trip and enjoy the warmer climate and scenery," she told her daughter. Shortly after the holiday, the weather had cleared enough for their plan of joining the caravan of guests in five carriages off to a southern part of the world.

The best and shortest route was through the Riverside Village. Lord Thomas experienced an unnerving moment passing through his birth village. Fortunately, Cybilia had no knowledge of where he was born, he never told her exactly. Why would she ask, besides, his humble home stood off the main road.

Along the trip, each evening they stopped at the homes of friends. All horses needed rest and fodder. Lord Thomas had noticed that these people had friends along the way, no problem to travel whenever they so desired. Now mind you, these friends were not mediocre villagers... they were rich as well. *Hmm*...thought Lord Thomas, *such friends are hard to find, unless one is also rich. I must take notes and remember their names.*

On days when the men and the women rode in separate carriages because, men talk about women; and without doubt, women talk about their men. Lord Thomas felt a bit antsy, insecure, not quite on the same level yet with these rich and notorious merchants. These men were unlike his old friends of long ago, with them, he was loud, tough, and sure of himself.

However now he had to adjust to a different level not only with these men but he had to tiptoe around his father-in-law. He tried to learn and obey. Listened well, now and then having few questions. Seven and a half days on the road the caravan traveled. Stopped along the way many times for the night and overstaying with friends. The further south they rode it rained, the ruts and deep puddles made the ride rough. Overall, nothing frightening or critical had occurred to annoy their wives.

Cybilia noticed the air each day a bit warmer, the climate changing, surely, winter had not reached this far south.

In the distance, Cybilia saw the sprawling villa and grounds of "Lotus Flores Vista." Cybilia's comments made him think she would rather live in this part of the world. For a while, she annoyed him by her excitement. On the other hand, perhaps it would be best to be far away from his memories of the river and that stifling house where he was born, and most of all, his brother. This was a world of different customs, food, and apparel. It began to intrigue him, having consumed too much food and wine, failed to ask the name of the largest city. A thought ran through his mind, *a good place to visit someday but alone.*

Cybilia was familiar with the road leading to Lotus Flores Vista Estate. This place, for her, meant something. She had told her husband been had here before, several times as a teen. Uncle Lorenzo changed the name of their estate now, which was about ten years ago.

"Have you been here since then?

"Oh yes, one summer before I met you Thomas..." she said smiling. "With my parents. Uncle Lorenzo and AlaKara his beautiful wife told us about their trip to Japan, I... that summer was very hot," Cybilia said, turned her head to the window and stared out. She came away with many memories, now she began to wonder whatever happened to that particular person she had met and had spent so much time together. Cybilia dared not mention any of it to Lord Thomas, why he might assume too much. Accusations might fly later.

Lord Thomas and Cybilia walked into the cool parlor where the furniture was of such elegance he had had never imagined existed. Cybilia embraced and kissed on both cheeks by Uncle Lorenzo's wife, Lady AlaKara, a very attractive woman. Her smile and sparkling eyes one could not easily forget. Lord Thomas bowed and kissed her fingertips noting rings on every finger. He held his breath, his teeth clenched unable to whisper a proper greeting. Lady AlaKara intelligent, observant, took his hand and led him to the dining room for refreshments. Lady AlaKara turned her head and asked, "Cybilia dear, you did not forget to bring those tasty mushrooms from Mother."

"Oh of course I have not forgotten, Aunt AlaKara. These are the best of the lot. You will not find any poisonous ones, our girls know the difference." The two women went off to the parlor. In the dining room on the sideboard, stood glasses filled with wine. Waiters brought in platters of freshly prepared finger sandwiches and bowls of fruit. Cybilia thirsty drank a large glass of tea. Lord Thomas reached for a glass of wine and dropped onto the dining chair; thinking of what Cybilia said, "*poison mushrooms*," but suddenly a hand gently placed on his gave him to understand it was not the time for wine, instead a glass of tea came up to his eye level. He turned his head to see who was beside him; Lady AlaKara loomed over him; her low cleavage exposing her bosom; disarming him with her smile, looking into his eyes. He was caught at his bad manners; embarrassed he rose slowly from the chair, and apologized bowing repeatedly, mumbling that the trip tired him out completely. She walked away glancing back at him once. Truly, the whole trip did tire him out, and he needed a glass of wine to relax. He was tense, being in such a circle of riches. Lady Ala Kara invited her guests for early dinner, during which, wine flowed bottle after bottle, and Lord Thomas noted that the wine came from the Prozattis winery. Late into the evening guests relaxed on sofas, sipped wine in groups, their conversations hushed; erupting suddenly into chatter of objections, buzzed for a spell and then came loud laughter. Some guests were coming in late after dinner to join the party, others retiring to bed for the night; or those preferring to sleep in their own beds and being neighbors were leaving.

Uncle Lorenzo found Lord Thomas and Cybilia alone on the veranda enjoying the evening's warmth. He sat with them for a while avoiding the question why either one chose not to engage in conversation with their guests. Rather said his day was long and tiring and wanted to know if they wished to see their bedroom, Cybilia said she was tired and was ready to go to bed. Uncle Lorenzo led them to the far end of the villa where it was most quiet. Cybilia being tired paid no attention of the size and condition of this bedroom, though drunk, Lord Thomas noticed it right away. Began to grumble, that he was given the worst room and that he will ask why in the morning, as soon as he laid his head on the pillow, he was asleep. Cybilia she too exhausted fell into dreamless sleep.

Several days later, they took trips to the large city, touring, buying beautiful souvenirs for those back home, while absorbing the change of climate.

On other days, men walked along the huge lake on the property, smoking pipes, talking business. While women talked about romance and lovers, music, rouge, petticoats and dresses. Lord Thomas had one thought in mind: *mushrooms*. He must get more information but cautiously ask questions. At dinner, mushrooms served one serving spoon each. The moment he tasted them he was sure mushrooms would serve his purpose. No need to dwell on this now, he had plenty of time. One question he had to ask Cybilia, where had she stored them in the carriage.

Young men each morning served breakfast and elegant dinners; one could never have imagined out in the country such privacy and luxury.

Cybilia was in seventh heaven, while Lord Thomas felt uncomfortable. He seethed within. If it were up to him, he would rather have young girls serve his breakfast and dinner. This was a first for him, of course he has never been this far south in his life, now he much rather be in his old stomping ground, for some reason he noticed Cybilia and one of the servants exchange glances too often. Grant you that fellow was handsome. Each time at the table, Lord Thomas discreetly observed from the corner of his eye and thought, *yes, he has an eye for her. He is glancing at her, but why only her? The other women were very attractive, several of them were beautiful, he agreed, perhaps because Cybilia was the youngest of them all. Well in time, he will find out why.*

Lord Thomas was envious. He had to make her forget those young men. When the silent night disturbed by snoring now and then, Lord Thomas felt in the mood, but Cybilia explained politely she would rather not tonight, perhaps another night. He lay next to her for a while and then began touching her at first gently; she pushed his hand away, asked him to stop. He lost his temper and with force overpowered Cybilia; pinned her down, she struggled; he smothered her with kisses until she stopped struggling, he whispered what she wanted to hear until she submitted to him completely. In the silence of the night, no one heard the moans of ecstasy, height of passion, of pleasure in the bedroom at the far end of the house. Lord Thomas wished for a son this time. They were last to rise out of bed being late for breakfast.

Because of his envy, his deceptive concern for Cybilia's parents insisted they should return home. Inwardly as much as he wanted to stay, his aim was to keep Cybilia away from those young waiters. Stubbornly, Cybilia insisted on staying longer, she was enjoying herself with the circle of women. Lord Thomas repeatedly reminded her of her parent's health. Lady AlaKara overheard his concern and agreed with him, they should go home. Cybilia insisted that nothing is wrong with Father. However, at the end, Cybilia stopped whining allowing him his way. On one condition, they will go home if he goes to the city and finds a silver silk shawl for mother. Lord Thomas reluctantly agreed. Together with uncle Lorenzo two days, later early morning rode away to the big city. The city happened to be a bit over an hour each way. After many hours of traipsing from store to store, and the market, they bought a silk shawl. The two men arrived late in the day just in time for dinner. Tired and hungry Lord Thomas marched to the silver tray on the sideboard and poured himself a large glass of wine. Lady AlaKara watched him from the doorway, his back to her but did not stop him. He drank one glass then another, after which he poured one more. She noticed his sour expression; turned on her heel and walked into the parlor and sat next to Cybilia. Lord Thomas had not noticed the two women, but heard quiet voices. He listened to their conversation a minute and then walked in on them. Cybilia and Lady AlaKara turned their heads to him, but neither speaking directly to him.

"Ah..., my wonderful ladies relaxing and having a private chat?"

"Yes we are, and yes we need privacy," Lady AlaKara said. Lord Thomas bowed slightly and walked out through the house and into the garden. He sat and thought, *"I helped myself to their wine without anyone's permission. So...I am family now, I should be free to help myself, if no one is around. I will apologize later. Perhaps she had seen me that is why the cold shoulder."* Early morning they set out on their journey, saying goodbye was quite hard for Cybilia she wrapped her arms around Lady AlaKara and wept. Lord Thomas impatient stood by. Uncle Lorenzo gripped Thomas's hand wished them a safe journey home. The carriage rolled on jarring and jerking in some areas. Cybilia napped since they had to rise so early. Lord Thomas engrossed in thoughts looked out at the scenery. Their need to stop turned out quite often because that is what Cybilia wanted, passing through a village or a town; she wanted to go sightseeing. Lord Thomas stewed waiting in the carriage, whereas Cybilia excitedly purchased small things for herself and others. Back on the road, he made a comment that too many things on the floor, no room for his legs. Well then, we shall make room. She gathered everything off the floor and placed it between them. Now he had to lean more into the corner. Lord Thomas was thinking, "*She is aggravating me. She is becoming rebellious, I wonder where...perhaps I am the cause in some way...I have been pushy and rude lately...who has she been talking to, but why stand against me, hmm.*" Coming home seemed longer than going away from home. They stopped at her friend's country home to spend the night and visit during dinner. Conversation went smoothly. Slept well and next morning early having all they needed for the road drove away. Cybilia showed signs of exhaustion, napped long hours. Lord Thomas sat and he dosed now and then. Half way home, he asked.

"Cybilia, where do these mushrooms grow?" Cybilia surprised by his question had to collect her thoughts.

"What mushrooms are you talking about?" she said.

"Those mushrooms came to mind at dinner at your Uncle's. They were delicious. Who had picked them?" he asked.

"Oh the girls in the kitchen, I do not know exactly which ones," she replied.

"And how do they know what shape and color they are?" he said.

"Well one learns from an expert."

"I have no recollection of having any for dinner since we have been married."

Cybilia had a perfect explanation to his inquisitiveness; "Father avoids mushrooms, always had a very severe gastro-intestinal disturbance, and therefore they are never served."

Lord Thomas said, "I have discomfort with cabbage; surely, that is never fatal, or is it?"

Cybilia laughed sincerely and said, "Father loved cabbage, but lately he refuses cabbage as well when Flora serves. Why Thomas you have not paid attention at what Flora cooks every day, what is on your mind? Are you worried about something?"

Lord Thomas felt embarrassed and said he did have something important on his mind and for now, this topic is over. Cybilia abruptly cut off sat silent but her mind wandered from one thing to another. After a long day, stopping at one of Cybilia's friends cottage for the night he had many thoughts and decided to check the kitchen at home for these delicious morsels. Next day, they were on the road again, he seemed in deep thoughts and Cybilia did not disturb him, thinking he was tired and needed rest. His questions did not surprise her at all and she had no reason to doubt or suspect him of any wrongdoing. As the carriage rolled on and the temperatures cooled, she reminisced about their visit with Aunt and Uncle, and such great company in thought remained in that lush warm environment all the way home. They returned to their cold white wonderland and days of work. In addition, for Lord Thomas though he had more spare time, since it was winter, kept his mind on poison mushrooms and perfecting his plan, one thing worried him whom should he trust.

As weeks passed, months passed Lord Thomas eyed his employees and kept an eye on his father-in-law, old Prozatti now sat at home resting. Cybilia spent a lot of time with her parents since returning from the villa, began feeling queasy in the mornings, leaving her husband alone. Whenever he came to the main house from the winery always popped into the kitchen and asked Flora what she was cooking for dinner. Flora's answer satisfied him, since not always, she stood by the stove, but had Attenna or other girls cook. *Aha that is a good thing to know*, he thought. In conversation, Cybilia asked him, "Why do you go to the kitchen so often?"

He had one good reply, "Well, I never learned to cook and at one time, I was in trouble for that, now I want to learn to cook. Your Aunt's dinners were delicious my dear, do you object?"

Cybilia and her mother looked at each other smiling, and she said to him, "Why that is fine with me, you will serve me breakfast in bed every morning. You will be my special butler." Cybilia grinned.

Marianna kept her eye on him and later she told Cybilia that, "What I noticed was not pride of learning but anger, because he in his mind thought you made fun of him, weigh your words daughter."

When a driver came back from the market, he told everyone in the kitchen what he had overheard, a group of men talking which caught his interest. As he repeated these words to the whole crew, curiosity opened their eyes and mouths wide.

"Why, imagine, he said, that in a small Kingdom of Magda, hundreds of miles away from Riverside Village, ruled by King Clemens Bantar heard of a certain special wine and of a fellow who acquired riches in a short time and the questionable acquisition of it all." For a minute, they all stared at him. Then one of the men said, "Surely it is not our wine."

"Yes, well it could be or perhaps someone else, we know of many," Attenna said.

"Such news travels quickly, faster than birth of babes or death of the old. Human weakness is to whisper and gossip," Flora the cook said and dismissed it all sending them to their duties. Lord Thomas' success reached many an ear.

His servants overheard such gossip at the market during each spring and summer, informed his Master. Lord Thomas overlooked trivial gossip but those more impressive he shared with Cybilia. She was shocked, mortified. He laughed, seeing her mortified expression, shrugged his shoulders.

"Do not fret my dear. A man must plan his future; do whatever it takes to succeed. People look up to you then. I amount to something now, I am not weak and meek, like my brother, he will never become successful, why... how could he succeed, he has no backbone, no ambition, but he has a lot of dirt under his nails! Ah, he is like a church mouse. A peasant he is... and always will be," he said grinning.

Cybilia held her breath, unable to speak, words escaped her. Lord Thomas forgot himself and declared aloud what should have remained unsaid. She should have never heard his degrading view of his brother, to her it was most degrading and cruel. These were red-hot iron words, which singed her memory, for life. Thomas worked and prospered with each passing season as time marched on.

Shortly after the holidays, everyone began to prepare for spring. At the beginning of April, winter had its last fling. Temperatures dropped, crippling freeze held. Heavy snow had fallen, wind whistled and moaned, drifts high against the houses and stables, which was a good thing, kept animals a bit warmer. Splitting trees resounded like crack of lightning or explosions across the sleeping valley.

This was the last blast of heavy winter storm before spring. To chance a trip to visit Kathryn in such weather would be foolish, dangerous, and best to wait and let it pass. Kosta ventured out to check on Aunt Olivia though, made sure all was well with her. He stacked firewood indoors in the hallway, near the fireplace, by the tub anywhere room aloud. Dried wood burns warmer. She would not endanger herself struggling to bring it in then slip on ice, and injure herself. Returning home checked on his animals. His firewood stacked against the walls of the barn now completely covered with snow gave extra protection from drafts. He felt the difference when he entered it was warmer. He inspected for foxholes round the chicken coop, he worried less the chickens in the stone structure were safe. Inside, straw scratched into piles, chickens like to cuddle together to keep warm. One thing Kosta had trouble with collecting eggs each morning. The stench made him feel queasy. He had to bear it all until spring had no other choice. By the end of winter, Kosta repaired all the small things, which, sat all summer undone, and now had time to carve.

At last, with the arrival of spring, everyone scurried around outdoors. The temperature warmed the earth; awakened out of its dormancy; the familiar scene reappeared, profusion of flowers, green meadows, fragrance in the air sweet and fresh; swarms of insects buzzed and birds sang. At first chance, after snow melted, Kosta ignored the wet and soggy soil, rode quickly to visit Kathryn and her mother. Kosta reined his horse to an abrupt stop and jumped off in front of the house. Ran up to the door and knocked sharply. Kathryn threw the door open seeing him after the harsh and long winter she threw herself into his arms, tears of happiness flowed.

"I missed you so much, winters are just too long to be away from each other," she said.

"Kathryn who is here? Kathryn!" her mother called.

"Come, Mother is waiting..."

"Kathryn wait I must pull these muddy boots off first." Kosta embarrassed a bit stood in his old worn out socks. She glanced at his feet and smiled; she took his hand and led him to the parlor where her mother sat on the sofa. Kathryn went and found a pair of sheering boots for Kosta to wear.

"Mother Kosta came to visit us," she said. Kathryn's mother looked deeply into the eyes of her future son-in-law not regretting her blessing at all. The three of them had lunch and talked several hours. Kosta returned home happy. Now that spring is here, they will visit frequently to make their wedding plans. He walked into his home and first time it hit him, he is planning a wedding with Kathryn but not thinking and not seeing the mess he lives in. Without hesitation, he ran not walked to Arkushin who through the years became like a father to him, asked for help, which now he needed badly. Several days later, he rode to visit Michael and asked for help, which Michael had never refused.

Kosta's work around the premises began. First, Kosta and Michael whitewashed the house, Aunt Olivia and several women scrubbed down everything inside and organized as best they could. The grass began to grow back filling in bare spots, Kosta and Arkushin raked the area, and the women loosened the soil in the flowerbeds and seeded summer flowers. It seemed overnight spring flowers popped out of the soil and it is the first time that Kosta had noticed them. All these years he worked hard, and learned how to survive alone. Flowers bloomed every spring he had looked at them but never really noticed their wonder. Those that his mother had planted he ignored, but not intentionally. But this spring he felt alive and everything lived around him.

The barns and stalls had a face-lift. Everything sparkled clean. Kosta looked at the improvements and realized in what shabby condition and surroundings he had lived before. Thanks to his helpers, his true friends and neighbors his heart burst with pride. Now Kathryn would not be embarrassed to live here with him. He felt like shouting aloud how much he loves her.

Nineteen: Kosta and Kathryn Wed

May, the beautiful month of May, the month they chose to marry. Wild flower arrangements would be made of lilies of the valley and ferns. The profusely blooming lilacs would stand in containers throughout the house.

Kosta fought with his feelings -- should he or should he not invite his brother? Then, after having a lengthy discussion with Aunt Olivia, Ahnut's son hand delivered an invitation to his brother to be sure he receives it. Later his brother could not tell a lie, "He had not received an invitation." Ahnut's son retuned empty handed, Lord Thomas and his wife were away for several weeks. Kosta waited many days but received no reply.

The style of the wedding gown, made simply yet elegantly, laboriously sewn by Michael's mother, Beatrice Hartigan. Since Kathryn's mother, Grazine Wiltran, though suffering from crippling arthritis of her hands, still insisted to help at least with as much as was able with her daughter's wedding dress. However, after a few days of sewing caused her unbearable pain, she then had engaged a friend to assist Michaels mother Beatrice in the progress of the dress, which when finished was beautifully fashioned of fine fabric of lace and ribbons and very stylish.

The wedding arrangements and preparations were moving smoothly though much effort and time taken for the happiness of these two lovers between daily chores and work in the fields. However, compared to his brother's wedding, Kosta's wedding will be simple. Regardless of its simplicity, what matters most is everyone will celebrate this special day.

Kathryn looked closely at her face in the mirror, "Mother, look I am too pale. No color at all, my whole body is pale! I cannot wait to be out in the sun, I love the warmth of it. I feel healthier. Thank God for sunshine." Chatting away excitedly while Grazine, her mother sat in a chair, smiling, observing her daughter.

"My dear girl, you are pretty enough to marry a prince. Do not worry. Kosta loves you just the way you are, he is your prince, you know!" her mother said.

"I want to look my best for him. You know I love him very much mother, have you been outside? Lilacs are blooming and the lilies of the valley...those are my favorite spring flowers; so delicate and fragrant. I love all flowers as a matter of fact; they make my soul sing!" Kathryn almost shouted from happiness. Her mother felt happy for her daughter. She respected Kosta and loved him as her own son. Kathryn had arrangements with a woman as a live-in caregiver; otherwise, in her condition she could never survive alone.

On the wedding day, both the bride and groom were very nervous, and jumpy from excitement. Rabinna helped Kathryn to dress. All her friends were there chatting away; making sure everything was done to the brides wishes. Kathryn's mother and Michael's parents and brother were there. Both Grandmothers cared for the four-month-old Rebecca. Rebecca was born in the dead of winter, when the wind howled and snowdrifts piled high. Rebecca came into this cold world in the middle of the night. Michael's nerves frazzled because he knew nothing about childbirth. Thank the Lord no complications, having no choice reluctantly assisted delivering his own child. At one point he felt queasy; about to fall to the floor, but held on to one thought, *do not embarrass yourself, she is your wife, and it is your child, fool!* Rabinna told Michael what to do with the umbilical cord, he was scared to death, and his hand shook so hard he kept asking Rabinna how and what he should do next. She urged him to hurry; reminding him to tie the umbilical cord with the twine, which sat in the hot water. Michael was done and sighed with relief. The room was very cold. His newborn baby girl screamed as he wrapped her in a blanket. Baby Rebecca stole Michael's heart when he held her in his arms before he gently laid her next to Rabinnas. He had one more unpleasant task; the placenta; after explaining to him why; he had followed her instruction and done a good job on that part. After the whole ordeal was over; Michael opened the back door and vomited; Rabinna heard him heaving, she laughed. Now his baby girl is four months old. *Ah, she is a beautiful and a good child, I am proud of my girls,* he thought.

On this day, Michael glanced at the Grandmothers Grazine and Beatrice and smiled as they sat on the front bench, Grandmother Beatrice held in her arms sleeping Rebecca, waiting for the ceremony to begin. Villagers filled the Church of Hope. The bell tolled. Michael and Kosta stood at the tiny alter waiting for his bride to join him. “Look at her! She is beautiful!” Kosta whispered to Michael.

“I know, but which one...my baby daughter...or your bride?” Michael grinned at Kosta.

“Ah Michael, they both are beautiful, indeed,” Kosta whispered.

Arkushin, Kosta’s neighbor walked Kathryn down the aisle. Kathryn loved Kosta and it shown on her face. Kathryn looked stunning in her simple wedding gown of lace and ribbons. Kosta glanced at Aunt Olivia. She caught his eye and smiled. He was nervous. Arkushin and Kathryn stopped at the front pew; he released her arm and Kathryn reached out to her mother and bent to kiss her on both cheeks. Her mother moved to tears; with difficulty raised her arms to embrace her daughter. Kathryn took one-step over to kiss Lady Beatrice, Michael’s mother. Kathryn and Aunt Olivia together walked up to where Kosta stood; she took Kathryn’s right hand and Kosta’s left and their hands grasped tight. Aunt Olivia gave her away in a simple way and to all onlookers this was different but beautiful. The minister raised his arms for silence and began the ceremony. Rabinna and Michael stood at their side, as they were best man and maid of honor. The little church crowded with villagers eyeing the bride and groom. They exchanged those same vows as before at their engagement at Christmas, one could hear sniffles; many wiped tears with handkerchiefs overcome by emotions, to most of the women, this ceremony was not just the ordinary, but very touching indeed.

Everyone gathered at Kosta’s home since it was too small to accommodate all, many sat outdoors. The villagers brought benches, chairs and tables and settled down to munch on the elaborate feast prepared by the village women. Others sat on logs, eating and drinking, children sat on the grass and ate disregarding all else. Aunt Olivia was the greeter, at the gate inviting everyone who came to celebrate this happy occasion and partake in a buffet style menu inside or outside. From far the gathered guests heard a faint sound of music; turning their heads to see where it was coming from. The happy sound came nearer and louder, musicians from the near village rolled in on wagons and played jolly tunes. Kosta and Kathryn did not expect a band of musicians! Who was it? Why it was Paul the cobbler, Kosta had a surprise of his life; Paul smiled and embraced his young friend, Kosta grinned and said, “So you received my invitation, I am so glad you are here, come meet my bride.”

They walked into the house and Kosta introduced his bride Kathryn to Paul.

"Yes I received your invitation and you know I would not miss this occasion in the world." Music always brought laughter, lifted spirit and joy to the young adults, children, and the old as well.

The day was sunny, temperature perfect, when an elegant carriage rolled slowly along the road then turned into the front yard through the gate. The coachman slowed the carriage; many friends and neighbors sat and stared pointing and commenting. Children ran chasing each other oblivious to the incoming carriage. The coachman tugged the reins to the left leading the horses cautiously to the west side of the house. The coachman stepped down and opened the carriage door. Lord Thomas and Cybilia had arrived for the reception. Cybilia pregnant...had a difficult time to step out of the carriage, but for the help of the coachman, dressed in his uniform colors, black pants, white shirt, dark red coat and a red hat. Lord Thomas donned his light beige silk suit, now a bit snug. Shirt with white lace and his fancy black shoes; which he wore on his own wedding day; his long hair tied back. He stood out among the simply dressed villagers and they took notice gaping at him and his wife trailing close behind. Rightfully so, he knew he would. Disregarding his wife went on briskly to congratulate the newlyweds. Aunt Olivia noticed them she rose from the chair to greet them.

"Oh Thomas, Cybilia welcome, nice of you to come to your brother's wedding; the Bride and Groom are inside the house," she pointed to the door. He has never met Kathryn before. Behind him came up Cybilia breathless, she stepped in front of her husband, opened her mouth to introduce herself to the new bride, when Lord Thomas took her elbow and led her away.

"Kosta, she needs to sit down, she feels lightheaded. She is in a delicate condition, as you see," he said over his shoulder and proceeded to walk his wife to a chair. However, chairs were scarce not one available anywhere.

"Wait here my dear, I will find a chair for you." Lord Thomas, walked outdoors, glanced around and espied a boy sitting on one near the wall of the house. He walked up and said, "I need this chair for my wife, boy." He reached for the back of it and tipped it forward, the frail boy fell to his knees. Slowly rising, began to cry and hobbled away to find his family. Arkushin the neighbor observed this scene, ran up lifted the boy into his arms and carried him away. Lord Thomas paid no mind at the icy looks Arkushin gave him those nearby seeing it all froze, silently stared. Cybilia in the meantime introduced herself to Kathryn they stood waiting for her husband to bring in the chair. Lord Thomas came in with the chair, Cybilia sat down.

Kosta welcomed his brother; introduced his bride Kathryn; Aunt Olivia stood on the side watching and Cybilia had her eyes on her husband. Lord Thomas stood very erect and eyed the bride from head to toe, impressed by her angelic simplicity, *beauty and innocence of a little girl,* he thought. Her long hair loose, but for two braids plaited with ferns and lilies of the valley crowned her head. On her left arm from wrist to elbow coiled on the sleeve were the same flowers. She smiled sincerely. It was evident that this young woman had an inbred intelligence and taste. *Unfortunately, she is poor. A rich girl would never marry a simpleton like my brother*, he thought. The beauty of the bride struck him like a bullet between his eyes though; he stared at her. Kathryn extended her hand, he raised it to his lips, kissed it once, made sure their eyes met, he kissed her hand again, held it a bit too long, not averting his eyes.

"Where did you ever find such a pearl?" he said to Kosta.

His eyes still on Kathryn... suddenly burning prickles ran through his body, feeling envious...Kathryn, in her simplicity glowed, but oh so much more sophisticated then his rich wife. Kosta smiled with pride from ear to ear, exclaimed, “Why, I found her in the forest, she was lost or chased by a man or animal and when she saw me, she fell right into my arms.” Kosta did not overlook that icy look, and that false grin on his brother’s face, which remained singed in Kosta’s memory for many, many years.

Cybilia was unaware of what took place at the introduction. Interrupted by Aunt Olivia approaching with a chair and sat next to her asking how she felt; perhaps she needed food or drink, Cybilia thankful for her concern replied, “Yes I am hungry and thirsty, thank you.” Aunt Olivia walked over to the table and loaded a plate with a bit of everything on platters and in pots. Aunt Olivia, with her back turned to the bride and groom unable to see the whole scenario, because of people milling about or she would have something to say to Thomas if not at that moment then later. When Aunt Olivia sat down next to Cybilia, Kathryn and Rabinna brought plates of food and sat down next to the pregnant woman, plates held on their knees to eat before all the food would disappear, it has been hours since breakfast, they were famished.

“Oh your dress is so beautiful yet simple. Kathryn, your dressmaker is very good. Who is she?” Cybilia very politely asked.

"Mothers... both our mothers worked on her wedding dress," Rabinna replied, a bit irked.

"Rabinna, they are very gifted such talent and imagination, I love your coil of flowers on your arm! I wish to be friends with all of you. After all, we are family," Cybilia said seemingly sincere.

In the meantime, the coachman brought in a large sack of flour, a large sack of potatoes and large sacks of wheat, barley and rye; politely asking Kosta where he should store it all. Kosta instructed him to carry it all into the cold storage on the side of the house. In addition, Lord Thomas handed Kosta a leather satchel of gold coins. Kosta did not expect such generous gifts, and was at a loss for words.

"Kosta, how on earth did you manage to prepare all this food?" Lord Thomas inquired.

"Everything you see on the tables; all sorts of dishes of meats and vegetables, and cakes, the whole village cooked or baked for us; with Aunt Olivia's help, of course," Kosta replied proudly.

"Well, good for you, it is clearly evident people like you," Lord Thomas said stretching the sentence.

Cybilia stuffed herself with just about every dish on the table. As she talked with Aunt Olivia and Rabinna, Lord Thomas observed her, seething, but keeping his tongue behind his teeth, at that moment said nothing. The time slipped by, soon they must take leave or they will arrive home in the dark of night. Cybilia was not anxious to leave and she said so tersely to her husband. Kosta, Thomas and Michael sat and talked for an hour, when out of the group of people came Kosta's neighbor, Arkushin, in his arms carried the crippled boy, he sat the boy on a chair and without waiting in front of everyone he described quite loud of the rudeness and disrespect for a crippled boy. Arkushin faced Kosta and Michael, not once did he glance at Thomas. Kosta unaware of what had happened earlier was shocked, began to apologize to the boy. Arkushin raised his hand to interrupt him turned directly to face Lord Thomas.

"You Thomas should apologize to this child, not Kosta, he is an invalid since birth, and you have no regard for others, only your comfort. You were born here and have grown up here, now you have no regard for others!" Arkushin spat on the ground picked up the boy and walked away not looking back. Silence fell. For a while, no one spoke a word. Cybilia held her food in her mouth unable to chew; saliva drooled at the corner of her mouth, stricken with shame. When she swallowed, tears pushed forth, she stood up and announced to all.

"Forgive me Kosta and Kathryn but I must go home, forgive me, good luck to you." She did not acknowledge the rest of the people, slowly marched to the carriage.

Lord Thomas followed her, never looked back. When they drove away, Cybilia knew why he was fuming, but dared not speak.

"Cybilia, I cannot believe that you mingled with these peasants. You belittled yourself being too chummy with all of them. They are beneath your standards. They are uncultured peasant people! Did you not see the way they all were dressed and their behavior?" Lord Thomas screamed at her, his face contorted. She jumped, startled, and swallowed hard, for an instant shocked and then she screamed back at him truly angry, "Then why did we come all this way! I am with your child. You did not consider my inconvenience at all. I see that now! Why are you screaming at me, I have done nothing wrong I spoke with Kathryn and Rabinna! After all, they are family, and, Kosta is your only brother and I surmised you grew up in that house! You apparently have done something to offend that man, and that child...you failed to notice that when you dumped him of the chair..."

Now he abruptly interrupted her.

"Since when you are such a down to earth friend to them, consider your status, your dignity!" Lord Thomas shouted.

"I am a friend to everyone, not only to high society, my dear husband, but you on the other hand, who were you before...?" Again, he interrupted her.

"Now that is enough you must stop!" Lord Thomas grabbed her hand and squeezed it, Cybilia cried out from pain. Unjustly accused, felt her husband was treating her as a servant or a slave. She wept all the way home. For two weeks thereafter, they did not speak to each other, and avoided each other. Cybilia stayed at the main house with her mother, who showed signs of illness, which worried Cybilia. Lord Thomas being very busy visited them every few days out of necessity and courtesy to his mother-in-law. Cybilia's mother surmised trouble, but did not pry, waited for Cybilia to tell her of the problems arising between them.

Cybilia unexpectedly went into labor at the main house. Her parents stressed by her screaming ordered the servants to carry Cybilia out into the carriage. In a few minutes, savants carried her up the stairs to her bed. She travailed for days. The midwife declared to Lord Thomas that she has never been in a situation such as Cybilia's, and she will do her best to deliver their child, but he should not blame her if anything tragic happens to both of them. The midwife sat by the bed and wept, while Cybilia moaned and screamed.

Lord Thomas walked over to the main house to check on his in-laws just to escape Cybilia's screams and inform them of her progress. After an hour or so walked back, patiently waited for the ordeal to end, hoping the child would be a son. Sleep was impossible, so he drank glass after glass of wine, waiting and thinking had he caused this early labor, if this is his fault, she will not let him forget it and she will change toward him surely, which will cause her parents to look at him in a different light. At last, at dawn of the second day, a son was born. The midwife in her arms carried the newborn to Lord Thomas. He was asleep on the chair by the fireplace, though the fireplace was dark. She nudged his shoulder lightly to wake him.

"Lord Thomas, your son," she said in a low voice, laid the bundle in his arms; he looked at his son's face and kissed him gently on the forehead. Held him for a few minutes and handed him back to the midwife. Cybilia slept, the child slept in the cradle. Lord Thomas fell asleep in his favorite chair. Later that morning, Lord Thomas greeted his wife with a kiss, a flat "thank you for a fine son. I am sorry you had to suffer so much, he is a good-looking boy."

"Yes that he is. Thomas let me sleep, I am tired... ah, I need my mother, send for mother to come to me, please," Cybilia said and closed her eyes. Lord Thomas left the bedroom and walked into the kitchen, one of the girls was busy cleaning. Lord Thomas said, "Go to the main house, Lady Cybilia is asking for her mother, now go! Go quickly."

Lady Prozatti arrived in a carriage, went directly to see her daughter. What they were discussing no one knew. Lord Thomas hesitated to ask and Cybilia did not talk about it.

Cybilia's strength improved in weeks. Their newborn child cared for by a newly hired nanny. Months later Lord Thomas insisted on a date for a big celebration of their first-born son. They had a few spats about a name for their son. Cybilia wanted a name of Italian origin, Lord Thomas insisted on Jacob. At one point Cybilia asked him, "Did your father have a middle name, or your grandfather, to name your son after?"

Lord Thomas thought a while and said, "No, my father never mentioned names, and if he had, I was not there." At the end of their argument, they named their son, Mark Jacob Komarod. She protested insisting it would make more sense to wait, celebrate his first birthday. Besides, she needs time to fit into her dresses again.

She would be embarrassed parading around overweight, guests staring at her, especially the women. Lord Thomas agreed. As his son's first year neared, Lord Thomas, while in bed thought of his brother Kosta and Kathryn, reluctant to invite his peasant brother, he felt it would mar his image. Kosta lived without a suit or a good pair of shoes all his life. He remembered those grimy work boots he wore, he recalled the revolting feeling whenever he saw them standing at the back door on a straw mat, small wonder these boots were never cleaned, that would have been a futile task.

On Mark's first birthday, the house was crowded with guests; all of them were Prozatti's friends. A guest by the name Bastamo, a thin short of stature balding man popped a question.

"Thomas your brother, will he honor us with his presence today?"

Lord Thomas quickly replied, "Ah my brother...unfortunately, no, ah...he is busy working to provide for his, 'clutch' of children, they are hatching like ducks."

The guest Bastamo smiled sourly and moved on having a *clutch* of children himself, feeling that that remark was rude, a distasteful way to speak of his only brother, at the same time thoughtless disregard for his guests. The guest Bastamo repeated the disrespectful remark to a group of guests; they were aghast, insulted, it had not taken long to demean Lord Thomas's character. Before long, the whole parlor pealed with laughter. Lord Thomas overheard remarks, *"children, ducks-hatching,"* more laughter, eyes darting at their host, heads turning, staring.

Cybilia, her mother and several women sat at the dining table chatting. Sir Prozatti and Bastamo his friend sat on the sofa in deep discussion in their native Italian language, now aware of what went on. The guests congregated, chatting, drinking and munching on appetizers served on silver trays by servants walking from room to room-overheard remarks aimed at Lord Thomas. Soon the kitchen staff prattled of their master's unfortunate slip of his tongue.

When Lord Thomas walked into the kitchen, the servants stopped talking. They fumbled with whatever was handy. Their awkwardness piqued his anger at that moment. He thought, *definitely later I will have a talk with these gossiping broads. As to these guests, guests..., I must have a list of their names. One day they will pay for their insolence and ridicule; now, he will smile at them all, revealing not, that he is aware of their comments.* Over time, he not only learned to control his anger but also, thought twice before he spoke.

Having exhausted the "*clutch*" subject the guests turned their interest to current events. Little Mark Jacob awoke from his afternoon nap wailing, and promptly received mother's attention, thereafter Lord Thomas with son on his arm walked from group to group to impress his guests. This action rubbed his guests the wrong way and on their faces evident belittlement of their own sons. Soon after, the guests began to leave. Paulo and Marianna Prozatti bid them goodbye, thanked them for coming, and promised to see them soon. Before they walked out Paulo Prozatti took Lord Thomas aside and said. Thomas your behavior, overexcitement, offending guests by parading with your son, do you not realize these people also have children. And your unacceptable remark made it very compromising; indeed, you need to weigh your words, my boy, especially not knowing anything about these guests or their positions. Lord Thomas blushed up to his ears, and fortunately for him said not a word in protest, instead apologized meekly. Sir Paulo walked out of the parlor, mumbling of being overtired. Cybilia and nanny without hurry were gathering and putting things in a large bag to carry out to the carriage, it has been a long day; time their son seemed a bit cranky time to put him to sleep. Lord Thomas riveted to the floor stood in the doorway, watched on the sideline, feeling washed. The parlor was empty of such important, intelligent, and, educated guests. The servants sluggishly picked up cups or a glass to take to the kitchen. Lord Thomas glanced around and with a sour taste in his mouth shouted.

"Well! What are you waiting for! Clean up this mess, everyone has taken leave, so do not stand there gaping...clean up!" he shouted at the servants. Lord Thomas tried to hide his disappointment and the rudeness of his guests. Convinced he was faultless. Cybilia had observed but did not discuss the matter with her husband, fear of a clash outburst of opinions.

As to his first-born son, Lord Thomas loved him from day one, loved his wife less. He said when they have a second child, he would invite Kosta, but fewer guests.

At that, Cybilia thought but *all those people were my parent's guests. Yes..., they came to celebrate our sons first birthday, first grandchild. Thomas strutted like a peacock*; *yes I realize he is proud of his son. But showing off too much, it was embarrassing."*

What she thought, she would not say aloud. The Prozatti winery prospered and Lord Thomas prospered. Storage bins filled. Prepared for whatever calamity came along. Cybilia had nannies to care for her son, while she rested in bed frequently in the afternoons, and evenings spent alone. Her husband stayed out. It became obvious to Cybilia that he will never change. Apart too often, he was out much too much. Cybilia became despondent, suspicious and unhappy.

Twenty: Together

Kosta and Kathryn began their life as husband and wife in that little house. Kathryn organized and rearranged, as she cleaned she hummed. She was happy even though they had started from practically nothing, but for the few gifts received, for which they were humbly grateful. Their greatest gift to each other, themselves, their love and respect, for as long as they lived on this earth.

Working in the field practically all day, in the evening Kosta carved. Kathryn after finishing chores knitted or mended.

Each Friday, market day, Kosta was away all day. It surprised him how much the home improved not only in cleanliness but how roomy, and it was all because of Kathryn. Saturdays at dawn, they went fishing to the far bend where the creek ran deeper. Kosta sat on a blanket watching his line for a big fish to bite, on the other side of the creek in the reflection on the water he noticed something hopping from limb to limb, he looked up at the tree, and there among the branches were big black birds.

"Kathryn, look up at that tree; do you see those black birds? he said.

"Yes I do, why are they here I wonder. So many I should count them." Kathryn counted thirteen.

"Thirteen, thirteen ravens, Kosta those birds are not black birds, they are ravens. Kathryn exclaimed. As they were observing the ravens Kosta's line tugged, he jerked it back and the line went under moving to the center, he was sure he caught a big one, enough for a large family's dinner.

"Kathryn we should try to catch a small one for us and, this one we should give to Arkushin."

"Yes why not. Kosta it is so peaceful here; now watch I will catch a small one for us," she said.

"Oh you do that, and I will take a nap." Kosta kissed her cheek, fell back on the blanket and closed his eyes.

Suddenly Kathryn shouted, "Kosta help me, quick, Kosta!

Kosta sat up to see Kathryn struggling with a fish, which tugged and led her along the bank of the creek then pulled the line out to the deep. For a while, Kosta stood watching his wife maneuvering her line, for a minute he wanted to let her pull it in herself but from the way her bamboo rod bent, he realized that that fish must be twice as big as the first one. He ran up to her and together pulled it out of the water. Kathryn fell onto the grass trying to catch her breath.

"Well...woman, you have done well for a first-time. Your fish is larger, look at it!" Kosta held both fish and surely, hers was bigger, now it was time to go home to cook and share. As they walked, Kosta glanced at the dark water where the willows grew. No matter where he happened to be, water brought bitter memories of his parents, what a difference it would have made on their wedding day, he looked and smiled at Kathryn he was sure they approved.

Occasionally on Sundays, they attended services at the little Church of Hope, afterwards a short visit to Michael and Rabinna and on the way stopped by to check on Aunt Olivia. On alternating Sundays, omitting church services they rode to Kathryn's mother to check on her; each time Kathryn noticed her mother's health failing. Months swiftly passed. Kathryn's mother passed away in the spring of the first year of their marriage. Kathryn and Rabinna grieved together for both parents. Their father killed by a fallen tree several years ago. Now with mother passing, their sisterly bond bound them closer. They worked hand in hand prepared for and endured all seasons; to them their closeness could never be broken no matter what obstacles stood in their way; they were alone, just the two of them, though they were now married, still no other siblings existed.

Kosta and Kathryn not once received an invitation from his brother. Kosta had no need to wonder why, he was a peasant, a simpleton, leading a simple life, but being blood brothers his meager life should never be an obstacle, or should never make a difference.

Ah, but surely it does! Lord Thomas over time acquired everything of "*the best quality*" of their time. He also had been hiding a *secret*, a secret of *envy*. Lord Thomas often thought: "*where in the world had Kosta found such a beautiful woman*?" whereas, his wife was a bit homely; she had been pregnant and had put on some weight, the longer he looked at his wife, the more faults he found in her which made him angry.

"Time will come, things will change, I'll see to that." His tightened fists turned his knuckles white from anger. Strange *envy* had crept into his being which one day will reach its crest, without a doubt. *It did not seem fair, after all I have become, I am Lord Thomas rich and notorious, Kosta a poor peasant and just a carver*," he was thinking. With accumulation of best things in life

Lord Thomas had, his attitude and behavior proved to be childish, because of his ridiculous *envy*.

Kosta a struggling poor man, carved, tilled the soil, reaped whatever the harvest produced, sold at the market as always. Had an attractive wife, a small house on a strip of land, deeded to both sons, but the older brother gave up his half rights of ownership to his younger brother legally recorded, before marrying Cybilia the rich girl.

Kosta and Kathryn only had love for each other. Is this a good enough reason for his brother to be envious?

Kathryn at twenty-two at last had a baby boy. Kathryn realized and understood that naming their son David after Kosta's father would stir his memory of the tragedy. After many names to choose from, they decided to name their first-born son Mathew, Kosta's face had a happy expression now, proud of her and his newborn son.

A *second* child after two years a daughter was born *Tessana* named after Kathryn's great-grandmother.

The *third* child, eighteen months after another daughter was born, named Jasemin.

Fourth child Jason a son was born two years after Jasemin.

Fifth child a son named Kras Oliver (after Aunt Olivia) born exactly one year later after Jason. The *sixth* child a daughter was born one year and three months after Kras Oliver. They named her Marla after Kosta's grandmother.

Years of bearing children had stopped as if her body had said "enough." Their children fared well, grew healthy and beautiful. Kosta and Kathryn cared for them as best as they knew how, plus Aunt Olivia eagerly helped. Her life took on a new meaning, exciting with so many children around her. Then unexpectedly after five years, Kathryn became pregnant. Their seventh child a daughter named Rozaline (Rosie) from the day she was born her little cheeks were the color of pink roses, and the color never left her cheeks as she grew. Kathryn named their baby girl after her mother-in-law's younger sister. Within seventeen years, seven children came into their world and the little house accommodated them all. As the family grew, their need to feed and clothe their children each year became difficult. The clothes for the boys and the girls handed down from one to the other.

It was clear and frightening as the seasons passed; they had less and less supplies in the pantry, and less space in the house.

It had to happen one evening, when Kathryn sat on a stool milking the old cow. The cow seemed agitated; Kathryn barely managed to milk only half of what she used to give. What was the reason, they had fed her well. She barred the barn door; picked up the milk pail went into the house; leaned against the door and looked at each of her children. At this moment, they sat at the table talking about something quietly. She sat the bucket on the cold stove and said, "Kosta go take a good look at old Blaza."

Kosta saw the concern on her face without a word he ran to the barn. He was gone just a few minutes suddenly barged back in and slammed the door behind him. "Kathryn, I will have to sleep in the barn, the cow is down," he said quietly; Mathew seeing serious faces of his parents walked up and asked what was wrong. Kosta told him what was happening with the cow. Mathew said he would sleep in the barn too. Wrapped in blankets they sat on a bale of hay watching the cow. Kosta dozed off, how long he did not know. What had awakened him was a loud grunt. That grunt was her last, old Blaza croaked. Mathew was fast asleep on the hay. Kosta came into the house, everyone was asleep he had to wake Kathryn and tell her the cow croaked. She was beside herself, she whispered.

"Is it not enough for the harvests to be meager, now the cow croaked? What are we going to do now? Is Mathew sleeping?" Kosta whispered.

"Yes in the hay." His arms held her to close him.

"I must ride to Michael, he will help me with the carcass," he said.

"Let Mathew sleep. Give yourself some time before making coffee; do we have any coffee Kathryn?" Kosta asked.

"Kosta we are out, perhaps Michael could give us some, ask him," Kathryn said.

Kosta did not reply, put on his heavy cloak, saddled his horse and rode away. Riding up to Michael's home, he jumped off the horse practically at the front their door. Ran a few feet and rapped on the door, the loud noise echoed in the quiet of the night. It took a while for Michael to wake and open the door. Seeing Kosta said, "Come in Kosta, what happened?"

"Michael, old Blaza croaked. I stayed in the barn, but then dozed off, when I heard a loud grunt. I opened my eyes she was flat on the ground, dead. I came to you to get help with the carcass, and chopping up the meat." Kosta talked while Michael dressed in warm clothes, the night was chilly.

"Wait here I must tell Rabinna," he said and walked away.

"Michael can you spare some coffee, if you have..." Michael raised his hand and nodded. When he returned he pressed into Kosta's palm a small leather satchel and said.

"Kosta here take this, you will need to buy a cow. Your children need milk and coffee for you."

Though this occurred past midnight, they were busy until sunrise. Chopped and portioned meat stacked and ready for the two families and a stack set aside for Aunt Olivia. They worked well together between them was true friendship.

Each day, Kathryn's heart cringed and ached, for she knew well, that, while this supply of meat lasted what of the future days and months, what then? At the market, Kosta purchased a cow, same breed and named her Ruba, guaranteed to produce plenty of milk.

Rabinna and Michael, helped with provisions as much as they had to give, they proved to be unselfish and truly devoted friends. Arkushin also contributed with provisions. Kosta depleted of energy beyond his endurance. Many evenings Kathryn found him in the barn on the hay dozing. The house was crowded but to build a larger home was out of the question, without necessary resources, not even a small addition. They loved their children equally, they were wonderful little treasures, these children were gifts from God; to live for, work for, give all they had of themselves, a sacrifice no matter how difficult; watch them grow into handsome good men, and beautiful women. Now when they need good nourishment they are facing hardships. Kathryn worried for their health. The money saved from the sale of carvings, bought a calf, a goat, some grain for seed, and sacks of flour for bread. Kathryn cooked well and knew how to stretch each meal, but that was not enough, not for a large family.

Kathryn stayed up late sewing or mending garments for anyone and anytime, she accepted from these people whatever they offered for her services, but mostly milk, bread or cheeses. In fact, the girls were eager to learn to knit and mend. Tessana learned quickly, stayed up right along with mother. Even little Rozaline 'Rosie' tried to mend, but soon gave it up, her sewing was unacceptable even to her own self.

The first-born son Mathew loved to be with his father, he had talent and the desire to carve, just like his father, and grandfather. Kosta observed his son's boyish face concentrating on the object in hand; Mathew observed the precision and speed his father through practice worked with, and the result, an amazing piece of art. Jason and Kras played with the carved figurines, sometimes they too tried to carve, but when they nicked their fingers and felt the pain, saw blood trickling, they refused to pick up a carving blade ever again, so they went back to playing.

Kathryn walked into the chicken coop quietly one morning, hoping to collect eggs, she noticed one of the chickens in the corner nesting in the straw, her heart jumped with joy, a hen, she must be caged to be safe, Kathryn whispered, cautiously walked up to peek.

"Yes, yes, she's sitting on eggs. Oh...God... thank you!" Kathryn whispered and backed away, ran back to the house shouting.

"Children listen, we have a hen sitting on eggs she needs a nesting place! We will have baby chicks, isn't it wonderful?" Hearing such news the children cheered.

Kosta walked into the house at that very moment, they all chattered at once about the good news and that a hen needs a nesting basket.

"That is great news, anything else that is great news you have for me." He glanced at Kathryn. She blushed, staring at him.

"I have news for you, but not now, I will tell you tonight, after all the children are in bed," Kathryn said. The children looked up at their mother, with questioning expressions on their faces.

"Why not now, mother?" asked Jasemin, "so we can be happy all at once." She glanced at her siblings.

"Yes, yes, why not Mother?" the children demanded.

Kosta nodded slowly in agreement.

"All right, if all of you prefer it that way...I will tell you...we are expecting a baby. We are given one more, brother or sister...we cannot tell...ah...the Lord knows how much we love children."

Kosta's heart palpitated, at one instant he felt, as if it will actually stop beating, *Oh God, one more, I knew it,* pretending to be happy; he wrapped his arms around Kathryn and held her tight. This action she understood. Kathryn bore children from a young age, now she is near forty, Kosta was concerned for her and the child's health. Surely, in their hearts they would not love this child less.

During spring and summer, Kathryn worked right along with Kosta. Children helped as best as they could, especially the boys. The girls' main responsibilities were the house and feeding of the fowl. Kathryn over-worked needed much rest, some days walked home early in the afternoon. Kosta never complained, he understood how difficult it must be for her to work in the fields, she was in a fragile state.

Summer months with unending tasks to complete slipped by quickly. Autumn came with its fiery pallet of color but only briefly without a chance to paint the world for all to admire. October rushed in with freezing rain, which seemed a bit too soon;

surprised everyone. To conserve firewood, many a night blocks of peat burned in the hearth otherwise the home would be cold and damp all night. The goose and chicken feather quilts were thick and warm, each morning the children waited in beds until the house warmed up. Mathew and Tessana jumped out of beds dressed quickly then one by one dressed the others.

Kathryn's pregnancy seemed easy she had not experienced much discomfort; she knew the time was near and she anticipated it any day or night. On a very cold November night, contractions began. Kosta stoked the fire in the hearth to heat up the house. This night was very different. The children were awake. Tessana held Rozaline in her arms; with Kathryn's scream, Rozaline covered her ears and tears slid down her cheeks; Tessana whispered, "Mama will be fine... soon you will see a miracle." They waited patiently for a tiny infant to join their family, bring joy and in return given tender love.

Kosta mounted the horse bareback and sped over for the midwife. It was time. With the midwife beside her Kosta sat at the table waiting.

Kathryn travailed long hours, she tried to muffle her screams with a pillow, and the children wide-eyed waited for their mother's pains to stop. Kathryn despaired why she could not deliver as easily as her other babies. She was not as strong, that is true, and she was older, after many hours, an unbearable contraction seized her, she gathered her last bit of strength and gave it all she had and the miracle happened, a boy, one more son. Kosta held his son in his arms, a healthy boy, thankful for that, but in his heart he hoped it would be the last child, not enough room or food in this small home, although he loved them all. Kathryn rested after such an ordeal. With her son wrapped in a blanked at her bosom suckled. She slept. Kosta sat with a hot cup of water and honey until sunrise. The children slept. Kathryn remained in bed for much longer; her return to health was not as quick as with the others.

Therefore, each morning Mathew dressed the younger children. Tessana cared for the newborn, Rosie at her side every minute. Marla, Jason, and Jasemin busy in the kitchen making breakfast, and Kras sat at his mother's bedside, watching her sleep. Kosta saw his sons' worried look.

"Son, I see you love your mother. Are you worried about her?" Kosta asked.

"Yes Father, I worry, and I am thinking what it all means. Father, I do not understand all this," Kras replied as he looked up at Kosta.

"Kras when you are older, you will learn to understand it all. I assure you, you will. You know, I see your concern for your mother, and I am proud of you and your siblings. You are all so much help to us," Kosta said.

Kathryn appreciated those moments of rest, relieved of most of the tasks; with her instructing; her children were capable to manage. She could rest to regain much needed strength.

Twenty-One: Angel

Their newborn son slept, waking only when hungry. His little cheeks twitched as if smiling. After a month, the baby slept longer still and nursed less. The children kept muttering that he sleeps too much.

"Now listen here children, let him sleep. He is warm in that quilt, you must realize he still is too fragile to be carried, you must wait at least six months, and that means until spring," Kathryn said. Rosie the youngest impatiently said, "But mother, six months is such a long time to wait, I want to carry him...now." Mathew sat at the crib and looked closer.

"Mother he is barely breathing, is that all right?"

"Yes, he is fine, please best not to wake him, when he is hungry he will wake up screaming. All of you were just like him, at one time...but none of you remember," Kathryn said. Rosie sat by the cradle and watched her little brother sleep.

"Mother how do we choose a name for him?" she asked.

"We all will decide on a good name for your little brother," Kathryn replied. Tessana announced she wants to be baby Angel's '*Nanny*' to give mother much needed rest.

One early morning Tessana awoke from a bad dream. She dressed and walked into the kitchen wiping away tears.

"Tessana sweetheart what upset you?" Kathryn asked.

"Mother...I had a dream that our little Angel was naked and was with other little babies...and...they held hands hovered over the crib, smiling." Tessana sobbed. Kathryn very concerned put her arms around her daughter, held her in her arms until Tessana stopped.

"Mother...our little Angel...will not be with us very long." Tessana began sobbing again. Kathryn's heart beat faster and she said. "Tessana my sweet, why do you say such a thing, he is so tiny he needs his sleep; overall, he seems to be healthy. He is just a newborn, he is a little Angel, but as you see, he has grown already. Tessana he will be fine, please do not worry, you are like a little mother. I see you care for little Angel very much, thank you for helping me with all the children." Tessana leaned on Kathryn's chest, her arms around her mother's waist, but did not reply.

"Mother I would like to name him "Angel," Tessana said in a half whisper.

Kathryn's eyes filled with tears.

"Yes, we will tell the children. But do not tell them your dream," Kathryn said, and kissed Tessana on the forehead. That day, everyone agreed it was a very proper name for tiny newborn brother.

However, the joy of a newborn son was short lived, they realized that something was dreadfully wrong with little Angel. He was not responding to Kathryn's touch, suckled only for a little while then slept. Weeks later, Rabinna and Michael dropped by with Rebecca, Kathryn discussed the condition of her child, but Rabinna could not give her any advice. None of the neighbors could give her advice. The village doctor examined little Angel, he too had no solutions.

"He refuses my breast. He must be starving," she said.

Rather nonchalantly, the doctor said to her, "Small wonder...it is winter and normally everyone tends to sleep longer, especially newborns. Let him sleep." Kathryn thought for a minute then said, "But Doctor, we are not a quiet family, we do make quite a bit of noise, and he sleeps through it all." The doctor walked up to the crib and took a second look. He touched little Angel's hand the baby seemed in deep sleep. He turned to Kathryn, "he is fast asleep, he is adjusted to noises, you see babies ignore noise after a time, do not worry, he will be fine," the doctor said.

Little Angel some days seemed to be improving, he had grown and gained weight, as he should, other days he reverted to the not eating and not sleeping routine. Kathryn was at a loss of what to do, and she worried; many nights she could not sleep; she lay and listened for any distress; none came. On a very cold march night, Kathryn awoke feeling odd. The room in total darkness, children were asleep, she strained to listen, peer into the darkness but all was silent. The cradle stood near their bed, the baby warmly wrapped in a quilt, asleep. She reached down to make sure he was covered, but as she touched him, pulled away. She tapped Kosta's shoulder.

"What is wrong?

"The baby is ice cold and lifeless, oh Kosta... he is dead!" Kathryn cried.

They got out of bed. Kosta lit the oil lamp in the room and leaned over the cradle. Kathryn uncovered the baby took his tiny hand in hers; it was cold and lifeless.

"He must have died sometime after we all went to bed. Poor little Angel, he made no sound..." Kosta whispered. "Our son has gone to heaven to join other little angels, just as he truly was an *Angel.*"

"When he was born, Tessana and Rozaline wanted to name him little Angel," Kathryn whispered tearfully.

"That he was Kathryn. That he was. He did not belong here, his visit with us was short, and you labored long with him. You felt joy holding him close to your breast, our joy was having him among us for a little while, an Angel sent from heaven, but he could not stay. How sad, we will never know him, but surely he will not be forgotten, my darling...it was God's will..." Kosta broke off.

"He uttered no sound when he departed, how will the children take this?" Kathryn whispered. Kathryn's silent tears fell as she held little Angel, they did not speak for a while. Kosta wrapped his arms around her as she sobbed, her face pressed against his chest. They just stood there, he held both of them tight then he said, "Lay the child down... he is no longer with us. Cover him and let us get back under the covers, you will catch a cold." Kathryn laid their child back into the cradle, covered him, and slid beneath the quilt. Kathryn rested her arm on Kosta's chest, soon she fell back to sleep. He stayed awake, his thoughts were about his little son and he questioned; *why must fate throw such obstacles into peoples' lives? Dangle a bit of happiness, when they reach for it and grasp it, in a moment that happiness becomes a bitter gut wrenching parasite.* Kosta held Kathryn in his arms until dawn. Their little boy—Angel... was only four months old, just short of two months and it would have been a warm and sunny spring.

That morning when all the children were eagerly up and ready to greet their little brother Tessana was first to be up, came to help with breakfast but noticed that mother seemed very sad.

"Mother you are crying, what is wrong?" Tessana asked.

"Tessana, your dream...became real. Little Angel has gone to heaven." They wrapped their arms around each other and wept. Kathryn told the children their *little brother had gone to heaven.* These sweet and caring children were shocked. Tessana looked at her mother knowingly. This was a day of sadness, indeed. The lifeless baby Angel lay in the crib resembled a doll. One by one faces streaked with tears walked by the cradle, each one touched his tiny hand and whispered, "*goodbye forever, sweet little Angel.*"

On the day of the funeral, it was windy. Air intermixed as the sun rays streamed down through the slow moving clouds. Aunt Olivia stood with the children, she held Rosie by the left hand and Jason held Rosie's right hand. Neighbors, in silence watched; many felt the same sorrow losing their own children or newborn. Ahnut and Arkushin with the ground still frozen had difficulty digging a small grave not far from the house on a sunny knoll, dotted with spruce trees, which the family chose to be a cemetery. The priest from their church prayed as they lowered the tiny pine coffin into the grave. Kathryn refused to throw cold earth on her baby and the children refused as well. Aunt Olivia said she must let him go but Kathryn was ill with sorrow, she leaned on Kosta's shoulder, tears trickled down her cheeks; he held her close as she shivered. Their children surrounded them to express their support. At every chance, he uttered words of comfort to her and their children. He himself choked back tears. Arkushin and Ahnut with shovels filled the grave with cold earth.

Through the years, all children born to them had lived. This child being born into this family and dying caused them great pain of loss. The fresh grave filled and covered a small cross at the head pushed into fresh soil; it was over, there was nothing else to do but go home. The children walked close together not speaking. Not one question asked, once indoors just moped around the house. Tessana and Rozaline (Rosie) cuddled together whispered something to each other and wept. Mathew felt angry; being deprived of a little brother; unable to understand; and no one around to ask; to explain why; to justify the reason, or, whom to blame.

Time and work will ease their sorrow; minds occupied with daily routine gradually will lessen pain. Nevertheless, little Angel will always live in their memory, although his visit was short.

Seasons came and went and time moved on. Kosta's thoughts were of his children, as with each year greater need of daily essentials became reality. Rabinna and Michael shared food as much as they could. One night, the fox devoured and maimed many chickens, only a few lucky ones survived. Empty eggshells scattered in the coop, perhaps someone neglected or accidently had not secured the door for the night. It must have been an oversight of a child, punishment and truth useless after the fact. Several pigs, sold at the market for sugar and flour, several chickens, matches, and one pair of shoes.

Each time he looked at his children, one question came to his mind: *how will I feed all these children*? Kosta could not find a solution. He found himself in the barn more often than before, to think. Each year was the same as the year before. He was beginning to think and believe someone cursed him. What had he done to go through so much hardship and grief? Things were happening to them, as if huge obstacles lay on their path of life, which they could not move out of their way to get ahead; they were retreating backwards into a desperate situation. This winter they hit the bottom of the barrel from which they could not with his large family scramble out of into the safe zone.

Kosta and Kathryn had little to say to each other, their saddened and concerned faces weighted down by their situation. What future awaits them all? How will they survive all those forthcoming years without food? The children grew somber. Mathew watched his sisters as they huddled together and his little brothers sat on the bed, what they were thinking he could not guess. He too was found in the stable piddling around the horses, the kittens voiced their need for food and his dog Choppy looked into his eyes as if asking; *any bones left for me*? They needed proper nourishment, or else they might contract an unexpected illness and perish.

At night, Kosta held Kathryn close to him, each grasping for that feeling of security from each other, until they fell asleep.

The children never complained though, Mathew now sixteen. Tessana is three years younger, now at thirteen. Jasemin twelve and a half understood their situation. The younger ones Jason, Kras and Marla and Rosie noticed the change in their parents. They whispered among themselves that mother and father must be angry at each other because they are not talking or laughing as they used to. They were hungry. Jason ransacked the pantry finding sacks empty on the floor.

"Mother is not cooking, because the sacks are empty," Jason whispered to Kras. Knowing this it made no sense to complain. The following months, Kosta stared at decreasing supplies in the cellar, foreseeing starvation. Children's systems will not resist illness, he cannot lose his children, but he will, if he does not get help from someone, somewhere, but where? Thinking desperately perhaps, Aunt Olivia would help... with enough for a week or two she always had before. The thought of asking her hurt his pride, but she was his only salvation, for his children.

Many a night unable to sleep Kosta went back in time to count how many of the bad harvests they had and the good in between, but none as disastrous as these last several years. Rain and frozen fields. Fruit on the ground, discolored, iced over, now inedible. However, Kathryn picked the best fruit she could find and cooked it with a little bit of honey, the children loved it and ate with a slice of bread as a filler. It became so bitterly cold it was impossible to attempt any harvesting. They waited for the rain to stop, when it had stopped people ventured out to the fields harvesting what was still good; out of nowhere strong wind freezing rain whipped at their faces and hands, no other choice but pickup what lay on the ground and go home. Crops destroyed, disaster reined again everywhere. Kosta stared out of the window in horror. *"Slowly we will starve. We will starve this winter. I must get help."* He struggled with the thought of going to his brother for days. All these years his brother's visits were few, his brother had absolutely no interest in the survival of Kosta's family. He lived in luxury. Fields stretching far over the horizon surely produced abundantly; with minimal losses, if any; had reserves for several winters; not just one winter. His large home well heated, bellies full, and his brain wine happy.

Kosta had reservations and feared his brother's ridicule and belittlement. He did not mention his plan to Kathryn. Unfortunately, this was not his choice to make or Kathryn's. Starvation decides.

"Surely he has feelings. Would he ask me to leave without allowing me to explain my situation? He will laugh at me that I know as he always had when we were growing up. That eerie raspy laugh makes my skin crawl," Kosta thought.

Twenty-Two: Kosta's First Visit to His Brother

Kosta prayed for courage that night, sleep evaded him. The final decision had to be this night, go to his brother, or not. Just as he fell asleep, the rooster crowed. His rest was short, time to get up for the morning routine in the barn. He stood in the barn all alone staring into space. He knew he had to go. He had no other choice.

On that cold morning without telling Kathryn, he set out on a visit to his brother. He sat on the wagon with his head tucked in his coat, the wool shawl wrapped around his shoulders, tears trickled down his cheeks. He felt alone, disappointed of himself. His life seemed hopeless, he gave up his portion of a meal to his children, to save them, so did Kathryn; he knew her heart ached, her stomach cramped from hunger, she herself would rather starve than allow her children to suffer. That is why he loved this woman so much.

Kosta's feelings and spirit were down. The distance to his brother seemed much farther than ever before, and it was cold. At last, he pulled up to the gate, tugged on the rope, the bells piercing tone resonated in early quiet of the morning. He waited, a sudden shudder shook him; it must have been from the chill. It took minutes for the butler to appear in the doorway.

"What is it you want, who are you?" the butler asked tersely.

"I am here to see Master Thomas. I am...his brother." The butler stared at him as if trying to recognize; but after a moment motioned with his hand to follow. Kosta followed into the foyer.

"Wait here, I will announce you to Master Thomas," he said, and shuffled away.

"Is the Lady in?" Kosta called after him.

"Yes," muttered the butler, not looking back.

Lord Thomas came in dressed elegantly, dashingly. Expression of pride glowed on his face. Kosta's courage sank into his gut, feeling very small and out of place as he stood in the foyer. Lord Thomas came up shook his hand, inviting Kosta into the formal parlor. Lord Thomas sat down across the room on a sprawling chair evidently his favorite. His brother's stare made Kosta feel uneasy. Lord Thomas eyed Kosta face. Cheeks sunken, eyes rimmed with dark circles and he seemed to be half the size than he was; *what became of him? What of his children and Kathryn they look like him too? Things are not going well for Kosta. He did not look like his brother, but a stranger, unrecognizable. Hunger made him come.* Lord Thomas thought. They sat, neither spoke. Kosta choked on his feelings. To avoid his brother's eyes he glanced around the room. Lord Thomas after a moment asked.

"Would you like a cup of coffee, or tea?" he asked smiling.

"Thank you very much I would appreciate a cup of coffee, yes," Kosta replied. *It must have been last summer at Michael's home I had a good cup of coffee,* Kosta thought. Lord Thomas called for the servant, told him to bring coffee and cakes.

"And so... what brings you here on this dreadful day, has something happened?" asked Lord Thomas.

"In my life something always happens, but nothing good..." Kosta replied his head and eyes downcast.

The manservant came carrying a tray with coffee and sandwiches, the aroma permeated the room as he sat the tray on the dining room table. Lord Thomas said to Kosta, "Follow me," and he followed behind his brother into the dining room. Lord Thomas took a seat and pointed to Kosta to sit across the table from him. Kosta glanced at the cushioned seat thinking he might stain it. He wore his old work pants; those were the only pants he had. He sat down, carefully picked up the elegant cup of coffee, and inhaled the warm steam bursting with aroma, sipped the coffee slowly, his taste buds exploding with delight. Kosta closed his eyes. Moments later he spoke.

"Thomas my brother, it... ah... has been many years since I have seen or heard from you, I have extended invitations to you many times. You never replied. I guess you were too busy. I..." Kosta tried to say.

"Yes unfortunately I have been busy and am busy," Lord Thomas interrupted, stressing the word busy.

"Your life is very different from mine. You have prospered well, I am glad for you. I came to you because you are my brother... I had no one else to turn to... my life is one great misery. I am in distress and desperate, I came to beg you for help, for my children..." Kosta trailed off, his voice quivering.

"Kosta do not be offended but you should have been more careful, having so many... ah... times are hard and very unpredictable," Lord Thomas interrupted again.

He spoke but his left cheek lifted up as well as his lip appearing strange.

"I love all my children. Our children given to us by the good Lord, and, the good Lord took one of them from us. I am asking for them, not for me. We will not survive this winter. The harvest was bad, as you know...many villagers are in the same situation...Aunt Olivia needs help too..."

Kosta struggled to go on, but after a moment said, "I have depleted all means of support. I will do anything for my family." He looked up at his brother Thomas. "Please my brother, I need help, could you...have a heart... help your only brother...I will repay you someday. Or I will give you all my carvings..." His voice trailed off, looking at his brother's healthy face. He lowered his head and could not say more.

For a brief moment, an uneasy silence hung in the dining room. Kosta, though unnerved and ashamed, noticed this quiet; the whole house seemed to be deserted; as if everyone had gone, he wondered where Cybilia, her parents and their son were.

Lord Thomas leaned halfway across the table smiling, and then burst into that awful raspy laughter, it bounced from wall to wall, to Kosta's ears it was deafening.

"You... You will repay *me*! There is nothing you have that I want as payment from you, my brother. Nevertheless, come back tomorrow. I will prepare a wagon full of provisions. You will have enough to last the whole winter. As to the repayment, not to worry, I will think about it!"

Kosta could not believe that truly his brother will help! He sat staring. Kosta slowly rose from the chair grasped his brothers hand and held it tight.

"Thank you, thank you from the bottom of my heart. I will come back tomorrow, thank you. Oh, may I have another cup of coffee, please?" Kosta choked on that plea.

"Ah yes of course!" Lord Thomas called the manservant. "Prepare a large basket of food to take home for his children, throw everything into it, make sure, you understand?" When the manservant brought in a large basket filled to the brim, Kosta was surprised. With trembling hands lifted it and walked out setting it into the wagon. He heard his brother call out.

"See you tomorrow brother! And come early!"

Kosta, elated, felt no cold, shed no tears, only wore a weak smile on his face. "*My children will eat well this winter, thanks to my brother*," this was his only thought all the way home. Feeling guilty, he did not tell Kathryn about going in the morning not to give false hope. He must wait to be sure his brother truly delivers provisions as he promised.

Kathryn asked no questions when he came home with the basket of food. Mathew and Tessana rummaged through it putting everything onto the table, Kathryn cut nine slices of bread spread each with butter; Kosta sliced nine pieces of smoked ham everyone sat and ate. Kathryn warned them not to eat too fast, rather chew slowly but children ate greedily for they were hungry. Kathryn assumed all this food came from their best friends, Rabinna and Michael deeply moved silently thanked them.

In the meantime, at the estate in his bedroom, Lord Thomas deeply concentrated on the *'repayment'* from Kosta for the provisions. Since his brother is begging for food...well he cannot be that heartless, refusing help and people hearing about it his image would suffer. Not to mention his wife, she would be cross with him. It irked him to think that he was subservient to her. Grant you he was rich, still he felt not all of the wealth he lived in was his, not his at all. He told himself that the time will come with patience and planning.

Kosta anxiously waited for dawn. He slept fitfully, having all sorts of negative thoughts. At the first light he quietly slipped out of bed, dressed quickly it was very chilly in the house. He lit the stove, boiled water for a cup of hot water with honey. With his cup in hand softly walked to check on the girls, all four huddled together in one big bed. He looked in on the three boys. They too were huddled together in the other bed, wrapped in the down quilts. He looked at Kathryn, so beautiful, so desirable he wanted to kiss her, to touch her face, but hesitated, backed away, afraid of waking her.

The early morning chill cut through him, as he sat on the wagon, his old skinny horse was barely moving. He made a promise that he will feed his horse extra oats or barley, for sure, if provided by his brother. The poor thing deserves it. After all, he will pull the loaded wagon.

The old horse ambled slowly, no sense beating those old bones to go faster. He arrived at the estate, surprised to see the gate stood wide open for him to drive in.

The front door swung open and there stood his brother waving his arm, inviting Kosta in for early lunch. Next to him stood a little blond girl, about six or seven, holding Thomas's hand. "*Thomas had a daughter, when? I did not know they had another child,*" Kosta thought, as he walked up to the door. As he entered into the house, Lord Thomas said, "Well you arrived just in time for early lunch. Come in meet my daughter, Shara. Her name is really Sabrina. We gave her a nickname Shara. She is six now." Then he turned to Shara. "This is your uncle Kosta, he and I we have something important to discuss, now please go." Shara curtsied and without a word walked off.

"Shara is a beautiful girl. I did not know you had another daughter," Kosta said a bit caught off guard.

"Yes, two is enough, she looks a lot like Cybilia...she is a spoiled child...by her mother. Come in, lunch is ready," Lord Thomas said. In the dining room, the table was not set for two, but for twenty people, unbelievable, this is lunch? The coffee extra special, Kosta thought, oh *my God, Bacon and eggs, freshly baked bread and fresh butter, cakes and fruit*." Kosta's nostrils inhaled the wonderful aromas and his mouth salivated. He asked his brother if his in-laws, Cybilia, Mark, and Shara would join them. His brother replied, no, they have had lunch already.

While eating their subject of conversation was about their lives and families in general. It seemed to him the atmosphere was quite pleasant and at ease and the lapsed years came together as if yesterday. Thereafter, the table cleared away, Frunn served pastry and coffee. Sipping the tasty brew, Kosta wondered why this display of rich foods; was it simply to impress him? Perhaps prolong his time being there, since it has been so many years since. Kosta paid no attention to time; time had slipped by swiftly now realized that it was late afternoon, by the time they load the wagon; besides the horse is old; it will be dark, and his horse will be exhausted; I pray he does not drop dead in the middle of nowhere.

Lord Thomas leaned over the table, seeing Kosta in a daze punched his arm speaking in a low tone.

"Kosta, I know exactly what you need and how much you need for your family, as you know yourself, it will require many sacks of wheat and barley and flour, plus for your horses, hay. You know, you have a big family, I thought about you last night. I will give you all you need, but you must repay me, as you said, you would do anything for your children, right?"

Lord Thomas stared into Kosta's eyes from across the table for only for a split second. *I just snagged a fly in my cobweb* he thought. Kosta felt fear surge through from head to toe, he had no clue of what his brother had in mind and did not ask. He noticed something strange about his brother's eyes; his left eyebrow lifted higher than the right; giving him a wicked look, or, was it his imagination.

"Yes, yes...I will do anything for my family," Kosta replied with a bit of skepticism.

Lord Thomas stood up quickly and went up to the window.

"Your wagon is loaded, look Kosta, and a second wagon is loaded," he said not looking back. Over the wide doorway of the dining room and windows hung heavy velvet drapes, at times drawn for privacy stood Cybilia. Kosta noticed her and was about to rise and say, "good day Lady Cybilia," but Cybilia instantly placed her finger on her lips, to be silent. She nodded her head, her hand waved for him to go. Kosta stood up and walked to the window, and there he saw his wagon stood full of provisions, "Thank you," Kosta whispered.

"Now look over there, a second wagon is also loaded for you. As to the repayment, we will...but..."

"I will repay you, whatever you want!" Kosta interrupted his brother.

"Good, then it is agreed! You will repay me right now, will you not?" Lord Thomas spun around. Kosta froze, suddenly confused.

"But, how can I repay you now, I have no gold, Thomas, I have nothing!" Kosta replied fear tightened his chest.

"I do not need gold, I have barrels of gold. I want something other than..." Lord Thomas glared at Kosta with that piercing look, stared him down, his lips pressed tight. Silence fell. Kosta looked away his eyes fell on the two wagons, food for his children. He looked up at the sky, the sun has dropped low it seemed to rest on the mountain peak. Soon darkness will fall. A shiver and a chill ran up and down Kosta's spine.

On the poplar trees, growing along the lane, among the branches thirteen pair of eyes watched.

"What do you want from me? What do I have that you want? You are rich. You have everything under the sun, what do you want!" Kosta cried out, alarm in his voice... what do you want from me! Thomas I do not understand, but whatever it is, you shall have it," Kosta lowered his voice and stared back. Lord Thomas eyed Kosta smirking. Hidden behind the heavy drape Cybilia listened, she heard every word. She waited for the moment for them to leave. She needed to hear more and see what will happen. However, to her disappointment unable to hear what they were saying she had to leave her hiding place. Frunn could or would tell Thomas that she eavesdropped.

"Ha! Then come. It shall be done as you agreed... then come." Lord Thomas grinned. They went outside, the wagons were loaded, Kosta forgot his fears, thanked his brother, several times over again. He heard bad things about him, but this is mind-boggling, his family was safe. He gripped his brother's hand and even kissed it, Lord Thomas jerked away from Kosta's grip, shouting not to kiss his hand. Kosta felt a rush of tears, but suppressed them. Lord Thomas told Kosta to go and wait in the barn they need to talk. Kosta walked into the dim barn, when his eyes adjusted there stood a small chair close to the beam, on which he sat, it wobbled, Kosta waited, it seemed hours. Finally, his brother entered the barn. Two servants walked in on silent feet shortly from behind, undetected by Kosta, Lord Thomas talked too loud, and nodding his head, which seemed odd to Kosta. *Thomas never jerked his head like this. Perhaps he developed a nervous spasm,* Kosta thought.

"Now you have enough food for your children, and now you will pay me for these provisions."

The jerk of his head was a signal to the servants to do their job. Kosta felt a rope around his neck that pinned him against the beam, these men, worked quickly, he grabbed onto the rope but it was too tight he could not breathe. The men roped his chest, tied him with the chair to the beam. Kosta struggled to get free, he wrestled to stand up but the weak chair collapsed under him. Now he sat on the barn floor. The noose around his neck pulled away a bit but still held him. The two men who overpowered him stood behind him he could not see their faces. Kosta was shocked. His heart beat violently.

"Kosta, you agreed to repay me with whatever I want, right?" Lord Thomas grinned repeated the question.

"Yes," barely whispered Kosta. The men loosened the rope a bit.

"Then you will give me your right eye!" said Lord Thomas.

"For God's sake you want my right eye? Thomas what are you saying! I am your brother! How could you! I need my eyes to carve!" Kosta shouted, horrified.

"Give me your eye.... otherwise I will remove all the provisions! Your children will starve! Do you want them to starve! Do you understand?" Lord Thomas shouted at him. His face took on an evil snarled expression. He glared, lips twisted to the side.

Kosta trembled but had no choice only to give in. His family was more important than his eye. He stared into his brother's eyes and said, "Take my eye if this act will give you pleasure! Good God, evil has possessed you Thomas! God help me! God help you! Go ahead, but remember you are doing this to your own brother! You will never wipe my blood off your hands and you will not sleep—" Suddenly silenced by a blow to his head, Kosta's head jerked back;

assured he was unconscious they proceeded to remove his eye. The men untied the ropes and laid him on the ground face down.

"Turn the wagon around and into the barn. Load him under the front seat of the wagon, take him home, and remember what I told you," Lord Thomas hissed at the servants. The servants were shocked and horrified, but said nothing, just nodded their heads, eyes averted, they feared their Master. They obeyed.

The servant's wagon moved ahead faster followed by the old horse with the other man. By the time the first wagon drove very slowly into Kosta's yard it was already dark. He turned the wagon around at the corner of the house and began unloading the sacks.The other fellow driving Kosta's wagon with the old horse pull in front. At last, the old horse pulled in slowly. All the provisions were unloaded off the first wagon. But from the second wagon with Kosta under the seat, only half of the sacks were unloaded. Together now these men slowly drove out of the front yard making the least noise down the road. At the crossroad sped away back to the estate.

The sun had set over the mountains. The valley now stood in darkness. Mathew heard the rumble of a wagon, and a whinny of a horse; thinking father had returned...with a lantern in hand ran outside through the back door; by the dim light he saw the sacks on the ground. Quickly Mathew ran back into the house, calling everyone. Rosie held the oil lamp shivering in the chill evening. All of them struggled to drag the smaller sacks into the pantry, excitedly chattering. Mathew noticed father was nowhere in sight.

"Mother this is strange. Father dumped these sacks on the ground at the back door and went away, not saying goodbye?"

Kathryn puzzled by such a bountiful delivery.

"These sacks on the ground must have fallen off, the wagon overloaded. It is a wonder that the horse did not croak along the way," Kathryn said.

Kathryn prepared a good meal for the children, but all the while, she thought of Kosta. *"Where is he? Who was here, who had delivered all of this to them, who? But... where had Kosta gone. Where is the horse and wagon?* For a moment a horrible thought crossed Kathryn's mind, her heart cringed*; perhaps he left us! Perhaps he will never return!"*

Tears flooded her eyes. She let them flow, hoping that was not true, that he will return. Kathryn waited, going around the little house cleaning.

Instinctively Mathew went up to the window, moved the thick curtain aside, nothing to see it was too dark. Then the dog ran to the door barking; he wanted out. Mathew opened the door and let him out; the dog ran into the darkness barking. Mathew followed stepping cautiously ahead noticed the wagon and the horse on the ground.

"Mother, Mother!" Mathew shouted running into the house.

"Mathew what is it, why are you shouting?" Kathryn ran up to him concerned.

"Mother, the horse, he is dead!" Come quickly, get the lantern!"

All the children sprang away from the table and ran outside, Tessana held the lantern high. Neither Kathryn nor the children heard the final grunt when the old horse dropped to the ground, but the dog heard it.

"Mathew you must take these sacks in; the boys will help. At sunrise this will not be here, you know that. I know they are as hungry as we," Kathryn said. They worked quickly with the load for the night was chilly. When half done, all ran into the warmth of the house.

"My God, the horse is dead!" Kathryn gasped holding the lantern. She looked at Mathew he took the lantern from her and said.

"Mother we need to unload everything and drag it into the barn else it may be gone by morning."

"Yes you are right, we should; animals from the woods will come during the night." Sack after sack came down from the back of the wagon and dragged into the barn; darkness did not stop them. Rosie led the way; she followed their dog; behind her Mathew and Kras dragged a sack of potatoes. As they past the pile of sacks Mathew stopped.

"Rosie, come a little closer here with the lamp," Mathew said. Rosie turned back handed Mathew the oil lamp he lifted it high above his head; and there they saw more sacks. Mathew shouted.

"Mother please, come over here quick!" all of them ran to Mathew to see what was there.

"Oh my Lord, what is all this?" Tessana said.

Kathryn was lost for words.

"Well," she said, "we must drag all this into the barn too. But... who was it..."

Tessana turned to Mathew and said, "We must hurry I am freezing!"

"Well yes, drag these here first, they are in our way," Kathryn agreed. As fast as they could, all sacks were stored in a corner of the barn. Sweating and shivering Mathew and Jason dragged smaller sacks to the back end of the wagon. They reached for the last three and what they saw shocked them, beneath the wagons bench on the floor laid Kosta.

“Up here, Mother up here, father is here, he needs help, come quickly!” Jason screamed. Kathryn calling Kosta’s name, crawled up onto the wagon seeing Kosta slumped unconscious she cried out to Mathew.

“Shine the light here, oh my God your father’s shirt is covered in blood,” she cringed.

“Oh my God, is Father alive?” Tessana shouted to Mathew.

“Yes he is alive!” Mathew replied. The rest of the children began to shout,

“Mother, was father here all this time, mother?” Jason shouted.

“He will be sick!” Jasemin began to cry.

“Who did this to him mother?”

“Mathew, we need to get him into the house, shine the light here Mathew! Look at all the blood and his body is ice cold. What happened to his cape! Hope to God, he will not die of pneumonia. Oh Kosta; Mathew run next door for help, no, wait ask three men to come get him off the wagon; we alone could never manage. Then ride for the doctor,” Kathryn spoke quickly with distress in her voice.

"Yes Mother," Mathew nodded, ran down the road to the nearest house for help; his dog followed. Minutes passed then Arkushin and three men ran up jumped onto the wagon, quickly and easily lifted Kosta’s limp body and carried him inside, laid him on the bed. Kathryn told them, “Mathew must ride for the doctor.” The other two men left knowing soon the doctor would arrive. Kathryn covered Kosta with a quilt.

Tessana brought a bowl of warm water and a cloth. Kathryn gently dabbed at the dry blood, wiped his forehead and cheek, for the children’s sake she stayed as calm as possible, still her hands trembled.

His shirt ripped, bloody on the right side, but no visible wounds. She felt a bump on his head, someone had attacked him, she surmised. Kathryn gently continued to wash his face.

“Mother look at father’s right eye!” Tessana knelt close and whispered.

Horror gripped Kathryn when she leaned to take a closer look at his face.

“Do not say anything, you will frighten the youngsters, we have to wait for the doctor,” she whispered back.

"We will find out someday. Why and who...we will know, that I promise you," Kathryn said. Meanwhile outside, Mathew explained to the neighbor.

"The horse is dead, father is hurt, and Doctor is needed immediately." The neighbor saddled Mathew's horse and together they galloped to the doctor's home. Within half hour, they halted at the doctor's front door. Mathew slid off the horse ran up and banged on the door, ignoring the late hour. When Doctor Sobraya opened it, he stood in the doorway, listened as Mathew explained what has happened.

Doctor Sobraya seeing his distress said, "Wait here I need my cape and medical case." He threw a cape over his shoulders and pulled a winter hat on his head, with medical case in hand, waved and said to Arkushin, Kosta's neighbor, who sat on the horse waiting.

"Thank you, but I will ride my carriage."

Arkushin turned the horse around and galloped back to Kosta's house. Not far behind, Doctor Sobraya and Mathew pulled into the front yard, reins pulled sharply halted noisily. Mathew ran into the house, Doctor Sobraya followed. Mathew took his cape and hung it on a hook behind the door. Kathryn's face streaked with tears ran up to him, to thank him for coming. Tessana took charge of the younger children; she told them to sit at the table and not make a sound. She will warm up milk for them and boil water for tea for the doctor and mother. When water began to boil, she poured it into a teapot to steep, filled a cup for the doctor and one for Mathew, and for mother adding a spoon of honey to each. Kathryn sipped the tea while Doctor Sobraya examined Kosta. The children wide-eyed sat and sipped warm milk. None of them wanted to go to bed, yet. Doctor Sobraya found the lacerated bump on his head, which bled profusely, after so many hours passed, blood had clotted and now crusted over, and the wound on his face...Doctor Sobraya knew immediately what had happened. Mathew observed*; one day I will be a doctor...*he decided...*I know Doctor Sobraya will help me, he promised he would.*

The doctor thought, *who would do such a horrible thing*? Doctor Sobraya motioned for Kathryn to come outside. She listened as the doctor spoke.

"Kathryn, he lost his eye, it was not in a fight, I must tell you as I see it, you must be strong, and I will tell the children. This act was by force, restrained by several men. I know and see it as a fact. You know Kosta's strength. He would win a fight with many men. Have you noticed the welts on his neck, those are burns from a rope, and straw in his hair? This happened in a barn. That is how I see it, but whose barn? This is a tragedy and a puzzling situation. He will come out of it all right, I assure you. However, it will take some time to heal and adjust physically and psychologically. Give him time, but the children must know."

"Kosta must have left the house early this morning. When I woke up, he was gone. I do not know where he had gone. We waited all day," Kathryn said.

They stepped back into the house. Mathew sat on the bed next to his father. The other children sat at the table, sad and frightened faces. The doctor noticed the expression on Mathew's face.

"Son, you noticed your father's condition, do not worry, he is strong, he will be fine," Doctor Sobraya said.

"Mother, whoever had done this horrid thing to my father! They will pay!" Mathew faced Kathryn.

"Children listen your father must have been in a fight. You all know your father is strong. He could lick many a man in a fair fight, but this was not a fair fight. He lost his right eye. Your father is strong and tough, he will recover and he will adjust. Now, you must not go around with long faces. Now promise you will help mother as much as possible, promise?" The Doctor looked at all of them.

Tessana put her arm around Rosie, her face streaked with tears. Rosie wiped her eyes with her dress and whispered, "I will help Mother." The rest just stared, afraid to say anything or even move. When Doctor Sobraya was leaving, Kathryn offered grains, for she had no money. The doctor refused.

"Kathryn, I know your situation. You need not pay me, and remember I am here to help. You and Kosta sacrificed much caring for the children. The good Lord will bless you all." As the door closed behind him, the house was in total silence. Kathryn sat on the bed. Kosta coming around moaned. The last thing he remembered, being with his brother and his servants in the barn. He opened his good eye, saw Kathryn, she was weeping. Kathryn looked around the children were gone. She leaned down and kissed his cheek.

"Kosta, I worried about you, thank God you are alive. You must be in terrible pain, but you must not sit up, Doctor Sobraya was here, he said for you to stay in bed, do not raise your head. I must see to the children, I will come back shortly, rest now."

She went outside, and she could not believe her eyes, Mathew took charge of unloading the remaining sacks from the wagon, poor little tots, they struggled so hard. Kathryn felt proud of her children. When the wagon was completely unloaded, they stood around staring at the poor old horse, not knowing what to do.

"Come in, it is too cold out here. The horse will be here tomorrow. Michael will help us," Kathryn called to them.

Kosta felt his sore right eye and realized what his brother had done to him, *aha..., so this is what he wanted for payment, my sight, he really did it, that coward, that skunk...!* Kosta realizing his eye gone forever, his whole body began to tremble, hands shaking, clenched the covers tight. His mind screamed out uncontrollable rage. He lost consciousness.

Next morning when Mathew and Kathryn walked out the door to do their chores, what they saw shocked them. Nothing lay on the ground but the hide and the head. Kathryn stood gasping. Mathew stood speechless. Kathryn gathered her self-control said to Mathew.

"We must cover up all this mess, dispose of the head somewhere, no, the ground is still good to dig behind the barn, we will bury it and mix in some manure to keep the dogs away, come we must do this before the others wake."

Mathew picked up a spade found a soft area and began to dig while Kathryn milked the cow, thinking, *the rest of the animals can wait. They must bury the horse's head it cannot wait.* She called to Mathew to come and carry the milk into the house while she dug deeper. She wondered as she dug what was keeping Mathew so long, when she glanced up Kosta was coming with him.

"Mother, Father wanted to know why you were out here so long and so I had to explain..." Kosta waved at her and said, "Let me dig a while, you take a break."

"Are the children asleep?" Kathryn asked.

"Yes, fast asleep," Kosta replied.

"Kosta you should not bend over, please, if you must help go and fix breakfast. Please!" Kosta agreed and went into the house. Kathryn dug another foot or so in that time Kosta having breakfast done came out to help Mathew clean up the mess. The head and hide they dragged behind the barn, to where Kathryn was busy digging; suddenly Kathryn cried out. "Kosta stop!" she dropped the shovel, ran up to him, staring at the bandage red with fresh blood. Kosta did not realize the wound had opened.

"Father I think you need to go inside. We will finish," Mathew said.

Mathew shoved the hide and the head into the pit and covered the pit with dirt. No need to question or wonder who gutted that scrawny old horse and that was that.

Several weeks later, Kosta's throbbing pain eased, but he had no desire to carve; instead uselessness slipped in, trivial duties irritated him. Soon into his mind crept the state of depression. He sat at the window and stared out. Now and again, the scene stood clearly in his mind of that evening in the barn, remembering his brother's twisted face, his heart hammered so loud he heard it in his ears. He spoke little to the children. They tiptoed around the house like little ghosts, afraid to speak aloud, or laugh. Kathryn and the children worked hard to keep up with the chores.

Weather changed, dark rainy days moved in now. Sure sign temperatures will plunge and winters grip will last for long months once again. The wind howled all through the night and whipped the sleet into trees, poles and dips; as it fell it changed into snow wet and heavy. Children shrieked with excitement, after breakfast they dressed and ran outside to make a snowman. Days were shorter and nights long and cold. Jack Frost etched the windowpanes obscuring the outside world. At least this winter they will not be hungry. Kosta with time and Kathryn's help realized his family needed him and he must overcome this dreadful self-pity and reclaim his strong self.

Kathryn asked Kosta if he was up to carving with Mathew small animal figurines for the poor children. Kosta agreed. He recognized that Mathew had inherited his talent; many evenings when the wind howled outside, Kosta told to block the hearth, too windy, all the heat escaped out the chimney. They sat by the wood stove and carved, mother and daughters were learning together to knit and sew.

Nights were long. Days dragged unbearably. Kosta and Mathew had carved enough toys for the village children, and delivered to all before Christmas with Arkushin and his son Brodin. On the way home from the last drop-off Mathew rosy-cheeked exclaimed, "Father did you see their eyes sparkle, how they smiled?"

"Yes son they were happy especially those in great need," Kosta said.

"Did we forget any one, Father?" Mathew asked.

"I hope not," Kosta replied.

"Father up ahead that is Arkushin and Brodin, let's race him home!" Kosta snapped the whip and the horses galloped.

"Father faster, faster! Surprise him, oh Brodin looked back and saw us, Father go faster!" Kosta snapped the whip again and the horses galloped faster. The two teams were running, neck-to-neck, then in a moment, Kosta's team raced on and passed Arkushins team by three-lengths and was far ahead heading home. Mathew laughed from joy and kneeling on the seat waved back with his arms at their neighbors. Brodin waved laughing too.

"Father do you think we will have more horses before spring?" Mathew asked.

"I hope so, we need at least one, and I have inquired already, nothing yet," Kosta replied. Since their horse croaked, Kosta had to ask neighbors for the use of their horses; on Sundays, the children wanted to visit Aunt Olivia.

Children scraped the frosted windowpanes to see out, but saw nothing only snow. Kosta could see they were getting bored and were counting the days until spring. Kathryn told them amusing stories and played simple games with either buttons or sticks just to pass the time. Kosta and Kathryn began to plan the spring gardens inviting the children's suggestions.

"But, how will you plow the fields without a horse father?" Kras asked.

"Ah...let me think, now, aha! I think I have a solution," Kosta said.

"What is the solution father?" Jason asked, all eyes on their father, while he took his time to think.

"Aha very simple, I have the solution...: Kosta stopped eyed each one; they waited none wanted to ask what is the solution. Then Kosta raised his hand and said loudly, "Aha! I do not need horses, not one and not two. I have seven! I, have all of you!"

The children's jaws dropped and mouths open wide, then clamped shut. Wide-eyed stared at him holding their breath.

"Father...*US*, plowing the fields...how?" Tessana cried out.

"How... well, I will harness all of you together and you will pull the plow," Kosta said with a very serious expression on his face.

"Mother did you hear that? Mother where are you!" Rosie jumped up crying out nearly screaming. Kathryn came in within minutes carrying a basket full of veggies and meat from the ground cellar. She looked at her children, all big eyed and mouths open, Rosie's brows furrowed.

"What is happening here, what is wrong with all of you?" Kathryn asked.

"Mother, Father is going to harness all of us and we must plow the fields!" Rosie cried out almost in tears.

"What? Hmm... your father wants to harness...all of you? Well now, that is a good idea. You see, you have to share the load of work like the horse, if you want to be fed like the horse, and I will be the one with the whip behind you!" Kathryn sat down at the table. Kosta glanced at her and both began to laugh hysterically.

All seven children eyed their parents then looked at each other stupefied, assuming their parents were mad? *Yes, they are mad*! When both parents stopped laughing, Kathryn wiped her teary eyes with her apron. Took on a serious look, "Well children, now it seems to me all of you had a good picture in your minds."

"We... we really thought father was serious, but he was making fun of us," Mathew said.

"Yes and we fell into that joke, like mice into a barrel of pickles, or you know what!" Kras said laughing. All at once, they laughed hysterically. However, Rosie glared at those laughing, eyebrows pulled together, lips pressed tight, she was not happy.

"Why are you frowning so, Rosie?" Kosta asked.

Rosie made tight fists and shook them above her head.

"Father I am small, I will not...not, not plow. I am not strong...no *NOT* the plow! That is not fair! I will not plow! Father, you must get a horse! I will not drop dead like our horse did!" Rosie's fists flailed in every direction. The others watched and then burst into laughter again.

Now this seemed very serious, and Kathryn hushed them, then said to Rosie, "Now Rosie dear, we are not serious. We would never harness you or any human being. Look outside. It is not spring or summer, it is winter, and we have been in here all these months with nothing to do. Father wanted to make everyone laugh, perhaps it was a bit frightening to all of you, but at the same time *funny,* imagine all of you pulling that plow, if you imagine, it will be very *funny.*" Of course, everyone agreed not to take it so seriously. Children counted days for spring to come, to run outdoors and play in the warmth of the sun.

When spring winds blew the winter freeze out of the valley, temperatures rose and warm rain melted away all the snow. Then snowmelt cascaded and flowed down the mountains saturating the soil to awake it to life. Beneath the dead vegetation new lush green prairies appeared, splashed with wild flowers. It seemed trees burst into green foliage overnight. Flowering shrubs bathed in blooms in colors imaginable as far as the eye could see. The fragrant and fresh scent of it all permeated across the countryside. As for the villagers backbreaking toil beckoned. Spring was beautiful, but inadequate in nourishment for survival.

During summer frequent inspection of the fields showed promise of a bountiful cornucopia of staples to sustain them all. The villagers as per their custom always celebrated a Thanksgiving for the harvest, regardless of the outcome. Discussions among men went on for hours about the future improvements for their families and the community.

People traveled through neighboring towns and villages, heading to markets but along the way trading with the villagers, sometimes engaged in heated bartering over necessary purchases. Markets buzzed with people and stories, rumors about strange happenings, curiosity and caution got its attention from many in these crowds. Was it true? Gypsies are and will be gypsies, what sort of terrible monsters were they? Are they coming to peaceful villagers as themselves or are in disguise? Who knows, anything is possible. The old witches could not, and would not reveal. After all, they belonged to a different cult. They listened, said nothing but later discussed among each other. No one knew of the outcome; not even them.

Kosta heard of the wolf who liked music and one night told the story to his children, oh, how Rosie clapped her hands at the end when the wolf was free, and the rest of them applauded with her.

"Father, if that man would play his violin outdoors at night would the wolf hear it and come to listen? Jasemin asked.

"That is a good question, I do not recall hearing anyone say, if the man played at night or not, one day I will ask and we shall go visit, listen, and wait, perhaps that same wolf would come, not real close mind you, but close enough for us to see him. Be patient, I will find out," Kosta promised. Rosie, Jason and Marla jumped for joy. Now, the supplies they had rationed for the spring planting waited. Kosta through spring hand in hand worked with Michael and Rabinna. Children's responsibility was, to keep up with the weeding, chasing birds away and small creatures out of the garden. Even with that, they had fun. They kept in mind, and often talked about *the plow*.

Kosta and Michael became close friends, like brothers, avoiding the subject of what happened to Kosta. For Kathryn and Rabinna it was enough to glance at each other. With time, their domestic animals multiplied, and several more horses bought. The children were glad when another calf was born, overjoyed to see the chicks hatch and observed mother hens care of her brood, and the goslings, those tiny downy yellow puffs, waddled after mama-goose to the creek, tripping over their clumsy little feet. Kosta watched the performance of his children, and was proud of all them, especially Mathew. "Ah, handsome lad he is," he said to his friends. They agreed.

"You must keep your eye on the girls, boys surely will chase and ogle them," Michael said, and they laughed. Kosta adjusted quite well over the summer without his eye. Yet, many a night he thought about his brother, his feelings wavered between hate and pity, but the strongest feeling of pain was beyond comprehension, *why, brother against brother*. Knowing these, feelings someday would pass. As always one day, justice will prevail. They will meet again, surely, but for now, he must work hard and live with it each day. This year harvest unusually was generous all storage bins and pantries full. Kosta wished for a thoroughbred horse, his inquiries paid off, one day he found a young stallion, never had a saddle on its back but with Michaels help broken him in; when at the market Kosta displayed his carvings to his surprise many sold and were in demand by those understanding talent and fine art. They were thankful believing Faith had improved their life a bit. The following years, passed somewhat less stressful; now and then troubles disrupted their peaceful life; but were short-lived.

Twenty-Three: The Guilt

Lord Thomas a self-disciplined man developed great self-control and ruled Prozzati roost with an iron hand; up to the moment of that awful evening. His act of violence against his brother out of jealousy, within months, made him insecure. Passing strangers at the market made him feel uneasy, frequently glanced over his shoulder as if in fear of being followed or recognized. The image of his brother's face haunted him frequently. The cruel deed he had committed stood before him; followed him like his own shadow.

His moods changed from day to day, he bellowed at the servants for no reason. They cringed. His booming voice echoed through the house as he degraded Cybilia with offensive names. His children Mark and Sabrina hid in their bedrooms in fear of physical injury; which happened quite a few times before; now, a handy man with a list of trivial repairs required by Lady Cybilia always hung around close to guard them. Lord Thomas had noticed and questioned the man what he was doing, at which time the handy man showed the list of repairs. Otherwise he would suspect his wife of some sort of conspiracy against him. Cybilia wept many a night sitting alone at home. Her husband was out drinking at the 4 Hoofs Inn.

Lord Thomas desperately tried to erase the memory of his brother's bloody face. Saturating his brain with wine only fogged his memory. Kosta's words echoed, "*my blood on your hands...*" His friends asked about his brother, but he shrugged with an excuse of being too busy to visit, besides, they lived quite a distance away, and having too many responsibilities in running the winery. Returning home inebriated fell into bed still fully clothed, only the shoes came off his feet. Sleep overtook him quickly. The nightmare returned, the bloody image jolting him out of sleep. Guilt followed him like a spirit. The uncertainty of his brother's welfare drove him insane. He could not openly ask anyone about Kosta. He could never visit Kosta and his family. Even if he could muster some courage to face him, he could not.

The men who acted out this cruelty forewarned by their master never to disclose to anyone what they had done. The moment he hears about it they will pay the consequences, from that night on they kept distance not only from everyone else but each other.

Cybilia often wondered what had happened between these three men. During years of working together, they got along well. However, lately it seemed animosity crept between them. Perhaps a silent squabble for a higher position in this household, feeding animals and daily cleaning of stables is not pleasant. Surely, such a dirty job may cause one's loss of self-respect. She hesitated to question them their reason why the somber faces and avoidance of each other. Had they a valid reason to act this way. She decided not to discuss this situation with her husband; it was best to let it be. The three of them should resolve their problem themselves. Paulo Prozatti had built a large home for the men each had their own room. Younger girls slept in the main house with all the women. The Prozatti were good to their workers were respected by everyone. Cybilias conclusion, position, and seniority... it must be so...she dared not mention this to Lord Thomas. She observed them whenever possible. She tried to understand the change in her husband. She tried over the years to please him, but nothing worked. He was distant, stayed out late into the night. Cybilia, despondent and disappointed, questioned herself what went wrong. Squabbles, yes they had but those were unimportant; surely should not ruin their life. *What were they lacking, absolutely nothing*! He was in control of the winery business. Her father entrusted everything to him. Her parents were ill and aging; her father needed relief managing the estate regardless of all the hired help.

She heard about Kosta's accident with the eye. *To Kosta such an accident happened, how terrible! Was it an accident... was it? He lost his eye...hmm...* she kept thinking...recalling years back, comparing her husband then and now. Their early years of marriage, he had caused her misery, now buried deep in her memory, and she felt a stab at her heart just thinking about it. He was a deceiver from day one. She realized how naïve she had been in her youth, blinded by his charisma. He had swept her off her feet; she fell for him as a stupid moth attracted to a flame, and the flame singed her wings. He charmed all but one of the servants. Every aspect of their life had to be his way, his reasons and explanations always seemed reasonably logical, Cybilia recalled. Something had completely altered his behavior, and his attitude towards her. She once loved him. Her love of late no longer burned strong towards him, as when she was young and foolish. His touch no longer awakened desires within her as before. She felt the distance between them widening. The years had also altered her, from observation she realized he had not detected her change, preoccupied with his own self.

Cybilia grew up with nannies, tutors, cooks and servants. Many moved on. Those devoting their whole lives with permanent positions remained until old age. These old servants knew the complete life of the Prozattis. Together they had accomplished to what is at hand now.

With empty hands, Marianna entered into marriage. Paulo inherited these acres of land and having knowledge continued improving the business of winery. Marianna worked right along her husband from the start and together they labored hard and succeeded now deserves to live a comfortable life. Prozattis respected their employees. Young and old looked upon as an invaluable individual. The oldest cook, Nina had taught all the newcomers to prepare and serve meals to the liking of their masters. Now, Nina disabled, unable to walk, a cane supported her frail old body. Nina sat in the kitchen overseeing the young girls in their schooling; being an unmarried woman, devoted her lifetime of service to Prozattis. Moreover, if they clearly showed their discontent or behavior, they had a right to. Marianna always was there whenever end of life came. They were cared for, not ignored, dismissed from employment, or forsaken in their old age. The servants masked well their dissatisfaction in some situations, which arose, many a time; but they clamped up tight to suppress their opinions.

Cybilia noticed they lost respect for their young Master. Their false cheerfulness and politeness carried out immediate orders. Sometimes accidently overhearing their conversations made her rethink things. These servants had plenty to say among themselves about him, she detected insecurity, fear, not one word of praise but demeaning disgust.

Twenty-Four: joseph

Joseph, one of the most trusted and devoted servants, resigned, his reason to leave was a shock to all, a reason not very clearly convincing.

"You must have a good reason to leave us. Have we mistreated you in any way, have we done you wrong, or is it someone else that has hurt you?" Cybilia insisted on an answer, but Joseph remained silent. Cybilia promised she would not tell anyone, especially her husband.

"Your cause of leaving shall be known only to me. And your secret shall remain here..." she laid her hand on her chest, her eyes filled with tears. Joseph shook his head in refusal, his sad eyes too full of tears. He kissed both her hands and whispered, "My Lady Cybilia, please take care of Mark, little Sabrina and yourself..." He stressed, "*be careful...God Bless you.* Promise me, you will not tell. I must... leave early in the morning, my Lady be careful."

Joseph was ready to leave Friday on the market day to avoid his master. He had not considered that perhaps someone else be sent in his place, which Lord Thomas many a time had done so before, perhaps to confuse. Josephs fear for his life urged him to run. On that morning, well before dawn, Joseph up and ready stepped out noiselessly through the back door and headed around the back of the barn, knowing if someone saw him it would not matter, no one would be curious. He would slip out unseen leaving the long way.

"Mother I was in the kitchen looking for Joseph but he was not there and he is not in his room." Cybilia caught off guard stared at Mark, remembering what Joseph told her the evening before.

"Oh I do not know where he is. Perhaps he had gone to the market," Cybilia replied averting her eyes.

"Why did he leave Mother?" Mark asked.

"Joseph left us? Why?" Shara happened to walk in on their conversation asked visibly upset. Only the other servant James knew why Joseph left, but was not about to tell. The rest of the servants could not say why, even if they knew would not admit it.

James when questioned but had no explanation, he said to Lady Cybilia, "My lips are sealed, forever."

When Lord Thomas found out, he needed to vent. Cool his nerves. He rode his stallion Star hard for a while, on his return he questioned the servants what time Joseph had left but no one could say, because they truly did not know, they were innocent. Lord Thomas's suspicion..., Joseph escaped and was on the way to his brother, and he knew where Joseph's brother lived and how far. Two weeks before Joseph left, Lord Thomas hired two men. These were ruffians, would do anything for gold and a warm meal, well suited for any job Lord Thomas had in mind. After discussing payment and given directions they knew without question their mission and warning of the consequences if they fail.

Joseph walked to his brother's house, which was the fourth village away. Joseph estimated at least nine to eleven hours from the estate. Joseph would be safe unless unforeseen reason and would be home late in the evening. He hurried, keeping out of sight choosing area of easy concealment. Joseph looked up, the sky, clear. By his own shadow, he figured still early morning, far from noon. After hours of walking, he needed to rest. Finding a nice spot off the road and about to sit down, heard voices, instantly Joseph dropped flat to the ground and crawled into the nearest bushes. Three men on horseback past by eyeing the area, one of them spoke, Joseph immediately recognized the voice, and his heart began to flutter.

"He is an old chap, could not have reached his brother's house yet, I wager a few pieces of gold he is around here somewhere, we need to ride through the woods often he might be resting by a tree." The others agreed.

They rode through eyeing the bushes. Joseph's heart pounded so loud, he was sure they could hear it. Joseph had crawled on all fours into the thickest underbrush at a fallen tree, with difficulty squeezed against the base of it, from decay, half-crumbled leaving an open hollow at the underside, with his bare hands he raked at it not caring what crawling creature he infringed upon. He listened. The huge fallen tree smelled of rot, the inside of this tree had decayed for that he was grateful. Ants crawled around him and on him, through the small holes, which let in a bit of light. He remained in hiding for a very long time, when the three men rode around the bushes and the fallen tree Joseph's heart almost stopped, he clamped a hand on his mouth from fear, breathed through nostrils. Eyes closed waited.

Lady Luck was with him, they did not take the time to search the dense part where he squeezed into the crumbling tree trunk. If they had good scout sense and looked, there were broken twigs and fresh leaves as evidence someone had done this, but Joseph had not thought about concealing his little trail, he remained motionless. After a long wait not hearing talk or horses trotting peered out to be sure, he thought he was safe. Then Joseph realized he could only see from one side. He waited what seemed to be hours, all around him was quiet. He figured the three men were gone. Just when he was about to crawl out into the open area he thought, *what if they are sitting on the other side of the tree...I must wait longer...I must peek to the other side, find something to chip a hole through.* Carefully at arm's length groped as far as he could reach for a small but thick stick, he found one, moved it in slowly to test its freshness it crumbled half-rotten, useless. He eyed every twig hoping it was fresh. He saw one farther away from him, on his belly without a sound crawled forward, hand trembling grasped it, backed up like a crab into the hollow it was fresh and hard. Joseph now rolled onto his stomach feeling much discomfort. He poked gently, listened, it was too quiet, no sound of men or horse's, *surely, they are gone, but what if...they tied their horses and crept to the tree, waiting for me, jump me and kill me.* Joseph thought perspiration dripped from his face and he felt it run down his back. He chipped, poked the bark his fingers pulled away small bits and kept them inside, he managed a small peephole; determined to open a large enough hole to see through the bushes from all sides Joseph pressed the bottom and the rotten bark gave way, he smiled, *I did it, now look if they are out there,* he thought. However, that side was extremely dense. Joseph with both hands moved aside the tall grass and peered through, "Clear...no sign of them, or horses. Oh, that is good. They have gone on ahead," Joseph whispered to himself. He crawled out, tried to stand up but his weak knees dropped him to the ground, to calm down he sat a bit. Joseph brushed ants and leaves from his sweater, picked off the chips of rotted wood from his hair, and picked ants out of his shoes. After a cleanup and a short rest he walked on, the ant bites on his legs, arms and face burned. Weariness forced him to sit down again. He had to wait. The three men hidden in the shrubs far ahead of him also waited.

Joseph proceeded slowly through the outer edge of the woods, feeling more secure of not being in the open as before, and if he stays alert or feels danger, retreat quickly into hiding. He has circled the second village now, not seeing anyone near the woods, continued on to his brother's home.

I wonder if my brother was at home to receive my message. Too bad that young man's horse overloaded with so many bundles. How stupid of me, I should have escaped on a horse, not walk, now I am in danger! If God is with me, I should be at the house very late this evening, at the rate I am going. It is about noon now... he was thinking. Feeling hungry, out of stress and fear he failed to bring with him food early morning. He reached into his pocket brought out a half a slice of bread; *well this will do for a while.* His going was very slow and it was getting darker, now the sun did not penetrate much through these trees. He stopped for a moment and looked up trying to see the sky; *on the dirt road, I could guess the time by the cast shadows, but that would be dangerous.* Joseph thought. Stepping lightly he heard a loud snap. His heart pounded. He crouched down, on his knees crawled over to a bush and waited.

Soon a dark shape appeared a moose came very close to where Joseph hid. What a relief. Joseph observed the animal as it tramped by. He continued onward to his brother's home.

The three co-workers now Joseph's executioners relaxed hidden in a thick copse. Waited, waited for Joseph. As hours slipped away, the wind picked up the tops of the tall trees swayed, with the sudden drop in temperature, Joseph felt chilled through his thin sweater; if it rains; he will be soaked, without shelter of any kind in sight. Thunder rumbled, than lightning clapped and streaked across the sky, it seemed right above him as it struck a tree somewhere close. Joseph had to find a hiding place if it rains.

The three men were sure that Joseph should be approaching soon, but Joseph still stepped carefully over the thick forest floor. He realized that the storm actually is a blessing, as each rumble will muffle his run. He had a chance to head them off, if he hurries. At night, any little noise echoed more intensely than at daytime so it seemed.

He pushed through the thick forest, each stride wider as the thunder rumbled, and the lightning struck. The storm without rain moved on; but not fast enough. The forest was still dark. He happened upon a narrow path. Joseph knew this path, when he and his brother walked through it hunting. He smiled just thinking about those times. Out of breath, the need to rest urged him to sit a spell. The sweater wrapped tight kept him warm somewhat. He stretched his tired legs and leaned against a huge tree trunk. Joseph closed his eyes and listened to the rustle of the pines, and dozed off. The crash of a fallen tree startled him out of his nap. Joseph alarmed stiffened for a moment realized he was safe. Now sudden hunger rumbled in his stomach. This morning, he had nothing solid for breakfast, and that half a slice of bread earlier was not nearly enough. He reached into his left pocket, empty, in the right pocket the other half was still there. He savored each bite as he chewed. Without a drop of water, but enough saliva moistened, the dry bread calming his hunger. Joseph figured when this path turns sharply to the right, the lake and his brother's home should be in view. Joseph's arms crossed on his chest, prayed, thanking the good Lord that he was still alive, but exhausted. Curled in a fetal position on the ground, his arm for a pillow rested his head and fell asleep, the pines whispered.

Suddenly awakened by the hoot of an owl, he sat up. It was dark. His fingers felt soft pine needles. He blinked, realizing he had fallen into deep asleep. He felt rested though, but those men out there are waiting, he must avoid them. He continued on, his hands trembled, heart fluttered erratically, he stopped to listen, but heard nothing.

He was sure that the pursuers turned back and had given up their search for him.

Cautiously he inched to the edge of the woods, crouched, observed, turned his head from side to side and listened. Then his heart jumped and chills ran through him; he heard in the distance voices.

My pursuers, still waiting for me, surely they must be! Oh God, where do I go from here, where do I hide myself from these killers? If they kill me, my brother will never know masters plan to do away with Paulo and Marianna, but I know. Joseph fearing for his life crouched behind a dense shrub.

Perspiration from his forehead ran into his mouth, he licked the salty drops. With the sleeve he wiped his forehead, he remembered his sweater, and said to himself; thank God my sweater is dark green it blends with the vegetation. How long he sat and listened for voices he did not know. Then silence. *Now*...he thought *I must go to the lake.*

Just as he was about to walk out to cross the road, again heard voices. Joseph crouched in the shrubbery and listened.

"I think he will walk the road, it is too dark in this deep forest," one of them said.

"Yes and get lost, we are wasting our time, we should head back home," said another.

"I will not go back home, why, so the master would chop us down, you remember what he did the last time we failed, oh no I am not going home," the third one said.

"Hey you are talking too loud, hush now, we should ambush him not just ride back and forth, he may be old but he is not stupid," the first man said. The three men rode on.

When the voices of the riders faded, Joseph ran across the road to the lake, pushed through the shrubs and saplings, stepping over clumps of reeds, his shoes sank deep into the fetid muck. The fishy smell drifted in the air, but first he peered around to make sure these men had not double backed again to seize him near the water. Crouching low listened for any voices. Bent over he waded into the cool water. He cupped his hand scooped some water brought it to his mouth, but the fishy smell was so strong he could not drink it. Joseph was thinking; *it was well before dawn when I walked out the back door of the estate. Walking takes so much time. I should have planned my escape. Lark and I could ride out to a safe place for a day or so. I wonder if my pursuers had visited my brother asking about me. They need to kill me. I know too much. But, what I know I could not tell anyone for as long as I live, I am old, soon enough my time will come. They are chasing me to make sure I do not tell my brother what my master had done to his younger brother, yes it is so.* Joseph cautiously walked on avoiding open areas. He leaned against a huge tree to rest for a little while and analyzed his situation; *one thing I must do when I am close to the road, but how am I to cross the road? The prairie, as flat as a table, my pursuers will have a perfect view. I must wait to be safe, ah, but it is dark, too dark to see, I am too frightened to think rationally, if only I could last, oh I am so tired.*

The three pursuers hidden had a clear view. The directions were clear a turn in the road to the left, in the middle of a meadow off the road stands his brother's house. Again, Joseph forced to sit due to his legs, leaning against a tree, thankful that so far he had evaded his pursuers. In darkness stood his brother's home, he was that close, now. *Soon I will be safe, soon. Just cross the road. One thing seems odd, Lark failed to leave the light on. Late as it is, still the light should be on, unless he did not receive my message, or, something is wrong.*

Confused, tired and frightened, not knowing what to do, he sat dazed under a tree. All around silence, *perhaps my brother got tired of waiting; had fallen asleep; it just cannot be this late. My pursuers must have gone back to the estate to report to Master Thomas that Joseph was lost in the forest. I feel I am safe to go home*, Joseph thought.

Joseph crossed the road and cut through the prairie, walked slowly to the white fence surrounding the property, pushed the gate, it swung open, *not latched* that puzzled him, *always for the night Lark latched it.* Reaching for the front door handle, it too was unlocked, *the front door also open he must be asleep*, he thought. As he stepped in carefully, he heard strange shuffling, strike of a match, in a moment the oil lamp lit up the room dimly, to his horror, he recognized the three pursuers standing behind the chair on which Lark his brother sat, gagged, hands tied behind his back, a rope wrapped across his chest and the chair. Joseph froze; *that is why I heard nothing on the road...they came into the house to wait for me.* Joseph stood in the doorway.

"Joseph, come in... we have been waiting for you," one named Speshno said.

"Just do not scream or make any foolish moves, your brother will suffer if you do," Betra the second man said.

"We just want you!" Piabat said, from the dark corner, he was the tallest of the three, muscular, well-developed. He seemed to be the leader of this gang.

Joseph's adrenalin surged; he felt no hunger and he felt no exhaustion; rather moved in a slow pace keeping his eyes on the men's faces.

"Remove that gag, my brother is not the one you want. I see you obey your master well, so did I, and now I will die for carrying out his orders. You are foolish to follow his orders. You will end up like me. I know you have to kill me, but do you know why I ran away? You do not know what I have done, and why my conscience is killing me," Joseph said.

"Oh spare us your sorry version. Master Thomas told us what you are capable of," Betra the fat man said removing the gag. The three of them stood quite close together, Joseph turned up the oil lamp to brighten up the room, not looking at his pursuers said.

"It is time I suppose for you to do your job, before I die I would like to share a glass of wine with you as my co-workers, and, my brother, mind you it is not our master's wine, but world acclaimed." Joseph glanced at Lark and raised his eyebrows. The three executioners ignored his facial expression they were used to it.

Fortunately for Joseph these men were young and were not too bright, suspicious yes, murderers yes, but, the mention of wine sounded good, it surely would not hurt, they had a long day, what they had in mind would not take long, besides, it could wait. They do need a drink, one drink or two, or a whole bottle it does not matter now.

"Do you mind if I sit down. I am tired."

"Of course sit down, we do not mind at all, but you must tell us where you keep the wine," Betra said grinning.

Betra the shortest of the three, with long greasy hair, a fat mustache and a crumpled hat, in a few steps grabbed Joseph by the hair and slammed his face to the table.

"Tell us where the wine is, now!" Betra hissed.

"Hey untie me and I will take you to it. One of you come with me, we need more than one bottle!" Joseph's brother Lark shouted.

Just the mention of *many* bottles of wine, Speshno untied Lark, followed him to the kitchen where stood an oil lamp. Lark was about to reach for it when Speshno grabbed it and said, "I will carry it, you just lead the way." In the barn, Lark opened a storage door and pointed out the bottles, "these are the best that is why we store them on the bottom shelves. Lark picked up two bottles and handed them to Speshno.

"No, you hold them I will get the rest myself," Speshno said setting down the lamp.

The moment Speshno bent over grunting from being overweight reaching for more bottles. Lark struck Speshno with the bottle on the head with great force. The blood spurted as he crumpled like an empty sack of potatoes to the ground. Lark with the sharp neck of the smashed bottle slit the man's throat. Dragged him out behind the barn, dropped him by the wall. Lark picked up the lamp and the wine and walked into the house carrying six bottles and roughly rolled them on the table, some clanked together.

"Hey, not so rough you will break them, where is Speshno?" Betra gestured a warning, pointing a fist with a knife.

"Nature calls to private duty," Lark replied, standing the bottles upright.

Piabat went out to look for Speshno. Joseph glanced at Lark his brother then at Betra with a meaning for him to run. Lark understood and quickly said.

"Let me get some mugs from the kitchen." He set three mugs on the table and asked, "Joseph, where are the rest of the mugs, we need two more."

Joseph after a moment said, "I hung several on a hook a long time ago, I guess they are still there, go and look." Lark ran out the door, he ran around the house as fast as he could to the neighbor across the field. Lark banged on the neighbor's door, the door opened and Lark screamed; he needs help his brother was inside with three men and they were about to kill him.

Minutes dragged, Joseph and Betra waited, keeping an eye on Joseph pointing a curved knife at him. Suddenly the door opened Piabat ran in with bloody hands.

"What is going on here, what did you do?" Betra shouted at Piebat enraged.

Piebat sat down at the table and said, "Speshno is dead! I did nothing!"

"How did it happen?" Betra shouted and hit the table with his fist.

"His throat was cut, must have been with a bottle." Betra stared at Joseph.

"Well well, your brother is smart, but do not worry we will get him, after we have some wine and fun with you." He laughed like a hyena.

Betra opened a bottle and filled the mugs, and at that moment when the pursuers clanked their mugs, Joseph dropped his cup to the floor. The two killers laughed heartily.

"Joseph, are you too weak to hold that mug? Death is staring at you, fear of dying ha?" Betra said amused.

"No, I am weak from hunger, would you like to have some good bread with that wine. I gladly will get it. At least let me die on a full stomach." Joseph's amusing and wise last request, had not fooled them, they knew he is stalling. They glanced at each other and admitted that they too were hungry.

"Well if you put it that way, why not, go get the bread and do not tarry, it will not do you any good," Betra said.

"Yes, one minute or one hour will not matter, that is our order from the big master himself," Piebiat added.

Joseph in one hand had the bread and the bottle of oil, in the other a knife. A step away from the table dropped the bread and oil bottle. The two executioners startled stood up. Betra in an instant stooped down to pick up the bread, Joseph said, "Oh, let me help you, I am a clumsy old fool." Joseph bending to pick up the bread in that moment in a quick succession stabbed Betra in the belly several times, he fell.

Before Piebat realized what took place Joseph knocked over the table the globe shattered spilling oil as it fell to the floor. The room went dark for a minute. Then the linen tablecloth burst into flame. Betra on the floor did not move. Piebat stared at the flame. He raised his arm to protect his face. The linen tablecloth burned quickly, flames snaked and streaked and licked, in an instant, the flames caught his linen shirt. Piebat unknowingly stood too close to the table, shocked, screamed, swearing, beating at his shirt, backing away. Joseph picked up the oil bottle off the floor and smashed it to the floor, and ran for the door. Piebat determined to kill him aflame ran after Joseph, grabbed the back of his shirt threw him face down, in the struggle Joseph's clothes caught fire. Piebat being stronger sat on him, grabbed Joseph's head and viciously smashed his face repeatedly to the floor; knocking him unconscious. The interior of the small house rolled with smoke. Piebat coughed, inhaling the thick smoke, his hair and back ablaze collapsed on top of Joseph. In minutes, the house and the thatched roof blazed. Lark and the neighbor ran to the burning home, unfortunately, they could do nothing, but watch in horror as it burned.

Joseph found courage, a quick decision to save his brother Lark. He could not escape death but made sure his pursuers did not escape death either.

Three bodies charred found in the ruins at dawn. Joseph, Lark's brother was one of them. Lark knew to whom the other dead bodies belonged to, three bodies buried in the forest by Lark and his neighbors. Joseph rests in peace beneath his favorite Linden tree. Larks better judgment told him to avoid at all cost that certain MASTER. Rumors were; Poor Joseph lost his way in that thick forest, possibly devoured by wild animals or, perhaps died of a heart attack in those woods, after all, he was old.

The Master's hand reached out for Joseph and had Joseph's blood on it. As to his three executioners, no one heard from them, since that day they went off to capture Joseph, they never returned. Their master never questioned anyone nor mentioned their names. *Thereafter his secret was safe.* The three servant executioners did not receive the reward as promised by their master, a twist of fate foiled by Joseph, their reward, to perish in the fire.

In time, the truth will be unearthed. Mother Nature regurgitates unjust acts, especially when the innocent perish. Therefore, eventually the puzzle solved; complete full circle, such is the law of justice. Justice is persistent, no matter how much time elapses.

The other partner in crime, forced upon him by his master, the servant who had remained with Lord Thomas was warned, keep silence or hang. So he understood, and he would never disclose the event that took place, on that awful evening, never!

Lord Thomas did relax a bit, became more like his old self, speaking to his wife congenially, freely and openly, and had stayed at home more than usual. He read his books but in the back of his mind, his thoughts were not of Joseph, though he was sure since Joseph was his scapegoat he is free to expedite his plan. Concerning the others as the wheel of time revolves, strange things do happen. The wheels of evil plans are in constant motion as well.

Frequently the same nightmare returned... the one, which tormented Lord Thomas from the first night of that cruel deed.

He dreamt that someone came at him with a hot iron and gouged his eye out, and the pain was real, his nostrils filled with the smell of burning flesh, his own. He awakened screaming, sprang out of bed clutching the bed sheet, thumbs pressed into his eye sockets, covered in sweat. Cybilia startled by all this screaming, ran into her husband's bedroom, for she no longer wished to sleep with him in the same bed. She tried to quiet him a bit, Thomas shivering from fear held on to her.

Fear kept him sleepless and many bottles of wine stood empty on the floor where he sat and drank before bedtime, his brain buzzed then fogged over. From time to time he remembered why he was in his favorite chair in the parlor and alone. Hope, it was hope, hoping that the wine would mar or erase that nightmare. No such luck, haunting continued to irritate him. He became angry with himself, angry for being foolish. At the market place, he noticed people stared at him and whispered, unable to hear what they said felt his hair rise on the back of his neck. His skin crawled; he assumed people knew of what he had done. Fear, chased by fear, he jumped onto the cart and sped away, back home. He was angry, for losing his self-confidence.

His power and control slipped. He felt like a fool, small and very insignificantly unimportant. He felt that everyone could see right through him, he desperately masked the waves of emotional rage within him, which he could not allow to surface. With perspiration glistening on his face, he shoved his trembling hands into the pockets, nerves taut like violin strings. Paced around the parlor disturbed, confused, unclear thinking. He sharply ordered Frunze to find James immediately.

"James! Come Friday you are to take the produce to the market. I forbid you to speak to anyone about our lives, do you understand!"

James felt anger surge through his veins but his master would never detect it. James never questioned, but accepting the order as always, casually. As time went by James began to detest his master for what he himself had become. Some fine day it will surface and his master will pay. James from that day on walked around with a tiny smirk on his face. No one asked, and if anyone did, his reply always seemed satisfactory and logical, without question.

After many months of struggling to overcome those fears and the inescapable awareness of his deeds in waking hours and at night, he could not allow this weakness, this nightmare to take over his senses. He will have and must have control of himself and in time return to be his normal self. Was it all normal?

Twenty-Five: Cybilia

Cybilia sensed the fear as well, but it was not for Lord Thomas, but for herself and children, Mark and Shara (Sabrina). Why this fear, what was the problem with her husband? Urgency forced her to seek someone who would understand this sort of situation. Yet, she could not bring herself to do that; the possibility of her husband's madness would bring untold consequences.

Her nights were restless. What horrible plans had he in for her, since the unfortunate eye incident that happened to his brother, she wondered had he anything to do with it? Since then he has become a raging bull.

She began to think back, relive those months and years. She remembered that morning, when they had breakfast together, when the servant mentioned his brother's accident with the eye. It was the evening before his brother was here...late. They were discussing something and Kosta seemed to be agitated. Following morning, Cybilia at breakfast observed her husband; yes, now she was sure, he was acting different, on edge, very restless, but now he is calm and pleasant. Just the mere thought, Thomas, her husband would do such a thing made her tremble.

Run away, take the children and flee, but then, he would realize that she knew if she and the children would leave.

She could not go to her parents they were deceased now for several years. She suddenly recalled the stone calmness on her husband's face at her father's funeral, as if a heavy obstacle removed out of his way. He seemed glad that her father was dead. She recalled when father died..., thinking, remembering, yes now she is sure, not even a year after Joseph left and never heard of again, and those three men they also were gone, hmm...,

Her father suffered of cirrhosis of the liver, according to doctor's diagnosis; and her mother suffered right along with him as she watched her husband die slowly. Father suffered six or eight months before he took his last breath. She also recalled her father protesting to the doctor that he has no pain at all; but feeling weakness by the day. She remembered how seldom he had visited her ailing father, his excuse, preoccupied with all the responsibilities of the estate since the load of work fell on his shoulders her father fell ill and he found little time to visit his dying father-in-law.

Several years later, her mother died of heart failure, she just simply fell to the floor and died, their doctor assured Cybilia that it *was* her heart. Cybilia never knew of her mother's condition, her mother wished to keep it from her, so the doctor said.

When Cybilia's mother died suddenly, she recalled how distraught she was and out of her mind. He had not offered to console her, not a minute to hold her in her arms, or speak with her but if only for a second. Cybilia was beside herself. She was alone now, no siblings to share her grief with, her cousin and Uncle Lorenzo being far out of the country and never knew of their deaths until months later; she recalled, when at her mother's funeral her husband had that same calm expression on his face, just like at her father's funeral. Not once did he whisper a consoling word to ease her sorrow. He had not shed a tear for either of them. After all, her father had entrusted him with his lifelong business, an opportunity of a lifetime. He became rich on their sweat. She also recalled the women in the kitchen were talking about some drops, which were hidden, when she entered they stopped talking and all scattered out of the kitchen like mice facing a fat cat. As much as they respected her and liked her, none, none would talk about those drops. Cybilia after time felt she knew what they were. How did she come to realize what they were, she remembered, it was in the fall while she and Flora were discussing what was needed in the pantry, three of the girls with baskets were ready to go mushroom picking, Flora stressed and warned them to be very careful and not pick the wrong ones. Cybilia recalled asking, "Flora these girls do not recognize poisonous mushrooms by now?" Flora told her, "Once when they brought a basket full of deadly ones; I set the baskets outside the back door and came back into the kitchen for the matches to dispose of them quickly. To this day, Lady Cybilia, I will never know who took one basket; I burned the other two baskets myself." When questioned no one new, and Flora said she felt uneasy for a long time since. Cybilia from then on kept busy with of all things learning to sew which kept her in a large room at the guesthouse.

She realized what he was all about, and she felt trapped. Every time she faced him at dinnertime breakfast or lunch, she felt ill at ease. Mark conversed with his father freely. However, her questions, Lord Thomas ignored.

Shara pointed at her father with a fork and said quite loudly, "Father, why are you ignoring mother's questions, you do not look her way as if you are blind in the right eye, and deaf in the right ear!"

Thomas dropped his fork, stood up and glared at Shara, "How dare you speak to me with such mannerism, I shall not tolerate insults and disrespect from you or anyone else, now go! Leave...now!"

Mark came to Shara's defense. "Father, you know Shara...she means nothing by it...she speaks before she thinks." Mark spread a big smile on his face. Shara insulted, glared at Mark.

"And you think you are so wise, huh, Father does not hear how you talk!" Shara stood up and walked away from the table.

"And what did she mean by that, Mark? Perhaps you would explain." Lord Thomas glared. Mark's eyes were on the plate, did not reply.

"My family is in turmoil! What is happening here?" Cybilia shouted, she pushed her chair back from the table it scraped loudly, she jumped up and disappeared into her bedroom, there she began to pace and think; *what to do now...and where to go?" I have no one to talk to, and no one to trust. I wish I could visit Kathryn and Kosta, seek their advice, if not that, just to talk with them would help me. Relieve my stress. Nevertheless, that is out of the question, impossibility.*

Frequently, very frequently whenever she was alone in her bedroom she felt the presence of her mother's spirit. Her peripheral vision caught a faintly glowing silvery sort of mist flowing across the room. Perhaps that was a sign to beware of him, her husband. Perhaps her mother tried to tell her, *the cruelty committed against Kosta was his brother Thomas.* When did Cybilia come to realize all this...the instant recollection of certain things, which happened..., now clear in her mind. Suddenly she felt chilled to the bone.

"What drove him to it? Evil heart; he has an evil heart. How blind I was then, I had two children with him, oh God! Will they become like him also?" she whispered and began to pray. She paced that evening in her bedroom very distraught. Suddenly heard footsteps, her emotions chilled. Standing in one place, someone knocked, she waited; who will enter her bedroom. Thank Goodness, it was her son. Mark, not waiting for reply entered. Mark noticed his mother had a questioning look on her face.

"Mother, are you alright?" Mark asked.

"Mark, I am stressed, I questioned certain things; discovered things going on here, but, I cannot explain to you at this moment," she said.

"Mother, it will all work out well, you will see. But I do have a question of importance to ask you," he assured her.

"What is so important that you must know, Mark?"

"Mother, do you remember that morning when Joseph went away? Well, he came into my bedroom and said that he left something for me with James. I asked James, but he claims he does not remember anything from Joseph for me. Could you find out, please, it is haunting me. I need to know what it is." Cybilia hesitated, after a moment, she stammered, "Son, of course I will ask James, I am sure he will remember, the moment I will ask him." Cybilia patted his shoulder.

"Thank you, Mother I appreciate it." Mark walked out. Cybilia was just about to go out and look for James, there came, another tap on the door, thinking it is Mark again. She opened it and faced her husband. She lost her voice, looked startled. Lord Thomas smirked at her, entered not waiting for her to invite him in, glanced around, sat on the bed and motioned for her to come and sit beside him. Not wanting to cause any suspicion, she sat next to him. Lord Thomas sat looking at her but not speaking, suddenly he wrapped his arms around her and pulled her to him, Cybilia forced to fall backward and Lord Thomas lay on top of her, kissing her. She struggled to free herself, but his weight pinned her down and he said in a low voice.

"Why you are avoiding me, you are planning something...conniving excuses? Stupid reasons of not joining me in conversations or outings..."

"Now you wait a minute, When I ask you a question, you pretend you do not hear me, you are avoiding me!" Cybilia shouted into his face.

Lord Thomas stared at her.

"Well you never come to the distillery. It is your business; after all, you are the sole heir, you should have interest in it. I have information from a trusted source of what has been going on. By the way; I must tell you; I engaged legal counsel; by which, I shall benefit much..."

"What are you talking about, what information, who is the trusted source?" Cybilia exploded with fury.

"Aha! Pretending you know nothing! How long has it been? Ha, too long, and as you know I have my rights as a husband. Are you rejecting me because I am a bit overweight and perhaps indulge excessively? Are you feeling repulsion towards me? Well, I will have you by force if I have to, you are my wife and you must and shall submit, or, I shall accuse you of adultery and you shall stand trial," Thomas wheezed sarcastically.

"Thomas, have you gone insane? I have never been unfaithful to you!" she stammered, her breath short and shallow, feeling faint. Horror seized her. She had no choice. To scream would be useless. No matter what else she would say, he would fulfill his desire, and so he had done just that.

Cybilia infuriated to the point of hate and repulsion at that moment, provoked, she was on impulse ready to commit murder. Unfortunately, she had not the strength to compete. When her husband left her bedroom, she fell into her pillow and cried bitter tears. Still infuriated sat on the bed wide-eyed knowing what had to be done. Quickly went to bathe. She then dressed, went in search of James. She found him in the kitchen with a cup of tea in his hand.

"What is this 'something' that you have for my son from Joseph?" she asked rather harshly. James for a moment stiffened.

"Lady Cybilia, forgive me I completely forgot. I will bring it, if my Lady would not mind waiting for a moment. I apologize. Ever since Joseph left...I forgot, having so much work to do," James nervously replied, ran off to his room. After a while, he came back and handed Lady Cybilia a small rolled-up burlap cloth tied with twine.

"Why did you withhold this...this rolled-up cloth from Mark?" she asked angrily.

"My Lady, forgive me... but, ever since Joseph disappeared...,my mind has been preoccupied..., it simply slipped my mind and I forgot." James repeated again shrugging his shoulders. Cybilia still angry with her husband, unable to calm down, insisted, "Mark had asked you several times for whatever Joseph left for him and you denied having anything for him?"

James mumbled repeated apologies to Lady Cybilia. At last, she excused him, warning him not to ever do it again, as she left the kitchen. James agitated and nervous, quickly shoved trembling hands into his pockets, forced to drop into a chair and relax a bit. He wondered, what was in that package? Will it reveal what happened that night? As to Joseph, when he went away that morning, no one ever heard from him, or his brother. Strange, no one inquired about Joseph. No, from the day he had left no one at the estate ever mentioned a word concerning Joseph. However, James had a feeling who knew.

Perhaps he should go far away like Joseph. To a place where Lord Thomas would never find him, perhaps he should go and inquire Joseph's brother or neighbors and from there decide. James planned his getaway, waiting for the moment when his master is away for several weeks, as others have done before. His plan of escape came to life known only to him.

Cybilia was curious, what was in this rolled-up burlap from Joseph for her son. She should not peek, for now, she will forego her desire to know, besides, she will find out later, one way or another. She knew what sort of relationship her son Mark and Joseph had. Those times she watched them as they went fishing, she saw a bond of grandfather and grandson, of that she was sure.

Twenty-Six: Mark and Sabrina (Shara)

Cybilia found Mark at the stables and handed him the burlap cloth. She was proud of her son. She could not believe that he was nearly eighteen, she felt older because of him. *"Nonsense,"* she thought, *"that is the way of life, and that is why we have children, they are the continuance of our existence, and God forbid for my son to become like his father."* Mark took the burlap cloth.

"Mother, if you do not mind, I need to go for a ride," Mark said, kissing his mother's cheek.

"Of course I do not mind, be careful." She handed to him a blanket, which, he always used when going riding. Cybilia watched as he swung his leg over, mounted bareback, and rode off.

Mark for a moment felt the rhythm, the speed, the breeze against his face. He truly felt connected to nature out in the open fields, the vastness of the land, he leaned forward low, keeping his left arm on the horse's neck, and right hand held the reins. Being this close to his beloved animal thrilled him, eyes closed, his nostrils inhaling the moist scent, he felt the surge of power in his beloved steed. He headed straight for his secret oak, in his pocket burlap wrap held a secret. Across his legs a blanket.

Beneath the giant oak tree with its sprawling branches low to the ground, the thick shade of it was so comforting and secure, and the soft breeze so welcoming, it embraced anyone who cared to relax in need of seclusion beneath its canopy. Mark loosely threw reins over a low tree limb; spread the blanket on the grass stretched out comfortably on it, beneath the huge oak. He closed his eyes, relaxing. Then reached into his pocket for the burlap roll, untied it, and unwrapped it, inside was a small piece of white cloth folded with the corners towards the center. He unfolded the white cloth, one corner marked with a black dot, one red and two circled with black ink; on the white square cloth, attached a triangle piece of black cloth; and, on top of the black, a triangle of red cloth. On each corner yellow dots, in the center of it were two large yellow dots, one yellow dot crossed off... Mark stared at these two pieces of cloth and could not imagine what they signified, why would Joseph the loyal old servant leave to him a mystery of three pieces of cloth.

Besides, he believed that this was valid; otherwise, Joseph would not let it be a secret. Joseph although a stranger, an employee of many years, became like a grandfather, and they bonded a strong relationship from the day Mark began to walk. Together Joseph and Mark did so many fun things. They went fishing, horseback riding. They went to the market together. Joseph taught Mark how to do so many things, which his own father never took the time.

Mark sprawled on the blanket, smelled the cool grass, closed his eyes and let his mind drift back to the times with Joseph.

"Why did he leave these three small pieces of cloth for me, what do they signify? How will I ever solve this puzzle?" he thought.

Mark laid there for a long time, until he felt the dampness creep into his bones. It was time to return. Riding home, he made a promise to Joseph and to himself that he will solve this mystery, no one will know, especially his mother.

"How do I tell mother that it is a small "significant" Joseph's rusty fishing hook with which a long time ago I caught a big fish. Yes, that is exactly what I have to tell her and show her the hook, first I must find one, let me see, where are they? Also I must never change my story, or she will get suspicious, mother is like that," Mark was thinking. On the way home, he decided to stash the rolled up cloths in the horse's stall.

From that day on Marks mind was completely preoccupied with unraveling the mystery. What puzzled him the most the two dots in the center of the red cloth, one crossed off. Someone told him red color meant love, white is purity, but the black ink dot bothered him the most. Mark's emotions and expressions checked well, much like his father, always smiled, when he recalled those days when Shara was seven and so spoiled, she was at that time a little brat. His sister Shara was four years younger, now fourteen, still very gullible. When she was seven the servants told her scary tales, to see her frightened face with eyes as big as owls to them it was funny, the poor child developed fears and phobias. When Mark and Joseph planned a fishing outing, Shara insisted on going with them, but Mark always ordered her to stay home. Shara would telltale on him, just to get mothers pity and attention. Having a vivid imagination, many a time followed and annoyed the servants with questions.

She stayed up nights fearing the creatures from the stories, believing they will snatch her out of bed while she slept.

Mark to avoid his sister ran to his secret place. Mother always calmed Shara with hugs and kisses, milk and cookies. Shara insisted for the youngest servant girl to sleep in bed with her. It was an unnerving nightmare not only for Shara, but for everyone in the house as well. When Lord Thomas and Cybilia had just about enough, all the servants, cooks, gardeners, grooms, those coming to work for one day going home in the evening they had been told not to tell Shara scary tales.

At the market, Mark had accompanied James that day. As the hours rolled on, James espied a canary and purchased it for Shara to keep her occupied. James took the chirping yellow bird in a fancy bamboo cage to Lady Cybilia; Mark followed him to her room.

"Well James I declare this is a nice gesture, Shara should love it, surely," Cybilia said. "Now James go find Shara and tell her to come see me, I have something for her." James found Shara in the kitchen talking with Nifta. James said, "Miss Shara, mother wants you right now." Sabrina wanting to know why and James had to tell her in a roundabout way. She ran up to her mother's room wondering what James was talking about, what surprise waited for her. Sabrina barged in without knocking, startling her mother. Seeing the chirping little yellow bird, Shara clapped her hands and smiled from ear to ear, she loved it. She named him *Sunflower*. Shara sat by the cage and watched it hop around and tweet.

Several months later, Shara left the window open but only half way hoping the canary learns to sing from the wild birds. That afternoon a storm passed through with gusting wind, since the cage sat on the table beside the bed; the draft toppled the canary's cage to the floor.

Shara sitting near her mother on the sofa remembered the open window; she jumped up and cried out, "Oh no!" and ran up into her bedroom, the cage lay on the floor. She screamed for her mother. Cybilia came running. The bird at the bottom of the cage lay still. Cybilia gently picked it up, wrapped it in a linen towel, and handed it to her heart broken daughter. Shara wailed. Cybilia tried to explain how fragile these birds are and told Shara to put the bird back in its birdcage.

"Will Sunflower live, Mother?" Shara asked.

"We will know in the morning my dear girl," her mother replied. Still spoiled Shara would not relent and continued to lament driving everyone into a state of frenzy.

Next morning Shara found Sunflower, her canary dead. She was sure that the goblins killed her bird, everyone objected to that silly notion, telling her it was the cold draft.

"No, the goblins killed my bird!" She held the dead bird in her hand all day long, stroking its feathers and crying. Lord Thomas had enough of her unruly behavior. On an impulse walked up to her jerked the dead bird out of her hand and threw it out the window, pulled Shara to a chair sat her down and said, "You...Shara need a spanking, but instead I will say this, if you do not stop all this nonsense, I will give you something to think about, one more sniffle...or tears...and you will feel the power of my hand, do you understand?" Shara sat stiffly; looking at her father teary eyed nodded and muttered, "I am sorry Father."

Next morning, at breakfast a big discussion erupted; the subject; Shara's behavior, of course, Mark was not at fault. Shara was causing this commotion. Mark listened, but realized that parents pointed their fingers in his direction! Why was he to blame? That is ridiculous; she is a spoiled brat that is all! Mark decided to talk with his sister, if she is scared now she will be frightened more after they talk.

"Shara, would you like to go for a walk and try to catch butterflies and pick flowers for mother?" Mark asked her.

Shara's face lit up; she was ready to go with her brother any time he asked. When they were far enough from home, he began talking about different creatures that live far away in deep woods. Shara immediately began to object to the subject she horribly despised. Mark kept talking, on and on not paying attention to her.

Shara at one point covered her ears and said she will run away if he did not stop.

"Well, why do you hesitate, just run off to the forest or just keep running until some demented person..."

"Mark what is demented?" Shara interrupted him.

"Demented means, crazy, or not normal," Mark said, "in many cases demented individuals hurt other people, preferably little children. One like that could kidnap you and keep you prisoner or murder you, which means you will never see us again, if you run off, that means you do not love us!" He trailed off into silence.

Shara contemplated, then with a questioned look on her face she asked, "Mark if I do run away then come back, where will you be?" Mark did not reply for a moment. She waited impatiently.

"That depends when you will return, if ever, by then I would have grown old, mother and father would be dead. And you would also be old and all alone." He pointed towards the dark woods.

"In those forests, live all kind of fierce animals, you think listening to scary stories is frightening, mind you, they are only stories, but if you wander into those forests and the animals find you, than my dear little sister is when you will be a big dinner to those wild things." Shara quickly grabbed his hand and held it tight.

"You will not leave me here alone are you Mark?

"Yes, I will leave you right now, if you continue to scream and create commotion in the house. Everyone is very upset, just because of some silly ghost stories you heard from the servants. Just remember this, the animals in those forests avoid people, live their own lives, but when hungry to survive they kill. They care less if you are a good girl or a screaming brat, if they are hungry they will eat you. The ghosts or goblins did not kill your bird. The cold draft killed it. Canaries are very delicate, sensitive to temperature changes. Day and night you babbled on and on about it, you refused to go to bed, you did not care for others feelings, just your own. Oh yes, I need to mention those vicious animals rarely leave a trace behind, not a shoe or piece of ribbon from your hair, not even one hair for someone to recognize that it belonged to you."

Shara said nothing for a long time, just held his hand tight.

"Mark I promise, I will be good now. Please take me home, I want to hug mother and father, and everyone in the house, and tell them I am sorry," she spoke meekly.

"We shall see, but do not break your promise, or you know what will happen to you," Mark said very sternly; down the narrow path, he led her home. She was then seven. Shara apologized to everyone for misbehaving. From that day on, Shara changed, at night, went to her bed and slid under the covers, but her fear remained within her, realizing the consequences for her behavior.

Twenty-Seven: The Ravens

Summer, beautiful summer was ending.

One day a group of children played around their favorite tree and noticed that it was dying. The children ran and told their parents. Many parents stood around it perplexed, wondering what is wrong with this tree.

"One evening, a long time ago I...I heard voices in this tree. I ran home scared to death, thinking the tree spoke to me," one man said.

"Ah, you had too much to drink and you imagined it all!" others said. Of course, the man insisted that it really was the truth.

"One evening I saw strange birds swooping around it....and I am telling the truth," a woman said. Were these villagers jesting, or really telling the truth?

"Perhaps the witches put a curse on it, who knows...years ago an older woman whom the villagers accused of witchery, she and her house hit by lightning burned to a heap of charcoal," a woman spoke in a low voice.

Those were the times when people believed in superstition, ghosts and sorcery, witches, potions and curses. When out of the marshes fog drifted forming strange shapes, they believed those were spirits; restless lost souls wandering on earth. They questioned everything as they whispered. Candles lit and prayers said for many hours to avert misfortunes, earnest prayers to the Almighty for protection for their families. The old tree stood divided, one-half dry, leafless, branches fell to the ground, the other half dense and green. Eventually the green half also stood bare and dry all was left of it was the short trunk.

Thereafter, no one paid any attention, preoccupied with daily work.

They flew in on a gloomy late afternoon. There were three.

Then five swooped over noisily, perched on the top branches.

Five more flew down and settled on the middle branches. In silence but alert hidden in the denseness of the huge oak tree, waiting. The one perched on the lowest branch was their leader.

These were the selected thirteen by the Council of the Elders in the invisible paradise. These were the thirteen chosen, committed to a lifetime assignment: observe, judge and bring justice.

The sun dipped over the mountains. The valley shrouded in darkness.

Mamut their leader said, “Good evening my Brothers!”

“Good evening our Leader!” in unison echoed a greeting.

“Good evening my Brothers, we meet again, all accounted for?”

“Yes, all here!” the reply came by all.

“What news do you have to share with us tonight?” the Leader Mamut asked.

Abimust Raven Number One said, “My Leader, I have traveled far and I have seen many problems. Frustrated people do not know how to solve many of them.”

Benoki Second Raven spoke, “I have learned that a Royal Princess is very ill, no one has found a cure. The king, King Osckarion Bantar ruler of Magda, a kingdom on the mountain, desperately is seeking someone to save his only daughter.”

Kotur the Eleventh Raven spoke, “In the Town of Roses, there is an enormous crisis, the water wells are low, soon to go dry. Suffering will follow.”

Denos Raven Number Three said, “One morning in a small village, feathers of many colors fell from the sky noiselessly. The people were frightened, but only one boy disobeyed and paid the consequence.”

Erissot Raven Number Four spoke, “Denos, do you recall the boys name and do you remember exactly what happened to him? The family was to seek a solution from the witch, what was her name, was it in...”

“Erissot let us discuss the current problems at this moment, if you do not mind,” Mamut their leader interrupted.

Erissot Raven Number Four spoke, “I do apologize, my leader. In the west village a woman’s leg is very ulcerated she needs help, soon.”

Fijuron Raven Number Five said, “I have heard from a source of an unfortunate accident during winter on the river, this tragedy, created suffering for two brothers; who are grown men now, and up to the present time the situation is getting... actuality it is getting out of hand. Something unfortunate will occur if nothing is done to correct this situation.”

Raven Gromu spoke, “Dear leader, my name is Gromu, I am young and I have little experience, this time I have nothing of importance at all to report. I request your consideration for me to be one of the brothers. Permit me to remain, to learn and observe. Surely I will not disappoint you in the future.”

"Aye, please do consider his age, why, he is just a fledgling out of the nest as you see, he does have stamina and eagerness given a chance, let him be one of us, I will take him under my wing and teach him what he needs to know, my leader," Insemir Raven Number Seven said.

"Let him learn and realize what goes on in the world," another spoke.

"As time goes on he will see how justice is done, and what it really means," another interjected in a low voice.

The Ravens cried out to the Leader Mamut, then silence, nothing stirred, as they perched on the branches, even the night creatures were silent. They waited.

"Very well, let him stay with us, over time he will learn, as it took time for all of us, after all we are older now, we do need young enthusiastic, energetic brothers to join us, he will stay," Mamut their Leader said.

Hatuii Raven Number Six said, "Have you heard? In an unfortunate marriage hate and jealousy is prevailing."

Insemir Raven number seven spoke in a melodious voice,

"My Leader, I have seen an old man living alone, very lonely, but well to do, he surely will die of loneliness if no one is willing to take care for him, we need to find a family that is loving and caring, their reward will be great, to be sure."

Jemolai Raven number eight said, "Ah, mm...Mamut my dear Leader, I regret to announce that as you all know I am old...the time has come for me to retire to my resting place. I am overjoyed that a young Raven...ah...what is your name...?

"Gromu, my name is Gromu!" Young Gromu interjected.

Jemolai Raven number eight continued, "Ah yes...Gromu, has joined our brotherhood, and is willing to continue our work. I spent my whole life on discovering situations and finding solutions. For me it has been a great privilege and honor to be part of this group of Brothers. Therefore, I assign Gromu to take my place among you, my Brothers."

Leader Mamut sighed. His voice projected sadness, as he spoke they listened respectfully.

"Yes, I truly regret that our brother is indeed retiring, we will truly and sincerely miss him, but as we all know such is life, we do what we are capable of achieving, which is sometimes very difficult, but nevertheless, we must go on till the end, that is our destiny. Tonight we will have our discussions, consider all reasonable solutions. Find the one and only individual who with great dedication will venture out to solve these problems, forsaking his family, sacrificing all he possessed for the betterment of those who suffer. The only one who is willing and believing in faith and love, charity and compassion, and is pure of heart. We must get our rest, now, and at dawn, we will bid our brother Jemolai farewell, then we will fly away in search of more problems, we will meet again to discuss solutions. We are aware of our natural sense of instinct. We have inner clocks for time and inner sense of direction from time immemorial. We know when to meet again. Continue my brothers, Krugg do you have any news... speak I am listening."

Krugg cleared his throat and said, "My leader at this time I have nothing to report."

Mamut to that said," Very well, perhaps next time we meet you will have something of interest to tell us, continue, who is next?"

Kirree Raven number nine spoke up,

"My brothers, I have observed, one of the two brothers in a village has been abused and deprived of sight in one eye, by a cruel deed. This individual sacrificed his sight for his starving family. A brave man, a loving father and husband, I say it takes great courage, very few are as brave. This evil deed is to be without a doubt justly punished. No one should be so cruel to one another, especially to a brother."

All the ravens began chattering at the same time.

"How cruel...outrages! Unthinkable!" Someone cried out.

"He is an individual without a heart for sure!" Another vocalized with a screech.

"Where did this happen?" one of them questioned.

"Who is this person?" another asked.

"What a shame!" another cried from a top branch.

"Does anyone know who he is?" one of the older ravens asked.

"Tell us where does he live?" a pleasant voice questioned.

"I am outraged! Has he many children?" concerned spoke one more.

"Heaven's sake, what has he done to deserve this!" retorted still another.

"What a terrible crime! Such evil must be punished!" sadly, spoke the old one.

"What direction is that village? We will go get him now!" Cried out to be heard the young one, Gromu.

The Leader Mamut raised his voice, "Brothers, brothers quiet please, you are too loud it is midnight, control yourselves! SILENCE you are Ravens, not hens in a coop!"

They all quieted down, only the rustling of the feathers were heard, the frogs began their evening serenade, the crickets chirped, and the owls hooted somewhere in the forest.

Lornven Raven number twelve, asked the leader, “Our Leader, how soon will we have solutions to all of these situations...?”

“Excuse me...when is our next meeting and where?” Young Gromu interjected.

“Yes, yes please tell us!” another said.

They were shouting again in unison.

Mamut shouted, “SILENCE!”

After a moment, Mamut the Leader cleared his throat and spoke in a hushed voice, “We have gathered here tonight to tell each other of all the problems, situations which had occurred, we will not have solutions for these and other problems until we meet again, I will travel far, I will have a meeting with the Council of the Elders, they will instruct me. To the question put before me by the young one, have you already forgotten, that we have from the beginning of time, an inner clock that directs us exactly where to go, and when we shall meet, so for now let us meditate and rest, goodnight my brothers, goodnight.”

“Goodnight our Leader!” they all replied in unison.

Silent was the night, only a single chirp or a hoot echoed now and then somewhere in the distance.

What solutions could they possibly come up with these Ravens? They were big black birds, one would ask; yet they had the power of speech, emotions, and pity. They also understood human emotions as well, their anger, hate, violence, cheating, cruelty, even love... why were they so concerned about human problems, what power, instinct, directed them to undertake such a remarkable task, which takes years to solve. To them solving these situations were difficult, time mattered. They were dedicated to work long and hard for necessary justice to prevail. After all, they were the thirteen chosen Spirits.

When at dawn the warm sun lit up the sky, the chill of the night dissipated. The rising sun brightened a new day. The Ravens one by one awoke greeting each other. They noticed that their Leader was not among them. They began to mutter not understanding the reason for his absence. Suddenly Mamut flew in perching on a branch, they greeted him warmly, but they had questions.

“Where have you flown off to, our leader and when?” the higher ranked Raven Lornven asked.

“Well, I flew away long before dawn, all of you were snoring, ha, ha, just a short distance to someone with a problem, to check if things had improved. You are aware of the brother disfigured by one of his own, as you recall we talked about him last night. He has been deeply depressed. Presently, I must say, his confidence somewhat has improved."

"What of the other?" one of them asked.

"Were we really snoring?" Jemolai asked.

"His future is uncertain." Ignoring Jemolai, Mamut said, "Now we must be off to soar our separate ways, farewell till we meet again."

Mamut their leader Raven Number Thirteen flew away.

One by one flew away in different directions. The mystery of it all shall remain a mystery. As the years move on, lives change, feelings change. As time moves on *nothing* is ever the same.

Jemolai the old one, his time as a Raven was over. Jemolai the Chosen Spirit must retire to the invisible paradise unseen by the human eye. One Raven remained perched on an old tree limb, seemingly asleep, far from the oak tree on which the Ravens had their last meeting. He could no longer fly away with his Brothers the Ravens, several days he sat motionless; then one morning was gone. Upon the return of the Ravens, he will be no longer a Raven Brother, but a memory. His feathers shall be scattered into the four winds. His bones shall turn to ashes to be as one with mother earth as she gathers all ashes.

Time moves on.

Twenty-Eight: The Murder

On the outskirts of these dark forests things happened.

At one time, a house and a small barn stood atop a high mountain on a large piece of cleared land. The only occupants of this house were Sean and his sister Marysa.

The story goes that, Sean was extremely jealous of Marysa, she was a beautiful young woman. Young men from the village called on her, but her brother Sean turned them away. She became a prisoner in her own home. He claimed none of these young men were good enough for her.

"I will keep my promise I made to Mother before she died, that I will take care of you," he said and he was doing just that.

While Marysa gathered flowers and berries in the woods down in the valley, one day a handsome young man rode by on a horse, and many times thereafter. The young man's name was Christian; whenever Christian rode down that trail and Marysa was near he halted jumped off his horse and they talked. As Fate has it, they fell in love. From then on, they met secretly in the woods at the same spot where they met the first time. She always told her brother Sean she was going to search for berries. At least Sean did not deny her that pleasure. She returned with a full basket of berries or mushrooms, one day she held an apron full of gooseberries, her brother's favorite. Her brother Sean never thought or suspected that a man could be waiting in the woods for his sister.

Then, one afternoon Sean on horseback came upon a shocking scene, Marysa sat beneath a huge tree embraced by a young man.

Sean did not react, slowly turned the horse around and returned to the house. He removed the saddle then walked his horse to the fenced small pasture hung the saddle up on a peg went inside the house and waited. When Marysa came home, he did not mention seeing her with her lover. This went on for many summers. Sean observed, blind with jealousy. Marysa disobeyed. He was to choose a husband for her, but she found one herself. *Who was he*? Sean knew nothing of him. Sean's wish was to find a girl to love, and be cared for in return too, unfortunately; none of the girls liked him. Sean's appearance repulsed the girls. He was frustrated and raging to see Marysa and her lover together. Even though they were only talking. When she returned home one day, with a full basket of berries and flowers, he confronted her then about the man. Out of fear, she denied it all at first, but when he told her he had spied on them for a long time, under that huge tree in an embrace, she began to cry, "Please, I love him and want to marry him...he is the man I love." Sean enraged struck her several times across the face.

"No! You are not going to marry the one you desire, you will marry the man I choose, me alone! What is his name?" he yelled, struck her face again.

"Never will I tell you his name, if you are going to treat me this way!" Marysa through tears screamed. Sean stopped. Her mouth and nose bled. The blood dripped onto her blouse, her hair disheveled by his grip. Sean spent of anger, dropped into the chair and propped his chin on his fists, stared into space.

"Why do you hit me? I am your only sister. I would never stand in your way if you loved someone," Marysa spoke softly to him, "I will run away if you continue to beat me. You cannot control me...I am a grown woman... Mother will curse you from her grave."

"Mother and Father are dead. I am not afraid of them... they cannot hurt me, and I will do with you what I want! End of conversation!" Sean shouted back.

He could not let her abandon him, not ever. He was so angry he did not speak to her for days.

Marysa kept to herself in her bedroom, she began to write about Sean's cruelty, being very cautious. Started at every noise, fear shook her, quickly hid the diary under the pillow lay down pretending to be asleep. When all seemed to be quiet she resumed her writing. She had to find a way to get it out of the house secretly. She thought of bringing a basket of berries to the elderly woman, at the foot of the hill, a short distance, but a rough descending trail Marysa had visited her quite often with mother. Perhaps, just perhaps Sean allows her a short visit. After all, that woman was their parent's friend. One day she asked Sean if he would like to go with her to visit old Lody, he told her, "I never liked that old bitch, she gave me goose bumps." Marysa asked if she could, he allowed her a short visit old Lody the elderly woman.

She stopped meeting Christian. Christian realized something had to have happened, it was not like her, all those times she met him without fail. Christian spied on a moonless night; the house in total darkness, all seemed quiet. From where he stood behind a tree from that distance he could see her moving about in the candle light. He ran from tree to tree than up to her window, tapped lightly once, Marysa walked up and opened it and whispered, "Go away quickly my brother will kill you and me if he catches you here, he said he would." Christain whispered, "Come away with me, he will not find you, we will go away from here, come to me, I love you."

"No Christian, not tonight, perhaps in a few days, I love you too," Marysa whispered and closed the window slowly so it would not make its raspy noise.

Christian's suspicion was correct so he came again, he observed, again she stood at the window, then a candle light flickered and Christian saw a man come at her waving his arm and screaming, she walked away from the window and the candle light must have been extinguished the window turned dark. Not knowing what took place inside backed away and disappeared into the darkness. Christian surmised him to be her brother. Marysa said just the two of them lived in that house. Her parents were dead. Christian believed she was in some danger. As many days as he waited, she never came, but at night, he spied, hiding in the woods. During the day, her brother allowed Marysa her outing, berry picking, but kept an eye on her from the top of the hill. Christian was heartbroken.

Sean spied for months to be sure she was alone, only then permitted her to roam the outskirts of the woods, but specifically told her, that she cannot venture into the woods farther than his line of vision from the hill and that she better be quick berry picking, or he would beat her.

"Why not come with me, watch me, help me, you never do, you know," Marysa said with basket in hand walked out. She did not care as long as she could be out of her brother's sight. She found a patch of wild strawberries she sat on the ground and picked ripe ones without hurry. When she walked into the house, Sean waited with a whip in hand.

"Why were you gone so long, you disappeared from my view, did you meet someone out there?" He glared at her.

"I sat down—what...am I supposed to pick them standing up? You were watching me from the hill...it took longer that is all. Here, look, these were small, a full basket just for you!" she quickly replied.

He hung the whip back on the hook behind the door. She stared at it.

"Were you going to whip me for picking berries for you, Sean? You have lost your mind! Do not think that you will get away with such brutality! Someday you will be very sorry, remember! If you continue, the truth will be known sooner or later, and you will pay!"

Trembling from fear, she ran to her room and locked the door. Pacing the floor thinking, "*How to sneak my dairy out, now, the basket... no, not in the basket, Sean might inspect it...find it...and beat me, oh my Lord, I know what to do now! I must wrap the diary in a scarf, wrap it around my belly under my skirt, Sean will never see it.*" Her heart raced uncontrollably but she must carry out her plan before something terrible happens to her. Sean was not himself...his eyes large and glassy, as never before, as if possessed by a demon. Several days later, while she prepared breakfast she said, "Sean I would like to visit old Lody again, momma's friend, to cheer her up with some berries." After Sean thought about it, he said, "yes."

Marysa in her room tied the diary to her belly with a scarf, put on a full skirt, went to the kitchen to fill the basket with berries. Sean sat at the table deep in thought. She wrapped a shawl around her shoulders and started for the door. He jumped up and followed her out, in a loud voice he said, "Just you come right back, I know exactly the time it takes to walk over there, come home in an hour do you hear!"

"Yes, I hear. I do not own a time piece, but I will be back soon!" she shouted back. She walked at a slow pace then faster and when she was out of sight she ran, and ran, out of breath she ran down the path to the house and pounded on the front door, after a minute old Lody opened it. Marysa ran into the house and dropped down onto a kitchen chair, breathless. Old Lody surprised to see her out of breath asked.

"Marysa what happened, Marysa?"

"Ah, I ran, I am scared of my brother. He seems odd. Sick," she said out of breath.

"Marysa sit, relax, I just boiled tea have a cup, now tell me what is going on with him?" Old Lody shuffled over to the stove touched the stew pot it was cold. Old Lody added small kindling to the still glowing ambers in the stove; poked around a bit, and they burst into flame. She added small dry branches. It was not very long before the aroma reached their noses. In just few minutes, a bowl of stew sat before Marysa; and old Lody brought a bowl for herself.

"I only have few minutes, I must go back home soon, I must." She gulped down the tea and quickly ate the tasty stew. She took the bowl and spoon to the dishpan and quickly washed, dried them and put them on the shelf. She came back to the table took old Lody's hands and kissed them.

"Thank you for the tea and the stew, it was good as always. If ever my brother comes asking you if I came to see you, please say yes...tell him I was...and please...never tell him what I am about to give to you for safe keeping. Better still I would like to bring back a bowl of your stew, he might not come than." Old Lody agreed and filled a bowl with stew. Marysa lifted up her skirt, untied the scarf revealing a small diary and she said, "Put this in the basket and cover it with the doily. If anything happens to me, you must give it to the young man. His name is Christian, send for him. Promise you will send for him, you must give him the basket...promise!" Old Lody promised.

"Will you come again soon?" Old Lody asked.

"Yes. If I can I will, I promise!" Marysa replied.

Lody observed Marysa closely, noticing an old discolored bruise on her cheek.

She took the basket, promising Marysa she will call on Christian.

Marysa ran out, this was the last time elderly Lody ever saw her. She examined the diary wrapped in a cloth tied with a ribbon and the young man's name written on a piece of paper; *Christian, his house is white with green shutters and a white picket fence with many flowerbeds.* She covered the diary with the doily and sat the basket on top of the cabinet, then sat down at the table and tried to unravel the mysterious visit, the basket of berries and the diary.

Marysa came home on time, gave Sean the bowl of stew which he ate, but did not comment if he liked it or not, and all seemed fine. She went to bed before dusk and at once fell asleep. Next morning, she worked in the garden for hours, hungry and weary, sweaty the day was hot and humid. She washed up prepared a sandwich and ate it. She laid down for a short nap. Before she fell asleep, she wondered if Old Lody had given Christian the diary, was Christian reading it this moment.

Her brother Sean was sitting on the ground leaning against the huge oak tree far out at the end of the property, a rake and a shovel at his feet.

That afternoon he unlocked Marysa's room with a spare skeleton key, entered her bedroom quietly, approached the bed slowly, and stood very rigid staring as she slept. His arm jerked; as he raised it high, it trembled and with great force stabbed her over and, over, and over killing her. He stood breathing hard glaring at her bloody and still body on the bed in a pool of blood; Marysa with her lifeless eyes open, stared blankly at him. Sean stared back at her and his chest heaved a rasping quick breath. Wild eyed, trembling and weak in the knees. He wanted to scream but could not. He backed out of her bedroom still gripping the knife, dropped into the chair at the table and stared out the window in a stupor. His white linen shirt now red, face, arms splattered with blood. He stopped shivering. He came back to her bedroom with the knife still in hand; he looked at it long than placed it on her belly wrapped her body in the bloody bed sheet and coverings, dragged her across the overgrown lawn to the oak tree. He shoved her body into the deep grave. Sean went back to the house and rolled up the wool and straw mattress carried it to the grave where he threw it over his sisters' body and set it on fire. The mattress burned completely. Sean shoveled the dirt back into the grave and then leveled the dirt. It was finished. Sean did not worry about freshly dug up dirt. The grass will grow back when the rains come, better still throw some flower seeds here, the grass and flowers will look pretty, besides, no one will know any different. No one comes here at all.

The silence unnerved him; he stood in the doorway his eyes scanned the property and then fell on the dark spot beneath the oak tree. The birds stopped chirping; was it because of him, or approaching darkness? Sean feared darkness. The sun's rays of orange and red streaked across the sky as it dipped over the mountains. He looked up; right above him, red clouds moved towards the horizon, to him they appeared streaked with blood, Marysa's blood.

The whites of his eyes were red. He stared at the clouds, and suddenly realized up in heaven above someone knew he had committed an unforgiving crime, a premeditated act, which will haunt him until his death. This day's sunset will be everlasting, never fading from his mind, all the days of his life.

He tried to cry but his eyes were dry. Fear gripped him of the thought, "*what if that young man spied and will come to inquire about her. What about that, old woman, ah what is her name...she too will want to know Marysa's whereabouts.*" This was not a dream. This was reality. He needed a good alibi. Nothing made sense. Sean backed into the house and closed the door behind him, locking it, it was dark inside with trembling hands he found matches and lit the oil lamp. Extreme mental fatigue suddenly came over him. "*I must try to sleep,*" he thought, but sleep was long coming, he lay motionless, thinking, "*when will it come, I must sleep. I am hungry... I forgot to eat. Marysa she cooked something, I should look and eat a bit, or I will have a stomachache.*" However, Sean did not rise to check the pots on the stove. Instead, his attention turned to rustling noises outside, beneath his window. His body stiffened, muscles taught, with eyes closed he lay a long while. The noises stopped but Sean still listened then fell asleep. His sleep lethargic, disturbing, restless, hearing voices, was it *Marysa? No not Marysa... she is gone*. Sean said through his restless sleep.

During the following weeks, he slept a bit more, fear ebbed somewhat. No one came looking for Marysa. Still, Sean stuck to one definite alibi if anyone should ask: *Marysa is visiting their Aunt, not sure, when she will return. We never had an aunt, well... so what else, I say...good enough aunt it is, aunt...name I need a name. That is logical enough for her absence.*

One morning awakening to a house too quiet, *where was Marysa*? He jumped out of bed and ran into the kitchen, *Marysa! Marysa, where are you*...! Sean ran outside and his eyes fell on the oak tree, his feet riveted to the ground. Marysa is there, that flowerbed, her unmarked grave. It all came to him why he had to kill her. "Her lover was going to take her from me. Now, no one will have her, I took care of that," he said out-loud, visualizing them in an embrace, which made him rethink the reason of her absence.

"She eloped with her lover. That is what I will tell everyone, that makes much more sense, and that is why I cannot stay in this house, I must go find her. Yes! That is a great alibi. I will be in the clear of all suspicions...if anyone comes snooping, asking too many questions, like the village Chief," he talked to himself aloud.

Many evenings when the setting sun turned bloody red, his fear and guilt came back. He sat at the table and stared until total darkness crept in. He was frightened, what was the meaning of this? Sean fought off this guilt. Conscience bothered him though; his nerves pricked, made him jumpy.

He buried her beneath the old oak tree. No one would suspect to look there. What justified her murder? No one questioned him or dug deeper of her disappearance. At the market, he wandered aimlessly through the crowds. When a friend pulled his sleeve, Sean jerked away, about to run, recognizing his friend Reigben stopped. "Hey...Sean...why so jumpy...what is wrong!" Raigben laughed.

"Oh, I was just thinking you startled me just now," Sean stuttered.

"What have you been up to lately Sean, and how is Marysa?" Raigben asked.

"She is gone, I woke up one morning and she was gone. I have no idea where, perhaps off with her lover. I aim to find her," Sean said showing a firm expression.

At that, Regben was shocked, Marysa to do the unthinkable, never. What Marysa had a lover? Who was he?" Raigben asked observing Sean's face.

"She ran away with her lover. It is...I cannot stay in that house. I am responsible...I need to find her. I will find her...I will," Sean said.

Reigben thought, why is Sean acting so strange now?

"Well, see you around, Sean." Raigben walked away lost in the crowds.

The truth is, Marysa's spirit visited him, disturbed his sleep...well then, his alibi must change.

Unfortunately, Christian never heard of her disappearance. Heartbroken stopped spying her house. Avoided his friends, said he was too busy. Until one day, tending to his roses a boy ran by shouting, "Christian, Marysa is gone!" Christian was stunned. "What did he mean gone, to where? How dare he, that little imp, how does he know, and who urged this boy to say such a thing," Christian mumbled angrily. After several days, Christian decided to ride up to investigate. Reins tied to a tree branch left his horse at the foothills began to climb up the well-treated path then hid behind a huge tree he observed. He waited a long time, but there was no activity at all. He stepped cautiously up to the window of Marysa's bedroom; he cupped his hands, leaned his face to the windowpane, and looked inside. Her bed stripped of bedding to a bare wood frame. He decided to go inside the house since no one was there; he grasped the door's handle and pushed, not expecting it to be open. He scand the room no one was in, quickly ran into her room. In the dim light, he saw what made him cringe. That empty bed gave him chills and an eerie feeling. A feeling of something terrible had happened here, in this room. *Marysa, went away... but why*? He thought. Fearing of discovery by her brother, he slipped out of the house and ran into the woods, down the beaten path, mounted his horse and rode away. From that day on, he spied her brother; he was there; very early in the morning or evening; who moved about in and out, but no sign of Marysa. Sean never knew Christian watched him from afar.

Sean dreamt of Marysa, he remembered upon awakening. She cried out to him angrily. *"You...snuffed out my life before my time. I am doomed. My spirit will wander this earth for eternity. Know this Sean, I will haunt you, you denied me life! You robbed me of love, my life! I will haunt you! I will haunt you! Find you in every crevice you might think of hiding!"*

Several nights later he dreamt of his sister Marysa, again, awakened covered in perspiration: *"Sean—Sean...you can hide from the law, but you...you cannot hide from me...you killed me! I will crawl into your brain...torment you with horrific scenarios...!"*

Sean truly feared sleep after these dreams and her words. He felt prickles run up and down his body. He knew she would. "Was I really dreaming? Was it real? No...it cannot be real it is only my imagination, that is all. Sean talked to himself, I must control myself, I do not believe in such things, ghosts and spirits, I will not dream of her again." Constantly talking just to hear his own voice; convince himself it was not true, but his sisters' words rang loud in his mind. When sleep closed his eyes, she appeared bloody, she yelled at him.

"Sean...hell is awaiting you! I will make you mad...you will not know if it is day or night! You will be shunned by people...thinking you are mad! You will never find love! I curse you! My curse will last your lifetime! Someone is watching you. I will tell the truth, you will not escape. Deaths eye is upon you, following you...and you will suffer much before you die...alone...forgotten. The same way you dumped my body in that hole under that oak tree, my body lies there, no one knows of this crime, my blood is on your hands. Look at your hands Sean! I will rest when they find my remains...Sean you are doomed! Justice will be mine."

Startled out of that dream, it was dawn, he jumped out of bed, trembling, looked at his hands, blood! He screamed. The expression on her face lingered...horrified him.

"I must go far away from here."

Raigben told his friends, "*Sean is jumpy, not himself, and his eyes were strange.*" Rumors began to spread through the village, about the brother and sister, up on the mountain. Raigben and his friends visited the Village Chief Pargoone, Raigben said, "Sean's story did not make sense."

Raigben, and Chief Pargoone rode up to inspect the house, Sean at that moment sat beneath the oak tree, for a split second he was about to run, but he closed his eyes pretending to doze. He sat still. Raigben called his mane and waved to him. Without hurry, Sean stood up, brushed off his pants and came into the house. The inspector explained why the unexpected visit. All seemed to be in order but, Marysa's bedroom, empty.

“Sean, did you whitewash Marysa’s bedroom recently?” Chief Pargoone asked.

“Uh, yes, aha recently yes,” Sean stuttered. Chief Pargoone eyed Sean closely.

“Why did you whitewash her room and not yours?” he asked.

“Uh, I uh, wanted it to be clean and fresh when she returns,” Sean stuttered. However, without evidence of blood Sean was not guilty of any sort of crime, he was free. As soon as Chief Pargoone and Raigben disappeared down the hill; Sean knew what he must do; he was not crazy, far from it; he killed Marysa out jealousy; he wanted control over her; in his mind, he hoped she would never marry; stay with him and care for him only. Gathering his belongings, a sack full of food rolled all of it in a blanket and sat it inside the pantry. Fearing the hangman’s noose remained vigilant all night making sure no one came to seize him while he slept. He saddled his horse and slipped into the darkness of the woods and disappeared, never to return.

Early evening Christian watched the house, now abandoned. Christian entered the unlocked house, walked to her bedroom, empty, the bedroom whitewashed. Puzzled he walked home with a heavy heart. Christian stopped visiting; it was just too painful her not being there.

Struck by lightning on a stormy night the house burned to the ground. Over time, weeds and vines overgrew the foundation, but the old oak tree remained standing like a sentinel guarding the secret beneath its sprawling canopy. On the rectangular flowerbed, forget-me-not flowers grew, as if to say, “*I am here, do not forget about me.*”

Christian, after Marysa disappeared, began to have strange dreams, he heard Marysa’s voice, glimpsed a mist flow by. He justified these happenings to be just an illusion.

Illusion or not...in the back of his mind one thought persisted...her disappearance. Christian stayed awake sometimes until dawn. He began to inquire. Some said the man up on the mountain went away. Others said the house had burned to the ground from a lightning strike. Christian walked up the hill to see for himself, the house was gone.

Christian never received the diary. Old Lody did not send for Christian. She waited, for him to come to her. At the time, Marysa gave her the basket she was then up in age, and had forgotten her promise to Marysa. The basket sat on top of the cupboard. Old Lody lost her hearing close to a year of Marysa’s visit.

Christian never knew Old Lody kept Marysa's diary for him. Then one day her neighbor not seeing Old Lody outside as usuall went to check on her and found her dead. After her funeral, the house went up for sale. Christian for some unexplained reason purchased the neglected home, began to clear out the usual clutter. He reached for a dusty basket on top of the cupboard filled with dried flowers. He was about to fling it onto the trash pile but, as he stared at the doily, hesitated; it looked familiar, curiously removed the dry flowers and slowly pulled the doily out from the basket. As he did so, noticed something wrapped in a cloth tied with a ribbon, a diary. Thinking it belonged to this old women dared not read it. He placed the doily back into the basked and set it back on top of the cupboard.

While he laid in bed that evening thought of the basket and Marysa; he suddenly recalled when he met her that afternoon, she walked through the woods and sang a song. Her basket with the doily was the same as that one on the cupboard.

Rising early the next morning, saddled his horse and galloped to the empty house he had purchased; he reached for the basket with trembling hands. Untied the ribbon and unwrapped it, turned the cover, inside written on a piece of paper was his name. This was for him, belated. As he read, tears fell on every page he turned. Now he understood the reason of her disappearance. She wrote of all the cruelties her brother inflicted upon her. He lost her to a heartless, controlling brother. The law will judge, sentence and execute him. He must show this diary to the authorities. Christian grieved, but time heals. He concentrated on fixing up the little house, knowing that is what Marysa would have wanted him to do.

Christian up on the hill sat beneath the old oak tree, remembering moments of embracing her, those, were precious moments together. She was gone, now. If only those blue forget-me-not little flowers and that oak tree could speak.

Twenty-Nine: The Castle

One day a stranger on a horse rode through Riverside Village, as his eyes took in the serenity, mountains surrounding this valley and the village in itself, the upkeep and the people nodding a greeting as he rode along, he liked what he saw. As he came upon a crossroad, not knowing which way to turn, a boy with big soft brown eyes stared at him and asked, "Are you lost sir?"

This stranger smiled and replied, "I guess you might say I am, I am in search of land, and you seem to know just by looking at me, you do know where I should go, am I right?" The boy, his head down thought for a minute then said, "Go up that mountain, way up and you will find what you are looking for, sir." The boy nodded and walked away. The stranger followed the dirt road up to the top, and found a plot of land, just as the boy had said. He fell in love with the panoramic view. He walked the length and width of the level plot. The stranger stopped to admire the only thing there, a massive old oak tree. The gnarled limbs sprawled low to the ground seemed to shield something. This tree meant strength in itself, claimed a space, and withstood all elements. Strangely, it beckoned to come closer, an invitation to rest, and peaceful place to meditate beneath its canopy. Beneath its dense, shade a relief from the summers' heat is appreciated. Escape from daily stress and toil. Relax, enjoy tranquil moments to reminisce and dream. Known only to one, this oak tree shielded a secret. The barn which housed one horse, crumbled to the ground, where the house once stood left no trace but a few timbers chard and mossy indicating a foundation, now overgrown with wines and weeds, a few pines had grown tall over time.

The stranger sat on the grass beneath the canopy of this oak for many hours, intrigued by the panorama and listened to the wind song in the trees. At last, when hunger became unbearable, he decided to head down to the village, he needed more information on this particular site. The boy sat on the steps of his home and seemed to be waiting for this stranger, now they met again. The boy gave directions to the Mayor's office. The mayor recognized this stranger as a rich man in his manner and dress.

Given all information on the property in question, it was for sale, for back taxes, since the owner's whereabouts were unknown.

Mayor's wife prepared a fine meal, offered lodging at their home and care for his horse, hours of conversation with the Mayor, the stranger gave his name as "Baron" but days later on legal papers signed his name disclosed and known only to the Mayor. The sum of gold he had paid was well over the taxes owed, and the value of that property. At the time of purchasing the land, no one mentioned of the unsolved murder, which occurred some years past. Although her body never found, the truth remains known only to one, that huge oak tree.

This appealing place was the right place for the new owner to build a huge castle in which he planned to spend the rest of his life.

Baron had a dream, a vision of the structure like no other, he spent many years searching the world over and had seen much, therefore, spared no change on the architectural drawings and planning of every detail, and it had to be huge and elaborate. Baron hired local men to build a small cottage on the premises for him, also several other cottages for his crew. Barnes stables, for horses, and a building for supplies. Master architects arrived, bringing with them approved plans, after deliberating on certain particulars work began. A beehive of workers scurried to excavate the basement. Many men walked beside the laden wagons of huge beams tied with ropes. Many teams of horses struggled up the hill. Wagon after wagon with all sorts of supplies and lumber carried from not only this village but from far villages and towns, anywhere where good lumber was available for purchase. In addition tons of stone. Constructing the huge one of a kind structure would take time. Four buildings connecting at center hall, each wing with a fireplace, sofas, bookcases, paintings and wine cases. All bedrooms were on upper level, three wings for guests and a master suite for Master Baron. They tirelessly labored to complete this intricate castle, craftsman completing their part of work were replaced by others, as the massive stone walls rose higher and higher with four towers, each wing a staircase leading to the top tower, the square room opened to the top of the world. This tower stood taller above the others, with apertures to the four corners of the world. The day Barons castle stood complete, he slowly ascended the stairs men following behind him inspecting the scrolled wroth iron sconces secured on the walls. Heavy drapes hung in the openings for protection from take wind, heat or cold. The entire group stood taking in the breathtaking views. Then the interior work began, walls textured, murals painted by skilled artisans. Baron inquired about a carver, needing benches for the tower made on site, and hand sewn down cushions for the towers. The small round heavy tables stood near the benches. Sconces secured the lamps on walls, for safety from fire, in every hall. The enormity and rarity in its size alone attracted the villagers. In this peaceful valley apart from the world, a rare architecture, visible far across the valley from the mountain had the people in awe. People passing through the village talked about it to others.

When the structure was finished and interior complete; after which silence prevailed as if it never began. The villagers wondered what came next and when. Then one day the main road congested with rumbling wagons of which made villagers take interest. Women and children lined the fences gaping at these overfilled wagons heading to the castle on the mountain delivering interior furnishings and wall hangings for the rooms, seemed never ending. Many village young men and women employed for positions such as cooks, house cleaners, gardeners, carpenters for constructing small structures, a butler, even lumberjacks. Villagers delivering to the castle an assortment of goods from the market for their effort were generously paid. Baron traveled to large cities to purchase paintings of famous artists, one in particular was Rembrandt. All the dining room items such as table covers, sets of dishes, silver settings, crystals and all necessary kitchen supplies, plenty of pots and pans and utensils. Wall tapestries, silk fabrics and velvets, for the window drapes, and matching down quilts. Every bedroom decorated fashionably matching bedding, came from large cities. Returning after months of absence Barons carriage led the long caravan through the village carrying skilled professionals to do the endless work at the castle. When at last every bit completed, it was finished, done.

Baron walked around and admired his home; he has accomplished his dream of a lifetime. And he knew why he had such an empty feeling in his heart, he ascended the stairs to the top where the table and down pillows on the couch waited for him to sit and watch the sunset; but one important thing was missing, he longed for a loved one to sit next to him. That certain someone for whom he searched but had not found. Tears rolled down his cheeks, which he brushed aside. He sat long after the sun had sat alone.

One day, he rode down to the cross roads to find that boy. Baron knocked on the door, the door opened and a boy stood in the doorway.

“Young man, do you remember me? Baron asked.

"Yes I do, I see from here what a monster you built up there." The boy tipped his head towards the mountain.

"Well, hop on I will take you up, I need your approval," Baron said. The boy lifted up onto the horse, shouted, "Mother I am off to the castle!"

Baron heard a woman's reply from the interior of the house. "All right Seth, but be back soon."

"Yes I will mother," the boy shouted back.

As they climbed the mountain road Seth glanced left and right and up to the sky. The areas sparse of tall trees cleared a picturesque vista, which put a smile on his face. This his eyes had never took in before, his young eyes saw a new world far, far beyond mountains and horizon. Seth's mother, on crutches unable to walk, and he, still too young to climb never strayed so far from home, and be lost. Baron saw the awe on this boy's face and was glad to have him, show him a different world from this high up. The closer they climbed, the larger loomed the castle. At the gate, the courtyard and huge entry door Seth gaped. The extravagant interior, riches, elegance, Seth swallowed hard. His eyes darted here and there amazed. Simena welcomed the boy and said she will serve lunch shortly. At the long table the two of them sat. Baron asked, "What is your name?" The boy visibly stuffed the whole sandwich into his mouth, replied chewing, "My name is Seth."

Baron asked, "How old are you, Seth?"

The boy thought for a minute and said, "Sir...I will have to ask my mother, but I think I am old." Seth dropped his eyes and stared at the last sandwich on the plate, he was about to reach for it and eat it, but stopped, Seth looked at Baron and said, "Sir, I need to take...for my mother."

"Of course, Simena will make more for you to take home. Now remember, come anytime you want to, do you have a horse?" Baron asked.

"No Sir, I do not have one, fact is, we have very little of everything." Baron took Seth by the hand, lifted a basket filled with food, and went out to the carriage. In the carriage, they sat with the basket between them. Seth's eyes admired the plush interior, he said, "Sir, this is so soft and pretty, what sort of fabric is this?"

Baron smiled and said, "This is velvet, and yes, it is soft and warm and pretty, someday you might own a carriage as this one, when you grow up."

"Oh that would be grand Sir, my Mama would like it." The carriage rolled jerked and swayed on the uneven road down the hill, it took but a few minutes and they were on the level road. They stopped at the house, which stood on the crossroad. Baron opened the door and helped Seth down the step. With the basket in hand, Baron carried it to the door. Seth looked up at him and said, "Thank you Sir!"

Within several weeks, a man rode in on a horse, leading a white horse behind, came up to the boy who sat on the front steps of the small house.

"Is your name Seth?" the man asked.

"Yes," Seth replied.

"Well then, this horse is for you, from Master Baron up at the castle." Seth stood up slowly, walked up to the white horse, solid white but for a brown diamond patch between the ears. Seth looked up at the man and said, "Please wait just a minute," and ran into the house. A woman appeared in the doorway on crutches with Seth beside her. She was smiling. "*It is a good thing for Seth to have his own horse, God Bless whoever the benefactor is,*" she thought.

"Well, go and thank him, lead the mare to the stable," she said.

The man led the horse to the small stable with Seth beside him. Inside Seth tied the reins to the post. Seth's mother hobbled out through the back door on crutches she walked around the horse and smiled, "Oh my... it is a mare."

"Mother a mare?" Seth questioned.

"Yes it is a girl horse. Now be sure to thank the good man." Seth ran out the door shouting, "Thank you, thank you very much!" The man sat on the horse about to ride away. He heard Seth calling to him. He did not turn but rode on.

"Mother, what are we going to do with a girl horse?" Seth asked his mother as he walked back into the house.

"Oh, Seth, just you wait and see, wait and see," his mother replied, smiling.

Within an hour, a wagon full of horse feed rumbled in unloaded by two men and stacked it all inside the barn. The woman perplexed had never met him or heard of that man. A stranger with a good heart, but a simple message of thank you was enough to the benefactor.

Up at the castle, festivities began when wealthy guests arrived in buggies and carriages, or on horseback through the main street of the village, rattled on up the high mountain road, every several days or weeks from far parts of the country and presumably the world.

The nearby villages buzzed with talk of the "Baron" and his guests at the castle on the mountain. These guests lulled around and celebrated with food and drink. What did they celebrate, Barons success and fortune, of course. Couples with their arms around each other, glasses of wine in hand sat on benches beneath the huge oak tree, relaxed, enjoying tranquil evenings in conversation sipping imported wine, now and again the quiet of the evening resounded with laughter.

At last, after several months of merriment, three quarters of his guests departed. Those remaining guests enjoyed quiet hours in bedrooms or reading books. For most part, the castle stood in silence. The servants kept busy cleaning up and replacing everything back to order besides their daily duties. Those were the times Baron submerged himself in his deepest thoughts. Whenever his guests were in seclusion, he walked through each room evaluating all he has acquired and accomplished, enjoying all of his possessions and his good fortune. Hours spent in meditation in the west tower; encircled by the stillness of the forest he watched the sunsets, intrigued. At times, he shared these moments with some of his guests those who wished to sit quietly with him. Still deep within his heart emptiness lingered, missing that someone to share all his riches and comfort with, life would be doubly enjoyable. Those feelings he never shared or spoke of with anyone. When his guests retired for the night, he sat long into the late hour alone with his feelings, then retired to his huge bed. As weeks passed guests departed by twos and threes, graciously thankful for his hospitality, promising to return perhaps next summer. Therefore, he and his crew returned to normal daily living.

He loved beautiful gardens, flowerbeds and shrubs, but most of all he loved those *'forget me not'* those tiny flowers among all the others in the flowerbed. Those tiny flowers brought back memories of long ago, but that *was* long ago, still he felt that pain. He would rather not dwell on those memories but squelch them deep into his mind, try not to let the past surface, but think of the present.

He meant to ask his gardener why in the world he had scattered these tiny seeds in the flowerbed under the oak, especially if he himself loved order. On a fine morning, Baron seeing the gardener working the flowerbeds approached him and said.

"Good morning Kirk Spence." The gardener on his knees looked up.

"Ah! Good day to you Sir Baron."

"Tell me Kirk Spence, why are these tiny blue flowers scattered so?" Kirk Spence replied nonchalantly.

"Sir, they sprouted after I planted all the others, I believe they grew here long before you acquired this land, they are called 'forget-me-not."

"The previous owners had planted them here, you think?" Baron said thoughtfully.

"Sir Baron, now that might be a positive assumption," Kirk Spence replied and smiled.

Strolling in the early evenings always led him to the oak tree. He took pride in the results of his hard labor and all those who had a hand in it. Whenever he thought he heard singing, he dismissed it to be the wind, especially while he sat in the tower enchanted by the awesome sunset. After a time he enjoyed the singing of the wind, together with the sunset he felt inner peace. Baron never realized that that soft singing which seemed somewhere far belonged to Marysa's spirit. Her body lay in the grave literally at his feet whenever he sat on the bench beneath the huge oak, how could he have known?

However, in the early fall guests arrived. The weather had been still warm and evenings calm. When weather turned, it rained for weeks, intermittent by only few days of sunshine. Tough warm and pleasant, to enjoy walks through the gardens, was an impossibility, soggy, slushy grasses and puddles crossed the lanes. Days became dreary and cold, much to guests' dismay, felt sleepy, all stayed indoors. Then during the night they were aroused by strange disturbances, most of the guests ignored them, but others questioned Baron.

"Patrick have you heard, what in the world were those annoying noises last night?" a friend with grayish hair tied in a ponytail asked.

"I could not sleep a wink; I will be forced to take a nap. Please wake me for teatime," said a redheaded woman, who being a friend of a friend, came along for a good time.

"Patrick the other night I heard singing...seemed very far away, did you hear it too?" A slim attractive blonde woman wrapped her arm about his shoulder; she seemed a bit snobbish though. Baron, ignored her touch completely, but listened to what she had said. Surprised at such questions and comments, Baron replied.

"I have not heard anything out of the ordinary. What you heard could have been settling, after all it is a newly built structure. Besides, I live here. As to the singing, it could have been the wind. Surely, my servants if they had heard anything unusual would tell me, no, I regret to say, I am not aware of such absurdity going on. And you my dear, you need another glass of wine, it is chilly a bit and you need a wrap on your shoulders, you might just catch a cold in your bosom." Baron smiled and led the blond woman to the fireplace. Baron motioned to Butler Ridiller to bring a wrap for his guest. Butler Ridiller when in the kitchen, mentioned to the cook their Master Baron has a first name, Patrick. Still no one dared call him Baron Patrick. The disturbed spirit instead of singing began to frighten the occupants and guests.

Someone ran up and down the stairs. Bedroom doors opened and closed. After consuming large portions of dinner, drank bottles of wine all the guests should sleep soundly. Loud scream reverberated through the castle, startled guests out of sound sleep, frightened remained in bed until daylight. Constant tapping on bedroom walls and windows was just too much to endure. Sleepless nights wore their nerves thin. All the guests within a few days after a hearty breakfast, scurried out of the castle like mice from a trap, drove away never to return.

Baron was beside himself, he could not understand the sudden change in his beautiful castle. No one mentioned ghosts in their cabins during months of construction, and no ghost in Barons cabin either.

His comfortable, serene, tranquil home became a mad house. He sent Butler Ridiller to the village to question the people, but Butler Ridiller came back without a stitch of information. Baron became very unstable in his behavior and manner to his servants residing at the castle, or rudely spoke to the people at the market whenever out of necessity had to be there.

Butler Ridiller irate grumbled to himself, yet understood Master Baron's predicament, his responsibilities too important and pay doubly profitable, having calculated well, a long-term motive up his sleeve, had no desire to move out, winter was upon them. Baron completely shaken, realizing winter is near, any day it could snow. That means staying indoors. The days will be short and winters nights are the longest. Perhaps plan a trip to a warmer climate, then return in the spring, perhaps by then all will change. Baron could not believe his castle was haunted.

On those rare warmer days, he strolled through his gardens, admiring what was left of the design, but now the flowerbeds with the collage of color and overpowering fragrance were gone. This change actually helped him forget the unpleasant remarks of his guests and the disturbances of the ghost. He sent for his gardener Kirk Spence and together began to sketch the flowerbeds for spring planting. Corresponding with many friends inquiring information for exotic or rare plants having lasting blooms, if found to be sent to him in the springtime. Desperate for conversation invited his entire staff one by one to dine with him and asked questions about their lives. Then, he dined alone. After several hours of meditation in solitude, slipped under the warm covers for the night.

In his dreams, a misty spirit flowed through his room; her arm outstretched pointing at the window.

Mornings found him recalling those dreams wondering why this spirit is disturbing his sleep. To avoid that spirit he chose to read. The screaming and rapping on walls continued, disturbing his reading. The spirit came no matter when he chose to sleep. After weeks of such disruption, Baron exhausted fell into a deep dreamless sleep.

On occasion in his dreams the spirit of a young beautiful woman levitated over the bed, always pointing towards the window, her face streaked with tears.

Those mornings found him sitting on the sofa in the parlor, a large room with many chairs, tables and lamps, sipping coffee, quietly engrossed in the mystery of his many dreams. His castle was surely haunted, realizing that to fear her he no longer should. "*Who is this mysterious lost soul and why is she here—I need to find out,*" he whispered.

The annuals, planted in the spring around the massive tree still not transplanted. Gardener Kirk Spence ran short of time to move them into the greenhouse. Temperatures dropped during the night and an early blizzard surprised everyone one morning. Gardener Kirk Spence ran out to save his precious flowers, too late, all were lost. He walked away merely sighing. The winter had arrived with heavy snow, whistling wind rattling whatever was loose.

Baron stayed in his castle alone but for the servants and the ghost, warmed by the fireplace meditated or read books.

Many nights the ghost was destructive, books and objects fell off the shelves. In her ironic laughter, could be clearly detected pain and sorrow as it echoed through the castle, everyone heard it and everyone was on edge. The servants covered their ears, horrified. Baron pleaded on many occasions with this spirit to stop harassing him and his servants, out of anger he yelled at her, to his dismay it had no affect on her at all.

Yet Baron refused to vacate the castle, all his employees remained with him. Trying to solve this mysterious ghost's presence, who she was and why was she so angry. He needed answers, but none came forth, who is holding back the truth, the truth. All the villagers talked about Baron's inquiries. Yet they knew little of what happened there on that mountain, besides, that was several years ago and now, forgotten.

One man knew partly, but kept silent, the time will come everyone will know the truth. Who was this? Christian. Marysa's lover Christian read her diary suspected she was murdered. Come spring he will pay a visit to the Baron and tell him everything.

Down in the village everyone not only Kosta and Kathryn struggled. Homes buried in snow half way up the windows. Villagers tunneled through from house to barn and stables. The wet firewood smoldered and crackled, giving little heat; children huddled together to keep warm. However, for the adults never ending daily chores waited.

Tessana and Mathew always prepared breakfast for the whole family. Coffee was ready; at least this winter they had food.

The wind on some days howled and whistled swirling and whipping at the windows instantly obliterating the view. They feared of losing the roof. Branches, treetops snapped landing close to the house. Children sat quietly and listened wide-eyed. To keep warm they stayed in bed and slept a lot.

Time dragged. This winter the blizzard continued for weeks, paralyzing the whole country. Residents of Riverside Village had no other means of communication, other than walking on snowshoes made of boards tied with ropes to their boots. High drifts covered windows and blocked doors. To reach neighbors house, who would actually dare.

Several months had passed, weather should have changed, another month and it would be spring, but the freeze held. Looking out of the frosted windows, they could not see a living soul. The children questioned, "How could wild animals survive such severe winters? What do they eat?" Their dogs and cats kept in the barn. Kosta checked the food bins every day, to his surprise his family has consumed quite a lot, a bit too much. He suggested to Kathryn, "Cut back on the portions, staples are getting low. We should ration from now on; or surviving the months ahead will be tough."

Kathryn explained to the children what situation they are facing, all of them agreed to eat a bit less, they were such wonderful, understanding children. On some days, the sun peeked through the slow drifting clouds and for a moment, the snow-covered countryside sparkled like tiny diamonds, tough the promise of spring still far off. Then, as days become longer and temperatures rise melt the snow and water will rush down from the mountains, renewing people's energy and enthusiasm. As it is expected every spring slushy puddles, mud and flooding. Nature will awake the sleeping earth; long awaited rainbow of colors will burst forth, all budding trees and flowers would unfurl their unique shapes and petals and fill the air with fragrance.

Oh, the wonderful spring, for which the children waited counting the days. In the meantime, as weeks, dragged, parents told stories of long ago, some amusing, some depressing and then there were those that raised the hair on their necks.

Thirty: Fire

Kosta throughout the winter had plenty of time to teach his son the art of carving. The girls learned baking and cooking. Now they were readying for spring. Excitedly Kosta and Mathew together walked over to the barn and checked on their implements, so much to do before spring bursts into full bloom and then planting time.

They were a happy family despite Kosta's loss of his eye. He was thankful they all survived another heavy winter without any major crisis. He loved to watch Kathryn at work with the children. She was so gentle and kind with a heart of gold. His other concern somehow, adding one more room to enlarge their living area for his family, but how.

One late evening while he and Kathryn discussed the spring planting, a sudden strong windstorm moved in. This was disturbing. Kosta looked out the window, the trees bent low. The family sat at the table listened, waited for this windstorm to pass, but to their dismay, after a while it turned into rain mixed with snow, very unusual, must be the last winter storm rage of the season. The family listened to the whistling wind; at intervals, suddenly they heard distressed cries of their domastic animals.

Kosta held the lantern inside his cape protecting it from going out. The wind whipped at him from all directions as he walked backwards and forward towards the barn. He saw the barn door swing on hinges and bang into the frame. Kosta sat the lantern on the ground and as he struggled to secure the heavy door, just an inch away of throwing down the bar, an abrupt gust jerked the door and Kosta lost his footing still holding the ring of the door in his hand. The gust of wind, tipped the lantern over as it rolled into the barn bumped into a chopping stump and cracked, spilling oil, and the straw caught fire. Kosta ran up and tried to stamp it out, but it was no use. He ran, unbarred the huge door on the opposite side of the barn, ran to open the horse's stalls, opened the cattle gates, next the pigpen, yelling chasing all of them outside. The dog ran to the house barking fiercely, Kosta blinded by the thick smoke; unable to breath ran out. Draft causing red-hot sparks swirl through the interior; now both doors banged open and shut. Sparks landed everywhere igniting dry straw. The interior aflame, soon the whole barn will burst into a ball of fire, not knowing if all the animals escaped, he could do no more.

He staggered reached the step sat and leaned on the front door. Kathryn feeling that Kosta had been gone a bit too long threw a cape on and stepped out the back door. She saw the flames shooting in all directions. She ran into the house shouting.

"Mathew the barn is on fire come help!" They ran out, stared in horror, everything stored in the barn for spring planting consumed by flames. Frightened did not feel the cold wind whipping at her, she screamed, "Mathew, dress the children, be ready, if the wind shifts the house will catch fire!"

Mathew ran in and saw the children were dressed and wrapped in their capes.

"Get into the wagon and huddle together, cover with blankets, I will bring the pillows for you," Mathew said to them.

The neighbors came running, filled buckets of water but it was no use. The intensity of the heat kept them at bay, the mix of rain and snow had no impact on the flames. All they could do is to watch as it all burned to the ground. The wind suddenly turned, sparks began to fly at the house, but fortunately, the thatched roof did not ignite, as if only to frighten them, then the wind turned back the other way.

Kosta sat on the step, no one saw him it was too dark. When he rested and was able to breathe easy, the family realized he was not around, Kathryn screamed his name, ran around the burning barn, Arkushin with the other neighbors stood stupefied watched as it all turn to ashes.

Kosta rose slowly walked to the wagon to comfort his children. Mathew turned and saw his father, ran to him.

"Where have you been Father?" Mathew asked.

"Son, I sat on the step unable to speak when you and mother ran out." Kosta coughed. Kathryn frightened out of her skin ran to Arkushin distraught, but when she saw her son and husband, she ran past Arkushin and into Kosta's arms.

"Why us, have we not endured enough? Heaven help us! What are we to do now?" Kosta said holding her. Kathryn's tears flowed as she clung to him but did not reply. Mathew went chasing after the cows, came back and tied one to the fence, then went off looking for the others, the horses were somewhere in the fields, it was too dark to see. Other neighbors rushed to help.

The children scrambled out of the wagon and went home, Tessana made hot tea. Still wrapped in blankets, children sat on beds. Mathew concerned said to the neighbor.

"Please take mother inside. She will catch her death if she stays out any longer. She will not listen to me."

"Kathryn you must go inside, your children are worried about you, you must come inside, come!" the neighbor spoke firmly to her. Kathryn went indoors sat with her children shivering uncontrollably wrapped in a blanket, sipped hot tea. What a tragic night. The neighbors stood and watched the smoldering ruins, speechless and sorry for the family. They doused the charred rubble with water to prevent rekindling.

They too were aware this could happen to them as well, and leave them in the same situation. They went into the house, sat down drank hot tea to warm up. It stopped raining but the wind whistled and howled less intensely.

The hour was late, Arkushin said to Kosta, "There is nothing to do tonight, thank the Lord you are all alive, I will lead the animals into my barn. Kosta we will come in the morning to help you. Good night children, Kathryn get some rest." Kathryn helped the children into beds while Kosta remained sitting at the table alone.

"What now? There is no grain left for the fields, and nothing to gather in the fall! Dear God what am I going to do? My children, Kathryn, my family is going to suffer again," he began to sob, and his heart ripped with sorrow not for himself, only for his children and Kathryn. He did not hear Kathryn and the children come up to embrace him, they wept with him. He hugged each one, said he loved them and sent them back to bed. For them it was a sleepless night. Kosta and Kathryn their arms tight about each other, lay in the darkness not speaking. Kosta did not see Kathryn's tears. Reality hit him hard, and he clenched his teeth. His need to scream fierce, but his voice refused to come out of his chest. At first light he slipped out of bed, Kathryn was asleep, he dressed and went out to check the ruins, the horses found their way home, stood along the fence, raised their heads when he appeared, came to him nickering, freezing and hungry.

The dog curled by the door did not move, but shivered, Kosta picked him up and slipped him into the house, the pets were forgotten, cats were nowhere around, they perished in the fire. The fire consumed hay and straw, tools and all the farm implements, all gone! Despair gripped his chest tight, he could not breathe, and he gazed at the sky as if searching for a helping hand from above.

With daylight, the villagers were up busy with the morning chores. Kosta looked all around, neighbors had their barns, but he... he had lost it all.

The lamp, the wind blew the lamp over, spilling the oil, now he remembered. That is what happened, he was alone, tried to shut the barn door, why did it swing open? Perhaps the latch was loose. Mathew was with me last night. Could he have left it unlatched? It was no one's fault, his or Mathews. No matter, it is too late, it would have happened regardless who was the last one here last night. Now I must figure out a way to provide for my family.

Michael and Rabinna arrived when they heard what happened, carrying two huge baskets of all sorts of foods.

They talked and planned. First of all a shelter for the animals must be built, the weather still unpredictable, the neighbors came in offering suggestions and help. Kosta accepted whatever they could provide. At desperate times, they were a united people. Within several weeks, the lumber, which arrived from all other villages, and the men power that came along with it proved unity and unwavering friendship.

Over a short time, with the weather easing off a bit, as if Mother Nature gave them a break. The new barn stood solid and strong, if the weather had not improved, their effort would have been a slow process.

Besides having work of their own these villagers helped Kosta. He in return, offered to make whatever they need, be it a new chair, bed or table, at no charge, he will be forever in debt for all the help given his family.

Tools of all kinds brought to him by strangers from other villages. This was an unbelievably charitable community not only this village, other villages close by as well, he felt proud to be part of it.

He in gratitude gave to all one of his carvings. They loved the gesture indeed. Piglets and calves were brought over and a few chickens, and even several kittens, the children were delightfully happy with the kittens. The following day a girl brought a puppy. That solid black pup took to Mathew immediately his name, "*Midnight*."

The kittens each had names. Rosie named her grey kitten Sootie like the ashes. Tessana named her white kitten Dot, since she had a pink nose and a black spot on her forehead. Jason wanted a kitten too. The girls let him have the black kitten. Pirate, Jason liked that name.

"Who is willing to care for the little piglets?" Kathryn asked.

"I would, I will raise them, and they will be the largest of all in the area. May I Mother?" Mathew jumped at the chance.

"Very well, the piglets are Mathews," Kathryn said.

Several days later, two wagons with food for the horses and cows rolled in unloaded and drove away. Neither Kosta nor Kathryn knew from who had delivered all that food. Two weeks later, a wagon rolled in, a man and three children from Kathryn's village arrived. Mathew opened the door for them as they came in carrying a rabbit, chicken and a pair of geese. Kathryn greeted them with a big smile, "Oh my good Lord, how thoughtful of you Kola, please come in and sit down here. Mara, so nice to see you and Alba you have grown, my, look at Kila you are catching up to the girls!

Kathryn called her children into the parlor, they came and faced the visitors; she introduced her children, Mathew, Tessana, Marla, Jasemin, Rosaline, Kras, and Jason. Tessana, as always set the kettle on for tea. Kathryn reminisced a bit with her old friend from her younger years.

"You have fine children Kathryn," Kola said, "and Kosta, where is he by the way?"

"Kola, so do you, how is Lorena, is she well?" Kathryn asked.

"Kathryn, we lost Lorena last fall during harvest, her heart failed." Kola lowered his head hiding tears.

"Oh, I am so sorry, no one told us." Kathryn's chin quivered and tears rushed out of her eyes, but she held them back. Tessana brought a tray with freshly brewed tea and cakes for the children. The back door opened and Kosta walked in, Kathryn waved him over to greet their visitors. The two men gripped hands.

"Nice to see you Kola, how is everyone in your family?"

"Lorena, she died last fall. Her heart just gave out," Kola said.

"Kola whatever you need let us know we are here for you and your children."

"Thank you both, my children are very helpful, they are good souls," Kola said.

"Kathryn, are you ready with dinner, Kola stay eat with us."

"Yes it is. I have been waiting for you to come home," she said.

After the meal, Kola and the children drove home.

"Kras, Jasemin and Marla come you have a choice of pets," Kathryn said.

Kras took the rabbit, Floppy. Jasemin took a chicken, Chuba. and Marla a pair of geese. However, Marla now could not think of names for them, all the children chimed in with suggestions, but none seemed to be catchy. Marla went to sleep.

"I have names for my geese. I bet you will never guess," Marla said at breakfast next morning. All looked at her wide-eyed waiting.

“I have no idea, what are their names? Rosie asked.
Marla looked at them and said smiling, “Meg... and... Peg.”

Thirty-One: Lord Thomas - Waiting

News spread quickly about the complete loss of the barns Kosta and his family endured. Brother Thomas listened and wondered when Kosta will visit again. *"Perhaps I should be the one to visit my brother, see what he needs, but no...I will not, I will wait...here."*

Lord Thomas felt positive...and thought..., *he will come begging. His brood of kids eat everything in sight, so...come he will, strangers will help but not for too long. What should I demand of him this time, when he comes? He will surely agree to anything I ask, after all, does he have a choice.* He was endlessly preoccupied with ideas, imagining his brother on his knees begging for food. He smirked at the thought that Kosta will crawl and beg. He felt power, having complete control over all and everything. *What if he does not come to me, what if he manages on his own or with the help of his friends? That will not look good at all, people will talk, and my reputation will suffer...* Thomas was thinking as doubt infringed on his positive thoughts.

He enjoyed hearing praises from his pals on his generosity to someone who was in great need. However, one thing his pals were not aware of, it was his brother in need and his pals will not find out of the terrible deformity he inflicted on his own brother, they never will. Oh, that made Lord Thomas upset, he clenched his fists, his teeth grinding, almost having one of his fits of anger; "he must come only to me for help, no one else!" he said aloud and hit the armrest of the chair he sat on.

The servant just at that moment was passing by and saw the expression on Lord Thomas's face and heard his outcry, it did not surprise her at all. She and all the other servants were used to their master's fits.

Cybilia tiptoed around the house purposely avoiding him frequently, keeping busy. She dreaded to be in the same room, fearing her husband's anger and tantrums.

Cybilia, Shara and Mark together frequently saddled up their horses and went riding, just to be away from *Father* and his moods. The three of them enjoyed riding horses and picnicking under the huge tree. They also browsed all day long at the market, Shara and Mark stopped at every kiosk, asking questions and buying things for themselves and once in a while for “father” a trinket or a pair of slippers from other countries. Cybilia relaxed with her children being away from home. Forgetting there in that enormous house sat her husband of whom she terribly feared. She could not completely understand why but time will tell all.

With little responsibilities, some days spent lounging around playing games, or plainly lethargic, or pleasure of reading far-fetched fables. They never thought of anyone but their needs. Never asked how their uncle Kosta and his children fared, to them it seemed as if they never existed. They felt no hunger, or cold, they had it all. They never handled pitchforks or a shovel and never cleaned the stables. These self-centered spoiled people will never understand the connection between man and soil.

It never occurred to either of them what would happen if they suddenly became poor and ragged, if they had to beg for food and work from sunrise to sunset in the fields to make a living with their own hands, why...they would perish quickly.

As weeks went by Mark overheard the servants whisper about the misfortune happening to a large family. Mark questioned Flora and she told him what she had heard from others. Mark asked her if she knew who the family was and she told him in confidence, it is your uncle, your father’s brother. Their loss of everything they owned in a barn fire. Now, faced with not only lack of food but gone were all reserves for spring planting. The realization hit him hard and he began to dwell and feel different towards those much less fortunate. Mark at dinnertime remarked, “We are very fortunate to have good people to work the fields and all around our property for our benefit. I never realized before what comfort and ease we have each day, all done for *us*. But others do with so little.”

What Mark said irritated Lord Thomas, he understood very well what it was like to be poor but now he has no worries, except for one thing gnawing at his mind, and that is Kosta. Mark noticed father’s sudden sour facial expression and the way he bit his lower lip whenever Mark broached that subject, he was puzzled, but hesitated to dig deeper.

“That tragic fire happened to Uncle Kosta it had destroyed all crucial tools and implements. Now he must start all over, I feel sad for his family, it has been years since we have visited...them, or seen...I wonder how old all the children are...now..." Cybilia trailed off. Lord Thomas never carried any of their conversations further, as if he turned a deaf ear. One could not overlook how quickly and nervously he cut his meat and chewed, eyes darting from son to wife to daughter.

"I have been wondering how they are surviving, do they have enough to eat, those poor children... Mother, the weather is quite fair now, we as family, we should visit them, and... perhaps they are in need of food," Shara exclaimed.

Neither of the parents answered her questions. Cybilia dropped her head and did not look up at her daughter. Shara irritated and perplexed turned to Mark, but he also did not respond. Finally, Shara broke the silence.

"Well, I guess I will have James take me there. Since I cannot get any answers, seems as if suddenly everyone has gone deaf!" Shara's heart had softened from the time she heard of the fire at Uncle Kosta's. Besides that, she could throw a nasty tantrum, to get her own way. Lord Thomas stated with his fists on the edge of the table.

"Sabrina! (Shara her nick-name) If you try to go that far you will be sorry, first of all it is still too cold, and James has his obligations to ME," Lord Thomas said icily.

Shara asked a direct question of her father. "Father, you do not care what happens to your brother's family? Do you?"

That question flared up his anger like never before, upset at a very reasonable question asked by his daughter, one thing was clear, it hit a raw nerve.

Lord Thomas, stood up quickly, the chair crashed to the floor, his face contorted, glaring shouted, "No one else is more important than my family, no one! I worked hard and I am working hard for everything we have! They have to work for their own survival. Do you understand! If he really is in dire need, he will come to see ME... you will see...I am sure he will come begging from ME!" Realizing that his sudden outburst of temper not only disclosed his feelings but also the lie of working hard for what they had now, purely out of line, he excused himself and stormed out of the dining room.

Cybilia, Mark and Shara stared with mouths open. They sat for a while not speaking. Shara began to cry, she could not understand why her father would not help anyone else but himself.

Mark checked his anger, slowly stood up and walked away from the table. Shara and Cybilia sat in the dining room and whispered something; the house cleaner was unable to hear any of it.

Somewhere out in the orchard Lord Thomas walked briskly. Fists clenched, he needed to relax and take complete control of his mind, lost in the surroundings he walked farther and deeper into the orchard. When his nerves settled, he felt his shirt cling to him damp with perspiration.

He returned to the house, in his room changed into his nightshirt, before he went under the covers, he downed several glasses of wine, which as per instructions to his butler, the carafe was never empty. Having disturbing thoughts too irritated to sleep, he slipped out of bed and paced the floor in circles half the night, at dawn he dropped into bed and slept in his robe.

For Cybilia, Shara and Mark lives were becoming more and more somber and insecure.

Sometimes seasons pass quickly and others drag on seemingly never ending. However, these villagers were ready for spring's arrival. From old people to small children all waited for spring, except for one family. Empty bins meant spring sowing would never happen and summer meant living on charity, fish, and wild life or empty stomachs. Kosta contemplated many days and nights what to do. Thinking of Michael and Rabinna how much they have given in food and support, but they cannot feed them year after year. His brother Thomas came to mind, but Kosta rejected that thought, feeling that he will mock him and call him names as before. Kosta visualized his brother, that laughter irked him to no end, however, where else could he turn to...*I have nothing. He does not care for my carvings. He said so. I only need a sack of grain for one plot to carry us through. The vegetable gardens do not produce quickly enough, and if the harvest is rich, I will return what I borrowed, God I owe him..., I promised to return a portion every fall until I return all of it. Perhaps he will help us, again. He knows of my misfortune, is he that heartless, yet I know how cruel he could be. Kosta dwelled on that thought of asking for help, but deep down reluctant to do so...I should look for a job somewhere. Perhaps all this will turn around. I am a fool, I am hoping things will change, but hope is the mother of fools. I must find a way to earn money. I will not go to him, not just yet.* Kosta forestalled, withheld these plans and thoughts from Kathryn. His main concern, his children were hungry and he could not wait too long.

"Have you heard what is going on at the castle," Michael asked bringing food for the children.

"No, what is happening over there? Kosta asked.

"Our rich Baron is having a lot of trouble with of all things, a ghost. All of his guests packed up and left. That is what people are telling me, everyone is afraid the castle is haunted. Rumors are going around that he sees a ghost of a young woman in his dreams, and he goes crazy, every day he destroys a piece of furniture. The servants are prattling of this all over the village. Soon he will be out of furniture to sit on. Kosta perhaps you should go see him, you never know he might hire you, make furniture for him. That is something to think about, just do not hesitate too long before somebody else grabs it.

"Are you serious? All this is going on at the castle," asked Kosta, "you know Michael, I think I will go, perhaps he will give me that job. I will take some of my carvings to show him, I will be able to purchase grain, God! That is great news, thanks to you!" Kosta's face lit up and he grasped Michael's hand.

"Kathryn must hear this." They both went inside to tell her of a possible way to earn money. Kathryn listened, a smile appeared and a glimmer of hope in her eyes, to hear about a job at the castle.

"What a wonderful idea, thank you for telling us about him, we are so preoccupied with finding a solution to our problem never thought about anything else, you are truly a wonderful friend." Kathryn hugged Michael.

Thirty-Two:

Work at the Castle

The following morning Kosta was on his way to the castle, his only breakfast a cup of strong hot coffee and a slice of bread. He walked up the steep hill feeling nauseous that piece of bread did not sustain him for long; at last, he stood at the door of this massive structure. He raised the heavy knocker and brought it down several times, the noise echoed, Butler Ridiller opened the door. Kosta walked right in, Butler Ridiller noticed Kosta's pallid face and asked.

"Are you here to see the Baron?"

"Yes, I am here about a job," Kosta replied.

"A job, what sort of a job?" Butler Ridiller kept asking.

"I heard that he needs some furniture made, I am a carver and a furniture maker. Is it possible, or am I too late?" Kosta heard hammering echoing through the castle.

"Perhaps someone else has been hired for this job," Kosta said.

"Oh that pounding, the gardener is trying to adjust the kitchen door," explained Butler Ridiller.

They entered the large parlor, elegant but very few pieces of furniture stood around, they found Baron sitting on a small chair, Butler Ridiller whispered something in his ear. The Baron rose and came over to greet Kosta.

Baron was a very handsome man, and best of manner, pleasant voice, but in his eyes there lingered sadness. The two men looked at each other for a moment, Kosta taken aback a bit, *a rich Baron coming up to greet him.* They shook hands.

"Welcome, to my humble castle, what are you here for?" Baron asked politely yet in a very sophisticated manner.

"I am here to inquire, if you need..., I will come straight to the point forgive me but the news is going around that you need some new furniture made. I am a carver and a furniture maker I really need a job, my barn and everything I owned went up in flames, "Ah yes I heard," Baron interrupted.

"I have a family of seven children, and no means of support....

"Ah, yes and you have seven children," Baron interrupted.

"Yes we have seven wonderful children...here are few of my carvings, please inspect them. Also I have brought sketches of the pieces I have done, as for the quality, ask the villagers." Kosta handed the carvings to Baron. He stood having nothing else to say.

Baron looked at the sketches and inspected the small carvings carefully with great interest. Then he rang for the butler, told him to prepare a big brunch. Baron asked Kosta if he would like to see the lower part of his huge home; of course, Kosta said he would love to and so they walked through each of the rooms; Kosta impressed with such quality and elegance. At one moment, he pointed at a high back chair, many spindles, carved armrests, and said, "Sir Baron, I made this chair for you."

Baron stared at Kosta and after a moment, he rolled up the sketches and handled back to Kosta. Baron waved Kosta over to follow him into the dining room and suddenly exclaimed, "I thought your voice sounded familiar and face, but for the patch. What happened to you?

In the dining room, they sat across from each other munching on all sorts of tasty canapés sipping wine. Talked about many problems and gossip, but Baron being aware of all of it was not concerned at all.

"About the patch over the right eye... Kosta what happened?"

"Ah Sir Baron, I really would rather not talk about it, one day I will tell you, I give my word," Kosta said.

"Please forgive me, I had no right...but I must tell you; my castle is haunted. The presence of the ghost irritated my employees and my guests. There is a mystery about this ghost. I have seen her clearly in my dreams. She is a beautiful young woman, she weeps, points to that huge oak tree, no one knows why, I am not afraid of her, rather accustomed but not afraid. She seems to ask for something. I do not hear her voice, and I cannot read her lips, it is frustrating, and maddening. It is beyond my comprehension who and what it would take to release her spirit from this bondage, or a curse, and let her rest, but where is she buried? Who is she? This is a puzzle...which, I must one day solve in detail," Baron said.

"She must have died before her time. Otherwise her spirit would have been at rest," Kosta said as he looked around the room.

"I want to help her, but how? She will not leave me alone. I am somewhat used to her making all that racked around the castle, and if she ever stops, I will know she is at rest. She makes me and my employees infuriated, but I am the one throwing things around, I have never done that, ever. As to my furniture, oh well, my precious possessions they became little bits and pieces, and I threw them in the fireplace. I am confused, by this never believing in ghosts, until now. The strangest thing of all I look forward to fall asleep and seeing her in my dreams, never did I think I would." Baron stopped and looked at Kosta, after a while he said in a half whisper.

"Do you think this is absurd, to miss a ghost, if she is not in my dream, possible, or, am I a lunatic? She is brutal sometimes, I see it in her face, but it is understandable, her spirit is frustrated, being that her life cut so short. Do you know of anyone to solve my dilemma?" Baron asked.

"No Sir, you are not a lunatic, you are curious, I think that is all," Kosta replied.

It was very evident Baron had no one to talk to freely, the servants refused to hear his morning tales of nightmares. Kosta surprised to be here for the first time, one on one; and the Baron bent his ear. Before he left, Baron gripped Kosta's hand and said.

"The job is yours, come anytime. I will pay you well."

Kosta was elated but perplexed about Baron's situation. After many hours conversing with Baron, then having a big lunch Kosta walked home down the mountain with a big basket of food. Kathryn wept when she heard the story of the ghost and Baron.

"It really is an unfortunate situation over there. Poor man is in a madhouse. Thank goodness for all his servants, it is a miracle that they remain with him," Kathryn said. They discussed the job and he told her, "I will be away several days, but not very far, just imagine for each piece competed I will be paid." Kosta's energy and the will to work returned to do a job he loved.

At the castle his days were busy, but their nights, disturbed by the ghost. Kosta looked like a ghost himself each morning. Both, Baron and Kosta laughed at each other at breakfast. Kosta finished several pieces, received payment, returned home, and on market day, Kosta and Mathew were off to purchase necessary supplies.

Mathew and Kosta selected carvings to sell at the market, which sold. With that money, purchased much needed bail of hay and a sack of grain. Kosta went back to the castle and as he worked, noticed Baron seemed a little peeked. Perhaps it was the weather, the chilly days still lingered, people waited for spring, something changed in the regular order of the seasons, a cool spring shortens growth and ripening, which means bad harvest.

"Odd changes always brought hardships to us before. We must be prepared for whatever comes, as long as there is food on the table and no life lost," Kosta thought as he worked. Kathryn and

the children looked well with healthy nourishment. Each time Kosta came home, to check on the chores but Kathryn Mathew and the children helped, all was done, he was proud of them. At dinnertime, they sat and ate quickly and cleared the table of dishes and girls took turns washing and putting away all the dishes and utensils. Kathryn and Tessana prepared hot tea and sweet cakes and brought it to the table, Tessana poured tea for everyone then sat next to mother to listen as Kosta began telling the story about Baron and the ghost.

Kosta described the way the ghost slammed doors, opened windows, and screamed. he said he was afraid at first, but each time he had spend the night she just irritated everyone and no one could rest.

Then Rosie the youngest asked, "Father, do you think the ghost knows where you live, and will she come here and scare us?"

"Well, I do not believe she will come to disturb your sleep, my little one, come let me hug everyone of you, I miss you. Kosta outstretched his arms and they all fell in with laughter. Kathryn loved to see them happy. She loved him and her children without measure.

One quiet evening someone knocked, surprised Kathryn started and the children sat bugged-eyed.

"It is dark out there...maybe it is a ghost?" Kras whispered.

Kosta opened the door to see a handsome man standing with a lantern.

"Come in, extinguish the lantern and tell us who you are."

The young man stepped inside the kitchen, Kosta closed the door behind him.

"I apologize for my late visit, my name is Christian. I need to speak with you about the castle. I have questions if you could have a minute; I need to know; tell me what is happening there." That surprised Kosta, who was this individual, why all this interest in the castle.

They sat at the table, the children observed him from the sofa. Kathryn tried to listen but the girls whispered, as all girls do.

"I bought the old woman's house. I am sure you have heard about the brother and sister who lived in that house on the mountain. Christian began."

"Yes Christian, we heard the story but we never learned the details," Kosta said.

"I loved her. We planned to marry, we met in the woods one day, from then on, we secretly met and she told me how abusive her brother was, she left a dairy for me. Unfortunately, the woman died and I bought her house. I found the dairy in a basked and I read her dairy every day. She disappeared one day, and her brother also after a time. The house struck by lightning burned to the ground, only the old oak tree stands there. I used to walk the grounds wondering what really happened." Kosta nodded his head, feeling sorry for this young man.

"Love does strange things to people, we know," Kosta said to him.

"Yes, and I fear the worst, I feel it," Christian replied with a fist beat his chest, clearly emotional. Christian was about to leave he said, "Please tell the Baron I would like to come and talk with him, I have a feeling the brother is guilty of committing a crime, and I, or we, if you are willing to help me find out, I would be forever grateful."

The work went on for several months and Kosta's family was doing well.

The fields seeded with a variety of grains. Gardens with vegetables, at last all set for this year. Sudden storms passed through flooding fields, rivers spilling over their banks. Rushing waters carried debris weakened the structure of the only bridge connecting the village. The road leading to the castle turned into a mudslide. When the sun dried out the fields somewhat, reseeding resumed.

Baron satisfied with his newly altogether different style of furniture paid Kosta very well. Kosta used the earnings to purchase necessary grain to reseed the fields. Kosta wondered what ruin Thomas experienced because of this storm.

Lord Thomas had problems of his own, though the estate itself sat on a rise, the apple orchards flooded. Yes, that storm had damaged everyone's crops. However, the valley vastly devastated.

Lord Thomas hording all things of quality had everything he desired. Dismissing his actions at times was a bit careless. Whenever he laughed, anyone familiar with it shuddered. His friends began to avoid him so much that over time he became a very lonely man, angry at that, his own children avoided him. He stayed out late at night, who knows where he wandered so late, as time went on Cybilia and the servants stopped wondering and caring they did their own thing. Cybilia had said to Mark and Shara, "We must watch him closely, more than before."

Her inner feelings kept her alert for their safety, she felt like a prisoner in her own home. In conversation of heirs and ownership, Lord Thomas slipped up exclaiming his sole ownership and his rights, so he believed. Cybilia an only daughter owned entire property. Lord Thomas realized he had nothing and his attitude changed; since then became quiet, thoughtful, and less explosive. After months of grimacing and pouting, exposed his bullish self.

Cybilia contemplated a long visit to Uncle Lorenzo with Mark and Shara. To avoid any abuse or violence, her husband's outbursts frightened her. He would not hesitate to commit a crime, as she was sure he was involved before, if not with his bare hands, by the hands of others. Her self-confidence slid low. Her decision at the end out of fear was to stay home. She will discuss this with her children, perhaps one day they will get away, if only for a visit to uncle Kosta and Kathryn, without Thomas.

Up in the sky, big black birds circled one late afternoon as Kosta headed home down the mountain on his newly acquired horse. "*Strange*," he thought, "*why are these black birds flying...no they are not black birds, they are ravens.*" As he descended lower at a bend, he was startled, ravens flew above, and others perched in trees, silent. Kosta kept his eyes on those on the trees. It seemed they were observing him. At some point he halted near a tree for a minute, will they fly away or stay. Kosta was close enough to see their black shiny eyes he counted thirteen. His horse stumped the ground, ready to gallop away. Kosta nudged, the horse trotted down to the valley, Kosta glanced up the ravens followed. Just when he was about to enter his home these ravens flew over the house. He could not sleep that night. *What sort of omen is this?* Feeling restless and hoping nothing tragic will happen to him. Denying, dismissing odd feelings and thinking they were only black birds, but they were not just black birds, they were ravens, but each time he closed his eyes he saw their eyes and that kept him awake until dawn. Morning found him quiet and thoughtful. He went out to the new barn and stayed there much longer than usual. As a youth, Kosta believed in superstitions, but now a grown man should not allow the appearance of a dozen birds concern him. *Still, why were they flying so low, why?* He tried to apply his concentration to the job at hand. Kathryn busy with the children had not noticed the change in her husband.

No one suspected that these birds would one day contribute to the welfare of someone in dire need of saving.

Rebecca and Mathew enjoyed fishing together. They had much in common, their ideas and ideals, their dreams. They discussed the unknown world beyond those mountains encircling their valley. The world to them seemed a fascinating place, their wish was to explore, travel and meet people. They loved the idea of venturing off.

"Just look and wonder what is around us," Rebecca said.

"Here we have wonderful mysteries and we have no way of finding out how all this works," Mathew replied.

"Why even the teacher is puzzled, he has never been anywhere else but here, how much could he know," Rebecca said.

"Rebecca, he must have lived and studied somewhere in the world, otherwise how would he know so much, knowledge he did not dream up! Yes, and he is old, we should not wait around but go see the world. I wonder if our parents will permit us to go, perhaps they would if we are together and you are my chaperon, or guardian, or something like that, what do you think, Mathew?" Rebecca said not looking at him. Her eyes were on the fishing pole. Mathew annoyed glared at her and burst out.

"What? You want me to be your guardian or something. Why, that is out of the question, when we are old enough, we will have servants and guards to protect us. You know by now, that I intend to be rich one day. You are a doubting Thomas, Rebecca!" Mathew said with a raised voice.

"Oh Mathew please do not be cross with me, it was just something that came to my mind so quickly, I did not think. Oh, that would be so grand to be rich, have comfort and worry-free lifetime, Oh Mathew, really you will be rich someday?" She looked at him with those soft blue eyes and he knew he had to assure her that he would.

Mathew stared at the water; there before him slowly the line moved from his right to his left and went slack. Mathew reached for the bamboo tightened his grip waiting, he watched as the bamboo arched and the tip dipped into the water. Mathew held on when the line pulled away' he jerked it back; by the force of the pull Mathew knew he had caught a big fish. The fish led that line down under then the whole body jumped out of the water into the air, frantically flapping turned and dove in the deep. Mathew held on, while Rebecca sat wide-eyed holding her breath, after, a long time tugging at the line to be free the fish bellied up, and was pulled ashore, they were both screaming from excitement.

"Some dinner this will be for all of us, Rebecca look! What a beauty!" Mathew shouted. They did not wait to catch another, though they would have, instead hurried home with their prize catch. Kathryn quickly cleaned the fish and told Mathew to get the fire going, Mathew brought kindling and logs quickly started the fire.

"Could Mathew take me home I want to tell mother of the good catch, and that you have invited them for a fish dinner here!" Rebecca asked Kathryn.

"Yes, go quickly and tell them, yes they are invited," Kathryn said. Mathew with Rebecca sat behind him holding on to his shirt as they galloped on to her house. Mathew turned into the front yard and reined the horse at her house. Rebecca slid of the back and ran into her home. She announced that they must come to Mathew's home for dinner. Rabinna and Michael looked at each other and agreed their daughter found a companion. Invitation accepted. Kathryn and Kosta adored by Rebecca. Rebecca addressed them Aunt and Uncle and she felt like she had sisters and had brothers. They truly got along well.

After dinner, Kosta carried the fish scraps to the garden, dug a hole, threw in the scraps and was about to cover with dirt when a shiny object caught his eye, he picked it up, it was a wedding ring. Kosta went into the barn and slipped the ring on the nail.

Next day in the barn he examined the ring, this he could not believe, how uncanny, not in a million years, the ring in hand had an inscription: *David and Liana forever*. His eyes filled with tears, he whispered; how many years has it been since they perished in that river, how many! The recollection of that night stabbed at his heart. That evening he told Kathryn.

"How ironic, after many years my father's wedding ring surfaced out of the belly of a fish my son caught."

"It is better not to tell the children, let it all be as it is," Kathryn said.

All summer Kosta had two jobs, at home and at the castle, almost all of the required furniture was complete, that meant he would have no income. Perhaps try other places. While completing the last chair he felt sad. Baron noticed Kosta's sadness.

"Now look, do not feel this way, you will come again soon, I would love to meet your wife and children, let them run all over the castle and make some noise. It is like a tomb, here!" Baron exclaimed.

"Oh are you sure, you want my children to come?" Kosta asked surprised.

"Absolutely, I have no other visitors, the ghost drove them away. I am sure the children know about the ghost. Perhaps she will not bother us, since they are children. We will have plenty to eat. They will enjoy my monstrosity of a home...if you could call it that."

Kosta excited could not wait to tell his children of the invitation to come to dinner at the castle. The moment he told them, they jumped up and down creating an unbelievable, commotion laughing and screaming from happiness. Mathew rode to tell Rebecca, she was ecstatic.

One Sunday well before noon, dressed in their best, seven chidren sat on blankets on the wagons floor rode up the mountain. As the wagon rolled, higher and higher Rosie was edgy and expressed her fear.

"Father, will the wagon roll back, will it if we go higher?"

"Rosie, this is like being a bird flying high, look at the world how huge it is; you can only see it like this from up high," Mathew quickly replied to calm her fear.

"I would like to be a bird and fly!" Jason said.

"Oh Jason, even if you had wings you could not fly!" Marla had to interject her opinion.

"Marla, you always seem to think I cannot do things right!" Jason a bit perturbed came back at her. Tessana stopped their squabbling. Kras and Jasemin sat mesmerized by the scene before them. Rebecca was so impressed she glowed from excitement. "Mathew is this...how...it is to be rich...is to own a castle? Are you going to build one, on a mountain?" she asked him. Mathew just grimaced, but did not reply.

The wagon stopped at a spot, which opened to a panorama unseen by their eyes. They stood up in the wagon and gaped at the vista from the top of the mountain. Then they drove up the courtyard, all heads and eyes looked up at high walls built of stone reaching up to the sky. Kosta stepped down of the wagon walked to the heavy door and rapped hard with the wolf's head knocker. Kathryn stepped down and the children jumped off the wagon walked up and stood in a group behind Kosta; after a long wait Simena the cook slowly opened the heavy door recognizing Kosta smiled.

"Simena, my wife Kathryn and my children," Kosta said to her, the children curtsied. Simena smiled and said, "Come in, come in, welcome. Master Baron will be glad to see you." They cautiously tiptoed into the foyer, it was so grand, mouths gaping, amazed. Kathryn warned them, "If you do not close your mouths, you will swallow flies for sure, if any were in here." Therefore, they walked with their mouths closed. Holding hands, eyes darting at the mirrors, rugs, iron brackets on the walls for the lamps, and the heavy velvet drapes on tall windows, they stood before the paintings, Marla whispered, "How was this done? I want to learn."

"Ask the Baron, he might know," Tessana replied.

So many things their eyes had never seen, from around the world. Baron waited for them, he was impressed with this little '*clutch*' of children. Unfortunately, he never had a family of his own. When they entered the dining room, Kosta introduced his family to Master Baron. Kathryn impressed, also admired these riches, riches, everywhere!

Kosta pointed out all the furniture he had made; she was so proud and literally speechless.

"Now seat yourselves and then you will tell me your names," Baron said to them. The huge table was set, with large bowls of fruit. The children sat and gaped when the servants brought in platters of meat and vegetables and the aroma of tea in silver carafes they took it all in and could not believe their eyes that so much food existed, much less in their reach to be eaten.

"All right now, before we begin our lunch tell me your names," Baron said.

Kosta glanced at Mathew.

"Sir, my name is Mathew I am the eldest. I am Tessana Sir. My name Sir is Jasemin. Jason Sir. I am Kras Sir. Marla Sir. And I am Rosalie Sir." They stood waiting to be seated. Master Baron bursting with emotion clapped his hands and said.

"Kosta, Kathryn you have a beautiful family, and very intelligent, now go ahead help yourselves."

The lunch served early, they ate and ate and ate. Baron beamed with satisfaction and pleasure. He withheld questions or urging them for conversation but allowed them to eat as much as they wanted. After the children had their fill, they sat at the table feeling uncomfortable glancing at each other as if saying 'we want to leave the table,' but knowing well just to leave would be very impolite. Baron could see they had enough and were antsy to go outside and explore.

"Go now and play, just be careful do not go too far, and do not go near that old huge tree." Baron waved them away towards the door. They all ran out and in unison chimed a cheerful, "Thank You!"

Kathryn wondered why they were not to go near the tree. She was just about to ask, when Baron offered his reason.

"My gardener Kirk Spence worked tirelessly at the flower beds and children will be children, speaking of the oak tree, when Kirk planted the bed of spring flowers shortly after the 'forget-me-not' sprouted in that bed, I wondered who had planted them there under that oak tree."

"They should stay away, as to those flowers, I would say, must have been the young woman who lived here," Kathryn agreed, she had many questions on her mind, but dared not ask. Her expression gave her away. Baron knew she was curious, to know his past and why he settled here. That has to remain for later. If ever he wishes to disclose to them or anyone else for that matter he will do so.

"Shall we go for a walk up to the tree, and sit a spell. I want you to see those flowers," Baron said, rising from his chair.

Kathryn and Kosta followed him out to see the grounds. The children ran around the grounds like squirrels, hopping like bunnies. Kathryn seemed to be on cloud nine, all this overwhelmed her, riches and all this space, comparing to their little shack. Time flew by quickly, for the children had fun. At one moment when they were running up and down the stairs, Jasemin heard a whisper. She ran to Kathryn and whispered in her ear.

"Mother I heard a whisper upstairs."

"Perhaps a maid is up there," Kathryn said.

Jasemin insisted that no person was up there.

Baron overheard her, and told Jasemin who was upstairs. Jasemin clung to her mother and refused to leave her side.

Baron explained to Jasemin that this ghost was young and beautiful and that her soul was lost here on earth, someone harmed her and she cannot rest. Even though Jasemin was just a child, she seemed to understand.

"Sir, are you afraid of the ghost?"

"No. Only sometimes when I sense she is angry. Jasemin go find your brothers and sisters, I want to show you something, hurry," he said. Jasemin ran to find them, shortly they all gathered in the parlor.

"Come with me, it is almost about that time." Baron climbed the stairs. Kathryn and Kosta followed behind the children as climbed the stairs behind the Baron. On the walls, in large iron coils oil lamps hung, giving light all the way up to the west tower. There before them opened up a breath-taking panorama, as far as their eyes could see, below them stretched the forest and far on the horizon blue and purple mountains. The sun was setting. Their eyes drank this scene and Kathryn's eyes filled with tears, this she never had time to see, not from their little home. No one spoke but stared in awe. Baron felt joy and sorrow, joy seeing these children mesmerized by this vista, and sorrow, unable to hold in his arms his only love he had lost a long time ago. This visit to the castle children will remember, for the fun they had, enormity of the castle was a reality not a dream. Baron made them promise to come back anytime, and they said they would. When they arrived back to their tiny house feeling different somehow, here they were born and here they must live. Villagers hearing of their visit were envious, of course. Kathryn thought about the Baron and said to Kosta,

"He must be lonely, alone up there. All the riches will not give him happiness, riches give comfort and a full belly but not happiness, unless, he has someone to share them with; someone to love and be loved in return."

"How true, but still it is such a security to be rich, not wanting for anything," Kosta added.

"Loneliness disarms a person, lack of interest in their surroundings, because of depression, tears, and solitude. How many lonely people do you know of, or visit, those alone, lonely, perhaps without a family, their only companion...solitude," Kathryn said.

"One person I know of is my Aunt Olivia. I know she is lonely, never married. She told me once, while she lived in a foreign country she was in love, but she never told me in detail of what really happened," Kosta replied.

"Do you think she will ever tell us of her experience?" Kathryn asked.

"To devote ones' life for others, but never realize their own dreams. And then to know that the last chapter of life is ending, is very sad," Kosta added.

"I must tell you, my mother before she became debilitated preferred to be alone, never complaining. She was blessed with a strong constitution of mind and character," Kathryn said.

Kosta respected Kathryn's opinion, and was proud of her knowledge she had compassion for others. She also inherited her mothers' strength and endurance, no matter what she has to face.

"Baron is alone. Having all the riches he ever wanted or needed, he is alone, unloved and unwanted," Kathryn said to Kosta.

"His guests never returned; the ghost frightened them off. I am sure he realized they were only his friends when he provided a full table served by a peasant girl, a comfortable bed, wine, laughter and pleasures. Baron told me all about his friends, while I worked there," Kosta said.

"They were not true friends or companions. Such fickle friends he could do without in his life. Our children gave him more happiness at least for a few hour...did you notice?" Kathryn asked.

"Yes I did notice, but that ghost's presence is a very annoying distraction. The servants are mere servants following his orders and they are loyal, I assure you. Kathryn while I worked I wondered, how did he acquire all these exquisite artifacts and why did he settle here in this part of the world, far away from rich social circles where he surely was accepted," Kosta said.

Many a night Kosta and Kathryn broached that subject, had questions but no answers, and that was as far as they could get. Where did he reside before, where was he born. Where was the rest of his family, that, only he could and would answer if he so wished.

The Baron will continue to live among them, like a king ruling from afar without ever acknowledging he has a kingdom.

Thirty-Three: The Harvest

Summer days were not idle for these people. Large projects or small had to be finished because as summer ends, it would be time to reap the harvest.

Kosta worked with speed and sweat from sunrise to sunset. Preparing the storage bins. Cleaning out where needed, Mathew and the children helped. Unexplained feeling of urgency hung in the air, they hurried every day to get it done, the fields were long and the backbreaking loading and unloading of the wagons must begin. Each day the distance to their home shortened as they began their harvest from the far end of the field. The days were warm and evenings pleasant, yet something was amiss, something was going to happen, no one could explain that eerie, uneasy feeling. September and part of October slipped by without a drop of rain, but the moaning and whistling of the wind till dawn kept many awake.

Mathew in the morning asked, "Why is it so windy lately. I was awake all night; I am like a rag this morning without restful sleep." The younger children also complained and had similar questions.

Concerned for the animals in the new barn memories of the previous fire made him cringe. Kosta felt uneasy, especially when he carved in the barn. His skin crawled, and hair bristled on his neck. He glanced around but saw nothing. He placed the carving on a beam and with the little blade in hand quickly went home.

Whenever conversing with the neighbors they admitted that they too were aware of something unusual. At dusk, they all kept themselves busy indoors. Most of the children were afraid to go outdoors. What was happening?

Such weather changes usually brought out the worst fear, backbreaking toil was not over. Then the weather changed, the last week of October mornings were crispy and by noon, very warm, in spite of the occasional strong wind blowing for several hours when loading wheat onto the wagons. The debris blew into their eyes and hair, and grain scattered to the ground, but they kept on working to the finish. The fruit trees laden with delicious fruit were picked clean. When the work in the fields ended, they breathed a sigh of relief and prayers of "*Thanksgiving*" never forgotten.

Lumberjacks hurried into the woods because their main job was to supply firewood to everyone for the coming winter. Even young teens contributed time to load and deliver to each house, the unloaded wagons returned for reloading. This went on for days chopping and hauling, back and forth until every house had cords and cords of firewood stacked against their houses.

Up on the mountain at the castle everyone worked while the wind howled and whistled many a night. Baron Patrick in his library read his books, his mind quite often drifted to the mystery of the ghost. Then he thought of the time his heart was broken losing that someone he loved and will love until his dying day. He was a bit bored just staying indoors so much, not having anyone to discuss his favorite subjects. He did mention to cook Simena of the sudden change in the weather, she quickly replied.

"Sir, weather is always unpredictable. It is the end of autumn and winters around the corner."

"Is it now? Then better get ready for it, and do not forget to fill the pantry, full. I will inspect everything later," Baron Patrick said to them in conclusion of their usual meeting in the kitchen.

"Oh Ridiller, on the way back from the market stop at Kosta's home, I am inviting the children for dinner."

For days, he went around and checked for depleting supplies and reminding them to be sure to replenish empty bins. When all items on the list for winter were completed and checked off the servants relaxed, went about their daily chores. Baron Patrick resumed his solitary existence in the library reading. The ghost stayed away for a while though she disturbed his quietness, and amused him knowing there is afterlife, he missed her. What a moment it would be, a moment in time, as their spirits met.

Suddenly he blinked back to reality.

"No... I am not ready to cross over, not yet, what if I have not earned heaven, but hell! Oh well, realistically I do not believe in demons. Ah, the human mind very capable of isolating a single thought or idea and creating an out of control web of hideous nightmares. Ah...but I have had dreams of a perfect paradise in a dream, so I will take the paradise anytime," he said to himself. There were times when Baron allowed his mind to tangle his thoughts into such a tangled web, causing insomnia and confusion.

When the newly hired helper, Dirks, entered master's bedroom early mornings and saw his master's disorientation and disheveled appearance, he was shocked. Master Baron's room was topsy-turvy. Dirks ran down to the kitchen and called master's private and faithful servant Ridiller for help, they both could not understand what is wrong. Fearing for his health, they tended to him nonstop, until Master Baron had enough of their overbearing attendance became too irritated and harshly said, "I am not yet an invalid, leave me alone!"

Ridiller instructed the younger fellow Dirks to go fetch Kosta.

"You know how well they got along together all summer. Perhaps he could come and check on the Baron, and yes invite them for dinner, the whole family, do not forget," Ridiller said. Dirks dressed warm and off to the village he rode to ask Kosta since it was urgent to come and check on master Baron. When Kathryn heard a knock on the door surprised to see Dirks, she invited him in out of the cold.

"Dirks what brings you here?" she asked. "Did you ride down?"

Dirks said, "Yes," and explained why he came. Just then, Kosta walked into the house. Dirks repeated what was happening, was about to leave recalled the dinner invitation, Kosta agreed to come visit the sick Baron with his family.

All the way up the mountain to the castle wrapped in blankets, the children huddled together. Kosta felt chilled to the bone, Kathryn shivered, the wind whipped around and whistled. The higher they climbed the colder it was, they could not wait to get out of such a dreadful cold and have some fun and learn about the ghost again from Master Baron.

Entering the castle, they found Master Baron in the library as usual reading his book. What a great pleasure it gave him to see his friends.

"Kosta, good thing you are here, I missed you though it is a dreadful day. Good God lets have some good wine, could the children have a sip, too?" Baron asked cheerfully.

"Yes, thank you, it is very windy, we are chilled," Kosta replied.

In addition, Rosie said, "I am still shivering, my nose is frozen."

"Well then we need a sip of wine so your nose will unfreeze itself!" Baron Patrick smiled and touched Rosie's nose lightly." The children sat at the table sipping wine from tiny crystal timbles, now and then a slurp a smak of someones lips and ahh slipped unintentionally of course while the grown-ups attention, was discussing something important; actually did not hear any of it, since they sat at the other end of the long table. Simena quietly walked in from the kitchen took the wine bottle and topped each tiny crystal timble for each one. She whispered, "Just a little bit more to warm up your frozen toes." Simena tiptoed back into the kitchen. The children glanced at each other and Mathew said, "We need to gulp this down before mother notices our glasses are full." At once, as if syncronized they lifted up and gulped it down. Rosie began to caugh. Jason's mouth opened wide but nothing came out for a few seconds then, "ah, ah, ah!" came out and his eyes wide. The rest looked at each other and laughed. The girls came in from the kitchen with platters of food setting all on the table. Baron Patrick, Kosta and Kathryn came and sat down next to the children to share the brunch. As all the other times before, they thanked Baron Patrick amd wemt off to play throughout the castle. They had fun. Rosalie not as shy as the first time was more talkative, and so were the others as well.

Suddenly Kathryn said, "Kosta remember the invitation, Celebration of the harvest."

"Ah yes, I had almost forgotten if you are well and wish to join the villagers for a celebration of the harvest, next Sunday, you are welcome."

"Wish to! Kosta I would love to go down to the valley. I would not mind at all, but what about the weather, it is horrid out there!" the Baron exclaimed.

"Ah the bad weather, I agree it is cold, bundle up, do not worry, the celebration will be at the Village Hall, followed by a drink and a quiet time at the home of our Mayor," Kosta replied.

The time had come to head home, Kathryn and the children sat in the wagon waiting. Kosta in the kitchen assured Ridiller that Baron is fine; in a low voice, Kosta asked Ridiller,

"Your Master Baron, does he have a first name? If you know do tell." Ridiller shook his head.

"Keep an eye on your Master Baron, do not worry, he is not ill. He probably had nightmares. You must prepare delicious meals for him," Kosta instructed the servants.

But on the way home he felt concerned, Baron did look a bit peaked, not himself at all, he will discuss it with Kathryn at home, she will know what to do.

The horses trotted at a fast pace down the mountain, Kosta's head tucked in the winter cape he leaned a bit forward to hide his face from the wind. Kathryn sat with the children under blankets no one noticed the ravens circling overhead. The day of the celebration of course had been prearranged a long time ago, so Kosta was not fibbing at all. Kosta in person visited Mayor Maurice Treashone, to inform him of the Barons attendance, the Mayor was surprised and very pleased, at that moment proposed a visit to his home for a spell after the celebration.

Baron arrived at Kosta's little house, Kathryn blushed, embarrassed, for a rich man to step foot in their little cluttered home. Nonetheless, seeing the Baron the children squealed from excitement, ran up to Baron clung to him. The boys, Jason and Kras sat on the seat with the coachman, the girls inside the carriage with Kathryn. Kosta and Mathew rode the wagon to pick up Aunt Olivia on the way, as they all entered the Village Hall villagers gaped when Kosta introduced Baron to Mayor Maurice Treashone. Mayor Treashone walked up to the podium, hushed all present villagers raised his arms and began.

"Attention my wonderful citizens, we have a special guest among us, may I introduce to you, the honorable Baron from the castle on the mountain." They applauded feeling honored to have among them a distinguished persona such as the Baron. With the Mayor at his side, the villagers stood in line to shake Barons hand, he met farmers with wives and their children, young men gripped his hand hard and women curtsied, smiled, crowded around him asking questions, made him feel as one of them, the attention and the remarkable simplicity of these fine people, astounded him. Many were well dressed, others wore their simple best; none looked overly shabby. Kosta led Baron to the large table where Kathryn sat with Aunt Olivia and the children. Kosta introduced Aunt Olivia to the Baron.

Aunt Olivia and Baron for the longest moment looked at each other as if a glimmer of recognition of the past had suddenly appeared. Baron held her hand, kissed it.

"Olivia... my pleasure," Baron said, still holding her hand, she tried to pull back but he held it.

"Kosta it gives me great pleasure to meet your beautiful aunt," Baron said. Kathryn and Kosta stared at them. Aunt Olivia was composed but rather stiffly replied, "Time is passing it has been said long ago. Thank you." Baron kissed her hand again. Kathryn unable to grasp the meaning of her reply at that moment, perhaps if Kathryn could observe a bit longer, but were abruptly interrupted. Baron whisked away by the Mayor to a group of men for discussions. Baron turned his head many a time towards the table where Aunt Olivia sat to make sure she was still there. Crowds of people blocked his view. Once the crowd dispersed, at the table no one was there. Impressed with the villagers, their food, dancing and singing pleased him immensely. The day was ending and the celebration over; it was time to return to his castle. Baron thanked all of the villagers and Mayor Maurice Treashone, his wife Collette for such a wonderful reception. Unable to locate

Aunt Olivia concerned him, wondering where had she gone off to and why. At this point, he could not ask, a strange feeling of loss lingered. Their wine glasses clinked to a toast to the Mayor Treashone and his gracious wife Collette. Kosta and Baron took leave.

"Where are the children and Kathryn?" Baron asked.

"Kathryn and the children are in the carriage. Mathew took Aunt Olivia home in the wagon."

"And how are we getting home, walking?" Baron smiled.

"Oh no, Arkushin my neighbor is driving us home, any minute now." Kosta noticed his quietness but dared not question the reason.

"Kosta I enjoyed today I had no idea that I...I never imagined that these villagers were so united and sincere. I thank you and Kathryn for a lovely day, your children are wonderful, and, I am happy I met Aunt Olivia."

Baron on the way to the castle in his carriage sat thoughtful.

In his castle, he sat down in his large overstuffed high back chair, the fireplace glowed, and its heat warmed him, as did the wine. His mind seemed to be preoccupied, with the past, that woman's face and what she had said. What made her say that? She does resemble someone, I...but that has been so long ago. Her comment that day...just that one, seemed to mask something, something, which I cannot place at this moment.

Kosta chopped wood when a messenger handed him a letter from Baron. Kosta read it to Kathryn and the children,

"Thank you for including me in the festivities, and meeting Aunt Olivia, I regret not seeing her before she left. Do come again, no need of an invitation, also never forget to bring your Aunt Olivia with you, thank you again, Baron."

"He must be thinking about her," Kathryn said.

Baron in his luxurious castle was in another world, his own. The enormity of the castle made him feel small, yet he felt secure. Very often, his thoughts drifted to that day he met Olivia, something about Olivia, her eyes, or was it her voice. It is a shame the weather is changing and soon he will not be able to venture out to see Kosta and his family, particularly Kosta's Aunt Olivia, an older woman but beautiful, she caught his eye. She sparked his feelings. How would he feel seeing her again? She seemed rather familiar, her eyes, though years have passed, he saw a glimmer of recognition, and that remark, time is passing. "Oh heavens, it cannot be, or, could it? How, could that be possible after all these years? I must find out, or I will go mad, could it be possible, her, here? All this time, she was here, lived here? Her name is the same!"

Baron after several weeks not hearing from Kosta wondered should he send a servant with an invitation for dinner again, their friends too, and to be sure include Aunt Olivia. Anxiety and the waiting made him restless. Baron called on Dirks sent him with an invitation in hand to Kosta.

Dirks returned bearing good news though not very clear, Baron listened as the servant recited Kosta's reply, a bit concerned not knowing who had a "small incident" but no name mentioned. Kosta apologized, they will be there, and he corrected himself...meaning they will come...but not until the second Sunday.

Cook Flora was to plan a menu for Sunday's dinner.

"Sir, how many in the party?" Flora questioned her master. Baron thought for a minute and replied, "Eleven, counting Michael, Rabinna and Rebecca. No one moment, seven children, parents, and Olivia, ten, plus friends three...yes now, thirteen, plus myself, fourteen."

"Very well sir, all will be taken care of." Flora disappeared into the kitchen.

Thirty-Four: The Migration

Black birds flew high over the valley the second time.

Gliding, hovering, they observed the area flying over Lord Thomas's estate several times. The time of the year for birds to migrate had passed with temperatures dropping below zero, without supply of food very few birds would survive.

Cybilia sat at the window, observing this flock of black birds flying in an unusual formation. Flying high, swooping down, up again, and again, which caught her interest and she watched as long as they were in her sight, she was intrigued by them, she has never seen a display as this before, it being very cold outside.

Shara entered her mother's room.

"Did you see the birds?" her mother asked.

"Birds, what birds, no, I did not see any, why?"

"I observed a flock of them they were odd looking, big and black, they seemed to be searching for something. I wonder why they are still here. I have never noticed them here even in the summer. Have you?"

Shara looked at her in wonder. "Why would you be so interested in black birds, Mother?"

"They are different. Odd, never have I seen such black birds. They were huge. I am telling you Shara, they seemed very odd, they gave me the chills," Cybilia answered. Shara left and suddenly there was a crashing sound. Shara ran in the direction of the crash.

Cybilia jumped off the window seat, ran to find her daughter staring at a broken frame, torn canvas of a painting on the floor, how could the painting have fallen off the wall? The wire was not broken and the nail still sat in the wall.

All the windows were closed it could not have been draft.

They stared for a moment. Cybilia led Shara away to let the servant clean up the mess. Their backs to the windows... they never noticed drapes slightly rippled by invisible hands. *"Sabrina, oh Sabrina is throwing a tantrum again screaming. Screaming?"* Mark thought. This was the start of something stressful and disturbing, for one particular individual, this ghostly visitor would muddle his mind and try to break his spirit, and bring him down to his knees. Everyone began to feel odd, the chilly rooms. Missing objects, creating distrust among the servants.

Mark also felt something odd and unnatural lingering in his room. There were moments while in deep thought about Joseph, as he pondered over the mysterious cloth from Joseph, now and then a feeling of foreboding and feeling a chill touch him, ever since Joseph went away. No one had heard from him or of him since then. Is he alive? His brother Lark had not inquired of Joseph's whereabouts. Father never mentions Joseph's name, since then. Mark wondered who had a grudge a reason to harm Joseph. Mark continued to try to unravel the mystery of the package, but could not solve it. Mark often felt his father had rejected and abandoned him, since he stopped talking to them. Father kept to himself. Mark felt bitter. He began to dislike his life in this cursed house. It was not a big home but a structure that is all, now. It no longer was a happy, noisy, fun and secure home. Lately his Mother seemed to be very irritable as well. She stepped lightly, always looking over her shoulder, no matter where she was. No one noticed this change, and no one offered to help with this situation. Clearly to Mark, confusion reigned this household. If it is Joseph's ghost, then Mark wants a sign. Perhaps too soon to reveal this mystery, one day he must. Now and then, he glimpsed a weaving vapor across his room, but in a blink of an eye gone, nonetheless he felt uneasy. Marks concentration distorted; the girls ran down the hall screaming to Lady Cybilia, in the kitchen things are reshuffling.

Lord Thomas irritated with all women constantly yelling would leave the house and be off to 4 Hoofs Inn to drink. His friends talked their usual family talk and mentioned Kosta and his family, for they knew of their problems; triggered curiosity of how they fared lingered. Lord Thomas replied curtly, "I am too busy to listen to gossip." His drinking pals changed subjects not wanting to ignite his demeaning and explosive side. Because they knew, he cared little. When one of them mentioned the ghost in the castle, Lord Thomas ordered three drinks and downed them one after the other. Unfortunately overconsumption of wine could not drown what he felt.

Returning home late, he muttered. "All this commotion about the ghost, those women jump at a pin drop. I have...no fear...I fear nothing. I ignore all ghost talks, period. I am in control of me...ha nonsense!" Lord Thomas barely balanced in the saddle. His horse knew the way home. However, inebriated, still remembered to secure his horse Star into his stall, and checked water bucket. Then noisily grappling in the barely dim house managed to find his bedroom; slipped his shoes off, and fell on the bed in his clothes.

When the servant opened the drapes in the morning and woke him too early, he chased her out, muttering foul words before falling back to sleep; rising before noon for lunch. The house was quiet and empty, walked into the kitchen, all were gone but for the one cook's helper, the girl who looked at him suspiciously, his nerves twitched every time he saw her. Something about that girl bothered him. He ordered her to prepare lunch and told her to sit with him at the kitchen table. She set plates of his lunch before him and sat across from him watched as he ate. The kitchen quiet, all others went out to their responsibilities. At one moment, he swallowed what he chewed, took a long drag of tea then asked her; "Cybilia and the children are not in the house; do you know where they are, he looked at her. The girl said she did not know.

"I see," he said, what other questions were in his mind he kept to himself.

As time passed Lord Thomas' face turned brutal, dark rings under his eyes, his skin grayish and wrinkled, and his demeanor changed, he despised everything, and bellowed at everyone in the household, instilling fear. Mistrusted his manager, questioning every move he made, except James.

James had that little quirky smile and always overly courteous, nonchalant attitude, which exceedingly irritated Lord Thomas, especially that sly look. Lord Thomas contemplated a plan to oust James from his estate. He watched James at every opportunity. Gave him nasty orders to do, which the others would dislike, but James performed everything to a tee, Lord Thomas did not like that either, or that slight mockery coming from James.

Some evenings while in bed he heard inaudible whispering. Other times clearly he heard incomplete sentences like, "*woe is...*" and "*doomed... you dammed...*" and then, "*time will come, your back... you.*"

Such instances drove Lord Thomas mad, especially when he heard, "murder..."

Thirty-Five: Inferno

Unexpected extreme cold gripped the valley, and this was not even start of winter. On such a dreadful night, it was unthinkable for someone in their right mind to venture out, perhaps a mad man, a recluse or a demented person, if lost on such a night would perish quickly. And on this night, a shadow of a man stepped stealthily along the side of the structure so as not to disturb the resting animals, cats curled up deep in the hay would not hear an intruder who tiptoed along the side wall to do them harm. All dogs and cats slept indoors on nights such as this. However, this sudden freeze was unexpected. The man trembled, feet numb, his sheep boots and wool socks barely warm for such freeze. His shawl wrapped around his face iced from his breathing. He carried a bag of oiled straw and in his pocket matches. He noiselessly stuffed the straw under and in between cracks of the huge barn door, reached into his pocket for matches, knelt on the ground his back to the wind. Held his breath, as each strike of the match died out, he tried again, and again. His hands trembled but he struck again, this time the flame licked the straw and flared. Adding more straw his hands over the flame warmed them a bit. The barn door barred from the outside none of the animals should escape. He crept away as the flames began to lick the weathered door. The dry wood began to glow and sparks flew. The fire was doing its job. The man moved to the dark side of the house crouched near the wall stacked with firewood and watched as the flames crept under the door and into the barn. Mathew's dog Midnight opened his eyes, perked up his ears listened then growled hearing desperate animal cries for rescue.

Midnight jumped onto the bed, barked to wake Mathew, but Mathew patted the dog's head told him to stay, to go out is too cold. Midnight ran to Kosta and barked.

Out in the barn pigs squealed, cattle bellowed and horses neighed, flames licked the bales of straw on the ground near the inside door reaching for everything it its path.

The shadow of the man became but a silhouette in the glow, as he watched smoke began creeping through the cracks. He waited for the inferno. He then retreated into the shadows. Without a doubt this job well done. Watching from the distance, he knew that what he has done tonight will be vivid in his mind all life long, and he will pay dearly. Either way tonight this act was not his choice, tough this cruel deed carried out by him out of fear, subconsciously opposing, his submission to this was not his weakness of character. Opposition would bring him unbearable punishment, sudden death.

Kosta in his sleep heard the dogs bark reached out to pat the dog, but could not wake. Suddenly Midnight pawed at him hard. Kosta feeling pain jumped out of bed, the room lit up by the fires red glow. His heart raced, he screamed “FIRE!” to wake his family.

They all jumped out of their warm beds in their night clothes ran to the kitchen and out the door. The flames blinked through the barns cracks, smoke poured everywhere, the interior engulfed in flames completely. “All our precious animals are overcome by flames!” Kathryn screamed.

The girls screamed ran towards the flaming barn, calling their cats, tears streaming down their young faces. “Kathryn, go inside with the children, NOW!” Kosta ran to the back of the barn still untouched by fire, flung back the bar, struggled to push the huge door open. The cats sat in the corner meowing, Kosta ran in and grabbed two, threw them out the door the rest followed. From what he could see, the flames and smoke now concentrated on the other side of the barn. The horses, he had to get to the horses. The smoke now rolled from top to bottom, horses rearing, snorting, and kicking in fear. Kosta’s blood turned to ice, he forgot fear, he freed the horses, and they ran out. The cows’ heads were overtaken by the heavy smoke, Mathew ran in to help, he too tried desperately to unlatch the cows doors, only a few were pulled to safety, those near the start of fire stood frozen in place eyes bulging breathing in the smoke. Mathew’s decision is to leave them, but get to the pigpen. The pigs ran around their pans squealing. Mathew crawled on his belly to the pigpen; reached up to pull the rope loop off the latch, Mathew rolled pulling the door to the side, just as the pigs ran for their lives, heat seared their backs; survived by Mathew’s bravery.

The flames were closing in on the cows in the rear enclosure. Their fierce bellows hoarse from suffocating smoke. Their eyes bulging with fear. Kosta desperate to rescue repeated, “They cannot burn, God they cannot burn!” he screamed. Extreme heat singed his arms and face, he dropped to the ground, crawled, reached the latch, pulled, doors swung back, and Kosta yelled,

"*HO! HO! HO*!" His throat burned from heat and smoke. The way to safety was clear the cows ran out of the burning barn.

"Father, Father where are you?" Mathew screamed hearing his father's voice.

Kosta had collapsed to the floor, with his last breath and strength inched his way out, lungs filled with smoke cut off his breath. Safety he could not reach. Mathew dropped to the ground, seeing his father down crawled to him grabbed by the shirt, inch by inch pulled with all his strength tried to drag his father to safety. Mathew overtaken by smoke collapsed near the exit, still holding on to his father's shirt. Kathryn and the children now dressed were out screaming, the neighbors came running to help.

"The other door, the back door, they are there!" Kathryn screamed to them. The neighbors ran to the back, finding Mathew, Arkushin dragged Mathew away from the barn door. Arkushin with his fist hit him on the back several times, Mathew coughed, gasped, cried out, "Father...father in the barn... save him!" Arkushin crouched to glimpse where Kosta lay, crawling on fours like a badger holding his breath, grabbed Kosta's arm and dragged backing out as quickly as he had strength out into the open. Cresteron and Lester ran up grabbed a hold and dragged now both men. Arkushin himself wheezing managed to say, "All is smoldering... soon...will burst into flames, must move him to the house." Cresteron and Lester half-dragged Kosta to the house, on the floor, turned him face down hit him on the back hard, sat him up and rocked him. Kosta's body limp, no response. Again, they turned him face up now, pushed on the belly but no sign of life. "It is no use son...we have tried..." Arkushin said. Mathew and Kathryn pounded on his chest. "Kosta wake up!' Kathryn yelled. After minutes what seemed to be hours, Kosta spurted out a breath and began gasping. The children sat huddled together on the bed to keep warm, the cats were with them. The men helped Kosta to a chair, with difficulty gasping for breath. Cresteron sent Lester for a bottle of fire brew. Lester came back and said, "Pour him a large glass he needs it." Kosta drank and coughed, soon warmed by the fire brew now able to speak. They thanked God for his life. "Where...are the...animals, are they... alive...or dead?"

"Father they all ran out and they are alive, you and Mathew saved them!" children cried out. Kathryn poured tea for everyone.

"As I ran around the corner...I saw a man...retreating into the shadows, I wanted to give chase after...but he...slipped into darkness. Then the...children and Kathryn ran...out into the...cold, screaming," Kosta said to Cresteron.

"Are you sure?" asked Cresteron the next-door neighbor.

"Yes, but I...had to save my live stock. I will find him...later," Kosta said coughing.

"Did you see his face?: Lester asked.

"No was...too dark, why... why us again... my God! Why again?" Kosta said, lost control of his emotions, hung his head and cried bitter tears.

Other neighbors came running. "No one short of a miracle could survive in an inferno as this," someone said. They stood far from the searing heat and watched in horror as the structure collapsed on itself to the ground, flames and sparks flying in all direction. The four neighbors jumped away quickly running into the house. They sat down glanced around the room. "Kosta are you strong enough to come outside for a minute?" "Yes, is something going on out there?" Kosta asked. The group walked out, in the distance the sky glowed, three different areas of the village. "Look around, three more fires, and you were the first," one said.

After the shock wore off, they all went out to gather the frightened animals, which were sheltered in nearby barns. The children cried when Kosta told them none of the kittens survived. Unfortunately, that night, the barns destroyed, two of them happened to be Kosta's friends, the fourth was just a one of the villagers. This was not going to pass without investigation of who ever caused these fires. The villagers kept a vigil until dawn and several nights thereafter.

The half-frozen man reached the edge of the woods his horse waited covered with blankets. Out of sight in the dark, the man raised his stiff leg with difficulty slipped it into the stirrup, his cold fingers barely able to grip the pummel, shivering pulled himself up slowly, swung his right leg over the saddle, and rode away. When he returned to the stable barely at grey dawn, first thing, he rubbed down his horse and covered him with blankets, gave him oats as a reward for being good. Then quietly entered the servant's quarters, tiptoed to his bedroom, slipped under the covers dressed as he was, waiting for sunrise. He shivered, unable to sleep, his feet and hands were numb, so were his ears and nose. Shivering under the down covers remembered the stashed bottle of wine. Slowly got out of bed, shuffled over to the secret nook, reached for the bottle, it was gone. Alarmed, thinking his Master had found it, but no, here it is in a new hiding place, he sighed relief, sat on the bed had difficulty uncorking it, as it popped noisily, he did not care if anyone heard. He raised it to his frozen lips downed half of the bottle at once. He sat and listened. After a few minutes he gulped downed the rest. The empty bottle pushed under his bed. He covered up waiting for the wine to warm him and sleep to come. However, his sleep would not come easy. He envisioned his criminal act, and why, it had to be not one barn, but three. He could have knocked on Kosta's door in the middle of the night, explain why he came, expose the person giving the order, but he could not. He could never go back to his master's house, he could have ran off, had the opportunity, but for one good reason, he could not, and that reason was his *woman,* that girl in the kitchen, many a time his Master eyed her, she had told James she feared him. James whispered, "I will protect you Lanar, I will protect you, fear not my love."

At early dawn without knocking, the master walked into the bedroom, his servant was fast asleep with his clothes on. An empty wine bottle was under the bed. He knew that his faithful servant had carried out his order.

When James shuffled out of his bedroom, it was nearly noon, feverish chills racked his aching body, and he knew that he had caught his death. In the kitchen, Lanar warmed up a bowl of soup, and fixed a sandwich for him, then, she gave him hot rum. He slowly shuffled to the parlor to give his Master the details of his mission. His Master satisfied with the report, stressed harshly,

"It better be the truth, or else. Now stay in your room for several days till you feel better."

"I shall tend to him myself," Lord Thomas told his servants.

Lord Thomas was thinking... "*he should hang. Better yet, he will suffer unusual consequences for a time, and then, disappear without a trace.*"

The guilty party that had a hand in the destruction of several barns will be a mystery to many people. During sick days, the Master poured glass after glass of wine, and rum, James already drunk, drank not only to forget his awful deed, but could not refuse his Master. "Drink, this will help you recuperate faster."

When the servants were out of the house on errands or the orchard, two strong men carried the semiconscious blindfolded servant to the barn. They cut out his tongue to keep him from talking. Back in his room James lay on the bed barely conscious his mouth open blood drooled onto the pillow, his master removed the soiled pillow brought another. Since James could not write, he could not tell of the deed his Master forced upon him. This poor servant was unable to eat for the pain, loss of blood and loss of weight. Lanar who took care of him knew something was terribly wrong, and one day she asked. "James what is wrong with you?"

James only shook his head, and tears ran down his cheeks. Lanar wiped away his tears and kissed his cheek, out of compassion for she loved him. Recuperating, James the faithful servant promised himself that one day his Master will pay and those with him as well, for what they had done to him, everyone will know, that is a promise before he dies. James was never the same again. He wandered all over the property, babbled incoherently something but no one paid attention, seldom did he complete a required task. His Master overlooked it, knowing the reason for James's behavior. Besides, he feared nothing and no one.

Time finds a way to uncover the truth. That is true justice, as it should be. As it was from the beginning of time and, the beginning of human frailty and cruelty inflicted on each other, the strongest survive and the poor, good people perish.

As it was, Lanar concluded the reason James acted out of his mind. On an evening while everyone retired to their rooms, Lanar slipped into James's room, sat on the bed, took his hand and said, "James, open your mouth, please." James shook his head, "No."

"All right then I am leaving in the middle of the night, tonight. I do not want to end up like you.

James gripped her hand tight, moaned and opened his mouth, to make her understand with his finger demonstrated a sewing motion to his tongue. Lanar gasped. She whispered, "Master Thomas did this to you?" James nodded, Lanar wrapped her arms about his shoulders and wept, he wiped away her tears and she kissed him. Slipped out of his room and tiptoed back to her bed. Lanar realizing to leave she could not. She loved James, she needed to keep an eye on him and their master, to tell anyone in this household, she could not, confused and frightened, she stayed on to be with James.

Thirty-Six: The Hunt

Desperate for survival, after the horrible fire Kosta wrestled on the one decision to go again; plead with his brother for help. Not only was he embarrassed to face him, he feared his brother. Present circumstances gave him no other choice, or else they perish of starvation, they lost their most valued possessions, their only life support, grain. Now all of it was gone.

It took days, then weeks to gather the courage just to think of his brother much less to go to his brother's estate. He stalled. The feeling of foreboding kept him at home. He could not swallow the little portions of food their friends brought. He gave it to his children. Michael once gave him a bottle of wine and now he sipped it whenever the hunger became unbearable. Kosta felt guilty not telling Kathryn about the wine, she too was starving. The children were huddled together most of the time.

Mathew's feelings raged within him, but he said nothing.

Kosta gave in, and when the children were asleep, he reached for the bottle and said, "Drink it, the warmth of it will kill the hunger a bit and help you sleep."

"Where in the world did you get this wine?" Kathryn asked as she drank from the bottle.

"Michael gave it to me just a few days ago."

"That was very nice of him." Kathryn cuddled close to him and said, "Hold me."

Kosta wrapped his arm around her, laid awake; when she breathed evenly, he knew she was asleep. Kosta contemplated going hunting with Mathew and the trip to his brother.

Mathew rode over to Rebecca's home, discussed their situation over and over again, the two of them considered going to the castle to plead with the Baron, but changed their mind. "He probably only has enough for himself and his servants," they told each other.

Midnight, Mathew's dog had enough sense to go and catch anything that moved. He brought home a rabbit. Kathryn skinned the rabbit, chopped it into small pieces, Midnight patiently waited and after a while received his share.

Kathryn asked Kosta and Mathew, “If you went out hunting on a day like this, would you have any luck getting a dear or a wild boar?”

“Last night I planned to go out, but because of the cold weather not wanting to,” Kosta replied.

“Our dog did not think of the weather, hunger urged him on,” Kathryn interjected and smiled. They quickly gathered their gear dressed and were ready to go out. Kosta said to Kathryn, “As I was saying, to venture out today is a bit risky, besides all the animals are in their own shelters deep in the forest.

“Be very careful do not go deep into the woods,” Kathryn called after them.

Together ever so watchful for anything that moved, after many hours of waiting and walking Mathew spotted a buck, they crouched being still. The buck stood, head high in an open prairie as if waiting. Mathew sighted and hit true. Today they were successful, a buck, they dragged it home. Mathew described in detail on their luck. The girls were sad, saying, “He was a father of a little fawn or a baby buck.” Kosta tried to explain how desperately they needed food.

“You know that buck sacrificed himself to us, otherwise he would have been far away and deep in the forest, it was the will of God.” Truly, he himself believed it. Children had a good portion of meat on their plate, chewed slowly enjoying each tasty morsel to make it last. Mathew went next door offering a piece of venison, but Cresteron declined. “Mathew we have plenty, thank you for your good heart. Mathew, keep it you have a large family.”

Kosta wrapped a large cut of the meat for Aunt Olivia she too was in need of food. That night the children slept soundly. As weeks slipped by Kosta and Kathryn discussed the matter of the barn, and how will they save money for the necessary lumber. The good neighbors cannot and will not keep their horses and cows all winter, this was becoming a dilemma. He should go to Michael and consider taking the horses to him.

“Kosta are you forgetting that Michael’s barn also went up in flames? Kathryn said quizzically. Kosta looked up at her flustered, “My God! I completely forgot!”

Kosta and Mathew arrived at Michaels home and Rabinna served tea with honey. Rebecca and Mathew immediately went off to the bedroom and began talking.

“Winter will be soon upon us. We still could dig deep enough and erect a good size stable,” Kosta said to Michael. “It will be impossible for the men if they tried to build the barn later when the freeze comes," Michael agreed.

"To complete it quickly we need all the men from the village," Kosta said thoughtfully. Rabinna chimed in, "Just think about it, yes it is cold, but the ground is not quite frozen it has only snowed once and once that night a strong freeze, what if you cut down enough trees to at least build an enclosure with a makeshift roof. That would give the animals shelter."

The two men looked at each other and laughed. Michael said, "of course it would, we have spoken of the same thing my dear." Rabinna blushed.

The men gathered from villages, had worked tirelessly and put up a structure in no time as planned. It stood away from the house for safety. The interior walls stacked with hay and held up by pilings and saplings up to the rooftop, separating the animals. The saplings and straw used to cover the roof. A wealthier farmer delivered sacks of grain as gifts to Kosta's family. Stacked inside wherever they had room. "Cut more saplings and put up a fence around the stable. Your horses and cattle will have their own yard. Make sure it is high enough and far from this shelter, you know just in case someone tries again," Cresteron said.

"Aye, we should get to it right away," a younger man agreed. All the men stood and stared at this crude structure when it was finished. They looked at each other and laughed.

"Now we go build another, for Rabinna and Michael, this will do anytime," they all agreed.

The horses and cows returned to their make shift stable. If not for these animals, Kosta will butcher for food or sell if he needs to. One thought crossed his mind,

"If it should happen again, whoever comes will set the house on fire too. Who had done this to him? At that time of night, it was too dark to find any tracks.

Thirty-Seven:

The Spider is Waiting

Lord Thomas completely relaxed and lounged around in his favorite chair, seemed to be whispering, his lips moved. The servants thought, surely he lost his senses.

Oh, but they were mistaken. Lord Thomas absolutely did not lose any of his senses he was in his old world, he had to satisfy his long time revenge, known but to him only.

He walked around the house admiring all of his possessions, proudly told himself that he will have much more. He will be the richest man in the entire world. He...Lord Thomas... the poor peasant boy who emerged from the dung and poverty ambitiously created a kingdom of his own. "*Lord*" a nickname his mother had given at birth suited him so appropriately, now.

His little smile gave him away. He waited for that one certain visitor. He was ready.

James was ill for many months. He refused to take any sort of medication from anyone but Lanar. He could not locate Lanar anywhere, her room empty all her belongings still neatly lay in place, as before. He was now mute unable to ask, besides no one understood what he tried to say, he walked the grounds his normal tasks undone, looking, looking for Lanar. He just wandered around and sometimes wept. He sat in his room, when Alanda brought to him his meals; James would take her by the hand and walk to Lanar's room pointed at her belongings. With his arms waving in desperation, trying to get Alanda to explain to him what happened and tears rolled down his cheeks. Alanda after many times avoiding his questions told him, Lanar went away. James's eyes grew large and with angry fists beat his head, shook his head his mouth open trying to say, no, no. Alanda grabbed his arm jerked it hard and with her finger on her lips ordered him to be hush. She would take him back to his room making sure no one sees them, waited for him to eat his food, and gave him a large glass of wine. She whispered, "Lay on your bed and rest." In his extreme depression, he relived his life and his deeds as if reading chapter after chapter in his book of life.

Alanda reported James' progress to Lord Thomas. His order was to leave James alone.

James no longer smiled as before, realizing that that little smile had betrayed him. That little smile his co-workers were so used to, now he wore a deep frown, in his eyes sadness. That certain spark was gone. His attitude changed towards his working companions whom he constantly pestered and teased, before. They were used to a jolly man, since then he dragged his feet, slouched forward as if carrying a heavy load on his shoulders and his eyes downcast, as if he feared that someone could tell what he had done.

"Something is bothering James, he refuses to speak, points to his throat, as if in pain, he is not the same, absolutely not himself. What happened to him, Mother?" Mark remarked.

One day Mark approached James and bluntly asked him what was wrong with him. James with his head down muttered something his hands rubbed his chest, indicating to Mark his chest ailing but he did not speak, he pointed to his throat which meant he had a condition which bothered him for a long time, James longed to disclose to Mark his secret pain. His awful deed, the harm done to others he cannot carry that burden alone anymore or hide that fact from Mark, but how?

"James, why do you not speak to me? Do you feel ill? Where is your pain? What are you trying to tell me?" Mark questioned, time and time again.

James did not know how to explain. James took Mark's hand and walked to Lanar's bedroom. He pointed to the bed and then his eye, as if asking, where is Lanar?

The expression on his face was fear, sheer fear, eyes darting around in fear of someone watching. Mark at first did not understand what James meant. "James you want to know where Lanar is. Is that it?" James nodded. "James, Lanar quit her job here, went home." James wide-eyed his face wrinkled shook his head, "no no!" his arms waving, shuffled off.

Mark grabbed his arm and swung the old man around and when James faced him, Mark saw the tears streaming down this old face, "James, James what is it? Tell me please!" However, James could never speak to Mark again.

Very upset with the reaction from James, Mark went quickly to talk to his mother on the slightly ajar door Mark tapped and walked in, Cybilia sat at the desk jotting down something in her diary she closed it as Mark approached.

"Mother what is wrong with James? He has changed from a jolly man to a shuffling blob of flesh. He seems to be dying right before our eyes! I need to know what happened, what is wrong!" Marks loud demanding voice echoed through her room, Shara came in just then and she wanted to know why James had changed.

Lord Thomas hearing loud voices cautiously approached to overhear Cybilia saying something in a low voice. He peeked into her room Mark and Shara were with her.

Cybilia motioned for them to sit down and said, "I have asked several times about James, the cook explained to me, that James became ill and had lost his voice, that is why after many months he cannot talk, they all told me the same thing. I believe them. Have you forgotten, a few months ago, we all stayed away from him in fear of being infected? James' sneezing and coughing, burning up with high fever, Father confined James to bed, ask Alanda, she catered to him," Cybilia explained.

"Mother, that is absurd! No one ever looked this bad in this household as long as I remember! Ridicules reason! I do not believe this at all!" Mark highly irritated burst out at his mother. Shara agreed with Mark shaking her head, adding.

"Mother, Mark is right, think back, Alanda did not catch his sickness, besides it was not Alanda caring for him, it was Lanar, and where is Lanar, what happened to her, does anyone know? There must be more to this, we will find out somehow." Cybilia stared at them, a feeling of suspicion crept into her mind.

Then she said in a hushed voice, "Be careful who you ask, especially those men; they are crude and the kitchen help are close-lipped, fear for losing their job. You know how father has been lately."

"Mother I see you have no concerns for James at all, why. And where is Lanar anyway?" Shara asked. Cybilia looked at her daughter and replied, "Shara, I am concerned but he has overcome all of his ailments, he will be fine now, he will spring back, when Lanar returns. Father told me she had to leave for several months, but she will be back...to tell you my true feeling...she will not be back."

Lord Thomas barely understood what she said to them in that last sentence but he smiled, turned and quickly tiptoed away. *"Hmm...my children are concerned about James...well...well...I will solve their concern for them soon..."* he thought.

Cybilia, Mark and Shara were not aware that someone eavesdropped.

Mark puzzled over this simple explanation; his gut feeling refused to accept it, there must be more to this. Mark kept thinking back, *I have seen James having colds before, why, all of us had at one time or another, a cold, but none looked as bad as James is now. The cook had all sorts of remedies, but this...this is not a simple cold ailing James.*

Mark knew down deep that there is a different reason. "*Hmm...Joseph and Lanar disappeared, now something is dreadfully wrong with James,*" Mark thought.

He will keep asking, must get an answer, no matter how long it will take.

Considering which of their servants would be willing enough to inform him, and of course substantially compensated. He began to snoop around the kitchen. His pretense was of being a bit hungry. The best place to snack of course was the kitchen.

Observing the kitchen help, he inquired, "Who is that shy girl, and when was she hired, and where does she live and how large is her family?" Questions asked had not been routine, as the master's son he had every right to question. Within weeks, he had all the answers, now he was ready to uncover the secrets of Joseph, James and Lanar.

Nifta a peasant girl newly hired, shy, one day confronted by Mark listened intently to his detailed instructions.

"Do not ask all your questions in one day, just now and then, you know, just wondering why and how and who, do you understand? Consider each question before you ask any of them, then when you have information, find me, we will then arrange a meeting under the huge tree, I will go riding, do you know which tree?" he finished. "No. I do not, Sir."

"I will take you there, do not worry," Mark said.

She was willing to help Mark because her family was poor and needing her help.

Weeks passed, Nifta avoided Mark, not even a glance at him whenever she served dinner, Mark was puzzled, but said nothing, he kept asking her for more of this or that, he kept trying to meet her eyes, but she did not glance at him, knowing that he was trying to catch her eye, purposely averting her head.

"What was wrong? Did someone frighten her? Perhaps the senior servants warned her of him, do they think falsely of him? Why, I should wait for a few days longer, perhaps she has no information." He kept reassuring himself and waited, as several months went into spring now. Then one day, Mark sat in the library reading a book when Nifta tapped on the door, asked permission for a day off, her mother was ill and needs help quickly, could someone take her home.

The way her eyes darted he understood what she meant, he agreed to take her home on horseback. Mark told her to get her things and in a few minutes, he will saddle his horse. She nodded and went back to the kitchen. After a few minutes, Nifta sat behind Mark as they rode down the road out of the estate. Reaching a small rise making sure they were out of sight, Mark turned the horse towards the big tree in the meadow. Nifta slid off the horse. Mark dismounted pulled a blanked from behind the saddle and spread it on the grass.

“What did you find out? Anyone protested that you were going home?” he asked.

“Yes,” Nifta nodded.

“Why did they? Who objected, tell me. Do not be afraid of me, you are able to talk I assume, speak to me freely.” He smiled at her.

“Sir of course I am able to speak. I...am afraid, not of you of course, but...them. You see, I found out that James will never speak again, his tongue was cut out, what he knows will never be told, besides he cannot write, he tries to tell me by pointing towards the distillery and showing me his mouth, and I figured it out, when these men were drunk—”

“Which men, do you know their names?” Mark interrupted.

“I heard them talking about Joseph and those three men, who were sent to find and kill him. I pretended not to hear, I was just rocking and pretending to talk to myself, I know they think I am a little daft, and so they ignored me.”

Mark interrupted again, “Where were you at the time they were talking about Joseph?”

Nifta smiled, then quietly said, “Master Mark, I was in the stable looking for anything of interest and found a piece of cloth which is used to clean, and I held it up and laid it down on my knees and kept twisting it, and humming a tune, you see I knew they were in there. One man looked at me and said to the other, “I think she is not right in her mind” Sir, I must pretend or they will do harm to me too, sometimes I think they are planning something anyway. They think I do not know the difference.”

“What were they doing there? Mark asked.

“Nothing, they were sprawled on the hay drinking. But when I heard what they said about Joseph, I started to dance and waved the cloth and I skipped and whirled, all that time my eye on them, I danced all the way to the kitchen,” she said.

"Did they come after you?" Mark asked.

"Ah no sir, I am frightened, wondering if they suspected I heard and understood what they had said. I have to tell you, I have never been with a man and I do not want to be harmed by one, especially them." Her voice trailed off, she cast her eye down embarrassment.

Mark observed her closely as she talked. She was attractive, and graceful, certainly intelligent, far from being a bit "*daft*." She was only acting the part. Her voice was very sweet, her strawberry blond hair scintillated in the dappled sunlight. He found her captivating, why, almost seductive. "*No wonder these men are contemplating crime, she must be protected, especially now. She has been in the kitchen and I did not pay attention until I needed information about James and Joseph's disappearance. Now she is facing me, and I like what I see in front of me, who is she?*" Mark was thinking.

"I want...young miss, we have been here a while and I do not know your name," Mark said sternly. She looked up at him with watery blue eyes, as blue as the sky with a bit of sadness, "Nifta is my name," she whispered.

"Nifta is a fine name, is that your real name and where is your home, Nifta?"

"My home is not very far, I walk to work many times," Nifta replied.

"I see. Do you have brothers or sisters?" Mark inquired.

"Sir, I...have no brothers or sisters, I am an orphan...she replied lowering her head...a family took me in when my parents died of a fever. They had six children of their own. I have been with my adopted family all my life. They are good to me and I need to help them financially," Nifta concluded.

"Your adopted parents had six children when they took you in," Mark wanted to know.

"Yes sir...six, but two died, now only four plus myself," Nifta said.

"When did my father hire you? Mark asked.

"No sir, your father did not hire me, your mom did...I mean Lady Cybilia...when Lanar left," Nifta replied.

"Why did Lanar leave, do you know the reason?" Mark asked surprised.

"Sir, you must have known that they loved each other, James and Lanar, but she was...was...oh, I cannot tell you, forgive me, now I must go home, please take me home." Mark wanted to know more, but today, time ran short.

“Come I will take you home.” He stood helped her up to the saddle, he mounted behind her. They rode at a fast pace, she jumped off the horse and ran into the house not looking back at him.

Mark turned his stallion around and galloped back to the tree in the meadow. There he slowly mulled over every word she had said, he wondered and tried to analyze the whole situation, and could not completely understand why all of this happened for what reason. He dosed off for a moment, awakened by shrill noises above him. He looked around, above him among the branches black birds peered down at him. “What are these big birds doing here, why, they disturbed my nap! Just as well, time to get back home. He should not stay this long, must keep an eye on everyone, perhaps father is too lax, servants do what they want. Fact is father is hardly ever around. Mother is too preoccupied with herself. Shara is just a frolicking brainless girl. I am the only one concerned with what is going,” he mumbled to himself on the way home. He felt it was his responsibility to look after the estate or else it could be dismantled without notice, like the ants on a picnic, carrying away crumbs piece by piece until all gone. Nifta did not come to work for several days. Mark wondered why.

“Nifta mentioned *they*, who were *they*?” He was completely engrossed in thoughts about what Nifta had told him. Why was Joseph murdered and James maimed for life? The one question always screamed in his head, *why?* These men, Joseph and James whom Mark respected and looked up to and who since Mark was a little boy were his teachers of many things and his best companions.

He swore to search for the answers for as long as it takes. Mark made a promise, not to himself but to Joseph and James.

How inconceivably cruel of these men were they born this way, or were they that weak of character to be easily swayed by evil, as time and years went by? Why be so cruel to the weak, inflict pain, watch them suffer and die? Life is hard enough without being tortured. These sadistic brutal men were the kind that their Master hired to carry out his orders. All along, these cruel drunkards finalized a plan to torture and rape Nifta. She would not live through it, precisely their plan...pleasure...and then no witnesses. No treachery the two were in this together, no treachery, each knew the consequence.

Thirty-Eight: Escape

Nifta returned to work after several days. Each time these two men came around she shivered, fear urged her to escape to a far village for safety. She explained the situation to her adopted parents and pleaded to promise never to tell anyone of her whereabouts. She will send word wherever she settles. They agreed with regret of losing her. She swore she would help them financially, somehow she will, she promised, and they believed her. Her adopted parents wished her a safe journey when at grey dawn she went away.

Nifta walked mainly through woods and prairies staying of the road. After several days of walking her food basket was empty. At last, she came upon a small home on the outskirts of a village, small but well kept. Hunger pangs forced her to stop at a home to ask for bread and water. The individual who opened the door was shocked to see a young woman on foot and the day was dreary.

"Please sir, help me, please, I am so hungry...please help me..." Nifta begged and feeling weak dropped to the ground, her head to her knees. The man at the door helped her into the house and walked her to a chair at the table, she trembled. He gave her a glass of water. Nifta drank it greedily and said, "thank you sir."

"Sit here I will prepare a sandwich for you," he said. She looked around amazed at how clean the place was and wondered if he was alone, perhaps married with children, but where are the children and the wife. The man came back with a large sandwich on a plate set it on the table in front of her. Nifta reached for the sandwich and devoured it in a few bites. The man observed her closely, amazed.

"Tell me what brings you here and why?" he asked her.

"I cannot tell you anything right now. Please do not ask me. I appreciate your help, now I must leave," Nifta said rising from the chair.

"Where are you going?" he asked.

"Sir...I do not know yet, I just need to keep going," Nifta answered.

"Why not stay here for a few days, I will do you no harm, I assure you. Enough room for both of us, perhaps you will be of help to me, as I will be to you. A glass of wine will do you good." He handed her a large glass of wine. Nifta drank the wine; which warmed her and somewhat became drowsy. She asked if she could nap for a while on the cot. "Yes, of course, go lay down you look tired," he said. Nifta fell on the cot and closed her eyes.

"Yes, sleep my pretty girl," he whispered. He sat and watched as she slept and noted how familiar her features were, a close resemblance, the girl he loved and lost, but for her hair not of the same color.

Nifta slept soundly. The young man also slept, but lightly, waking often to see if she was still there on the cot.

In Nifta's dream those men were calling her name, she tried to run, run away from the estate. She woke up in the middle of the night drenched in perspiration, and disorientated. She fell back onto the cot to think things through. That young man, who sat in the dark watching her, was Christian. He waited for sunrise.

At the estate when Mark went into the kitchen asked the cook, "Do you know where the new girl is, ah her name is Nifta?"

The cook hesitated. "She is not here anymore."

Mark was stunned.

"But she was here just a few days ago, did she leave?" Mark visibly upset. "Yes, she left. You might just go and talk with her parents, she could be at home." The cook gave him a questioning look. "Do you know Mark, where she lives?" Mark was beside himself, he said. "No! Tell me." Fearing for her safety Mark did not waste time, saddled his horse and galloped to Nifta's house to question her parents.

"She was home for one day, when we woke up at dawn she was gone," Nifta's father said.

The servants tight lipped, if their master asked for information, would never admit knowing what they know, anyway. Mark did not tell his mother of his plan; Shara cared less, preoccupied with self-image, comfort, and constantly pampered by her servant; in her own little world, the bedroom. At the estate for now, the turmoil has subsided to everyone's surprise.

Thirty-Nine: Decision

The change was in the air, one could smell winter. Surely, winters are unpredictable; it could swing either way, dangerous freeze or much snow. However, food shortages this winter seemed to be the last straw for this family. Kosta having no other choice, the decisive moment is now. One more time he and Michael sat down and discussed options of where to go for help, after all his barn also burned, and they were short of supplies, though with one daughter, still anticipated difficulty for the long winter as well. They decided to visit their friend Baron, perhaps he would help with food, in return, they will work free, no matter what was needed to be done and no matter how little he could spare for their families.

On a good day, both set out on horses to the castle. Butler Ridiller let them in and they followed him to the study where Baron Patrick sat reading and writing something in a huge ledger. When Butler Ridiller harrumphed and coughed, Baron looked up to see his two friends standing in the doorway.

"Come in out of this horrid weather, you need a warm up, a large glass of wine! How is Aunt Olivia, is she well? I am glad to see you!" Baron exclaimed rising off the chair and gripping their hands in a strong shake. Kosta taken aback a bit, replied, "We are holding on as best as we can, and Aunt Olivia is much better now, she has been unwell for a long while. She is sending her apologies again for her absence to your dinner invitation. She wishes you well." Baron was thoughtful for a minute, "Come let us sit in the parlor by the fire, you need to warm up," he said. Rang the service bell, Butler Ridiller entered the parlor, Baron ordered lunch.

Baron looked at Kosta and said seriously, "Kosta your Aunt Olivia, ah, she is planning to visit me one day soon is she not?" Kosta stammered not sure how should he speak for his Aunt not knowing her feelings.

"I suggest you invite her again, you know how women are at these games."

The three men sat in the dining room now, as they ate, Baron listened to their situation and proposition. Baron Patrick had been aware of the tragic fires, agreed to help. Both men were in disbelief that it turned out so well for their families.

"The good Lord is watching over all of us, even though we suffered such terrible losses, we will be fine," Kosta said on the way home.

"Yes, you are right we have a wonderful generous man up in that castle, we will be forever grateful, to be sure," Michael agreed.

"But Kosta, what about that other family, whose barn had burned too, has anyone helped them?"

"Oh yes, Arkushin told me his brother and friends from the other village rebuilt it for him, they are fine," Kosta replied.

The two families lived together in Kosta's home since it was much closer to the castle. This combining and rationing of staples should suffice through the winter for them and the animals. Mathew was pleased to have Rebecca so near, never ran out of subjects to talk about. The younger children sometimes complained that they talk too much, because they could not join in the conversation.

Rebecca and Tessana became close as sisters; helping to dress, the younger children and worked hand in hand in the kitchen. Kathryn loved her as much as she loved her own children, and Rabinna worked the chores with Kathryn. Baron Patrick supplied provisions. Each visit to the castle the Baron Patrick inquired about Aunt Olivia's health, and each time at home, Kosta mentioned it to Kathryn.

"Why not have her go and stay with the Baron for a while, it seems to me he would like to see her. It would not be so lonely and boring for either of them. They are adults and up in age individuals. You know what I mean," Rabinna said.

On a Sunday Kosta and Kathryn visited Aunt Olivia, hoping she will agree to go for a visit to the castle. Aunt Olivia listened.

"Yes, I will go if you so wish, I appreciate your concern besides in your house there is absolutely no room not even for a mouse, much less for me," Aunt Olivia replied thoughtfully.

"You are absolutely right, or for another cat or dog, but we will patiently wait out the winter, and we will visit, the children love to frolic in the castle." Kosta laughed.

Within days Kosta and Aunt Olivia were riding up to the castle. Kosta noticed Aunt Olivia seemed a bit restless, but carried on a conversation pretending all is well.

Butler Ridiller opened the heavy door seeing Kosta with Aunt Olivia on horses. A biased expression of surprise and disapproval plastered all over his face, Aunt Olivia was not to his liking. To conceal his displeasure Butler Ridiller became overly courteous to them, which Kosta did not overlook since this was not his usual manner. He carried the small bag of her personal things as they followed him as he stopped in the doorway of the parlor; he announced, "Master Baron, guests have arrived, and with Sir Kosta a lady."

Kosta and Aunt Olivia followed behind the butler. Baron sat in the high back chair facing the fireplace, his back to them. The moment he heard Kosta's name he rose out of the chair and turned surprised to see Aunt Olivia. Baron folded his hands in a praying fashion as he walked towards them.

"Kosta, what an unexpected pleasure...my God...Aunt Olivia, welcome...do come in, please!" Their meeting again seemed to Kosta that surely this man and this woman had a past, from the way Baron took her hand and the way he kissed it. Kosta had never observed any man kiss a woman's hand with such tenderness. Baron led her to the comfortable chair on which he had sat. Their unexpected visit surprised and excited him. Wine and lunch was prepared immediately.

"Olivia I am so pleased to see you again, it seems years...since we had—"

Aunt Olivia interrupted him..."Oh yes it seems that way...at the harvest festival... I do remember, are you well Baron?"

"Yes I am well, you were under the weather so I understand, I should have known..."

"Well you know, time changes us a bit, and makes us a bit feeble. But you look well."

Kosta in a hushed voice said, "Sir Baron please forgive my asking, is there a possibility, with your agreement of course, for Aunt Olivia to spend the winter with you here at the castle." Baron smiled broadly, and in his eyes joy sparkled at such a proposal.

"Of course...with great pleasure, Olivia may stay forever if she wishes to!" Baron exclaimed.

When asked if she will stay, she replied, "Yes, for a little while. Perhaps even through winter." As she spoke, her eyes fell on things of interest, the riches all around. Although she was not rich, sitting in this parlor in a castle did not feel out of place. On the contrary she felt very at home, which surprised her.

Butler Ridiller observed them hidden behind a doorway, wondering who this woman was, and why was she here to stay. Several hours later Baron Patrick took Aunt Olivia on a tour through the whole castle, answered all her questions. He either held her elbow up the stairs or held her hand as they walked from room to room. Kosta followed them noticing that being a Lady not objecting to his polite attentiveness. Before Kosta left them, Baron provided provisions for the families for which Kosta was grateful. On the way home Kosta visualized Aunt Olivia's poise and how she absorbed Barons attention.

"I cannot wait to see the outcome of this meeting," he said out loud on the way home.

When he entered his crowded little home everyone looked up at him wanting to know how the meeting went. "Very well, I think they will not be bored with each other, and she will not be hungry with him. I must say, I noticed a hidden mystery about them. Something I could not detect, Aunt Olivia was a perfect Lady and the Baron very attentive, indeed, even held her hand going up the stairs," Kosta replied.

Rabinna and Kathryn said, "We must pray to the good Lord to give them happiness and peace. Since both have been alone so long. Perhaps the ghost will leave them alone for a while, give them a good night's rest." Winter came, gloomy months dragged on, what was anticipated had not occurred, this winter seemed the mildest of all previous winters they remember. The younger children were restless and oftentimes they fought for space or food. Whenever possible they all crowded into the wagon and rode up to the castle for a visit to break the monotony. Since the winter was mild, Lord only knows what spring will be like; and spring months still far off, even then late in March or April it would snow instead of expected sunshine and warmth. As winter dragged, the family rode up to the castle, often. These trips broke boredom, eyes shining, smiling, and glad to have such a grand place to spend a day. Whenever sunshine peeked through the clouds every child's face lit up anxious to run outside to play. Springtime had that same old grind, but at least fresh air and sunshine was a pleasant change, bringing forth life to their world after a long dreary cold winter.

During the night, the last day in April, so late in the season unexpectedly it snowed. After several weeks and warmth, the snow began to melt, icy water rushed down the mountains, flooding the lower fields. Everything was at a standstill, a stalemate for how long remained to be seen, people waited for the land to dry. Delaying plowing and planting.

Mathew and Rebecca could not wait for a good day to fish. Kathryn cautioned how unsafe the riverbank is, now. The force of water eroded and loosened the soil, ripped out many trees, and at any moment, the bank could collapse under their feet. Rebecca and Mathew understood this was a dangerous time. They heeded her warning. These teens felt cursed, and they expressed their opinion to their parents. Each outing they had ever planned something delayed them and they were furious. On this particular day, Kathryn observed them, and decided to tell them about Mathews grandparents. She began the story as she heard from Kosta, the tragic loss right there on that river, and she pointed out to them that perhaps Mathew's grandparents are protecting them from danger, especially in bad weather.

They listened and began to believe, Rebecca cried true tears of sorrow. Mathew regretted the privilege of never knowing his grandparents. These two teenagers exhibited understanding, obedience and intelligence. Kathryn was proud of them, also her concern grew for them.

Forty: Lasting Love

Christian the young lover of the murdered girl, Marysa, daily read her diary. Longed and wished her alive and with him. He was determined to solve the mystery of her death. Now Christian and Baron talked, many hours on the bench beneath the huge oak tree. Never suspecting her body rested at their feet. "I believe Marysa loved this oak tree, she points to it in my dreams," Baron said.

"Yes, she did, many times while she was alive she had said to me, I like to dream my dreams beneath that tree," Christian replied.

They sat on the bench in silence trying to understand the meaning of it all and why such things should happen.

Aunt Olivia remained at the castle until spring. The ghost did not disrupt them as much as when Baron was by himself. Baron one evening told Olivia about his friends visiting, having fun, and why they left never to return, because the ghost frightened them. Whenever Christian visited she observed them talking on the bench under the tree. She wondered what they had in common. "Baron, everyone addresses you as Baron, do you have a first name?" Aunt Olivia asked smiling.

"I would rather not...it is well with me, no need for them to know it, yet," Baron spoke slowly as she looked at her. Baron read her questioning expression one evening as they sipped wine by the fireplace, he told her the story of why the ghost is wandering and disturbing their life. However, he did not mind, he felt sorry for her and Christian.

Aunt Olivia understood. Years ago, when she was young she was desperately in love. She lost him, but her love for him never died, and now each day being together with Baron she relaxed and her feelings awakened from years of dormant sleep and she longed for his embrace.

Baron felt he knew her. A wonderful feeling moved him when they were just inches from each other, her voice and her eyes were the same although she has changed with age. Avoiding embarrassment and rejection and perhaps anger, he kept his feelings to himself, but knowing that day will come she will understand and forgive him.

Now Olivia revisited her past where she saw him young, that hairline, and those lips. Though that sparkle in his eyes was lost, the upturned corner smile did not. She knew him, and her heart beat a bit faster, she began questioning his past. He gave her very descriptive replies, wanting her to know it was him, she smiled, visualized those places, but at times she was disappointed. "*Had he forgotten or is he purposely holding me at bay, but why? Time is slipping away. Perhaps he has not recognized me yet, or is afraid of me*," Aunt Olivia thought. Concealing her feelings and many evenings retired early excusing herself as being, a bit tired. "It must be old age, and a long day," she would say. Baron never detained her, escorted her upstairs. "You must rest, sweet dreams." He kissed her hands, and asked, "Would you allow me to wrap my arms around you and hold you a moment?" Aunt Olivia smiled and said, "You may, but not too long."

All servants liked Aunt Olivia, they agreed, "she belongs here, she is perfect for him." All but one, Butler Ridiller, he had no opinion either way.

"Whatever made you chose to live here in Riverside Valley?" While having lunch Aunt Olivia surprised him with this question.

Baron did not reply, instead he said, "Walk with me and I will tell you, after lunch. But dress well, still chilly out."

They strolled to the oak tree and sat on the bench. Baron, silent for a long while, he gazed far on the horizon; and was about to begin; Aunt Olivia broke the silence,

"Forgive me but it is too cold for me, perhaps the green house is warmer."

"I agree, let us go inside the greenhouse," Baron said. They sat on an old bench without speaking, it was so quiet in the greenhouse, the plants still dormant and the air smelled earthy.

"I ask you...Baron began, if you have been married, you must have loved that man. If you loved a man and lost him to whatever circumstance, that love for him never died. Life then being alone seemed meaningless. Nevertheless, life has to be lived; it does not matter where the road leads.

Some individuals take their grief to the grave. Others go in search, with time forgetting what it was they were searching for; still others create a life of riches of immense proportions, believing they will find love. As it happens, when a new love comes along, ones first love still has a place in the heart. One must move on and not look back. I traveled the world, and I searched, never once wavering in faith that I will find the one I loved."

Aunt Olivia put her hand on his arm and asked, "Why did you lose your love?"

"At that time of my life, I did not understand why I must enter a pre-arranged marriage. Marry a woman my parents had chosen for me, ignoring my heart's desire. I rebelled. I opposed and lashed out with words I often regret. My parents forbade me to see the girl I loved. They could never understand my feelings. Baron paused...She was my life...he said. I had written her a letter and I will never know if she ever received it or read it. Gillian my trusted friend delivered it. Who took the letter from you, I asked him. Gillian told me it was her brother. Baron Paused for a long time then he continued...I waited months for a reply from her, but none came. One day I announced to my parents that Gillian and I are going away, far to the ends of the world. My father jumped up from the table grabbed my shirt collar and said; "You have disgraced our family with your rebellious behavior. You are to leave now! Your foot shall never cross this threshold. This front door to you is forever locked, never come back...my mother's tears I see even today. Regretfully she never uttered a word of protest on my behalf. If she only knew how crushed I was."

Baron Patrick sat with his elbows on his knees staring at the ground. He never saw the tears on Aunt Olivia's face.

"We traveled," Baron continued, "around the countries, we accepted menial jobs, earned pennies and saved them. We were fed had a corner to sleep in, we moved on and luck was with us, we came upon wrestling matches, we observed but that was not for both of us. Gillian and I later joined the gypsy caravan. They are a free people, traders, nomads of the world. They told us stories from around the world, not only did we earn money but I learned much from them on trading, mingling among the wealthy. Learning to live, learning to survive.

"We traveled north to a large city bustling with many foreigners, trading went on not only at the largest markets the likes I have ever seen, but also in the grubbiest places of that city. I settled there for ten years, worked in the fields for a very prominent farmer. In my spare moments, I read any kind of book I could get my hands on. I came across a small book with drawings of natives with pearls in their hands, as if beckoning to me, "this is your destiny, come this is your fortune." With luck after many months of inquiry, hitching rides on anything with wheels, we arrived at a seaport, earned food and lodging on ships loading and unloading merchandise of all sorts. After many weeks of waiting, at last, the Galleon set sails and we were off to the south-sea islands. I have never sailed on any sea vessel. This Galleon was impressive. The voyage at sea took months, horrific rocking, raging storms, crashing waves, and vomit. I stared at the horizon where the sea and the sky merged. I saw nothing else but the vast ocean all around, nothing else. At last, an island loomed on the horizon and everyone roared, anchor dropped into the sea and in dinghies, we rowed to the island, a wonderful paradise, isolated from the rest of the world, surrounded by water, with beautiful people, generous, happy and free.

"White beaches, and clear salty ocean water, so clear one could see the bottom and the fish of many colors. The natives dove into the depth of the ocean in search of precious pearls for which in return I paid the natives well by teaching them the language and to read books, they were as much in paradise in books as they were on their island. Thirteen years later, I was leaving that island and those wonderful people. They stood on the beach and waved as the dinghy carried me to the moored ship. I returned to Europe. I made a fortune from the sale of the pearls. I had comfort but not love. My love has been in my heart...but not in my arms," Baron paused.

Aunt Olivia sat staring at him in disbelief. "Then, all these years you never married?

"No, I never could. I was always looking and waiting. Where is she, is she alive, did she marry? With a fortune in hand, I began to visit small towns and villages. None pleased me. I decided to spend the rest of my life in solitude and hopefully in a peaceful setting. I traveled to many places, sometimes settled for a while, looking for her. Then I came here. The moment I entered the village I felt a sense of excitement. These mountains surrounding the village and this valley attracted my attention. I heard singing. Someone's angelic voice resonated, seemed to be everywhere. A feeling tugged at my heart. I saw a boy, oh about twelve years old, leaning on the gate of the fence. He looked at me and said, Sir you seem to be lost. I said yes you might say that I am I asked him if he knew of any land, imagine asking a boy...and he said, go up on that mountain and look. I rode my horse up here and I became mesmerized by this panorama. I hung around for several hours; I sat beneath that oak tree, I felt peace. Going back down from here, I met the boy again, I asked for directions to the mayor's office, the boy pointed but said nothing. The mayor informed me I could purchase it for back taxes. The mayor and I came up to this mountain. The moment he saw the view, the serenity of it all he said, you found your home. I told him that exactly. I was immediately interested in this lone oak tree, its age, the sprawling corona, in its tranquil shade one could dream. Now it is mine."

Aunt Olivia interrupted by placing her hand on his arm, "Yes you brought us some excitement and that noise resonated down to the valley, and you employed many people in need of work." Baron glanced at her, "well, all that noise was unavoidable, but look what the best craftsmen and many people had built, this castle, I call this a looming monstrosity...I call it my home and I love it, and," Baron paused, "I would love to share this tranquil setting with the one love that is in my heart."

Aunt Olivia hesitated for a minute then asked, "Whatever happened to your best friend?"

"Ah Gillie...! Ah, he fell madly in love, married a gypsy girl. I went on alone."

"Your life was full of adventure, and life threatening, I admire your courage," she said softly.

"Olivia, did you ever marry?" Aunt Olivia did not answer.

Baron looked up and saw the tears, and instinctively said, "Alas my love, why the tears...?" Aunt Olivia's tears slid down her cheeks, Baron reached up and touched them. For a moment they looked deep into each other's eyes and she softly spoke,

"Patrick McGrubshin I never received your letter. I would have run away with you, if I knew you were waiting for me out there. I never stopped loving you. I...after fifty years still love you, none other."

Baron Patrick caught his breath, his chin quivered and tears filled his eyes.

"Oh Las...the moment I saw you...at the festival...I felt I knew you, but I dared not cause you stress. You said, "Time is passing, it was said long ago," my heart skipped a beat...it was you...I used to say that to you." He took her trembling hands kissed them tenderly as when they were at the festival. Oblivious to their surroundings with bursting emotion Baron Patrick embraced her and held her, his chest heaved from emotion and tears streamed down his cheeks.

"My sweet love, at last I found you! Oh...how I love you!" he whispered tenderly kissed her lips igniting their long lost feeling of passion.

Aunt Olivia pressed close to him and replied, "My love for you never died, Patrick. Patrick, we lost a lifetime!"

They felt this moment as if years rolled back to when they were in love and young. Their paths of life merged after all these years, now they sat embraced, afraid to let go, else be apart again. "Olivia you are shivering, let us go in for a cup of tea with rum." Baron Patrick and Aunt Olivia arm in arm walked back to the castle.

Flora and her helpers were observing them from the window in awe. Flora said, “Well God Bless them, this is a new beginning for them,” Dola said. “We must tell...” but Flora clamped her hand on her mouth and said. “No, do not be a bunch of magpies. Nobody tells! Not a word to anyone, you hear?”

Forty-One: The Change

Kosta and Kathryn lived a complicated life, for all their life's misfortunes, struggles, enduring and overcoming adversities. Their lifestyle remained the same, in fact, in a worse position than ever! The children were growing up with less.

From constant worry, Kosta's hair turned slightly grey at the temples, and his physique lost its brawn. He was not the same in appearance and expression. His eye sank deeper into his brow, his cheeks more prominent than ever before.

Even Michael noticed the change and became concerned for his friend. Michael moved his family back to their home in the springtime. Michael discussed the situation about Kosta at length with Rabinna. Neither one could think of a solution to the situation they were in.

Kathryn noticed the change not only in her beloved husband, but in all of them as well. She went about her daily tasks.

"Why is father so glum? We are worried, he looks so different." the children whispered. "Keep busy with whatever you find to do," Kathryn said.

Everyone became quiet and the little home had lost its cheerfulness. Rebecca was not there to chat away with Mathew. They all prayed for a better tomorrow.

Kosta realized that all his hopes and expectations for his hard work were in vain, all. All his undertakings failed! His carvings were meaningless to him now, and of little importance to anyone. They were not selling as well as before. Oftentimes he wondered why.

He worked in the fields and stopped thinking and planning of ways to get ahead.

Through the past winters, their children battled colds. He and Kathryn overcame their own ailments. Though the farm grew in quantity had less to eat.

With the help of the neighbors and good friends the barn constructed twice, without them, he could not have built it himself. Baron never let any of them down. However, now they were on their own, now working the land hoping as always for enough to live on. The years of struggle and strain caught up to him, and now he was giving up. His strength gone, he has lost the will to go on. He disappointed his beloved Kathryn in so many ways, yet she stood by him through it all, never complaining.

His brother stripped him of his vision in the right eye..., he dared to be so cruel, why is he so heartless and cold? Kosta could not comprehend why his brother hated him so much...he sleeps at night in comfort and contentment without as much as a second thought of what goes on in my life. he said to himself. Why wonder, now he had the best. He has forgotten how it feels and what it means to be in need. Succeeding he did, grant him that, the question remains by what means had he acquired it all. Now comfort has dulled his feelings. He has much surplus stored, where others barely survive on crumbs. Kosta confused, no place to turn, thoughts crowding his mind, Kosta never in his life had been envious of anyone's success. Kosta toiled in the fields, his muscles numbed by the strain. His sons tried to work right along and do their best to keep up. Then all of those feeling left him. He stared out into the far horizon, his mind blank. At night, he laid down next to Kathryn not speaking. He drifted off to sleep but waking often in the night. "*What am I going to do, what to do, where to go*!" His mind in complete turmoil, his brain turned on and off with intermittence of quiet and then fury. This went on for weeks. No one knew how to snap him out of that state of mind.

Mathew begged his father to carve a bit with him but he refused. The younger children asked him to tell them a story he, refused. Many evenings he walked alone along the river not knowing why he was there, or what he was looking for.

He had a few good days when he was almost himself and his children were happy, and so was Kathryn. There were nights they talked until dawn, discussing, discussing all plans possible. Those were the good moments, when he was his own self.

Kathryn's trust never wavered, she believed in him now as she has from the first year together. Many nights she reminded him how much the Baron has helped them through the winter. He should have more faith and be grateful. "We will have enough you will see, this harvest will be good," Kathryn assured him.

Forty-Two: Patrick and Olivia

Baron Patrick and Aunt Olivia were inseparable. They truly wanted to recapture their youth and love. Spring hours spent watching their world come alive, reading, talking, laughing, as they had never laughed before. The castle echoed with their voices calling for each other. All the hired help smiled and winked in a knowing way. That was good, happiness lingered in every corner of the looming castle on the hill. The summers spent outdoors in the surrounding greenery and flowers, and many days and evenings up in the towers watching sunrises and sunsets, mesmerized. When the days grew shorter and cold, now fall and winter were approaching. Aunt Olivia needed to spend some time in her little house talk with neighbors and to secure it for the winter. Baron Patrick offered to go along to help her, but she insisted on going alone, also she reminded him Kosta always was there to help.

"My darling Las, you must come back and spend the winter here with me. I will dry up like a prune without you!" Baron Patrick quipped in a boyish gesture. Aunt Olivia always giggled when he acted in that funny way.

"Why Patrick you have not forgotten, you called me 'Las' my nickname of long ago. I will hurry to get things done, talk to my neighbors to watch the house for me, tell them where I will be all winter and I will come back and be with you from then on." She patted his cheek.

"Oh darling Las, I will count the hours and the days. Hurry back I need you, I will miss you, remember I love you now more than ever." He covered her face with kisses, then both her hands. Baron Patrick helped her into the carriage, and it rode away.

Baron Patrick walked back into the castle. The sudden silence made him realize how much he needed Olivia.

In the valley on the way home, she stopped to visit Kosta's family. The children surrounded her with questions about her stay in the castle with Baron Patrick. They begged Aunt Olivia to stay for a while they missed her as much as she missed their company. She wished they had come more often for a visit. Kathryn and Aunt Olivia had many private conversations out on walks and Aunt Olivia agreed that the time spent in the castle was pleasant, Baron Patrick is a fine man and she liked him.

"Aunt Olivia his first name is, Patrick?" Kathryn surprised asked. "Yes, Patrick," Aunt Olivia answered. "We only know him by "Baron" all these years. He never told us his first name or last, I wonder why?"

Kosta explained how much work they all had. They promised to come soon. Aunt Olivia rode on to her home, the children waved to her from the doorway. When she arrived at her home, she instructed the driver to go on back to the castle saying she will return with Kosta's family.

While working around the house her thought was not only of Baron Patrick but also of her feelings for him. She also was concerned for Kosta, he looked out of sorts something must be amiss. She reminisced of her love Baron Patrick again..., when we were young he had asked me to marry him, and when I asked, what season would you choose Patrick, he always said, Christmas, festive, very memorable. However, that never happened, our world and plans and love abruptly interrupted and he was gone. Through the years my hopes of seeing him again past like each sunset passes over the horizon, and my hopes passed into darkness. Now after all these years we are back together again. Why now, why not years before so we could have more time, why now? The reality of being old made her cry. "Oh...a lifetime has passed. Now so little time remains for happiness. But I will be thankful if only for a while to be with him, I love him so much," she thought as she worked.

One week passed. Two weeks had gone by Aunt Olivia sent a message through Kosta "*wait for me I will return soon.*" Baron Patrick anxiously awaited her return.

The first snow flurries fell. When the wagon pulled into the courtyard and the whole family jumped off and ran to the back of the castle to the kitchen. The excited cook cried out, "At last, what kept you away so long, we missed you!"

Cook Flora hugged and kissed them, then prepared a meal for all of them.

Aunt Olivia fell into Baron Patrick's embrace he held her tight and said, "I was afraid you would never come back, love."

"My dear Patrick, forgive me, but it took a bit longer than I expected. But from now on I am yours here to stay and make you happy." Olivia kissed him, her arms around his neck. They forgot that the whole family stood and gaped at them. Kosta and Kathryn glanced at each other and Kosta said, "I had a feeling they had a past. Something she said to him at the festival when they met, remember?"

"Yes I remember, she never talked about her past, now here it is, it caught up with them," Kathryn replied and squeezed his hand. The castle on the hill echoed with activity and laughter for days. Then at dinnertime Baron Patrick said to them,

"May I please have your attention everyone? I have an announcement to make," he turned to Aunt Olivia took her hand and with Komarod's family watching he proposed to Aunt Olivia she gasped, and was about to say..., "Patrick, please...,"

But Patrick interrupted, "Christmas, I love Christmas you will be my bride for Christmas." Kathryn and Kosta with the children were overjoyed, applauded. Rosie jumped from her chair ran to Aunt Olivia hugged her and cried out,

"Aunt Olivia you will never be sad anymore, Baron Patrick will make you happy." Old Simena brought in a platter of cakes for them. Rosie jumped up at the table and shouted. "Simena, Aunt Olivia and Baron Patrick are getting married!" If Simena had not been close to the sideboard, she would have dropped the plate on the floor. "Oh good Lord, bless them, it is about time!" she clapped her hands and went back into the kitchen, suddenly all of his staff barged in and shouted congratulations and applauded for a few minutes. The children sat gaping. Kathryn said, "Kosta these people love them, what joy, they are sincere, but someone is missing." Kosta glanced around, surely one person was not in the crowd, Butler Ridiller.

On Christmas day, the parlor decorated in its holiday décor, in the fireplace embers glowed, many candles burned brightly. On a silver tray, a decanter with red wine and two crystal wine glasses sat on a round table covered with lace tablecloth, waiting for the bride and groom. The kitchen buzzed with last minute inspection for perfect presentation. The dining room table in its festive display of fine china, crystals and silver candelabras, waited. Kosta with his family upstairs also waited, when the loud knock echoed through the quietness, someone had arrived, possibly the minister. Within several hours, all the guests invited had gathered in the large parlor, sipping wine and munching on horde ours, waited. Butler Ridiller nervously traipsed around the castle checking for who knows what, he had been observed by Michael and Rabinna with knowing glances, their inkling was, Ridiller did not approve of this union. He from *day one* was Barons *butler*, he was important, but now...a *woman* invaded his space. Ridiller was not sure how many positions this woman would change, if she is allowed to change, women know how to change things, pull wool over the man's eyes and have it their way, always.

Upstairs the bride and groom were about to descend down to the parlor, Aunt Olivia's hair was braided and wrapped around her head and forehead a bit. Her dress a silk salmon color shimmered in the light, and on her neck, she wore a string of large pearls. She smiled into the mirror, she felt younger and beautiful. She touched the pearls with her fingers, remembering that one day a long time ago. In the Barons room, the groom dressed in his Sundays best, admired his image in the floor to ceiling mirror. "*The day has come, my dream and wish come through, for that I am grateful, Lord, thank You,*" Baron thought. Baron came down the stairs and everyone applauded and shouted, bravo, congratulations!

Shortly after Aunt Olivia carefully stepped down the stairs, she blushed, "*I suddenly feel nervous as young brides do, anticipating, wondering of my future. Today, I am not a young bride, I am older, not knowing when, or how long...no, I will not doubt, as of today I know my future.*" Aunt Olivia shrugged these thoughts aside, she came down those stairs gracefully, Baron Patrick came towards her with outstretched arms, and she with hers and they embraced before the gathered witnesses. The village minister, Papa N'Poposh began.

"Attention everyone, today you will witness the shortest ceremony in your life, as time grows short. Patrick and Olivia after many years apart reclaimed love rightfully theirs, at this moment, now, I am empowered to pronounce them, husband and wife. May their life and love bloom for as long as it has and continue for a long time...May God Bless you today and, always." As they held hands, Aunt Olivia surprised hearing the minister proclaim their life's story, she could not hold back her tears. At last, she stood next to *him*, whom she loved, today he is hers, and she is his. For her age, she looked stunning, as Baron Patrick looked at her as her tears slid down her face, felt compassion, love and joy. He uttered these words to her as he brushed her tears, "Olivia my Las at last, our love won, we are together and no one will separate us, or tell us how to live." Baron Patrick kissed her hands and then they kissed wrapped in each other's arms. The whole group hooted and applauded.

Mary, Olivia's friend cried tears of happiness and so did all the other women. The guests seated in the dining room, "now dinner is served," Butler Ridiller said coolly. The guests seated were, Michael, Rabinna and Rebecca Hardigar. Kosta and Kathryn Komarod, their children Mathew, Tessana, Jason, Jasemin, Kras, Marla, Rosalyn (Rosie). Also were invited the village Mayor Pillar with Gritcha his wife, the Village Constable Maurice, Collette Gradeau and their teenage son Monty, Christian and Nifta sat next to the minister Papa N'Poposh. Twenty guests plus 12 employees, two, were privileged to join the dinner party, gardener Kirk Spence, and old Simena.

Everyone cheered and toasted glass after glass of wine in honor of the newlyweds.

Flora the cook noticed the sour grimace on Butler Ridiller face. He was unaware that she stood to the side of him. Flora tugged at Lipkas sleeve, the girl looked up at her, Floras eyebrow raised her expression meant do not speak, Lipka did not question they just backed away and out of sight.

"Watch out for the butler, from the looks of it, he is very unhappy with Master Barons love, I am not positively sure, perhaps I should not say any of this but, I feel deep inside that they are both in danger," Flora whispered.

"Flora...I heard him say he hates Lady Olivia, I did, when I was in the pantry he came into the kitchen talking to himself, I hid behind the door, and waited until he left. I slipped out of the kitchen and went to my room. What are we to do now Flora?" Lipka whispered, Flora whispered back in her ear... "Tell no one just yet. Let us observe him for a while. Then we will decide what to do," Flora said thoughtfully.

"Flora I will not tell anyone, I promise," Lipka replied with her hand on her heart. Flora heard her name called. Quickly she found herself at the dining room table.

"Flora my dear, are you and the rest of the girls finished in the kitchen?"

Flora big-eyed blushed, said, "Yes Master Baron, we are done." Baron Patrick waved his hand and said, "Now have everyone in here this minute, join us, this day is special for us and all of you."

Flora ran into the kitchen and shouted, "Everyone to the dining room, now, and you too Ridiller, Master Baron said so!" They all came and sat, dined with the guests and the bride and groom, a handsome pair admired by everyone. Many would cherish this memorable moment this Christmas.

After dinner, conversations among all the guests rang out with jolly laughter and much wine. Kathryn said to Rabinna, "We must ask Aunt Olivia about that string of pearls."

The two women approached the bride, "Aunt Olivia you look beautiful and those pearls are huge!" Rabinna exclaimed.

"I love that black one in the center, very exquisite piece, Baron Patrick kept them for you all these years," Kathryn said and wanted to say more but Aunt Olivia stopped her.

"Oh no, these are mine...I found these in a jewelry shop years ago...in a very large city, I only bought the string of the white pearls," Aunt Olivia explained.

"But you never mentioned a word about your life, all these years," Kathryn said.

"Well then, Baron Patrick gave you the black pearl?" Rabinna questioned her.

Aunt Olivia's friend Mary walked up hearing the mention of the black pearl. She began to tell them about it.

"Last night, while we were sipping wine, Baron Patrick said to Aunt Olivia, "My lovely Las, I have, through the years kept something for you. Always hoping I will see you again, stay right here I will be right back...he left her, when he returned his expression calm, he said, I had forgotten a very important piece, just slipped my mind, I am so sorry."

Out of his pocket he brought out a black velvet little bag out of which, a large black pearl brooch fell into his palm, he knelt on one knee and asked, will you wear this tomorrow?" Mary told them.

"And I said, yes! This morning while we talked about this black pearl broach, I recalled my string of pearls. I retrieved them from my case and clipped them together. What Mary said was all-true, Mary sat across from me by the fireplace. Aunt Olivia smiled, seeing the women wide-eyed, gaping.

"Will you tell us where and why you bought these pearls, please," Rabinna pleaded. "I will gladly, now that all of this is out of the bag, but not tonight, tomorrow," Aunt Olivia said.

Forty-Three: Breakdown

Kathryn at home retold the story of the pearls to Kosta. He listened with interest and said to Kathryn, “I am sorry I...never bought you anything all these years, I am ashamed, forgive me!”

“Kosta, we are talking of a love story of a lifetime, the way it is predestined, I have nothing to forgive you for. I know our life, our struggle, and Kosta I love you, just YOU!” Kathryn kissed him hard.

As weeks slipped by, Kosta became quiet as if something bothered or worried him. He seemed not talk about anything at all. This after a while irritated Kathryn and had one day an emotional outburst, not being able to withstand the way Kosta withdrew from her and the children, seemed to be tearing him-self apart. She expressed her opinion loud and clear. Sometimes she did not care if the children were present she raised her voice to say what she had to say.

“Kosta, you must try to control yourself, concentrate on what we have here, now, and make the best of it. We will survive! You must not tear your heart out like this! You will not be any good to us if you become ill! Kosta do you hear me!”

Kosta listened without replying, walk out of the house and go for his walk along the creek. He needed to be alone.

“If only they have not perished that night in that cursed river! Would it have been different? My family’s way of life, would it be better? How could it have been different? Being alive how could they have made a difference in my life? I cannot imagine, I just cannot think. My brother...would he have been more compassionate to them, be a bit more caring, I do not care for myself, but for my children. Why would he care for my children? They are not his children they are mine! I am responsible for them! I am! I am!” Such thoughts churned in his mind constantly.

Kathryn worried that he would harm himself. She followed him to the creek, hidden out of his sight observed him. She only saw a lost, lonely man alone with his thoughts. She felt sad, and sorry, this was her husband, a lost man because of a life laden with struggles. Now he struggled within himself. She loved him even more now and, she will love him until she dies, she knew that.

Making sure he is all right, she headed back home without him ever knowing she was there, watching him.

All those nights and days that she had prayed seemed to be in vain. Her prayers not heard and not answered. Her thoughts and feelings were as Kosta's and whenever she observed him at the creek, she ached with the same pain as he.

If Fate chose an individual for whatever reason, only to keep that individual down on his knees for all of his or her lifetime? When does this misery end, when one dies?

Too often, the scale of justice is off balance, could justice not only be blind but deaf? As it happens in so many cases, many lives are never the same. The self-confidence and courage seldom return to broken lives.

"From my observation and calculation of the crops yield put together, again the harvest for this fall will be inadequate," Kosta told Kathryn, on one of his good days.

"We will be careful for the months. The children and I will portion out again as before," Kathryn replied.

This is life's cruelest act of a sadistic deed, a show of power inflicted unjustly on a humble man, a man who happens to be of his own biological blood. Without a second thought or regret for the act, or disregard for the others. This is not fair and unacceptable for any one human being on this earth to be disfigured this way, not only the physical body is affected, also the spirit. She felt his thoughts, his desperate feelings.

The conflict of emotions suppressed for so long within, kept mounting into an eruption of anger. She followed him again, she observed him from afar, her chest tightened when she saw him drop to his knees. His clenched fists beating at his chest, staring up at the dark sky, the stars twinkled but he did not see them...the creek gurgled flowing down to the dark and forbidding river far off where it whispered, beckoning...urging anyone weak...to come. It would be a refreshing moment to plunge into the depths of it, to find solitude to end this torture such as it is. Kosta was deaf to his surroundings, his mind in great turmoil. Beating his chest until he felt the pain, he fell to the ground pounding and tearing at it with his fingers, his face contorted from rage, he shouted, "I worked all these years from sunrise to sunset and you gave me little to nothing in return...only stress... you hypocritical deceptive FATE. I had faith! Now my faith is wavering! Why me...why...I do not understand, I never asked much of you...only enough to make my family... happy have enough to eat! What have I done to live like this and my family suffers?"

He did not care if anyone heard him, or seen him in this state, or those bitter tears he shed this night, if any one witnessed he cared not. He did not care if any one heard his sobs. The rage within had to be released out of his chest.

On that dark night, his energy spent brought him down, and he stayed down until his chest stopped heaving and he could weep no more. Kosta felt the damp ground, yet could not rise. Prostrated and motionless he laid there for a long time.

Kathryn hidden in the brush, watched as her beloved husband crushed lay there on the ground alone. Kathryn unsure of his reaction, out of the shrubbery approached slowly, called his name, no response. She called to him again and he stirred, lifted his head and saw her, he cried out to her, "Kathryn, Kathryn!"

She ran up reaching out to him and with cries of concern embraced him, and without anger or shame, he fell into her arms, sobbed like a child. She kissed his tears. They talked for several minutes than walked home. The damp night chilled them to the bone.

Kosta was not feeling well the next morning. Kathryn had done all chores with the boys. The girls were like shadows moving quietly about the little house so as not to wake their father. They knew that he had gone through a very trying time last night.

"Mother what happened to Father, after Christmas, after Baron Patrick and Aunt Olivia's wedding, something happened to him. I wish I could understand and help him. We all want to help but how, he does not speak to us. Mother, what have we done wrong? Tessana asked. "No you have not done or said anything wrong, none of you, circumstances have caused this turmoil in your father. We must be patient, talk to him even though he will not answer you, but he will in time, you will see," Kathryn said, and hugged Marla and the rest of them. Several days later as Kosta stood at the window staring out. Rosie walked up and asked, "Father, what are you looking at?" Kosta put his hand on her shoulder and said, "I am staring at a tree."

"Oh, which one Father, where?" Rosie asked.

"The one across the creek, the one looking half-dead," Kosta said slowly, thoughtfully. Something stirred within him, he stared at it, and suddenly knew that this tree should have toppled to the ground and decayed years ago, but as if in testimony of determined survival, it struggled to stay alive, withstood over the years all the tortures of the elements, now it seemed to be shouting, shouting to him.

"Look at me...I stand alone...I endure. I stand against all elements...the heat, the cold and the draught. I live on...my strength is in my WILL...no matter how much it hurts...I live on! YOU must live on... YOU must take it all... all the abuse that comes your way... take it all. YOUR greatest reward for being strong and tall is your WILL. Your WILL lives within your heart...driven by determination and courage... you forge forward...you will win and gain what you aimed for...but at the end...the legacy you leave behind will surely be recognized and will live on, all else remains as is."

Kosta turned and looked at his family. It was not the end, not yet, now he knew.

On the branches of the dying tree, the Ravens flew in on silent wings and perched for the night.

The Ravens were there for several days observing everything that went on, and they were sure that what was predestined unavoidably to happen was their assignment to be there when it does. They were ready. It took years to make the right choice, they traveled the world in their search, after many meetings with the elders they concluded that the worthy individual resided here in this little village.

The choice was unanimous. Soon it will be dawning.

Forty-Four: The Surrender

The choice was not his. What was predestined must be. With a feeling of urgency, Kosta felt it was time. He had to make that visit again. His heart sank with the thought of it. He cared not for himself anymore, but only for his family.

He sat them down at the table and told them of his decision. Kathryn gasped, grabbed his arm to object, but he waved her objections aside.

"This is the day I have chosen to go to my brother for help, and I want you to know that I despise the idea. I struggled against it but my decision stands. As you have experienced over the years we struggled and fought this meager life, always being short of everything," Kosta said.

"But Father, we are grown up enough to help you in the fields. We do not have enough seed for planting, but we will go and earn the grain, you will see, please do not go." Tears rolled down her cheeks, Tessana said no more.

"It is spring and it is time to plant. If you go we will be lost without you," Jason spoke up too.

"I will help too, Father," Kras said. Marla and Rosie looked at Kathryn wide-eyed, Marla said, "Mother if Father does not go and bring us food we will be very hungry."

"My kitty will be hungry too. I guess Father has to go and bring food for us and the animals." Rosie with a frown on her face said.

Kathryn could not believe the way her children understood the situation, she looked at Kosta his expression of love for his children so very visible, as he paid attention to their reasons of him going. He raised his hand and they fell silent waiting for him to speak.

"I thank you for your effort to help me. Listen all of you. It will take too much time for you to earn enough money to buy grain for planting. The sowing time will pass and as you know, the growing season is short. The fields will not produce enough grain plus other staples we need for this coming autumn and winter..." Kosta stopped, looked at them, Kathryn had tears in her eyes. Tessana eyes full of sadness.

Mathew stood up and expressed his opinion, "But Father, we are not children anymore, we will plant and gather enough, you will see! You cannot go to him! I will work hard with you, please Father, do not go, I beg you!" Mathew's voice became louder with a tone of fear. Kathryn upset held back her tears, the children were crying. Kosta continued... "Do not fret, it will work out, you will see I will come back to you with enough provisions, I am sure Uncle Thomas will have pity on us...."

The word "pity" struck Mathew's nerves like lightning. He jumped up and actually screamed, "We do not want his 'pity!' We will make it without his pity!"

"Father we should go to Baron Patrick, he will help us, he always does," Rosie spoke up. Kosta covered his face. He felt like a failure and was ashamed.

"My dearest family...I cannot continue to live on constant handout. Baron Patrick is our friend and I cannot take advantage of his generosity any longer, we must keep him a good friend and appreciate his good heart. From now on we must stand on our own two feet, today is the last time I will go to my brother, the last time, I promise you," Kosta said firmly.

Kathryn stood up and walked away from the table, she was trembling, visibly trembling from fear, her face ashen. Kosta made his decision to go, and that was his final word. The little home became deathly silent, no one moved and no one spoke a word. They just sat and stared into space before them. It was still early in the morning, enough time to go to his brother's estate and back.

He embraced every one of them, but Kathryn stood as if frozen in one spot. He walked over to her and gently put his arms around her and whispered, "Kathryn I will be back, I am going to see if he will help us, perhaps he will laugh at me, ridicule me like he used to, either way I will come home tonight, if he does not help we will find a way. Remember I love you, all of you, and I ask your forgiveness, for I have failed you!"

"Please come home to me, to us, please! You never failed us!" she hid her face in his cape and wept.

"I do intend to come home, why would you say that? Of course I will come back, I must leave now." He kissed her lips. Kosta walked out into the early morning and stepped up into the wagon and as he looked back, they were all there, standing in the doorway...his heart heavy, a strange feeling surged through him, but he shrugged it aside, he was on his way to his brother.

"My brother will laugh at me, deride me, and belittle me, make me feel small again. Regardless of all these negative feelings, I must overcome. I will not turn back," Kosta spoke to himself aloud.

It was the beginning of a new week, people were busy coming and going about their business. At last, he arrived at the gate of his brother's huge estate; the servant recognizing Kosta's name, went to his master and said his brother is waiting at the gate.

Lord Thomas was quite surprised.

"What, a visit from Kosta this early in the season? Something unexpected occurred! Let him in, and brew some fresh tea, prepare hot ham sandwiches, oh yes do not forget the cake!" Lord Thomas ordered the servant.

After a little wait at the front door, the servant led Kosta to the familiar parlor through which they walked into the dining room. The table was elegantly set with fine china, Kosta observed. Lord Thomas stood waiting; greeting Kosta with a smile and a handshake, which to Kosta seemed quite sincere.

Lord Thomas not surprised at all by his brother's shabby clothes. Evident lack of improvement and progress, life was not as it should be, but no matter, politely Lord Thomas invited Kosta to sit down and share a little brunch.

Kosta felt out of place, in spite of his awkwardness sat down and stared at the bounty of food the servants brought to the table. Lord Thomas observed his brother and knew that Kosta came to him for help. For the second time, it seems a bit too soon.

"What brings you here Kosta? How is your family... keeping well? Perhaps you have some good news for me! I have not seen you for several years now. As you see I am getting along just fine." He finished eyeing Kosta.

"Yes, many years have passed. Children have grown quite nicely, even though we had many problems, no doubt you know it all. You are looking great Thomas life is good to you. I am positive you know exactly why I came to see you. We do not need to guess or pretend," Kosta said dryly.

Lord Thomas was eating his sandwich and sipping tea. Kosta just sat there. For some reason he could not touch the food.

"Kosta eat, you will feel much better, you have come a long way; I am sorry I made you feel uncomfortable, forgive me. Please, eat your sandwich," Lord Thomas said firmly. Kosta not looking at his brother began to eat the sandwich, oh how wonderful it tasted, his taste buds exploded with such delightful delicacies and the tea so aromatic, so delicious, he forgot himself and gulped down quickly like a hungry wolf, he was very hungry without a doubt. The servant placed a piece of apple cake in front of Kosta, he would not let that pass him by, he ate one piece and asked for another, all in all he ate four pieces of this delicious apple cake, and was not embarrassed at all.

They toasted together, a good glass of wine, Kosta felt so melancholy that any moment he felt he would burst into tears, but thank goodness, he was able to control his emotions. For a while, they sat not speaking, and Kosta realized that this scene right here and now is the same, as the first time. His heart began to beat faster, he needed to get away but was riveted to the chair, in his mind whirled the scene of the previous time. His hands began to sweat, and he was at a loss for words.

Lord Thomas began the conversation about the weather and the outcome of the harvest. Kosta only heard parts of the sentences. Feeling jittery, he forced himself to talk. The butler leaned into the doorway and announced.

"Master Thomas...Ah, Lady Cybilia, to greet the guest." Cybilia walked in with a strained smile, her poise stoical as if expecting a confrontation, which to him was visibly evident, she was hiding something, immediately he noticed that in her eyes that sincere twinkle was gone. Kosta rose, took her extended hand and kissed her fingertips. "Kosta what a pleasure to see you again...is your family well?" Cybilia asked.

"Thank you, my pleasure Lady Cybilia, you look wonderful. My family is as well as it could be expected," he replied.

Cybilia sat down at the table and kept looking into his eye. Not acknowledging her husband, who sat and glared at her, disapprovingly.

"Cybilia we are in conversation of deep concern, you barged in unannounced. You are aware how much I dislike this kind of interruption from you, or, anyone else," Lord Thomas spoke forcefully through his teeth. Kosta taken aback a bit by his brother's tone, was not sure if he should interject his opinion on behalf of Cybilia, No... he must not. Kosta glanced at both of them, but neither looked at each other.

"I am sure children have all grown healthy and beautiful, I must...I mean...we must visit one day and get our children to know each other, it has been several years since we have seen them, that would be really nice, would it not? Thomas?" she said as she glanced at her husband.

"You do agree my dear Lord Thomas, do you not?" she asked again, stressed the Lord Thomas, which sounded odd. He just nodded his head in approval. The sudden tension felt by all. Kosta broke the silence.

"We overcame calamities, with the support of friends and work at the castle. We survived, that is, until now." Cybilia had no more questions. She heard what she came to hear directly from Kosta, and now she saw for herself, all she heard was true.

Lord Thomas hated her interference, and those questions what was her point? The look in his eyes gave him away. He did not offer her any tea or sandwich. Cybilia helped herself to a cup of tea a sandwich and apple cake. Before she left, she took Kosta's face into her hands. "God bless and watch over you and your family," Cybilia said.

Kosta observed her moves, and concluded the cause of that strain, a wedge between her and Thomas. She left as suddenly as she had come in. The dining room became silent.

Lord Thomas began to mutter something and cleared his throat.

"Well then, shall we get to business...brother?" asked Lord Thomas.

Kosta shuddered; felt trapped. *"Why was he feeling this way? What is his brother up to?"* Kosta's thoughts rushed through his mind. Lord Thomas said that it was getting late and they need to go, he rang for the servant, James came in, seeing Kosta James took a step back, averted his eyes at objects in the room, he acted uneasy. Kosta noticed this and thought it odd, but said nothing.

Lord Thomas instructed James to load the wagon with provisions for Kosta's family and to deliver right away. James nodded and left the room. "*He knows the way to my house?"* Kosta thought.

"Well now brother, now we must come to an agreement on repayment for the provisions, you know that is part of the bargain, right?" his brother said.

"Yes I know. I will be ready to pay as much as you want, I will, but in time. I need time from you, come fall I should be able to set aside for you several sacks, and thereafter...until I am caught up. I have not forgotten the number of sacks you gave me before, plus what you give me today, plus extra, and I will give you all my carvings, but only as collateral. If you so wish in gratitude for all of your help, when I return all I owe, I will take back my carvings, unless you would like to keep those you like. You are the only one in position to help me. I am grateful from the bottom of my heart, I truly thank you." Kosta looked down into the cup.

"Kosta my brother, no need to return any of these sacks to me, and I do not need any of your carvings, they are not important to me, all I need from you is your other eye." Lord Thomas laughed that same guttural, grinding eerie laugh. Seeing the fear on Kosta's face, he laughed saying, "Kosta I am jesting of course!" and again his laugh made Kosta's skin crawl.

Kosta stared at Lord Thomas speechless. He felt that he had to leave right now, right this minute. He must get away from his brother, who is half-crazy.

"I cannot subject myself to such cruelty! How could he even think of such a thing to say, I will be blind, I will be useless, might as well die than to be blind!" soberly he thought.

He gathered his courage and said, "What sort of man are you? Put yourself in my shoes and realize what you are asking me to do? I will be useless to my family and myself! How could you do such a thing? Thomas, why do you hate me so much, why?"

Kosta stood up to leave. Lord Thomas said in a quiet voice.

"I was just playing on your nerves, I did not mean it, but if you are hurt and afraid, then go. Go then, and let your children hate you for not providing for them with all necessities through the years. I told you a long time ago those silly carvings of yours will not supply you and your family enough food to live on. Go then and starve. You are a failure. You are as a man, a disappointment to Kathryn and your children. Go! Go home to your meager existence.

However, know this: if you give up to me your other eye, they will respect you for your ultimate sacrifice. You will survive and your family will live well. I promise you that if you would do this I will promise to provide for them for as long as it takes to be on their own, as adults. Now that is a long time, they are still young children. Kathryn will love you regardless of your condition. She will care for you no matter who you are and what you have become." Lord Thomas finished his critique, a guilt trip reaching down to Kosta's core. Thomas sat down at the dining table, and patiently waited.

Kosta's mind reeled, he was shivering, he listened but his nerves were out of control. *My brother is out of his mind! He does not make sense at all. He will or he might not keep his promise. Thomas said before that he was just "jesting!" Now he is talking as if he wants my eye. Never to see my children's faces and Kathryn's beautiful face! No! I cannot go through with such an idiotic deal! That is insane!* Kosta thought.

"Put yourself into my situation my brother Thomas, would you give up your eye to be useless to the world and your family? Tell me truthfully! Give up the talent that the good God has given you, depend on others, what if the others abandon you, where would you be, and Cybilia, do you think she would stay with you or go and find a new life, and your children grown up leave to lead their own lives, and you...

"Enough that is enough, now you are putting me in your place, ha! How wise you have become!" Lord Thomas shouted.

Kosta stifled a quiver in his voice, he stopped, in a while Kosta continued.

"You said that... you were just...you are insane! I must go home, I was so wrong believing that you having so much would stoop so low, and to become so cruel to your only brother. Why do you hate me so much? Why?" Kosta's voice rang out and he hung his head on his chest. He could not look at his brother's face, if he had, he would have lunged at him and strangled him, he could not have controlled his anger, and he would have killed him with anything in his hand, and was ashamed of his outburst.

Lord Thomas with a smirk spoke very slowly, "Go on home...you sniffling coward. A simpleton, when it comes to the support of your family and their future. Father was never ambitious. Kept his nose to the ground, you are like him, not a spark of ambition in your veins. You always liked Father. Slow and humble. Without ambition, your nose is to the soil, and those carvings, ha! That collection of figurines will not feed your clutch of children. Kathryn must be blind to your lack of ambition! Your lack of aggressiveness to claim the fortune that is rightfully yours in this life, without any progress or improvement for the future you and your Kathryn and those children will parish! Starve! You, you are letting them down! Go! But remember what I am telling you, I will write a promissory note to give to Kathryn, of how long and how much I will provide for them and you."

Lord Thomas ending his derogatory criticism of his brother, face flushed, but temper controlled, remained seated.

Kosta did not know what to do and what to think. He had to get some provisions for his family, but not at the cost of his only eye. His mind in turmoil from the words his brother threw at him; those were daggers not words plunged right into his heart; the hurt he felt at this moment; the confusion he could not stand, most of all that heartless man sitting across the table, he could not believe was his own brother.

He was walking out the door, he had to get away right now, or he might just be foolish enough to give in to this idiotic act.

Lord Thomas just sat there and whispered, "*You will be back, I am sure you will!*"

Kosta jumped onto the wagon and sped away, he needed to get away far, far away from his brother. Horses galloped, wagon rattled. Kosta frustrated snapped that whip over them.

He was half way home, when he had slowed the horses down to a slow pace, and began to think about all that his brother had said.

Those cruel words jabbed at his heart like daggers, words echoed in his mind that he was, "*useless*" and a "*failure*" and that, "*his nose was to the ground, just like father, Disappointment... failure...no ambition! Children*...he called my children a "*clutch*"! How dare he, calls them a "*brood.*" *The nerve, how dare he*!" Kosta's anger mounting cried out. He heard these words ring in his mind.

What am I going to do! Where to go, My God help me, I need help right now! He whispered and then began to cry aloud, his voice carried across the countryside. He began to cry bitter tears of despair. The horses ambled along, and suddenly he knew he had to make that choice now, he had to go back and renegotiate with his brother. He turned the wagon around and was on his way back to his brother. The gate was open. Someone stood in the open doorway, his brother Thomas was waiting. He knew Kosta would come back. Kosta stepped off the wagon, walked up. "*Yes he has come back*," Lord Thomas thought.

"You knew I would be back?" Kosta asked.

"Yes, I knew you would be back! Let us go inside," Lord Thomas said smiling, in the parlor they sat down.

"Listen Kosta I should not have been so cruel to you, you do not deserve to be treated this way, I am sorry. Glad you came back, I was hoping you would and you did." Kosta stared at his brother.

"Why yes... you should be apologizing, you hurt my feelings. You are brutal. I came back to negotiate an agreement with you, you should be sorry! I...you were trying my nerves when you said all that, you are jesting, are you not?" Kosta spoke icily, his fists in his pockets.

Lord Thomas hearing Kosta's icy tone taken aback, laughed.

"I am not going to hurt you. I should not have used my scare tactic. As pertaining to the repayment... you should not worry, not to worry at all, your wagons will be loaded and ready in a few minutes.

Kosta could not believe his ears....is it possible my brother had a heart after all. His anxiety slackened a bit. Lord Thomas and Kosta shook hands. "*How strange,* Kosta thought, *but then my brother is a bit strange ever since he married Cybilia.*"

"Come let us have a toast, "to brothers" a glass of good wine, like two brothers." They went into the dining room, the bottle of wine and two goblets sat on the table, waiting.

Several hours later they were still drinking, Kosta having no opportunity to drink much, for one thing never could afford it, having a glass of wine with the Baron several times, and months ago he shared a bottle with Kathryn, a gift from Michael. The wine tasted very good, went down smooth. His brother, filled both goblets to the brim, neither completely empty. Kosta's head buzzed, he became so relaxed, his arms and legs felt heavy. All tension and frustration drowned in the wine, along with the reason why he came. For once, the two of them were really, as brothers should be. They laughed, told each other stories, some were funny, they laughed hysterically, but the horror stories spoken in hushed voices, thinking, trying to grasp the meaning of these horror stories.

Lord Thomas swayed in his chair, propped his head with his arms, he winked at Kosta. He seemed to be just as drunk, slurred speech.

"Ah, brother... I feel...feel good having you here. We should have had drinking sessions like this one a, a long time ago. Ah...the wine is good...makes you forget all your troubles. And you know...Cybilia does not drink, like us, *she slurps!"* and he laughed. He had a way of acting the role of a drunk, yet his evil eyes in the shadow of his brows alert. Lord Thomas like a spider knew exactly when to pounce at the innocent unsuspecting victim. Yes, Kosta was an innocent victim.

Kosta never had time to socialize, drink with strangers just to be intoxicated. Neither at the Inns or at home with his friends, never with pals such as his brother Lord Thomas associated with over the years and, possibly he still does, and often.

At one moment, Lord Thomas just dropped his head on the table and was out... Kosta sat there staring at him. Unable to think or utter a word, his tongue lazy refused to move and seemed too thick....his brain a sponge saturated with wine.

Lord Thomas remained in that position for a while. The time slipped by and Kosta did not realize the late hour.

When Cybilia left the two brothers in the dining room, and stepped into her bedroom locking the door, she cried bitter tears. Kosta to her was so gauntly her heart cringed at the thought that his children and Kathryn look the same, as he. She liked and respected Kosta, to her he was gentle and kind, she felt so sorry for him, but everything was out of her reach to help him and his children, she felt for Kathryn, knowing now what pain she is going through seeing her family hungry, watching Kosta weaken each day. Suddenly she heard a knock at the door. She quickly dried her eyes and ran to open it. Shara stood there wide-eyed and disturbed.

"What is the matter Shara, what happened you seem to be afraid my dear, come in!" Cybilia spoke in a hushed voice.

"Mother, Mark has gone somewhere, no one knows where! What is happening in this house, I am afraid! Mother, did you see Uncle Kosta downstairs, they are both drunk! I never thought that my own father would make Uncle Kosta so drunk! How terrible! Mother... where is Mark, Mother?" Shara kept throwing all these questions at Cybilia, and never noticed her mother's eyes.

Cybilia walked over to the window to hide her eyes from crying.

"Shara I believe Mark went to the other village to see someone, as I understand from what he was telling me and had been planning some time ago, do not be afraid, he will come back soon." Cybilia's explanation well taken, Shara joined her mother at the window. They stared into the grayness, Cybilia, with her arms around her daughter stood for a moment not speaking. Shara broke the silence as she spoke in a low voice,

"Mother Uncle Kosta is here very late, why do you think Father is keeping him here so long?

"Well, they both have matured...I think father misses his own brother, so tonight they are, I believe bonding as brothers should, they need this time together," Cybilia explained.

"Perhaps you are right, Mother" Shara was growing up and understood much more nowadays. She left her mother's bedroom but instead of going to her room, she carefully edged closer to the dining room to see what was going on. She watched hidden behind a huge drape which hung over the door, they did not see her, she heard her father say something of a sort, "it was time to go and take care of business, it is late."

Kosta was very drunk, and everything around him appeared double. Lord Thomas helped him to his feet, and they staggered out of the dining room. Lord Thomas led Kosta to the barn. The wagon stood loaded high with an assortment of sacks. Kosta tried to speak, but his tongue refused to function, his heart beat violently. At one moment, he just reeled and fell to the ground.

The servant scrambled up unto the wagon and rode away slowly to Kosta's house. A horse tied to the wagon, for the return.

This was one of those nights no one would ever forget.

Forty-Five: The Waiting

Kosta's never returned as he promised, which frustrated Kathryn. After many hours of waiting, the house was quiet children slept, but for Mathew and Kathryn. Mathew was nervous and he expressed his concern.

"We will wait, I hope nothing unexpected happened, we must wait," Kathryn said.

They waited far into the night. Something upset him and he could not understand what and why, ready to jump on his horse and go find his father. Kathryn fell asleep at the table, head resting on her arms. Mathew sat a while in the silent house and fell asleep as well.

When the sun came up the next morning, Kathryn and the children were tired and achy from their awkward sleep positions. Kras walked outside, saw the wagon and the horses still hitched standing in the middle of the yard, ran in calling.

"Mother, come here quickly! The whole family ran out and saw the horses and the loaded wagon but no sign of Kosta anywhere!" *What happened? Where was he?*

Several hours later wagon unloaded, provisions stored in the barn and some in the pantry. Kathryn could not believe her eyes, "*so much... so much...enough for the whole year, what a great supply, but for God's sake where is Kosta, this is the middle of spring! We need him here it is time for planting. Why is he staying away! This means, now the children and I must toil without him! He will not return! It means that he has abandoned us!* She thought.

She began to pace aimlessly around the kitchen, worried and confused, all she could think about was Kosta and why he did not come home! Then she walked outside, she was heading for the creek, where he used to go when he felt distressed.

She walked along the path, the rushing water shimmered, lapping against the rocks, she stood and stared, and she heard what seemed far in the distance, someone calling her name, she looked in every direction, but no one was there. She was puzzled. Again she was sure someone called her name, was it Kosta or someone else playing tricks?

She ran home breathless. Jasemin stood in the doorway when Kathryn ran up to the house.

"What happened to you out there, Mother you look frightened, and you were gone so long."

"I walked to the creek for a few minutes to think, but something frightening occurred and I ran home," she explained. Jason curiously asked what frightened her.

"Well, as I walked down the path, I heard my name called, it was your Father, it sounded so eerie...I ran home, thinking he had come home," she said.

All day and night, she kept thinking about Kosta. She could not understand why he left them to fend for themselves. Sudden feelings of anger surged through her, why would he do this to them, she felt confused; I need to go and search for him, something happened... someone beat him and robbed him on his way home like last time, dumping him somewhere.

Kathryn's fitful sleep made her jump out of bed and walk in circles. Holding her head and pulling her hair. Anger, disappointment, despair engulfed her, her heart ached but she could not cry, near dawn she fell onto the bed dead asleep.

Mathew and Tessana always were up first and always prepared their breakfast. Mathew said, "Do not wake mother, she has been up all night, walking, walking in circles.

"She is very worried, I am too, what happened to father, Mathew," Tessana asked.

Kras joined them rubbing his sleepy eyes, "Is father back, Mathew?" he asked.

"No, he is not back, but do not wake Mother, she is tired, let her sleep," Tessana replied.

When the rest of the children woke up and were dressed. Mathew and Tessana served breakfast to them in silence while Kathryn slept, in a deep, deep sleep.

Forty-Six: Darkness

Kosta had been unconscious through the night until noon of the next day. When the warmth of the sun awakened him, realizing he was somewhere out in the open, he listened but then slipped back into semi consciousness for several hours. He tried to think while he was awake but nothing seemed clear, recalling bits and pieces of what happened, his head ached, unable to lift it up, drifted in and out of his drunken stupor and slept all day.

The sun had set it was the second night. Suddenly the cold and the dampness brought him back to full awakening. Surely, it must be nighttime, it was too quiet, now and then an owl hooted.

Disorientation overtook him again, his throat dry, hard to swallow. He tried to remember what happened. He felt dampness of the ground. Kosta rolled to his side carefully, reached out to feel what was around him, his head ached worse when he moved. He rolled on his back, Kosta thought, "*my head aches from that wine, I need to stay still, but it is so cold. Where is my cape? It is so dark, hard to see anything, must be a moonless night.*" After a while, he tried to sit up but could not. He touched his temple. He felt pain. He was hurt, very badly, "*have I fallen off the wagon being drunk*?" He could not remember falling anywhere... "*how did I get here,*" he wondered, he tried to open his eye, gently touched the left eye socket, and cheek then as he felt the right side of his face he felt crustiness. *"This must be mud on my face,"* he thought, moving his fingers up to the right eye when a terrible pain shot through him, still, he had not realized the real cause. Suddenly Kosta heard grunting, he lay very still trying to discern the direction of the noise.

The thought hit him that the grunting and sniffing could be wild boars or wolves.

"Oh...God...not the wild boars or wolves! They smell me, or the blood, it must be blood on my face. When I fell on something, I have a cut close to my eye. I cannot move... the pain... what am I to do?" Panic seized him, his heart thumped so loud he felt it in his temples." *Am I blind, did he gouge my right eye this time..."* With trembling hand, he touched his eye again and the pain hit like a knife. Within his head he screamed, his lips tight. It was then he

realized to his horror his right eye had been gouged. He wanted to scream, but was afraid of the animals around him.

He could not cry... the excruciating pain kept him rigid. He tore at the dirt and weeds that grew around him and under him, the noises he heard stopped, he listened. Suddenly he felt something moist and cold touch his hand, he held his breath, unable to see what sort of animal was standing above him, he was beyond his fear... "*whatever happens, let it happen, it is the end anyway, this is the final moment...makes no difference!*" Kosta thought and waited. However, this animal sniffed Kosta's body, his face, but this animal did not attack, instead dropped down across Kosta's legs. Kosta did not move a muscle. *"This animal is a wolf, a lone wolf...waiting for me to die then will devour me*!" Suddenly Kosta heard more growling...coming closer and closer...he lay motionless, straining his ears, he was surrounded by a pack of wolves, yelping, yipping, growling and snarling. Kosta was their prey and they were here for the kill.

Wolves. His heart pounded like a hammer against his chest, yet he could do nothing, but be motionless, pray to God to take his spirit before they eat him alive. He was freezing and in great pain. But to his utter surprise, instead of harming him, the pack of wolves laid down around Kosta, one of the wolves laid his head on Kosta's chest to keep him warm. When drowsiness overtook him, he gave in to a deep sleep until next dawn.

The morning sparrows chirping, cackling of birds woke him and the sun warmed him, but he felt the cold dampness rising from the ground. Awake tried to recall last night; *the wolves, they were with me last night, are they still here?* To lift up his head he could not. "*No, they must be gone,*" Kosta thought. His outstretched arms felt only grass, he was, alone. The shirt smelled of the wild*; "the wolves kept me warm all night I remember now. It must be Divine intervention. God's Mercy that led them to me, I have never heard of such an incident, ever in my life, but it happened to me and no one will ever believe me, that is if I live. I believe....* Kosta thought and felt a strange peace within.

He tried to think back what took place at his brother's home. His memories flashed back. The whole evening with his brother at the table and all that wine, now he knew.

"*My brother... kept pouring wine, so much wine... and I was foolish to drink it.*" He recalled the conversation he had with him; "*my eye... my brother wanted my eye. I refused! I walked out of his house and I was on my way back home... why did I go back to him, why! Yes now I remember, I went back to beg him for a loan of provisions... I offered him my carvings and give back more than..., oh... kept pouring that wine... so much wine! I have been a fool as before, to believe in the sudden change of heart he portrayed to me. I have been ignorant, a fool...but he is worse than I, he is a coward... he could not face me...look me in the eye, like a man..., he had to get me drunk first...to gouge out my only means of survival...I will never carve again, or see my family's faces again! Where am I? Wherever I am...no one will find me! My brother...is a despicable coward! He will suffer from now on...his guilty conscience will not let him sleep, if he has a conscience, what he did to me, will follow him to his grave."* Kosta dozed off, when he awoke again his thoughts returned to his brother.

"Thomas was not as drunk as I was, he was acting, pretending...that must have been so...he waited for me to pass out...and then he did with me what he wanted. Ah...to be so naïve...believing he had compassion...I bared my soul to him...I believed in my brother. What possessed him to be so cruel! It is too late now much too late for questions or explanations. My poor Kathryn...what will happen to her and my children."

"Oh my God, I pray you will help them, send someone to help her and my children, please," Kosta out of despair cried aloud.

His chest began to constrict and heave from sorrow, not for himself but for his loved ones; the sun rose high. Hunger pangs getting stronger, not knowing where he was, much less try to crawl to find his home. Very slowly, he turned his back towards the sun, a sudden thought of Kathryn entered his mind..., *"what is she thinking, my children, Baron Patrick and Aunt Olivia, my friends Michael and Rabinna, do they know...oh my God, do they assume that I walked away from them and disappeared...but I could never abandon them. Mathew... my son must hate me, all of them tried to stop me from going. I hope Mathew had not gone to Thomas, asking what happened to me. He would never get a true answer anyway from Thomas."* The pain hit him again from the change of position. He tried not to move. Any movement caused pain. All sorts of thoughts and scenes flashed in his mind, fear, doubt, questions and no answers.

"Here, I will die, this must be my destiny, to die alone somewhere far out, away from the village no one will find me!" Drowsiness came over him he fell asleep again.

This was his second day alone.

His dreamless sleep, minimized the agony of being alone, in pain, desperate, kept him from panic of dying alone, and his family would never know what had happened to him. “*Surely, one day my brother’s terrible secret... of this crime will emerge like a nightmare and justice will prevail.*” Between dozing and hallucinating, unable to comprehend why his brother, his only blood brother... *“Why...do this to me?”*

Forty-Seven: Strange Omens

The amassing of earthly possessions overpowered the mind of this cruel brother. Strict control over everyone made him feel he has the right to judge who is to prosper, to live and love. The evil entered his heart long ago, when he was still a youth, and in time, his heart hardened to a block of ice. The madness gradually had overtaken him, the evil shone in his eyes, his family suffered.

However, Fate can turn and punish severely an evil person. Fate gives, and Fate will take it away. Only Fate and time will tell when.

Lord Thomas did not believe in ghosts. However, something was affecting him to an extent that he walked the nights fearing sleep. He did not see anything or hear any noise but a feeling lingered around him as if some spirit was present, breathing on him. He imagined that if he should fall asleep he would die. As the days went by he became a raging bull, anger and memories of his brother stood in his mind fresh as if it all took place yesterday.

The wine did not drown or block his memory of all deeds he has committed, in fact, all of his evil deeds kept creeping into his mind, which, when his mind was sober and clear, all acts were *justified* as, Master's right to have control and power.

Then he began to hear voices at night, whispering now and then, knocking on doors and walls as if someone walked by and each step was a knock, when he heard a knock at his door he would reply "enter" but no one entered.

Cybilia Mark and Shara avoided this mad man constantly, always having an excuse of some sort not to be around.

The ever-watchful eyes of the thirteen Ravens observed and listened. They flew high above the estate.

Time slipped by.

Lord Thomas content with his worldly riches, never had noticed the Ravens, he never took time to observe nature like other people, the sky, the clouds, birds and flowers. If anyone ever asked, his reply was always the same,

"I have no time for such trivia as observing nature, let others waste their time. It is my privilege to take from nature what I want. That is my only desire and interest."

This feeling lingered. While he sat in his favorite chair, a slight touch of his hair; made him aware of an unnatural presence; he was alone. He quickly jumped up, briskly walked to his bedroom and closed the door. But here again, that feeling had entered his room, and, is with him now, beside him, goose-bumps ran up and down his body, his hair bristled all over him.

The thought of his brother, and what he had done to him was constant. He imagined someone had found him, and took him home... and his brother in delirium exposed him to everyone..., Kosta would tell where and who the criminal was...his rich brother, had done this to him. *"What if he is still ALIVE out there?"*

This was too much of a strain. He seemed to be in another world, he stopped paying attention to his surroundings, the staff noticed, his wife and children noticed. Their MASTER was losing his grip on reality.

One morning Lord Thomas had his horse saddled, went off riding. A ride to the cemetery, but he was not sure which one Kosta was taken to, that meant that he had to go to several of them. As he approached the first cemetery, a large gathering of people stood around a coffin and an open grave. He stood for a while and observed. Too far to recognize any of the people, but mourners glanced in his direction. That is not what he wanted to see, or to be recognized by those people. He rode off to the next cemetery, which was a good distance away. The time wasted looking began to irritate him. He spurred his horse, the startled stallion reared up and Lord Thomas nearly thrown to the ground. He swore, called him a, *dumb animal* and used his crop, whipped him, Star, his stallion galloped at full speed. Lord Thomas realized that this was not going to be easy. To ask his men which cemetery they dumped his brother would surely be a mistake.

"No use asking those two, they would not reply, they were, no longer around," he mumbled and rode back home.

In his bedroom, he picked up scattered papers off the floor. He glanced at the full-length mirror to see a smeared letter clearly recognizable as...

Chills ran up and down his spine, what panic seized him only one can imagine.

Lord Thomas collapsed onto the floor prostrated, his eyes shut dared not look, remained in that position for an hour or so, when his fear subsided he stood up and looked at the mirror. The smear was still there. He was dumbfounded, he was not sure what to do, clean the mirror himself or call Cybilia or the house cleaner, "No, not the servants, they gossip too much, I will call Cybilia," he spoke out-loud.

"I will get to the bottom of this prank! I will find out who had such nerve to frighten me. Beware...whoever it is. This has never occurred before, not the first time I gouged Kosta's eye, but then it could not be them..., and Joseph and James are gone, dead. I refuse to believe in ghosts! I must think about the other men, first I will ask them about this, then I will decide what to do with them. If these signs disappear than surely they are guilty but if these pranks continue of course that will prove they are innocent. That will save their hides otherwise their heads will roll. Perhaps Cybilia..., she has been acting strange lately." Lord Thomas theorized, as he was looking for Cybilia. Lord Thomas, unable to find Cybilia or his children in the house, went out to the stable looking for those men. They were not around either, he stopped a youth and asked where were the two older men, one with a pony tail and the other with the red beard, the young man shook his head and said all he knows is that they are dead and I am a new hired help. Lord Thomas suddenly recalled what had happened to those two men. He turned and stormed out of the stable. Out on a country road, a woman on a horse rode away, having a short visit with Flora, Francine and Sebastian greeted her warmly entering the kitchen, she came for a short visit with her friends at the estate. She galloped away down the lane quickly. Once out of sight she slowed her horse to a slow trot. Master Thomas never knew she was ever there. No one would tell him.

Forty-Eight: Despair and Panic

Kathryn walked around the house in a daze. The children were quiet. Mathew walked to Rebecca's house and when she opened the door asked, "You walked here?"

"Yes, I just... Father did not come home from visiting Uncle Thomas," Mathew said.

Rebecca pulled him inside and led him to the table. He just sat staring blankly. It was a total shock to Michael and Rabinna. When Mathew said, "Father did not return, just left the wagon in the yard in the middle of the night. Leaving us and disappearing? Where would he have gone on foot?" His eyes filled with tears.

"This calls for a meeting, alert everyone, could something have happened to him, and he is out there somewhere alone?" Rabinna said.

Their meaningful glances to each other understood. They must go see Kathryn immediately. The three of them and Rebecca jumped onto the wagon and rode on to Kathryn's home. This was almost the middle of spring and each day warmer. This day was unusually calm, hot, and miserably humid.

When they entered the little house, Kathryn paced the floor.

Michael had to stop her in her tracts to bring her back to her senses. She embraced him, Rabinna came up to her and put her arms around her, Kathryn sobbed. The dark circles under her eyes were lack of sleep. She looked so haggard. They felt so sorry for her. No words would console her now, the search had to begin soon, the plan had to be put in motion, time, was running short.

"Kathryn, I will ask some of the neighbors to go with me and search for him, Rabinna will stay and help you, so will Rebecca."

She could not think of anything to say, she was aware of them being with her, and aware of only one thing, Kosta did not come home, and it is the third day already.

Michael went over to the neighbors. Rabinna prepared dinner, not needing to ask Kathryn if the children were hungry. Rabinna's simple questions revived Kathryn, for up to now was just in a state of shock.

The children whispered to Rabinna that mother talks to herself, and that she has not eaten anything for the last few days.

"Why did you wait so long to come and tell us your father had not returned, it has been two days now," Rabinna whispered to Mathew.

"Mother wanted to wait a few days, she was sure that father would return home...soon...any day, you know Aunt Rabinna father drove over to Uncle Thomas, I am embarrassed to say, for provisions for this year," Mathew replied.

Rabinna understood, did not broach that subject to Kathryn at all, when dinner was ready they all sat and ate in silence. Kathryn nibbled, shoved the food around on her plate. In this situation and her condition, nourishment was necessary to build up her strength.

The hours dragged on, Rabinna encouraged Kathryn to eat she must have strength, she seemed to drift off, nodding now and then, she looked around stared at each one of her children. The youngest of the girls, Rosie suddenly began to cry and wail at the table, everyone stared at her stunned, unaware why. Kathryn jumped up and ran to her, she held her close.

"Why are you carrying on like this my sweet, tell mama!" Rosie's tears ran down her cheek, through sobs she said, "Momma, Momma...Father is not ever coming... back home, I know..., I can feel it! Something happened to him, Momma I feel it!" Rosie screamed, holding her head.

Kathryn and Rabinna continued to comfort the child, but Rosie kept on crying and mumbling about her father not coming home.

The rest of the children stared at her, and doubt crept into their hearts. The day was ending... night time, darkness, dampness, the wind began to whistle and they all knew this night would not be a pleasant one.

Michael and Rabinna with Rebecca returned home. Children slept but restlessly. Kathryn promised Rabinna that she would try to sleep. When in bed, she closed her eyes. Without Kosta, the bed was too big it bothered her. In the dark and silent house, she heard the restlessness of her children, besides that, again that mumbling, moaning, and whispering something inaudible came from whichever direction she turned her head. She slipped out of bed and paced around the room, wringing her hands and whispering to herself; it is windy, it must be the wind, if not the wind, I must be mad. I will go mad. What is going to happen to me... where is he...why did he leave us?

This night was the same as the night before, that same voice whispered something, she concentrated on several words though somewhat inaudible; *come...come...*and then, *go...go...no...not here! Save me! Come!* She thought she is going mad. This was the third agonizing night. She had not slept well at all. Kathryn talked to herself.

"Why am I hearing this voice? Where is Kosta? Perhaps I should visit Thomas and ask him; 'When did Kosta leave your house?' I should go and look for him...but where? If he really has gone away and left us to fend for ourselves then by now he is far, far from this village."

The wind whistled lightly through the trees. She stood at the window, listened, thinking, *"but it is not the same. Wind does create eerie sounds of laughter and cries, never words as I am hearing."* Kathryn sat down on the bed with a shawl on her shoulders, stared out the window. Her eyelids grew heavy. Her body stressed though she fought sleep then fell on the pillow, slept.

Many ignored this type of an evening, but others who perceived over time through intuition such lamenting sounds as those, were omens of pain and sorrow.

Forty-Nine:

The Third Night - Solutions

A trembling body still lying on the ground, thirsty, hungry and aching, not knowing his whereabouts, that trembling body was Kosta. He tried to keep awake, hearing strange noises, which seemed to be above him. He strained to recognize what these strange noises were.

The wind chilled him through and through, his legs, nose and ears felt numb. At least they did not ache like his head. Completely fatigued, waited for the end, how many more days until he surrenders his spirit. The silent clouds drifted over the area and it rained, refreshing but cold drops fell and hit his bloody face, causing pain on the open wound, he covered it with his hand. Greedily licked and swallowed every drop that fell into his mouth, his clothes wet, water seeped underneath him. Rain fell heavy enough to soak everything, not enough to relieve his thirst. Now, he shivered more, the early spring nights still were very cold. Rustling sounds above him seemed to increase.

Kosta paid attention to these odd noises though shivering. These noises were much different somehow. He distinctly heard whispering. Who could be whispering here? Kosta laid still. He heard flapping of wings, now. He curiously listened. For a moment, he forgot his pain. "*Were they large birds? I must be close to a tree. I wonder what kind of birds these are,*" he thought. Suddenly a loud squawk pierced the air.

"*I was right it is a bird, or birds,*" he thought and listened not twitching a muscle.

Then he heard more sounds, noises, it seemed a large flock flew in at once.

Why are they here? The whole tree must be full of them, what kind of birds are they, I hope they do not see me. I am sure by now my shirt is very dirty I should blend well with the vegetation.

Now and again, he heard more whispering. *How could birds whisper? Strangest thing I have yet to hear, birds whisper. How could that be*? He listened.

Suddenly he heard someone speak. Kosta almost cried out, surely someone is out searching for him and are about to find him, whomever it is they will take him home. However, no one touched him or called to him, or called his name. Kosta waited and waited no one came near him. Then, more whispering, now, shrieking, as if angry, warning tones, this is unreal. He was sure something was going to happen.

Fear stricken, Kosta shivered thinking, *"Oh, my...God...Perhaps they are here to tear me apart! What should I do? I must be still, hopefully, I will not be...but my shirt is white! Surely, they will see it."* Kosta remained motionless.

Kosta realized there were many different tones of voices, now. *It must be nighttime. Am I delirious, or, am I dreaming? Of all the extraordinary, beyond my comprehension, my belief, this is happening when I am in this condition to hear voices in the middle of the night, this, no one would believe, but me...yet, here I am and I hear voices. Why are they here*? Kosta thought. Suddenly he heard a loud voice.

"Good evening my Brothers."

"Good evening our Leader Mamut!"

"Is everyone here?" their Leader Mamut asked.

"Yes, we are all here, our Leader Mamut!" they all answered.

"Good, we shall begin. The night is long. We must disclose all the pertinent information tonight. We will give all the solutions to the problems we have pending. We searched, as you are aware, for an individual worthy of this mission. I am glad to announce that now we have found the perfect one for these important problems and their solutions," said a voice, it was their Leader Mamut.

"I am Number One Raven Abimust, may I speak?"

"Yes you may begin Abimust."

"Thank you dear Leader Mamut, I have the solution and am ready to discuss it tonight."

Their leader Mamut interrupted Abimust Raven Number One. "Now listen for a moment, before we begin, first and foremost I must explain about the misfortune of our chosen individual. Through no fault of his, our chosen individual has become an innocent victim at the hand of his own flesh and blood, who through greed and obsession for material possessions lost his senses. Moreover, never had considering those less fortunate or deprived. True, he acquired all of his treasures through his ambitious desire to possess material things and power. True, he had no fear to take charge of his own destiny, but the difference is that destiny had given him all what he desired. He was aware of receiving an important gift to know the difference between greed, generosity and willingness to share his fortune with others. Unfortunately he disregarded that gift, and continued to be selfish."

The night dark and silent only interrupted by words spoken by their leader, the Ravens listened.

Kosta was listening too. From the sound of these birds, he perceived there had to be a tree not far on which they perched, and these birds spoke; these were strange beings out of this world in the form of birds. No one would understand or comprehend what presently was taking place here and now.

Kosta not knowing exactly of whom they were talking about, hunger gnawed at his stomach, but he listened, being very still on the ground.

They murmured at first then the whole flock of them squawked and flapped their wings, these birds became angry and created a loud ruckus at which time their Leader Mamut had to quiet them down, they were too loud, their shrill voices reverberated through the silent night.

"Brothers, brothers quiet please, we have just begun, settle down. We have so much to discuss, time is short!"

The Ravens did not hear him. They were irritated, he shouted "Silence!" The Leader Mamut was upset as well at the situation between these two brothers, the reasons one day would surface but not today.

"Speak...Benokai Raven Number Two!" their Leader Mamut ordered.

"Dear leader Mamut, I have, that is Abimust and I have acquired the solution to the problem of the King's daughter—"

"Princess Alexia," interjected Abimust Raven Number One.

"Yes, Princess Alexia, the little princes being very ill. Her condition is grave... a..."

Abimust interrupted, "a sleeping condition which is a coma, which could be terminal."

"For which we have found a cure," said Raven Benokai Number Two.

"What is the cure and how far is the kingdom?"

"King Oscarian Bantar's domain is at the top of the fourth range of mountains to the west," Abimust interjected again.

"Continue, and Abimust please do not interrupt," Leader Mamut ordered, "speak Benokai."

"The cure should be a concoction prepared from the tree frogs boiled in chicken soup that is the magic cure which will cure Little Princess Alexia. The King is offering a sack of gold to anyone who is willing to undertake the healing process, slow reversal of coma." Benokai Raven Number Two and Abimust chimed together, "that is all, thank you."

"Good solution, it will work," comments heard from some of them.

"Coma, oh, that is a grave situation..." one said.

"Kotur, Raven Number Three, what do you have to tell us."

"My dear Leader Mamut, you recall the last time we had this meeting, our concern was about the Town of Roses, where the wells are dry, and the people are in a panic for loss of water. All the vegetation is withering. They bring water in buckets from the river, a good distance away, creating hardship and strain on these people."

"Have you the solution to this situation, tell us."

"Yes. I do have the solution, guaranteed to work, absolutely guaranteed. Dear Mamut, the old well is in the center of the town, from the old well walk East 200 paces. Find a young willow branch with a cluster of seven at the tip, spread like fingers. This willow branch will quiver and bend at the spot to dig for a new well. As to the payment for the service that will be resolved in the future." Concluded Kotur Raven number three.

Praises of "well done" from one of the Ravens and all followed.

"My Leader Mamut, may I interject a question, before I forget?" Raven Denos asked.

"Yes, go ahead Denos Raven Number Four."

"Will the colorful feathers appear any time soon?"

"The matter of the feathers is not important at this time, we have urgent issues to discuss time is running short," their Leader Mamut answered.

"Not important, not important," whispered the others.

"Erisot Raven Number Five, speak, what have you found?" their Leader Mamut spoke sternly.

"I have found an older woman with an ulcerated leg, she lives all alone and she needs immediate attention."

"Clarify the correct solution?" Mamut said.

"The solution is: one has to gather wild garlic and squeeze a bit of juice, gently rub all around the wound, around the wound mind you, otherwise it is very painful...find the plantain plant and make a plantain poultice as a dressing, change it every day, and drink hot wild blueberry tea with cinnamon and honey. Definitely, this will cure her leg. The same road leading from the City of Magda, will after many days come to a fork, take the left turn follow to this woman's home, it is the fifth house on the east side of the road in that village."

Fijuron Raven Number Six had a question. "What ever happened to the two brothers that lost their parents that winter night on that river?"

The Leader Mamut cleared his throat and said very clearly, "You all remember when it happened... I am sure, the older brother gouged out the left eye of the younger brother, and the anguish, pity, tormented him, in time adjusted, presently he is doing fine. We will discuss his condition later. My brothers please continue."

Gromu Raven Number Seven spoke. "My Leader Mamut, I am the young inexperienced member, newly commissioned, and I am still learning your ways and I truly enjoy the responsibilities we undertake. I am grateful to be a new member of your brotherhood, thank you."

"You are welcomed by all of us, learn quickly, and you will gain much knowledge," their leader Mamut spoke to the young Raven.

Hatuii Raven Number Eight spoke, "As we all remember from the last meeting, the hate continues to flourish in the other unfortunate marriage, and now even the children are dissatisfied and severely affected, very sad situation, indeed. The ending of this unfortunate family will be very tragic. I have heard the elders Olymar, Smetos and Gleryk discuss their case, very unfortunate."

Insemir number nine spoke quickly and distinctly. "I have found an elderly man in need of care. Although he needs care, he has a gift, which will be of dual benefit. This is the last of the missions on the chosen one's journey.

This elderly man resides on the same road on which the chosen one will be returning home from his missions, he will come to a small neglected white house with yellow shutters, the last house out of the village. This poor man needs to be taken care because of his fragile bones, he cannot do much for himself, but many others come to his aid. It will take some convincing for our chosen one, to move this needy elderly man from his little home in which he lived all of his life with his wife. The most important is that the elderly man has to reside with our chosen individual and his family, this will be the most trying and dangerous journey for both. Encounter unexpected problems along the way, a trial of courage and endurance. They both must survive this last journey through treacherous terrain, which will be the final test. I believe I am correct in concluding that if anything goes wrong, the consequences will be painful and regretful."

Their Leader Mamut congratulated all of them for such excellent work.

Kirree Number Ten interrupted the conversation to mention the loss of one of their brothers Jemolai.

"Yes, let us have a moment of silence for our departed brother Jemolai Raven Number Eleven his spirit soars in the spirit world of our paradise."

They were silent for a moment in respect to the departed brother.

Mamut their leader spoke. "At our next meeting we will be joined by a young brother, his name is Sankuol. The elders speak of him highly. Sankuol will be Raven Number Eleven."

Lornn Number Twelve spoke. "Now my brothers we need to discuss the situation with the abused brother. Listen to our Leader."

They made strange flapping and rustling noises, then silence.

Kosta listened to the strange noises, but all was quiet again. He tried to put this puzzle together. What was this about? He could not understand why all of this was happening. He tried to remember all those problems and solutions. "*Who is the one to solve them, surely not I..., I am blind! Do they know I am here? What if these mysterious birds, they must be birds, are not aware that I am here and I am not to hear all of this, what will happen to me then. Oh my head...the pain, I am dying of hunger, soon it will be over, I cannot go on much longer.*"

Kosta did not move, afraid of being discovered, and as a spy would be torn apart by these creatures. The silence of the night was broken when Mamut continued, a slight breeze rustled in the trees.

"My brothers, we have come to the conclusion of our meeting. Lastly, I must speak about the humble character and his sensitivities as our chosen one. His love and devotion is evident in his ultimate sacrifice for his family.

"The Elders Olymar, Smeto and Gleryk after lengthy discussions had decided that he is the chosen individual for these special assignments. His heart is pure. His honesty, humility, and devotion, with these virtues he earned to be the Brother of Light.

"Here among us he is... he is at this moment very helpless... you see my brothers... he is the same individual, who to save his family from starvation, surrendered his left eye in order to receive provisions, *as a payment* his older brother demanded. The older brother as you know is very wealthy, to give up a few sacks of needy staples would not make a dent in his bins, but the hate and envy, of which we are not sure of yet, the reason, turned his heart cold and evil lurks within. He has joined with the demons, and he has become the Brother of Darkness.

"The second time the needy brother turned for help to his wealthy brother. I feel that, if I may state my opinion, his foolish pride prevented him from receiving food from strangers. His decision was to go back to his only brother.

"The evil older brother, heartless and cowardly made his brother very drunk then proceeded to gouge the right eye. No means of earning a living or ever seeing the faces of his family, without his sight he is an invalid with a broken spirit, a useless man. He has a talent of a true carver.

"His family is very broken-hearted and worried. He has been absent now for three days. The Elders Olymar, Smeto and Gleryk at the last meeting decided to restore his eyesight. Energized with power to fulfill the obligations of which we are discussing. He is our chosen one for these missions.

"Therefore to restore his sight he must have faith, never weaken or falter else he will be lost... he has to find a small cluster of carpophore puffy mushrooms which are all around him. Break them open and rub his eye sockets, his eyesight, shall be restored.

"He must remember all the solutions to these problems, which we have discussed. He must hurry to reach the fourth range of the mountains first and all depends on him to cure the Little Princess Alexia. We FORBID him to go to his family NOW. There will be time enough for Fate to reunite them later. We are done. Now we shall depart to whence we came," their Leader Mamut concluded.

Kosta listened to the Ravens discussing the problems, then the solutions. He absorbed all of it like a sponge.

When they mentioned the puffy mushrooms he began to feel around him on the grass, some of the weeds were tall, he cautiously groped for these puffs, being very alert, he paid attention as these strange voices talked about him, and to him, he understood. Yes, yes he understood!

Their meeting was over.

Kosta intrigued by these speaking creatures, unable to see them, realized they are birds, what they looked like he will never see. He lay listening, all around was quiet but for a light breeze, leaves rustled now and then.

The Ravens, one by one, flew off into the darkness without a flutter.

The last one called out a shrill "caw, caw," that echoed into the silence.

Fifty: Morning After

Kosta remained motionless on the ground, absorbing what he had heard. “This must have been a dream, a delirious wishful dream to have eyesight and see again and be home with my family.”

Instead of panicking, he began to think. Now soberly thinking, that this was not a dream, he was awake throughout their meeting, what he had heard was very real, not fictitious. He will do precisely as instructed and do whatever it takes to have his vision back.

However, in order to see he must have strong faith for it to happen, he must not doubt, otherwise he and everything else in his life will be lost.

He groped around for those small round puffy *carpophores* mushrooms, he felt something, yes a cluster of the puffs, and began to pull them out of the grass and squeezed till they popped and with a trembling hand nervously rubbed his left eye, nothing happened, darkness.

He waited, then sprinkled the sore eye, very gently, the intensity of the pain lessened but nothing happened. He waited still in darkness. Hunger gnawed at his stomach. He shivered from dampness. He was not giving up, not just yet. He did not want to die. The Ravens instilled in him strong hope. They said, “*Not to doubt or all will be lost.*” He closed his eyelid and began to think of his family. Gradually drowsiness overtook him, he felt as if he was falling, falling into the dark bottomless bowels of the earth. Deep sleep blocked all of his senses.

While in deep sleep, nothing mattered. His family must manage their life on their own. Nothing bothered him, the pain that tugged at his heart reminding him what his brother had done to him, or what the Ravens had said, and not the cold which chilled him to the bone.

The clouds drifted across the sky and the moon shone brightly illuminating the crosses and the limp body in slumber between two grave mounds. Kosta suddenly awoke instinctively opened his eyes and saw the night sky, the stars and the moon. He was still alive. He propped up on his elbow and looked around. The huge oak tree stood not far from where he was. Was this a miracle or was it magic? It didn't matter, he was alive and he had vision just like the Ravens said. He fell asleep again. The hours passed as the moon walked across the sky, the morning sunrays warmed him. Awakening from deep sleep a bit disorientated. The bright light of a new day made him squint. The shocked realization, bewilderment...this was real, as he slowly raised his hands to his face, he shut and opened his eyes again, his hands, he saw his hands he will carve again. He looked up at the blue sky, and all around him were crosses. Three days he was here on this cemetery ground, laid by the servants or was he dumped between two grave mounds.

"This is a miracle, or is this a dream? Did I die and had gone to heaven? I must be dead. No...this is real...I can see...I must not deny what I heard... during the night I woke up and I saw the sky and the moon," he said aloud. He sat up, got to his feet without effort. He stood for a little while, shocked that this is where he was while he was unconscious and bleeding. He began to shake convulsively. The fact is; this was done to him by his blood brother, this, he could not fathom. Too much, too much to comprehend, but in his mind is one question, *why?*

His knees buckled under him, he sat down again, held his head between his knees, and stayed in that position for a long while. Strange, he forgot hunger, or cold, and he said, "My God, this is a miracle! I am alive, I did not starve, the wolves did not devour me, and I have my vision, I SEE! God I am able to SEE!" he whispered.

Now, he was up on his own two feet and marveled at his recovery, he believed.

Then he noticed on the grass by the tree, black shiny feathers. He stared at them, walked over and picked up all of them. He counted thirteen feathers, *so they were birds!*

"Without a doubt, they were Ravens...thirteen of them," Kosta said aloud.

Each one of the Ravens dropped a feather as a reminder they really were here last night, and what he had heard was real, as real as his eyesight. Now he must do what they instructed him to do. It was all up to him now.

He held these feathers in his fist and promised to keep them for always. This cemetery was far from the village, an uninhabited section, situated close to the forest, since this was early dawn he has seen no one, and no one was about to see him.

He wasted no more time, began to walk in the western direction to the fourth mountain range. He felt no fear of this long journey, or fear of hardships, which he will encounter along the way. Going west is to lead him to the Little Princess in the City of Magda.

How he knew where to go he did not know himself, something, someone led him. There were moments his feet never touched the ground and his surging energy never diminished. His mind was strangely alert and in high spirit.

He walked with an unusual stamina, he did not tire, trip over tree roots and gravel stones, nothing seemed unusual, jumped over fallen trees and waded through streams, and cool water refreshed him. He walked all day, and at sunset came to a hut at the outskirts of the woods. A lone woman greeted him at her front door.

"You must have walked all day," she said, "from the looks of your clothes, you surely have encounter some vicious animals. Look at your shirt!" She pointed at his shirt.

Indeed, he looked totally disheveled, the shirt had stains of blood and mud on it. He completely had forgotten that his shirt was bloody, at first he was lost for words, especially explaining about the Ravens, he could never utter a word of what had transpired last night never, ever. Anyway, who would believe him, he agreed with her about the encounter with the animal.

He asked for something to drink, she poured a large glass of milk and he drank it fast, tasty and wonderfully refreshing. She asked if he was hungry, in fact, now he was feeling a bit hungry, she gave him a large slice of bread, he told her he had no money to pay her, also asked her for small burlap sack, which he desperately needed.

Without hesitation, she went inside and after a minute she came out, gave him a small burlap sack. Kosta thanked her and was on his way. She waved and called out to him, "Good luck on your journey."

Kosta now crossed two mountain ranges, walked all day and through the night. He was by some force pushed on, sleep evaded him, never even thought about wild animals, did not encounter any, as if some invisible shield protected him from danger. He scaled steep cliffs of the third range with dangerous crags into which he almost fell when he lost his footing. Nevertheless, kept on and on towards the fourth mountain range. To count days, Kosta picked little stones at sunset. Thirteen weeks and many miles have past. He crossed three mountain ranges, without his awareness, some unforeseen power advanced him this quickly.

For any other individual this journey would have taken several years of travel.

Soon, very soon he will arrive at his destination. His eagerness mounted thinking of the ill little Princes, and soon he will be able to cure her.

Suddenly he recalled back what were the necessary ingredients for the cure, "*Ah, yes...the little tree frogs he must not forget to add to the soup.*" He walked on in a faster stride.

Up on the mountain tops, during the day the snow gleamed brightly but the nights were chilly, it was still spring, the farther west he walked the higher the elevation and the colder the air. The bloody shirt too thin to give warmth, he wished he had his cape it would keep him warmer, he wondered if it is still at his brother's house.

When it came time to rest each night, he chose to crawl under a spruce tree, if he found one. With his hands raked up leaves or needles. Crisscrossed tree limbs, pushed them into the ground for sturdiness, stuffed layers of leaves between. Small branches and twigs stuck where needed, atop all that more leaves, held down with more branches, a simple tent for protection from the wind, or detection by wild animals. Not too solid but at least something, he shivered, the ground being damp, Kosta crawled out and went around and raked with his hands piles of needles to make a softer bed. He tried to comprehend what really was happening, why at the beginning of his journey, he felt no hunger or cold, but now being much closer to his first assignment, he is feeling hunger, weariness and cold, what has happened to him, nothing is making any sense.

The rain woke him up in the morning, which chilled him more, he ran to keep warm. Driven faster and seemed to be in a trance again. Kosta stopped to rest and to search for something to eat, berries would suit him fine. Soon he should be there. Surprisingly his thoughts of the previous nights erased. Mid-afternoon, in the distance, appeared the looming castle high on the mountain, the Kingdom of Magda.

Fifty-One: Kingdom of Magda

Kosta came upon homes built at the base of the mountain and up on slopes, higher and higher all the way to the castle. This was the Kingdom of Magda, he climbed and observed through the winding streets all the way to the top, as he turned to look down his eyes took in a scene of quite a large settlement. The little streets looked like ribbons winding around small homes, busy people passing him by, yet, none paid attention. He surveyed the area searching for a lake or stream, where the tree frogs should be plentiful. Kosta strolled back down through the streets and turned in the direction of the woods where he hopped to find a lake. He came upon a marsh overgrown with reeds among which saplings of willows fought for space. Since it was still early in the afternoon Kosta returned to the outskirts of the town to inquire where to find a bit of food. A group of boys approached him.

"Which one of you will lead me to a place where I might have something to eat?" Kosta asked. The boys stared at him speechless.

"And who might you be, looking like that?" A tall boy measured him up and down pointing at his dirty and bloody shirt.

"I have come a long way and as you see I had a life threatening encounter, you see I won," Kosta without hesitation said. They looked at each other then at him. The tall boy whispered something to a chubby boy, who immediately ran off. The boys surrounded Kosta but did not speak just eyed him up and down, they seemed to be waiting for the chubby boy to return. The boy came running breathless, and again they whispered.

"Well, have you boys decided what I will eat and where?" Kosta said sternly.

"Come with us," said the tall boy and all of them marched Kosta down the street, which wound around several houses and then stopped in front of a nice cottage, and pointed for him to go in. Kosta thanked them and the boys ran off. Without hesitating Kosta knocked on the door and a man opened it and glared at Kosta.

"Well, what do you want, and who are you? The man wearing an apron asked.

"Pardon my intrusion, are you the proprietor? Kosta asked.

"Yes I am, enter," the man replied waving his hand, and held the door open.

"As I told those boys, I had come a long way and I am hungry, could you spare me a slice of bread with cheese and some milk or tea?" Kosta waited.

"Well come in, I will feed you." Inside this cottage, a table stood dressed and ready for clients. On the outside, a young woman served an older couple bowls of soup. She glanced at Kosta. The man led him to one of the tables outside and told him to sit. In a short time, the man came carrying a bowl of soup and a large slice of bread with cheese, and a glass of ale. For a moment, Kosta forgot that he had absolutely no money to pay for this meal. He explained this to the man before taking a bite of the cheese.

"Do not fret about money. We mean to please, who you are and why you are here, however, we know, and we aim to keep an eye on you," the proprietor said.

"But how do you know who I am?" Kosta almost shouted completely perplexed.

"Do not be afraid, eat," the man said and walked away.

"Who told you?" Kosta asked.

"Gypsies," the man replied without looking back, "they know everything."

Kosta finished the delicious meal and drank the ale. It was time to go down to the marsh to catch the tree frogs. Along the way down, he was surprised that no one paid attention to him as if he was invisible. However, to dwell on that he had no time.

As he walked along, he noticed the tall boy standing in the middle of the narrow street. When Kosta came to him, the boy joined him and without hesitation said.

"My mother and a neighbor were talking about a gypsy fortune teller that walked through the streets and was telling the people that someone was coming soon to cure the Princess. They were laughing at the gypsy. My mother told the neighbor that sometimes the gypsies tell the truth. They know, perhaps a stranger will come and cure the little princess. Are you the stranger she was talking about, we have never seen you here before, is it possible it is you?" the boy asked Kosta.

"Well now it might just be the truth and I might be the one!" Kosta said smiling.

"Now you are in trouble!" The boy stopped and eyed Kosta from head to toe.

"Why am I in trouble?"

"Well... that chubby boy's father... works at the castle and said anyone that claims to have a cure for the King's daughter and does not...cure her...his head falls off!" the boy exclaimed.

"How many tried and lost their heads, do you know?" Kosta asked.

"Oh...many," the boy replied, "very many, their heads are hung on trees in the forest!"

"Well then I better go now, by the way what is the name of your town and your King's name?" Kosta asked the boy.

"HUH! This is not a town! We live in a Kingdom, ruled by our King, Clemens Oscarian Bantar. You come here not knowing?" the boy said and walked off before Kosta could say another word. Kosta headed to the marsh in search of the green frogs, repeated the name of the King, *Clemens Oscarian Bantar*. For several hours he rested in a well-hidden shrubbery at the edge of the wetland, he had no other choice but wait for the early evening. Just when the sunset sank beyond the trees, the frogs began their evening song.

"To hear them is one thing, but to catch them is tricky," Kosta said to himself. So much so, Kosta finally managed to catch several tightly tied them in that small sack.

Now he was ready to see King Clemens Oscarian Bantar, even though it was rather late, he decided to go and at least try to get into the castle, to get some sleep and start the cure in the morning. He followed the streets up to the castle, just as he was close enough to the gate the guard shouted, "Who goes there!"

"I must see the king immediately, open the gate!" Kosta shouted to the guard.

The guard did not believe him, the guard on the tower ran to inform King Clemens Oscarian Bantar that some kind of lunatic was at the gate and it could possibly be a hoax or do harm to the little Princess Alexia.

While Kosta waited across the moat, King Clemens Oscarian Bantar ordered his guards to unbolt the gate and seize Kosta. Guards with swords led him inside the castle walls, obeyed and faced the wall. King Clemens Oscarian Bantar approached, "Now turn and look at me," the King said. Kosta turned and faced the King in tattered clothes and dirty. The King did not look him up and down, did not comment on his appearance but ordered the guards to free him. Kosta respectfully bowed to the King and said, "Your highness, forgive me for such an intrusion, for the late hour...but the matter is urgent...I came from very far, I am here to cure your daughter, little Princess, Alexia."

King Clemens Oscarian Bantar closely observed Kosta for a few moments and understood. Even though Kosta looked ragged and muddy, something in his eyes made the king believe him. The king ordered the guards to escort him to the kitchen and serve him supper. Thereafter escort him to the king's chamber, the time did not matter. The important matter is the little princess. Kosta had a good meal, again, relaxed a bit and then escorted to the Kings chamber.

The little sack was with him at all times, Kosta did not explain to King Clemens Oscarian Bantar of how he learned of little princess's illness. King Clemens Oscarian Bantar did not ask for details. Only one question the king asked Kosta.

"Where is your horse?"

"I walked all the way."

The king understood. "I am sure you are tired, so I want you to sleep well tonight. First thing in the morning prepare the cure, now I will show you to your room," the King said.

Kosta never in his whole life has seen such luxury as this. Kosta washed up and changed into the nightclothes the servant laid out for him. He stretched out in the huge bed feeling luxuriously comfortable, thought about his family, he missed his children, what are they feeling right now, his brother had he delivered the food, what if he lied, what if they are suffering great hunger, what if they are ill, he cannot help them now. Not now, he has so many more problems to solve which will take time before his journey takes him back home.

He wished to have his lovely Kathryn right here beside him. She will never know until he is back home what really happened to him, how he missed her at this moment, and she is heart-broken and the children sad. Mathew must hate him for leaving...perhaps they will hate him when he returns. Are they assuming he left them to fend for themselves, absolving himself of all responsibilities? Such thoughts crowded his mind until he forced himself to change to positive thinking and hope for the best. At least he was hoping that they thought of him being alive, even though they do not know where he is.

He awoke with a start, the room still in darkness, the castle silent. He barely found his way to the window, to a faint sliver of light peeking through the drapes, pulled them back, a new day on the horizon, he was in the castle and had a job to do. He dressed quickly and followed the aroma of breakfast to the kitchen. When he entered, cooks, and corpulent servants were bustling about preparing breakfast for the King and the whole crew including the guards. Kosta explained why he was here, quickly the pots and ingredients needed sat on the fire. Kosta watched for the soup to bubble then glanced about, quickly dropped the frogs into the boiling pot.

Suddenly King Clemens Oscarian Bantar walked into the kitchen. All the servants bowed and chimed all together a "Good morning your Highness!"

Then Kosta recalled the Raven's words, *to have courage,* now the magic soup was boiling and just about ready. Kosta asked for a bucket to discard the ingredients, when he was done he took the bucket out to the moat emptied it all for the fish.

The liquid poured in a large covered bowl carried carefully to the bedroom of the sleeping princess. Kosta asked politely not to be disturbed. King Clemens Oscarian Bantar without protest obliged. She was a beautiful frail child, he wondered how long she had been asleep, and he prayed that his magic broth worked.

He approached the bed and took in the scene again recalled the Raven's words, '*he should not have any 'doubts,' they chose only him,*' he felt self-assured. He propped the sleeping child on pillows. Sat down at the edge of the bed, little princess Alexia lay with eyes closed, her blond curly ringlets draped her pale face; with her lips slightly parted slept peacefully. Kosta with great patience carefully moistened her lips with the liquid, waited between each drop.

Morning turned into night as time ticked away. Kosta continued this process drop by drop.

One thing entered his mind and that is; cook a fresh pot of soup, but the ravens never mention anything about cooking fresh soup, he rationalized for a while, but surely, fresh is important, I must use my common sense, I will to this immediately. Kosta hurried into the kitchen and instructed the cook to prepare all the ingredients in a small pot, but do not start until he returns. He walked out of the castle, ran down to the marshes to find the green tree frogs.

King Clemens Oscarian Bantar tapped lightly on the door and entered, Kosta was not there. His little princess propped up, still slept. Alarmed called the guards, *"quickly go find that man, go*! The guards scattered through the castle. In the kitchen furiously questioned the cook and all the servants gathered wondering what is going on. "What is happening that you are in such an uproar, the man went out for a little while, is the princess asleep in her bed?" asked the head cook. The guards replied, "Yes, she is."

"Well then clam up and calm down, he will be back."

Then the king ran into the kitchen very agitated, seeing his guards instead of looking for Kosta sat at the table having tea and cakes. The cook said, "Your Majesty, Kosta is out looking for whatever he needs for the soup, please calm down and have some fresh cakes."

The cook was right, within several hours Kosta walked into the kitchen, everybody was there waiting for him.

"I am glad you returned! Next time you must leave let someone know I need to be informed," the king said, then added, "have some tea and cakes."

"Forgive me Sire, I was preoccupied, I assure you it would not happen again, I do need to go out every second day," Kosta said.

The King observed the tender way that Kosta administered the freshly cooked magic broth. His heart went out to him. "*Who is this gentle man? Where did he come from? No matter, there will be time to ask questions later, my only wish is to have my daughter, little Princes Alexia back alive and happy,*" the king thought.

Kosta sat without speaking, just motioned to the King to leave. King Clemens before leaving said to Kosta, "her name is Alexia, she is seven years old."

"Yes I know," Kosta replied.

The time dragged very slowly. Little Princess Alexia slept. Kosta could have given up, but he held in his mind those words he heard that awful night: *"do not doubt, but believe*" so he sat at her bedside, and having the broth warmed up kept up the feeding drop by drop.

Everyone in the castle waited, not once did they mention the newcomer with his magic broth. No one questioned if this simple magic broth will work, neither did anyone say his head would roll too, if it does not. Everyone kept busy with daily tasks.

The day she stirred and moaned Kosta knew she will live and will be well. She opened her eyes every day for a little while and was fully awake on the thirteenth day. This was the most joyous and memorable day in this Kingdom, especially King Clemens Oscarian Bantar, and Kosta.

She stared at Kosta, recalling memories, it seemed a long time before she asked, "Who are you...where is my father?" Kosta pulled on the rope, to signal King that his child is awake. The king ran into her bedroom and seeing she was awake, cried tears of joy, embracing his little girl, she was back from the sleep of death, and the credit was all Kosta's. King Clemens Oscarian Bantar forgot his royal position and embraced Kosta out of joy and gratitude slapping his back hard.

"Today is a day to celebrate, trumpets must blare, and messengers dispatched with the wonderful news of the Royal child's recovery throughout the country." The King shouted and rang for servants. At least a dozen came running, guards, cooks and maids. King Clemens gave to each an order and they ran off in different directions; knowing what each one of them must do. Only one remained in the bedroom with little Princess Alexia, her responsibility tending to her every need.

Kosta pleaded with the King to let him go home, but the King insisted for him to stay for the feast, like none other. Kosta stayed, Princess Alexia and Kosta were the celebrities. The King gave Kosta and enormous amount of gold. The merriment lasted three days dancing, and singing, the children gathered around Kosta, and the group of boys he had met the first day, gripped his hand and the tall boy gave him a big hug "we are glad you did not lose your head," they said laughing.

All of the townspeople were overjoyed, especially when the King from gratitude gave an order for each of his loyal subjects in his Kingdom to come to the castle and collect a gold piece one for each member in the family. The Royal Knights went out to the countryside, proclaimed to the people the Kings order.

After the townspeople cleaned up the whole town, everyone settled back to relax. Kosta needed to journey on to the second urgent assignment.

The King had insisted on answers to many questions now, Kosta forced out of courtesy to explain, having to dodge the truth; gypsies know everything and he had strong feeling; and this feeling compelled him to come this far and save his child. King Clemens Oscarian Bantar accepted his reply without questions; still would not allow Kosta to leave. Kosta felt he had to sneak away during the night but then changed his mind. He decided to stay. As days dragged on, in his mind, the other problems urged him on and he was determined to do all of them just as instructed by the Thirteen Ravens.

He was a celebrity, people swarmed around him with lots of inquisitive looks and demanding answers to their curious questions.

Little doubt they had, these simple people, gullible to boot, you could tell them anything, and they would believe, but not Kosta, he had never told a lie in his life, some facts were omitted and unsaid, much less lie about something as important as the cure.

Did he lead them to believe that the simple broth cured the child? Yes! The sincerity in his voice and the simplicity of his character proved to be the truth.

His brother, on the other hand, most likely would have embellished the cure to be something out of this world, an ancient concoction of some Asian Monks, who prayed over the sacrificial ashes of chicken claws and leaves, ashes scattered for secret ritual.

The city buzzed with the news and echoed into the distant towns and villages, that the Little Princess Alexia is alive and well, and that a stranger from some village from the east cured her. Yet news had not reached his village or Kosta's family, who mourned his disappearance, or his demise. What if the news should reach them, what effect will it have on them? Why should anyone assume or believe that it is he Kosta, it could be anyone, any man. His name is not important, because no one knows his name, but King Clemens Oscarian Bantar. The only important news will be that, little Princess Alexia King Clemens Bantar's daughter was cured.

What of his brother Lord Thomas, how would he react to that fact, that, his blind brother supposedly devoured by vicious animals piece-by-piece carried away, bones snapped and splintered by sharp fangs? Suppose his brother hoped, his delirious, blind, crawling, groping and grasping brother to find his way, but to his misfortune fell into a ravine, or a creek, or wandered off far enough to fall into the river to drown.

Then news, to hear of a man from the East village cured a little princess? Never in a million years would Lord Thomas believe that this man would appear out of nowhere alive and well, and his name would be Kosta? Found in a far country achieving such complicated deeds, never! Never ever would that be a fact! If it were to be true, that he was back and alive, Lord Thomas would sneer and refuse to accept such an asinine story, call it a hoax, someone playing a dirty trick just to drive him mad.

This once in a lifetime miracle, a magic of nature's wonders, the mystical phenomenon that sometimes occur, but only to the chosen. Dreams and visions have many meanings, difficult to understand or be able to analyze and heed. Evil spirits do harm, whereas the unseen gentle spirits warn and protect.

Fifty-Two:

Suspicion - Retribution

Far beyond the four mountain ranges to the east, at the little house, Kosta's family's faces were sullen; laughter that once echoed now silent. The children refused to play outdoors, and conversations that Mathew carried on with Rebecca ceased. They merely existed it seemed, but endless silence and gloom lived on.

Kathryn's eyes lost their sparkle. Her hair that once flowed freely now tied in a knot proved that her nerves are in a knot. She could not free her feelings of this terrible loss, the awful realization that Kosta was gone, drained her whole being of life, now she existed only for the children. Yes, they had plenty of food for the table, but every meal she prepared made her aware of his absence and the fact from where the food had come from. There were times her mind for a moment cleared, thoughts turned to that morning. The morning Kosta went to his brother, she wondered why that same day Kosta just disappeared. She recalled the first time, he had gone to his brother, he came home unconscious bloody under sacks of grain; without an eye, and this time he is gone. Her mind returned many times to this same thought. She cannot accuse the man, cannot prove anything and yet her suspicion gnawed at her mind. She imagined gossip about her, never thinking that just maybe these people worried about her and hoped for Kosta's return. Her stomach in knots unable to swallow any food.... she just could not swallow!

Rabinna many evenings tried to console Kathryn, which only brought on a deluge of tears.

"How will I manage alone without him? What is going to happen to us? The children will grow up and go away, settle down and live their own lives. I will die alone." She could not express it all to Rabinna, with difficulty through tears and sobbing she uttered, "Rabinna why did he leave us, I do not understand why, I worked with him all these years, and when he was away at the castle, I worked it all by myself, the children helped little, and I gave my heart to him. Forever...I was forever his, where has he gone Rabinna, please help me to understand why, and what on earth, have I done wrong to deserve this!"

Rabinna tried to speak but Kathryn again bombarded her with questions to which Rabinna had no answers.

"Have I not been a good wife and lover? Did I not show him enough affection? We have seven children constantly around us, we just cannot be so open and free!" she carried on.

Rabinna at last was able to stop her for a little while to give her some answers.

"Kathryn, why not show your children your love for each other, it is natural, love instilled from childhood will flourish among them, and they will respect and love one another. After all, you had seven children together. I am sure the older ones understand life. Kathryn I do not mean to sound negative, but we also tried all these past months to understand what happened. What reasons did he have to abandon you, and all of his precious children? We have discussed at length, Michael and I feel that he did not leave of his own accord, not in the least! You know he loves all of you. You must have faith that he is alive and will come back." Rabinna paused. "If he was dead...Rabinna began again; someone would have found him by now, and you would be informed, and look here, until now we have not received absolutely none bad or good news. You must soberly think this through, with Mathew you can talk about it, he will explain to the children they must live with hope. Look at your children, you think you are worried...they are depressed and sad. Kathryn you must show them your strength and give them love, they need you, they are as lost as you...." Rabinna's voice trailed off, tears rolled down her cheeks.

Kathryn stopped sobbing. She paid attention to words of truth spoken by her sister. Rabinna was right. The children needed their mother now, who else is there for them to turn to. They suffer as well as she and miss their father immensely. It is hard to live without him. He made them laugh. He showed them how to do so many things ever since they can remember, but now they are lost. Kathryn looked at her children and her heart filled with compassion. She realized Rabinna was right. She stood up from the bench they sat on, and called her children, "Come to me my sweethearts, all of you, we need to talk, and I need to embrace you!" They came one by one, and she hugged each one, from the youngest to the eldest, they sat next to her and their eyes absolutely had no sparkle. Kathryn's heart sank even more for being engrossed with her own grief; she overlooked them; their sadness and loss. She said, "I am so lost, lost in my grief. I lost my strength and hope, and all of you were just as lost. Today your Aunt Rabinna opened my eyes and I must say I am ashamed. Just this minute I recalled what Baron Patrick had told us, "Never lose hope. However, things, not always work out for the best. Sometimes, life will bring surprises you never dreamed could be possible..." The children listened as she continued. "If life throws a curve and knocks you down on your knees that does not mean you stay on your knees. You gather your strength, stand up and keep going." Your father had done just that many times, took a deep breath and kept going, he had courage, overcame fear...I cannot tell you where he is or what happened, we will survive and endure and our faith will be stronger because of that." When she stopped Rosie, the youngest of them all asked.

"Mother, does this mean that Father will come back to us, and bring us surprises?"

Kathryn had to smile, "perhaps that will be so... let us not lose faith."

"I must ask you to forgive me for neglecting you... just when you needed me, but because of the terrible loss we have to endure... I only thought of myself... which was selfish of me, I became a blind person to my surroundings...please forgive me." The children loudly said they forgive her, and their voices became heard, and there was a bit of cheer in their life.

Up at the castle Baron Patrick and Aunt Olivia were extremely concerned for the welfare of Kosta's family. He could not believe that Kosta would just up and leave without a word of justifiable reason to anyone. All he remembers is hearing from the servants that Kosta visited his brother. Since then no news, Kosta vanished. Normally news travels fast, but not this time. The weeks kept passing. Baron Patrick encouraged Aunt Olivia to stay with Kathryn and the children to help them cope. He did not mind; he would come off the mountain and come fetch her if he misses her too much.

Aunt Olivia stayed for days at a time but her presence made Kathryn cry the more when Aunt Olivia admired the flowers in the garden and the vegetables, it was springtime, the world buzzed with life, but where is Kosta. Aunt Olivia always parted with a heavy heart. In the past several months, she herself did not feel up to par, her breathing gave her some difficulty, but she never admitted any of this to her husband or anyone else. To mention her problems would not be helpful at all. After all she and Patrick are getting old, so why bother. Her life with Baron Patrick was magical, such a warm and wonderful person. The lost lifetime they should have had together while young never happened, no sense to dwell on it. Nevertheless, what time remains together now, they must cherish. Their love is keeping them young and alive, although in spirit only.

They slept together in that huge bed. They always ate together, strolled together. On pleasant days they rode to the countryside for a day, it did not matter where as long as they enjoyed being together. Aunt Olivia visited small towns in which she had never been and had bought things her eye fancied, nothing was out of Olivia's reach, on the contrary, everything was within her reach.

What puzzled them also the supplies of provisions, delivered periodically to Kathryn, which came from Uncle Thomas of all people.

On a day Aunt Olivia visited Kathryn it was humid and stifling. It was difficult to breath for everyone. Kathryn noticed the pallor on Aunt Olivia's face and the rivulets of perspiration at which she dabbed often with a handkerchief. They sat in the shade of a tree on the side of the house. Then Rabinna with Rebecca arrived to join them. They had a wonderful time talking about the children how well and fast they had grown.

"Yes they have grown, that means we are that much older," Aunt Olivia said smiling. Of course, they all agreed to that true statement. Kathryn through tears said, "My son is seventeen, that means I am seventeen years older and now I am alone."

"Kathryn, do not cry, look around you, you are never alone," Aunt Olivia said.

"I am here and Aunt Olivia and all the children, and I know Kosta will come back to you soon, he must be alive, for what reason he went away I cannot tell you, but put your trust in faith and God," Rabinna chimed in."

I cannot forgive him for leaving us, I cannot!" Kathryn said angrily. Rosie came up to Kathryn drenched from perspiration,

"Mother I am so hot, I want to go swimming in the creek," she said. At the mention of swimming all eyes turned on Kathryn. Rabinna laughed and she cried out,

"Well... why is everyone still on the ground, come on!" Aunt Olivia stared at them, "What do you mean I should go in with my clothes on...?"

"Aunt Olivia we always go in our shifts, the children will not mind at all!" Rabinna said and laughed. In no time at all, they were in the water splashing and diving. No fear of drowning the creek is shallow.

"Mathew!" Aunt Olivia waved him over and said, "Mathew I recall while I traveled people made rafts out of bamboo, too bad we do not have bamboo growing here."

"Bamboo, I have never heard of such trees," Mathew said. Rabinna listened and said that she had heard of it, but no use talking about it if there were none here.

"Aunt Olivia, Baron Patrick would know where to get some, would he not?" Tessana said. Jason put his two coins in. "Aunt Olivia could you ask Grandpa Patrick somehow get it for us, please!" The other children just listened could not imagine what the others were talking about. Aunt Olivia said she would ask him, I am sure he knows everything about bamboo, after all the time he spent on the south islands.

Refreshed in the cool water the children ran into the house to change into dry clothes. For the three women it turned out to be a dilemma; Kathryn's clothes did not fit Rabinna or Aunt Olivia, their solution; while dresses hung out to dry, the three women wrapped in sheets prepared a big meal for the hungry crowd. At the table, the children wolfed down the food. Talked with their mouthfuls about the fun in the water, and they will do it again till summer ends.

While Aunt Olivia visited Kathryn and the children, Marysa's ghost in dreams appeared to Baron Patrick. In his dream at last, he heard Marysa's voice. Clearly, she said, "My brother Sean murdered me. I loved Christian. My body lies at the foot of the bench beneath the oak tree." Baron Patrick abruptly awoke to the quiet of the night. His mind held on to the dream and those words trying to grasp their meaning. Early that morning Baron Patrick sent a servant boy to the village to find Christian.

"Do not come back without him, the matter is extremely urgent," Baron Patrick told him. After several hours of waiting, the servant and Christian returned.

"Christian come let us have some breakfast and I have some important news for you." Baron Patrick led him to the dining room. At breakfast Baron Patrick in a low voice explained, "Last night Marysa came into my dream again. Permit me to tell you from the very beginning. At first, we heard noises and screams we were petrified. In my dreams she was a young woman, I was disturbed. She tried to tell me something, pointing to the tree, but I never heard her voice. She was angry. Disturbed my staff, after a time we ignored her screaming and commotion. I tell you...when my guests overstayed she frightened them so much they never came back, not one. Last night she came again, and this time I heard her speak. Christian...what I am about to tell you...is horrific. Sean her brother murdered her out of jealousy, she wanted to marry you. She told me where her body lies, beneath the flowerbed near the oak tree. Remember the last time we sat on that bench and we talked about her," Baron Patrick concluded.

Christian's heart cringed and he began to weep. After the outburst of tears subsided, and emotions calmed he said, "I have had dreams also, she sang in my dreams. She was never angry, I felt her near me very often. My feelings were correct, she did not forsake me of her own free will, all those dreams and appearances, meant something, she tried to tell me Sean murdered her. I wonder where he disappeared to." Christian clasped his head in his hands and sobbed. "Oh my God, oh my love had to die so! Marysa, Marysa..."

"Her murderer has to be found and brought to justice. You are free to go in search of this murderer, you have a lifetime to go and look for him," Baron Patrick said.

"But where am I to go?" Christian asked.

"Your feelings and the spirit of your beloved will lead you to the murderer. You will find him, one way or another," Baron Patrick replied. They agreed for Christian to go in search of Sean, the murderer. It matters none how many years it will take to find him, faith would fare the murderer well if he died before Christian finds him.

Christian headed to the constable's home to seek his counsel; Constable Maurice Greadeou listened to Christian's story and became thoughtful.

"Christian I feel for you. Spending half of your lifetime searching the world for that sort of scoundrel, no, I would say, do not waste your life, no, do not go! Think about it. Besides you do have a woman, now to care for, she seems to be good-hearted, stay and make a life with her. In the meantime, I will make contacts with other counties and villages. I know what he looks like I have talked with him before he went away."

The greatest satisfaction and fulfillment in Christian's lifetime, before he closes his eyes forever would be to hear that justice caught up with Sean the murder.

Whenever Aunt Olivia stayed with Kathryn, Baron Patrick alone sat on the bench under the huge oak tree and meditated. "Life is a road of searching, constant searching. I have searched and by chance found the one I was searching for, that is all I need, I love her and I know she loves me. At least, now I know what ending awaits me. I do not want to see my sweetheart go before me, my heart will burst and I shall follow." Baron Patrick sat alone and thoughts ran through his aging mind. He thought about Marysa. "Her spirit will no longer wander on this earth in distress." Baron smiled for he envisioned himself meeting this beautiful young maiden as "spirit to spirit" on the other side. "Ah yes the evidence is right here, her wandering soul will have peace, and her remains are right here below my feet," he said to himself and smiled again and, with that smile, he walked slowly to his domain, to retire early for it was a stifling day, and he felt drained. He needed to sleep and dream. Aunt Olivia shall return tomorrow.

Fifty-Three: journey Home - Town of Roses

Kosta accepted the sack of gold from the King, and humbly asked the King for just one more thing to help him on his long journey, a horse, and some food.

Since the next town is quite a distance away and it is very urgent for him to be there. The King gladly granted him more than what he asked for, not one horse, but four, a comfortable carriage and all the necessary supplies.

Kosta tried to refuse such a generous gift but the King insisted, after all his daughter Princess Alexia is alive and well, he deserved the best. Kosta rode away in a carriage fit for a King. The City of Magda was far behind him, the sun slowly dipped towards the horizon, the gusty wind still carried winters chill. He had to wrap a newly acquired cape over his shoulders for warmth. Along the dusty road, the carriage rolled and rattled. Kosta could not imagine the effect his appearance will make on his family after his long absence. He will stand before them, alive. If he could fly to them, he would. He has caused them anguish, uncertainty and shame, desperately he wished to wash away their pain. His thoughts were only of his family, blocking out all sounds around him.

He was unaware of what was ahead. The horses suddenly began to slow down to a confused trot and sidestepping as if trying to avoid an obstacle, or a disturbing scent in the air. The sudden jolt of the carriage startled Kosta back to reality. He scanned the area, the horses snorting, stomping nervously raising a cloud of dust.

He heard sounds, without a second of hesitation his gut feeling urged him to flee. The whip cracked, horses galloped fast leaving the lurking danger far behind. Kosta reined in to ease the exertion. He turned off the road spotting a lake, unhitched the horses by two walked them to the lake for a much-deserved watering.

The trip to the town of Roses was uneventful which made him relax, now and then thoughts of his family put a smile on his face.

The evening dusk shrouded the countryside, time to find a place to sleep and rest the horses, but as he traveled on for miles and miles nothing around but open land, forests and lakes, no sign of villages or farm land between the City of Magda and the small town of Roses. He slept in the carriage, while the horses grazed and rested. At dawn, the happy chirping of many birds woke him. He sat for a while glad to be alive. Breathe in fresh air and admire the beautiful world around him. He had looked at the beauty of the world all of his life, but today he appreciates it much more.

As he rode through the wild countryside, a small settlement came into view. He stopped to purchase supplies and ask for directions to the town of Roses.

"Just follow this road on and on but, look out for thieves along the way especially being alone," the man said. Kosta handed him a gold coin, and rode on.

He found the small place and purchased necessary supplies. On the way he thought about, Kathryn, *my Kathryn if only I could send a message to you that I am alive and well.* She probably would not believe it, thinking it was some heartless joke.

This idea kept coming back again and again, he rationalized it could be done, as soon as he is in the Town of Roses, he will somehow send a message, but having no clue how far he still had to travel or how long all these assignments would take.

He has accomplished the unthinkable, unbelievable, and all because of the *Thirteen Ravens,* their feathers found on the ground that morning, his evidence.

Kosta smiled, "What will my brother Thomas say and do when he hears of the great knowledge I received that night at the cemetery," imagining his brother's expression, yes, he will hear of this soon enough," Kosta said aloud, "how will Thomas react to seeing my face and my eyes, which he gouged out and left me blind to die? How did he feel after he committed that cruel deed? Did he sleep well? Nightmares, how often does he have nightmares, I wonder...for sure I endured much more than nightmares. Mine was not a nightmare but reality, and excruciating pain. I endured all and now I am myself, a whole being as before, this day forward I and my family will have an enchanting life." Kosta on this long journey alone needs to hear a human voice so he talked aloud.

The horses galloped each day covered a lot of territory past through towns and villages; fed and watered well to maintain their endurance on this long journey. Little villages supplied all his needs. He paid well for meals, rooms, and boarding horses. Fell asleep thinking of the solutions to the problems remaining ahead.

A sudden storm interrupted his sleep, strong wind and the downpour of rain drummed loud against the windowpane. Kosta listened until it passed. At first light, he stepped quietly out of bed and dressed, was about to go outside; instead peeked out the window streaked with rain. Someone was by his carriage, Kosta watched. The man opened the door and peeked in, there was nothing to steal, quietly closed the door and walked off, *his clothes tattered*, Kosta thought, *perhaps a homeless man.*

Kosta decided to go out and inspect his carriage for leaks, as he stepped out the door, the man stood by the wall of the house. Kosta pretended not to see this ragged man, peripherally observing. The man walked over but halting a few feet away.

"Good morning sir," the man said.

Kosta unaccustomed to such formal greetings stared at the man.

"Well good morning to you likewise, some storm passed through last night!"

"Yes, this happens quite often around here, Sir," the man said. Kosta eyed him, not very old; beard yes, long hair, yes...

"Are you by any chance heading to the Town of Roses?" the man asked.

"Ah the fact is, yes I am," Kosta replied.

"May I come along...though I am in these rags, I am not a thief, and, Sir...there is safety in numbers," the man spoke politely.

Kosta observed him, as they stood and talked; his hands and nails are clean, which meant he did not work hard. There was something, something about him. He decided to take him along.

"Have you eaten breakfast?"

"No Sir, nothing for the last two days," the man replied.

"What, nothing? Where have you been last night when they served supper?" Kosta questioned.

"I was out there in the stable. No one knew I was there, or they would have run me off," the man said.

"Where did you come from, I mean where is your home?" Kosta asked again.

"I actually live at the outskirts of the Town of Roses, we have a very bad situation there and I left to seek some help, I could not find anyone to come to our town and help find water, I have been away from home for months," he explained to Kosta.

"How strange that we should meet here, I am on my way to your town. I will take you along," Kosta said surprised at hearing the man's story.

"By the way what is your name?" Kosta asked the stranger.

"Sir, My name, is Eloy Plonner," he said and bowed.

"My name is Kosta. It is a pleasure meeting you, Eloy." Kosta bowed and they both laughed at their gestures. The man's eyes twinkled, smiling from ear to ear. Kosta seeing this stranger's happy face felt comfortable.

"Sir Eloy, I need to feed my horses, do you mind helping me, then we shall have breakfast," Kosta said.

"Absolutely sir, get right to it!" Eloy cheerfully replied.

Soon after they fed the horses, they went into the house for breakfast.

The woman of the inn eyed the man and was about to refuse service. Kosta said to her in a hushed voice, "Madam, we are both hungry and, you are the proprietor of this public Inn are you not?

"Yes, I am running a public place," the woman replied.

"Last night I paid for a room, did I not?" he asked.

"Yes you did, but I should refuse anyone who is not presentable," she pointed at Eloy.

"Your reputation will suffer if you refuse service to us. After all, customers have made you Madam successful, and...customers surely can ruin you. I will pay for both of us we are not beggars. Besides you should not judge us by our looks," Kosta said confidently.

The Madam of the inn felt embarrassed and blushed to her brows, realizing that Kosta was absolutely correct and apologized. Eloy downed his food quickly having nothing in his belly for a few days. Kosta ordered another serving and Eloy swallowed that too. They had their fill of good food and were off to the Town of Roses. Along the way, Kosta found out a lot about his passenger. Why his clothes were tattered and what his profession was that sustained his way of life.

Eloy a teacher of horticulture, interesting, having knowledge was the key to teach. So many fields and gardens needed someone to show an easier way of toiling.

"Sir Eloy, you are a Godsend, you are indeed needed, and I am sure you are sought after," Kosta said with certain excitement.

"Thank you sir, you are very kind, I am needed that is true. Unfortunately, I am only one. Many the likes of me are in need to instruct many people. Some people are leery learning something new, they are set in their old ways. The results are fruitless, and disappointing. Do you not agree?" Eloy Plonner said.

"Yes, I do agree, we had our share of disappointments. It is the truth. Having this knowledge, which you share with others, is admirable, my hat to you Sir Eloy. Where did you acquire all this knowledge, if I may ask?"

"My father and, grandfather, through trial and error, handed down to me perfected unmistakable knowledge and process of the horticultural expertise that I hold now," Eloy explained.

The horses galloped along the narrow dirt road, after days of travel, meals, slept in rooms in odd places, or in the carriage in woods, or open prairies but the water for the horses cost him many pieces of gold. Many hours of conversations, and when they ran out of subjects to talk about each dozed, for a while. At last, they neared the Town of Roses, Eloy asked Kosta to let him out on the outskirts of the town, and Kosta agreed.

Eloy stepped down, bowed, turned and walked away.

Kosta forgetting what they said before about helping each other watched him walk off.

The horses trotted on and Kosta a bit puzzled shrugged off the odd feeling about his unusual passenger who disappeared after a while into the distance. The instructions from the Ravens he recounted in order one more time.

First, he must find the willow tree, straight ahead, he recognized willows, but many were old and dry. Nevertheless halting the horses jumped off to look for saplings, but to his disappointment as he scanned the area, saw nothing. Where else could he find willows!

He was about to ride on as he viewed the area one more time he espied a green patch, instinctively pushed through the thick overgrowth and there stood a young willow. He was amazed to see one with a cluster of seven not wasting time cut it off, ran back to the carriage, and rode on into town. This was his lucky day. As he rode he saw a group of men gathered at the dry well, seemed to be discussing something. Heads turned hearing the rattle of carriage and four white horses heading at them. Kosta reined up right up to the men, horses stomped raising a cloud of dust. The group of men circled around him with sour faces. Kosta stood on the step his eyes looked at every face; then introducing himself, inquired about their Mayor.

"Our mayor passed away weeks ago," one man said.

"What business do you have with our mayor?" an old man asked.

"I will go for the mayor's wife, if you need to speak with her. She is in charge now," a young man, as slim as a bean, said and walked away. The rest of the men stood and stared at Kosta, expressions of curiosity, Kosta had to explain; "I am here to solve your water problem. I would like to start, but first I need to tend to my horses, do you have any water at all?" Kosta said.

"We haul water from the river in buckets by the wagon load, but I will bring some for your horses, they will not be thirsty," another said.

Kosta counted off two hundred paces to the west, the dowser did not twitch. He counted off two hundred paces to the east, holding the dowser before him, "*I must be counting wrong*," he thought," *it has to be two hundred paces, is my stride too short or too long...I will change my steps...*"

Kosta lost himself for a moment. "*Why is it hard to go two hundred paces*? He had to rethink the instructions from the Ravens, "*ah yes...that must be my mistake...yes...I am going about this the wrong way.*"

"I need a man to help me here!" he shouted to the people standing around and watching him. Out of the crowd a man stepped out, walked up to Kosta, he was none other than Eloy Plonner, his passenger. Eloy apologized for his sudden disappearance. "Oh it is you, great to see you again! But how...ah, never mind, I am glad to see you!" Kosta excitedly exclaimed.

Eloy and Kosta walked off the 200 paces. Kosta held the divining twig with a cluster of seven horizontally, the dowser began to quiver and its tips bent downwards. Eloy waved his arm to the bemused bystanders, who were watching these two fellows looking for water with twigs? This they had never seen before. Why they almost laughed aloud...but when Eloy waved and called to bring spades to dig, all the men came running. They dug and dug, taking turns drenched totally in sweat. They dug to a depth of twelve feet deep and width of eight feet.

Kosta said that was deep and wide enough. Now the men had a questioning expression, where is the water? Kosta stood there for a moment and then said, "Before we go home to rest, one more important thing we must do, collect as many large stones as possible and stack them around the opening, so no one falls in, even an animal, now hurry." The men gave each other a knowing look and jumped onto the wagon, they sped off within an hour the wagon rolled in filled with good size boulders, those men who waited for them unloaded, stacked the stones and boulders all around the open pit. Tired, sweaty and thirsty stood waiting for Kosta to tell them more.

"Thank you, you have done a great job, now all of you go home and rest. In the morning you will find water in this well." They stared at him with doubtful expressions.

"Come early in the morning, the well will be full. Now I would appreciate a bed for me and a shelter for my horses...I will pay for lodging," Kosta spoke firmly.

Suddenly they murmured something to each other and shuffled away.

The Mayors wife came up to Kosta and Eloy offered them lodging and food.

"Thank you, you are very kind we will accept. My deep condolences on your husband's passing Lady...Lady I do not know your name," said Kosta bowing and kissing her hand. Eloy did not know her name either; he too expressed his sympathy.

"Thank you Kosta, Eloy, for your sympathy. I am Belinda the widow of Mayor Ensmon York. The unexpected death of the Mayor created stress among the town's people.

After dinner, they toasted to the well with a glass of wine.

"May it be full in the morning!" the Mayor's wife Belinda said to them. Eloy surprised at the mellow taste of the wine asked, "Where did you acquire this wine Lady Belinda?

"At one time the gypsies passed through our town and had many bottles of this wine, my husband, may he rest in peace, bought from them all they had." She smiled at both of them. Kosta glanced around the room, seeing the bottle asked if he could look at the label. She stood up quickly and stepped over to the sideboard, handed it to him and Kosta stared at it.

"My God, this far away...my brother's wine?" Kosta said.

Eloy glanced at him and Belinda. No one spoke; Kosta was speechless for a long time, just staring at the bottle.

"I will leave you until morning. I am going next door for the night," Lady Belinda spoke and rose from the chair. Kosta and Eloy understood and retired to their beds, after a tiring day fell sound asleep. Kosta was up at dawn, dressed was ready to go out to check on the well. Lady Belinda was busy in the kitchen fixing breakfast; she smiled seeing Kosta in the doorway.

"I hope you slept well, you must be thirsty and hungry. Well, I have prepared breakfast for both of you. Please sit, the coffee is ready."

She walked over to the small table bringing the coffee in a porcelain pot; poured three large cups, the cream and sugar sat on the table. She went back to the kitchen for the platters of eggs bacon and bread. Kosta heard Eloy entering her home and melodiously almost like singing a cheerful greeting "good morning!" a happy expression on his face and a twinkle in his eyes.

"Ah my good man, have you been to the well yet?" Not waiting for Kosta's reply continued, "you should go and take a good look...you will be shocked out of your hair."

"What do you mean, what is wrong? Perhaps I better run over there and take a look, the way you say that, I..."

"Oh do not worry Sir, sit, I am just teasing, nothing is wrong. Everything is as it was yesterday. And a large group of people are on the way to see you." Eloy laughed.

Kosta did not know what to make of all this, why are they coming to see him, for a split second....But a loud rap on the door startled them. Belinda flung the door open, about a dozen men stood there, behind them villagers. She invited them in. Two sat down, others stood around the table, they were silent for a while, staring. Kosta studied their faces.

The tall man began to speak. "We do not know who you are; and we appreciate all the effort you have shown to produce water. We do understand your confidence; ah..., we want to believe in you. We regret to say it is not happening. There is no water in that hole in the ground... that is the well..."

But a younger man interrupted him saying, "And we cannot pay you for your good deed. We are short of not only water but provisions too, summers are short, and our crops will be almost zero. Until we replenish all we need."

"Sir, you must understand, we cannot let you leave us until the well is full," spoke the thin young man.

"Come next harvest, we will be back on our feet again, if we have water. We will not forget you, the day will come we will compensate you well..." Kosta raised his arms to stop them from talking.

"Now listen here. I promise you water will come, since it had not rained it might take another day or two. I must leave as soon as possible, I need to get back to my family, and I have been gone too long."

An elderly woman pushed through the crowd who pressed through the doorway trying to listen what these men said.

"Let me pass, please let me pass, I know something you do not!" she shouted loudly. The crowd stepped aside and she walked into the house, she apologized to Belinda the Mayor's wife, walked up to the table and said to all those men.

"Now listen, a week ago I was at the western market and I learned something very important." Silence fell they listened. Eloy and Kosta taken aback listened, she continued, "As you well know gypsies are everywhere, and they were at the market that day. I heard them say; "a man from the east arrived at the Kingdom of Magda and cured the King's daughter, Princess Alexia...now I have observed this young man," and she pointed at Kosta, "he must be the one... I feel he is telling the truth and we must listen and be patient, let him go home to his family." Everyone stood not uttering a sigh just glanced at each other.

Then the tall man seated said, "Agreed, we will wait for the water. We wish you a safe journey Sir Kosta. The man came up, shook hands with Kosta, and thanked him.

Kosta taken aback, protested for so much praise, "it is your effort, you have done all the work, by the way, make sure you build a solid wall for the well..."

"I will make sure of that, not to worry Kosta," Eloy cut in.

"Thank you Eloy. I am not asking for any payment, my deed was an obligation as I was instructed to fulfill for my fellow men in great need, so as long as the well is full to capacity I shall be happy," Kosta politely replied.

The men returned to their homes as they bid him a safe journey, thanked him again as they walked out. Breakfast, prepared by Belinda very early the following day Kosta readied the horses, with a bit of supplies for the road The Mayors widow hugged him and said, "The meal is on the house. We will not forget you, for what you have done for us. God bless you." Kosta climbed up onto the carriage, sat down and looked around, the villagers still slept. The sun has not risen yet. He was ready to ride on to his third assignment. Eloy stepped up from the other side of the carriage and said, "Kosta, why not drive around the well, before you leave to see if..."

"I had the same thing in mind Eloy." Horses ambled along without much noise. Kosta stopped and both jumped off walked up to the well leaned on the boulders to look. The bottom appeared dark, too dark to see their reflection. Eloy said one way to find out if water came in." He found a small stone and threw it down, they listened what they heard put a wide smile on their faces, a big splash.

They looked at each other and Kosta said, "I need another stone."

"I will find one for you." Eloy brought a hand size and Kosta threw it down a big splash echoed.

"The water is filling up the well," Kosta said still leaning on the boulder. Eloy replied, "Yes it is, life will buzz now in this village."

"Eloy, I must go now," Kosta said.

Eloy said, "Take care, my friend, safe journey." Eloy turned and walked back to Belinda's house. The Town of Roses now is his town, gladly, he, will educate and restore the shortages for these people. One never knows...perhaps Eloy Plonner is to be the next mayor, and the widow Belinda, the new mayor's wife.

Fifty-Four:
Lady Kora Swirtz

Kosta rode alone to the next assignment and time dragged; he missed Eloy and their conversations.

"*I must send word to my family that I am alive and well and I will be home soon*," Kosta thought. Coming to a fork in the road, and for a moment hesitated, which one to follow, but recalling the directions by the Ravens, the road out of the Town of Roses, to the left will lead him to the third assignment. He took the left and continued from the looks of it this road well used; he was on the right track. The horses galloped at full speed. The day was sunny but a bit humid.

Kosta eyed the countryside, not one farmhouse around, but forests, lakes and prairies, a good place to rest. Horses need to rest and graze. He turned off the road, a good distance ahead the lake glistened. Stepped off the carriage and stretched his whole body, he pulled the horses to a tree tied the reins on a limb and walked to the lake, looked around, not a soul in sight, a good place to submerge completely into this clear cool water, quickly threw off all of his clothes and waded into the water. Kosta played in the water for a while, scrubbed his body vigorously. The clothes had a scrubbing as well and were not quite dry, but Kosta dressed and lay on the seat of the carriage, to rest. "*What a joy to be able to see again*," he thought gazing at the sky, his chest bursting with gratitude. Whatever took place that night at the cemetery transformed his life. He felt a surge of happiness like never before. Life was going to be good, he was thankful, he smiled and dozed off. When the sudden jerking of the carriage woke him, it was twilight. Kosta had not thought why the horses were nervous he did not notice the eyes of the Ravens watching but had realized the horses needed water. Unhitching two horses led them to the lake, then, the other two drank their fill. Now he needed to eat, checking the back seat found a sack with bread and cheese and about a dozen apples, four baked. Kosta ate the baked apples first then feeling full ate some of the cheese and bread. The rest saved for next morning. Now, he settled for the night, slept a sound dreamless sleep. In the morning, chirping birds and the jerking of the carriage awakened him. Kosta felt rested. His team of four white horses rested and watered well, now was time to move on. The endless road led him through areas unknown to him existed, hills, mountains, rocky bumpy dirt roads, he wondered had he lost his way...nothing around no one in sight, until he passed the dark forest, a small village came into view. Arriving at this village, the street was empty of life, no one to inquire about the ailing Lady with an ulcerated leg; for that, matter is this, the village he was looking for. Now moving along slowly glancing into every window and yard if someone at least was inside the homes, no one, what a disappointment, in the middle of the day and not one individual appeared. Out of nowhere down the road a man came toward him and Kosta halted when the man neared the carriage; Kosta asked "Sir, is this the village where Lady Kora Swirtz resides?"

The man had not changed his pace or looked up just pointed, "There, that small house with a log fence around it, down the road," he said and kept walking.

Kosta drove slowly ahead considering the dust raised by the horse's hoofs. Kosta pulled the team to a slow amble. All along the road, not one house had decent fencing. Seemed to be in need of much care, the reason why such neglect he had no time to dwell. He approached the little house with the log fence. Drove into the back yard and stopped under the shade tree to be out of the sun, all day long the hot sun bared down on him. A little dog ran out barked, and then ran back to the front door. A middle aged, woman leaning on a cane appeared in the doorway, wearing a long skirt, a blouse with puffy sleeves, an apron and a scarf wrapped around her head.

"Good day to you my lady," Kosta greeted her as he stepped down slowly down the steps.

"Is it possible to buy a drink of water for me and my horses?

The woman greeted Kosta with a smile.

"Good day to you too, I am Kora, Kora Swirtz. Please help yourself at the water well, find the well at the far side of the house, the bucket hangs on a peg," Lady Kora said.

"Thank you kindly. By the way, is it possible to buy a noon lunch, Lady Kora?" Kosta asked.

"Well now, you are in luck, I just fried a nice piece of pork and eggs, you are welcome," Lady Kora said.

Kosta led the horses to the well and cranked up the bucket full, drank greedily. The horses also had their fill.

Lady Kora used a cane to get around. For a moment, she leaned on the edge of the table waiting for the pain to subside, she placed an extra plate a spoon and a mug on the table, just as Kosta walked in.

"I see you are in need of medical attention on your leg," he said.

"Yes, it is very painful I am at a loss of what to do. We do not have a doctor in our village. Everyone travels to the next village, which is far. As you see, I am alone," Lady Kora said as she sat down heavily on the wooden chair.

"Have some lunch with me, please help yourself though, you see it is hard for me to get around," Lady Kora said.

Kosta walked over to the pots and began to load his plate, not only pork and eggs, chicken and potatoes and beans from the garden. He sat down at the table, ate it all, and mopped up the plate with the bread.

"Thank you, very delicious. I have not had a meal this good in weeks, you are a good cook, these vegetables, are from your garden? Kosta asked.

"Yes, I have managed to plant and gather myself for years but now, as you see I am unable to work," she explained.

"Forgive my question, but where is your husband, or your children?"

Lady Kora hung her head and said, "I have no one."

"I am sorry. Do not fret I am here to heal the wound for you, in a few weeks it will be as good as new, and you will go dancing!" Kosta smiled seeing a surprised look on her face.

"Who are you, where are you from? You came directly to my house, you must have known about me, who told you?" Lady Kora asked.

"Yes I knew about you... that is why I am here... I was sent by someone... someone passing through..." Kosta said as he chewed a second helping of tasty chicken.

"Most of my neighbors are afraid of me. They think I am contagious leper. I feel very lonely at times," Lady Kora said softly.

Kosta said nothing.

Thinking back to that night and the Ravens, he could never tell anyone about these mysterious birds, everyone would think that he lost his mind. The problems will be solved, he will go home and be happy with his family.... that is all he ever wanted, love and peace, raise happy children and grow old together with Kathryn.

After lunch he asked Lady Kora to show him the wound, he looked at it as she removed the wrapping. The wound was horrific, seeping puss, deep and raw. The odor hit his nostrils and he recoiled from it. Kosta jumped to the window and threw it open, and opened all of the windows in the house.

"I am sorry, this unbearable smell, I cannot do anything about it." Lady Kora's eyes filled with tears, she dabbed at them with her apron.

"Whatever began eating away your flesh must have begun a long time ago. Do not cry you will be fine," Kosta said. He thought of the Ravens cure, he knew what he had to find.

"Rest your leg on this chair and wait for me. I need to go and search for something, I will be back, meanwhile you stay right here or, better still go lay down in bed right now, but do not cover the wound, wait for me, and I will be back," he said to Lady Kora.

Kosta unhitched a horse, led him to the side of the carriage from the seat threw one leg over onto its back, and took off to look for the wild garlic.

The prairies were far from the village the horse galloped fast past the small houses. When he reached, the prairie jumped off and searched for the wild garlic, as he walked on through the tall grass, his horse trailing behind came upon a small creek, along the low banks of this creek he found the wild garlic and the plantain, now he had to look for the wild onion. Keeping his eyes to the ground found none. Time slipping, he must find the onion!

Then he came up to a small patch of trees, there he found what seemed to be a burned down cottage. Lo and behold, there on the side of the ruins a patch of wild onion grew. Now, one last ingredient, blueberries, and after a long search he found all the ingredients he needed, he cried out, of course no one heard him, "I found them!"

Kosta not used to mounting a bareback horse, and these horses were at least two hands taller than his horses at home. Of course, if there is a will there is a way, finding a stump helped him easily mount his horse. Lady Kora napped while he was gone. The moment, he walked in she awoke and was glad to see him.

"Did you have a good nap, Lady Kora, in a few minutes I will have tea ready for you, relax for a little longer," Kosta said. Kosta steeped blueberries he handed her a cup of the strong blueberry tea and she drank it. When Kosta gently applied the poultice she began to weep, the pain was so unbearable.

After several hours or so, she felt relief and stopped crying. Kosta knew right then that he has done the right thing for this woman. She fell asleep soundly. It was obvious she did not sleep much from the constant pain.

Kosta watched her sleeping and dosed off himself for a while in the chair. He woke up and she was still asleep. He had to be on his way, time is wasting, next assignment waited. He was about to wake her and tell her, but she awoke a minute later and with the most compassionate eyes said, “I feel so much better now. I feel the pain has lessened much, thank you for your help, I did ask where you came from, but you did not reply, but no matter, now, one thing I know that you are blessed and Fate will be good to you and your family,” she said.

“It does not matter where I came from. I came to help you as was meant to be so. This was the most crucial moment. If I would have been delayed several days, you would have been in real danger of losing not only your leg, but also your life,” Kosta told her.

“How can I repay you, I have no jewels and no gold. But be assured wherever you may be, my prayers will be with you,” Lady Kora said. Tears of gratitude slid down her cheeks.

“You must remember to drink the tea and make the poultice. I will show you how to make it before I leave. No need to pay me, what is important, is that you are well and happy, no more pain or tears, I must be on my way it is urgent,” Kosta said touched by her sincerity. Lady Kora understood and assured him she will daily follow his instructions.

“It will take about six to nine days, by then the wound will close up, but you must drink the tea and keep the leg elevated. Now I really must be going, God bless you, I will think of you.” He rode away to his next assignment. He was impressed how she managed to keep her home clean, in spite of her pain. These neighbors stayed away because of fear, Kosta felt disappointed, everyone cared only for their own, not one showed compassion for her. Dismissing the fact that one day, they too will need help. How sad.

Kosta looked back at the village as he rode out into the open countryside. He began to concentrate on his final assignment, recalling the instructions to all the problems, suddenly he realized there were no instructions...not for this last assignment. It was all up to him to resolve this situation with this poor man.

His nerves gave him a jolt. He searched his mind to do the right thing. How to approach this man, the way home is long. The terrain ahead could be rough and hard, this will be a challenge for him, and could he do it? Engrossed in thoughts the road ran through the forest, soon it will be dark, he realized he had no food for this journey or oats for the horses. It is important to stop where the horses could graze, and he must rest, not finding solid food but a slice of dry bread in his basket. He chomped it down, washed it with a cup of water, water he had.

Kosta had no idea where this road led. All he remembered was to go east, morning sun, shines in his face, by noon it is right above him, afternoon on his right shoulder, and at sunset, it will set behind him. That is how he followed the road by the sun. Kosta puzzled at times, "*this must be magic, the work of the Ravens, no, none of this is magic, this is real, and the Ravens were real.*" He pulled off the road near the edge of the woods.

The horses grazed. Kosta walked off a short distance found a patch of shrubs and there he found an abundance of wild blueberries and wild strawberries which he quickly picked and ate a good portion of them, the rest went into the basket. As darkness settled over the forest, all life fell silent. Kosta stepped into the carriage and saddled down comfortably on the padded seat. On this moonless night, he channeled his hearing for any danger, soon dozed off.

Sometime during the night, the horses nickered and stamped, the carriage rocked and swayed waking him with a start, too dark to see what was out there, whatever was there spooked the horses they galloped across the prairie. Kosta being disorientated thrown from left to right. In the darkness grappled for the door handle as the carriage rattled on, he managed to push it open and held on for his dear life as he struggled to climb to the top seat. The carriage rolled across meadows ridges and bumps, shrubs snapped he slid to the seat. He pulled back on the reins sharply brought the horses to a halt. Never in his life had he experienced such a jolting ride and abuse to his body as this, never. Whatever spooked the horses must have been close by. I must have fallen fast sleep, fresh air, and riding all day, what frightened the horses?" Kosta talked to himself, feeling uneasy. He turned the horses around and parked closer to the road. He stepped down led the horses to a tree and secured the reins, stepped back into the carriage and closed the door.

This unexplained uneasiness he experienced surprised him, why in the world was he afraid to be in an open area on a meadow at night in a carriage, he sat there feeling angry with himself, for he was not a coward. However, why should he not be afraid, if encountering danger he is empty handed, he had no weapon at all of any kind, not even a stick to fight with, man or animal. Horses nickered again. Kosta strained to see into the darkness, but saw nothing. As he dozed on and off, it came to him, "*an owl must have swooped down silently a bit too close, it is a bird of silent flight.*" Kosta only was half-right.

Horses were spooked, but not by an owl. The Ravens were watching his every move, where his assignment took him; they were there. They were not his stalkers, but protectors.

Kosta slept soundly until dawn, when he opened his eyes canvassed the area for any sign of trouble, none. He stepped out of the carriage stretched his limbs in every direction to relieve the stiffness. He looked up at the sky, clear. The sun felt warm, it will be a hot day. He must hurry to find food and water. The carriage rolled eastward. The road curved over hills and unfamiliar unusual topography. Many fallen trees blocked the road, which Kosta moved out of the way. These villages were far in between, a much longer journey then to Magda. *Had he gone the wrong way...I am extremely thirsty and the horses frothing, they need water. There must be a village or town, perhaps a small settlement along this road. This is such a desolate and uninhabited area.* His eyes took in the countryside saw *nothing but wilderness! God Almighty where am I*? Kosta thought and a bit agitated at himself. Without noticing the road turned into a smoother stretch, which stopped the jerking of the carriage, Ah, now this is a well-used road, civilization must be close, good, "thank God!" he said aloud feeling relieved.

Another turn and a few more miles and there emerged a tiny village. Some homes nicely kept and here and there a few vacant crumbling overgrown with weeds and shrubs. He drove into the yard of the first nicely kept house. Stiffly stepped off the carriage and walked up to the door, knocked. A young woman cracked open the door, eyed him up and down, her expression purely puzzled, "a carriage fit for a king but in clothes of a peasant," she mused.

Kosta noticed her confused stare and explained. "I have traveled for days, I and my horses need water desperately, please spare us some." She invited him in and handed him a large glass of bitter tea.

"Oh this is the best from the whole trip that I have been on! May I have a little more?" Kosta politely asked.

"No not now, you will have more after you watered your horses." She led him out back to the well. The horses drank from the buckets.

"Young Miss...I need to know is this the village of the old man, the one in great need of care," Kosta inquired.

"I know of which man you are talking about. His house is at the far end of the village, yes, he does need a lot of care, his bones are brittle, so they say, everyone is helping him as much as time allows, now look at our village, poor, not enough money, and the young and able men went off to look for work elsewhere." She stopped.

"Are you living here all alone? Are you not afraid? Kosta queried.

"No, I am not afraid. This is my village and my home. I manage fairly well. I grew up here, and I have a feeling I will die here, where else should I go? I help the older people around here, what will happen to them if I should leave. She replied.

"Do you have brothers and sisters here also, and your parents, they live close by?" Kosta asked.

"Brothers and sisters, oh yes I do, but they had moved away some time ago. I do not hear from them, they must be faring well, or else they would have come back. You know how life is, when one has all the comfort, there is no room in ones thoughts or feelings for others," she said sadly.

"How true" Kosta replied. "There under that young birch tree, that little cross, who is buried there," he dared to ask her.

"That little cross...there lies my little friend a cat, he was only a little kitten...had no chance to grow up," she paused.

Kosta curious needed to know. "What do you mean if only he had a chance to grow up?

"My brother, before he went away took my kitty out to the woods and killed him," she said.

"What? Kosta was shocked. "I am truly sorry...that was cruel of your brother to do...living alone here at least you need a little friend, like a cat, definitely...your brother did not think of your feelings at that moment...life is not fair many a time. But why did he kill your kitten?"

"Never told me the reason...just went away after a while, but it would be nice to have a dog for protection. Wolves and large animals come around quite often."

"Well, you will have a dog. Forgive me but time is passing and I must be going, I have a long trip ahead of me, I will think of you, be sure of that, farewell," he said to her. She nodded and turned to go inside her little home.

Kosta took a handful of gold pieces from his hiding place in the carriage and walked back to the front door and knocked, she opened the door and he saw that she was crying.

"Take this. This is for your hospitality and your honesty." She smiled clutching the gold in her hand.

Kosta jumped up onto the carriage and drove away.

Fifty- Five: The Old Man

Kosta pulled up close, believing this to be the old man's house. He stepped off the carriage and stretched his limbs. He went up and knocked on the front door. No one bid him enter. He knocked again, but no one seemed to be in; without waiting, turned the handle on the door; unlocked. He stepped into a dim house, waited a moment to adjust his eyes. Kosta called a greeting to whoever lived there, as he walked slowly through the kitchen, no sign of pots or dishes on the table, no smell of any kind of food. He entered into a dark living room, drapes closed, Kosta walked up and pulled back the drapes and opened the window. From the looks of it, no one enjoyed this room, many chairs sat on top of the table and pieces of fine furniture moved in clusters, evidence of thick dust on everything, no one dusted or cleaned this room, or the house for that matter. Perhaps whoever lives here is out...*hmm.* Kosta peeked into the bedroom, there on a bed slept a grey haired old man. "*He is sound asleep, either deaf or dead,*" Kosta thought. He called out again but the man did not stir, Kosta leaned over him; he was alive; shallow breathing proved it.

Kosta sat on a chair hoping the man will wake, but waiting is not going to feed and water the horses. He went out to the horses, a chance to glance around where to board them, the barn stood empty, no animals or food. Kosta wasted no time, backed out of the yard and sped quickly back to the house and that girl. Knowing she would sell oats, the young woman surprised to see him come back, listened as he told her what he needed, she gladly obliged. Kosta returned to the old man's house and unhitched the horses leading them into the stalls. He found couple of buckets filled them with water from the well and left in the barn. Then walked back into the house, the man was still asleep. Checking around found a nice cellar, good supply of food, but not the kind for a long journey. Without waiting for the man to wake Kosta began to cook. The aroma of food permeated through the home, it tickled the man's nose, he opened his eyes, at first, expected one of the girls cooking dinner, to his shock a young man came into the bedroom when he called the girls name.

"Well sir, at last you are awake...that is good, dinner is about ready," Kosta said and smiled. The old man said not a word, but glared. Kosta sat on the chair leaned forward and said, "My name is Kosta, I will serve dinner and you need not be afraid of me. I am really a friendly fellow, now be ready when I bring your plate."

The old man could not decide if he was amused or scared, his hand came out from beneath the sheets. He pointed a long thin white finger at Kosta and asked.

"Where did you come from? Who are you?" The old man's voice was a bit hushed.

"I will gladly tell you who I am and why I am here at dinner, if that is fine with you, sir," Kosta said and headed for the kitchen.

While fixing the plates Kosta thought...*what do I to say to remove this man from his home, why... he will feel evicted...I must take him back with me, how will my family accept him...a stranger, in our small house sick and old who needs care. She has little care for herself, with seven children. Will she forgive me...gone so long...come home with an old man. I have no choice...my last assignment, I must, God...I must do this...my life depends on this old man. She knows nothing of what is going on, or where I am now."*

Kosta carried the plates in and set them on the night table. Pulled up a chair to the bed and sat down.

"What is it you want?" the old man asked, holding the sheet up to his neck.

"I need nothing from you. I would like to know your name though...I came to help you. Sir, is the front door always unlocked? I walked in you were asleep. You never lock it?"

"No, I do not get out of bed much. It needs to be open in case someone comes to help me," the old man replied.

"You must be lonely. Do you have a daughter or a son?" Kosta asked.

"No...unfortunately never had any. Do you have children?"

"Yes, I do, seven." Kosta smiled seeing the old man's eyes grow big. "Please eat your dinner. Yes, I do have seven, three boys and four girls. I love them and my wife dearly," Kosta said, chewing bread.

"You must love your wife very much, yes," the old man said, reaching for the plate.

"My wife yes I love her. Unfortunately my children have never known their grandparents."

"Oh...why is that, if I may be so blunt," he asked, taking a bite of bacon.

"My parents died when I was fourteen...now, since we are talking about grandparents I would like to make a proposition to you," Kosta said.

"What kind of proposition?" the old man asked.

"Take you home with me, I assure you they will welcome you, give you comfort, and all the care you need," Kosta replied.

The old man kept eyeing Kosta, suspecting him of being a foxy thief or a murderer. He considered, "*This man entered my home and sat waiting for me to wake, if he is a thief or murderer he would have done me in or robbed me while I slept. Therefore, he is not that sort of a character, but why this sad story?*" The old man thought.

Kosta realized his words were not of strong conviction and absolutely without meaning. Kosta sat and observed the reaction of the old man.

"You are hesitating. I see that, you are afraid. You have every right to be afraid. I am a perfect stranger who walked into your home, and is giving you a sob story, that his children have no grandparents, and that you could give happiness to many children, not only mine. You could you know. You would feel fulfilled as never in your entire life before. Children are a wonderful gift. Unfortunately, you never had children, so you missed all that happiness. All our children gave us a reason to live." Kosta watched the man's stone-cold face had no change, but the chewing motion. He knew he must choose the right words to be convincing, he must accomplish this last assignment well, and after a while, he began again.

"Have no fear... I am not here to hurt you in any way. I must tell you that I have come from very far, and I must bring you home with me. It is an urgent matter. It is time for you to have someone to look after you. Think about it for a few days, we have time and on the other hand, we do not. My family is distraught over my disappearance...You seem not to believe me, I see from your expression, but it is true. I will tell you the whole story. What happened to me a few years ago and, why I am here with you, also, I must tell you, you are not the only one I had helped. You will surely hear of the little princess Alexia, she was asleep for months, no one else were able to cure her, but I, and then the town of Roses, where the wells were dry, I helped those people too, and the woman with the ulcerated leg. Now, if you are able to get out of that bed, go outside and take a good look what is standing out there, perhaps you will consider... but now we must eat, I am hungry, I am sure you are too."

After dinner, Kosta picked up the dishes, washed them in the pan, threw out the dishwater outside and set a pot for tea.

The old man observed Kosta, speechless. He closed his eyes and must have been mulling over what Kosta had said. The man dozed off because soon after he snored. In the meantime Kosta went out to the barn, surprised found several eggs. *"These will do for breakfast,"* he thought. Kosta heard a cough as he stepped into the kitchen. The teapot spurted boiling water all over the stove. Kosta found tea in a small canister, poured boiling water over the tea leaves into two cups and a sugar bowl. Kosta brought it to the bedroom. The man lay on the bed still with the sheet up to his chin, with eyes still closed said, "I am not going anywhere... with you... or anyone else!"

Kosta was not surprised at all, this is sudden, and this poor old man is afraid, being uprooted after all these years, unsure of where he would end up, with whom, where he would live and under what conditions.

"Give me a good reason why not? What quality of life have you had here up to now? Look around, gloom and loneliness that is what I see, you deserve better. For breakfast, I found eggs and bacon, but we need bread. I brought tea for you. Sip, might be too hot, smells good," Kosta said in low voice.

The old man opened his eyes very wide and in his quivering voice despair, "This is my *home!* Forsake my home and never to *return*? It is part of *me* and I am part of this house and everything in it, this is my life! You do not understand that, I gather. Take me out of here and my heart stays here, I will be empty inside without my house!"

Now both were silent, then Kosta spoke, "All right now, first I must say; you were hungry and you ate like a starving wolf. You need good wholesome food; no need to be at someone's mercy, as you are now; you need real human contact not once in a while someone comes in and you hear a voice and see a smile; and then they leave. Day after day, if I would be in that bed, I would go stark crazy. From the looks of this place; you do not have much help; you do look undernourished and feeble, alone you cannot manage; and you will die alone. All these possessions here will remain standing as they are now. Look around...is all this so important? You lay here withering away. Nothing on this earth, objects or a house is that important that you cannot leave it; go to a better life. All of that is material, all this you accumulated over the years, amid all this I see nothing worth staying for, and none of these objects will serve you as you feel they will...you, your health, and your soul are important. You will be content knowing you have done the right thing, for yourself, no one else."

The poor old man listened as Kosta went on.

"But with us...you will become stronger and happier...you will not be at the mercy of others, as you are now...we will care for you well. I also must mention that you owe me nothing in return, just agree to come along with me. That is all I ask. I will go tend to my horses...you think about all I have said and proposed...I will not be gone long." Kosta took his cup and walked out of the bedroom.

The old man stayed in his bed and contemplated what to do; *it is true I do need help, but who is this handsome young individual? He seems to have a good character. Sincerity shines through his eyes. He tells like it is...truth ...and in him I see good nature...he has opened his heart to me...perhaps, I could and should go with him, I would entertain his children, I love children, I could tell them so much, and teach them so much...I worry though...will they put up with me and my ailments?*

Kosta came back into the house.

The old man now sat up the skin on his thin arms white as snow, seldom felt the warmth of the sun, if ever. He pointed a long thin finger at Kosta and said, "I see the honesty and trustworthiness in you...I have decided, I trust your words...one more thing I must say, you, you sure can cook!"

"Yes I can cook, are you hungry? We just ate. But I will fry more bacon and eggs in a little while." Kosta laughed.

"Yes, I am famished! Are you sure, you want me to go along with you, what was your name? I will not be a burden to you and your family?" the old man asked.

"Kosta is my name. I give you my word, that my family will welcome you warmly."

"Kosta, I forgot to tell you, you must go down to the root cellar, on the north side of the house, find that door, plenty should be in there, unless someone helped themselves to it all." He interrupted shaking a finger in the direction of the root cellar.

By the time the meal was done cooking the afternoon sun hung quite low on the horizon, soon darkness will shroud the countryside, candles or oil lamps need to brighten the rooms. The small table in the parlor would not be too difficult for the old man to sit at. Kosta cleared all the clutter off and dusted with a cloth from the kitchen, the full plate, spoon and a fork carried to the table. He realized he needed a pillow for the old man to sit on, Kosta turned to go fetch one off the bed but to his surprise, the old man sat up with his legs dangling off the bed waiting for Kosta to help him. Kosta noticed the socks had holes on the toes, and the nightshirt crumpled, long to the floor, needed washing. Kosta carefully helped him over to the table to sit down on the pillow, the old man smiled, had that twinkle in his eyes, he was happy.

"Mind you, it is a pleasure to have real company, share a meal...," he said before emotion cut him off. Kosta glanced at him but did not reply.

" What is your name. I have been with you all this time and you have not told me your name, so what should I call you, after a while Kosta said, "Grandpa?"

"Well..., I would rather not...I..., my name is funny. Many people made fun of my name, I will not say aha...a... but a long time ago, I had an incident, oh but I cannot talk about that either, not now... I will not mind, "Grandpa" will do, for now."

Kosta wondered, *"What could have happened that traumatic that he does not want to talk about it. I will find out sooner, or later."*

"Kosta did you find any spy-rots down in the root cellar?" Grandpa asked.

"Spy-rots, I have no idea what that means, Grandpa," Kosta said.

"Ah forgive me, I misspoke, that used to be our code word for spirits," Grandpa said.

"I will go look, be right back."

Kosta went out to the cellar, it was pitch dark, simply feeling for things in between things, felt something cool and smooth, it must be the bottle, and it was, well... *"now he will sleep good tonight, poor old fellow,"* Kosta thought.

After having two small glasses of wine, Grandpa's eyelids drooped, he retired to bed. Kosta sat on the chair next to the bed. After about twenty minutes or so, Kosta cleaned up the dishes, pots and the whole kitchen; then heard his name called, peeked into the bedroom, grandpa raised his arm and said, "I forgot to drink my tea, and closed his eyes again. Kosta heated up the tea brought it to table next to the bed.

"Grandpa, drink it or it will be cold in a minute.' Kosta said.

"Kosta what should I take with me? Gold, wait do not forget the gold," he said to Kosta and sipped tea.

"Gold... where is the gold?" Kosta asked.

The man for a moment had to think...

"Oh the gold...ah...yes it is hidden in my bed...I think...yes, that is where it is...come quickly, look here." The man pointed to the right side and under the thin mattress. Kosta began groping under the mattress and found a small sack tied with a string and handed it to Grandpa.

"In the morning, after breakfast I will tell you something, now I would like to sleep. Thank you Kosta."

Kosta retired on a sofa in the parlor. It was good to stretch his legs and have a pillow to rest his head on.

"There is another sack bigger than this one in the barrel...no wait... it is on the top shelf in a basket...in the pantry, go find that one too," Grandpa said, after they breakfasted on eggs and bacon.

Several days later early morning the same young woman drove up in a wagon full of horse feed and a loaf of bread, the one he talked with when first entering the village, Kosta paid her with his own gold. Old man, Grandpa, invited her in for a cup of tea. She stayed and chatted for a while, then went on home.

Later after chores done and meals prepared Kosta went to the pantry, looked into the barrel, found nothing. He called out.

"No...there is no gold in this barrel! I will look on the shelf!" He looked into the basket, empty. He took the basket with him to show it to old man Grandpa.

"Oh no...my gold is gone!" he shouted.

"Perhaps you changed the hiding place! Think, where could it be? Who came to see you last, do you remember?" Kosta asked. Grandpa was so shocked he could not speak. "I do not remember," he mumbled, closed his eyes to think.

In the meantime Kosta went back to the pantry, he moved everything on the floor, then in the corner covered by burlap he found a little barrel, in it was the gold. As he lifted it up, he was surprised it was quite heavy.

"*Where in the world did he acquire so much gold*?" Kosta thought. He carried the small barrel to Grandpa's bed.

"I found it. It was in this small barrel." Grandpa was hilariously happy, clapping his snow-white hands.

"How much do we need to take with us?" he asked, as Kosta sat the barrel of gold on the bed.

"Take all the gold, but only a few of your belongings, not much room in the carriage."

Grandpa looked at Kosta's face for a long time as if trying to find an evil streak. Then he said, "I am not ready to go just yet. I must think about my life here, in this house. In a few days I will be ready."

Kosta not surprised at all, but he preferred to be on the road now, he wanted badly to be home with his family. The "several days" turned into weeks, but Kosta patiently waited. He felt that to rush this poor old soul might throw him into panic, and he waited for that moment. Grandpa did not mention of being ready to leave. He felt content. Kosta tended to him hand and foot; it was a good feeling. However, knowing that to keep Kosta here with him too long, meant his family waits, which was not fair. Then, one afternoon he shouted, “Well...I am ready!”

“Let me help you get dressed,” Kosta said excitedly, at last. It took very long to convince him. Food was the most important for the long journey, the gold and small momentous together, insisting on taking his small tables and tied them on top, Kosta agreed, disappointed. Still he packed whatever Grandpa wanted. However, when Kosta carried him outside his eyes grew large, he gasped, the carriage stacked with small tables on top and bundles stuffed here and there embarrassed him. Suddenly he realized that this was not a wagon, but a carriage fit for a king, but no king ever would stash furniture on such a fancy. How true were Kosta’s words, nothing material is worth keeping. When he looked inside the small space left for him with his important items packed into the carriage, sitting on quilts and wrapped in a down quilt, he seemed uncomfortable and claustrophobic.

“Kosta take all those tables from the top and I will give you things from inside too, you sat those aside far from the house.” Kosta removed everything from the top of the carriage and bundles from inside and set it far from the house. Grandpa pointed to the house and said.

“Kosta now set it on fire!”

“What, whatever for? What about the food in the cellar, why not give it all to that girl; she baked bread for you! Kosta exclaimed.

“Too much pain and loneliness will remain, whoever will want to live here might be affected by its loneliness,” Grandpa said with candor.

“Are you sure you want to set it on fire?” Kosta questioned concerned.

“Yes! Let it go up in smoke! Let me watch...I want to see this miserable, oppressive dismal residence of mine together with all those lonely years and dust, let it blaze, it shall be no more, but a memory of my past. Memory...memory of my past, oh no not yet, wait! I must go get my memory of my past! Kosta please fetch my burlap wrap under my mattress at the foot of my bed! That cannot burn! He shouted shaking his finger at the house.

“Where do you keep matches? I used up those you had in the cup when I cooked. And I will get your burlap,” Kosta said.

"Matches, oh...I do not remember where they are! Go and search the house...perhaps where I keep the lamp oil...hurry! I want to see the fire! It will be spectacular! We have not had a good bonfire in years around here!" he shouted excitedly.

Kosta went back into the house and looked around, what he noticed was the furniture and small items, accumulation of a lifetime, now the time has come to turn all of this into ashes, which in reality should be left for those who often helped him to survive. Kosta walked out with the matches and the small burlap wrap. The burlap was so old it just about crumbled to bits, in it a small painting.

"Is there anything that you would like to bring out and leave for those who took the time to help you?" The old man thought for a moment.

"Yes you are right. If you do not mind bring out the small items that you can carry and set them on the side, the pots and dishes and things in the pantry, perhaps they will serve someone in need. Indeed, you are a thoughtful person. Oh bring out the table and chairs, too, and anything on the wall!"

Kosta quickly carried out as much as possible outdoors, a good distance away from the house, as he rushed in and out of the house, had a thought, why not have that girl come and take what she wants, especially empty the cellar. Old Grandpa sat and watched. Kosta walked up to the carriage and expressed his thought. Grandpa listened and agreed. Kosta hopped onto the carriage and drove to the girl's home; when she opened the door, she was surprised to see both of them. Kosta explained what Grandpa wanted her to come and take whatever she needed. Gladly she followed them back to the house. She loaded her wagon with everything useful, kissed the old man's cheek and sped home.

Kosta went in with the matches without another glance he spilled the oil all over the bed and set it on fire. He ran out of the house, the man stuck his head out of the carriage and waited for the flames to consume his house.

They rode away a short distance, stopped and watched. Kosta realized that when the Ravens were discussing this man's situation, they never mentioned anything about burning the house...chills ran up and down his spine, perhaps he made a mistake...and now this trip might turn into a disaster. However, at this moment whatever happens let it happen, they watched. Soon smoke came through the chimney, and then through the front door, the thatched roof burst into one enormous ball of fire.

Grandpa's eyes sparkled with satisfaction, no need to shed tears...he watched his past life turned into ashes. Slowly they pulled away, farther and farther away from the burning home. They were on their way to a better tomorrow. When they looked back, the smoke billowed to the sky drifting on mild wind.

The distance to his home shortened by each day, he encountered problems of the wheel breaking down, fallen trees, downpour of rain which slowed their pace considerably because of flooding, in some areas the dirt roads looked impassible, but carefully they were able to overcome all obstacles along their journey.

Grandpa's pain was excruciating, he moaned continually. Kosta thought, "*If only I had an herb to ease his pain, but I have none.*" He tried to think, sometime before, before all of this happened, what did Kathryn use to relieve pain?

Worst of all, ruts in the road jostled the carriage. Kosta drove slowly to avoid deep puddles not knowing how deep they were to be stuck in such a rut alone would have been impossible to get out. Kosta feared the old man had already broken some bones and might not survive this trip. He needed a doctor to check him thoroughly. He surely will ask for one in the first town or village they come to. They rolled on for days; it was a good thing they took all the food with them, Grandpa insisted on taking along a jug of milk, which clabbered after a few days, from the jerking. Kosta let him enjoy all the clabbered milk, which he ate with a spoon. The horses grazed along lakes and creeks they happened upon.

Besides Grandpa's pain, Kosta's concern was, how his family will greet not only *him*, but old *guest* too. The nights were very uncomfortable sleeping on the driver's seat. It was not enough that the nights were humid but also blood-sucking insects buzzed and bit all night long. At dawn, flies and no-see-ems were bothersome. Once on the road with constant breeze was bearable. Wolves and a pack of boars ran across the road, the horses panicked, nickered, reared, Kosta managed to keep them from running wild.

Other days, Kosta and Grandpa rested in the shade, while horses grazed. Kosta decided to ride half the night for them and the horses. Kosta halted somewhere not knowing how much time had passed, it was time to sleep and horses needed rest. When the sun lit up the sky, they moved on until the sun stood mid noon, they rested in the shade for a bite to eat, especially coming upon a large lake, both submerged totally to refresh and wash their naked bodies off sweat and odor. Kosta rinsed all the clothes while Grandpa munched on leftovers. It was about time to find fresh provisions, for the journey home was long. Grandpa's basket was about empty. Kosta's basket had enough for both for a few days. Then a village came into view, for some reason this area seemed familiar to him.

"*This is odd...have I been here before? I need to look around, this is uncanny, I have a strong feeling I have been here before, now I remember, I was here with my father,*" Kosta thought. What triggered his memory were the trees, the tree limbs entwined creating a tunnel over the street. He inquired about a doctor. He found the home, now at which he was intently staring. A woman stepped out the front door.

"Is this the doctor's residence?" Kosta asked.

"The doctor lives in this house, here...yes," she pointed at the front door. Kosta's mouth fell open.

"My God now I remember. My God I am close to home, just a day or two, and I will be home," Kosta said aloud, heart beating faster.

"How far is it to Riverside Village?" Kosta asked this woman.

"It may take you a few days, we have had much rain and the bridge is under water, by the time you get to it, it might be passable again. You might want to wait here for a day or two to be safe," she pointed at the old man and said.

"Your passenger is awfully pale, better hurry."

Kosta thought about this earnestly, *it would be foolish to take risks, being this close to home.* "I guess no one is going where I am going," he muttered, but she heard him.

"Fear not, you need a runner? If you need to send a message I know one fellow who is going in the morning, he is taking the long way but he surely will be there before you," the woman said.

"Yes definitely, is he going to Riverside village?"

"Yes he is to your village and beyond," she said.

"Beyond where, how far?"

"Well, all I know he mentioned some estate, gypsies and some news...I do not remember it all."

"I need to send word to my family that I am coming home. However, right this minute, I need to see the doctor. This passenger of mine is in great pain," Kosta replied.

"If you stay at the doctors overnight, in the morning I will send the fellow over to you, give him your message then. Good day to you, good luck." The woman went on her way.

To Kosta it was an incredible recollection of days he spent here with his father and, now he recalled the doctor's constant demand of perfection of my father. No wonder he had erased it all from memory.

He knocked on the beautiful front door, the door his father carved so long ago. The door flung open a man with a frown splattered on his face stared at Kosta.

Yes! What is it?" he said gruffly.

Kosta explained what was happening to the old man.

"Come inside the house." Kosta entered and his heart beat like a drum. He looked around thinking, "*soon very soon I will embrace my beloved Kathryn and my children, although this last assignment is a bit trying. Nevertheless, so far I have managed to overcome obstacles.*"

Though he could not recall doctor's name still remembered how scared he was being with his father here in this house. Kosta followed the doctor to a small room where he would examine the old man.

"I cannot help him much, but I will ease his pain with herbs, which will diminish his pain considerably."

"Well thank you doctor, perhaps he will sleep better tonight."

"Yes he will. Our beds are comfortable enough even for him," the doctor said.

Fifty-Six: The Plot

Weeks slipped by. Months went by, no improvement in Kathryn's condition. Every day sadness and tears, weight loss, dresses hung on her. She was slim before, now she was much too thin.

Rabinna, Michael, and Rebecca were concerned. They talked about her constantly. They feared for her mental health. She seemed to be withering away more each day. What should they do to cheer her up a bit? Mathew and Rebecca caught a large fish for dinner for a change. Kathryn had no objections at all, if they go fishing. For their safety, now she had no concerns at all.

Kathryn's head ached, burdened with sorrow. Kosta was constantly on her mind.

She never told anyone what she dreamt, or that he called her name, but upon awakening, she felt worse.

She imagined his spirit was calling her. She felt that he wanted her to die and be with him for eternity. When the children brought her flowers, she just smiled gave each a hug and kissed each of them on the head. At those times when thinking rationally, the clear fact was she had children to live for therefore she could not leave them orphans. Kathryn talked with them, fed them and cared for the livestock with the boys help. Nothing helped at other times. The children feared their mother one day would fall over and die. The provisions periodically provided. Knowing Kosta was dead; Uncle Thomas kept his word.

However, nothing mattered. Nothing would change the loneliness within her. Kathryn lost hope and faith and no one could help her.

Mathew and Rebecca one day set out to visit the Baron at the castle, the brass wolf knocker echoed loudly off the heavy door, when the servant opened it she recognized them.

"Ah...Kosta's children...if you are here to visit the Baron unfortunately he has been in bed with some illness, please do come back some other time."

Mathew and Rebecca returned home and while all of them sat at the table having their supper, Mathew related their visit to the castle to Kathryn, rest of the children listened disappointed, and began to chatter creating a buzz.

"Mother... oh Mother...Baron Patrick is ill we have to go see him! You must help him!" Rosie called out to Kathryn above all that noise.

"We will go visit our friend Baron one Sunday after church, agreed?" Kathryn with little concern calmly said to the children. They all together chimed a loud.

"Yes Mother!" When Sunday came, Kathryn felt ill could not attend church. All the children sat quietly trying not to disturb their mother. Rosie wondered when mother would feel better, so that everything will return to normal in their life. Weeks passed, children hoped mother would take them to the castle. Kathryn felt strong enough and told them that they would go after church in the wagon. They rode up to the castle. Mathew knocked several times, but no one came. He rapped harder with persistency. At last, a young girl opened the door apologizing.

Kathryn was perturbed but did not reply. Kathryn and the children marched right in. as they passed by the girl, she stepped aside. She followed them through the courtyard into the castle, and then disappeared into the kitchen. Kathryn and the children marched up the stairs to the Baron Patrick's bedroom. Kathryn stopped in the doorway. The children stood behind her. Her eyes adjusted to the total darkness and she saw the big bed and motioned for them to go, they tiptoed around the bed. Just then, one of the servants appeared when Kathryn was about to pull back the heavy drapes covering the large windows. The servant ran up to help her pull the drapes open but only half way, the window remained closed.

"Butler's orders are not to open the windows," she said.

Kathryn ignoring the girls comment opened it anyway.

"The air in this room is stifling." She stared back not believing her ears and eyes as she stepped up to the bed.

"Children our friend is gravely ill, unrecognizable. He has aged much since father has been gone. Why...what has happened, what is wrong? Why did you not send for me or a doctor and where is Lady Olivia?" Kathryn confronted the servant.

"The doctor visited here several times, but said there was little he could do for the Master now," the servant said.

"What has he eaten today?" Kathryn asked.

"We served him chicken broth. That is all he wanted, my Lady," the servant said politely.

"Where is Lady Olivia?" Kathryn asked her again.

"Lady Kathryn...Lady Olivia has been gone for two weeks now. When she came back from visiting you... Lady Kathryn, she received a message, something about her house, she has not returned," the servant explained in a whisper. Kathryn stared at the girl, her mind reeling.

"What is going on here, look at your MASTER and tell me there is nothing wrong with him!" She pointed to the bed. At the foot of the bed the girls stared at Baron Patrick submerged up to his neck beneath the covers only his face was visible, to them he looked dead.

"Open all the drapes and the windows let some fresh air in, it is stifling in here," Kathryn ordered politely.

The servant obeyed. The bedroom filled with fresh air and bright light, the room immediately became cheery. Kathryn motioned to the servant to come out to the hallway. Kathryn asked her.

"How long has your master Baron been ill?" The girl looked a bit flustered but said, "Well...if I am not mistaken...I overheard, about two months...oh but Lady Kathryn I must go now." The servant girl glanced around and ran off. Kathryn came back and sat on the edge of the bed staring at the sick Baron.

"Just look at him, life is drained out of him visibly even at this moment. Baron Patrick, do you hear me...this is Kathryn...the children are here, wake up!" she spoke loud and clear. The children stood around his bed waiting for him to awake. Again, the servant girl appeared in the doorway.

"Mother, the girl is here," Mathew said.

Kathryn walked up to the girl and gave instructions.

"Please go to the kitchen and boil water, throw a cup of dry blueberries and let them steep for ten minutes. Make sure the tea is very strong and stir in a tablespoon or two of honey. You seem to be new here, what is your name?"

"Oh, my name is Lira, my Lady Kathryn."

"Lira, how long have you been here?"

"Ah, just about a month Lady Kathryn," Lira replied.

"You do remember my instructions, I want you to make the tea, only you, go now quickly." Lira nodded and went down to the kitchen.

Watching her old friend so ill and frail, Kathryn forgot about her own loss.

"Mother, that servant girl, where is she from? She is so different, her dark skin, black hair and those big black eyes. All the girls around this area are pale comparing to her, have you noticed?" Mathew said. Kras added a few words on the subject.

"She speaks funny. I did not understand what she said to mother."

"Well Mathew, ask her when she brings the tea. She is beautiful. I would like to know how she happened to come and work here at the castle," Kathryn said to her sons.

"Children we must care for Baron Patrick for as long as it takes for him to recover, do you agree?" she spoke softly. Mathew and Rebecca quickly jumped at the chance to stay and care for him. Undertaking such a responsibility without hesitating seemed a very noble gesture of these two young people. Kathryn agreed but they will only remain with Baron Patrick for one day, they must come home to help her with the chores.

No sign of life stirred from this sick body lying in that bed, Kathryn waited, children waited.

Then Lira came in and said that the tea is ready and Butler Ridiller will bring it shortly.

"Mother will he wake up?" Rosie whispered. Her hands folded in a praying pose.

"Yes, I hope he will," said Jasimin, and the boys also chimed in hoping he will wake up. Kathryn was glad to see the children so concerned for their friend Baron Patrick, after all they visited him quite often over the years, they were very close, he was their Grandfather and they were his adopted children, they gave him joy at times when their laughter echoed through the castle. They chased each other up and down the stairs. The whole place was alive when they visited. Aunt Olivia and Baron Patrick are married and they both are very happy. Now she is missing, something is very wrong here!

Baron Patrick looked around through slits in his eyelids.

"Olivia? Olivia are you here, Olivia!" It took several minutes to recognize who stood at his bedside. Ah, the children came. A faint smile lifted the corners of his saggy cheeks.

"Kathryn...children...oh I am glad you are here...I thought I would never see you again...Kathryn where is Olivia? Kathryn, my sweet children...I am so pleased...forgive me...but I am not well...as you see...some weakness confined me, in this huge bed...I feel very *small*" Baron Patrick closed his eyes. After a while, a trembling hand emerged from under the covers reaching out to Kathryn. She took his cold hand in hers and held it. Mathew leaned over and asked, "Sir, are you able to sit up for a while, and have some tea."

"Yes, please prop me with pillows, but no tea...or food," he said weakly.

Just then Butler Ridiller walked in carrying a tray with a teapot, cups and chicken broth, he sat the tray on large rectangle table next to the bed.

"Hope you are feeling better, Sir Baron, we worry about you," Butler Ridiller spoke curtly. Baron Patrick nodded his head without speaking. Butler Ridiller turned and walked out of the bedroom.

Kathryn poured some tea into a delicate porcelain cup, she handed it to Baron Patrick, which he rejected, with a trembling hand. "No, no I do not want any tea or food!"

"Why, what is wrong? You must eat to regain your strength, looks to me you have lost a bit too much weight!"

His facial expression showed fear. His finger to his lips, "Kathryn, I am in danger here!"

"What are you saying? What danger?" Kathryn questioned in a whisper.

Kathryn glanced at all of them knowingly. They acknowledged they understood.

"They...they want me dead and buried here and Olivia too," he whispered.

"Who wants you both dead, and out of here, who are they...?" Kathryn asked in a very low voice. Kathryn motioned to Jason.

"Son, go down the hallway and watch for anyone coming and let us know quickly."

Jason stood in the doorway of the bedroom and then moved out into the hall pacing back and forth watching like a sentry. Jason observed Mathew and the girl Lira at the top of the stairs, but did not interrupt their conversation.

Kathryn turned back to Baron Patrick. "Now, who wants you dead?"

"All of them!" Baron Patrick said with irritation.

"How do you know, who are you suspecting?" Kathryn pressured him with questions.

"I had many warnings, but I refused to believe it to be true, I shrugged it off, and told no one..." Baron Patrick whispered.

"Who warned you? Kathryn held his hand she felt it tremble.

"She did!"

"Who is she? I do not understand" Kathryn continued.

"She came in my dreams so many nights to warn me...that girl's spirit... I should have considered her warnings...more seriously, but...I chose to ignore her...I should have said something to Olivia..." he trailed off and closed his eyes.

"But sir that is impossible, they all love and respect you! Why would any of them do away with you, you gave them so much to better their lives!" Mathew interjected.

Baron Patrick opened his eyes and spoke with difficulty,

"My dear boy...that is the reason, old and alone...the loyal servant feels...in return for his...or her lifetime of services, to possess...what he or she believes... should belong to them...upon my demise." He closed his eyes again.

"Yes that is true, quite often it changes their attitudes and lives," Mathew said.

"It was their choice to dedicate themselves to a lifetime of service!" Rebecca quickly added. Kathryn could not believe this. Though the tea had cooled, she poured a cup and sipped it anyway.

Baron Patrick opened his eyes, and saw her sipping the tea, his hands shook, he stuttered trying to warn her that the tea might be poisoned, to stop her it was too late, she drank it all. The children watched their mother, but she had absolutely no reaction to the tea.

"You see, all is well, you are not in any danger, I am alright, you must have some chicken broth and tea, or I will spoon feed you," she smiled. The children looked at each other.

"Are you sure...you are all right?" Baron Patrick questioned.

"Yes I am, but the tea has cooled too much, I will call for Butler Ridiller to make a fresh pot, then will you have some? You will feel much better," Kathryn politely said to him.

Mathew went off to the kitchen and requested a fresh pot of tea for the Baron. Lira came up to him and said she will do so gladly. After a while, Lira walked in carrying a fresh pot of aromatic tea, she filled a large cup with broth, which also cooled a bit, but Baron did not mind, sipped half a cup of broth, then had some tea.

"Are you feeling any better?" Kathryn asked.

"Somewhat, but I feel a little sleepy again...I feel as if I am floating away..." His eyes closed and he fell asleep.

Kathryn and children sat watching him nap.

Kathryn could not believe that he was in such great danger. Nevertheless, she did not ignore the possibility either. After all, he is getting old, but where in the world is Aunt Olivia? What if, Aunt Olivia too had been drinking poisoned tea, and no one knew. Kathryn recalled Aunt Olivia's last visit seemed distressed. Kathryn's heart began to pound.

"That butler, what if he really is slipping something into the tea...not the first...but the second teapot...there should be something to counteract the ingested poison or sleeping potion.

This must have been going on for a long time. I must find out soon," she whispered to Tessana.

She recalled the conversations they had and the story of that day he had arrived at their village, resided at the constable's home, many skilled men constructed this magnificent castle, and furnished. Many servants hired for positions. Kathryn recalled the caravan of guests riding through the village, in elegant carriages up to the castle. The merriment went on for weeks. Music and laughter echoed. Than the ghost frightened the guests, they quickly packed up and departed never to return, nor had written to inquire of his welfare, as far as they were concerned he could be dead. From then on, the castle became as silent as a tomb, the servants walked quietly. Baron Patrick became a lonely man. She recalled when he told them that, she, Kosta and the children made him feel he belonged. Now Kosta has disappeared without a trace. For some unknown reason Aunt Olivia is also missing. In addition to all happening, now Baron Patrick is ill. She and the children are on their own. Everything is happening all at once. She sat thinking deeply.

Baron Patrick opened his eyes, the bedroom bright with candlelight. He looked at the family surrounding his bed.

"Kathryn...you and Kosta...your children gave me...many happy hours. Now...you and they...are depressed and lost...without the pillar of their life. Oh but my dearest children...as time goes on...all will do well. As you grow...you will overcome obstacles..., which...at times...life throws your way. I know...you will be strong, and I am proud of you. I enjoyed the company of the ghost...more as time went by...we communicated. However, I ignored her warning...now I am at the mercy...of someone to do me harm." Baron Patrick smiled and closed his eyes.

Kathryn wiped her tears, she and the younger children needed to return home it was late in the afternoon chores awaited.

Jason came into the bedroom and whispered something to Mathew and stepped out again, Mathew leaned towards his mother and whispered that the butler is in the library dusting off the books, should it not be the housekeeper's job? Is he eavesdropping...? Kathryn did not react. She said to the children in a clear and happy voice, loud enough for the butler to hear, "Children we must say good-night to our friend and wish him well, time to go home, it will be dark soon."

She glanced around the room and called Jason. Was she imagining or did she see a shadow move away from the door. Where was Jason?

Mathew ran to the door and checked the hall but saw no one. He ran down the stairs Jason was talking with Lira.

"Jason we are leaving," Mathew shouted.

"Be perceptive and discrete," she whispered to Mathew and Rebecca, "you have to remain in the castle and keep watch over Baron Patrick. Rebecca I will inform your parents of your decision to stay. I am sure they will not object."

Mathew and Rebecca agreed to do so. Butler Ridiller seemed perturbed when told that Mathew and Rebecca are staying for a few days with Master Baron to entertain and bring him up to date while he is bedridden. Kathryn, Jason, Kras and the girls scrambled into the wagon and rode home. As night encroached on the castle, eerie darkness entered into each room, it was very unnerving. Mathew and Rebecca at first felt uneasy, they remained at Barons bedside.

The oil lamps illuminated the walls and the staircase; still there were many dark corners.

Rebecca an observant girl noticed things that Mathew never would. This night, the mystery of Master Baron's illness, perhaps could surface. Butler came into the bedroom and told Rebecca and Mathew.

"Dinner will be served shortly, please go down, I will come down with master Baron after I have dressed him."

Mathew and Rebecca ran down the stairs directly to the dining room. The long table was set for four, which meant the Baron will sit at the head, and their place will be at his right. After some time, Butler Ridiller cautiously descended the stairs, in his arms carried Master Baron. Butler Ridiller sat the ailing Baron on the chair to the left, butler sat down at the head of the table. Tonight he was the Master. The true MASTER was only a guest at this table. Rebecca observed but said nothing. Servant girl Lira walked in with a large platter of roast beef garnished with greens plus vegetables and potatoes.

Lira placed several cuts of meat onto the plate for Butler Ridiller.

Then she came around to Rebecca and Mathew and served them. Placing the platter on the sideboard marched off into the kitchen.

Lira returned with a prepared plate from the kitchen for Baron Patrick, Rebecca surprised pretended not to notice.

Her brain worked overtime. "*Why is the butler at the head of the table*? *Why was the Baron's plate of food prepared in the kitchen, why not eat the same food as we are*?

Rebecca also observed that Butler Ridiller did not have to make requests from the girl for service. The girl seemed well trained in directives.

Baron Patrick did not look up, or speak. He slowly began to nibble on the small portions on his plate. The glass of wine he did not touch, the tea he did not drink.

Rebecca observed without speaking, the silence was deadly at the table and, she began to feel very queasy, she felt that if she does not excuse herself right this minute she will vomit right onto her plate.

Rebecca quickly stood up and excused herself running off to the kitchen. Butler Ridiller asked what was wrong!

"Oh...she likes a lot of salt with her meal," Mathew quickly replied.

"I see," Butler Ridiller mumbled.

"I like pepper," Mathew said excusing himself.

Butler Ridiller nodded, slowly chewed, looking at the dinner plate. Rebecca pushed the kitchen door and entered, the staff sat anywhere or even stood having dinner, but their menu was different, besides a different menu, also enjoyed two bottles of red wine, mugs filled to the rim. That also puzzled Rebecca. She startled them, when they saw her all froze in motion. A minute later Mathew came charging after her.

"Is something wrong in the dining room Miss Rebecca?" one of them asked.

"No nothing is wrong. Rebecca likes a lot of salt and I like pepper, where would I find them?" Mathew said.

Rebecca glanced around at those plump faces and said, "Yes, I love salt."

The cook stood up walked into the pantry and brought out the salt and pepper, and handed to Mathew. Rebecca tried to choose one she could relate to freely. The youngest one will have to do. Rebecca motioned to the girl to follow, no one objected, the girl walked right behind Rebecca out of the kitchen,

"Come with me, you will take back the shakers, are you new around here?" The girl followed Rebecca and Mathew out to the dining room.

"What is wrong, Miss Rebecca?" Rebecca did not reply. She just stood by the table waiting for Mathew to pepper his meat, he handed her the saltshaker. She sprinkled her meat and potatoes and all the vegetables. The young girl stared at them and so did Butler Ridiller. Rebecca handed the girl the shakers.

"Thank you, please take them back to the kitchen, oh...yes, before I go up to my room I would like a large glass of warm milk please, will you take care of that for me?"

The young girl nodded. Mathew forced his well-peppered dinner down, and so did Rebecca. The food on Barons plate barely touched. The butler carried Baron Patrick up to his bedroom and put him to bed. Rebecca and Mathew stayed in the room exchanging few words with Baron Patrick. Through the open window, the bedroom filled with crisp air as they waited for the girl to bring the milk.

"What is going on here?" Rebecca asked the girl in a low voice as the girl followed into Rebecca's bedroom and closed the door behind her.

"What do you mean Miss Rebecca, I do not understand." The girl began to twist her apron with her fingers.

"Sh...speak quietly. Master Baron, what is wrong with Master Baron? Why is he treated this way?" Rebecca whispered.

"Oh...you see...Master Baron is ill, so Butler Ridiller figured that he should take over everything and it will only be his way, so we were told, and Butler Ridiller also said, "that is exactly what Master Baron wished him to do." The girl nodded her head.

"You say that was Master Baron's order? The butler told all of you that?" Rebecca questioned in a whisper.

"Yes Miss Rebecca. We must obey, do what Butler Ridiller orders us to do, or we lose our jobs."

Rebecca noticed the girl's sincere look on her face. This was a perfect moment at which to ask many questions, and the girl was willing to tell her everything.

"Ah, tell me this...do you know what medications Butler Ridiller is giving to Master Baron every day?" Rebecca asked.

"The only one thing I noticed is... that is, a small bottle of some kind of...I believe I heard them say was...a...for the heart and the nerves...I cannot recall the name..."

The girl tried to relate all that she has noticed in the kitchen while she was working there.

"Who was talking about the medications, was it the cook, or the maids, tell me quick. Do you know where they keep the bottle?" Rebecca asked.

"Yes, I do, I will show you in the morning, I will try to bring it to your room...or perhaps you better come down to the kitchen...they might miss it...I must be very careful, you know," the girl whispered.

"I am very glad you are so observant. What is your name?"

"Lucinda Nell, Miss Rebecca," the girl replied.

"May I call you Nell?"

"Yes Miss Rebecca, I do not mind, I should go now...Butler Ridiller might wonder where I am, Miss Rebecca."

"Yes go back, you are right. I will come down in the morning. Oh Nell, one more question. Who hired that girl Lira, and who told you my name?"

"Lira...? Your name...Flora told me. Butler Ridiller hired Lira, Miss Rebecca, the gypsies came one night and dropped her off here."

At dawn Rebecca went downstairs slipped into the kitchen and was snooping in the pantry when one of the cooks came in and saw her.

"Miss Rebecca what are you looking for?" the cook asked.

"I like honey with my coffee in the morning," Rebecca replied.

"I must warn you Miss Rebecca, never to come into the kitchen looking for things while no one is about," the cook sternly said.

"Why not, I had to help myself, since no one was here," Rebecca said.

"Well, Butler Ridiller presently is the MASTER of this castle. Miss Rebecca, nothing slips by him. We have to obey all his orders." The cooks icy stare startled Rebecca.

"What? What about Master Baron, he has nothing to say anymore?" Rebecca pretending surprise.

"He is too ill to run this place, soon he will be dead, we all know it, and you will see that he is weaker by the day, and observe the color of his skin, it is grey, Butler Ridiller says that is because he is so old, soon it will be over." The cook's eyes cast down finished speaking and began to walk away.

"But...she will take care of the castle after the Baron passes." Rebecca called loudly after her. The maid stopped and looked at Rebecca over her shoulder and said, "Why there is no one else but 'Master Ridiller' of course, all of us will stay on as nothing happened."

"I doubt that very much...the Baron's wife, Aunt Olivia his heir," Rebecca said tersely.

"Yes Miss Rebecca, that is correct, but she is not...here...at this moment, by then..."

What do you mean, "By then?" You do not expect her to come back!" Rebecca alarmed questioned.

"She has been gone several weeks we do not know where she is."

Upstairs Mathew watched from behind the heavy drape, next morning as Butler Ridiller readied the Baron for breakfast. Butler

Ridiller was not aware of Mathews presence being sure Mathew went searching for Rebecca.

Butler Ridiller after positioning the Baron in bed, reached into his pocket and out came a small dark bottle, he counted off several drops into the cup with water, which he brought close to Barons lips. Baron refused to drink averting his face to the side. Butler Ridiller sat the cup on the side table and walked over to the chair picked up a pillow, which he raised and pointed to it. At that moment, the Baron raised his thin arms and shook them in protest.

Mathew's heart began to drum, and his throat tightened up, "that is the reason the Baron did not speak at the table, or drink anything. That is what is killing him. The butler is giving him poison! Drop by drop! What is this, poison? He must alert Rebecca, they must be cautious, or he will poison them too." He retreated further into the shadows, as he noticed Butler Ridiller looking around the room, as if sensing someone being there. Sneaking out of the room now would not be wise the butler would see him. He must observe what happens next.

The sun has not risen yet but Rebecca alone tiptoed through the dark halls, and looked over her shoulder often. She climbed to the top of the stairs, nearing closer to the bedroom, felt eerie, her skin crawled and chills ran up and down her spine.

Her intuition warned her of something dangerous waited ahead, she halted at the Baron's bedroom door, and noticed Butler Ridiller standing over the bed, she froze, and observed his actions. Mathew watched from behind the heavy drapes.

Suddenly a gust of wind flung the window open with such force it slammed against the frame, the glass shattered, flew like bullets at Butler Ridiller. To protect his face he raised the pillow, ran up to the window to close it, at this opportune moment Rebecca took two steps and entered the bedroom.

Butler Ridiller surprised to see her, called out.

"Oh...Miss Rebecca come help me pick up all this glass, sudden wind forced open the window, the glass on the floor in pieces!" he was caught off guard.

"Oh! No, no you might cut yourself, the housekeeper should sweep these small fragments, Sir Ridiller go fetch her," Rebecca said.

Butler Ridiller quickly walked off to find the housekeeper or anyone to come do the cleanup. Mathew slipped out from behind the drapes. Rebecca surprised but glad for she knew Mathew had observed.

"You saved my life... you saw what he was about to do, I knew you... were behind the drapes. Mathew you must...tell your mother! You must! Please...do not leave me alone here...I am in danger... I told you!" his voice quivered.

What should they do now? Mathew poured the glass of water with the poison quickly out the window, ran to his bedroom and refilled with fresh water from his pitcher, ran back set it on the table next to the Baron Patrick's bed.

Rebecca and Mathew discussed Baron Patrick's rescue. The plan was to tell Butler Ridiller about Rosie's birthday and that mother requests his master's presence for the weekend. They waited for the butler to come back to the bedroom to take Baron Patrick down for breakfast. The housekeeper with a broom and a dustpan came in to sweep the glass, followed in by the butler. Rebecca noticed a small cut on his lower lip, quickly reached for the glass of water, dipped the handkerchief and in mid-air, she brought it to butlers lip. Horrified, the butler hit Rebecca's hand, the glass fell out of her hand to the floor and Rebecca staggered back.

Mathew lunged at Butler Ridiller from behind knocking him down. His face hit the area rug. As fast as Ridiller fell, he scrambled up and disappeared out of the room.

The housekeeper stood gaping not believing what she just witnessed. Mathew picked up the broken glass and also picked up a small brown bottle, it fell out of the butlers pocked when he had fallen. Baron Patrick did not utter a word until the housekeeper left with the dustpan full of glass. For lunch and dinner the cook, Flora brought up the plates herself. The next day at breakfast, Rebecca said to the butler they are taking Master Baron to the birthday party for Rosie and said mother requested the Baron's attendance. Butler Ridiller eyed them suspiciously and thoughtfully, he complied. Mathew to ease the tension, which like a dark smoke cloud hung over the table, added smiling, Master Baron will be gone just for the weekend. We will bring him back.

Two mornings after having had breakfast, Baron Patrick wrapped in a blanket was carried out to the carriage, with another blanket around his knees. Mathew and Rebecca appeared a few minutes later carrying some of Baron Patrick's essentials. Rebecca slipped next to him. Mathew jumped onto the carriage and slowly rode away, not causing suspicion. They snatched Baron Patrick from certain death at the hand of Butler Ridiller. The Baron reached for Rebecca's hand and squeezed it weakly. She knew he understood what they had done. They pulled up to their little house and the children surrounded the carriage, glad to see Baron

Patrick. Kathryn surprised had questions, but she was shocked hearing at what took place, agreed they definitely did the right thing. Rebecca in detail repeated what the cook had said about Aunt Olivia. Mathew galloped to find Aunt Olivia, he found her at home. Hearing from Mathew what has been happening with her husband she quickly came to be at his side. Kathryn asked why she had been gone so long.

"Butler Ridiller informed me that he knows someone interested in the purchase of my home and will come within a few days or weeks. I had so much to clean, Kathryn you have your hands full. I did not want to burden you with my work. Patrick recommended I sell my home, since we are together, married. Butler Ridiller must have overheard our conversation and sent me on a wild goose chase, it has been weeks, and no one has come to buy my home," Aunt Olivia explained.

"Aunt Olivia how long has Patrick been sick like this?" Kathryn asked.

"Patrick has complained a bit that he is tired, weak, and he sleeps longer, past breakfast, his mood changed, you know, I really felt I was the cause of it all, now I understand, it is the butler. Oh my God, Kathryn, what are we going to do?" Aunt Olivia began to cry. Kathryn put her arms around her and held her, truly, she did not know what they should do, but someone must know, how she wished, Kosta were here with them right now.

Baron Patrick entertained by the children had no idea what the women were talking about, or what they were doing in the kitchen.

"Kathryn let us serve lunch everyone must be hungry, especially my Patrick."

"Yes, Rebecca said he only picked at his food, afraid to eat, poor soul," Kathryn said

Baron Patrick and Olivia went to spend time together at her home, and had a doctor examine Patrick, the doctor's diagnosis was a weak heart. Aunt Olivia prepared healthy meals and made sure Patrick rested, and in those weeks away from his castle Patrick began to regain a bit of energy, more color on his face, and they were happy. Discussing the situation of the butler, they concluded to wait and see what transpires, Baron Patrick said one day that butler will slip and fall. Like a fish into the net.

Mathew knocked on the door, Olivia opened it, seeing Mathew at first a bit alarmed, but Mathew assured her nothing was wrong, just a short visit to see if all was well.

Mathew asked Baron Patrick should he go to the constable and have him come and discuss the matter of the butler and his attempt to murder him. After a thought Baron Patrick said yes notify the constable, make sure he keeps that little brown bottle in a safe place as evidence. Mathew visited the constable before going on to see Rebecca.

One afternoon Butler Ridiller appeared at Kathryn's door perturbed and demanded the return of his Master back to the castle. Kathryn a bit apprehensive yet apologetic said, "Of course, but the decision is up to Master Baron and Aunt Olivia when they wish to return to the castle."

Butler Ridiller blinked too many times hearing that Aunt Olivia was with them.

"But Madam, I am only concerned for my Master's health," he blurted out.

"Aunt Olivia and Baron are not here. They have gone out of town," Kathryn said eyeing his face closely.

"When will they return?"

"I did not ask, because it is not my concern. We will see them when they come back, that is all we can say."

Butler Ridiller without a reply excused himself and headed back to the castle cursing all the way. Kathryn frightened worried not only for Barons safety but Aunt Olivia's as well. Under the watchful eye of Aunt Olivia, Baron Patrick regained a little strength, and he warned Olivia of suspecting the butler poisoning not only him but her also. Butler Ridiller waits like a cobra for an opportune moment to deal a lethal dose.

Instead, the lethal dose would come to him. The law knew the truth and they had the little brown bottle. They too were waiting for an opportune moment to seize him.

Fifty-Seven: The Courier

Grandpa curled up on the seat in the carriage, waited for relief, then dozed off.

"It is unfortunate, but that is all I have to offer, I have little knowledge of such conditions, by the way, you look a bit familiar, what is your name sir?"

"Well doctor, I remember my father carving this front door, this here cabinet, and the fancy carved table. One thing I do not remember doctor is your name," Kosta said. The doctor eyed Kosta with a frown on his face trying to remember, then he shouted from excitement.

"As the sun shines in the heavens, Kosta Komarod, it is you! Why, you are the spitting image of your father! What an unusual circumstance, how wonderful to see you. You have your father's talent, so I hear. I loved his work. I have told so many people about him and now you. Unfortunately, I heard that something unknown happened to you, now you are standing before me, it is a miracle! Whatever happened to you?" the doctor spoke quickly and called to his wife, "Victoria, come and greet the famous carver. Ah yes, my name, well of course you would not remember. You were here on the last day your fathers finishing and cleaning up. Ah..., yes. I am Doctor Slovick Blaitmann."

Kosta bowed out of respect to all women, kissed Victoria's hand. Moreover, he realized that the news of his disappearance traveled all through the country. Kosta said it is a pleasure Lady Blaitmann." Doctor's wife smiled and agreed that he is the spitting image of David. Kosta said to the doctor, "Today I cannot tell you the reason of my disappearance, but when I am back with my family, I will return with my wife and children for a visit. It is urgent right now to send a message to my wife and find a place for the night."

The doctor said to Kosta, "We will put you up for the night. You do not worry about anything. When they walked, out to the carriage to help old Grandpa up the steps the doctor's mouth hung open when he saw the most beautiful carriage he has ever laid eyes on, excitedly shouted.

"Kosta you are successful I see, what a beauty, life must be good, I am glad, very glad for you!" Grandpa sat on the bed in a small room having some bitter medication or herb, which made him drowsy. Kosta was in the adjoining room. They retired after a hearty evening meal.

The next morning the young fellow arrived at the doctor's home, and Kosta gave specific directions to him repeating several times the name Kathryn Komarod and seven children, tell her: "I am coming home, and I will explain what happened."

The young fellow hesitating a bit said, "I will try to remember." The doctor quickly wrote down the message and handed it to the fellow.

"Now go tell them quickly, tell them in a few days he will be home. Go now!" the doctor said to the fellow.

While Kosta traveled along the way fulfilling assignments given to him, the news preceded him quickly. Name or description not mentioned, only of the good deeds done by a man who had come from the east, somewhere across the four mountain ranges. The gypsies told stories about the King's daughter little Princes Alexia's cure in the Kingdom of Magda. The water well filled to the brim in a small town of Roses.

They talked about the woman's cure of the ulcerated leg in a small village.

The saddest news spread like wild fire of the old man, who perished in the fire of his own house. A mystery to the village people when they found some of his possessions outdoors, saved...perhaps for whoever needed or wanted any of them.

Kathryn also heard these rumors but such news had no connection at all with her missing husband and father of her children.

Engulfed in grief she barely functioned each day. The children were very helpful with the chores. They tried to cheer her up, but no matter what they said or did, the sadness never left her eyes, her spirit low, it would take a miracle to bring back her smile and sparkle into her eyes, as she always had before.

Mathew encouraged his siblings to help, to make her smile a little. They were good children. They tried their best, but many, many nights gloom hung in that little house.

The youngest daughter Rosie wept because she missed her father. Marla held her in her arms consoling.

"I miss father so much, and mother is sick, and so sad, what will happen to us if she dies too, what will happen?" Marla comforted Rosie as best as she knew how.

Kosta was unaware of the news preceding him. Along the journey at each stop, some people impressed by the carriage pointed at him asking, "*Who is he?*"

At the estate of Lord Thomas Komarod, the kitchen buzzed with the news. Servants talked of all those problems solved by a man who came from the village somewhere far to the East a village situated by a river. This had no effect on Lord Thomas at first, suddenly all his nerve endings electrified his brain when he heard news of this stranger, then uneasiness roiled in his brain intensified each day, curiosity grew, he began to inquire, but had no definitive answers. The news was a seed planted to take hold and grow into questions in his waking hours and fitful nights...

Question...*who,* questions...*which village*? There were villages scattered all across the country, but only two largest settlements divided by the same river where he was born, the Rapid River. Why was he so concerned about this man? Nevertheless, whenever his conscience threw little darts of fear his concern gnawed at him.

After such a long time of Kosta's disappearance, he was able to relax, feel the power over his domain and his notorious name widespread was only his. He enjoyed his peaceful days, without any worries. Now something new came up and he must deal with. He instructed his servants to find out all the news, especially question the gypsies, why such interest to know about these gypsies, what were they up to if they were in the vicinity? Flora had suspicious feelings, but of course kept her mouth shut.

The closer the road led him home, the faster Kosta's heart beat in his chest. The anticipation almost made him cry out from excitement. The horses galloped, a trail of dust followed. Grandpa bounced in the carriage, muttering, but held on, hoping soon this trip will end, and he will relax, get to know his new family. They were about one and a half days trailing the young fellow on horseback with the message to Kathryn.

Then abruptly the horses halted, nervously fidgeting, began to back up, stumping, nickering in fear, shaking their heads.

Kosta raised up to see why the horses stopped, the scene before him turned his stomach, there in the middle of the road, lay two bodies, whatever was left of the young man, and the horse, the young man mauled unrecognizable, the horse partially devoured.

Kosta's stared stunned, hands trembled and chills ran through him. He scanned the area for danger; *what lies ahead if he should continue on, should he turn back or keep going!*

He thought, "*No! Turn back, back to the crossroads. Flee! Go back! Flee away from here*!" His instinct screamed for him to go back, get away as fast as possible. The remote area thickly overgrown, this narrow road turning around will be difficult. One side of the embankment soft and slippery from the rainfall of several days past, he tugged the reins to steady the horses, then after maneuvering several times turned the carriage around and galloped away.

The whip arced and cracked above the heads of the horses as they galloped until they were out of danger. At least Kosta felt they were safe. He arrived at the crossroad, turned onto the road leading long way, however, longer does not mean safer, but at this point, had no choice, at this moment, determined what had taken place on that other road behind him was very clear the choice made for him.

Grandpa had no questions, what he saw, he feared, curled up on the seat lay silent.

"*What a horrific ambush! Ambushed by some vicious animals, not one, but many,*" Kosta thought. "*if we would have come upon that attack our remains would have been scattered too, seems they had...no chance. No chance at all.*" Kosta shuddered, the scene in his mind clear, impossible to shake off. "*With God's help I will make it home. I will have to face my family without the news from the messenger. I hope that they will understand and forgive me for the pain I have caused them. However, it was not my choice. I had to complete these assignments, and only then I could return home,*" Kosta was thinking.

Time dragged, the road was rough, both were tired, and hungry, the old man held on, covered to keep warm. The afternoon sun slipped down towards the horizon, time to stop somewhere off the road and eat the bread and cheese the doctor's wife gave them. Kosta was sure the old man was starving. Spotting a huge tree and enough space for the carriage, he parked there. The horses grazed.

Kosta reached into the basket tied to the seat. He stepped down handed the bread and cheese to Grandpa. They ate greedily, washed down their meal with a cup of water.

Kosta noticed from the old man's eyes darting in all directions and his expression of concern for their safety, yet not a word about what he saw.

"Are you feeling better, since the doctor gave you the medicine?" Kosta asked.

"Yes, much better, but when it wears off, the pain will be back," Grandpa replied.

"Hopefully we will be home soon. I am worried about one thing, how my wife will react seeing me again...alive," Kosta said.

"What do you mean, alive?" Grandpa puzzled asked.

"I will tell you all about my experiences when we get home," Kosta said.

"Well now...I will wonder about what you just said...that is a very serious and puzzling statement, you know," Grandpa said.

"Yes I know, everything that occurred on this trip is not as troublesome as the moment when I see them, I assure you. You will be surprised," Kosta said.

"Kosta please help me get out of this nest, I need to stretch my legs," Grandpa pleaded. Kosta helped him out and down to walk around and answer natures call, then settled back in the carriage, to them time was precious, must keep on.

The sun sat and darkness engulfed the whole countryside. Horses ambled along. Grandpa slept.

Kosta had time to think what to say to convince his family that it was really *him*, in his own flesh. He will tell them where he has been and why.

His first stop would be at Michael's home, Michael and Rabinna will understand without hysteria, Michael is rational and strong, he will be more composed.

The moon slowly rose above the trees; cast its silvery light on the road ahead. The horses ambled along. It was so peaceful, not a living soul in sight. The forest on each side of the road stood dark and forbidding. Now and then, a wolf howled or an owl's hoot echoed somewhere far. He has been on the road for such a long time, has accomplished so much, weariness and much needed sleep began to take hold of him. Kosta fell asleep, slumped onto the basket next to him, the reins wrapped around his hand; Grandpa slept lulled by the ever-rocking motion of the carriage, and at one point, the horses stopped, hung their heads, the time nearly midnight. On one side of the road prairie merged with the horizon, across on the other side grain field illuminated by the moon. Pine forest far in the distance its fresh scent drifted on the soft breeze.

They slept soundly for several hours. When a loud clap of thunder shocked them out of their sleep, and a downpour washed over them from the sudden storm. The horses spooked and tried to gallop away. Kosta jerked the reins, controlled the horses and slowed them down.

Soaked, but refreshed since the night was warm. Sober in body and mind glad they were alive and safe. The moon now, obscured by heavy clouds in the darkness the road barely visible. What made Kosta alert was the silence. He feared that the rumbling of the wheels would attract wild beasts.

Grandpa tried to sleep after the storm. The pain returned. The hours passed, soon, it will be dawning. Clouds moved on and the moon high in the sky shone brightly. Even though the sun had not risen yet, Kosta felt the warmth of the day approaching before the light. His uneasiness dissipating as the morning mist warmed by the sun, soon daylight increased, and the world resounded with the familiar chatter of life.

Several wagons passed them by, he knew soon they should arrive at a village. He drove into the busy street and stopped to inquire about feed and water for the horses and food for themselves. Having gold, everything is readily available.

Kosta asked a man how far it is to the Riverside Village.

"I am not sure but I think not more than half a day, or less," the man replied.

Kosta's heart began to pound from excitement. He had been away for so many years. Now the moment had come. With bellies full, men and horses were back on the road heading home. Now his mission was complete and he was free. It was time to enjoy the company of his best friends, time to embrace his children and his beloved Kathryn. This traumatic change in their life happened because of his brother, and the Thirteen Ravens. He was determent to fulfill the assignments according to the plan. He persevered through all seasons, but he does not remember days of cold rains, and snow and those winter days and nights on his way home. All he remembers are the sunny and warm days. What ever happened, how had the weather changed, as if he skipped those seasons, how could he; only one thing could have happened is that the Thirteen Ravens had power to change all things relating to him and his journey, because he wanted his life back with his family, his time to live, and live he will.

His feelings towards his brother were dead, other than deep-seated memory of the cruelty.

Ride, he must ride to Michael and Rabinna first. Tell them what had happened.

That morning, Michael was busy planting flowers for Rabinna in the front of the house half shaded by the huge oak tree. Startled by the sudden clatter and snorting of horses, he looked over his shoulder to see a fine carriage and four white horses entering through the gate, *who is this?* Michael saw a stranger sitting atop the carriage, a bandana on his forehead. Kosta looked at Michael and smiled, then stepped down, took a few steps towards Michael and said, "Michael it is I, Kosta." The unexpected long-lost friend stood before him alive, but Michael's face took on an expression of shock, confusion, and then anger. This emotional moment Kosta will not forget. Michael for a few moments stared, brows furrowed, walked slowly towards the friend who stood near the carriage. In a moment, the truth will be of recognition and reunion.

"Kosta...Kosta is it you? How could it be...you are alive?" Michael asked greatly surprised.

"Yes Michael I am alive, very much alive!" Kosta cried out emotionally.

"Rabinna...Rabinna! Come quickly RABINNA!" Michael shouted. Rabinna ran out to see what was going on.

She felt faint from the sight of Kosta. The look of great awe and unbelievable sight, he was truly back and alive. Then her surprised look took on an angry demeanor, she turned on her heel and walked quickly back into the house.

Kosta and Michael embraced, slapped each other's backs. Michael asked questions.

"Michael not now, it is not the right time. I will tell you everything, but later, first I must see Kathryn and my children."

They walked into the house, Rabinna cried from anger. She was lost for words, he looked well enough, she did not notice that his face was normal, that the patch was gone. Michael held her in his arms calmed her down and turned her around to face Kosta.

"Look, take a good look at his face, what is different!"

Rabinna caught her breath, her hands on her mouth, she just then realized that Kosta's eyes were both normal, his beautiful blue eyes.

"How could this be, Michael?"

"Kosta will tell us all about his life while he was away later, but first he wants to see Kathryn and the children," Michael said to her. Rabinna ran up to Kosta and embraced him.

"Oh my dear Kosta...Kathryn is beside herself, she is just a shadow, she is not a woman and mother as you have known her. She has been fading away from loneliness. She has resigned herself to an early grave, the children see that, and it makes them so unhappy. But today you are back, I want to know all about your adventure, it looks to me it... turned out... Kosta...your eye...how in the world..."

Rabinna could say no more, tears filled her eyes. Kosta embraced her and looked at Michael and the other nodded his head. Michael came up and put his arm around Rabinna and she leaned on his chest.

"It is a miracle that you have returned now, but she will be shocked...she will be very angry...it might kill her...but we must somehow tell her...that you are well and alive, but how? You must know that there were times that we were very furious at you. There were times when we really believed that you abandoned Kathryn and the children, to save face, but we all had hardships, your disappearance we could not comprehend. We had no inkling what had happened to you. I do hope you forgive us for thinking the worst of you. All these years you were missing, it was pure chaos for them, for us as well...after all we are your closest friends, and Kathryn is Rabinna's sister. You have absolutely no idea of the mental strain and anguish all of us endured," Michael said.

Kosta did not mind that both of them stared at his face, and after a while he said, "My dear friends, I will tell you the whole horrific story later. But at this moment please help me with my passenger friend out there in the carriage."

Rabinna ran up to the carriage and peeked in. The tired old man was napping. Not disturbing the sleeping man, they went indoors and Rabinna boiled water for hot tea, cut thick slices of home baked bread with butter and honey. Kosta hungry ate greedily. They sat and discussed a plan, how to break the news to his family. What will they do or say?

"They might just run me off, after all the grief I caused, but the truth is, I did not cause this, someone else did," Kosta said.

"Michael, you need to bring Mathew here to help with a difficult project. He will come, Kathryn will not object, we have asked before, let him see his father first, then, all of us will go to your home." Rabinna's suggestion sounded good.

"Excuse me, but, I need to check on my passenger, surely he is awake, he might be uncomfortable, it is warm today," Kosta said, went out to take care of Grandpa. Michael rode away on his horse to bring Mathew. Rabinna began preparing lunch. Kosta assisted the feeble old Grandpa to literally crawl out of the carriage and slowly walk into the house and sit at the table. Grandpa seated on a soft pillow at the table slowly chewed fresh bread with honey, washed it down with milk, savoring the taste.

Fifty-Eight: Unexpected Stranger

Kathryn felt calm that particularly pleasant morning, she decided to visit an ailing neighbor and then walk over to Rabinna's for a cup of coffee or tea and a chat. It has been several weeks since they have seen each other and she did not mind the hour walk. She entered a small house to visit with the neighbor.

Michael spurred the horse hurrying to fetch Mathew, passed right by the small house into which Kathryn just entered. Kathryn stayed only a few minutes since the woman seemed to be doing well.

"I will come back in a few days or so, right now I am on my way to visit Rabinna," Kathryn said and walked out onto the street. As she walked, a farmer with a loaded wagon of hay drove up.

"And where are you off to this fine day, Kathryn?"

"Well Iandoll, a good day it is, I am on my way to Rabinna for a chat and some tea," she replied smiling.

"Well then I invite you for a ride, since you seem to be walking in my direction," Iandoll said. Kathryn accepted his invitation gladly.

"Iandoll thank you, this lift will give us time to talk." When the wagon stopped at Rabinna's home, with an appreciative thank you, Kathryn carefully stepped off the wagon. She noticed the elegant carriage in front of Rabinna's house. She was stunned. Just for a second she hesitated to enter, she stood staring at the carriage. Rabinna seeing her through the window ran out to meet her, nervously wringing her hands.

"Kathryn what a wonderful surprise, I did not expect you this morning! Come in please... come in! Have some tea or perhaps you would prefer coffee, if you wish, I will make coffee right away, come Kathryn!"

Kathryn noticed Rabinna's nervousness, and she asked, "Who is here? Someone is visiting you from a far city I gather... tell me who is it? Do I know them? Have I ever met them?"

Rabinna did not answer. She just kept staring at Kathryn.

"What is the matter with you Rabinna, why the silence?" Kathryn kept eyeing her, thinking how odd to see Rabinna behaving in such a restless manner. Rabinna took Kathryn's arm.

"Come, it is someone you must meet!"

Suddenly, as Kathryn stepped over the threshold in the kitchen she froze unable to move a muscle. Her eyes did not play tricks on her, she saw two men standing at the table, a very old man, and a middle-aged tall man, and now they were walking away from the table, the younger man...tall, well built...something about the way he walked.... Kathryn saw only the side of his face, not the profile, but that black hair tied in a ponytail. Her mind flashed back the image of Kosta with the patch on his left eye the last time she saw him before he vanished...but this face could not be her husband's face, how could it be possible! Yet, she felt strange. The man that just walked away stirred within her that long lost...that feeling which only Kosta could unveil within her, could he be...*Kosta!*

Her heart thundered in her chest, she barely could breathe.

"Rabinna," she whispered, "Who is this man? He looks so familiar!" Rabinna noticed the pallor on Kathryn's face; this worried her. She took Kathryn by the arm and tried to lead her to the table and have her sit down, but Kathryn's feet were riveted to the floor. Kosta preoccupied with Grandpa did not notice them standing in the doorway. When Grandpa comfortably rested in bed, Kosta walked back into the dining room to sit down and wait for Michael and Mathew. He was looking out the window, when suddenly turned his head and saw them. Kosta looked at Rabinna then at Kathryn, he stood up a bit too quickly and the chair fell over crashing to the floor.

Kosta recognized her, he took one-step towards her, and he stopped. At that one moment, when they looked at each other and their eyes met Kathryn tried to say his name, reached out to him, but the ringing in her ears came; all sound around her stilled; she felt herself falling... she fainted. Rabinna grabbed her to ease her fall.

Kosta in just a second was beside her. He fell to his knees, raised her gently by the shoulders and held her close to his chest. In his arms she felt as light as a feather, she was thin, her hair tied in a knot at the nape of her neck, on her face he saw worry and pain, it had lost its radiance. This was Kathryn. His beloved Kathryn, she suffered because of his absence. Because of his brother, they all suffered. The choice was not his. He was compelled to go, determined, fulfilling the assignments, all for the miracle of sight and return to his family. All those months turned into years, sacrificed for Kathryn and his children, all that time he was gone he thought of nothing else but his family. He and they had survived through this horrible ordeal.

Today, this day, for him the plan did not work out as he planned.

His heart cringed, and he wept at the sight of Kathryn in that condition, at her frailty, her simple drab dress.

He wanted to scream and swear at all that despair which had befallen his family, and wished he could turn back the time. An inner voice reprimanded him for his feelings of doubt and anguish at that moment, "*Time will replenish all that was ever lost.*"

He held her and felt pity, pity for his beloved Kathryn and the children, and desperately wanted to beg her forgiveness, she rested on his chest, he loved her before with his being and his soul, but now he would die for her and his children again if need be. Rabinna deeply moved, as she watched Kosta's compassion and love pour out to Kathryn. Anxiously awaiting Michaels return with Mathew.

Arriving at Kathryn's home, Michael rapped on the door. Mathew opened the door, surprised to see Uncle Michael. All the children called him "Uncle" since they were little.

"Hello Uncle Michael, please come in, you rode your horse?" Mathew exclaimed.

"Hello Mathew... is your mother at home?" Michael asked.

"No, Mother walked over to check on the neighbor, do you need to speak with her? Is something wrong?"

"No...actually I need you to help me with a project, you are not busy, are you?"

"I will come and help you!" Mathew answered and called to his siblings that he was going over to Uncle Michaels. They rode back to Michael's house. Michael could not show a need for urgency, yet the urgency was there.

However, as they approached Michaels home, Mathew surprised to see a carriage with two pairs of white horses.

"Uncle Michael you have company, such a carriage must belong to a king!" he curiously exclaimed.

"Yes it surely does look like that, huh?" Michael chuckled. However, when they walked into the house they had the shock of their life. There, down on his knees was Kosta holding Kathryn what seemed to be an embrace, but Kathryn's limp arms hung at her side and her head rested on Kosta's chest, Rabinna was crying.

"How did she get here so soon? We did not pass her on the road! What happened?" Michael perplexed and shocked, cried out at the scene before him, he looked at Rabinna.

Rabinna through sobs explained, "Kathryn arrived by a wagon unexpectedly. She...she recognized him...they stared at each other and before he could reach her, Kathryn just fell to the floor."

Mathew saw his mother in the arms of a stranger ran up grabbed the man's arm and screamed.

"Let go of my mother! What are you doing?"

At that moment, Kosta looked up and their eyes met. Mathew wide-eyed stared. Kosta did not utter a word, Mathew not fully recognizing him, accustomed to the patch. This was a face with healthy eyes. Mathew's brain kept switching images of his father before and now, and suddenly he screamed.

"Father, Father it is you! Oh my God, Aunt Rabinna, Uncle Michael it is Father!" He fell to his knees threw his arms around Kosta's neck flushed from excitement, sobbed. Kosta put his arm on Mathew's shoulder and whispered, "Mathew my son, Mathew it is I."

Michael then ran up to assist Kosta with Kathryn. Her limp body he carried to the sofa. She seemed to be dead. Kosta held Mathew in his arms; they spoke not a word, no need for that.

Rabinna dipped a cloth in water and placed it on Kathryn's forehead, hoping to bring her to consciousness. Kosta kept stroking Kathryn's hand and whispering her name.

Michael pulled Mathew aside and seriously said, "Mathew, I never thought that your mother would be the first one to see your father. I brought you here for you to see him first. We did not expect her this morning. We had no idea for either one to appear here today. I did not see her anywhere on the road...Mathew...your father will tell you what happened to him, be sure of that, but right now we have to attend to your mother."

"Uncle Michael, where was my father all this time, did he tell you?"

"I have no idea. He had no chance to tell us, with him came an old man, very old, come, I will introduce you to him." They both went to the bedroom where the old man was napping on a small bed, Michael touched his shoulder the old man opened his eyes seeing Mathew.

"Hello there young fellow, who are you?" he asked.

Michael explained who Mathew was and the commotion that took place in the other room, and the old man nodded his head knowingly.

"I am not surprised at that at all, seeing Kosta alive."

"What do you mean...alive?" Michael questioned the old man.

"Oh, he will tell you all about it. Just give him a chance that is all I ask," Grandpa replied and smiled.

At last Kathryn opened her eyes, she stared at Kosta and Mathew who were looking down at her. Kosta was weeping openly, she reached out and touched his face... it is him...and oh...those eyes...her beloved Kosta...but where and how...why...just an illusion...illusion. She lapsed into unconsciousness again.

Michael saw the need for a doctor, he sped away on his horse to fetch him, after a short time they both walked in, and the doctor examined Kathryn, with smelling salts woke her, this time she was fully alert. Kosta held her, his heart beat fast like a drum. Kathryn in a dress worn and faded clung to him, tears rolled down her tired face.

"Kathryn...forgive me...my love...forgive me...I will explain it all at home...we must go home now, I need to see my children," Kosta whispered.

"It was not meant to be this way, the plan failed. You caught us by surprise. No one expected your visit...nevertheless at last you are together!" Michael said to her.

Rabinna said to Kathryn while going out to the carriage.

"He will tell you all about it later, now go to your children."

"Rabinna what a miracle, it is a miracle. He is whole, his eyes, his left eye was gouged out remember...now he has his vision, it is a miracle," Kathryn said still in a daze.

"Kathryn I am sure he knows by what power all this transpired, and, he will tell us, unless he cannot disclose it not even to his family."

"Rabinna, will we ever know who was responsible to inflict such misery on us?" Kathryn asked. Kosta and Michael walked up holding Grandpa by his thin arms. Mathew peeked into the carriage, which was loaded with the old man's belongings. Mathew sat on the edge of the seat to give Grandpa more room on pillows and a cover over his knees.

Kosta kissed Rabinna's cheeks and gripped Michael's hand firmly. Kathryn sat next to Kosta. They drove on to the little house where the children waited for their mother and Mathew. The clatter created by the carriage prevented a conversation between them, attracting many curious onlookers, wondering who was rumbling through their village in an elegant carriage fit for a king! The carriage turned into the front yard, the neighbors recognized Kathryn as she stepped down and Mathew emerged out of the carriage, and an old man waved at the onlookers, but none thought that the man with the reins was Kosta. Kosta wore a patch on his left eye. Concerned for Kathryn and her children in his absence the neighbors tried to hold up her spirit with words. Feeling sorry for the children and wondered what awaits them in the future. Children ran out to see mother standing at the beautiful carriage, they were truly dumbfounded! Now when Kosta and Mathew led Grandpa into the house, Kathryn followed behind them.

"Father is back, look no patch...he is alive, oh my God!" Tessana whispered. Rosie ran up with outstretched arms screaming, "Father, Father you are back! I was afraid something bad happened to you, I cried a lot." Kosta picked her up into his arms and held her. They all ran to him chattering loudly the boys crowded around him hugged and clung to him.

"Father we will not be hungry anymore?" Tessana cried out.

Kosta wrapped his arm around her and kissed her head.

"No child, we will never be hungry from today on," Kosta told her.

"Come children, remember this day, father has returned!" Kathryn said to them.

In the little house, Grandpa sat on a pillow at the table. The children's questions rang out all at once.

Kosta raised his arm to quiet them down.

"Children I would like to introduce our visitor but unfortunately all through the journey he refused to tell me his name, perhaps now he will," Kosta said to them.

"Children...I am an old man, but your father has a fine way of convincing not only me, but I am sure anyone he meets, that is why I am here. My name is Horacio Chappaniac. I came from very far with your father."

They stared at him. Mathew spoke first, "Sir Horacio Cha...p...pa...niac, ah... am I pronouncing correctly your name Sir? My name is Mathew, and these are my sisters, Tessana and Jasimin, Marla and Rosie, my brothers Jason and Kras."

The children all chimed together, "Welcome Sir Horacio!" When he smiled exposed but a few remaining teeth.

"Thank you for your kind heart, all of you...he said, I have been saved by your father from tragedy and I will try not to be a nuisance. To tell you the truth I do not like my name much. In fact...whatever name you choose to call me by will be fine with me," Horacio Chappaniac said to the seven children.

"The circumstances were critical, the ultimate decision had to be, Sir Horacio Chappaniac is to stay and live with us," Kosta explained to his family.

He looked at Kathryn she glared at him wide-eyed, he was sure that after she knows the real reason why this old man must stay, she would understand.

Kathryn and the children welcomed Horacio Chappaniac into their simple and very crowded home.

"I like your name Sir; it is impressive and has distinction," Mathew said to Horacio Chappaniac. Sir Horacio grinned from ear to ear, immediately liking the boy.

"Distinction bah...just a captain of a pirate ship, that is all." He grinned again.

Mathew's eyes popped, "Really?"

After the children told Kosta of their feelings and doubts while he was gone, they somewhat settled down and began to disperse to do whatever they were doing. Jason and Kras went off to their friends to tell them father has returned. Horacio had no choice but accept the small room off the kitchen, which happened to be the pantry. Private it was but dark and close to the back door; comfortable in comparison to his back home a bit better. Assured by Kosta this accommodation is just for a short time, he will figure out something soon. Horacio did not protest, but sat on the small cot and suddenly felt exhausted after such a long trip; slowly slid his feet under the covers closed his eyes and slept.

Kosta hushed the children reminding them of the old fragile "Grandpa "needed sleep. He stayed at Kathryn's side all the while helping with preparing dinner, at one moment he pulled her to him and cupped her chin looked into her eyes but that happy spark of life gone; she seemed withdrawn; she turned away from him.

"Kathryn my love...I am with you...come back to me...forgive me...I did not mean to cause such grief to you and the children...you must hear me out, then you will understand." Kosta could not wait to have her all to himself, in private, hold her close, and tell her about the day he had gone to his brother, all of it from beginning to end.

Kathryn could not hide from him her thinness or shabby appearance, she felt much older, her hair grayed! While his hair still was blacker than black, and those blue eyes, she loved! Every time he touched her, she felt that warm feeling within, but she could not bring herself to lean on him, hold him, as before. From that moment when she saw him, she wanted to run to him, but unable to move as if grounded. She remembers fainting, and when she came to she saw his concerned face, her heart raced, as if she could not accept the reality he was alive. What is happening to her now? After years of longing, wondering, waiting for that finality, the closure, now he is near her, that feeling of doubt has not released her yet. This is so foolish of her, this is not an illusion, that chapter of her life is done with. She must live again with him, for him and the children. Is she still angry? Tears rolled down her cheeks and she could not stop them, Kosta saw and ran up to her and wrapped his arms around her.

"Cry my love, but not from anger, or sorrow, but *happiness.*" He kissed her as he had never kissed her in the years before. Kathryn's knees weakened and he felt it, he crushed her to him. Mathew seeing his parents in such an embrace walked out of the house, smiling. He was to remove important things from the carriage and bring them in. Neighbors stood at the gate gaping at the carriage and the beautiful four white horses.

"Who came to visit your mother, Mathew?" they asked.

"Father is back from a long absence. He is well, and we are happy to have him back!" Mathew proudly announced.

"Where has he been so long?" one asked.

"Father will tell us what...later. He is with mother and the children," Mathew replied.

"Will you tell him we are glad he is back, we also worried about her, you know," the neighbor said.

"Thank you I will," Mathew replied.

They whispered and walked back to their homes, some were running off, most likely to tell the others that Kosta was back, alive, and that elegant carriage a must to see!

Mathew drove the carriage closer to the barn, unhitched the horses led them into the stable to feed, and a well-deserved rest. From the carriage Mathew removed Grandpa's belongings, set them on the side in the stable, just then Kosta walked up leaned into the interior and brought out a small leather bag and handed it to Mathew, the weight of it made Mathew curious and surprised, and he gave his father that look of "*What is this*?" "Take this and give it to your mother. Wait! Give her this one and this one," Kosta said and smiled.

Mathew did not believe his eyes, what he held in his hands was a fortune, and he knew it. Kathryn sat at the table sipping tea when Mathew came up from behind her and said.

"Mother, Mother look, this is for you!" She turned, seeing the leather bags, curiosity sparked, she smiled and reached for them.

"These are for you from Father," Mathew said.

Kathryn opened the bag and peeked in, put her hand into it and felt the cool pieces of gold a handful she laid on the table, in bewilderment they stared at the shining pieces.

"My God Mathew, how...where in the world...did father find all this gold?" she asked looking up at her son.

Kosta walked in on them as they admired the gold on the table. The rest of the children were outside playing. Kosta sat down with them.

He took Kathryn's hand and looked from one to the other wanting to tell them what happened.

"Mathew you are old enough to understand, but first I must tell you I am very proud of you, you were much help to your mother and your siblings, as I see it now. Forgive me, but what I am about to tell mother, I wish for you not to hear...not now...not today." Kosta gripped his son's hand.

Kathryn looked wide-eyed, not speaking, though her eyes were questioning he knew what she meant.

"Father, I do understand...you and Mother need to talk, about everything, she has been through so much. I will leave you alone...perhaps the two of you need to take a walk to your favorite spot. Mother you know where!" Mathew said and walked out the door.

Kathryn did not want to walk today, not to the creek, where the despair and heartache remained vivid in her mind, not now, she wanted to be home and she needed to be in his strong arms; held tight and hear his heart beat. She needed to wrap her arms around him and cry from happiness, within her, those old feelings stirred, her love longed for him.

He lifted her into his arms and carried her to bed. She lay close to him. He told her everything, every detail, he kissed her forehead, cheeks and neck, he stroked her hair, she responded with passion and tears. He told her how much he loved her and missed her and the children, how he worried, it was not his choice... all that transpired was predestined and he was compelled to go away and perform the assignments according to instructions, else he would have never been back as she sees him now.

Her head on his chest, thin arms wrapped around him, she listened, he whispered professing his love for her, and asking forgiveness for being away for so long. He held her tight and felt her boniness. He held back the tears and promised her that from now on everything will improve.

She absorbed all she could but a little overwhelmed, yet she was thankful to God and the mysterious magic of fate, to have him back, his handsome self, as he was before, whole, healthy, gentle and loving. Her beloved husband was back in her arms. She pressed against him and wept from joy, and for all the pain inflicted on them and their children, he kissed her tears. Kosta thought, *she is responding. She is coming back to me.* They slept.

Fifty-Nine: The Unnerving News

The news traveled quickly to all the villages and beyond, soon news reached the estate of Lord Thomas, Cybilia and their children.

Lord Thomas terribly shaken by the news lost control of his senses, he tramped around the house and out on the grounds thinking and mulling over the unthinkable news. "It must be a lie! It must be a jest! Someone is playing a trick at my expense! It is impossible for Kosta to be alive! Not in a million years could he have survived, how could he?" Lord Thomas kept on repeating to himself over and over the same thing!

"It is impossible and I will not believe it! How could this be possible...I will be dammed, but fear not...I will find out, I will send spies! I will...I will find out how he could have survived, and who saved him, why was it kept a secret from me...and why did he come back in that elegant carriage! I will find out!"

He marched with short steps amid the rows of the apple trees and kept talking to himself. The more he talked the more agitated he became. Hellish anger engulfed his being. "I will not rest until I see for myself. I will look at his face myself...with my own eyes. They say that he has his eyesight back...how could that be! I gouged them out myself, me...I did it to him...!"

He was completely engrossed in his fury, oblivious to his surroundings, unwary of the heavy clouds moving in, thunder rolled, and, suddenly torrential downpour came upon him. This brought him out of his agitating whirling state of mania. He ran home huffing and puffing soaked through and through, he was angry, quickly dunned his sodden clothes and left them on the floor, vigorously rubbed his wet body with a towel and dressed into dry clothes. Ran into the dining room, his hands trembling poured a large glass of wine. He sat in his favorite chair and drank one glass after another. Cybilia watched him half-hidden from the doorway, she surmised that he knew, the news must have reached him...what will he do now? She went to Mark and Shara to come and observe their father.

"What do you suspect is going on, look at him...he is in some mental turmoil?" Cybilia whispered.

"Father is oblivious to his surroundings," Shara whispered back.

"Is it the wine or the news?" Mark asked.

"What do you think about the strange rumors? Everyone knew that Uncle Kosta disappeared without a trace, now he has returned. Something very mysterious is going on, and I admit I am having very uneasy feelings..." Cybilia said. They agreed with her, they too felt odd. They stood and watched for a long while, hidden behind the curtain.

"Mother, I have noticed Father's behavior; he seems to be in a dreamland," Shara suddenly whispered.

"The way he talks and walks and drinks, and recently he has become very quiet...that is strange, if I may say so myself," Mark stated, Shara acknowledged same.

"It is a complete reversal of his screaming at everyone, controlling and monopolizing, always shaking his fist. Perhaps he is losing his mind. The news shocked him! I cannot understand his behavior. I am afraid to approach him," Cybilia expressed her fear. They tiptoed away to discuss this matter further in her bedroom.

Lord Thomas might have appeared that way to them as if he was a bit touched, but no one knew that his strange actions, his disconnected behavior from all the surroundings, one could only imply, but what went on in his mind was indeed a very sober compilation of things to come. He sat in his chair ruminating from the beginning, from the very first time that he had cruelly abused his brother.

The second time when his brother came begging for help, and he again committed that same cruel deed, he visualized each occurrence, his hair bristled; his brother was blind, bloody and unconscious that night. How could he be alive with complete sight! That is impossible...impossible! That must be some witchcraft...or, someone is impersonating Kosta, that must be so, but why would anyone impersonate him...?

Joseph, Joseph knew it all, he was there assisting me...then I had him silenced forever. Where is James now? Ah...yes...that coward could not live with his conscience...what had I ordered him to do...I seem to have forgotten...no, he was not there the first time. Was he there the second time, no...he was the one that set Kosta's barn on fire...and the other houses, ah, that must have been a sight...I can see it now...everyone running around trying to save whatever...James described it all to me. Thomas began laughing aloud, his eerie laugh. *Where is James...he is also gone...why that jester...always had something funny to say and he had that queer smile smeared all over his face...he could not live with all his deeds...he lost his senses, and hung himself, rather than facing life. However, with me, he had a good life, yes with me...I treated him the best...whether he realized it or not...he hung himself...ha! Good thing I had his tongue cut out, or he would have blabbed... a decrepit weakling. What is all this about my brother returning from the dead! Ha!*

Whoever it is will not enjoy sunshine for long! I will eventually have to pay a visit to my sister-in-law...and find out who this person is trying to muscle into his brother's family, perhaps he is an imposter. First, I must send spies they will tell me, but whom should I trust?

Lord Thomas talked to himself, sitting down on the benches or walking in the groves. The staff whispered among themselves that he has lost his mind. On the contrary, he was contemplating his future. His constant engrossment gave him away in that respect.

Cybilia also concluded that her husband was not well and needs help. However, she felt apprehensive suggesting to him of visiting a doctor, he might get furious, and scream. Brake things as before, when things do not go his way. Cybilia discussed this matter with her children Mark and Shara at length, but neither one could come to any concrete decision. The only thing they should do is continue observing him, than if things do not change they will act.

Lord Thomas had difficulty sleeping, vivid scenes of years past, kept him awake drenched by perspiration. For him mornings could not come soon enough, at least he could go out far into the orchard; sit there undisturbed; think and plan. A bottle of wine stashed away near his favorite largest and oldest tree in the whole orchard, which he loved. He recalled their first rendezvous, before he and Cybilia were married.

In his younger years, he stowed away to the orchards in the early evenings formulate all sorts of plans and goals to perfection, and then set them into motion without interruption.

At present his mind seemed irrational, in great turmoil, to think soberly and clearly was burdensome for his brain, most of the time oversaturated with wine, not only the news shattered his peace, his nerves were ready to snap. The reality...his brother returned alive and worst of all that is all he knew. No one knew Kosta told Kathryn where he had been, far over the four ranges of mountains where he cured a Little Princess, the daughter of a

King. Restored the shortage of water; and magically cured the woman's sore leg. Lord Thomas knew that the old man with fragile bones, of all blasted things, is residing at Kosta's home!

That chicken coop of his cannot ever accommodate so many...must be very crowded, like eggs in a basket. The day he disappeared...I was complacent, happy; nothing perturbed me at all...not even my wife or the children. Nothing disturbed my life...until now. Lord Thomas mulled over the news as he sipped wine.

"As of today things will start rolling. Rolling as a silent mystery does, and one day explode at someone's door. Ah, that will be a pleasure to watch. First, I need someone capable to undertake such a task. Must be cunning, cruel, and ruthless, a big brute. Someone who might be as I used to be...for gold is a lure and many will be available...and willing...and when it is done...first I must pay a visit to my brother...it is only proper...to welcome him back...I should take Cybilia, Mark and Shara with me. What if he refuses to see my family and I and I wonder if he told Kathryn what I had done to him. Why...they might arrest me...no, he is too forgiving, he will not turn me in. I will think about that later...but just in case, I need to be prepared. I need to visit the inns, drink with the fellows, and pull some tongues for information, it might not be as easy...I have not been visiting those places for some time now...but...if I do get what I want...and need to know...I will triumph again...he will not be a thorn in my side for long! The visit to my brother, yes we will visit them, all of us, bring some wine...and several apple tree saplings, I know he does not have any fruit trees. I should bring some apple-baked goods...that would be very impressive, for sure...

"Not much remaining in their storage bins by now...summer is almost gone. Those children must be fed...I wonder how they managed without him...he has been gone several winters...hmm that long...ha! Misery that is all they have left. Ha! However, I have succeeded...I conquered...I did it with planning and determination! Ha!"

Lord Thomas sat and talked to himself, planning the visit to Kosta, and family. Curiosity getting to him, his plans changed by the minute, absolutely could not make up his mind what to bring or what to say to his brother. "Perhaps I should discuss this with Cybilia, yes I will...but before I do...I must, I must go and see for myself."

For several weeks, he planned this trip, but did not discuss this matter with Cybilia. He visualized his brother's face with those blue eyes and his handsomeness unnerved him to a point of madness. He sat in his favorite chair thinking, thinking, and tried to imagine who had helped him. *Was it Sebastian? Where has Kosta been? How could it be possible? Impossible...someone is playing a trick on me...he is dead...he must be...what if the servants took Kosta to someone for help and recuperation. Thinking back, I did not ask which cemetery they dropped him off and how far, without telling me...what if..., is that why Joseph left. But I took care of him for good...and James, to avoid telling me the truth...hung himself...now it comes to me, they were not my faithful servants...not to me...not at all. Good thing they both are gone...dead, ha, never mind them. Now I must find out for myself. First, I must go and scan the area. Perhaps I will be lucky enough to see that carriage the people are barking about, I should go before sunset. Everyone is barking about the adventures of my brother and the fortune he acquired being away, how did he do it, where has he been so long? I cannot rest until I find out...I must!* His thoughts churned on feverishly.

It seemed to all the servants that Lord Thomas had withdrawn into himself.

Recklessly at the market, one of the servants said something to that effect, and the gossip spread among the people and to some of Lord Thomas's friends.

One morning someone came riding in on a horse to the estate, the servant announced to Lord Thomas that a certain friend of his is waiting outside to see him.

"Well invite him in, do not just stand there, go and invite him in!" Lord Thomas shouted.

"But sir, he refuses to come in...I did invite him...he wants you to come outside, to talk," the servant fearfully replied.

"Well who in the hell is out there! All right I will go and talk whoever he is out there, but it better be a good friend, I tell you!" Lord Thomas spoke in a loud voice and went up to the front door. There sat on a horse, an old friend from childhood days, and his facial expression grave. Lord Thomas took a long look at the man and suddenly shouted.

"Well I cannot believe my eyes. Jackoby...Jackoby! Is that you for real? Well come in, why are you still on that horse? What is the matter, you look as if you have seen a ghost! Get off that horse, I tell you!"

The man, slowly swung his leg off the saddle, walked up to Lord Thomas they shook hands and embraced. It has been years since they had seen each other, and of course, they have changed, age took care of that, nevertheless, they walked into the parlor and, curiously, Lord Thomas exclaimed.

"I am happy to see you after all those years, Jackoby, you are looking great!

"Well...thank you. You remember Midget...I received a letter from him sometime back. He wrote that you have gone mad, and, have done away with yourself...by hanging. But now I see you are still alive, imagine I traveled two weeks just to make sure you are alive," Jackoby said smiling now.

"You are not serious, who could have spread such a horrid story! I cannot understand, who? As you see I am alive and very sane, come let us drink to that, with my good wine." Lord Thomas laughed that same eerie way.

"Hashmar bring us some wine!" Lord Thomas shouted to the butler, who was standing and staring not believing what he had heard.

"Yes sir, right away," Hashmar slipped away into the kitchen for the wine.

"Your servant has an odd name, where is he from?" Jackoby wanted to know.

"I have no idea, he was recommended by a merchant at the market. He is a fine obedient fellow. I have no doubts about him," Lord Thomas declared.

The two old friends sat and reminisced about their youthful days, and when the day came to a close Jacoby retired for the night. Next day after a hearty breakfast with the family, Jacoby rode away with a handshake and a hug from Cybilia and the children and promised to return within a year. Jacoby rode down the lane not looking back, soon was out of sight.

Lord Thomas could not understand who could have been the one to spread such rumors, and he confronted all the servants, his children and Cybilia, none knew of such a horrid gossip. This disturbed him to the point he visualized himself hanging when he closed his eyes. It took weeks to rid his mind of this nightmare, and be calm enough to go to the market again.

Mark, Shara and Cybilia were concerned over his strange behavior. Lord Thomas drank too much and walked alone too much, and no one could talk to him and help him, refusing help, he said to all, "I will solve this myself, now leave me alone." He resumed planning the visit to his brother.

Sixty: The Horseman

Early afternoon Lord Thomas decided to ride to the village, to the house of his birth. "I must see for myself that gilded carriage. Is it actually there! In front of that house, the shabby shack, what a laugh! Yes...the same one that I was born in and grew up, and spent my childhood days with Kosta and my parents." He was thinking and recalling those miserable years, that is why when he was old enough he snuck out and stayed out from sunrise to sunset, but after a moment of thought he asked himself out-loud, "Was it really that bad? I was fourteen then, I despised the smell of manure and the cleaning, I was obligated to do the job; of course, I had to, after all, I lived there. Ah my parents...no I would rather not think about that life...no!"

The sun dipped down towards the horizon, long shadows stretched across the road, *darkness approaching it will be hard to see*, he thought, but rode on at a slow pace.

His thoughts involuntarily went back to his childhood and the deeper his thoughts, the more his desire to see his brother diminished, nevertheless, he rode on.

Riding through his village, passing same old houses, in the twilight still he could see how little it had changed, this was his village too, seemed as if time stood still, here and there were new fences, those broken long ago were never replaced, some still leaning as before, gaping. He felt odd. It has been years since he had been here. The long evening shadows converging on the village seemingly misty as if a mirage. Dim lights glowed through the small windows. Now and then, a dog charged, barked, circled the stallion ran back to his place in the yard.

Lord Thomas felt nervous, disarmed, he glanced around to see if anyone was watching him, but no one was out. He kept on. Someone called his name, looked over his shoulder no one was there, must have been the black bird mimicking voices and whistles. He was the only one on this strangely quiet, deserted and eerie road. This was dinnertime for these villagers, from what he still could see the fields and prairies recalled memories.

The stallion walked very slowly as if he knew he should. The soft dry dirt road muffled the thuds of the hoofs.

Vulnerable feelings stirred, going back in time, and he was; he took control of his unguarded feelings. *I cannot allow sensitivity to creep into me now*. He stopped at the road leading only to the right, a dead end; there stood his birth home, situated on a small rise, looked the same, but for a large barn and a huge horse stable and a well on the side of the house. With trembling hands twisted the reins, Lord Thomas stood for a moment, hesitating should he go on, or not; then barely heeled stallions belly, his horse ambled in closer to the picket fence and halted.

There it was barely visible from the road, yet in the falling darkness, the white carriage shimmered softly just enough to see shape and size. To enter the yard he had not the nerve. He stared at it and smiled, *so it is true*...in his mind he began to envision and wonder whence it came from...he must know. He had to know.

The house was quiet, no light in the window. Lord Thomas stood and took in as much as he could in the darkness.

Inside the house Kosta and his family sat at the table, he was telling them all about his adventures along the way home. Then he broached the subject about Baron Patrick and Horacio Chappaniac, the best solution for all, when suddenly their 'Faithful' watchdog sprawled on the dirt floor raised his head, perked up his ears, and growled. The dog stared at the heavy draped window. They noticed the dogs' actions, Kosta's finger on his lips meant all to hush, or move. He pointed to the dog.

"I need the lamp, please bring it, from the pantry," Kosta whispered to Mathew. Mathew brought the lamp and set it on the table. Kosta told Mathew to blow out the candle when he reaches the window. Mathew did so.

Kosta carefully moved the heavy drape and peered out. There at the fence, he espied a man on a horse, too dark to recognize who the rider was, but it was evident to Kosta that that was not just a horse, this animal a black stallion, a white star visible even in the darkness between his ears. This individual did not want anyone to see or hear him, or else would have been announcing himself loud and clear of his presence at the door.

Kosta told Mathew to light the candle, and when the room was bright, Kosta told his family.

"A mounted rider is at the gate. I will go out and find out who he is and what he wants." Kathryn was a bit apprehensive but did not protest.

Kosta opened the front door, walked several feet forward, and raised the lamp high. The light somewhat illuminated the yard and the mounted rider on a black stallion. Kosta did not ask who was there; he knew.

The man on the stallion surprised by the sudden light made no haste to retreat; his hands trembled; his heart raced when the tall man appeared. In the dark their eyes fixed on each other; they felt each other. Neither made a move; both were tense; riveted in place. Then the rider slowly backed his steed away and retreated into the darkness. Kosta stepped backwards and waited in the doorway until the rider rode away. Kosta had won. He stepped back into the house and bolted the door behind him.

Mathew slipped out the pantry door, ran around the house and took a good look at the rider, not expecting a confrontation between the two, still was ready. When the rider retreated, Mathew ran back into the house, in his hand carrying a loaf of bread and a knife, a snack before retiring, so he said, when asked. Tessana and Rosie ran for the milk and butter.

Lord Thomas' hands shook, his breath shallow, his mouth dry, he swallowed hard.

"Damn! I had to get caught, I stood too long and too close to the house...did he recognize me...? He did...I could feel it, no matter if he did or not...it could have been anyone riding by. If he did recognize me, then he should have said something, or should I have spoken first. Instead, we just stood there and waited, waited for what? Either of us did not want to acknowledge the fact, we knew, he knew and I knew, I came to see with my own eyes...damn...I had to be caught! He caught me snooping. Was it...that was Kosta...really Being here at night now, he will think I am a coward...why am I losing my composure unnecessarily. Perhaps he did not realize that it was I...perhaps. It is best to wait for a while with my visit, perhaps a few months, he might forget this night. No he will not forget, suddenly he slapped his forehead, how stupid of me...Star, my stallion, surely he has never forgotten my stallion, well, what is done is done," Lord Thomas muttered to himself, he was extremely agitated, his evening escapade failed. Perspiration ran from his pores through his whole body.

"Damn the nerves...I had to be caught!" he swore as he rode on. His anger mounting and his evil schemes began churning anew.

Lord Thomas did not return home immediately, instead he detoured to one of the Inns where he frequented. In fact, in his younger days he used to be a very regular client, with time and age he slowed his visits.

He entered to find some old friends sitting at a table drinking as usual, arms went up for him to join then. A cheerful greeting, an invitation for a drink, which tonight he really needed one or two. Immediately the group began to socialize as before.

Over the years, their habits seemed to have changed little, but for the looks of them, time and wine made many changes. In spite of it all, these men he used to drink with were jolly and glad to see him, with a round of wine, everyone updated the events of their lives...and after several more drinks, conversation seemed to lessen, they ran out of subjects to talk about, none mentioned his brothers return, as if they knew nothing. With that, the atmosphere in the barroom seemed a bit cool, tense. Lord Thomas felt it, the other groups of patron's laughter seemed a bit muffled and the conversation a bit hushed.

A woman bartender preoccupied elsewhere ignored his call for service. Her aloofness visibly irritated him, years before she never ignored him, tonight she had. The other fellows noticed this and glanced at each other meaningfully.

The hour was very late, time to head home. He had forgotten about his prize stallion out in the dark, hoping he was still there. Not one asked him to stay a bit longer, or "have another drink," as they used to do.

He stood up to leave, walked slowly towards the door. His six pals stood up and followed him. He glanced around the room and noticed that many eyes were upon him and the room became stilled. He reached for the doorknob, turned it, opened the heavy door and stepped out. The six fellows closed the door behind him.

He felt strangely at that moment. Deep in his gut felt kicked out, not welcomed here anymore. *That is absurd, we have been friends for so long*, quickly shrugged it aside. Still his attitude changed a bit, he turned his thought on a plan of returning one more time.

"The second time surely will be better. I must bring a present for the girl. It has been a long time since I stopped by, I must prove I am still their pal, ah yes, I will bring wine for them to take home, I will do so outside before we all go home, that will cure their uncertainty about me, thereafter, I will acquire needed information." He was thinking of the Inn, he and his pals had quite a bit of wine for which he had paid and felt that they had no ill feelings towards him this evening.

Since it was late, he took the well-traveled path through the sparse patch of woods, though the low shrubs covered much of the ground. Star abruptly halted in its tracks, stumped and snorted, this night was moonless. Lord Thomas felt Star's every nerve and muscle quiver. Fear shot through him, too dark to see, or hear. Lord Thomas spurred Star hard he sprinted forward unsteadily. At last, they were out in the open to gallop. At home, Lord Thomas could not shake that uneasy feeling which still lingered. He was thinking; *why was Star spooked, someone or something must have been near, the scent emitted by this invisible hidden being frightened him, but who?"*

Over the years, Lord Thomas known as the most controlling individual in the whole area. Because of his reputation, many feared him. Some workers cursed and despised his mere presence. Although they abhorred the sight of him, they remained under his employ. As for Cybilia, Shara, and Mark, servants felt sorry for them, it was evident in their actions that all aspects of life had changed for them.

Kosta and Kathryn discussed the grave situation happening at the castle with the children, but not the mysterious horse rider.

The dog, Faithful, growled now and then but did not run to the door, and Kosta did not react. Mathew asked many times about that night.

"Do you think it was someone from another village, Father?" Mathew questioned, and the rest of the children curiously asked why someone would come and stand in the dark, to them that seemed very odd.

"Son, it was just too dark, and the rider went on his way. I am sure many come by late at night out of curiosity, while you are asleep," Kosta said.

Kosta and Kathryn could not sleep, both knew who that rider was, they felt an imminent danger approaching, but when?

Kosta changed the subject and said to Kathryn; "you know Horacio Chappaniac throughout the whole trip would not tell me his full name. I asked should I call him Grandpa, he said that was good enough."

Horacio enjoyed all the attention from the children and being happy regained some weight quite quickly, but his bones remained brittle and care had to be constant. Unfortunately, the house truly could not accommodate all of them, his little bed in the corner of the pantry gave him a sour disposition, and he was becoming claustrophobic.

Several times, he suggested to Kosta to add on a room for him, but Kosta promised Horacio Chappaniac soon they would start building a huge home to accommodate all of them.

"Please build it as soon as possible because I might not live to enjoy my room."

"You will be fine, first we have to seed the fields, than all my help will be ready to build the new home, is that fair enough?" Kosta asked.

"Fair enough, I will wait patiently, and Kosta if I may ask for a big window facing the east in my bedroom, please, I love sunrise," he said.

Sixty-One: Kidnapping

Months had passed since Baron Patrick and Aunt Olivia both visited Kathryn and the children.

Then Kosta returned. So much excitement, Mathew and Rebecca rode to the castle to tell Aunt Olivia and Baron Patrick that father had come home alive and well. Mathew said within several weeks they will visit with father. Kathryn had described in detail what took place at the castle. That the butler tried to poison Baron Patrick, tricked Aunt Olivia with a lie and sent her off on a goose chase, to sell her home. Knowing the situation, Kosta, Kathryn and the children one morning drove up to the castle in the carriage. The wolf head knocker banged by Kosta resounded. Lucinda Nell opened the door, recognizing Mathew was glad to see him, Mathew simply said, "*My Father.*"

"Butler Ridiller is with Master Baron attending to his needs at this moment, come in and wait in the parlor, I will go and tell him you have arrived," she said.

After a long wait they decided to walk up and check things out, when they entered Baron's bedroom, the Butler was absent. What they encountered was unbelievable. The room was dark and the air was foul. They tiptoed to the bed. Kosta leaned over the Baron and only saw the grey hair, Baron covered up to his chin. Kosta became very angry.

"Mathew go look for Aunt Olivia, have her come here!" Mathew ran off peeking into each bedroom, but Aunt Olivia was not in any of them. Mathew wondered what happened to her, where is she? Kosta turned to Kathryn and the children.

"Stay here all of you, I will find the butler, I have something to say to him! Suddenly the butler appeared from one of the rooms and Kosta lashed out.

"How dare you, neglecting the Baron so, it is your responsibility to care for the Master of this castle! After all...!" Kosta hesitated to say what was on his mind. Butler Ridiller ran down the stairs towards the kitchen, with Kosta on his heels. The kitchen smelled of lunch being prepared, the cook and helpers, stopped working. They stared at Kosta, Butler Ridiller's face paled a grey stone, hands trembling, with his back turned to Kosta.

Kosta eyed the cooks and servants and said, "Are all of you in on this conspiracy?

Butler Ridiller replied hoarsely, "You should talk abandoning your family..." He never finished, Kosta grabbed him by the back collar swung him around and punched him in the mouth, the butler staggered fell against the table in the middle of the kitchen. The employees gasped, but dared not act in either's defense. Mathew stormed into the kitchen took in the scene, noticed that the girl Lira was not there.

Kosta stopped, checked his anger, his fist in the butler's face, otherwise he would have beat him to a pulp, and without another word took Mathew by the shoulder walked out and slammed the kitchen door behind them. Up the stairs, they ran to check on Baron Patrick and Aunt Olivia. Mathew stopped Kosta in the hall.

"Father this is what we have seen before, all of them are taking advantage of Baron Patrick. Mother and I told you all about this. Something...we must do something to save them. While you were in the kitchen I looked for Aunt Olivia but I could not find her anywhere, Father what can we do?" Kosta listened. Mathew followed Kosta and talked, trying to keep up with his father's quick stride. They entered the bedroom; it was very dark with the drapes drawn. Kosta quickly pulled the drapes open, the room lit up. He turned to the bed.

"The bed is empty! Father, Baron Patrick is gone! Mathew cried out, Father all the servants were in the kitchen...except that girl...she was not there," Mathew observed.

"In that case, Baron Patrick has been kidnapped. Now go find your mother!" Kosta said flatly. Mathew ran down in the direction of the dining room. Empty.

Kosta in the meantime checked every room, found no one, but, in the last one down the hall, a young girl stood on her tiptoes reaching to hang a heavy tapestry on hooks.

"Have you seen Butler Ridiller?"

Startled, she lost her balance, clutching the tapestry with the chair toppled to the floor, exposing a large door.

"No Sir...I...no...something wrong sir?" she said scrambling up to her feet still holding on to the tapestry. Kosta curiously eyed the door.

"What is behind that door?"

"This door...oh...a closet sir," she replied stuttering a bit. Kosta had tricked her with the question. He walked up to the door and opened it, yes, he eyed it from top to bottom, just a plain empty closet without shelves or hooks of any kind to hang things. He also noticed at the bottom a faint streak of light. Kosta glanced over his shoulder, the girl ran off, tapestry on the floor. Kosta pushed on the wide panel and it swung open to expose a staircase. This was an escape door. This is the way they kidnapped and carried out Baron Patrick. Aunt Olivia, where is Aunt Olivia? Kosta ran down the stairs to the opened door, the source of light to the closet. Kosta stood scanning the grounds. At the far end of the grounds, he noticed Kathryn and the children coming into view, Kosta wondered, *what in the world, why were they down that hill?*" He called to them but they did not see him standing in that doorway, instead entered the kitchen by the back door. As Kosta stood and looked at the properties perimeter, he heard a faint tapping.

"Seems to be within the walls, perhaps mice? Rats? No, the walls are too thick for mice or rats this was not an animal tapping. Too rhythmic, that rhythmic sound is a human." He glanced around there was only the staircase and two plank walls, weathered, chipped, smudged and as old as the castle. Kosta flattened his ear to the tiny crack. Tapping stopped. Suddenly Mathew came bounding down the stairs seeing Kosta, exclaimed.

"Father, Mother is back!" Kosta motioned for silence, Mathew repeated.

"Father, Mother is back, everyone is all right, what is happening, how did you find this door?"

"I will tell you later, right now I am sure someone is behind this door, but, there seems to be no way to enter, unless...Mathew let's push on each of these heavy boards, maybe with luck this is it," Kosta explained. They pushed without success. They pounded from top to bottom. When they stopped, the tapping began.

"Listen, Mathew the tapping again, we must find a way in!" Kosta leaned on the frame and the wall opened, Mathew grabbed the edge, tugged, it swung away exposing a large basement full of furniture and miscellaneous items. Kosta blocked the door to prevent it from closing behind them. The basement dark, damp, smelled musty, cold, barely lit by a tiny window. They cautiously moved around the room, the tapping and moaning came from a dark corner. Following the sounds found Aunt Olivia on the sofa tied up, blindfolded, and gagged. Her legs were on the back of the sofa with her shoes she tapped on the wooden trim. Kosta ran to her rescue, quickly removed the gag and the blindfold. Mathew untied her hands. She was weak, hardly able to sit up. She gasped and whimpered like a child.

"Mathew, bolt the outside door. I will carry Aunt Olivia upstairs, close the door behind you, we know how to open it now."

Mathew closed the back outside door. Kosta lifted Aunt Olivia into his arms; she was light as a feather; her head on his shoulder, shivered. He carried her up the stairs to the bedroom. She sat on the bed. Kathryn threw back the covers and Tessana propped Aunt Olivia up with pillows. The rest of the children sat on the bed close to her.

"Mathew, run down and have Lucinda Nell prepare a meal for Aunt Olivia. I need to speak with mother." Mathew, Jason and Kras ran to the kitchen. Minutes later, Kras ran in breathless.

"Father, Flora said...Lira the gypsy girl and the butler are gone."

"Who is Lira?" Kathryn told him about Lira.

"No wonder, a gypsy...she must have been involved with the butler all along. We found Aunt Olivia thank God, in the basement just in time. She would have died of starvation. No one would have known. That Lira she must have been involved. I walked in on her, asking if she knew where the butler was. I frightened her and she fell off the chair taking the tapestry down with her exposing that door, then ran off. I saw a faint light on the floorboard, I realized there had to be a secret way to that light, and I found it. Now, the question is; where is Baron Patrick? We must ask Aunt Olivia."

Lucinda Nell carried in a bowl of soup to nourish Aunt Olivia. She ate slowly, drank the wine, fell asleep. The family sat and discussed how to find Baron Patrick, perhaps he is still in the castle or had they abducted him and escaped.

Sixty-Two: The Extreme

The incident in the woods kept puzzling Lord Thomas. Something frightened the horse. What sort of a spirit or ghost could have...or did someone wait in the darkness. Through the years, someone did follow him. His every move, his every action and all activity penned in his book of life. The decision as to his merits of his good deeds and his malicious deeds waited for the right moment, the right place, at which time sentence of justice would strike. They were there always, unseen and silent, dark shadows in the night, listening and watching. That eerie feeling Lord Thomas had experienced, had been by those invisible eyes watching daytime and nighttime. Lord Thomas never suspected such an intrusion on his privacy. He concentrated on the visit to his brother. His evil mind kept on devising plans, but was unable to decide on any one in particular, not yet.

At one point, his decision was to shower them with gifts, especially the children. He felt that, that would be the civil thing to do. His attitude must be most gracious. Otherwise, he will never discover the secret. The return of his eyesight, and all that wealth of which he heard so much about. To portray his goodness, he smiled, talked with the servants, took interest in winery and concerns of the estate.

Cybilia, Mark, and Shara perplexed at this sudden extreme. Cybilia suspected something brewing behind her husband's conduct, masquerading as his true self behind that invisible mask. Cybilia observed. Whenever Lord Thomas insisted on having lunches and dinners at a certain time without excuses, everyone must be present. Togetherness, togetherness, family must bond is most important," he stressed. Therefore, the good side of him shined for the family, but privately in his warped mind set the wheels of his plan to roll.

Cybilia learned of her husband's fickle character, as the years passed she felt hurt and her feelings chilled so much she had no pity, or care. As far as she was concerned he could be dead, she would not shed a tear. When she was young, unrefined, fell in love blindly, his dark side hidden deep within. However, time does bring justice, as it always does, at the most unexpected moment.

Lord Thomas walked the floor nightly, rehashed each plan. Although, unable to attain solid information, just bits and pieces, which proved dubious rather suddenly, realized that his friends took him for an idiot or a fool. Nonetheless, driven by his evil greed to find out the truth, it was time to act. He had to know, after all, he caused the pain, not once, but twice to his brother. He chose the plan, which relentlessly pressed at him, stand face-to-face, eye-to-eye, ask by what power he lives and having full eyesight. How could it be possible, he was blind, ah, those blue eyes, mother used to say; Kosta, your eyes are as blue as the sky..., I took them out one by one..., since mother never said anything nice about my *eyes*! That night, my brother was intoxicated. The irony of it...at that time, I pretended to be drunk! Acting came naturally to Lord Thomas, absolutely, he was a good actor and he fooled many in his lifetime. "*The time is now! Harvest is months away. Everyone is taking it easy, now, for a while. It is time to visit my brother*," he thought. At dinner, Lord Thomas announced to Cybilia, Shara and Mark it is time to visit Uncle Kosta and family soon on a Sunday. Disbelieving, what they heard, glanced at each other meaningfully. "*What is this? A dead leaf come alive turning into a spring green after all these years...hmm*," Cybilia thought. She was aware of all those unfortunate mishaps to that family. Surmising he had planned it all and others had carried out his evil deeds.

They were waiting for that Sunday, however, which Sunday he never did say, as they recalled now. Lord Thomas now stalled that visit to Uncle Kosta. Something is amiss, but what it is no one knew and neither one asked, fear of bursting his bubble of anger, as it had burst frequently before. Therefore, they patiently waited. Several Sundays passed. After breakfast, Cybilia and her children went off galloping through the countryside on their horses. They relaxed in the shade of the tree in the meadow. Hoping for that long outing in their fancy carriage, of course unannounced visit to Uncle Kosta.

Sixty-Three: The Kidnapping Solved

Kosta noticed a few of the servants behaving oddly while he was at the castle; disliked his unexpected visits. Mathew, Rebecca and Tessana remained with Aunt Olivia from that first day of her rescue by Kosta out of the castle's basement. The three of them kept constant vigilance. She was still weak, fed three to four times per day to regain her strength. The village doctor examined her, stating, "she will recover with food and rest." Cook Flora and Lucinda Nell were entrusted to prepare all her meals.

While Kathryn and Kosta worried and concerned for his failing health. Where is and what is happening to Baron Patrick. Waiting for some news from their constable, but none came. From town to town, from village to village, the news traveled, the gypsies heard the rumor, *someone, had kidnapped the notorious Baron!* The gypsies forewarned, knew how to find the kidnapped Baron Patrick, but this must be worth their while or else they will not bother. Lira, at each stop had inquired of the whereabouts of Krume then steered Butler Ridiller closer and closer to the gypsy camp telling him that was the best way her group's leader was wise in such dealings and would get the highest ransom. If he does not receive what he wants, he knows how to dispose of anyone without a trace. Butler Ridiller fell for it and agreed to deliver Baron Patrick into the gypsy leader's hands. There were moments when Butler Ridiller asked her questions, but being a gypsy, she concealed her uneasiness and deception well and chose words to calm him. During the trip Lira feared of being discovered as a conspirator, the fact was she had nothing to do with the abduction at all, she realized how cruel and greedy Butler Ridiller was and she felt obligated in some way to rescue the innocent Baron Patrick and felt he deserved to be punished for his crimes. They came upon several campsites missing the gypsies by a day or less, than in the early evening they pulled into a very large camp, wagons and tents spread with bonfires burning for super's meal. Lira walked along the wagon questioning in gypsy language where she could find Krumes tent and his people. After passing many groups of people, she found him and his trusted assistants. A group of men sat around the fire smoking pipes and waiting for supper. Krume surprised to see her after months of absence. Lira introduced Butler Ridiller as her employer. While Krume and Ridiller discussed the plan of ransom for the Baron, Lira quickly ran to the bonfire where women were roasting freshly killed pigs purchased from farmers, she asked for tea to quench their thirst after such a long journey. Lira walked over to the wagon to check on Baron Patrick, he was resting, listening to the chatter of strange people wondering what will happen to him. Lira handed Baron Patrick his cup of tea, and told him the women will bring his dinner shortly and that they will tend to him with whatever his need. Baron Patrick thanked her and smiled feeling somewhat safer among these gypsies. Then she spiked the tea with a sleeping potion; wrapped a warm shawl around her shoulders and walked back to the bonfire. She handed Butler Ridiller a large cup, and he drank greedily; then she placed a plate of food on the ground in from of him.

"Drink and eat, the trip was long and we need to recoup our strength and we need sleep," she said to him. Butler Ridiller reminded her of Baron's needs. Lira said, "I took care of everything." She sat down on the tree stump just a step behind him. She glanced at him occasionally while eating her own portion and sipped tea slowly waiting for Ridiller to slump to the ground. After he fell asleep, she related the story what she had done and why. Krume listened then said, "Go take care of Baron Patrick and finish supper. You did the right thing to Butler Ridiller." After supper they sat smoked pipes and drank wine discussing sometimes occasionally an outburst of anger could be heard and then laughter what they were laughing about Lira did not hear, she was resting in the wagon next to Baron Patrick. Before midnight, Krume told her of their decision.

"Our caravan will go back; anyway, we were going in that direction. Deliver butler into the hands of the law and take Baron Patrick to Kosta."

"Oh Krume, Krume thank you, Aunt Olivia will be happy, they all will be happy," Lira said and fell back onto the mat next to Baron Patrick. She heard his rhythmic breathing. He was asleep. He was out of danger. The butler tied up was not going anywhere, not tonight. She smiled thinking, *this trip turned out well for now*. She fell asleep soundly.

While Kosta and Kathryn worried and waited for the law to solve the kidnapping, the gypsies were on the road for several days returning the ailing Baron. The butler tied up, gagged, blindfolded, in a sack up to his neck lay flat in the wagon, which jerked and jarred him in every direction from the speed of the caravan. No need for directions they knew the way. Baron Patrick sprawled on a thick mattress of straw. Next to him sat Lira.

"How much further...Krume?" Lira asked.

"Not too far. First, this slimy worm...this criminal needs to be delivered to the constable," Krume replied.

"Krume, please hurry...I am exhausted. I ache all over. I want to be...with my wife Olivia," Baron Patrick pleaded.

"We need to stop by first at Kosta's home. Tell them you are fine," Lira said.

"Very well, I want them to know I am alive. They must be worried...oh my dear children...I love them as if they were my own...all seven of them," Baron Patrick agreed and said, "Hopefully the constable has strong enough rope to hang his abductor."

"All I know...is...while I was ill...Kathryn visited with the children often...she told me...that Kosta had disappeared one day...and has been missing...for several years now. I wish he would come back," the Baron strained to speak.

He closed his eyes and rested, his thoughts turned to Kosta and his family.

"Soon we will arrive at Kosta's little home. Mathew, Rebecca and children will greet me. They are special. That criminal, Ridiller will be in the hands of the law. He will confess to the premeditated murder of me, and those conspiring with him, I will deal with them. Hire new servants. Then decide on the estate... Olivia, now it was time..." his was thinking.

The gypsy caravan rolled on. When they entered the village, people watched the wagons roll with a racket. Not all gypsies were trusted; but their music and the special miscellaneous wares they loved to barter for. This caravan rolled on, but halted at the first gate where a man watched them coming. Gypsy leader Krume asked for direction to the law office.

The man offered to take him directly to the law office, which was not far, the caravan stopped in from of the home of the constable, out of doors and windows many gaped at the parade of gypsies. The constable appeared in the doorway. Seeing gypsies on the wagons suspected something important happened.

The gypsy leader Krume explained who is in the sack and that the Baron is alive and safe. Ridiller the butler at once dragged off the wagon and dragged to the building in the rear of constable's home and office, dropped on the floor in the cell. The two men shook hands and the caravan rolled on to Kosta's house. A pleasant surprise when the long caravan pulled up in front of the house, curiously Kosta looked up wondering who arrived. When Krume the gypsy leader jumped off the wagon and walked over to the standing crowd, he said, "You must be the carver, Kosta."

"I am he, you have business with me?" Kosta spoke in a pleasant voice.

"You do not know me but I know of you. I have brought you someone that you were missing." Krume said grinning, white teeth sparkling. From among the bundles on the wagon appeared a silver-haired, thin man, a wrinkled face with a smile from ear to ear, the children shrieked from joy, seeing a familiar face they have grown to admire and love. Baron Patrick with difficulty attempted to scramble up and out of all those bundles. A young woman stood up to help Baron Patrick.

Mathew stood near the wagon recognized her. Lira, it was Lira.

"Father, look Lira is with him!" Mathew cried out to Kosta.

They both jumped up onto the wagon to help Baron Patrick. Mathew glared at Lira, seeing she was assisting Baron Patrick.

"Why are you here? You should be in jail with the butler! You helped him kidnap Master Baron," Mathew snapped at her.

"I did not help him. I joined him to save Master Baron!" Lira snapped back her fists on hips.

"Mathew, do not be rude, before knowing the truth! Lira come down off that wagon and come into the house. Ah, Lira you were the one in that room hanging that tapestry, you were there!

"Yes, I was there but I..." Lira interrupted tried to explain.

"All right we will talk later," Kosta said.

Kosta holding up the trembling Baron Patrick at the waste walked him to the house.

Krume the gypsy leader hearing the heated conversation spoke up in defense of Lira. As the whole family gathered inside the little house to welcome their friend Baron Patrick, Krume said to them.

"Now hear me out. Lira had done nothing wrong. She risked her life to be an accomplice in this kidnapping with butler. Lira was the one urging butler to come to us. When they arrived at our camp Lira told me all about it. She observed him and knew he was planning a terrible injustice to a good man. That is when we drugged him, tied him up and brought your friend to you."

"What happened to the butler? Mathew asked.

"We delivered him into the hands of the constable, he is in the cell. If you feel Lira cannot be trusted, she stays with us. Know this, she had said she loved the people and the work at the castle, life was rewarding being there, for the first time in her life she was happy and treated decently. Sir Kosta, you decide her future."

For a few seconds it was silent in the room, all at once the children shouted.

"Lira stays!"

Baron Patrick smiled. Kosta was glad that his children had made the decision for him.

Krume handsomely rewarded drove away.

"Kosta...I just realized...you are back home, you have been gone so long! Kosta where is Kathryn? Tessana and Rebecca are not here either," Baron Patrick asked.

"Mother," Kras eagerly chimed in, "Rebecca and Tessana are up at the castle with Aunt Olivia, they...." Kras stopped, looked at his father apologetically.

Kosta looked towards Lira. She lowered her eyes. He knew she would not speak of what had happened to Aunt Olivia, he was sure.

The boys and Rosie stared at Lira. They did not know what to say to her.

Horacio tiptoed out of his cubicle to meet the famous Baron Patrick. Rosie and Marla quickly explained who their guest was, and Jasemin introduced Horacio as their adopted grandfather, Horacio Chappaniac.

"What Grandfather? But I am your grandfather too!" Baron Patrick shouted.

"That is wonderful, now we have two grandfathers!" Rosie clapped her hands.

While Mathew and Lira prepared a good meal, Baron Patrick and Horacio were in a deep discussion of their past.

Kosta pondered how to break the bad news gently without upsetting Barons weak heart. Regardless how ill she is; it is unavoidable he needs to be informed what had happened to Olivia. The day still is long, enough time to eat dinner and tell him what happened, and then ride up to the castle. The children gathered their things and put them into the wagon. Horacio Chappaniac collected his belonging as well and waited. The children scrambled onto the wagon. Mathew and Jason sat up front, the rest sat in the back.

Baron Patrick scrambled into the carriage with difficulty. Lira sat beside him. Horacio stood in the doorway. Baron Patrick glanced his way and shouted.

"Horacio Chappaniac come, what are you waiting for!" Horacio skipped over to the carriage and sat next to Lira.

At the castle when they arrived, servants greeted their master, and cried from happiness. Lucinda Nell ran up to Lady Olivia's bedroom.

"Lady Olivia, Lady Kathryn, Master Baron is back, everyone is here! Come quickly!" she shouted loud enough for Aunt Olivia to hear, too weak to get out of bed she asked Kathryn, what is going on. Kathryn said she would go downstairs and find out what all that excitement means.

"Oh Master Baron we all prayed for your safety," Flora said wiping tears with the apron.

"Thank you everyone, thank you. Lira here is the hero. She saved me from certain death planned by Butler Ridiller."

"Lira...?" They all gaped in her direction.

A whirlwind of commotion erupted. Many of the servants disappeared into their bedrooms and packed their bags. Flora surprised yet said nothing, realizing those who are running out were as guilty as the butler. How odd, they worked here, and ate here, yet were criminals.

Lira ran up to master Baron alarmed and stood next to him. Kosta glanced her way, she pointed to the kitchen. Kosta nodded. Baron Patrick turned to Kosta,

"Please help me upstairs, I need to see my wife." Baron Patrick supported by Lira and Kosta slowly took one step at a time all the way to the landing; out of breath rested a bit. Kathryn was just walking out the door of the bedroom; seeing him and Kosta ran to them, embraced Baron, he kissed her cheek. She took his arm and led him to the bed.

"Stay with them. I need to go to the kitchen, something is happening there," Kosta said. Kathryn nodded.

Patrick's arms stretched towards his beloved Olivia as he approached the bed. She slept peacefully but so frail. He stood for a minute, with eyes full of tears, with Kathryn's help strugled onto the bed and fell next to Olivia.

"My darling Las...I am here...speak to me, my love," he whispered.

Aunt Olivia's eyes slowly opened, she stared straight ahead, as if dreaming, her eyelids closed

"Olivia my love, look at me, I am here," he said softly.

She opened her eyes again and turned her head to see her husband next to her.

"Patrick, Patrick, I waited for you so long...I was dying in that basement...Kosta rescued me...oh Patrick I am so tired." She closed her eyes. Baron Patrick began to weep.

"You must get better, I need you! God...I need her. Please God do not take her away from me, after all these years of loneliness, and searching for her. I found her at last. She is my happiness, my life. Olivia I need you!" he sobbed into the pillow.

Several hours had passed he slept next to her. When she awoke Kathryn has been there watching and waiting for them to wake. Now she walked up to the bed.

"Are you feeling any better, Aunt Olivia?" Kathryn asked.

"Yes, I feel stronger, how long have I slept? Not waiting for an answer she said, "Kathryn I had a dream. Patrick came back. He was right here next to me. He spoke to me so sweetly, as always."

"Oh, but Aunt Olivia he is back. Look, he is asleep next to you." Kathryn smiled pointing at her husband.

Aunt Olivia as weak as she was, sat up saw her husband and cried out, "Patrick? Wake up, Patrick!" She shook him, but he did not respond.

Kathryn ran to the other side of the bed. Checked his pulse, he was alive. Considering such an ordeal he needed sleep, deep sleep. They looked at each other and smiled.

"Let my darling sleep." Olivia leaned and kissed his cheek.

"Kathryn I am famished, please bring me something to eat." She settled back on the pillow, Patrick slept.

Kathryn went downstairs to the kitchen. All the employees stood in a group. Flora was telling Kosta who ran out with their bags.

"Those who are innocent will keep their positions," he told them, "and Lira risked her life to save Master Baron."

"Now Flora, please prepare plenty of food for everyone, we are hungry, I am sure you are too," Kathryn said. The children and Horacio Chappaniac sat around the table listening intently to a serious story. They were oblivious to the commotion behind their backs.

The aroma of food tickled Patrick's nose, he awoke, seeing Olivia cried out with joy.

Ah, my darling Las, you are awake and eating without me, from now on we shall eat together! Let me taste some of that, please."

Weeks later reliving the terrible ordeal both experienced, Olivia and Patrick were like two doves, always together! Love does conquer all. Peace had returned to their lives.

Kosta and the family returned home to their chores. Late that night they sat beneath a tree discussing the trying events and the successful conclusion.

Because of Kosta's love and patience, noticed Kathryn's depression had gradually dissipated. Kathryn's love emerging from the depths of her being, replaced her shyness, on that day of his return; she was embarrassed to be so thin and shabby. Now all that is in the past, here together from this moment on she will be loving, and passionate. That spark of life in her eyes will twinkle bright again, as it had when they met in the forest. She was his Kathryn now, loving him, her children and loving life. Together again they will work hard, and together raise their children. Nothing will stand in their way, they have conquered nightmares, which invaded and overshadowed their life, they withstood all of it, and now whatever may come they will stand firm against it together.

They lived their lives never suspecting that those same thirteen pair of eyes still watched them.

Sixty-Four: Going Home

Lira was given a position as Aunt Olivia and Baron Patrick's personal servant, a position she gladly accepted. Now she feels at home and, she works hard to please. However, her thoughts turned many a time to the butler and his evil deed. One thing a very crucial thing slipped her mind: that special bottle of wine. Kosta in conversation with Baron Patrick offered to find good and honest people to work at the castle, without hesitation he agreed, giving Kosta a free hand.

Kathryn was amazed at how well all this was playing out. Is she dreaming? At this moment her beloved husband is right beside her, she feels such happiness, beauty and peace around her. All her sorrow dissipated without knowing when. She needs to store all this into her memory, someday when there is time, she will think back twenty years perhaps more than that, to their first meeting. She will think of all the good days, and all the hardships, the emotional suffering her family endured until now.

At the present she had to manage what was at hand, she vowed one day she would find out exactly who had been in their life and who caused such misery. There were moments her intuition revealed to her who the individual was. Unfortunately, without proof she could never accuse. Today she knows and still she cannot do anything about it, it was not the right time. Baron Patrick and Aunt Olivia invited Horacio Chappaniac to live permanently at the castle. Good company for each other, Horacio Chappaniac accepted, overjoyed that at last he will have a spacious room of his own, and every morning see the sunrise. Lucinda Nell assigned as his servant. Indeed, to him she was a pleasure to look at!

The joy of his new life unfortunately would be short lived. Since being old and feeble, it was just a matter of time. Horacio Chappaniac lived with pain. Care and gentleness was crucial.

"Have you noticed how much time Horacio and Flora spend together? Most of his time is in the kitchen," Baron Patrick said to Aunt Olivia one day.

"My dear, they like each other's company, they have mutual interests. I walked in once on an intense argument, which quickly fizzled out with apologies. I am sure when I left they had a glass of good wine. I think they are a perfect pair, he is much happier these days," Aunt Olivia replied laughing. Days slipped by, weeks turned into months.

Baron Patrick after experiencing the near death at the hand of the butler became much slower and weaker, as much as he tried to conceal his health condition from Olivia, in time everyone noticed. Aunt Olivia many a night lay in bed next to Patrick, she listened to his laborious breathing. In the dark of night, she prayed to the good Lord to give them both a peaceful death. If he should die, she could not live without him, their love binds them now together as none other after all these years, and now, if only for a few more years, if only. She too felt weak more often but was able to hide it from him. Horacio old but observant noticed these changes in them and decided to send a message to Kosta and Kathryn, it has been several months since their last visit, much work in the fields down in the valley. Frequent messages sent to the castle with inquiries of everyone's health; to which replies came "all is well." Of course, if changes occurred surely, Kosta and Kathryn would be concerned. Kosta receiving the last request to come seemed urgent.

"It is time for a visit, otherwise we will send a note, expect a visit soon. I had noticed the changes in all three of them the last time."

"We need to go now," Kathryn said.

Baron Patrick and Horacio walked to the bench as always to have their talk and enjoy a pleasant morning.

"You know Horacio since we are all together...my home is no longer haunted. Ah, I forgot you never heard that story, have you?"

"Yes I have, the children told me all about that ghost. I am glad she has not disturbed us, especially Olivia, she would have been frightened," Horacio replied.

"Horacio, do you think...that when dying old...we...we are old in heaven?"

"Patrick, my opinion is such. God does not want old decrepit, wrinkled, toothless souls shuffling around heaven. I feel young in my soul, but my body is old. I assure you that once we die, our souls will be young and beautiful. I declare you and Olivia will be a grand pair in heaven," Horacio told his friend.

"Oh Horacio may it be so, may it be so. Horacio I must go...and take care of something important," Baron Patrick said in a low tone.

The two aging companions shuffled back into the castle. Aunt Olivia stood at the window and watched how these two waddled back and had to smile, to her they seemed to be like two little boys.

Like Kosta's boys, deep in some discussion of importance. Baron Patrick while retired to bed broached the inheritance subject to Olivia. Aunt Olivia at first refused to listen, but Patrick with sweet persuasion and kisses explained.

"It is important. I will rest easy when...the heir documents are in order. I do not want all my...possessions to be carried...away...by some strangers...piece by piece. You my love are my heir, no one else. Then, if anything happens to you...I feel that only one other person...Patrick did not finish, Olivia interrupted him with tears and protest.

"But Patrick I cannot be without you. You must make different arrangements, not me, I will die with you."

"Olivia, Olivia no, no...such foolish talk...you are to live and enjoy all these luxuries. Long ago I gathered all this for us...hoping above all hope...I would find you...here we are together, very happy...but my time is near, my love...forgive me, remember I love you." Patrick was short of breath, closed his eyes, within minutes he was asleep. Olivia wept on his shoulder. The reality was staring at both of them. The change for the better was not in their future. This was a definite conclusion to their story... "Love lost reclaimed." When the trees turned fall colors harvest was over. Aunt Olivia out of necessity left the castle after breakfast and drove down to the valley.

Patrick and Horacio after breakfast, shuffled out towards the huge oak tree leaning on their canes, to sit and enjoy the autumn morning and the fall flowers in full bloom. Baron leaned against the oak tree, meditated for a long time. His eyes closed, both hands held the cane between his knees. Horacio Chappaniac did not disturb him; he himself took to admiring the countryside in its splendor from the mountaintop,

"Ah, the good earth, what a wonder, a miracle that I am still here," he said. His old eyes filled with tears, he whispered; "thank you my good Lord for my long life." Though he accepted his pain, which seemed more and more bothersome, at times cursed his weak body, having no other choice but live with it.

Horacio sat admiring the surroundings. Thinking; of his old home; his lonely life; his home burning; and Kosta's children. He slept in the pantry on the cot, but now here he has a bedroom with a big window facing east to watch the sunrise each morning and the world beyond. Horacio seeing his friend peacefully napping was not sure if he should wake him. However, when a chilled breeze hit his bones, he said.

"Patrick it is best we go indoors. Patrick wake up, the wind is too cold." When Baron Patrick did not awake or reply, Horacio gently tapped his shoulder, still no reply or movement, then Horacio shook him; the cane fell out of his hands, his arms dropped to his side, head on his chest. Baron was dead. Horacio hobbled back to the castle trembling and shouting for help. Jonasen and old gardener Kirk Spence heard Horacio calling ran towards him. Poor old man hardly able to utter a word, his whole body as if convulsing, out of breath stuttered, "Come... help, the Baron is dead... there on the bench." The old gardener Kirk Spence assisted Horacio to a chair in the kitchen. Jonasen and two other men ran to the bench beneath the oak tree, truly hoping Horacio was mistaken, that the Baron is only sleeping soundly. They approached to see Baron Patrick's body had slumped onto the bench. Jonasen touched the hand it was cold, he placed his hand on the Barons chest, he felt no heartbeat, and when he raised his eyelid to his relief, life had not yet dimmed from his master's eye.

"Get the smelling salts quickl*y*!" Jonasen shouted.

With trembling hand Jonasen fanned the smelling salts under Baron's nose several times and then came a sudden jerk of his body, they sighted a relief. The men carried him to the bedroom and propped him up on pillows. Baron did not speak but wore a faint smile, happy to be alive. Indeed he was. Jonasen sent for Kosta, Olivia, and the doctor.

Horacio could not compose himself, irritable and trembling, babbled. The distraught Horacio, seeing Jonasen jumped off the chair.

"Jonasen is he alive? Oh God let him live, poor Lady Olivia." The cup of tea spiked with rum, trembling hands raised to his old lips, as he sipped, the tears began to flow.

"Jonasen is he...dead or alive?"

"He will live, how long we do not know. You saved him, in time you called for help," Jonasen replied. Horacio thought of his friend on the bench just a while ago.

"Such a short time since we met and we are together; life ends so quick no time to say good-by; what will I to do and where will I go from here...I am very old. Fear gripped his heart...am I next? Will I wake in the morning? Good Lord...I am all alone now! I must send a messenger to Kosta quickly notify him of Baron's close encounter with death." Horacio ingesting the tea with rum began to relax. He turned to Lucinda Nell. "Did anyone sent for Kosta?"

"Why sir, you gave us the order yourself, you do not remember?" Lucinda Nell replied. As if not hearing her Horacio repeated.

"Send a messenger, to come quickly. The Baron is dying. Baron Patrick is dying!"

The girl understood.

"Horacio is in shock, delirious," she said to Baron Patrick's servant Lira standing in the doorway at that moment, and she turned looked at Baron Patrick laying so still in his bed, suddenly horrified, ran around the halls of the castle, all the others continued to perform their duties; silently shed tears. Lira collided with the new butler, Misha Kronin, and screamed at him.

"Send for Lady Olivia! Where is she? Somebody go find her!"

"Calm down Lira, it has been done. Soon the doctor will arrive," Misha Kronin said in a baritone voice, having a strong accent. Misha Kronin held Liras elbow and led her into the kitchen where Flora sat her down and forced her to drink a large glass of wine.

In the bedroom, Baron Patrick lay on the bed covered up to his shoulders. Lucinda Nell instructed to sit on the high back chair and do not leave until the doctor arrives. Lucinda Nell sat fumbling with her apron, staring at her master. Baron Patrick coughed and opened his eyes. Lucinda Nell heard him cough, he was not dead, her eyes wide, she fell off the chair, unconscious. Lira tiptoed into the Barons bedroom, almost tripping over Lucinda Nell's crumpled body on the floor, Lira shook her, Lucinda Nell opened her eyes seeing Lira sitting next to her, cried out, "He is not dead, he came back to life and I heard him cough."

Kosta received the urgent message. Aunt Olivia happened to be with Kathryn having their usual girl talk. The instructions to the messenger were to have the Village Chief and a Doctor come quickly, emergency at the castle. Kosta will follow with Lady Olivia. Kosta dreaded that moment to see him dead.

"*But he cannot be dead! It must be a mistake, surely. What will happen, how do you tell a woman who had found her lost love after so many years that he had suddenly died? The doctor should tell Aunt Olivia. How will she accept it or react..., hard to imagine*. Kosta thought.

When they arrived at the castle, the doctor was waiting for them. The Village Chief escorted her up to the bedroom followed by the doctor, where her beloved husband rested peacefully on pillows, dozing. She gasped, ran to the bed and threw herself at him, her face on his chest.

"Patrick, Patrick! Are you all right? Talk to me Patrick!" What happened to you?" All present stood speechless, words could never describe the look on their faces now, or ever. Baron Patrick opened his eyes, turned to Olivia, and spoke softly.

"My darling Las I had one of those moments... a sudden blackout, I...I feel better now, do not cry, I will be fine in a while." One by one, they left the bedroom leaving Olivia with her husband. Kosta called on Horacio to ask questions of what had happened.

"Oh God, well, we walked over to the bench and sat down. I did not speak. I was mesmerized by the horizon and by the world out there. I looked over at him his eyes were closed. I did not want to disturb him. He liked to meditate at times, just like that. We did not talk. When it got cold, I said, we must go in and that it was too cold, but he did not reply, I spoke to him and I shook him and I realized he had died. Oh God, may he rest in peace, what will happen to Lady Olivia now? And me, what will happen to me?" Horacio babbled on.

Mathew, Rebecca and the children arrived with Kathryn the next morning. Kathryn found Kosta up in the bedroom, she saw Kosta kneeling by the bed holding Aunt Olivia's hand, her arm stretched over Baron Patrick's chest, her eyes closed.

Kathryn held her breath, what is happening?

"Kosta, Kosta I am here," she whispered.

Lucinda Nell, and Lira sat on a fainting sofa in the back. Lira jumped off the chair and ran up to her weeping quietly.

"Lady Kathryn...Master Baron had an episode with his heart, and, we all thought he had died. Lady Olivia...and Master Baron are sleeping now. The doctor told us he will be well after a good rest," she stammered.

"What? What are you saying?" Kathryn questioned the girl. "Kosta what has happened? Are they all right now?" she ran over to the bed. Kosta looked up his face streaked with tears. In the hall, Kosta described the scene.

"Kathryn, Aunt Olivia was beside herself. Last night when the chief and the doctor were here, I helped her up the stairs, we walked in when she saw Patrick she gasped. I was ready to catch her if she had fainted, but she ran with her arms outstretched to the bed and fell on him thinking he had died. Patrick woke up spoke to her. With their arms about each other now are asleep. When everyone left I spoke to her I asked if she needed anything and she said. 'I need nothing. I want to rest here with Patrick. Kosta please cover me, I feel cold,' I asked if she will come down, or have something brought up for both of them to eat. 'No, I am not hungry at all, thank you, but in an hour or so, Patrick will need some soup. You are so kind,' she said to me."

The children were in the kitchen, waiting. A large platter of the cakes sat in front of them. They munched slowly and sipped the tea without speaking. Rosie the youngest began to sob and the rest of them comforted her when Kathryn entered the kitchen with Kosta.

"Mother our friend is very ill! Will he die now?" Marla asked.

Tessana and Marla noticed the sadness of their faces.

"Father, what will happen now, Aunt Olivia will be lonely without Grandpa Patrick."

"Children listen, Grandpa Patrick is alive. He is very ill but will recover, please pray for both of them, please. Aunt Olivia is resting with Grandpa Patrick...they need quiet," Kosta said. Silence fell. They hung their heads.

"Mother, we need to see them. Please, I need to see them," Tessana spoke up.

Jason shocked sat with his eyes closed praying.

"Why! Mother why is he so sick!" Rosie cried out almost screaming.

"Rosie, please do not cry. They love each other, but they both are quite old... this time he will be fine, Aunt Olivia will not leave him alone. She is with him and they are happy. You know that we all have to die. When we are young, we never think of dying. Our young bodies function perfectly. With time our bodies do not function well, everything has a beginning and an end, flowers die...birds...dogs...cattle and horses...and people. That is the cycle of life, but we never know when that time comes...my dear children." Kosta could not hold back his tears as she spoke to them. Kathryn and the children sat together at the table, a scene taken in by the servants.

Horacio after weeks of lamenting of Barons illness, one day remembered that he has been entrusted with a package given to him by the Baron, that when upon their passing, Horacio was to deliver an important package to Kosta via his maid Lucinda Nell. Unable to get around, having difficulty remembering, after hours of searching his mind, slowly shuffled over to the hiding place to retrieve the package.

He summoned Clara handed her the package and instructed her to take it back to Baron Patrick.

Weeks slipped by Baron Patrick was up and about feeling quite well, he and Aunt Olivia always were together, closer than ever, due to such a close call of his heart failure.

Holidays came and went everyone relaxed went about household duties, this winter turned out to be mild, many invited guests arrived. New Year welcomed with wine, song and dance. Not one tear fell that evening all was well. Young butler Misha Kronin upon hearing the wolf head resounding ran to open the heavy door. As a butler had no authority to turn them away therefore invited them in, four individuals followed him to the parlor. Misha Kronin announced thus, “Baron Patrick someone unexpected has arrived,” and all faces turned, gasped at four finely dressed individuals uninvited stood in the doorway to the parlor. Aunt Olivia clasped her hands together with surprise. Kosta’s blood turned cold, it surged through his veins and hit his face, Kosta knew, Kathryn knew but his children did not know who they were. The host never could be or ever was rude, graciously invited them to join in the New Year celebration.

”And who has entered my home so unexpectedly this evening, may I have the pleasure of knowing your name Sir?” Baron Patrick asked.

Aunt Olivia stepped up to him and said, “Patrick this is Thomas Komarod and his family, Kosta’s brother. Grandfather clock rang out midnight and Father Time danced on.

Sixty-Five: Lost Love Reclaimed

That one evening after dinner everyone went off to do what they wished to do, especially the children, Kras, Jason and Rosie were visiting for several days. The kitchen maids cleared the table and snuffed out the candles.

Baron Patrick took Aunt Olivia's hand.

"Come my Las, let us enjoy the sunset tonight on the far horizon," he said.

Slowly they climbed the many steps, both out of breath, they sat down on the cushioned bench to rest, on a rectangle table stood a bottle of red wine and two wine glasses.

"Why Patrick Grubshin you always surprise me, you are so wonderful. That is why I love you so much," Aunt Olivia exclaimed.

"My darling Las, it is an occasion we cannot miss to celebrate," Patrick said and smiled.

"Oh? What occasion could that be...have I forgotten something? Blame it on my old age!"

They laughed.

"Forgive me but I have nothing for you, only my love," Aunt Olivia replied apologetically.

"It is an occasion to celebrate life. You are my life. You have been my life. Now as I see, you have kept that flame of love burning for me as well. I knew, I felt it, I prayed and I searched, now you are with me, my darling Las, Olivia I love you till my last heartbeat," Patrick said reaching to kiss her hand, and her lips. Olivia ran her fingers through his hair, she wrapped her arms around his neck and their lips locked in a long and passionate kiss.

"You know Patrick I never married because I only loved you. I felt no one in this world would or could make me happy. It has been an unjust destiny for us to live solitary lives till now, I am happy, though at times I feel sad and angry at life, we were shortchanged of happiness. We missed a lifetime together, but at other times I thank the good Lord for leading you to me," Olivia said.

They sat in silence for a while, mesmerized by the colors and wonder of the sunset, a magical sight, slowly dipping down over the horizon. They sat and watched until dusk displayed its cloak of mist, and when the mist dissipated, they sat in total darkness.

It was a warm tranquil peaceful night. Then the moon appeared to brighten the world for them. Baron Patrick and Aunt Olivia sat on soft cushions in the shadows of the west tower, the moonlight, as bright as day, their world taking on a mysterious scene.

"Olivia let us enjoy a glass of wine.

"My dear Patrick, how thoughtful of you, when did you bring this up here?" Olivia asked.

"While you were in the valley I asked Lira to bring it up here, she also was to bring some snacks. When I became ill, I forgot all about it, but tonight I wanted to be up here with you, to celebrate. I must tell you this is of good quality wine. You will enjoy the taste of it. I assure you. I have had many bottles of it at one time, when I was younger. Oh when I was young, do you remember when we were young?" Patrick handed her the glass and sat down put his arm around her and Olivia leaned to him.

"Oh yes do I! I thought about those times all my life, I relived each occasion when we were together."

"Have you now, I never forgot your kisses, your trembling and want of passion," he said.

"I lived for those close intimate moments, your crushing embrace. You respected me. You never defiled me, because you loved me. Oh Patrick if only we could...again...be young and fulfill all our desires," Olivia whispered, clinging to Patrick.

"Ah yes, moments of passion and ecstasy, yes my love, I wish we could, I would make love to you and we would have a dozen children." Patrick and Olivia laughed. "Yes, and they would have been handsome and beautiful." Olivia began to cry.

Patrick's heart ached with the same pain as Olivia's, they both loved children. However, those chapters of their life are in the past. Now as long as memory allows go back in time and reminisce. Dream of what never was.

"Olivia my Las, our life would not have been shattered into pieces if only you had received my letter. I was so infuriated at your brother I wanted to kill him. Thanks to Gillian I reneged on that intention, I surely would not have found you. I would have hung on a pear tree for a crime. Patrick stared into the glass of wine.

"After you went away my brother fell in love with a pretty peasant girl, she worked in the fields for us. Father discovered them on a haystack. Father beat him badly. My brother out of anger went away, like you. He had lost his love, and he paid a lifetime of sorrow, like us."

As they talked now and then, they sipped the wine. They felt warm and were in each other's arms. Sometimes she or he would remember something and talk about it.

"Did your brother return?" Patrick asked.

"No...Father died that year. We discovered that the girl died in labor with my brother's child," Olivia said. Olivia would say something of the present concerning some problem and ask how it could be resolved or something fixed. Baron Patrick listened, than told her that someone else will worry about how to fix it, that he pays for such repairs.

"Your father paid the price too. Many broken hearts and broken homes, anguish and sadness for all, how unfair," Patrick said. They sipped the wine and the hour neared midnight they sat in the west tower. All around them peaceful silence, the moon high and bright. Both became drowsy, their limbs heavy from the wine. Neither said they should go to bed. No one was looking for them. No one came to disturb them. They were all alone up in the tower and just the two in the world.

Lira awakened from sleep, sat up in bed and listened, someone was singing, seemed far, far away. She listened. Abruptly she jumped out of bed and tiptoed to the bedroom of her Master and Mistress. Lira peeked in, the moonlight beamed in bright enough to see every object in it. Lira tiptoed to the foot of the bed, no one slept in it. Her concern awakened fear in her; *where are they*? She had not seen them since dinner; *where are they?* Lira walked through the hall checked each room, some empty in others the children slept.

Lira turned to the stairs leading to the towers the door was wide open. She tiptoed to the top of the stairs. Clearly, she saw the bottle of wine on the small table and her master and mistress in each other's arms on the cushioned bench. She came closer, bent down to look at their faces they were asleep. She glanced again to the table, *where are the wine glasses*. Again she came closer to them, there, they seemed to hold the wine glasses still contained a bit of wine, now tipped to the side. Lira felt chills, she stood close to them and listened, the night silent, the world slept, she heard no breathing, she bent down close to their faces, if they were fast asleep, she would hear them breathing. She was unsure what to do, this was not like them, to be here since dinner no wonder she had not seen them. Without another minute, she ran down the stairs directly to butler Misha's room. She turned the knob, walked right in, tapped Misha on the shoulder, "Misha wake up, wake up, you must wake up!" Misha abruptly jumped up startled. "Girl what are you doing here!"

"Misha you must come with me to the tower, Master Baron and Lady Olivia something is wrong, hurry!" Misha threw on some clothes and together ran to the tower. Lira brought an oil lamp, the tower now aglow with light enabled Misha to inspect the couple on the bench.

"Lira look, they are holding the wine glasses." Misha left the glasses in their cold fingers.

"Do not drink that wine Lira, they are both dead. It must be left as it is for the Village Chief for inspection," Misha said.

"What are we to do now, how do we bring them down... how? We must wake Jonasen to help you!" Lira cried out.

"Do not fret Lira, it will be done! You do not fret. Now go and wake the others. What has happened here concerns everyone," Misha said.

Lira alerted the entire staff, they all went to the tower to see Lady Olivia and Master Patrick dead on the bench. Why, why did they die together! All stood speechless, having the same question on their mind. Jonasen came up and closely eyed the situation. Women wept and the others had that shocked stare.

"Well...it is dawning, he said looking at each ones face, I will ride and notify the proper authorities, this time it is real, both of them...in the meantime go to your daily duties. Do not say a word to the children and do not allow them to go to the tower. No one is to touch that wine, you hear?"

On the way back, Jonasen stopped at Kosta's home with the sad news.

Kosta and Kathryn rode up to the castle.

"Kathryn no one expected this tragedy. Baron Patrick recuperated quite well after the heart attack. He was fine and happy with Aunt Olivia."

What happened? Kosta asked..., why did Aunt Olivia die with him, perhaps a premeditated suicide?" Kathryn replied sadly.

"No, never, ever will I believe they had intentionally committed suicide, together? Why would they? Both loved each other and their life together much too much to die," Kosta almost shouted angrily.

"But listen, they were old and anticipated health decline. Either one refused to live alone again. Could it be so?" Kathryn asked.

"That boggles my mind, to be laughing one moment and the next to go up there and commit suicide, preposterous!" Now Kosta was angry.

At the castle, the staff sat around and wept. Kras and Jason teary eyed met their parents as they entered the kitchen. Kosta glared at Flora, "They know?"

"Yes, Lucinda Nell ran round the grounds weeping and screaming," Flora said and began to sob.

"Father they are gone, gone forever," Kras said and wrapped his arms around Kosta's waist. Jason fell into the arms of his mother.

"Mother I will miss them, I loved them, Mother," Jason cried.

"Yes my son, I will miss them too. But now we must pray for their souls, may they rest in peace," Kathryn kissed her son's tear streaked face.

"Where is Rosie, still...?"

The silence in the kitchen resounded with a bang of the door as it swung open and Lucinda Nell ran in, screaming, followed by Rosie.

"He is gone, gone, he is gone!"

"Gone? We know Nell, we know! Please compose yourself, please!" Greta grabbed Lucinda Nell by the shoulders and shook her hard.

"I found him up in the tower! He is dead!" Lucinda Nell shouted.

Jonasen stepped up to her swung her around and said slowly. "Why were you up there? Did you drink the wine? Ha!" Jonasen shook her shoulders.

"Nooo... I did not drink any wine, he did...I mean...Sir Chappaniac did."

Kosta hastily ran up two steps at a time to the tower followed by the rest of them to see another dead body. They stood with sullen expressions around the bench on which the body of Horacio Chappaniac lay in a fetal position. The glass from which he drank the wine lay broken on the floor.

They all held their breath. Suddenly someone said, "Poison!" Another said, "Butler Ridiller!" Someone whispered from far back. "Yes...his handy work, now I know."

All eyes turned to stare at the sad face of Lira. "You know? How can you be so sure it was?

"When I was hired by Butler Ridiller, he took me to the dining room and in the cabinet he showed me that bottle tied with a ribbon... a white ribbon. He told me when Master Baron and Aunt Olivia celebrate their anniversary, you take that bottle up to the tower, tell him to make it a memorable evening up there for them on their special occasion. Butler Ridiller hid the bottle in front of me, back of the cabinet; I knew where it was no one else," Lira said shivering.

The Village Chief declared Lira innocent of any wrongdoing. However, promised to make a thorough investigation, moreover since he has proof that it was poison proves also that the butler was the guilty one.

In the little Church of Hope, three open coffins, one woman between two men, stood in front of the dais, the three coffins encircled by a large flower display. Three reposed peacefully in eternal sleep. The little Church of Hope filled with villagers' inside and outside, those who were close, eyed the coffins, what they were thinking, no one knew.

Aunt Olivia's dress was the one she wore on that day she married Patrick. Her string of pearls, and the black pearl broach Baron Patrick gave her, her hair braided as on that day. She looked beautiful, her facial expression peaceful.

Baron Patrick also dressed in the suit, as on their wedding day, he looked handsome, though his expression seemed to show disappointment, as if to say, *why, why so soon, we still had life to live.* Horaccio Chapaniac's expression none other than pain, since that morning he drank the poisoned wine on an empty stomach.

When Minister Papa N'Poposh approached the podium to recite the eulogy, all eyes turned on him.

"The will to die supersedes the will to live," he began. "Many a time it is felt by natural instinct that the time has come, therefore, we, mortals succumb fearlessly, humbly into the arms of death to sleep forever. Everyone's book of life remains open, all actions and deeds inscribed there to the last day, the last hour, and the last minute is there. When the souls crossover to eternity; then; the books of life are closed. Those who depart before their time we could not explain or understand why. The sorrow befalls the living. I joined them in matrimonial ceremony, and Christmas would have been another anniversary. This man and this woman loved each other throughout their solitary lives, until they found each other here among us..., and reclaimed their love, short lived as it was. Today we shall give them up into the arms of mother earth, together. Ashes to ashes, this is the way of life's greatest unsolved mystery... yes unsolved. Ashes to ashes, may they rest in peace and celebrate eternity." The smoke from the incense urns, curled up permeated the air mystically.

Minister Papa N'Poposh concluded the eulogy. Mentioning little of their characters, he stressed their lasting love for each other, but mostly stressed their premature death. Too many of the individuals present felt each other's eyes wandering from one to the other, feeling that the minister insinuated more likely this to be a murder rather than a suicide. Which will remain, yes, a mystery unsolved, a stab of suspicion.

Three coffins, two wagons decorated with yellow flowers and black and white ribbons slowly moved from Church of Hope to the castle grounds, where two open graves waited, one for Horacio Chappaniac, the other for Baron Patrick and his wife Aunt Olivia. Three lives laid to rest, just a few yards from the oak tree. Their headstones face the west. So many people's lives touched by their good hearts, now that they are gone will not be the same.

As the Komarod family stood over the graves, as a last good-by everyone threw flowers into the coffins. They were last to leave the gravesite. Rosie held in her hand three yellow flowers, out of nowhere, two yellow and one white butterfly landed on her yellow flowers, Rosie cried out, "*oh look*" and they saw. These butterflies fluttered barely touching the petals of each flower the children held, everyone held their breath. These butterflies hovered low for a few seconds over the graves then flew up and away. No one spoke, but looked at each other knowingly. The staff and those who were still there saw, and they too understood what these butterflies represented.

"Marla, which one you think was Aunt Olivia, the yellow or white," Rosie whispered. Marla was about to reply, Kras cut in, "the two yellow were Grandfather Patrick and the other Grandpa Horacio."

"Oh...how do you know which yellow butterfly was Grandfather Partrick?" Jasemin asked Kras. All of them looked at Kras for an explanation.

"Well...because Grandpa Horacio always lags behind, ah, when he was alive," Mathew cut in, everyone heads turned to ogle at him.

"I guess you would know... Mathew he sat on your flower the longest, he liked you from day one," Kosta said.

In the castle, gloom hung like a heavy rain cloud; such a sudden demise of these lovable people; depressed everyone. This day there were no echoes of voices or laughter, only silence. This will take time to adjust. Kosta called a meeting to assure the employees they still had responsibilities here, and all will stay on. He will come back tomorrow. Lira handed Kosta a fabric wrapped roll.

"Master Baron instructed to give you this, if anything happened to him." Kosta shoved it under his shirt. If the children see, they will want to know what it was. At home, he went to the pantry, placed the package on the top shelf, and threw a sack over it. Walked out the back door straight to the stable; preoccupied with grief stood in the doorway, what was he looking for or why he came, he could not figure out so he turned back home; at the table sat down, the children did not question but sat glumly. Rosie began to sob. After a minute, she asked, "Father, where did they go?"

"Who?" Jason asked Rosie. Rosie eyed Jason with a frown.

"What, you do not know who I am talking about?" Rosie said irritably.

Mathew interrupted, "Now Rosie and Jason stop. Father will better explain, later."

And so the time slipped by, and Kosta forgot about the fabric wrapped roll, having dual responsibilities now to do many chores at home and at the castle, and always listening to his children's questions and repeating his adventurous life away from home so long ago. The anguish and disappointment of Baron Patrick and Aunt Olivias passing always lingered, hard to forget, hard to adjust. In their mind and body, a certain turmoil and unrest gripped everyone, silence and peace prevailed only when everyone was asleep.

Sixty-Six: The Will

Kosta while in bed unable to sleep recalled that New Years Eve about midnight when his brother unannounced came calling. *Whatever made him decide to come; and so late; one reason only;* Kosta surmised, *someone had to have told him what went on, besides snooping at night trying to see with his own eyes the truth; that he is alive and well; and had to see the elegant carriage. Baron Patrick and Aunt Olivia were gracious hosts, fed them well. Though his health seemed fair, tired easily which I knew would cause a relapse, I prayed for him. We stayed up way past everyone's bedtime. Thomas's eyes wandered all over the place; he drank wine like a thirsty dragon; disregarding where he was and who he was. I noticed Baron Patricks glances while conversing with guests. I was embarrassed up to my gills. My brother made himself at home. All this time when I returned and am home he did not come, afraid I gather of a confrontation or accusation. He came that night. He could not stand it any longer. I* wonder *who informed him, I wonder. Cybilia seemed uneasy. She stayed near Kathryn, Aunt Olivia and Rabinna. The boys sat in a group and Sabrina socialized with the girls, they looked happy. I know one thing he will be fuming about the funeral and I wonder if he knew they were married. At both times I did not notify or invite them, but that was not my place to invite them to the wedding and as I recall now, Aunt Olivia had not mentioned him. She never spoke his name ever since I returned. Fur will fly, I know. The question is now, what happens who is the heir or heirs and where to find them.* Kosta's thoughts and visualizations upset him further and many nights he had not slept at all. His thoughts he did not divulge to Kathryn.

Lord Thomas learned of the sudden deaths of Baron Patrick, Aunt Olivia and supposedly the old man Kosta rescued. He felt insulted. After all, she too was his Aunt. In his private room paced, clenched fists and teeth grinding, boiling from anger. Why were they, not informed to attend the funeral to pay his last respect. After all, on that New Year's Eve he felt he belonged as one family. He was under the impression all was well now, why he also had discussed real estate with Baron Patrick, of Cybilias uncle and the villa, down in southern region. Baron Patrick listened as he described to a tee how charming Uncle Lorenzo's wife Lady...for a moment he forgot her name and had to think, "Ah yes her name, a very unusual name, AlaKara, yes very beautiful woman." Then he talked about the wine and taking vacations to warmer climates...of all things.

Had Kosta his brother intentionally failed to notify him and his family of the tragic deaths? Surely, he attended the funeral with his family! Lord Thomas had missed the privilege of meeting Baron Patrick personally throughout the years, and had never visited the castle. Hearing quite a bit from his spies of what went on around that area, surprised that Kosta had become Baron's friend, how had that come about and that Aunt Olivia became the Baroness, some sort of a love story evolved from their visits, at their age? He heard of the kidnapping and rescue of the Baron, and capture of the butler. This turned out to be a tangled web, a comical story, until now.

He wondered, what happens with that monstrosity of that castle; will it stand abandoned and go to ruin. Time will tell. By the time all those rich aristocrats hear about the owners passing, it will sit abandoned decreasing in value, a quick thought crossed his mind...*well why not...after all he was, the Lord Thomas and he was rich, rich, rich! He felt entitled to own such a prestigious piece of real estate...and I will be looking down at that shack where I was born in which my brother lives with his brood of kids...ha! Why not*! His imagination and curiosity began to run wild.

One afternoon unexpectedly two women and two men appeared at the door of the castle. Jonasen happened to be working in the courtyard he opened the door for them. "We are here for a visit with Master Baron. Is he in?" a blond younger woman asked giving him a downgrading look.

"Have you not heard seven months ago Master Baron Patrick and his wife Olivia had passed away?" Jonasen said.

"Oh, how unfortunate, we come at a time of mourning," the matronly woman said dabbing at her eyes.

"Oh, please forgive us. We truly have not heard," Jonasen assumed the matronly woman's husband said.

"We have traveled many days this long journey has been exhausting, may we impose to rest a while," the elegant Gentleman spoke up. The other woman turned to the young blond saying in a low voice, "I had not heard he was married, did you?" the blond woman shook her head, "No, how could we...it has been years since we have visited, you know that very well." Flora the cook came up and heard their conversation. Jonasen invited the unexpected visitors into the foyer gave a quick glance to Flora and politely asked the four individuals to wait. Flora briskly walked up to Kosta and told him people are in the foyer wanting to see the Baron. Kosta that day was repairing a loose hinge on the back door. Jonasen carried a brief conversation with the four individuals. Kosta dropped his tools and came to greet them. After introduction and trivial conversation Kosta said, "Of course you are welcome to stay, have dinner and retire for the night." One of the men said, "Thank you kind Sir, in the morning we shall leave." At dinner things happened, each time, these guests sipped wine and set their glasses down mysteriously they tipped over spilling wine. The meat slid of the forks the moment it touched their lips. Ladies earlobes tickled slightly, attributing such mishaps to tiny flies or mosquitoes. After dinner, these guests retired for the night, but their sleep disturbed by not only whispers, but also both women's feet and bellies tickled under the sheets. There were more than one ghost present, and the ghosts' laughter echoed frightening these visitors.

Kosta heard the commotion stood in the doorway of the bedroom. The two women seeing him screeched and ran downstairs. The two men stopped for a moment and apologized for the disturbance, then ran down the stairs. These guests fled for their lives into the dark of night not waiting for morning,

"Good Lord this castle is haunted and we are not welcomed here, we must leave." Kosta saw a man standing in the dark hall downstairs, he descended slowly to them, "Who is out there with them?"

"Jonasen is Sir Kosta," Misha Kronin said. Standing in the doorway, the three men watched as the carriage with the guests drove away down the hill. The heavy gate closed with a bang behind them, the tree men laughed as they went back inside. Kosta said aloud, "Now, you know that was not nice, frightening your visitors like that."

"Do you really think it was them? I mean Master Patrick and Aunt Olivia, of course Horacio too?" Misha asked.

"Oh yes, I am sure they were here, but do not be afraid, us they will not disturb, have they?" They all replied in unison, "NO."

"Well then we must go to sleep, good night." Kosta turned on his heel, walked slowly up to the bedroom and closed the door. The three gravestones engraved, lay waiting at the head of each grave by Kosta and Misha Kronin must drop them in the holes already dug early next morning.

In the castle, the only occupants were the servants. What is to happen now, this was a sad situation. Their fate fell on Kosta. The servants wished to stay on and work as usual. Their life was and is good here, comfortable, but for how long? Hoping someone will purchase this castle with everything and everyone in it.

Since the deaths of his Aunt Olivia, Baron Patrick, and Horacio Chappaniac, Kosta completely forgot to open the roll wrapped in cloth from Lira. One late evening while in bed, remembered where he stashed it. He slowly slid out of bed barefoot walked to the pantry retrieved it off the shelf. He thought it to be paper wrapped in a blue silk cloth, tied with a white thin ribbon. He sat down at the table, turned up the lamp, and pulled the ribbon to unroll the silk cloth. *So these are papers*, he thought. Top sheet of paper folded four corners on center, a seal held them together. Kosta gently unfolded it. His eyes grew big; keys and a gold piece were inside the folded paper. *What is this, legal papers?* He sat to examine them by the lamp light. He turned several sheets, and came upon a letter written to him.

My dear children, Kathryn and Kosta:

When you read this letter, I shall be forever gone.

Without absolute hesitation or slight uncertainty, my decision is final to whom I convey my possessions. In gratitude and as a reward. As to my family, all are nonexistent. I have been fortunate; blessed with good health; and reached a ripe age. However, my younger years spent in pleasures and drama; later years I led a solitary life. Until I settled here, through your unfortunate circumstances and dire need to survive, I found my lost love, Aunt Olivia, your Aunt. You know the rest of the story my friend. I, blessed with a fortune, comfort of material things, mind you very beautiful things, but the most beautiful among my treasures is my Olivia. Those items were pleasant to look at, but Olivia outshines them all. None of these items could give me love but Olivia. She filled my heart with love for which I longed for all my life. Those who were close or of importance, have been disappointingly short on friendship. Most proved to be fickle.

All legalities are in order and all rights reserved. Objections, if any heirs crawl out of the woodwork, legally have no rights at all to my castle and estate and to my one and final decision. My accumulation of expensive paraphernalia as beautiful as they are, stand cold and still. Today I do not care to look at them. Today they are meaningless. My remaining precious time I devote to my Olivia, to make her happy. My time is short and I hear my eternal home calling. I bequeath all I own to my wife, Olivia, to do with as she wishes, keep it all as a continuance of my memory. Therefore, my wife Olivia has legal rights to reside at the castle, which is a home for her now until she joins me. You are always honest and respectful and offer to everyone a helping hand.

I trust you will not be offended and will not reject what I am about to disclose to you. Do not be perplexed! This is our, Olivia's and mine decision and, it is final. From the day of my beloved wives passing, you Kosta Komarod and Kathryn Komarod and your children are as deserving sole heirs, none others. Reside in comfort as we have. Your life here will give more meaning to you and yours. I truly believe destiny led me to settle here in this region. Never had I imagined that I would ever find the love of my life. Olivia lived here. Life is such a mystery, I believe in life's destiny.

The recording of the legal title papers and the seal affixed in this township of Riverside Village in your names and your children's, therefore, as rightful heirs this testament of will not be challenged by anyone any time.

You hold a gold piece, with it you have a mystery to solve within the perimeter of this castle you shall have a bit of difficulty finding it. I assure you. Observe closely it is there. Whenever you decide to search for it, send the servants on a holiday. Kathryn and the children must be away as well. Children's tendencies are to divulge secrets thoughtlessly. They are only children. Your sons are special. Few will follow your footsteps, whichever road they choose will be successful in life. Your girls are angels. I loved them as my own. You were to me, a brother. I truly appreciated your friendship.

Kathryn grieved for you, but her courage and faith were as strong as her heart. When I fell ill, she saved my life. I regard Kathryn as my sister. "Tiny Pearl" my sister as I called her was eleven years old when I walked out of my home. "Tiny Pearl" how ironic. I returned once, I stood on the threshold of my birth home after many years... and visited my parent's graves, paid my respect and my last farewell. I learned that my sister had married and moved away. Separated by many years, I never could locate her. I never knew my one and only sister. Earl Rupert Grubshin is my brother, however fear not of him; where he resides there is no door for him to the outside world. May the Good Lord bless all of you, as He has blessed me by returning to me what I needed most, my lovely Olivia, we are happy though time grows short.

Forever yours
Baron Patrick Grubshin
Baroness Olivia Caraveadous, Grubshin

Kosta's hands shook. *What in the world, why did he give me this property of all people, why me? What have I done to deserve such a gift, it is a gift. I cannot accept this, I will have to give it away or sell.* Kosta's head reeled in surprise and shock, *all this left to us, and Aunt Olivia is gone. The castle is ours! With everything in it...is ours...oh...my...God...and the gold!*

Gold...gold, Kosta whispered. His head in his hands he sat until he felt his frozen feet hurting. Bewildered, he forgot to put away the deed, keys, and the gold coin. In his head what he read resounded. He left the table, slipped into bed and tried to asleep.

The room still in darkness but for the lamp dimly lit, hushed chatter woke him. He listened intently, than slipped out of bed, stood in the doorway, his children leaning over the table Kathryn talking. He realized what he had done last night. In a few strides stood behind them.

"What is going on? Why is everyone up so early, it is still dark! Kathryn I see you found the papers, Mathew did you read them?" He spoke sternly, a bit perturbed.

"No my dear, I just found these papers, and I woke Mathew, the girls heard us talking and they gathered here, we tried to be quiet. Mathew just glanced at it and told me it is a letter from Baron Patrick," she answered.

"I am sorry Father I... we should have waited for you till morning," Mathew apologized, and handed the papers to Kosta.

"Kathryn, please make us some tea... ah, no make a big pot of strong coffee. I surely need it and so will you, all of you."

"All of us, even I can have coffee?" Rosie said surprised.

"Yes, even you Rosie, but only this morning, understood?" Kosta said to them.

"Yes, we understand Father!" they answered in unison.

Mathew stoked the stove. Tessana set nine cups, sugar and milk on the table. Waited in the kitchen for the coffee to boil, Kathryn poured the hot brew into a porcelain coffee pot. Tessana carried the pot to the table and filled the cups. The children loved the aroma of coffee and eagerly eyed the brew. Kathryn sat wondering what was in the letter.

Her years spent on raising seven children and tackled daily chores. She felt deprived of education just like Kosta. Growing up she had attended school for a while until her father died beneath a fallen tree. She and Rabinna with mother worked hard to survive. Rabinna married Michael. Mothers crippling rheumatoid arthritis disabled her completely. All work fell on Kathryn's shoulders. She always wanted to read books. Kosta with Aunt Olivia's help and a tutor studied for months, learned quite well to read and write. When Kathryn confessed one day about not being able to read fluently or write, he walked with her along the creek and tutored her, after many months she no longer felt embarrassed, especially in front of her children. Their children received schooling and she was proud of them. They will never be embarrassed, or feel ignorant no matter where they are in this wide world.

The aroma of coffee permeated the whole room. They inhaled and sipped the steaming sweet creamy liquid slowly. Children's first cup of coffee and they loved it.

"What I am about to tell you, you will be shocked; surprised; and bewildered; stay quiet and listen; do not interrupt. Sip your coffee; no slurping please. On second thought mother will have the honor to read the first half of the letter; and then Mathew. But Mathew, do not read the last paragraph." Kosta folded the paper under and handed it to Mathew. Tessana leaned over mother's shoulder and followed her reading.

What the whole family heard was unbelievable, they sat wide-eyed with mouths open. Kosta folded again the letter and gave it to Mathew, Kosta nodded.

"Kras please read the last paragraph." That last paragraph Baron wrote about his family.

Kathryn sobbed and the girls crowded around her. The boys padded father's shoulder. None dared to speak for or against being the heirs. Reality had not registered. Yet sparks of hope twinkled; children's eyes darted at each other. They smiled. Kathryn observed Kosta trying to read his face, not a twitch of a smile. Kosta sat and observed them one by one. Kosta thought, *such luxury and wealth. Then who would dismiss the generosity of fate, reward for his family's suffering, their strong faith.*

Rightfully I should give thanks for such a gift, not for myself, but for Kathryn and our children, yes we will keep it, but not move into the castle yet. No one dared to speak. He noticed children's apprehensive looks and tiny smiles. Each one had shown a different expression. Father, after all had the final word of decision.

"Well my dear family, what should we do now, any suggestions?" he asked suddenly grinning. Rosie was always the first one to state her opinion; she looked at the others.

"Father," she said, "I think we should go now so we have time to decorate for Christmas." Kathryn laughed and Kosta laughed, all sat laughing.

"Could we Father?" Marla asked loud enough to cease laughter.

"Father, could I please have a bedroom to myself?" Jasemine pleaded. Kosta looked at them and said smiling, "If we do move, each one will have their own bedroom."

The children giggled shouting to each other. Kosta raised his arms and ordered a hush.

"Now listen here, it is easy for you to say let us move in, not so fast, what about all the work here, who is going to care for this farm?"

Kathryn spoke quietly, as she raised her hand to quiet the children.

"Now children, listen to me, I think I have a solution to our problem." The children paid attention as they plopped onto chairs.

"The move must be postponed until your Father and I have time to discuss this situation, then we shall tell you of the right thing to do," Kathryn spoke firmly, and she noticed that all of them fell into a slump. This is something Kosta never expected, or dreamed of in his lifetime, this was not real, he must be hallucinating but the papers were proof that this change in their lives was real. Could he and Kathryn adjust to a life in a huge castle?

Sixty-Seven: The Ravens

The Ravens by natural instinct flew in and congregated on a tree for their final meeting before winter. They were to discuss the outcome of the assignments. Mamut their leader spoke.

"Good evening my brothers."

"Good evening our leader Mamut!" they replied in unison.

"First on my agenda, I have an announcement. At the last meeting, I stood before the Elders Olymar, Smeto and Gleryk. After a long discussion, the Elders considered and reached the verdict, judgment and justice, the degree of pain to administer. Unfortunately, for the accused we the Thirteen Ravens are the executioners. Consider this is to be the worst moment of our assignment. As previously, psychological preparation is a must."

They perched on the same oak tree. The accused not mentioned at length this time.

Their leader Mamut continued, "I need every one's opinion on the performance of the Brother of Light, as we have named him."

Benokai, "He fulfilled the Madga solution precisely."

Abimust, "His honesty shone."

Kruegg, "I admire his bravery."

Kotur, "All requirements were complete."

Denos, "He believed."

"And his faith never wavered. Ah...at one point he wavered a smidge but was forgiven," Erisot reminded the brothers.

Fijuron, "I am amazed, he remembered it all."

Gromu, "He persistently forged onward. We calmed his fear, for a little while."

Hatuii, "His goodness was recognized by all."

Insemir, "He deserved all he received, plus."

Kerrie, "His performance was outstanding."

Lornven, "He is patient, but only to a point. Beware of his charge."

Leader Mamut interjected, "Yes he deserved it all, plus in his future lies much more for him."

"Ah yes, he was faithful. Dear leader are you ready to tell us about the other brother?" Kotur asked.

"No, not tonight, time is short, continue Kruegg we need your comment," answered Mamut.

"My brothers, since I first joined your brotherhood, I have not ever observed such devotion and compassion in anyone as this chosen one. He was justly rewarded and his future should be happy and tranquil," Kruegg concluded.

In unison they shouted, "bravo, bravo!"

Lornven, "His love holds true, he persevered."

Mamut gave them a brief input of what the near future holds in the lives of these two individuals of such dissimilarities in character.

"September will show the wavering of wills and strength, victory and defeat and final justice. The unfortunate demise of the man and the woman, as love joined them in life, their love is eternal, now. It grieves my heart as well as yours. Their friend has been relieved of his constant pain.

"True colors of the Brother of Darkness will surface. The light will shine only for the chosen one...this will be revealed...one day... but not today. Remember the spider weaves his web with perfection and, the entrapment is imminent for the unwary. The spider seldom suspects of being a victim of his own perfected trap," Mamut concluded.

After a short silence and a few loud sighs, what they heard they understood. Then the Thirteen Raven Brothers, with farewells, flew in different directions.

Sixty-Eight: Tarnished Pride

The villagers mourned the passing of Baron Patrick and Aunt Olivia.

Horacio Chappaniac was a newcomer, a stranger, but his name also spoken now and then. How they died and their true love story intrigued people. The village constable had not forgotten their case. Contemplating a resolve, Thomas needed more information from the staff. One day unexpectedly stopped in for questioning everyone, he was welcomed and catered to, no visible signs of guilt in any of them. They answered all his questions, some with a flood of tears, and truth.

Far where the wealthy Lord Thomas resided, having information on all the good news, gossip, and bad news, curiosity was his daily companion, and the wine second. Lord Thomas mulled the news, Baron's and Olivia's funeral most disturbing and insulting. Kosta failed to notify him of their passing. Curious to know who is and where are the heirs to Barons wealth. He also heard that his brother Kosta "was in charge," of funeral arrangements. *My brother...was that close to be Baron's companion? I wonder. I have not heard of such, not at all.* He needed more information and he needed a few good men to check things out for him. He should notify his wealthy friends. Rather quickly rejecting that idea, *no, why should he.* The owner of the castle has died. Surely, the property will sell, but at what price, hmm...As soon as all the information is at hand, he positively will inquire. That is exactly what he will do.

The information seems slow coming, his nerves twanged like violin strings. Unaware of what cause, still had to visit the 4Hoofs Inn. When he entered the 4Hoofs Inn, odor of spirits and smoke hung in the air as always. At the usual table, most of his pals were there, plus new faces.

"Well you got lonesome for us, did you not, Thomas?" Burly Jon asked.

"Yes...of course. I see knew faces, where are the others?"

"Oh, our three pals kissed the dirt, sudden, you know," Karl commented.

"What killed them so quickly?"

The barmaid stepped up leaned to his ear and whispered.

"Ale had done them in, the usual for you sir?" Glinis asked.

"No... I need something else tonight, let me choose," Lord Thomas followed Glinis to the bar. He reached over the bar for her arm and whispered.

"I promise to pay you generously if you collect what I need." The barmaid nodded. Lord Thomas returned to his chair. In a few minutes, Glinis set before him a large glass of gold liquid, he took a sip, tipped her a gold piece.

His pals were close-mouthed at first, and then decided to have fun, rile him up as they used to when they were teens, they remembered how he cheated and schemed, and none forgot his eerie laugh. That night at the 4Hoofs Inn, his pals bombarded him with farfetched stories, about the castle and the ghosts.

"Have you heard..., an attempt was made to murder the Baron? Gorink said.

"They arrested the butler," Burly Jon cut in. They thought Lord Thomas believed it all from his facial expression.

"I really heard all that, but besides that who has new gossip."

"But the plot was foiled by a friend of Baron's." Burly Jon grinned.

"Who was this friend?" Thomas asked.

"That we do not know we just heard the story." Gorink a newcomer cocked his head and grinned, their eyes on him.

"Thomas you are acting as if you have not heard any of this, why the whole countryside is talking. Your head must have been stuck in a wine barrel," Trayer said chuckling. After several hours of repetitive stories with an added "tis a fact*!*" and growing out of proportion, each scenario embellished a bit just to play on his nerves. His old pals knew how far Lord Thomas would allow such teasing before blowing his temper. Lord Thomas played along with their game. He observed every one of them and deduced none could he trust, they have changed; rather strong spirits had changed them. They are no longer the intelligent ambitious pals he used to look up to and admire. Their senses have drowned in the wine. The whole lot of them gave him a disgusting feeling.

That night his pals admitted they were teasing him. Lord Thomas was seething but showed little of his anger.

"I knew all along, you fellows had fun at my expense but now the joke's on you," Lord Thomas said. His pals had too much to drink by now, not fully understanding what he said laughed in his face; now his temper flared; he was no fool, he knew they were testing and laughing at him. The frequent visitors roared right along with his pals. This was just too much to bear. His fist pounded the table, swore at them with foul language, his voice boomed and their laughter stopped. Men at the other tables resumed drinking and conversed in a civilized manner.

At his table, his pals had their heads down and eyes stared at the glass or mug not speaking. Lord Thomas felt ignored, repugnance washed over him, but he knew he would have the last laugh. As he stood to leave, at the door, turned and laughed, loud, then louder. The place fell silent. All eyes on him, he slammed the door behind him. The six fellows watched him walk out with twisted grins on their flushed faces from overindulgence of wine. They stared at the door, perhaps they wondered, *will he come back in*, it has been a long time since they heard his eerie laugh, and their skin crawled.

"Friends...bah...these drunken fools are not friends of mine, losers, that they are, no ambition! No drive in those wine-soaked guts! I wasted my money and time, they will regret this, they will pay...they will pay sooner or later I will see to that."

Planning additional wealth to what he had, as if he did not have enough. One thing he was not aware of although in conversation one of the new man mentioned that someone has rights to the castle already but no names mentioned.

Kosta was the heir to the Barons estate. When this truth reaches Lord Thomas, it will hit him like a brick, he will definitely go insane.

Lord Thomas never went back to the 4Hoofs Inn, his contempt for his pals made his mouth sour, and so was his disposition, sour, anxiety drove him as in the past, unable to sleep and his days were riotous, yelling and banging this or that, even broke some valuable things that were special and memorable to Cybilia.

Mark and Shara were deeply concerned for the safety of their mother as well as themselves. They had been discussing of leaving for a long trip, where to... they were not sure, of one thing they were sure though, neither of them want to stay in this house with a raging and ranting father most of the time, and to them the question was...why!

"All the riches cannot give a true piece of mind. Riches become an obsession for amassing more, as if it was possible to bury it all in the grave to enjoy," Mark said one day to Shara.

"Yes, that is very true, but earthly comfort is no comparison to poverty, well, you know my choice. So at least while you are alive, be thankful and enjoy it, but I have learned, sharing gives me a feeling of satisfaction as I never had before. Do you feel the same?" she said.

"Yes, you are right, my compliment to you Shara, you have outgrown silliness and acquired intelligence. Now you are a beautiful young lady, bravo," Mark said to her grinning.

One evening, Lord Thomas alone leisurely sprawled in his favorite chair, one leg hung over the armrest and the other stretched out in front of him, sipped his favorite wine, nothing in particular on his mind, a blank state this evening. Something occurred to him, which made his hair bristle.

Relaxed completely, felt a touch, a gentle massage of his temples. Ah, felt good. His eyes closed enjoyed the sensation. Then this sensation slipped to his neck, down gently fondling his chest. Slowly moved to his belly, even though he was quite drunk, still did not reach the point of stupor, he felt pressure on his belly-button and then the sudden pain like a vise gripped and held, cut off his breathing for a few seconds, his body recoiled backwards. Everything began to spin. He sprang out of his chair when the pain was gone. Sobering instantly, eyes darting around the parlor, briskly walked to check behind drapes and every piece of furniture, but he was alone.

Heart racing, the glass in his hand cracked spilling the wine; he winced at the pain. He headed for the bedroom, when he opened the door the lamp was lit, he thought nothing of it, however, he noticed a chill in the bedroom, it should not be this chilly; he recalled down in the parlor it was chilly, it had followed him. Quickly he dressed into his nightclothes and slipped into bed pulling the covers up to his chin, blood seeped from the palm, he did not care, he wanted to fall asleep immediately, he listened for noises, eyes closed tightly, afraid to see someone, something, but surely, it would not be a living breathing human.

The following morning he recalled the incident of the night before, strange thing was as he thought; *"such a gentle touch! Perhaps Cybilia was playing tricks, to frighten me, pretending to be a ghost, but that is absurd. Impossible, because I jumped up too quickly and, there was no place for her to hide! That pain...oh what a terrible pain...how could a ghost have such power to inflict pain on a human flesh."* To mention of such an incident to anyone he had no intention. To be taken for an old fool or plainly imagining.

However, that evening in bed he heard a noise, clutched the covers, heart pounding, waited, no one came and noises stopped. He felt relieved and calm. He studied every object in view waiting for sleep. The oil lamp began to flicker, and suddenly winked out. Darkness engulfed the bedroom. Lord Thomas blinked into the darkness afraid to close his eyes, but all was quiet, he fell asleep not knowing when.

The next morning he awoke to bright sunlight. The drapes tied back and the window wide open for fresh air. He threw back the covers and leisurely stretched. Walked up to the open window, peered out, seeing no one around the grounds, wondered if it was noon, the sun was high.

"Well...at least I slept soundly. Good," he muttered. Then he recalled the incident and shivered. "Ah, but that was yesterday or was it the night before, that does not matter. This is a new day. I will not dwell on it, I have work to do I must get busy," he spoke louder. He turned to reach for his clothes, and suddenly something caught his eye.

The mirror, the mirror, something smeared on it, something opaque. At first, he could not make out what it was. He stared, hands trembled, he dropped whatever he was holding and backed-up to his bed and fell on it, as he stared at the mirror he distinctly recognized the letter "*M*" as if an invisible finger dragged across the mirror and below the letter "*M*" a noose. Lord Thomas lay paralyzed from fear.

"So... someone is in...ah... was in my room last night, oh God what am I to do now!" he whispered but only once. Fear clamped his throat like a vice. Unable to move, he broke out in cold sweat, and suddenly his mind was blank.

The servant knocked several times on the bedroom door, cautiously entered. Seeing her master lay in an awkward position with a dead expression. Quickly she ran shrieking to find Lady Cybilia.

All the servants came running towards the scream. The servant blurted out to them, "The MASTER is dead." Some hoped he really was dead; some peered over shoulders feared blame for his death for whatever reason. Cybilia entered the bedroom and smiled; the sight of her motionless dictator of a husband lay rigid on the bed. To her he looked comical, amusing and pitiful; "*Well at last something occurred to scare the hell out of him*," she thought. To help him come to his senses, she slapped him hard, which broke the spell; quickly he sat up, looked around, the room was full of servants at his bedside, staring. His demeanor changed into his usual hellish self, he threw them out of his room.

"Have you noticed the mirror?" he said harshly to Cybilia.

Cybilia replied, "No, what?" Lord Thomas pointed at it, Cybilia glanced at the smeared mirror, burst into laughter and walked out, her laughter echoed down the hall.

Lord Thomas felt embarrassed to be seen in his nightclothes, especially the servants! That was unforgivable. He must fire the servant who made such a commotion. Anger built up in him, quickly dressed and thought what he should say to Cybilia. *why...why did she slap me...still feel the burn on my cheek...how dare she...she was laughing...never mind her...I will deal with her later, I must find the maid.* He walked briskly down to the dining room. Cybilia and the children already seated having aromatic tea. They did not wait for him, Mark gave him a quick glance and Shara stared at him, Cybilia's eyes followed him, he caught a faint smile, which disappeared when he glared at her without a comment. After a long silence, he cleared his throat.

"Someone was in my room last night and marked the mirror, Cybilia you noticed. Who is playing such pranks on me? Whoever it is...I shall eventually find out; they will pay dearly for pretending to be a ghost!" His voice wavered, as never before. All three stared at him.

"Sabrina, (when angry Lord Thomas called her Sabrina) Mark, Cybilia what do you know of this?" he asked not waiting for a response from them.

"Father I know nothing of the sort, I went to sleep early last night, mother tucked me in. I must admit it was rather a strange night, I felt odd. Warm and cool air moved across my room. It was scary..." Shara trailed off.

"What Shara is saying is true," Cybilia second that.

Mark said nothing. Then he hedged his father with questions about that night's drinking.

"I was not completely drunk. I was just to the point of feeling good. Mark, do not ever question my behavior, it is not your place, do you understand?" Lord Thomas snapped.

Lord Thomas sat down hard on the chair. Cybilia poured a cup of tea for him. He sipped it. Suddenly that evening stood before his eyes oh...the hand oh... his face took on a very strange spacey stare. The three of them noticed and wondered what is happening to him, but said nothing.

"Ah...Father when are we going to visit Uncle Kosta and our cousins?" Sabrina asked. Lord Thomas heard her question, and now he had to answer soberly.

"I believe on Sunday, if the weather permits." He had a questioning look and eyed each one.

"Yes, we have been waiting and we are ready," they said.

The uneasy feeling lingered all day. This angered him, unable to shake it. He threw a cape over his shoulders and went out to the old apple tree at the far end of the orchard. From under his favorite bench, retrieved a bottle and uncorked it, took a long draw... "Ah... warming, hmm so good..." he said aloud. He sat alone, compiling plans; castle, wealth, and skipped back to the castle, what is within the castle; his mind whirling, thinking, that he could *own* a castle. His brother, well, his brother cannot do a damn about it. *First harvest gathering soon; we still have few weeks before autumn marches in with rain, and sleet, God, another winter.* He thought.

The castle stood empty but for the servants waiting for a new master. A few young girls moved on, a haunted castle is too boring. However, the faithful ones remained. One day Kosta's family rode up the hill in the wagon. The children were excited, they expected to settle in and decorate for the holidays. They ran to the back door, calling Simena's name, she clapped her hands seeing them.

"Good day Simena!" they exclaimed. The dog ran into the kitchen and Rosie carried the cat in her arms.

"Master Kosta and family are planning to spend the night here?" Simena asked them when Kosta followed the children.

"Yes we are. But why did you call me master?" Kosta asked. The cook just smiled, served a big platter of their favorite cakes. Thereafter, the castle resounded with cheerful chatter.

Sixty-Nine: The Visit

On a Sunday morning at last, the Thomas Komarod family was on their way to visit their uncle Kosta and cousins after many years had passed. Well before noon, the elegant carriage turned onto the road leading to the little house in which he was born and without hesitation ordered the coachman to pull up close to the front door. Lord Thomas told Mark to go and announce their arrival. Cybilia and Shara dressed in their finest Sunday apparel sat in the carriage. Mark gladly walked up to the front door and knocked. A young man cracked the door open.

"Good morning Mathew! I am your cousin Mark, Mathew we are here for a visit," Mark said.

"Ah...I am not Mathew...I am a caretaker. The Komarods are up at the castle!"

Lord Thomas hearing that jumped out of the carriage and in a few strides faced the young man.

"And what are they doing there?" Lord Thomas rudely questioned.

"Why sir, they are working there," the young man replied smiling.

"What did you say?" Lord Thomas boomed.

"Yes sir, Kosta Komarod and his family are there, Kosta...is Master ah... the... castle, did you not know this?" the young man questioned Lord Thomas.

"Who are you, and blasted, what are you doing in this house, Kosta's house!" Lord Thomas yelled.

"Who are you to the Komarods sir?" politely the young man asked.

"Who I am is no concern of yours! When are they returning, tell me! Be quick!" Lord Thomas retorted with indignation.

"They will come back perhaps tomorrow, who should I say came to visit?" the young man asked cleverly.

Lord Thomas seething, through his teeth said, "Tell him, that his brother, Lord Thomas came to see him."

The young man stepped back into the house and closed the front door.

Cybilia turned her head to hide a smile when she heard the news, "*what a twist of fate*," she thought. If her husband would see her smile, he would be verbally abusive or even strike her, when the realization hits him that a change transpired in Kosta's life, he will go mad.

Mark turned on his heel went back to the house and knocked on the door again, when the young man stood in the doorway, Mark asked, Are they heirs of the castle? Also I need directions to the castle."

Simple enough were the directions and a nod of the head confirmed to Mark who the heirs were. Mark settled back into the carriage, and whispered.

"Shara, ask father to go up to the castle and visit Uncle Kosta today, after all he does favor you."

Shara glared at him but shook her head and said, "Father it would be a waste of time to go back home, we have come this far. To miss a visit with our cousins would be foolish. We must go up to the castle, besides we are hungry and tired, I am sure Uncle Kosta will serve us lunch. The castle is up on the hill. Look!" Shara pointed up.

"Young lady you are disrespectful, speaking out against my authority, I will decide if we see them today or not. Besides I did not say a word to that effect." Lord Thomas said gruffly.

"I feel sad Mother. I truly hoped to meet them." Shara rested her head on mother's shoulder. At first Lord Thomas absolutely refused, but then, shouted to the coachman. "Go up to the castle!"

"Well, Father kept postponing much too long, it is his fault; always had excuses. Soon we will be greeted by an Uncle who owns a castle, I cannot wait!" Mark whispered to his mother.

"What a twist of events," Cybilia whispered back.

Lord Thomas suddenly feeling anxious could not wait to walk into that castle. His mouth twisted, possessive thoughts surged in his head. All the way up no one spoke, avoiding the subject of the new heirs.

As the carriage rolled up the hill, Lord Thomas thought; "*today, will be my chance to ask Kosta about his fortune. How his eyesight returned. Yes, that is a good idea.*" Now he will see with his own eyes. He called to his coachman to snap the whip and get those nags moving.

At last, they reached the top; Lord Thomas stepped out of the carriage and took in the breathtaking view. Excitement surged through him. He reached for the knocker in the shape of a wolf's head on the huge front door. He felt odd, nevertheless, he stood waiting for the massive door to open, and when it did, old Simena stood eyeing all of them and asked who they were, she learned that it was her new master's brother, she asked them to wait. Simena's discourtesy irritated Lord Thomas. He paced back and forth muttering something to himself, Mark and Shara just stood speechless. Their eyes wandering, taking in the enormity of the castle, mesmerized.

Finally Kosta and Kathryn appeared, with old Simena shuffling behind. The two brothers' eyes met and froze for a moment. Always the eyes tell so much more than one can imagine, or see, neither of the brothers said a word. Kosta did not flinch. Lord Thomas felt prickles surge through him. Still he too locked eyes with Kosta. If any other master of the castle other than Kosta faced them, an order to remove themselves off the grounds immediately would be proper. Instead, he invited them in with a smile, but Kathryn's feelings wavered. She felt evil was entering their new home. She disliked that feeling, but when she looked at Cybilia's face, realized at least she was not a threat, or her children, and she felt a little at ease. They entered and the riches hit Lord Thomas like a ton of bricks, this was not what he expected to see. He was staring, Cybilia tugged at his sleeve, "Close your mouth. You are embarrassing yourself."

Simena prepared lunch, which seemed to take forever, being old. Kosta led them into the parlor and rang for the butler. Who slowly walked in with glasses filled with wine on a tray, first he approached Lady Cybilia then Kathryn, Lord Thomas, and Kosta, was last.

Kosta raised his wine glass "welcome," and Kathryn said, "welcome" to Cybilia, Mark and Shara. Lord Thomas observed the butler from the corner of his eye; butler's impressive manner of service, slow and stiff yet precise. The conversation was only in spurts of questions and answers, nothing more. The years of separation without contact, or begin to reminisce of their childhood, that of course, too soon, too painful at least for Kosta, the distance between them so great that in this short time, here together could never be spoken of, "as yesterday." To Lord Thomas, the past he saw in the face of his brother, that night of the cruel act stood before him. Kathryn felt the tension and excused herself heading for the kitchen, then asked, "Cybilia would you like to come along?"

"Yes definitely!" Cybilia and Shara jumped at the chance, the three women headed for the kitchen. The surprise on the visitor's faces was evident, so many things in this kitchen, and many servants. Cybilia felt somehow small, but did not say or do to indicate her amazement, she pompously walked about peering with interest. The servants came in through the back door for lunch, followed by seven children. Old Simena said lunch is ready, served in the dining room, of course. When everyone sat down Kosta and Kathryn introduced their children. Cybilia Mark and Shara eyed each as they sat down across the table from their cousins. Lord Thomas was speechless.

First born to the last born stood and greeted their Uncle and his family. Mathew tall and handsome, perfect image of his father. Tessana named after her grandmother, a beautiful young Miss, long brown hair, and features just like her mothers. Jasemin, slim, graceful, yet a bit shy. Jason, alert, grinning, sat and observed. Kras observing his Uncle, feeling more and more distanced from the man. Normally he liked to talk complex things or simple with his brothers and adults as well, but not today. Marla, a beauty with eyes and face you have never ever seen, whose genes had she taken after. Rosie asking questions and curious about everything seemed a bit emotional, or is she soft hearted, as her father.

The guests sat at the largest dining table Lord Thomas had ever seen. He counted the thirteen people seated at the table and noticed that it could comfortably seat forty. The whole scenario astounded him. His brother and his children overcame such immense hardships, so amazing! Each time he glanced at Kosta, he could not bring himself to utter anything sensible, for once lost for words when at home all the arrogance spewed out of his mouth, like a torrential outpour of vomit.

"Whatever made you come for a visit after all these years?" at last Kosta asked.

Lord Thomas spilled a line of excuses, at which Mark and Shara gaped and rolled their eyes. Cybilia did not even raise her head; this to Kathryn was evident that Lord Thomas lied.

"Well, we...have been out of touch a bit too long and my children wanted to meet their cousins. When we stopped at the house, a young man told us that all of you moved up to the castle, and that was an unexpected surprise to us, you can imagine. You have done well Kosta, bravo! How in the world did you just happen to inherit such a prize? And all your children are nice and healthy," Lord Thomas blurted out.

Kosta smiled and nonchalantly replied, which his brother did not perceive to hear.

"I must say... we have not moved in, we are here for the weekend. I do have a harvest to reap and responsibilities in the valley. As to my family surviving, I must have earned it somehow, in the past someone watched over me and mine, I am forever thankful."

"Cheers to that!" All the children chided together then they laughed.

Lord Thomas insinuated that, that statement referred to him that Kosta was thanking him in a round-a-bout way; and so he loudly said as he raised his wine glass, "Perhaps someone's generosity gave a helping hand."

As he drank from the glass, he noticed that no one else drank to his toast. He felt offended, but controlled his temper and, chose his words carefully. "I must complement your staff, delicious lunch. Unfortunately, we need to head back home."

"No need to rush. Stay for the weekend. The lunch is not over," Kosta said slowly.

The servants continued to bring platters with meats and breads and fruit. They walked about the table exchanging dishes and the wine glasses were never empty.

"Very rich and impressive display...indeed," Lord Thomas said. His family wished to stay, even though he felt uncomfortable, soon the wine warmed and relaxed him and his discomfort drowned in wine.

The children conversed merrily, the wives chatted their usual.

Cordiality seemed to reign after so many years, brother observed brother. Unavoidably both relived that night. Though bursting with curiosity, Lord Thomas hid it well.

"*This must be some trick. Tonight when everyone retires, I will ask Kosta what is this enigma. The hours were passing quickly. Soon it will be nightfall*," he was thinking.

Kosta felt edgy, anticipating his brother will pry. When lunch was over, they toured the castle. Lord Thomas planned this visit unexpectedly to discover the truth, but not this, as much as he wanted to conceal his schemes churning in his head, overwhelmed by its wealth, his greed evident on his face. Kosta and Kathryn exchanged meaningful glances.

"Kathryn did you speak to Simena about dinner?" Kosta asked.

"No I have not, since we have guests," Kathryn replied.

Kosta excused himself and headed for the kitchen. Irmina was off on a visit in the village and Simena cooked. They were talking about the dinner menu when Kathryn came in, the conversation changed to the guests.

"They dropped in unexpectedly, who knew?" Kosta said to her.

"I feel uncomfortable; his roving eyes are rather unsettling. Have you noticed how impressed he is? I have a feeling he came with a purpose," Kathryn reluctantly said.

"I feel the same, I wonder..."

Overhearing their conversation, Simena spoke up, "Now Sir...you are aware that the ghosts are still in this castle, and they will act up. Have them stay, yes why not, let them experience one night at least."

"Pardon me Sir Kosta, for being so blunt, but your brother's interest, how I see it sir...he wants this for himself," Thomas's coachman at the kitchen table said.

Kosta and Kathryn did not feel offended when their servants expressed sincerity.

"I am very relieved to know your feelings. I believe you are right," Kosta told Simena.

The matter settled Kosta and Kathryn joined the families in the garden.

"Beautiful. This panorama is breathtaking," Cybilia spoke when Kathryn approached.

"What happened in the kitchen?" Thomas wanted to know.

"Ah, Simena needed the menu for dinner. They never make their own decisions for any meals," Kathryn explained. "*Bravo Kathryn that was smooth*," Kosta thought.

They traipsed the grounds as if prospecting purchasers, fascinated by its enormity, its elegance but especially impressed by the huge oak tree.

The sun slowly tipped towards the horizon, the air became a bit chilly. They headed indoors, settled comfortably in the parlor by the brightly blazing fireplace.

This place must belong to him, no matter what the cost or elimination of obstacles encountered. His curiosity could wait no longer; he had to pop the question.

"Well Kosta, when did you acquire and move in to this castle?" The question stunned him. He was lost for words, the right words. Kosta absolutely cannot tell his brother he and his family are the heirs.

In the meantime, Kosta's children were in the kitchen pleading with Simena if questioned about the heirs, to say, you know nothing, Simena gladly agreed.

Kosta looked at his brother then asked a direct question.

"Are you interested in purchasing this castle, if it was for sale?" Lord Thomas sat up straight and without hesitation answered, "Yes, absolutely yes, price is no object."

Cybilia shocked, stood up from the couch and walked out of the parlor. Shara followed her mother, and Mark stared at his father, teeth clenched. Kosta and Kathryn looked at Lord Thomas, no comment on the answer they heard. The silence was deafening, only the fire crackled and hissed in the hearth.

The butler appeared with a tray laden with glasses and a bottle of red wine.

Lord Thomas laughed. "Ah, perfect timing my man." As the butler lowered the tray, he reached for the glass without a thank you.

Kathryn waved her hand, no. Kosta held his glass but did not drink from it at all.

"Father, Mother wishes to speak to you," Shara said as she came in.

"Tell Mother to come talk to me here in the parlor," Lord Thomas replied.

Shara walked out visibly upset. Kosta wondered what was going on.

"I will go find out what is going on, perhaps Cybilia is not feeling well." Kathryn walked out.

The brothers were alone, neither spoke. Lord Thomas leaned to face Kosta, spoke in a low tone.

"Kosta forgive me for coming unannounced, things have been hectic of late, and time just slipped by too quickly." He paused, then continued, "I would like to talk to you about what happened...now that we are alone perhaps you could give me some clue...how and where have you been...after...what took place..." Looking at his face could not go on.

Kosta did not reply, after a moment of self-control, calmly said, "Today is not the right time for me to talk about what happened. It will take hours to tell you in detail, we must leave it at that. Perhaps the next time you come Thomas, come alone and we will drink to our health and future."

"*Come alone? By all means I will be back very soon*," he thought. "When would be the best time for me to come back, you know I am very curious to know the real story, because people talk and each time the story changes, what is the true story?" Thomas said.

"When you hear the true story, keep an open mind, you will understand everything," Kosta said sharply.

Just then, the women came with the children into the parlor. Mathew stoked the fire, flames danced. They sprawled relaxing in front of it exchanging words now and then. Soon dinner would be served and then shortly after everyone would retire for the night.

When dinner was over and the last of the wine sipped, all of them followed Lira to the bedrooms of their choice.

"Kathryn is it possible for me to be far from Thomas, his snoring disturbs my sleep. I am exhausted the next day," Cybilia asked.

Without replying, Kathryn took Cybilia's hand and led her to a very nicely decorated bedroom farther to the end of the hall. Cybilia would sleep peacefully tonight. Shara and Mark were in adjoining bedrooms and Lord Thomas in Baron Patrick and Aunt Olivia's master bedroom. Kosta and Kathryn decided to sleep above the servants' quarters. This will suit them well. Each of their children loved their own bedrooms. Kosta and Kathryn never imagined such luxury. Down in the kitchen a heated conversation was going on, what troubled them? Kosta heard the raised voices, concerned, he stepped lightly across the hall and down the stairs, he listened for a while, one of the servants was saying:

"Why is Master Kosta nice to his nasty brother? Did you see him eyeing Lira? He was undressing her with his eyes, followed her all over the dining room."

"Yes I noticed that too, good thing she did not look at him, or she would have been in trouble," interjected another.

"Yes especially the way she swings her hips and..."

"Ah, but...she is still young and naïve one must give her time," another interrupted. They all burst into laughter.

"You men are like hyenas, I saw you eyeing Lady Cybilia...she is some Lady; I saw your side winding glances," a woman's voice broke in. And another said; "but you cannot compare the two, our Mistress is an Angel, and she surpasses the other in beauty, I know one thing you might not have considered and that is her tender heart, observe them both together and I guarantee you, I know which one will win..." The kitchen went quiet, they were thinking. One of the men said, "You are right, I too agree that our Lady is more beautiful...I see more class in our Lady then the other, and have you noticed our Lady does not look down at us, like the other, I noticed several times already, that is my opinion."

Then another spoke, "You say we have roving eyes, had you not seen the visitor roving his eyes after all of you...my ladies, especially our young Lucinda, "they all laughed, some women began to hush them, "Hey, lower your voices we are too loud, someone might hear us, better be observant. But say nothing just like the young master Mathew asked us to do."

Kosta over heard that, Mathew asked them to pretend they know nothing when his brother questions them. “That was good thinking of Mathew, bright and quick, good children; I am glad Thomas did not hear what the servants said about the Ladies,” thought Kosta and, stepping lightly climbed the stairs back up to the room, Kathryn was in bed waiting for him.

“We have smart children, you know. I wonder what will take place tonight, if anything, I hope we will sleep peacefully,” Kosta said.

“Did you notice your brother how he acted all through the day?” she asked him.

“Oh-yes...very interesting...hard to understand him...he is two faced, I had that feeling all my life, but now it is clearly evident, to me at least. I wonder what will happen in the next few days. I see he is anxious to stay...and lull around in this luxurious castle. I know he wants it and, I know he wants to find out from me all about my magical return from the dead...wait and see, be very observant tomorrow, I have things to tell you, right now you would laugh and wake everyone,” Kosta whispered to her. Kathryn lifted her head and, “what kind of things you are talking about? Do I have to wait until morning? She questioned.

“Yes...you have to wait till morning, my dear,” replied Kosta and kissed her.

“And when will you tell him about you.”

“The next time he comes to visit, alone,” Kosta replied.

“Kosta, how do you feel being here..., sleeping in such a huge bed in a huge bedroom... we had so little space in our little house...this castle is so huge...such a change...it will take me I know a long time to adjust to this life...I think I am dreaming, tell me how do you feel?” Kathryn whispered to him in the darkness. Kosta was asleep.

Seventy: Midnight Stroll

She slipped out of bed and stood at the window, the night barely lit by the quarter moon. The white flowers stood out more than the rest slightly, as something moved, had she imagined it? There again someone walked by the white flowers, she stood and watched, soon out of the shadow she recognized Lord Thomas. What is he looking for? Should Faithful give him a chase? "Faithful, come to me." She pointed out the window at the man, "Faithful go play."

Kathryn tiptoed down the stairs, opened the kitchen door, dog slipped out. Kathryn left the door ajar and went upstairs to watch.

Faithful stalked, abruptly sprinted from behind to topple the man face down to the ground. Faithful stood on his back, growled than ran off.

Lord Thomas got to his feet, dusted himself off heading back to his bedroom; when suddenly out of the dark Faithful sank his teeth in his ankle, Lord Thomas froze.

"Let go you devil dog, let go!" Feeling pain, you dog, stop playing tricks with me, this will go on all night, how did he get out, did I leave the door open?"

Kathryn smiled. Faithful was having fun. He let go of the ankle and came bounding back to the room, panting, Kathryn patted his head, "Good dog, now go to sleep." He dropped next to the bed on a sheep hide mat.

"I am too tense to sleep, that man is contemplating something. Now Kosta must put up with him. Has he not suffered enough? I know Kosta will stand his ground this time," she whispered.

Lord Thomas examined his ankle on the bed, no punctures. He changed into his night shirt, walked over to the window inhaled deeply the cool night air, he thought; *ah, I will surely sleep soundly*." Turned out the oil lamp, and slipped under the covers.

The castle stood silent dimly lit by the quarter moon. Everyone slept well; the dog once raised his head, listened, sniffed the air, closed his eyes went back to sleep.

The dew shimmered in the bright morning sunlight. Lord Thomas fully awake inhaled the fresh air leaning out the bedroom window, his eyes absorbing the scenery. He felt excited at the top of this mountain in this castle. This exhilaration is what he needed and wanted, he must have it, no matter if Kosta had become the heir, dismissing it as a rumor. Being here with his family for the weekend meant nothing to him; he needed and will have the answer soon, perhaps even today.

And so, freshly washed and dressed, with an air of pomposity stepped slowly down the enormous staircase, marched into the dining room, there he found seated at the table splendidly covered for early breakfast were Kathryn conversing with Cybilia.

"Good morning Ladies, enjoying your aromatic brew. Oh this is a splendid day, do you not agree Cybilia? Kathryn?" He bowed low.

The two women glanced at him. Kathryn poured a cup of coffee for him. Cybilia smiled and nodded, neither replied. Lord Thomas added cream and sweetened it with two spoons of sugar, stirred it too quickly, the coffee spilled onto the saucer, and Cybilia smiled. Kathryn asked if he needed a clean cup.

"I am a bit clumsy this morning, I had a restless night. I also had a strange dream... unfortunately, what it was about I cannot remember at all." The conversation with the women absolutely bored him. After a brief silence, inquired the whereabouts of Kosta. Kathryn said he is in the green house.

Lord Thomas excused himself and wandered out into the gardens where an old gardener busily dug in the dirt. Lord Thomas tried to engage a conversation and asked if he was the gardener.

"This is not my garden, I work here."

At each question he yelled, "what, what?" no sense wasting time here, any information he needed drawn out of this deaf sulky old fellow, most likely would be useless. Discouraged Lord Thomas strolled in a different section of the garden there he came upon a greenhouse, another gardener fussed over some plants. The man seemed to be a bit upset. *Ah...great timing this might be a perfect moment to ask questions, usually anyone that is upset will give good answers, to relieve the man's stress.* Lord Thomas was thinking. With gusto walked up and in a loud voice interrupted the man's concentration.

"Good morning my good man, up and playing in the dirt this early?"

"Yes it is a good morning, but not for me, this work is never done," mumbled the old gardener not looking at the visitor.

"And what have you seeded?"

"I have not seeded anything, I am transplanting and the stems are brittle and I have broken too many."

"Well then plant a new batch."

"That is impossible, I am out of seeds. These were the last of them."

"And what kind of seeds were they that you are so concerned about."

"Cucumbers for pickling, oh never mind, you seem not to see the importance in gardening, begging your pardon."

"Cucumbers must be an important staple in this household," Lord Thomas sniffed.

"What do you mean? Sir, are you implying we are peasants? The gardener snapped.

"No, not at all, we also love cucumbers and onions and the like," replied Lord Thomas somewhat appalled at the straight forwardness of the gardener.

"I am in no mood to discuss this, if you forgive me for saying so," the gardener mumbled.

"Perhaps someone else upset you this morning not the cucumbers," Lord Thomas said laughing, his eerie usual laugh.

"Sir if you are implying about the new Master Kosta, the answer is no! No, the new Master is very kind he never upsets any of us." The gardener stood and stared at Lord Thomas.

"Is he really the new Master you say?" Lord Thomas smiled sheepishly.

"Why Sir, you seem to be acting strangely. Sir, did you not arrive here yesterday...?" the gardener smiled back.

Lord Thomas glared, *"this insolent peasant... he muttered, should mention this man's rudeness to Kosta."* Walking away, he thought, *"if my servant acted rude, he would have been in trouble with me."* He strolled through the grounds inspecting everything he stumbled upon, sat on the bench beneath the sprawling oak with branches nearly to the ground. Overcome by serenity he said aloud; this is what I need for my old age. I must have this at whatever the cost...closed his eyes visualizing himself as master of a castle. His thoughts were interrupted by a crash, startled he heard Kosta's voice behind him.

"Enjoying the view and the wonderful morning, brother?" Kosta calmly asked, Lord Thomas startled, derailed out of his concentration replied nervously.

"The view is breathtaking, hypnotically mystical. During winter, the scene here must be different then in the valley, serene wonderland, I am sure, charming, charming. What was that crash?" he asked.

"The crash...must have been the lumberjacks downing trees." Kosta sat down, not surprised at all at the anxiousness in his brother's eyes.

The moment his brother's boot stepped out of the carriage and entered the castle, it was all over his face what he came for.

"*My wealthy brother must wait for the truth. Let his nerves twist from tension and frustration as mine had when I had that breakdown. My veins were rupturing from rage. Not knowing where else to turn but to him. When my will escaped me, I dragged myself to him begging for food for my family. My brother had the audacity to deprive me of the most precious necessity for my life...my eyes. No, I will not tell him today. Let him wait as I waited, I have hardened my heart and will, but...it is to be so...I know deep within I am fair.*" These thoughts swirled in Kosta's mind. Something strange took place right there under this huge oak tree, it was rather comical to watch his wealthy brother squirm on that bench. However, Kosta's face remained carved stone.

The possessiveness for wealth and power as hard as he tried to hide was evident.

Kosta did not disclose who is or, are the rightful heirs, when questioned relentlessly Lord Thomas repeating what the gardener had told him, Kosta nodded.

However, this morning beneath the huge oak tree they were in combat of wills, submission of power, and control. Chosen words, gleam of fire in their eyes. Kosta aware of his brother's attempt to break Kosta's confidence, as was done to him once before. Kosta chose his words carefully, while his brother rattled on and on thinking that by talking, he would eventually get his brother to open up and tell the story.

Lord Thomas, could *not* break Kosta's will, now. The conversation was over. He realized Kosta hardened, like tempered steel, no longer meek and humble, as he had known him to be, from that tragic night when they lost their parents. When a youth of fourteen depressed and suppressed by poverty, no education, why, it never occurred to him to find out if Kosta ever did learn to read. With his nose to the soil throughout his life to support his brood of children, that is all he knew.

This morning he could not say or even think that. Today they sat together and they were on the same level of prestige. That is not what he intended to happen, not after all the cruelties he inflicted on his younger brother to break him, crush him, *his image*, the *likeness of his father*, make his family suffer, remove him from his own life forever. This will not be without a fight of willpower, and the power of gold plays great advantages over legality, so he thought. His younger brother now by Fate or deed has a chance to experience same power, a life of comfort and abundance. The rage within burned him through and through, a defeat he could not withstand.

The truth he must know and Kosta must tell him; *how in the world all this transpired, is this witchcraft, and if it is, I want some of it. My image cannot diminish. By what magic come rewards for suffering? What power is this, power of great love, believing and humility?*

With compassion, Kosta cared for everything around him, never held a grudge. Which of these virtues performed this miracle, he wants to know. Perhaps the witches had a hand with this miracle. They have done plenty of damage to people I knew of personally. Hmmm...perhaps it would be to my advantage to pay them a visit." These thoughts were constant as if possessed by Satan himself. His head ached and his brain burned. He must win. The greedy brother schemed, ideas grew then dissipated, and formed again, some were almost ready for action then fell into oblivion. This was the worst time in his life, unable to decide how to acquire what he desperately wanted. He did not need it, but he wanted. At the end, he will choose a plan at home. There he will contemplate in private. That was final.

The next several days were quite pleasant. The ghosts did not disturb the visitors, perhaps excitement of that sort would have been more fun, and Lord Thomas would have cooled his heels a bit of snatching this property from the rightfully appointed heir. Let it remain as it is.

Seventy-One:
The Last Dinner

The final night at dinner things began to happen. The butler and Nila were serving when suddenly Nila jumped away from the table, shrieked and ran into the kitchen. The butler set the platter on the table and ran after Nila. Nila's high-pitched screams threw her into convulsions. This sudden commotion, questions concerning her behavior whispered at the table. What happened? No one had seen anything.

"What made her jump and run?" Cybilia asked. Lord Thomas visibly irritated, frowned. Butler Jonason came running breathless calling, "Lady Kathryn please come quickly!"

Kosta followed them into the kitchen to find out what the problem was. Nila sat in a chair the other woman held her shoulders, the convulsions ceased. Nila opened her eyes, seeing everyone around her remembered what she had seen in the dining room, through sobs described what she saw.

"I saw a man behind Sabrina's chair waving his arms. I was frightened out of my skin."

"Ah, you are new here. You have never seen a ghost, have you?" Kosta smiled.

"No sir, I am sorry but I have never seen a ghost before. But I am all right," Nila replied.

"The ghosts are upset about something tonight. But that should not interfere with serving dinner, now get to it girl, the guests are hungry," Kathryn added.

Kosta motioned to the butler and returned to the dining table. Thomas asked what the problem was.

"Nila is new here. She thought she had seen a ghost. That is why she ran off," Kathryn said.

Oh's and Ahs echoed through the room. Nila and the butler resumed serving dinner, though Nila was visibly upset and embarrassed.

"Well," Lord Thomas sarcastically commented, "I was told that the castle's haunted but up to now I had not seen anything out of the ordinary, besides I do not believe in ghosts."

This was amusing to Lord Thomas until he raised his wine glass to his lips. A sudden jerk of his elbow wine splashed his face, ran down his neck, shirt stained red, at this he jumped up, everyone stared unsure what to do or say but waiting for someone to say something, no one ate, they all sat as frozen in time. At last, Kosta said to him, "Purely coincidental, I am sure." Lord Thomas became visibly enraged, his face as a ripe tomato.

"Coincidental or not, I demand a clean shirt," he muttered. Butler Jonason brought a clean shirt and asked Lord Thomas to wash up and change in the small bedroom. During dinner, Lord Thomas's napkin slid off his knee not once, not twice but at least ten times. This proved now a ghost was among them. The question is now what awaits them while they are asleep. Shara announced, she will not sleep alone she wants to sleep with her mother. Mark laughed at her.

"I will sleep no matter what the ghost will do, as far as I am concerned they can all go to hell! That is where they belong!" Lord Thomas mumbled.

Kosta thought that was quite outrageous of him, and rude; but did not comment.

When Nila served dessert, it happened again. Lord Thomas reached for the creamer. Then all eyes goggled at the creamer, as it rose into the air at least a foot by itself, tilted, poured the cream into the cup. Lord Thomas had chills ran through him. Cybilia wide-eyed from fear just sat still. She did not want to upset the ghost. Lord Thomas aggravated by these ghostly antics stood up and walked away from the table, everyone else remained seated.

Kathryn could not hold still anymore, and hold back what was on her mind so she began to talk directly at Lord Thomas: "As you said this castle is haunted, you have experienced it now! Let me say this, you have seen their action and have been touched by a ghost. Yes, by a wandering restless soul, last night it was quiet, but tonight she wants you to know she is here. We have nothing to fear, our departed friend Baron Patrick had much contact with this ghost...

"Why do you say the ghost is a she? Perhaps it is a he?" Lord Thomas interrupted. Cybilia stared at him, Kathryn continued. "I am sure you have heard the story of the brother and sister. They lived here a long time ago on this land. The brother murdered her because she fell in love. He was extremely envious. Unfortunately, no girl wanted him. On the day the law brings him to justice her soul will rest. It has been at least ten years since," Kathryn finished.

Lord Thomas listened and then he said.

"Yes I heard that story, but in my opinion this ghost should be helping the law find the killer, not stay here and intimidate people," he smirked.

"But it seems you are not aware of the reason she stays in one place, so it is said that; when one's life is snuffed out before ones time the soul cannot rest. That is the reason she is here and she is angry. Would you not be angry if you were in one place for eternity if no one solved your demise? Some ghosts are so angry they are destructive did you know that?" Kathryn explained.

"Since my parents passed away, I hardly ever dream of either of them and, they never appear, strange thing though the only time I felt my mother's presence was when I was very distraught and frightened," Cybilia said.

"And when were you ever so distraught and frightened my dear wife?" Lord Thomas glared at her, surprised at her statement and such frankness, in front of all the children and, even his own face, as if he had been cruel to her. Cybilia lowered her gaze and did not reply. All the children were very observant of both of the parents.

Shara, she was the defiant one, she had no fear of her father, suddenly recalled an incident and said quite loud.

"Father you remember, at the time when you were drunk, you broke Mother's precious vases from Grandmother, you were so violent and, you almost struck Mother, but I screamed, do you remember?" All eyes were on Lord Thomas and he felt very uncomfortable, he could not find words to defend his actions. He did recall that mid-day or was it in the evening, when he acted crazy.

"Well something must have triggered my anger, surely. Otherwise I would not have acted in such an explosive way," he muttered.

He felt at once under attack, anger escalated, realizing this he immediately suppressed it, could not show it here, not in front of everyone. Politely asked for a glass of wine, *nerves were a bit tight, he needed to relax*. Kosta poured his brother a glass of wine and for the wives as well. Tension no longer held everyone on edge, conversation stirred to daily matters.

All the children this night were close to their parents, they felt they should.

When the midnight hour neared, most of them were still awake, waiting. All was quiet on this moonless night. Dog slept soundly. Kosta relaxed, half asleep and Kathryn snuggled close to him in deep sleep.

Lord Thomas musing pleasantries, thinking while his wife slept next to him, ever since her pregnancy they slept in separate rooms, besides he snored. Over the years, their private meetings became infrequent, having her next to him had stirred his desire, he searched his memory, *when,* because of work and age plus the wine...realized, his inability... perturbed at that thought. More serious objective faced him. Surely, it will take months. However, in the back of his mind, lingered the irritable ghost and he knew that the only time her soul will rest and give them peace is when her brother is executed for her murder. In his mind, he enveloped himself as being here in this serene and enjoyable life. Greatly impressed with Barons imagination and class, *my loss, I did not engage his company throughout these years. Funny how time passes and what passes with time. Here I would have an easy and merry life indeed, this should be my way of life. Cybilia insulted me. I shall have a talk with her. I despise her outbursts. Why, that little homely wench I should send her and Sabrina away. Those two are twins. Even think alike. Mark is altogether different, evasive, never could have close relationship with him, is it I...or is it my son? My son..., I am proud of him he has my strong character. Sabrina (Shara) is flighty, like a dry leaf in the wind. I should discuss the management of the estate with Mark yes...a fine idea. What is keeping me awake...must be the ghost! Perhaps I should ease my tension, yes...perhaps Cybilia would drink with me, perhaps something might just happen after all these years, I do feel a bit amorous, hmm...*" after a moment he changed his mind. He moved to the edge of the bed, waited a minute then slid off and barefoot ventured downstairs in the dark. The dog in Kosta's room lifted his head, did not react but kept his ears alert.

Kosta heard someone moving around and wondered who is awake at this hour. He slipped out of bed walked into the hallway and in the darkness, cautiously stepped down the stairs, and saw, candle-light in the dining room, his brother filled a glass full of wine, drank one glass, then another and another, "*three glasses, he must be worried, how did he manage to find matches*?" Kosta thought. Then as if through mental telepathy, Lord Thomas turns to see Kosta standing in the doorway.

"Well, well, my brother," he spoke nonchalantly, "seems we both cannot sleep, perhaps we should drink...I mean, sit have a drink with me. That ghost is keeping me up. I helped myself to some wine...no one around, all asleep." Seemingly, a bit embarrassed. Kosta walked into the dining room, sat down, Lord Thomas poured a glass of wine for him and sat opposite, Kosta took a sip waiting for Thomas to begin talking, for he knew that is what he wanted, openly suggesting since he came to visit.

"At dinner all this talk about a ghost, it is irritating, I sympathize with you and the children, living with this ghost it will be very trying, if you know what I mean," he said cynically, "how will you live here with that ghost?" Lord Thomas asked.

"Thomas why does it bother you, we do not live here, it is just assumed. We have been here often for a visit Baron Patrick and Aunt Olivia, give children a bit of excitement and space. Do we not deserve a bit of a brake?" Kosta spoke calmly.

"But you said something to the effect that in your lifetime someone looked after you and you deserved this!" Lord Thomas almost shouted. Kosta raised his hand, to be quiet. For a while, they sat not speaking, Lord Thomas smiled as he thought, *ah, so...nothing is definite...I have a chance to fight for this property legally...*

Kosta also smiled for he could see through his brother, ideas whirling in his mind, now after all these years, four times in seventeen years never had need to be as a family, until now, he waited to see more of his character.

"Yes I said that. In part, it is true, someone had and I benefited from it greatly," Kosta answered.

"Kosta tell me now how did all this come about...your eyes and the fortune that you have acquired, I hear about it. You cannot deny it. Everyone is asleep. Here we are alone, talk, I want to know." Fingers intertwined so hard, his knuckles turned white.

"Thomas I told you I cannot tell you tonight, I have a reason and you should respect that, the right time will come, I will talk about all of it, not now. Not tonight, I have to go to bed. You should too." Kosta stood up and waited for Thomas to do the same.

"No, I will stay and think a while, do you mind, I am not sleepy, besides, Cybilia snores, not too loud but is irritating," Thomas said.

"Very well then stay, I will go...good night." Kosta walked away.

"You know, this waiting is torture," Lord Thomas said in a hushed voice.

Kosta only looked at his brother's flushed face evidenced with the excessive ingestion of wine, but did not reply, for he knew that would trigger a long discussion perhaps an argument, which would last until dawn. Kosta went upstairs. In bed listened for any disturbance from his brother's anger. He feared not for himself or his family, but for the young servant, his brother eyed her every move. Wine does disorient one's mind and one could blunder, she is young and attractive. I doubt he would, Kosta dismissed this thought.

While in bed, Kosta had mixed feelings of certain loss, at this late hour he would rather not analyze. All he wanted is sleep but kept visualizing his brother at the table with a glass of wine in his hand, the other drummed the table lightly. He turned on his side and wrapped his arm around his beloved Kathryn.

Seventy-Two: The Bloody Bed

Downstairs at the table Lord Thomas sat sipping wine, in his mind hearing Kosta's words. His hand trembled, could not think, but mumbled, now, *I must find the bed*, unsteady, but holding on to the banister carefully went up the stairs, shuffled down the hall to the bedroom, dropped onto a bed, his left hand grappled for the covers, reached over for Cybilia. Cybilia was gone! "Where is she now," he said, "ah, she is gone, good. I dislike...no... I hate sleeping with her anyway..." In his robe passed out. Then near dawn, screams echoed through the castle, alarmed everyone ran to where the scream came from, wondering, who is murdered? Lord Thomas sat screaming. Kosta, Kathryn, and Cybilia entered his bedroom, carrying lamps. Kosta sat the lamps on the dressers; Lord Thomas sat on the bed. The nightshirt had a large red stain. They stared.

"Whatever happened, and why are you in this bedroom?" Cybilia asked.

"I do not know...I woke up and felt pain and something warm and wet on my chest I screamed," he stammered. "I have no clue why this was done...to me!" he said, eyeing them accusingly.

"Done to you? Not I, I slept with Shara," Cybilia said.

"No Father, I did not do this to you," Mark said.

That dubious act falls on Kosta's children, and they all said.

"None of us would do such a thing to our Uncle. Why would we? We let the ghost do that." And they all smiled. Rosie tugged Tessana by the sleeve.

"I am hungry, walk with me to the kitchen." All the children followed. Lord Thomas held the shirt out in from of him. All three took a good look at his nightshirt.

"Any cuts on your hands, good no cuts." Kosta checked. Then Cybilia noticed something shiny, "Look at this Kosta," she cried out.

"What is that?" Kosta asked.

"Why...this is glass! Thomas did you take a glass of wine to bed with you?" Cybilia asked. Lord Thomas had a comical expression, as if a child caught stealing cookies.

"You must have, you broke the glass and cut your chest. Now that was foolish, you could have bled to death, you wine sucking fool! To drink that much, well what do you expect an old fool without a limit!" Cybilia scolded. Kosta picked up the broken glass, wine stains on the sheets.

"Lucky you, this could have been fatal," Kosta said.

"What are you saying? Cybilia how dare you call me an old fool! I do not remember carrying the glass to the bedroom. I think I left it on the table!" he said... if I did not bring the glass, if not, then who did? He was sober now, felt embarrassed.

The cut on his chest was quite deep, to bleed this much, but, it will heal quickly. After breakfast, a lengthy conversation ensued between the two families, while they strolled around the grounds, Kathryn and Cybilia wished to connect as a family if possible, after all these years, and for the children to keep in contact with each other.

As to the brothers nothing could change this quickly, time could not erase their bitterness. Wives observed and concurred, that, the sincerity between these brothers could never be.

Their eerie departure dragged until lunch. They stayed for six days and, really, it was time to go home. Kosta had a lot to do in the valley, cannot neglect the harvest. That young man glad to help with the chores while the family went up to the castle, Kosta paid him well. Michael, Rabinna and Rebecca will help Kosta as always through the years. Now the boys are old enough to share the workload.

After lunch, the two families said their farewells and in a moment, the carriage rolled and rattled down the steep mountain, disappearing out of sight and the rattle of the wheels faded away.

The family watched on their faces mixed emotions of sadness and relief. Kosta envisioned, "*This will not end well. I need to discuss this with Kathryn.*"

Kosta could see that some of the women wanted to comment about the visitors, but hesitated. Kosta asked the men if they were willing to come and help with the harvest, they complied, especially the young ones, with so many hands harvest gathering done in no time, and then they helped with Michaels harvesting. The extra helper's pockets jingled with gold coins when returned to the castle.

The two friends discussed the events that took place when his brother unexpectedly arrived. Kosta had to tell Michael about his confused feeling, his brother's insistence knowing the whole story. Kosta was concerned, his brother's obsession acquiring wealth, power to control.

Michael nodded then said, "Fate will decide the outcome of both of your lives."

Kosta thought about what Michael had said and, replied with sadness in his eyes.

"Michael...I never hated my brother, why is he so hateful towards me?"

"Kosta a long time ago, Kathryn told us that you were the perfect image of your father, and that is why he hates you," Michael said.

"But how did she know that, who told her?" Kosta questioned surprised at that remark.

"You need to ask Kathryn, someone who knew your father," Michael answered.

Never in his life did Kosta imagine anyone still alive who knew his father. Who was the last one, who...Aunt Olivia.

He tried to visualize his father's face and for a moment he did see the resemblance, he remembered the black hair tied back in a ponytail, especially at those times when they carved together. He remembered those blue eyes whenever he explained to him about his unique way of carving. He did remember his parents, oh how he missed them, he wished they were with him, but the years were full of problems and worry, so much grief. Yet he and Kathryn survived and the children have grown up nicely, he is proud of Kathryn, she held the family together.

Seventy-Three: The Move

Weeks slipped by time to make the decision.

Michael said to Kosta and Kathryn, "If you stay in this valley for another year surely you will crush their high hopes, or, make the move to the huge castle now. They are so elated having their own bedrooms. The privilege to be served and tended to like royalty, such luxury, but to deprive them of this chance will break their hearts." Michael was right. All-important decisions Kathryn and Kosta frequently discussed in their bed when the children slept. Although the children always came first regardless, what their final decision would be, what the good Lord has bestowed on his family, so be it. The day had come, the decision of the move was about to be revealed.

Rosie hopping across the room smiling, she had that feeling and she giggled and hugged everyone.

"Oh but wait I did not tell you of our final decision!" Kosta raised his voice. The din in the small room was unbearable. Each proclaiming that they know what that decision is. When Kosta raised his arm, they all fell silent.

"Now listen here, you need to sit down, hear our decision, and no interruptions for a moment." Kathryn and Kosta observed their children, and the expressions on their faces were unforgettable, it seemed the end of the world happened.

"You tell them what we have decided, I cannot," Kosta said to Kathryn.

Kathryn took a deep breath and, spoke very softly,

"You know children all of you were born here in this little house and grew up here; we have gone through hardships over the years, but we managed. We should manage future years, we will. Your father and I decided that...you must understand that it was very hard to make that final decision. We ought to be thankful, for our wonderful friend for loving and thinking of us and giving us such a residence as no one else could have, so we are going to, stay..."

Mathew interrupting his mother: "We are moving to the castle!"

Kosta raised both arms and said, "Mother was not finished speaking."

"Is it true? Are we going to live up at the castle?" Tessana asked smiling.

Kathryn shook her head, "Listen, settle down and let me finish!"

They listened.

"As I was saying, we are going to stay here for a few more months or weeks, depends how fast we finish what needs to be done. Then we will move."

"Few more months, Father, what must we do? Tell us and we will do it!" Mathew said.

"What about our animals?" Rosie jumped up and said.

"Oh I cannot wait!" Jason clasped his hands and turned to Jasemin, Kras and Marla together discussing the move.

Kathryn began to cry. Kosta held her in his arms. The girls also shed tears from happiness. From now on, they will enjoy comfort.

Therefore, the transition took place quickly, first they decided that everything in this small home had to remain as it is now with the exception of Kosta's tools for carving, Kathryn's basket for sewing and knitting, children's nick-necks, small animals resettled, and minimize work and travel.

The neighbors wept when they learned that Kosta's family is moving to the castle.

"But...it is only up the mountain up there, all of you are welcome. Come and visit just as you have done all these years here," Kosta said.

"When you need me I will be there for you, as before," Kathryn told them.

When she was in dire need, her neighbors were all there, and that she will not forget. The only one request Kosta and Kathryn had is for the neighbors to keep an eye on their little home. The neighbors gladly agreed to do so, and if any of them had any news good or bad, they would send a messenger to them quickly.

A storm of cold rain blew in, during the night, which by morning the countryside lay covered by blue crust of ice. On the day of the move, they prepared for a rough ride to the top. By noon, the ice had melted. Not anticipating problems they settled in the wagon wrapped in blankets, the dog and cat between them, half way up the mountain, it began to rain again. Under blanket's they huddled close. Kosta and Kathryn smiled at each other as the wagon slowly rumbled up the road. They were half way up when suddenly the front wheels of the wagon sank deep into soft mud. The horses struggled to pull the wheels out of the rut. Kosta shouted to Mathew that they should get out and push it.

"Father I will ride up to the castle for help," Mathew said.

"Yes Mathew you ride up, I will stay with the family just in case, unhitch the horse quickly." The children's blankets soaked through and cold water seeped into everything, they shivered. Kosta and Kathryn sat alone on the front seat covered with wet blankets. Their coats soaked cold water trickled down their backs.

Streams of rainwater ran down the horse's heads and bodies, whipped by gusting intermittent wind. The rushing water rutted out its path down the mountain, washed a wide and deep muddy pool, horse's legs sank deep in cold water as deep as the wagon wheels.

"Mother all the bundles on the floor of the wagon are sopping wet," Rosie whimpered.

"What is taking Mathew so long, he must come soon or we will freeze and die!" Kras whined.

"God please stop this rain, we are freezing, please help us, it is so cold," Tessana prayed earnestly.

"It is not letting up soon we will freeze to death," Jason whined.

"Stop saying such horrid things, Mathew will come soon," Jasimin scolded.

Suddenly the horses stumped nervously. Kathryn noticed their quivering muscles, snorted, reared, stumped the mud and shook their heads. Something spooked them. With so much pulling, pushing, and jerking the wagon turned sideways the back wheels inched to the edge of the hill. Kosta saw no other reason to be so agitated but the rain. He used the whip to force the horses to pull forward.

"What is taking Mathew so long?" Kosta said.

"It does not take that long to saddle a couple of horses," Kathryn agreed.

The horses now stood at an angle almost facing the drop off the mountain. Kosta cracked the whip, horses pulled. Kosta tugged on the lead to the right to safety. The horses gave it all they had, moved away from the drop and out of the soft trench of mud and rushing water, then the back wheels fell into the muddy puddle. Mathew and three servants from the castle came on horseback trotting down, with the power of eight horses pulled the wagon out and rolled on. The higher they climbed the better the traction, the wind was stronger as they reached an area with only scattered trees, the scenery opened before them and it was beautiful. Kathryn said, "*halt the horses here,*" she called out to the children to come out from under the blankets, to look at the world from this spot, at first Rosie cried loudly that, she is stiff and frozen solid and she cannot move. They laughed at her and said she was being silly, reluctantly they uncovered their heads and peeked out and were in awe at the scene before them, so peaceful. Snow covered the mountains. The horizon and sky blended. Below them, the trees shimmered like crystal.

They forgot the wind and rain and the cold. Their eyes drank this incredible scene. The world soon will rest beneath winters' white blanket of snow, soon.

They were three-quarters up with extra help reached the top quickly and headed directly into the stable. The children ran to the back door of the kitchen, threw off the muddy shoes and wet coats, the servants wrapped each one in dry blankets, all seven sat at the table sipping hot tea with a little rum. The women gathered around happy to see them, especially Simena, the children always clung to her, she was old and they called her their Grandma. The kitchen warm and cozy, aroma of cooking and something baking made them hungry.

Hot tea with rum tasted great, and the freshly baked bread and butter, delicious.

Rosie ate like a little hamster stuffing her cheeks with bread, washing it down with tea, as if she had not eaten a week. Describing in detail to them, how frightening it was up the road and the rain coming down in buckets. The servants laughed at her clowning when she was done she complemented and thanked them for baking tasty bread; Simena's cheeks were covered with kisses, that made her day happy.

Kosta, Kathryn, Tessana and Mathew entered. The servants smiled, mugs of hot tea with rum, waited on the table for them, a platter of bread, honey and butter stood ready. This was one scary day with an awesome view, intermixed rain and snow. The kitchen was a hubbub with everyone talking and laughing.

The move turned out to be a bit complicated with the weather turning nasty. However, to make the children happy Kosta, Michael, and several of the servants for days had moved all the horses and cattle and the fowl, settling down the animals took another few days. The holidays were just around the corner. Besides unexpected snow might come down by the feet, not inches, soon.

The holiday was so different, the enormity of the castle, the servants preparing so much for them, this was hard for Kathryn and Kosta to get used to, but the whole family truly was mesmerized, to them this was a dream. One important thing they missed, the chatter of neighbor's children knocking on doors coming and going, playing outside or just visiting. Then a day before Christmas half of the village was up at the castle, their best friends were there as well, "*enchanting*" they kept repeating, never imagined celebrating the holidays of all places in a castle. The laughter and the running up to the tower and down the stairs all day, the lunches and dinners then the children crashed into beds exhausted, slept.

Everyone gathered in the dining room, the table festively decorated. Aroma of food on large platters sat on the table. The village women worked hand in hand with the staff preparing and setting up the table. Candlelight danced with shadows on silver plates, and glasses filled with wine, elegant and romantic, aristocratic, such riches they have not seen before. The villagers asked if Kosta's brother was expected.

"No, not this year, our present guests are more important and we are grateful for every one of you, we would not trade any of you for one wealthy person, ever."

The women stirred to tears. The men gripped Kosta's hand and kissed Kathryn on the cheek, they were true friends and good neighbors.

One thing none of them had, those elegant expensive dresses the rich Ladies wore on festive days like this. These villagers wore their simple attire what they had considered their best, simple, plain, but clean, their good hearts shone like gold. Gold they had, time they did not to travel to purchase latest elegance of mode for their era, they will, someday. This was one Christmas all the servants were together as one family they dined and wined until past midnight. When they sang songs and carols Kathryn burst into tears, their voices hushed, they looked at her, and none spoke for they knew why she wept. Old Simena sat next to her; she wrapped her arms around her shoulder.

"Lady Kathryn cry tears of joy, Master Baron and Aunt Olivia are here no doubt, looking on and they are happy for you and the children," she said.

Suddenly the candles fluttered and the flames snuffed out one by one on the candelabra, then the second candelabra winked out, then the first relit. This was the show of the evening for all eyes to see, the ghosts were here. No one moved a finger, but all eyes darted from one to the other. Then the wine glasses jingled, everyone startled, jumped, laughed and some cried. Their children wide-eyed shivered never expecting this sort of evening, of which none will stop talking, surely. Calmed by their mothers later went to sleep after a long day, the rest of the guests slept on beds, or anywhere they found a comfortable spot.

"Thank you for your hard work, we appreciate all of you, now go sleep, leave the cleanup for morning it is very late," Kathryn said to the servants. Shortly after the castle stood dark and silent, everyone slept. The only disturbance was the echo of their snoring. The wind whined and moaned, the raindrops changed, large intricate designed snowflakes fell, by morning their world lay beneath a white winter blanket.

Seventy-Four: The Second Dinner

Across the country late into the night, someone was still awake. The wind howled and the sleet in waves whipped against the windows. Someone sat alone sipping wine scheming, visualizing, dreaming, listening to the wind, soon this sleet will turn to heavy snow. The obsession and curiosity kept him in a spellbound grip.

Ever since Lord Thomas returned home from the visit, his brother's words echoed in his mind. He walked in the night, dreaming strange dreams. At times needed to scream, falling on the bed, face in a pillow squelched it, because someone might hear him.

On some mornings warmly dressed, strolled among twisted dormant apple trees, dark from moisture having strange forms. Just for a moment Lord Thomas sat on the bench and thought he should withdraw from the purchase of the castle, now rightfully belongs to his brother. A voice whispered into his ear; "you backing off? You cannot allow him to be wealthier then you, can you! Do you want to be, ancient history, to your friends in your circle of high society, do you? What is more, you are notorious everywhere. You do not want your opinion changed, do you?" Lord Thomas, listened to that little voice and agreed to it, and the scheming spark glowed anew every day and night.

"Forego the scheming first find out where he was that changed his life around. Who had such powers? Is it witchcraft or magic? Who could possibly undo what he had done, who saved him? I will never believe unless I hear the truth," he mumbled.

The first winter storm had passed leaving the countryside bright with fresh snow. Lord Thomas asked the cook to have his breakfast ready he is going for a short walk.

It will be a long winter, as always, he thought. The breakfast smelled good he ate it quickly. As he sipped the coffee it dawned on him..., *winter, to wait until spring to know the truth will surely try my temper.* His nerves pricked him all over. Aware of his short temper he might snap. He must act soon. Lord Thomas decided that before the weather turns very nasty he should visit Kosta. Recalled his words that...I will tell you about my adventures, next time you come, and he said to come alone. *I wonder why alone. Never mind, it does not matter I will find out why when I see him. Perhaps I should bring a small token of appreciation, a bottle of my wine, yes that will impress them I am sure.* Lord Thomas stood at the window and thought for a while, curiosity mounting. One morning he announced to Cybilia, Mark, and Shara that.

"I am going to visit Uncle Kosta, alone."

Of course, they grumbled.

"Father I hope you realize that blizzards come out of nowhere, do you want to risk your life, freeze to death, you should wait until early March," Shara voiced her opinion loudly.

"Yes, I remember you telling us many people are found frozen to death in the spring when the snows melt, do not go now, what is so important for you to go right now? Mark frowned.

Lord Thomas thought, "Perhaps I should heed their warning, this time."

The long winter raged and dragged unmercifully, short gloomy days and long cold nights drove Lord Thomas insane, but controlling his patience, he endured. Holidays his family spent celebrating alone. The staff had their own dinner and celebration in the servants' quarters. When the servants sang carols, it upset him. Cybilia could not imagine why beautiful holiday songs should upset him.

He rode away early one morning in the first week of March after a hearty breakfast. Seated comfortably in his carriage, an extra blanket lay on the seat just in case of unexpected weather conditions. The coachman dressed warmly, the horses galloped, the sooner to arrive at the castle, avoid late evening darkness. Anyway, it would be rude, besides darkness is much unnerving. Lord Thomas dozed off dreaming. Suddenly startled out of his sleep, when the carriage hit a rut in the road it threw him to the side of the carriage. His head bumped hard giving him a lump too sensitive to touch. This angered him, his fists tight. Noonday, obscured by clouds, snow rolling in, he tapped the side of the carriage with the cane. The coachman halted, he stepped down and opened the carriage door. "How much further... Wait just a second nature calls!" Lord Thomas walked off several yards hid behind a tree.

"We are near your village sir and, soon we will climb the mountain," the coachman replied.

"Keep going looks like a storm is brewing on the horizon. I am tired and hungry and so are you, my brother is a good host, and he will feed us well," Thomas said.

They arrived at the gate of the castle, the coachman stepped down stiffly walked over and banged with the head of a wolf knocker. After waiting a while, a man appeared.

"Yes, who has arrived?" Butler Jonasen asked.

"Lord Thomas, your master's brother has arrived," the coachman said.

"I will announce you are here, if I find him," Butler Jonasen said, and closed the door. The coachman sat inside the carriage to keep warm with Lord Thomas.

"We have to wait until he finds his master," he said.

"What do you mean if he finds him, is that what he said? Perhaps he is in the village. We should have stopped to check there first." He was irritated unable to check his composure. He felt it would be embarrassing, so he tried hard to control his temper. He remembered the first time he belittled himself in front of that young man at Kosta's little house, well, actually it was his too; he grew up in it, surely his temper will not flare this time.

Butler Jonasen found Kosta and Kathryn in front of the fireplace with the children on the floor staring at the dancing flames.

"Sir, your brother has just arrived, he is in the courtyard waiting in the carriage, alone I believe, please come, he is waiting for you, or should I show them in?" Butler Jonasen said.

"Thank you, we will come." Kosta and Kathryn jumped to their feet headed for the front door. Kathryn glanced back at the children motioned for them to remain as they were. The door swung open and Kosta crossed the courtyard. Driver opened the carriage. Lord Thomas stepped out and walked into the courtyard greeted by Kosta and Kathryn. The surprise was evident on their faces, still their welcome sincere. They went into the parlor. The girls curtsied. The boys shook hands with Uncle Thomas, but Mathew, only bowed low.

"Welcome back Uncle Thomas," Mathew said.

Kosta was surprised at his sons' behavior, but said nothing. In the kitchen, the cook prepared plates of food for the hungry visitors.

"Oh you are not the gardener or a cook either?" Asked the coachman sipping tea, "I would never have guessed, this tea is perfectly steeped, soothing for a dry throat," he smiled at the woman, and she smiled back at him.

"Yes he is 'the' gardener and the best in this area. His gardens overflow with everything he plants, enough to last through the winter. He has been gifted with a great green thumb," Simena proudly stated as she nudged the gardener. Sudden rasping cough made her walk out quickly, she had to bed down for a while, she, over winter contracted a cough bad enough to keep her down in bed, Kathryn worried about her, the winter was severe to call on the doctor, was impossible.

The gardener being polite sat at the table to keep the coachman company, just sniffed and sipped his tea.

Kosta sat in the dining room to keep his brother company while he ate his lunch.

Kosta wondered what will transpire now since Thomas came unannounced and in the middle of this chilly day. *He must be mad with curiosity. He could not wait for spring I realize that, well I wonder how long he will stay this time.* Lord Thomas ate quickly, chewing, swallowing and washing down the good food with tea, he was hungry his coachman had forgotten the basket with snacks in the kitchen back home.

"Mother why is he here?" Jason asked.

"You should know why!" Tessana answered him.

"He scares me, the way his eyes jump around," Rosie whispered.

"I like Aunt Cybilia, she is nice," Kras said to Marla.

"I think Mark is very handsome, I think his character is different than his father's," Jasemin said, resting her chin on her hands, she was staring at the flames, relaxing on the rug.

Mathew glanced at his mother and they smiled.

"Mathew what do you think of Sabrina?" Kathryn asked.

"Since we are discussing your cousins, but be nice and be careful, Father may just pop in here any minute, so be ready to go upstairs. Do not forget to be polite."

"Oh Mother," Rosie said, "of course we will. We are not babies anymore."

They laughed. Rosie looked at them and said perturbed; "well, we are not!'

"Mother to answer your question about Shara, well she seems to be nice. But, I feel something strange...another thing puzzles me, why do they call Shara, where did that name come from..." he trailed off. Kathryn did not reply she just looked at her son and wondered what does he feel and why? The brothers walked into the parlor with wine glasses and Kosta carried one for Kathryn.

"A toast to our guest, Uncle Thomas!" and at that moment the children one by one began to leave. The three adults seated relaxing. Lord Thomas satiated seemed a bit sleepy. Kathryn sipped her wine and watched the flames dancing in the hearth.

"*How odd...*thought Kosta, *this red-hot fire reminds me of that winter evening when the barn burned...and then the second time...that man in the shadows...We lost everything...but thank goodness no lives were lost.*"

He was so engrossed in his thoughts, did not hear Lord Thomas talking to him, until Kathryn pulled his sleeve.

"I am sorry, it has been a long day and I am tired. The flames are hypnotizing and, the wine is making me drowsy. What did you ask me?"

"Never mind...we shall talk in the morning. I too am tired from this long trip. I will retire if you will show me where to sleep. I appreciate your hospitality very much, thank you," Lord Thomas said and they went upstairs. Kathryn remained in the parlor by the fireplace sipping wine. She waited for Kosta to come back down.

Before his brother arrived, they both relaxed. Now she feels odd. The night will be long. She was not ready to go to bed. She needs to make sure the coachman is comfortable too. Lira and Dola must be careful perhaps Simena should sleep with them. Surely, they will question her why. She will explain later after their guest leaves. Kosta came down and sat next to her and Kathryn jumped. "I am sorry I startled you, love. We should go to bed."

"I need to talk to Simena and the girls."

"Why? What is it about? Do you need me to come along?" Kosta asked.

"It is important to me. You know how I feel about your brother. My question is while he is here...am I wrong...to feel they should not sleep alone."

"Well...I know Thomas has a roving eye, but I doubt very much he would be foolish to make such a stupid mistake. You know what it would cost him. Kathryn if it makes you feel better, we will go and talk to them, I am sure Simena will watch over them, and I mean watch them," Kosta smiled. The quietness, the darkness, the moonless night seemed eerie, the temperature had dropped and it was cold, the air in each room hung heavy. One can only wonder how many will not sleep. Eyes opened staring, blinking, and waiting. Listening, listening for what? Something, something, tense, then darkness.

Kathryn cuddled next to Kosta afraid to break this eerie silence by speaking. Sleep closed their eyes near dawn, deep sleep, but short sleep.

The rooster awakened them, they were aware that someone had arrived unannounced last night and is in the castle. It was too quiet, each morning the laughter of children and the dog barking echoed through the castle, voices in the kitchen and the aroma of breakfast in the air made everyone cheerful.

But not this morning...it was tension, caution, whispering, yet the aroma of food drew everyone into the kitchen, the women acted different, quiet, they did not call to each other for "hand me this or that," but reached for such items themselves. Kathryn noticed and Kosta observed them all, wondering, *they feel it too?*

"This is a bad situation here, I must resolve this," he said to Kathryn.

"So... he said, tell me, Simena what is wrong. Why so sullen, so dismal, why, all of you are like shadows around here. This is not acceptable to us. You are not our usual happy crew! At least for the next several days all of you show that nothing is wrong. This is a morgue, now, not a kitchen! Please do not allow my brother to notice and wonder why this change. We would like to see smiles and hear laughter as before. Thank you."

Dola began to cry, "We have the same feeling, foreboding feeling, and we are afraid."

"Afraid of what?" Kathryn asked. They looked at the gardener.

"We must tell our master what is wrong." The whole crew nodded. They sat around the kitchen table and Simena told him.

"We fear your brother. We are afraid that he will buy this castle and we will either work for him, or lose our jobs, we truly fear harm for some of us." Kosta listened and when they had their say, he had to tell them.

"My brother came to find out what happened to me, where I have been so many years. This castle, I assure you, is not for sale, period! You should have no doubt, absolutely no doubt."

All of them relaxed, smiles appeared on their faces they promised to be more cheerful. Kosta's feelings lingered, same as theirs, but he could not admit this to them, before he walked out of the kitchen he faced them, and said, "One more thing. First do it for yourselves, and then for us. Whatever it is you feel, reject it, we must overcome all of it...and we will...it will pass...things will be fine...I know...you must believe in me, you did not fail from the start, so do not fail me now." Kosta whispered and they all looked at him. "Nothing will change...we will be together...so show your strength." They promised him, no matter what, they would not fail.

He knew what the problem was and he knew Kathryn was aware of this too. The days, evenings, and nights that followed were stressful. Lord Thomas was like Kosta's shadow. He followed him around everywhere and talked constantly. To some questions, Kosta simply had no answers. Which irritated Lord Thomas, he frowned. However, Kosta never flinched. He was expressionless, calm and composed.

Lord Thomas as hard as he tried to rile Kosta, to make him at least once show anger or explode, and expel his feelings, could not. Kosta's composed behavior Lord Thomas could not break, it was getting to him more and more, with each hour that he was spending there. The children were distant from him; they eyed him and whispered something among themselves. Spoke to him very little, keeping occupied with trivial things, as if those things were more important than their Uncle was.

Four days had that gone by, and soon it will be time to go back home.

Kosta had not mentioned anything about his misfortune and adventure and the fortune he had acquired.

Every time Lord Thomas looked at the face of Kosta the bloody image stood in front of him, aware what he had done to Kosta he needed to hear this time everything, he is here alone. It was time. Kosta was stalling. He felt it.

At breakfast, Lord Thomas unexpectedly threw a blunt question at Kosta. "Before I leave tomorrow I would like to hear the whole story of your adventurous long journey, I am here alone as you said before, come alone. Please I cannot stay much longer, so do not stall." His voice was tart. All eyes turned on him.

Kathryn cringed. Mathew's hands slid under the table and he clasped them tight. The younger children stared at their Uncle, unable to eat. The whole dining room fell silent.

"Why do you need to say it so bluntly, I gave you my word, I did not forget, just that I had to think it over, consider how you will absorb it all when you hear what happened," Kosta quietly said and smiled. Kosta looked at his family and smiled at them too, the girls had tears in their eyes and the boys had sour faces.

"Relax everyone, it is fine with me, your Uncle is curious, that is all. I think he should know the whole story, later on you will agree with me. He is my brother."

Within minutes, the children and Kathryn excused themselves and walked out of the dining room.

Seventy-Five:

The True Story

Lord Thomas sat at the table, while Kosta reached for a large bottle of wine, poured two large goblets and handed one to his brother.

"Let us have a drink my brother, this will be a long story, rather I should say, my true story. We should sit comfortably in the parlor, by the fire." Kosta looked deep into his brother's eyes.

"I detect a bit of mockery with this toast," Lord Thomas said.

"Forgive me if it seemed to you that way, but it was just...that...it was that moment," Kosta replied.

"Aha...before I start I need to go bring something very important." Kosta walked out and after a moment returned, lay on the side table a grey cloth rolled up, tied with a black ribbon.

"Well now...Thomas, I am sure you recall our childhood. Our way of life changed when our parents died, but we went on with our lives as best we knew. My complements to you...Kosta took a sip of wine...you fared well. Without Mother and Father I had a rough adjustment to a meager life, if not for Aunt Olivia, she was my only family... I should say our only family. I grew up fast and worked hard. I was the one with many obstacles in my life. No need to go into more detail, you know the story of my life. The day you married Cybilia we were there, uninvited. Aunt Olivia and I we stood in the back, among all other uninvited onlookers, you did not see us. Aunt Olivia was deeply hurt and offended but she never talked about it." Kosta stopped for a minute, looked into his glass, took a sip.

"But Kosta I can explain..." Kosta raised his hand to forestall him.

"Thomas no need to. I knew why, the reason I am bringing this up is, you hurt Aunt Olivia. I... did not matter. You did not need me in your life."

"But you did not understand what I aimed for, Kosta!" Thomas objected.

Kosta looked away and continued, "One day Kathryn came into my life and stole my heart. You know we have seven children. That land did not produce enough to support all of us. I recall my first visit to you. You knew my need, my misery. I accepted the loss of my eye, you disfigured my face, and I saw pain in my children's eyes, for me. I cannot and want not to make you feel guilty. I lived for my children, we enjoyed good times, but unfortunately, the bad outweighed the good. The barn went up in flames we lost all winter grain. The second fire I knew it was intentional arson. I saw the man running off."

"You...did you recognize him?" curiously Thomas asked.

Kosta looked at his brother thinking, *is he afraid I recognized the man, then it was his man, his action proves it.* Kosta continued... "no, it was too dark. Again during mid-fall, we lost everything second time, but we survived. Years of misery, worry. You were fortunate, very fortunate. You succeeded. I looked up to you, even though you did not think of me much of a man. Nevertheless, Thomas I worked hard. We were thankful for having little."

Thomas stood up and refilled their glasses, sat down, crossed his legs and his left leg began to swing.

"There were times I could not understand how Fate rules peoples' lives. The balance of fairness seemed none existent. Yet, to God or man I did not complain. I felt cursed, why should I be cursed, what crime have I committed? I cursed the soil I worked, which years of labor gave me little in return. I crawled to you, my only brother. You had done to me what you felt justified to do...you needed to do, to what I had agreed to...the first time. What you felt was fair the second time, well I cannot... and I was placed between the grave mounds, I was left there to die."

Lord Thomas nervously jerked his leg, switching left to right, his expression sullen.

"I was unconscious all night, that wine we drank together that evening...I knew it was morning the sun's heat woke me up...I sobered up, I felt the pain... unable to see where I was, I was sure I would die there alone, Kathryn and the children would never know what had happened to me. I began to wonder why... why...why did you punish me in such a way Thomas? If you walked in my shoes, would you still have?" Kosta asked directly looking at his brother.

Lord Thomas downed half a glass of wine, did not reply.

"In my mind I talked to you, I kept asking why...I slipped in and out of sleep. Hunger and thirst gnawed at my stomach. The insects attacked my open wound I covered my eye with my arm. I must have had millions of bites.

"But that second night animals approached and seemed to be all around me, I knew what animals they were, their snarls and growls as they closed in...I realized they were wolves. Surely, I felt they would rip me apart, gripped by fear I prayed to God to take my soul now. I dreaded dying that way."

Lord Thomas sat up straight and cried out, "Wolves, but..."

"Yes. Instead of killing me, these wolves settled around me and kept me warm. I slept a deep sleep," Kosta said looking into his goblet.

"Second day was the same. Not a chance of finding my way home, being blind, even if I could crawl, how far would I get. It rained. I caught a few drops of that sweet refreshing rainwater into my mouth, but not enough to sustain my hunger. I was in terrible panic, such as I have never experienced in my life, I tried to scream...but who would hear me." Kosta stopped and downed the rest of his wine and refilled his glass. Lord Thomas sat, listened and sipped the wine slowly.

"Here my brother is the mystery I could not comprehend." Kosta's eyes cast down, "I knew my fate. I had no other choice when I heard noises but to lay still and listen; I heard strange rustling and whispers. I strained to hear what or who was near; but I realized these whispers were coming from above, a tree, I did not know if trees were that close, how could I. Mystery magic or witchcraft I did not know...I was blind. Afraid of being discovered, afraid of being torn apart by whatever creatures were out there, I lay very still, the insects were fierce but I was forced to endure."

Lord Thomas sipped the wine and listened intently. From the start of the story his left leg was swinging, but now his right.

"Were you dreaming, or were you awake?" he asked.

To Kosta this meant his brother was irritated and uncomfortable by the complete description of the scenario. Now and then, he scratched his nose. His facial expression showed annoyance. A twist of his lips, or a lift in the corner of his lips, he turned the goblet full circle.

Kosta did not comment, he continued, expecting his brother to interrupt him soon. He did, in his voice Kosta detected boredom.

"Kosta, that is preposterous, what were these creatures saying, could you understand them clearly?" Lord Thomas leaned forward uncrossing his legs, reaching for the wine bottle, refilled both goblets.

"Yes I could hear them very clearly, these creatures returned on the third night."

"Really...these creatures were there two nights in a row? What did they talk about?" he exclaimed.

"Well, on the second night they talked about problems in different parts of the world. They named the towns and villages...and the kingdom of Magda where the little princess lay ill."

Lord Thomas seemed to be interested now, as he reached for the goblet sipping more often. Kosta noticed a spark in his brother's eyes, as he continued.

"They also talked about a tragedy which happened a long time ago, but they did not mention where. Their leader said they must choose an individual for assignments. Then they abruptly flew away. I waited. How odd I thought, these strange creatures could speak, had strange names, what intrigued me the most was they knew so much, where they came from I cannot tell you.

"Do you remember their names?" Lord Thomas asked.

Kosta did not reply but stared at the fire in the hearth.

"No. But I assure you there is God...you see, the night was cold, the ground damp, I was shivering, then I heard again the sounds somewhat different, so it seemed...I expected this time wild boars. I prayed to God I do not want to be torn apart alive. I held my breath, my heart drummed loud in my ears. Soon enough they were all around me, they sniffed my face and I knew the same pack of wolves came again they clung to me, kept me warm, I know they were wolves, their wild scent rubbed off on me.

"I was grateful for their warm bodies so close to mine, one laid on my chest as before and I slowly raised my hand and I touched him, he licked my hand. I needed food and water, and have my vision, go home, be with my family, instead, here I was sleeping with a pack of wolves. I knew I would die of starvation if no one finds me soon. That is a horrid way to die, I would not wish that on my worst enemy believe me. The third night the speaking creatures were back, again I feared for my life. What if I am not supposed to hear what they were talking about, they will kill me, believing I was a spy. But this night was different and I was the subject of their meeting."

"You...they were talking about you?" Lord Thomas exclaimed.

Leaning slightly forward in his chair he thought, "*this is bizarre. Kosta is fabricating all of it. I must hear this.*" He sipped the wine.

"Yes me. They knew everything about me, and when they began to speak, they spoke directly to me. I held my breath. I could not believe what I heard.

They knew I was there on the ground and that I was blind. They said that my eyesight will return, all I must do is to feel in the grass and I will find carpophores..."

Lord Thomas interrupted asking, "What is carpophore?"

Kosta glanced at the large grandfather clock, nearing eleven, one hour to midnight.

"I can tell you the name is imbedded in my brain, Bovista Plumbea, round puffy mushrooms. I was to rub my eye sockets and my sight will return. I must go to these places and solve these problems. Not only will I have my eyesight. I will be very rich.

"They forbade me to go home to my family. I must go directly on my journey and, when I complete my assignments then I will be back with my family. Although my family will suffer much, they will survive. They said, next time they return here, that is where I was on the ground, would be in the springtime, early springtime. I listened, soon they were silent, seemed to me that they too were sleeping, or perhaps they flew away. I began to grope all around me, I felt something soft and I pulled it out of the grass, I felt this round ball and I smelled a distinct aroma of a mushroom, I rubbed my left eye, and then gently touched my right eye; waiting for something to happen; but nothing happened. I waited. I felt a strange drowsiness come over me. I slept through the night deeply."

Kosta stopped for a moment, and that moment seemed long, as he stared into the fire.

"You recall it was spring when I came to see you...remember? And now it is spring," Kosta said and closed his eyes for a moment. Lord Thomas said in a hushed voice, "Yes it was, I remember well, I did have trouble sleeping after what I had done to you, but time took care of that, you were gone so long, at least three years now, is it not? I thought that animals had devoured you."

The silence made Lord Thomas uncomfortable, but he did not dare ask Kosta to go on.

"Sometime in the night I woke up, I said to myself, I slept long. As I opened my eyes, it was nighttime, I was looking up at the stars twinkling, and I saw the moon. Was I alive or had I died? I sat up and glanced around, yes, I was alive, and I saw, I was at the cemetery between graves. I blinked and fell back, this was no dream. This was real. I touched my face, no pain. I fell asleep again. Awakened by the warmth of the sun, I cried out, Oh God, I have my eyesight, just as they said I would. This was either magic or a miracle. I sat up and looked around, then I was on my feet, I saw the oak tree, at that moment I realized what I was, and now what I am. My body trembled. I dropped to the ground again with my head between my knees."

Lord Thomas skeptical to this far-fetched story listened, but did not interrupt. He was waiting for the true story's ending.

"I sat between the grave mounds and, I noticed those white puffy mushrooms which the creatures said I should rub my sore eyes to regain my sight. I remembered that after I had rubbed my eyes I became drowsy; I drifted off into a deep sleep.

I stood and stared at the oak tree. I noticed something black on the grass beneath it, I walked over there to look and, 'lo and behold' on the grass were scattered feathers, shiny black feathers, I realized then those voices did not belong to some creatures, rather belonged to the Ravens, as I picked them up I counted, there were thirteen feathers. I needed to keep these to my dying day.

I reached out to heaven and said a prayer for the miracle and life's mysterious magic. I could live a normal life again."

Kosta reached for the grey cloth tied with a black ribbon, untied it, spread that cloth revealing the thirteen shiny black feathers. Lord Thomas leaned forward and stared at those feathers, and no one could ever have guessed what he was thinking of.

Kosta rolled up the cloth tied the ribbon and set it aside. Lord Thomas had no questions.

"Off I went, believe me; I felt no hunger or thirst. Within me, some strange energy propelled me onward and, what would have taken months perhaps more than that to reach the fourth mountain range to the west, strange as it sounds I was there, actually, I counted the days, and weeks, you know it was thirteen, thirteen weeks to reach the fourth range. All the while on my long journey, I knew what to do, where to go. All this for my children, my Kathryn, for them I lived, and I loved them, and, I thought about you.

"The King gave me four horses, the carriage and sacks of gold, and the celebration went on for three days in my honor, I cured his little girl, princess Alexia. I had done what I was compelled to do. I was gone for several years. I did not lose my eyesight..."

"So all in all how many problems did you solve?" Lord Thomas interrupted.

Kosta took his time, took a sip of wine and looked at the clock, walked over to the fire and added several logs and returned to his comfortable chair and continued.

"Well let me see...total of four. The distance between each was great, and some were complicated, the Ravens said that one would be difficult to handle, it was, but I was determined, I refused to give up, I had to overcome obstacles, which I had a few. And so I managed, that is why I was gone so long."

Thomas stirred on the seat.

"And each time you solved a problem you received a sack of gold?" Lord Thomas asked.

"Yes, I tried to refuse, but these people insisted, so I had to take the gold..." he hesitated knowing he just told a white lie, but had no regrets, Kosta replied nonchalantly.

"The last assignment took the longest with that very old man. At first he refused to leave his house, but after days of talks, cooking and waiting his decision to come along with me, to live with us, my family, be a grandfather to my children, a grandfather they never had." Lord Thomas shocked jumped up in his chair.

"What? You had to bring an old man back with you to your house! That small house of yours, why there was no room for a mouse, much less for another human body!"

Kosta smiled amused, not at all surprised at that remark.

"Yes of course, I had to, that was one of the stipulations, if I did not, I would lose everything, plus my eyesight." Lord Thomas frowned and took a gulp of wine.

"What else did you have to do that was not pleasant, besides the old man?"

"Thomas...excuse me, I need to tend to the fire it is almost out. I am at the end of my story. I will answer any questions you have when I am finished, I do not want to lose heat."

Kosta politely said to his brother and, getting up out of his chair walked over to the fireplace, placed a few pieces of kindling on the dying embers, it smoked for a while and then burst into flame, Kosta then added more firewood, stood in front of it and waited to make sure the fire will flare and burn well.

After a few minutes, he walked back to the chair and sat down. Kosta glanced at his brother and noticed his brother engrossed in deep thought.

"*What is on his mind at this moment? Let him visualize from the beginning to the end what cruelty he had inflicted on me,*" Kosta thought.

Kathryn and the children enjoyed togetherness up in one of the library-sitting rooms. They too had a nice fire going, the girls loved to just sit around and watch it glow. Mathew and Rebecca were engrossed in reading, Kathryn with her head resting on the back of the chair with eyes closed thought about her life as it was years past to the present, those awful winters, lack of food. Miraculously all is well. In a few days Rabinna her sister and Michael will arrive, that will be fun.

Mathew nudged Rebecca and they quickly left the room, tiptoed down the stairs hid in a dark corner and eavesdropped.

Kathryn changed her thoughts to Thomas and Cybilia she was not sure what the future held, since the two brothers reunited somewhat in a strange way, after all these years. Thomas had only one reason to be here, that she knew, the mystery and magic of Kosta's regained eyesight. The hours passed. Downstairs in the parlor the two brothers sat and the conversation went on.

Lord Thomas was looking into his goblet of wine, as if something floating in it, he said, "I apologize for interrupting; I do want to hear the end of the story."

"Well, the elderly man was the last one on my assignment which was on my way home. When at last the elderly man decided to come along, he ordered me to burn down his house...and everything in it. That was some sight, and I observed him when his house burned, he said, that many years of loneliness and sadness are going up in smoke, he also said, that he did not want anyone else to have the same miserable life as his was, and it burned. The elderly man became ill. I stopped in a village seeking doctor's help...through him we sent a messenger to my family. The messenger died from an attack of vicious animals on the road. I came upon their remains we had to run for our lives.

"That truly must have been a hair-raising experience to both of you." Lord Thomas sighed.

Kosta thought for a minute and then glanced at the clock again.

"Yes I was never more frightened than at that moment, even the horses sensed the danger and they galloped away. Back home everyone thought I was dead and, as far as Kathryn was concerned, I was *dead...*" Kosta's voice trailed off.

The silence in the room was unbearable, neither one spoke.

Kosta did not want to reveal that that morning when he stopped at Michaels, and the plan turned out so badly and Kathryn fainting. No, that part he will not talk about, his brother heard enough. Weather he believes all of it or not, it does not matter to Kosta, everything he said was the "*truth*" it is up to his brother to understand it and believe.

Lord Thomas sat his empty goblet on the side table and rose from his chair; he walked over to Kosta and said in a voice, which seemed truly sincere.

"I am sorry for all I have done to you, and your family, I do hope you will forgive me." Kosta at first did not reply, for some reason he could not, all he could do is look at Thomas, he kept looking at his face, seeking sincerity, Thomas reached out his hand and Kosta stood up and took it, they held a tight grasp for a moment.

Lord Thomas said two words to Kosta and let go of Kosta's hand, "*thank you.*"

Still Kosta said nothing.

Lord Thomas turned and walked out of the parlor. Kosta sat back down heavily into the chair, and closed his eyes, perhaps he did not want to look at an empty room the fire burned down to grey ashes, and Kosta felt very empty within, as if he had just lost his brother forever. Same empty feeling as of long ago when he lost his parents. It was late into the night, but he could not make himself go upstairs, not yet. He refilled his wine goblet sipped it slowly. He stared at the wine and wondered, *what makes it so red*?

He heard footsteps and someone walked into the parlor, it was Kathryn, she came to him took his hand and, she led him out of the parlor and went upstairs. It was almost dawn. Shortly the staff will rise to another busy tomorrow.

Kosta relived his three days of pain and panic all over again that evening. Kathryn's hand held his. He felt such love for her, as he had never ever had before.

Seventy-Six: Agnostic Thomas

When dawn lit up the bedroom Lord Thomas was still awake, dressed and, ready to return home, his home, his wife and children. His mood full of mixed emotions and he felt as if those feelings were controlling him. He wanted to believe that incredible illusionary story, but then he had doubts. He almost convinced himself that someone found Kosta. Recalling that night he imagined, *perhaps the servant did not gouge out the eye. Perhaps he just had gone through the motion with small cuts creating blood flow, which streaked down his face, it was rather dark in the stable, he was quite under the influence of the wine too, and the servant could have fooled him. No, he had done it himself just as he gouged out the other eye...that is bizarre...magic. What magic*? His thoughts ran wild and he began to feel very restless, as if he had to get away from here. Then he smelled the aroma of fresh coffee. The girl served him a large cup of coffee and a slice of bread and butter, she offered honey but he waved her away and said, "Ah, Irmina a glass of wine would suit me better than honey. Will you please scramble three eggs each and some bacon, thank you." They laughed. The morning, was cool, during the night snow barely sprinkled the ground, though it was early spring. He needed to go out with his coffee to that bench beneath that huge oak tree, for the last time. He told the servants that, if their master should come, tell him I will be there on the bench.

He sat and sipped his coffee, shortly after Thomas saw Kosta walking up the path, last year's brown leaves sprinkled with snow underfoot. Red-golden leaves and flowers victims of the long winter freeze. The scene was different from the summer's happy colorful gardens. The trees still were bare, what remained of summers beauty here now remained dead all around. Upon arising that morning he felt a bit depressed. Was it Kosta's story? Could it be winters lingering gloom, still?

The two brothers sat without speaking, Kosta could not understand what had happened to Thomas, why the sudden quietness, it is not like him at all.

At last, Thomas spoke and his voice sounded somber.

"You have told me the 'real truth' I tried to feel your suffering and your pain, I realized I had done an unforgivable cruel deed, the unjust feeling of hate for you, I cannot explain why all this happened, but I know that I did you wrong, I do hope you will forgive me."

Kosta surprised to hear the spoken words of "forgive me," again observed Thomas, searching his face to detect any hidden deceit.

"Why did you hate me so much, Thomas?" he asked.

The answer came to Kosta as a shock, "Because you were the one with talent, compassion, humility...which I realized I did not possess, you are the perfect image of Father. I always felt that they loved you more. I remember when you were born, they devoted all their time to you, and I was on the sideline. I was in competition with you for attention and affection. You also have so much love in your heart, it shines right through you, which I cannot have...or able to display. I grasp for material things instead, I have amassed much, thinking these things will replace the love I yearned for long ago, but, could never possess...Cybilia is a good woman...she gave me a son and a daughter, but I feel nothing towards them anymore...I always feel angry and I do not know why.

"This anger makes me want to acquire more and more. I am possessed. Now...I have exposed to you...myself...and now you know my feelings. Know this, regardless of what I told you here and now...still, I do want this castle, I will pay any price, whatever price you want, say you will sell it to me."

This unexpected statement caught Kosta off guard. He was breathless. His brother's open confession and true feelings and observations throughout his lifetime Kosta heard, made him speechless. For some unexplained reason Kosta unable to protest to every word that his brother had spoken. His voice refused to emerge out of his chest to reply. Why did Kosta feel so oddly skeptical of his brother's omission of many facts? Kosta was aware of those things. It was best to let it all rest for now, in time all will surface.

Lord Thomas announced he was leaving before noon. He wants to go home. He will send word to inquire about the decision on the sale. Kosta had no words at that moment, and he could not look up at his brother but sat and stared into the ground.

Lord Thomas walked away not bidding him goodbye.

Kosta glanced after his only brother stroll away and wondered what is going on in his mind. Some of the things he said were not altogether true.

Kosta strolled to the castle, found his brother in the kitchen, having a basket prepared for the road. Their parting seemed cool, distant, in their handshake the grip was not there. Lord Thomas rode away in his fine carriage. He glanced back and saw Kosta standing in the gateway.

All the way home Lord Thomas thought about what Kosta had told him, this to him was an incredible story, rather his reality, experience of suffering, emerging out of it victorious.

Suddenly his evil self-emerged. Envy to possess what he rightfully should leave alone. He began to compile plans to acquire what he wished for, not by force but by events. He must choose a trustworthy servant, one who keeps a secret and nerves of steel. Visit his old pals at Hoofs Inn. Go fishing, now that appealed to him, so he told of his plan to Cybilia, Mark, and Shara. Cybilia and the children replied they would have to think about a trip like that, they wanted to know how long would they stay away from home?

Lord Thomas said, "At least a month." Cybilia sternly objected.

"Too long...leave the estate in the servant's care would be foolish. You know very well what could happen," she exclaimed.

"Nothing will happen! They have been with us most of their lives, they are faithful, they will plant on time, and besides they are paid. I want to go away," he insisted firmly.

"Why must you Father?" Shara asked him.

"I am tired of such long winters, and I am getting old, severe cold bothers me. I have not mentioned before, I do feel it in my bones," he replied.

Cybilia thought that that was a lame reason. He never wanted to go away to a warmer climate...he loved four seasons.

"What about summer, is it not hot enough? Cybilia asked smirking.

"Are we not visiting Uncle Kosta this year?" Shara questioned.

"We could stay with them for a few weeks, now that you two are friends again," Cybilia interrupted.

"The time will slip by faster. They are a lot of fun," Shara declared loudly and Mark quickly agreed with her, even Cybilia agreed.

"Perhaps you are right, I will...it is only early spring, we have time to decide about vacation," Lord Thomas said.

"If we spend the summer with Kosta's family, then you are free to go on your trip and stay until autumn," Cybilia said.

Lord Thomas looked at her and his son and daughter and curled his lip.

"Well I suppose I could be nice to my family and oblige their wishes, agreed."

Lord Thomas sat alone in his favorite chair sipping wine, dreaming of that day when he will be the wealthiest man. The whole world will know his name. What he desired, was fame. One day, his horse saddled, he trotted off to the cemetery, to check out the area, *the* space and the *oak tree*. Sebastian did not question just wondered. While saddling his masters stallion Star a week later, asked.

"May I ride with you master? I love to ride." Together they approached one of the cemeteries a bit too far from home but rode through it. Sebastian thinking his master is ill now is choosing a gravesite, his expression grave. Lord Thomas asked why the sadness? Sebastian told him the reason.

"Oh no, I am not ill, I am searching for a nice spot, this is too far from home."

"But who is it for?" Sebastian asked.

"Sebastian there is no 'who'... it is *why*, with a reason," Lord Thomas said.

"I know of a cemetery much closer to home."

"Oh, where the river runs to the east?" Lord Thomas asked.

"Yes, that one, my Aunt is resting there. Sometimes I sit and talk to her. I bring greetings from my mother," Sebastian said.

"Well then we should go there right now, it is still daylight," Lord Thomas exclaimed. Sebastian rode to the end of the cemetery. Sebastian meandered through the mounds to his Aunts grave. Lord Thomas noticed the huge oak tree, steered Star to it, rode under the oak tree, and called to Sebastian.

"I have a plan for something spectacular and I want you to be part of it."

"What...What sort of plan?" Sebastian concerned for his life at that. Lord Thomas circled the oak tree, and thought, "*just as I envisioned exactly as Kosta described.*" Feeling satisfied they headed home.

Seventy-Seven:

The Spring Blizzard

Kosta's family has been residing in the castle for one year now. Everyone got along well and the place rang with harmony.

The young fellow living in Kosta's little home delivered a letter to, *"K.K. Komarod Family"* from Lord Thomas. Kosta read the letter, Thomas's wishes for his family to spend the summer at the castle. The letter signed by each one of them.

Well now, Kosta and Kathryn over dinner discussed the letter with the children. Arguments were for *'yea'* and *'nay'* for their Uncles holiday visit, but after an hour or so unanimously agreed to invite them.

Rosie excitedly cried out, "Hey maybe the ghosts will visit us."

"Oh that would be fun! Should we call them out?" Tessana caught on to that and exclaimed.

"Oh yes let us do that, perhaps then Uncle Thomas will forget about buying our castle." All of them laughed until they cried.

"You know I do miss our dear friend Baron Patrick and Aunt Olivia, but I am sure they will give us a sign if they are around," Kathryn said.

Suddenly during the serving of the dessert, one of the candles on the table winked out, someone pinched it, all eyes were on it and then they applauded. A good sign, the spirits were within the castle, then surely during summer the show will begin.

That evening was most enjoyable for all, even the servants were happy.

"We should write an invitation to Michael, Rabinna and Rebecca Hartigard. Mathew you are good at writing letters, please write to them, and a reply to Uncle Thomas."

"Gladly father, I will do so in the morning," Mathew retorted.

Tessana smiled and said, "Oh yes he will gladly do so, because, that means Rebecca will come and they will be chummy again."

Kathryn reprimanded her. "Tessana how could you make fun of them...they grew up together, they are true friends, my dear do not make such remarks."

Jason put his two cents in by saying, “Yea...what about you Tessana...when Mark is here you stare at him, and you forget yourself, but I noticed that many times, and you blush!” Kras made a funny face.

“All right that is enough, all of you!” Kosta shouted.

It was getting a bit too loud. Now everyone sat quietly. Kathryn smiled at Kosta.

“You know we do not have little children anymore, just look at them they are young adults.”

“Yes I see that, and that makes me feel very old,” he smiled at the children.

Tessana hugged him and said, “Father you are not old, we are just catching up to you!” At that everyone laughed, dinner was over and it was time to do things before going to bed.

While in bed, Kosta expressed his feelings to Kathryn about his brother.

“I have an uneasy feeling, I am trying to push it aside, but somehow that feeling keeps creeping back, why, that I cannot place. Nevertheless, I never expected or dreamed that my brother would ever reconsider, wanting now to be part of my simple life. Growing up he used to sneak out early in the morning or predawn, be gone all day. I saw him leave. My parents were fast asleep...tired from daily toil...when my father was away on a job mother had done the chores, alone. My brother was out with his friends having fun and, I was still a weakling. I could read the hurt in her faraway look. You know...Mother never complained or ever told Father. Then they died. I was alone. My brother did not care about me.

“You did all the farm work, alone?” Kathryn asked.

“Yes, remember, on our wedding day that was the very first time he came. He acted and strutted like a peacock, and throughout the years, every invitation to any occasion we ever had extended to him, he always had excuses, important reasons not to attend. My humble life he clearly avoided, I always felt that he was simply ashamed of me, what bothers me the most is that “change of heart” I keep hearing it in my mind over and over, it reminds me of that awful night, I truly believed that evening he had a change of heart and was willing to help us. I do not like this at all, not at all. Now he wants to be back in my life?”

Kathryn listened and then said, “I understand what you are feeling Kosta. Believe me. I too have my reservations about him. Something is brewing in his mind, whatever it is, forgive me for saying this, but I see it in his eyes. Many years ago I saw the way he looked at me and I felt eerie, he is your brother, but this I felt than and lately too, since you are talking about him, I needed to tell you, I hope you forgive me for saying the truth."

Kosta knew exactly what she meant. No need to defend his brother or his innocence, what she had said he has known of his brother's wayward character long ago, before she had ever met him. However, he never dared to approach his brother on such a delicate subject, most likely his brother would have reproached him for suggesting such a thing, without a doubt, he would have denied it all.

He wrapped his arms around her and said tenderly, "You know I love you very much, I have from the moment I saw you walking through the woods, let us not talk about him anymore, we have said what needed to be said. Now come closer and hold me, I need you in my arms."

That year spring came to be the oddest of all spring seasons ever.

Not everyone enjoyed to be out in that weather, only out of necessity. The visitors expected never arrived. The family in the castle spent dreary days indoors having only the crew for company, but this they enjoyed, for it brought tranquility and a closer bond between all of them. Kosta was thinking more and more what is taking place down in the valley, and he wished he could ride down and check on his old little home and the young man that was caring for it.

On a clear day weeks later Kosta decided to ride to the village, he mentioned his trip to Kathryn but she objected firmly, he assured her he would be back before dark and, if all is well, he will ride over to Michaels and bring Rebecca, a nice surprise for Mathew.

"Are you sure you want to go alone, perhaps Mathew should go with you, the two of you would be safer, I would not be concerned as much," Kathryn said thoughtfully.

Kosta noticed that certain worried look. Kosta gave in.

"Well, so be it, find Mathew and ask him if he wants to go with me down to the village." Well, Mathew was ready in a second. The downhill trip was slippery, at one point Mathew's horse slid and landed on its rump after which hobbled a bit, down in the valley the muddy road helped ease the pain. If Mathew's horse should go lame, they would have a problem, fortunately the horse had not shown discomfort the rest of the way. They reached the little house, all seemed to be fine. The neighbors stuck their heads out the doors and waved to them as they passed on to visit Rabinna and Michael, and bring Rebecca with them up to the castle. When they arrived Rebecca ran out to greet them, the visit was short unfortunately, the sun hid behind heavy clouds, temperature dropped. They anticipated a long trip home.

As the three of them were half way through the village, Kosta saw dark clouds on the horizon, seemed to be moving in fast, Kosta knew the rest of the road would be hazardous. Heavy storm will come upon them; in such conditions as they are surely, they must hurry home.

No one was out this day but these three individuals on horses. The wind picked up swirled dry granules and whipped around them, heavy and wet snow fell, and the visibility close to zero. The accumulation of snow covered all tracks, but Kosta led them on to the castle, which was still visible, soon it too will vanish out of sight.

Rebecca's white horse slid, fell on its belly, Rebecca screamed as she fell face down into the piles of snow.

Mathew followed behind her saw her falling, quickly jumped of his horse. Her frightened horse struggled to rise but kept slipping. Rebecca's leg was in a precarious position. The poor horse was in a mud and snow patch. Mathew pulled Rebecca away from the horse.

Mathew screamed. Kosta with the wind directly in his face, wrapped with a shawl around his nose and ears, never heard. After some time he looked back. Mathew was on the ground barely visible in the patchy snow. He double-backed to help his son, Rebecca was unconscious. No way to calm her horse his front legs sprawled, the belly flat on the ground. The horse for some reason could not rise, or even grunt. At one point, the horse ceased to struggle, his neck stretched lay on the ground, motionless, dead.

Mathew noticed Rebecca's leg was to the side.

Mathew mounted his horse, with Kosta's help managed to lift her up and lay her across his legs. Her arms dangled, her wool hat lost, Mathew removed his shawl and wrapped it around Rebecca's head and neck.

Rebecca opened her eyes, all she could see was the ground and horses legs, feeling uncomfortable, she moaned, she kicked, but her left leg gave her a sharp pain and she cried out, struggling grasped Mathew's leg. Mathew halted, helped her right herself onto the saddle, confused and embarrassed asked,

"What happened? Oh my leg, it hurts! Why was I in such a precarious position?"

Mathew held her close.

"I will tell you what happened when we get out of this snow storm. Now hold on, I pray you will not get dizzy or we will topple to the ground together."

She sat sidesaddle, her head on his chest, her arms around his waist and held on.

The road up to the castle was steep and slippery. Their horses strained. They reached the courtyard and turned to the back of the kitchen. Kosta carried Rebecca, Mathew followed behind, the cook taking in the scene, cried out to the others to come and help their master. Rebecca sat on a chair at the kitchen table. The three shivered under blankets. The cook handed each a large glass of wine.

Kathryn came running into the kitchen and the children followed, seeing Rebecca in a disheveled state.

"What happened? Were you attacked by wolves?"

"Beneath the snow must have been ice, Rebecca's horse slid, his legs sprawled flat out and landed on his belly, unable to stand up. Rebecca was thrown, she must have hit her head on something she was unconscious," Kosta explained, "she must have twisted her leg, she has not taken a step yet. Unfortunately, the strain and struggle had killed the horse. This incident surely proves the horse had a health problem." Kosta shaken, drank the wine to calm down, but worried about Rebecca's condition.

Rebecca had plenty of attention and glad that she was all right.

"Mother, Rebecca does not remember what happened, which concerns me," Mathew said.

Kathryn examined Rebecca's head and found a bump on the right side, not wanting to upset Mathew but..."In this case we need the doctor as soon as possible."

"Mother, what doctor would be willing to come in this blizzard, especially up this steep hill!" Mathew declared with concern.

Kathryn agreed with him, they discussed this situation with Kosta. The decision was to closely observe Rebecca, and do not mention Silky, her horse. Rebecca listened to conversations, but it was evident that she could not understand. They noticed a slight loss of equilibrium. Her leg slightly twisted at the knee but after a few days, she was able to put her weight on it.

As days turned to weeks, Rebecca improved, to everyone's relief. Rebecca was Mathews love as he realized long ago, when he was a teen, but he never told anyone. Now he is a young man of twenty and he positively felt she was his only love.

On a clear afternoon, Rebecca and Mathew walked around the gardens, when she walked into the stables to check on her horse, he was not there. Rebecca questioned Mathew,

"I did not want you to know while you were recovering. What

happened that afternoon in the snowstorm, your horse slipped and never could stand up...Rebecca...it was his heart...he had health problems, no one knew."

She wept, saying that was not fair, that the wolves devoured him, that was terrible and, she cannot imagine that her horse Silky had died. She dropped her head on his chest. He wrapped his arms around her.

"Rebecca, this summer I will find a black colt for you. You will train him and you will love him. You two will bond as much or even more than Silky."

"You will get a colt for me, Mathew?" she asked looking up rivulets of tears slid down her cheeks. He could not stop himself from kissing those tears.

"Yes I will, just wait for summer, I promise you I will!" he said tenderly.

The spring was wet and cold, unusual, the children marked each passing day on a sheet of paper, warm, cold or rainy or sunny, and did not forget a windy day.

Seventy-Eight: Long-Awaited Spring

By the end of April, the weather changed. Much moisture and warmth in its air, the days were longer, and life was definitely stirring within nature and people loved it. When the April rains came, it was time to roll up their sleeves and begin the toil.

The valley transformed into lush green, the fields were dark and moist, trees in cloaks of green. The country bloomed.

The rattle of wagon wheels and clatter of carts and people shouting to each other, laughter echoed and song birds on the wing. Rivers spilled their banks rushing far to the sea.

What more could one ask for, live and work and love, blessed with another year, another day, and another hour to be thankful for.

Far from the hub in the valley at the estate, work went on as efficiently as ever.

Eager to set his plan into action Lord Thomas sat on a bench leaning against the house, mulled over the plan from start to finish. Fear pricked like fire through him for a split second, he ignored it. Just took another sip of his favorite wine. He imagined all sorts of scenarios and the reaction this would have on all, especially his brother Kosta.

With that, a smile stretched and curled his lips to one side of his face.

"*Ha-I cannot wait for all of this to take place. It will be my time to reign*," he mused.

At the house Cybilia, Mark and Shara stood at the window observing him.

Wondering what was roiling in his mind.

Of course, they would have never guessed of his perfected plan and absolutely no one will, but for Sebastian who vowed on his life to keep the secret. Knowing what had happened to the others who have crossed the master's trust and what their punishment had been.

One more time Lord Thomas needed to visit with his brother,

one more time to ask his final decision of the sale. Winter interfered and prolonged the plans Lord Thomas had. Now it was spring, in just a few more weeks, his waiting will be over, and his plan carried out. Lord Thomas wanted one more visit for the coming weekend to the castle, and all four of them rode out early, this time without the coachman.

When by noon they arrived at the castle, everyone who happened to be working outdoors was surprised to see the unexpected guests.

Tessana at that moment busy with the old gardener planting flowers around the huge old oak tree, happened to look to the front and there they were; Mark, Shara and their parents.

"The family Komarod has arrived again!" she whispered and the gardener looked over his shoulder.

"I cannot stand that man! He is a brute, without consideration or manners. My dear girl whenever he is around me I pretend that I am hard of hearing." She smiled, catching his meaning.

"Good, I am glad you thought of that trick," and they both laughed, working with the planting and replanting.

Kosta greeted his brother's family at the door arriving just after their lunch the table cleared of dishes. Kosta and Kathryn led them in and said, "Please come seat yourselves, I will order lunch, all of you must be famished." Of course they were, gladly waited.

The families sat at the table. Kathryn disappeared into the kitchen and Kosta excused himself just for a minute, so he said. Their children were nowhere in sight. After what seemed an hour, Kosta and Kathryn came and sat down to keep company munching on cakes as dessert and fresh coffee, while his brother and family enjoyed lunch.

Tessana this time was conscious of her blushing so she chose to sit on Marks side of the table, this way she avoided looking at Mark directly. The fact was she liked Mark, but unfortunately, he was her cousin, but still, he was handsome and she was attracted to him, like any other girl would be. His voice a soft baritone, his manner certainly edged a bit on aristocracy, on his mother's side, of course, she enjoyed listening to him speak and his hands in motion, that came from his grandfathers Italian genes. That is all, she did not care what Jason had said before.

After lunch, Mark strolled through the grounds, joined by Jason. Tessana did not see them approaching, not that she cared if he sees her working with plants, or had dirty hands. Tessana washed up and they strolled over to Mathew, busy working on an urgent project for the stables, so he had to forgo the pleasant walk with them. Rebecca always was at Mathew's side, no matter what he was working on. Mark mentioned that he had noticed Rebecca was Mathew's shadow.

"Those two grew up together and, they are inseparable. Rebecca Mathew and father were in the valley she came along to spend the holidays, caught in a sudden snowstorm made their climb difficult. Her horse slipped on ice fell, he strugled to rise but died. Father said. When Rebecca fell, she sustained few injuries. Her slight memory loss lingered, but thank goodness she is well," Tessana explained.

The adults sat up in the tower carrying on small talk.

"Coming up the mountain we noticed the remains of a horse," Lord Thomas mentioned. Kosta explained what had happened during the storm. Over the next few days all went well, the older children, that is to say actually they were young adults no longer needing to hang on mothers apron strings. Their discussions, life of their own and, making decisions about it.

Mark, Tessana, Rebecca and Mathew sat beneath the oak tree, seemingly deep in conversation, Mark stood up and began pacing, Rebecca kept reaching for Marks arm but he avoided her grasp. Mathew said nothing just kept on listening and glancing at Tessana occasionally.

Parents of these young ones watched from the tower, wondering what sort of hot topic they were discussing. That evening Lord Thomas eyed everyone seated at the dinner table and popped a question.

"So my dear brother, have you made a decision on the matter in question as we discussed before?"

Kosta was just about to take a bite of the bread, when he heard those words; he hesitated, looked at his brother and Kathryn, took a bite and with a mouth full said, "No!"

Silence fell and all eyes were on their full plates, and no one dared to look at the other.

During the night, Kosta and Kathryn were wide-awake unable speak or sleep.

In the other bedroom, Lord Thomas clenched his fists and mumbled something under his nose. Cybilia in the adjoining room wept, unexplained sorrow gripped her heart, which she could not control. After a while, her weeping ceased and she slept.

Up in the tower a loud noise disturbed them, what was that noise? No one dared to go up and check it out, something fell, a heavy object dragged round. Faithful, growled, listened but did not move.

Kosta and Kathryn did not sleep but were not afraid of the ghost up there making the racket. However, he had to smile to think how frightened his brother must be, and all at once, he gave out this loud laugh, which he could not suppress any longer. Kathryn jumped startled. She rolled over to Kosta and clung to him.

"What on earth is the matter with you, that noise above did not let me sleep, now you are laughing?"

"How funny, through the winter ghosts did not disturb us. Tonight just before my brother is leaving, well, what do you hear? I am very glad, very happy for the noise!" Kosta said. His arms around her, kissed her. Kathryn after a while had to admit that he was right, and she too smiled, thinking, *how funny...what they would say in the morning.*

At sunrise, everyone was up and ready for breakfast and a walk in the far gardens, especially the young, eager for sunshine and fresh air.

However, when Lord Thomas and Cybilia entered the dining room they looked ragged from lack of sleep.

"What the hell went on last night, whatever or whoever was making such a racket above my bedroom gave me a bad headache," Lord Thomas said sourly.

"Kosta do you know which ghost made that racket?" Cybilia asked.

"To tell you the truth, I have no idea which, they never talk or give their names. I have no idea what that was, but we will go up to the tower and check for clues. Thomas, do you want to go with me?" Kosta asked.

"I will go up there. I want to see for myself," Thomas replied.

Shortly after breakfast they all headed up the stairs to the tower, the dog was ahead of them and when Kosta unlocked the door. Their dog Faithful ran in and began sniffing the whole room.

Lord Thomas a bit relieved exclaimed.

"Aha...so...someone was here last night, look at your dog sniffing all around!"

Kosta pointed to the key in the door and said, "This door is always locked, I have the only key!"

Glaring at Kosta Lord Thomas spoke sharply, "Someone was in here last night making that racket, you heard it! So who was it?"

Kosta said angrily pointing out, "Thomas you seem to be accusing us of playing tricks on you. It was one of the ghosts. Stop worrying about the ghosts! Thomas, take a look at this view."

Cybilia stood with Thomas and eyed the world before them, mesmerized. Lord Thomas bellowed at Kosta.

"Kosta this is heaven, you did not show me this room, why not?"

"You were preoccupied, asking so many questions, you had other priorities, anyway we were up here yesterday," Kosta replied.

"Never mind do not remind me, ah, my fault. I must admit this is a timeless view."

Nothing changed, both were on edge, one could see the profound power of the two brothers. Lord Thomas did not receive an answer from Kosta, and all the way home he thought about that, and, fumed, his stomach cramped now and then, just the thought of going through what he had planned made him queasy, *no that will wait until I get home.* He wondered why Kosta hesitated answering to his invitation to dinner, years overdue. Anger grew as he evaluated his wife's friendliness with Kathryn. Daughter, and son; they behaved well, as aristocrats should. They dozed since last night the ghost deprived them of sleep. Lord Thomas sitting on the driver's bench was thinking.

Arriving home, Lord Thomas immediately called on Sebastian to discuss their secret plan.

"So do you have all we need? Especially the last, just a small cup that is all we will need, anything unusual occurred while I was gone?" Lord Thomas questioned.

"Yes...I prepared it all, but the last...I had to wait for your return. I will take care of it at the last minute," Sebastian replied.

"Good...we will set out when the rain stops. The ground has to dry. Make sure, just watch the weather," Lord Thomas said and Sebastian returned to his duties.

Lord Thomas was anxious, counting the days, but the rain did not let up, every other day it had rained not torrentially but enough to leave puddles. His plan again interrupted by of all things, rain. *This must take place by the end of this month. They will come. If not, then next spring? That long! A whole year I cannot and will not wait. I forgot about the ravens, I have not seen any at all,* he thought; *perhaps it is not time, I need to observe the sky, perhaps I will be lucky enough to spot them, than I will proceed with my plan.*

After two weeks, rain stopped it was the end of April.

Without a word to Cybilia dressed in old clothes since no one paid any attention walked out. He found Sebastian waiting in the stables with the horse. Lord Thomas made sure they had it all, together they rode one horse into the early evening, Sebastian smeared the chicken's blood on the eyelids for his master, between the mounds of graves Lord Thomas lay down, and he wore a white shirt just as Kosta. Anxiously waiting one hour, two hours, hours passed, his body shivered and he felt stiff, he whispered, "they should arrive soon, the hour is near, as I recall." Sebastian instructed to hide well and wait in the dense overgrowth.

The night chill and moisture crept out of the ground, and the wind picked up a bit, it was very uncomfortable, he recalled Kosta saying this is how it must be. Lord Thomas listened for any approaching sound or noise, those Ravens should be here any minute, but heard nothing.

Sebastian crouched in the shrubs strained his eyes peering into the darkness but heard nothing. Hours slipped by, no sign of the Ravens. Lord Thomas fell asleep, near dawn when he tried to open his eyes, his eyelids glued together by the dried blood. He rubbed off enough to open his eyelids. It was dawn. He sat up and looked around everything was the same.

"*I wonder if they were here last night, I fell asleep, and I snored*," he thought, "Sebastian! Are you still out there... then come here!" Lord Thomas shouted.

Sebastian chilled through and through came running, crouched down close to his master, he said, "Nothing happened last night, I am freezing and, master I must say you look a sight with that blood smeared over your eyes."

Lord Thomas said angrily, "Well I had to smear it on, you know that was the plan, the eyelids were well cowered, no one could notice, I was able to see well, that is until I fell asleep. One thing we forgot which was very important; water. How in the world could I go home like this?

"Master Thomas, you stay here and I will ride and fetch water, I will be right back,"

He ran for the horse but the horse was gone. During the night, he had wandered off. Now Sebastian had no choice but to run home. As he ran, he caught sight of his horse grazing. Sebastian headed for him and the horse again ran off a short distance. Sebastian cursed, but called to the horse impatiently,

"Hey, hey, here boy, halt, we must go home!"

Slowly Sebastian walked over to the horse and took the reins, mounted and galloped to the house. He ran into the kitchen, the cook glanced at him and threw a quick question at him.

"And where the devil have you been, look at you, a real scarecrow, that is what you look like."

"Woman...I need a bucket and a rag and that is what I need now and quick!" he raised his voice at her, he was serious and in a great hurry."Now you give me a second and I will get it for you!" she shouted back at him.

The cook handed him the rag and the bucket, they walked out to the well and when he mounted the horse she handed him the filled bucket, Sebastian galloped away. The cook staring after him wondering what in the world was going on.

At the site, Sebastian washed his master;s face. When he was done, they mounted the horse and returned home. They ate a good meal. Both of them ate nothing since the evening before. The cook dared not question her master or Sebastian, but she surmised that both of them were up to something together, but what?

Lord Thomas after washing up and changing clothes relaxed in his chair, after a while he dozed off. He had a dream that he talked with a strange creature. This creature beckoned him to follow, but Lord Thomas hesitated, this creature encircled by bright yellow light, came reaching for Lord Thomas, suddenly a bonfire glowed it grew high and wide reaching up to the sky and he felt its heat. Thomas walked backwards not knowing what was behind him. At that point, Lord Thomas woke up. He thought about this dream, he could not understand its meaning and would not waste time to analyze it, so he dismissed it. He planned to return in the evening to the same spot again at the cemetery, to wait for the Ravens.

At twilight, Lord Thomas was out there with Sebastian going through the routine. "Remember I will call you when it is all over. Nap but do not go to sleep, you must observe and listen, hide well, you cannot be seen, or both of us will be dead, understand? Lord Thomas said. He was ready and waiting on the ground, they both had a heavy supper, no need to wake up starving, waiting for their coming, the Ravens.

Lord Thomas thought, "*perhaps I am mistaken. Perhaps it is too late, or too soon. But I must wait a few more nights.*"

Sebastian crouched in the dense shrubbery well hidden waiting not knowing what is to take place. He promised to be there and wait for his master's call when it was all over. All those nights of waiting Sebastian assumed that his master lost his mind, fantasizing about some strange thing, several nights Sebastian fell asleep from boredom, to keep warm he brought extra clothing and blankets and made a makeshift tent, and waited, no one came, nothing unusual happened. Sebastian had no idea what he was waiting for, what was to take place, why here at cemetery at night, all night waiting, for what. However, he promised his master to be there for him, and he is. That night, as hours slipped by, the wind softly moaned and whined and these sounds one could not forget. Something strange and unexplainable seemed to fill the air.

Seventy-Nine: Ravens Returned

Every spring the Ravens appeared without fail, but they were seen by few.

In daylight, no one paid attention to birds flying high, so high their size never differed from the other birds. Gliding on silent wings with perfect vision, observed. Though well hidden in trees far from the villages at nighttime, no one knew they were there. How they came to know everything that went on, none could guess, or ever question.

The slight rustling noise perked up Lord Thomas's ears, he heard more noises, his heart beat a bit faster, he heard whispering, or was it the wind. Thomas strained to hear more, but nothing else happened. Whenever the wind blew harder, he thought that that was when he heard voices, but were they the Ravens. Thomas dared not open his eyes, it was cold and he shivered, but also it was fear, what if they discover him knowing he is a spy, and he will lose. After what seemed hours, and feeling very uncomfortable, the sudden rustling noises were loud, very loud.

What he heard was beyond his belief; still he did not dare open his eyes to peek into the darkness. When at last he heard a voice clear and authoritative, he knew then that, they were who Kosta said they were, *THE RAVENS*.

The leader spoke, "Good evening my Brothers!"

"Good evening our Leader!" in unison, they all replied.

"What news do we have to discuss this evening?" the leader asked.

"Our leader, we have gathered here to hear you tell us the solution to a problem we heard about," one of them spoke.

"Yes, I am here to do just that," retorted the leader Mamut.

"Will you please tell us what will—" being interrupted in mid-sentence by their leader Mamut who raised his voice and said, "Stop...of that we will not discuss tonight, do not mention it again, any of you!"

The leader Mamut continued, "As you all know the world is

corrupted by evil, the good suffer, grant you ambition is not wrong and decency is a virtue which so often is trampled on and lost, and it is only for survival. I will name a few of the vices, greed, murder, encroaching on others lives, cruelty to others, demeaning others, pride, gluttony, amassing material things which are artistically crafted but useless, adultery, also abortion, thievery, jealousy and the last one out of so many more...hate. Those I mentioned are never ever, rewarded! These are only a few among a list of hundreds of others. Every individual knows deep within his heart and soul which of these he or she committed in their lifetime and, for which they will pay a price. Eventually if not in this lifetime, then it shall be judged in the afterlife, none escape justice.

"Tonight I have decided not to discuss problems which are happening right here in this area, and tonight we also will forgo discussing the solutions to these problems, although we do have an individual who will be justly rewarded for all accomplishments, and of deeds done for others and to others. This particular individual distinguished himself through his own cunning ambition. To succeed through ambition is not a crime, not at all. Ambition is encouraged, that is, if it is accomplished through honest deeds and hard work."

Ravens perched on branches up in the huge oak listened. Here and there, flutter of feathers could not tell one from other rustling noises. For the longest time none of them spoke.

Lord Thomas heard every word and wondered their true meaning. He could not dwell on those words right now, later he will think about them, now he wants and needs to hear more of the problems and solutions for him to solve, but for some reason they are talking about completely different subjects, this is not how Kosta described to him when he was here. They are not talking about those puffy white mushrooms, something is wrong here and Lord Thomas was feeling a bit irked, but remained unmoving, his eyes closed. His position from which he could not raise himself to take a peak, Time elapsed. This waiting for him became unbearable. He had to look if they are truly here close to him. Unfortunately, his eyelids glued together with the chicken blood threw him into frenzy. His anger peaked, but knowing if he stirred or made a sound, they would immediately consider him a spy and do away with. "*Are these birds aware that I am near them, surely, they will not give themselves away,*" he was thinking, so the waiting game continued.

Suddenly one spoke in a deep tone of voice. "Dear leader Mamut, we are waiting for the decision, will the action take place tonight or do we come back tomorrow?

The leader gave no answer, silence again.

After what seemed an hour, their leader Mamut spoke. "We have waited long enough. Forgive me for tiring you in this manner. The hour is late we shall rest, for dawn will come soon. You all know very well that we have the solutions for those problems, which I will disclose on the third night, good night my brothers."

"Good night dear leader Mamut," in unison, they replied.

Lord Thomas could not believe what he just heard.

What?"I have to wait until the third night for the solutions. This is madness! I am so uncomfortable on this damp ground, and I am hungry! Nevertheless, I must be patient. I will try to sleep now, though it is chilly." Lord Thomas listened and waited and then fell asleep. Next morning, the sun's warmth awakened him, he felt better.

He tried to open his eyes but the caked blood dried, he has no choice but to remain motionless and wait. He felt anger and frustration, did not know if he should sit up and call for his servant Sebastian, was he still there hiding in the shrubs.

Sebastian hidden in the shrubs watched and counted as the Ravens flew away, there were thirteen of them, all was clear. Sebastian came running, calling out to his master with a basket full of goodies. Sebastian washed his master's eyes of the dried blood just enough for him to see. Thomas ate and drank tea. It was not the servants place to ask about last night.

Lord Thomas said to Sebastian, "Go home and bring a blanket, no wait, bring the sheep skin the large one on the sofa in the parlor, it will keep me warm, the ground is so damp, I will suffer of rheumatism later in my life, so go now and do not tell anyone what you are up to."

"Are you staying here all day, master?" Sebastian asked curiously.

"No, you fool, what am I to do here all day, just go now and get those things and bring them here for tonight, understand? And remember tell no one, I mean no one, or you will end up like Joseph and James...dead"

Sebastian walked to the wooded area where his horse waited. Mounted up and galloped home. He found the sheep skin and had some hot coffee and freshly baked bread with butter, the cook did not ask any questions but kept an eagle eye on him, soon Sebastian was on his way back to his master.

The cook called Franka told her that she suspected Sebastian was up to something, and instructed to cautiously go and find

Sebastian even if it takes her all day, she will explain to the Lady of the house if need be.

Franka hung her apron on a hook and went in search of Sebastian. She followed the hoof prints, which led her to the cemetery road. Franka cautiously scanned the area for anyone. She crouched in the bushes to avoid detection. Franka came upon the horse grazing. She knew Sebastian was nearby. Observing from afar, she saw her master and Sebastian sitting on the ground talking. What they said she could not hear. *Was she supposed to go back home and report to the cook?"* Franka was confused. Nevertheless, she watched for several hours. The time was passing slowly, she was very uncomfortable in the bushes, nothing out of the ordinary going on, she decided to head back home and tell the cook what she had observed.

Lord Thomas and Sebastian were busy preparing for the evening of the third night.

The sheepskin laid out on the ground was to keep Lord Thomas comfortable, but to their disappointment, it was too white and would be too noticeable at night. Sebastian went a short distance and ripped out some tall grass to camouflage the sheepskin, it worked. They were ready. Lord Thomas changed shirts and shoved the bloody one under the sheepskin. Threw on the clean shirt and they rode home to talk to his family and the staff as if nothing at all is going on, he also looked in on the preparation of fall production of wine. Cybilia preoccupied with employees had no clue, what her husband was up to for the last few days. Mark gave him a side-glance, but had no desire to converse with his father, just not in the mood.

The anticipation of the unexpected to come made Lord Thomas nervous and jumpy. His bloody shirt and his bloody face waited for nightfall. Sebastian walked back to his makeshift tent, to wait and observe.

Dusk turned into darkness of the third night, it was quiet. Lord Thomas strained his ears, listening...listening...waiting, but heard no sound. He thought about what the Ravens had said the night before, and all of this puzzled him, *this was not how Kosta reiterated his experience with these Ravens, something is different, but wha*t? He thought and waited. Sleep came over him. He awoke by loud voices; his heart began to beat like a drum. *What did I miss? Why did I fall asleep? Dawn, it is dawning. Too late,* he thought, *surely, I had missed the beginning of the discussion of the problems and solutions,* anger raged through him, but he listened. The next words he heard made him tremble, unable to open his eyes, he had to lay there and wait for the Ravens to fly away.

The leader Mamut spoke loud and clear, "Tonight my dear brothers we are here for the final moment of truth, and tonight we will expose the imposter who is among us." Lord Thomas understood that they discovered a spy, an imposter among themselves, how odd, "*What will they do with him? Most likely oust him from their group, or perhaps kill him*?" he thought.

The leader Mamut continued, "But first I have to tell you of a big problem which is happening right here and now, it is here in this area, as you recall a long time ago when we discovered the cruelty of an individual, a wealthy man, who acted as God and abused his brother, you do remember?

"Yes! We remember," the Ravens in unison replied.

"The abused brother today is healthy and rich because of his determination to fulfill all the assignments. He persevered, suffered and became victorious."

Then Lord Thomas heard murmurs and whispers, sort of objections.

"Very well now, I shall talk about the village with a big problem, en enormous swarm of bees settled high in the church steeple and no one is able to remove them, disturbed bees may become very angry, attack and easily sting a man to death."

"O" and "Ah" echoed through the oak tree, and flutter of wings.

Lord Thomas absorbed the problem now he wants to hear the solution and reward for such a dangerous task. "*the sack of gold must be huge, or bust*," he thought.

The Ravens continued to chatter among themselves for a while, until the leader Mamut shouted "silence!" and silence fell.

Lord Thomas anxiously waited for the solution to the bee problem, but the leader was silent. After what seemed hours, the leader resumed the conversation without disclosing the solution.

"My brothers, we cannot procrastinate any longer, one by one I need for you to state your name and if you are ready to execute the justice which is to be carried out, as ordered by our elders. First, I will explain the solution to the bee problem, which is, no one will climb the steeple, and the bees will sting no one. The solution is smoke...smoke will drive them out of the steeple...do you not agree that this would be the easiest and simplest solution, now, why no one thought about this, is beyond my imagination."

All the Ravens began a loud flutter of feathers and chattered all at once. Which irritated Lord Thomas, he too agreed as he thought about the bees that that was a simple solution. "*What about the reward? How much gold for each problem solved?*" he was thinking.

Unfortunately, Lord Thomas must remain in the same position as he was all night and wait.

Their leader Mamut said:

"Now shall we have our roll call? "Yes!" they all shouted.

Abimust Raven Number One, are you ready? Yes...came the answer.

Benokai Raven Number Two, are you ready? Yes...

Kotur Raven Number Three, are you ready? Yes...

Denos Raven Number Four, are you ready? Yes...

Erisott Raven Number Five, are you ready? Yes...

Fijiron Raven Number Six, are you ready? Yes...

Gromu Raven Number Seven, are you ready? Yes...

Hatuii Raven Number Eight, are you ready? Yes...

Insemir Raven Number Nine, are you ready? Yes...

Kerrie Raven Number Ten, are you ready? Yes...

Kruegg Raven Number Eleven, are you ready? Yes...

Lornven, Raven Number Twelve, are you ready. Yes...came the answer.

"I, as your leader say, yes! I am ready".

Lord Thomas dumbfounded, thought, "*What are they waiting for? What are they planning to do now? I need to know, my patience is short. Strange names, I counted thirteen, just as Kosta had said, thirteen.*"

When the leader began to speak, again Lord Thomas paid attention.

"At the start of our gathering here tonight I told you I will expose an imposter here among us, as you all are aware I have been consulting with the elders, Olymar, Smetos and Gleryk, their final verdict is, execution. This individual deserves nothing other for all the crimes he has committed, scheming, cruel deeds and murder. Tonight is the night. This individuals demise will be hard to accept for the brother, who long ago was abused in such an inhumanely manner, to deprive a person of sight and leave him to die is unforgivable. Therefore it shall be done and the book of life and deeds shall be closed...forever."

Lord Thomas listened and his skin crawled, those words aimed directly at him, they knew he was there and that he tried to trick THEM. To outsmart the *RAVENS* will not escape him tonight. He realized that they were talking about him; he was the imposter, confused and afraid unable to escape he remained motionless. To call out to Sebastian would be futile, and to run from them out of the question. He began to perspire, heart drumming from fear, but still he waited. The silence around him drove him crazy. His eyes closed wondered, "*had they left or are these RAVENS watching me. This was not what Kosta said would happen. This is madness!' I was set up*!" frightened and angry he thought," *I promise I will get even with Kosta for this and he will pay*!"

He had no choice but wait until Sebastian comes; he had to remain in this position, even though they know he is here.

Eighty: Sudden Strike

They perched and waited for predawn for a reason. Those bloody eyes must open to see justice done, by them. Suddenly the flapping of wings and horrible high pitch screeching broke the silence. They were right above him. They were on him. He opened his eyes. Arms flailing, fighting off these huge ravens in vain. The ripping of clothing, the screeching, powerful talons digging deep tearing; quick fatal strikes of their beaks tore bits and pieces of flesh and scattered, every inch of him. One strike at the jugular vein spewed blood like a fountain. The esophagus ripped open to silence a short-lived scream. The minutes ticked away. The Thirteen Ravens as commanded by the Elders worked with remorseless frenzy to destroy within minutes of what used to be a man's form.

In the shrubbery among the thickness of leaves, two eyes bulged out of their sockets watching in horror...

The Thirteen Ravens had worked to scatter, distort, but only leave but a contour. His arms and legs nearly cleaned to the bone scattered, this man's torso whatever was left of it lay in a puddle of blood, now it was over, now it was done. Silence prevailed, the sentence carried out. The Thirteen Ravens hopped around wings spread wide, looking for any witnesses, there must not be any witnesses...!

Sebastian curled in a fetal position, vomited. The urge to flee was fierce, but realizing the consequences he decided to stay hidden. The smell of the vomit drifted, horror-stricken, should the Ravens get a whiff of it, and he will be finished just like his master. Sebastian clawed at the dirt and grass to cover it; tears ran down his face and dropped to the ground, disbelieving what he had witnessed. After a while his trembling and heaving ceased.

The Thirteen Ravens hopped around with wings spread, inspecting their work of many years of waiting for this moment. The only part of the human form remained intact, was the face, a bloodless ashen face, spattered with its own blood, and the lifeless glassy eyes stared at the sky. The frozen expression of surprise and disbelief of this sudden strike, unexpected, but it was all over.

Beaks open wide dripped with blood, to their feathers and claws bits of flesh clung; their eyes wild, glowed red from exhaustion. The execution concluded without witnesses. On silent wings one by one followed their leader to the nearest pond to splash, submerge to rid themselves of clinging scraps of flesh, wash away all the evidence of their deed. One by one spread their wings to cool overheated exerted bodies. The leader scanned the area for any movement, for assurance no one spied. The thirteen Ravens returned to the denseness of the oak tree to rest. When the sun lit up the world, they took to flight.

These Thirteen Ravens circled above the remains and each one released a black feather. As they circled, the second time these Ravens transformed into thirteen spirits. Braids loosened black ribbons with pearls at the end dropped close to the shredded body for evidence that they were here and have done this.

In the living world, Sebastian well hidden in the shrubs on the outskirts of the cemetery crouched, listened and watched, to run now he dared not, as he was the sole witness of this supposedly "magical event," as was told to him by his master. Against the grey dawn, he watched every tree, every bird flying over, in horror recalling, dark silhouettes, fiercely mingled, hopped and jumped, tore at his master. He held his breath. The sudden rush of tears blocked his vision. His stomach churned a terrible need to vomit again, he swallowed, heaved unable to keep it down; he vomited. If discovered meant his demise as well. Sebastian curled up in a fetal position, choked on his inner screams, until the sun had risen high. His masters words rang in his mind repeatedly, "*Magical event*" and "*Victorious*! *This was not to be so. I was the only one to know his plan, his only witness. My master was to be victorious. so!*" Sebastian feverish, shivered, eyes darting, fear of discovery whispered; *if they find me, they will tear me apart. Just as they did my master, and the way he screamed, horrid!*" Sebastian in a state of delirium trembled. Sunlight assured his safety, so he thought, abruptly black birds flew out of trees it seemed hundreds. The sky was black as they circled. Heart pounding he waited, but they were not the ravens. This huge flock of smaller black birds converged on the body to feast. Still his eyes scanned each tree. None, Sebastian stood up his knees locked after so many hours of crouching on the ground, could not walk, as slowly as he could staggered from bush to trees; leg muscles weak, he kept on, half way home, able to walk faster, then he ran, ran in a great hurry to the estate. Breathless, Sebastian barged into the kitchen. All eyes fell on him and stared. His face streaked with tears, sweaty, stunk of vomit, clothes tattered and dirty.

"What on earth has happened to you?" Franka asked. He collapsed into a chair.

Franka handed him a mug of water, with trembling hands, he raised it to his quivering lips. He gulped the water greedily and banged the table with the mug.

Transfixed eyes into space he stuttered, voice barely heard quivered as he said, “Our... master...I...dead...dead...I...say, I...tell...you, I...I...saw...it...all!” he said, “told me to hide in the bushes... watch and wait. What happened next...to him was not to be...! Oh, not that way to die...oh, what a scene, pieces, pieces flying everywhere, ooh... terrible death! What a way to die! It is unforgettable! I will go insane! Horrible...I feel sick... I...could not... help him! Oh God...I could not help him!” Sebastian screamed. He dropped his head on the table, and pounded the table with his fists. The cook and everyone gathered around him, gaped at each other wondering what he was rattling about, the cook asked.

“What do you mean, watch, wait...dead...how?”

“What...How? Our master is dead?” he cried out.

“They killed him! They tore him to bits!”

“Did you kill him?” Franka asked.

“I... Me? Are you daft? I did not kill him, they did! You should have been there! You would have seen what they did to him!” he shouted, jumped up off the chair shaking.

The men tried to question more, who were “they?” but Sebastian said he must find Lady Cybilia, she *must* know. His face pale, streaked with tears, face wrinkled with emotion tried as best he could to describe as a witness to the scene. Lady Cybilia listened in shock. She felt a constricting pain in her bosom, swooned and fainted. Sebastian caught her fall. Placed a pillow under her head and staggered out of the parlor for help to lay her on the sofa. She remained unconscious for a long time. Mark and Shara informed of their father’s tragic death. Marks comment;

“Father always was obsessed with material things. Fate has dealt him a surprising blow.” Mark turned away and wept. Shara ran around, screamed envisioning father torn to shreds. When time elapsed, the servants went to gather the remains of their master. All they found was the bloody skull. The rest of the bones picked clean of flesh, some carried away by the wild. Swarms of blood sucking insects buzzed on the site. The servants stared, riveted, breathless. The memory of this nauseating scene singed into their brain like a branding iron to remain until they die. The most unbelievable were the eyes, untouched, evidence of the chicken blood now dried on his ashen face. The Ravens intentionally left them whole, for him to see and experience his last moments of life.

His lifeless eyes now portrayed surprise, despair and the horror of unexpected sudden strike.

Cybilia half-sane, her mind whirled, too fragile to go to the scene, neither could Shara, they stayed close together at home. Mark had to go and witness for himself, after all this was his father. Whatever he had done in his life had no reflection on his own character. Mark his first born, was now the heir and master of the estate, he will rule now.

Mark found and picked up thirteen black feathers and the black ribbons with the pearls.

News of this horrible death spread like wildfire. Shock and disbelief were a constant topic among the people. The constable arrived to the scene but little was left of him. His pals from the 4Hoofs Inn heard but refused to come to the place where it happened, a need to remember him as he was then and not now. The question was always the same,:"who and why?"

The castle stood looming enormously in the distance on the mountain. Spring has definitely arrived, though late this year. The valley and the world came awake to a season of beauty, warmth and much toil. Summer will follow with its charm and pleasures.

On a busy day, Mark rode in on a horse. When he entered the kitchen with a somber expression, everyone knew something was terribly wrong, but none asked what happened, butler Jonasen found Kosta in the stables, by now Mark sat in the dining room with Kathryn and Tessana, old Simena shuffled in, she herself near the grave, her illness devoured her. Mark shocked to see her so small and shriveled, but had no comment.

Kosta with foreboding entered and saw Marks eyes full of tears.

Kosta embraced Mark and the boy burst into tears, this was not expected, a youth confident and proud to crumble like this.

"Mark what happened, calm down a bit, and tell me, what is it?" Kosta said.

"Uncle Kosta it is father...he is dead...so sudden..."

Tessana stared at her cousin feeling something foreboding, something in the room with them, but what?

Kosta poured glasses of wine, handed it to him and said, "Mark, drink this, it will ease it a bit." Mark gulped down some, took a breath and said, "The Ravens shredded his body. They killed him."

Tessana clamped her mouth with her hands and tears welled in her eyes. Kathryn stiffened entwined her fingers squeezed until her knuckles were white. Simena crossed herself, closed her eyes seemed to be praying. Butler Jonasen stood frozen in place. When the reality hit Jonasen, he turned and ran into the kitchen there he told everyone what happened.

Kosta sat not speaking, his mind was not with him, it was far by the oak tree, he knew that something like that his brother would do and he knew why.

Mark, after hours of grieving with them, described exactly what was left of his father.

Kathryn deeply concerned for Cybilia asked how his mother took the news, Mark said she seems insane, at this time.

"You should be with her, you are strong, although we fall apart for a while still we collect our senses gather our strength and keep going, you Mark, are her strength now, go to her and Sabrina, remember we are with you, always," Kathryn spoke softly.

"Yes, it is rather late; one can only imagine what is going on at home. Thank you Uncle Kosta, Aunt Kathryn, thank you, Tessana."

Mark was leaving when Kosta said to him, "In time the pain shall pass, and then you and I will talk, then you will understand."

Thomas' grave dug not among the other graves, his remaining bones and the head placed in the coffin and buried beneath the oak tree. The carved gravestone, just his name as it was, Thomas Komarod.

Cybilia for hours could not control her trembling, imagining the horrid scene, no one thought she could be strong in such an adverse situation, but she was.

Although for hours unable to focus, accepted what had happened, now gone, she must go on alone with her two children, nothing else to do. Cybilia stayed in bed for several days, thinking, thinking, and then, having nightmares. Shara cuddled close keeping her mother sane.

"So it caught up to him, his schemes and control, well now, he thought he was untouchable, no one is invincible, but now, I wonder where is his soul," Cybilia said to her daughter.

The Master and Heir of this castle sat alone and grieved, up at the tower. He clutched the black thirteen Raven feathers and black ribbons with the pearls, found at the gruesome site of his brother's remains. Mark delivered the thirteen feathers and thirteen pearls on ribbons to his Uncle Kosta, assured that only he knew their meaning.

Tears trickled down Kosta's face from sorrow, not seen by anyone else. Kosta wept silently for his now deceased brother the one and only blood brother. Growing up Kosta looked up to his brother, trusting and forgiving all those nasty things done to him, until he grew up alone realized how selfish his brother was and learned what it meant to have and not have. His brother had much, by marrying a rich girl and through scheming and his greed to amass and possess the best. Having more than enough still he wanted more, and that more was the castle which now belonged to Kosta and his family. His brother wanted to take that away from him too.

He endured all of his life not having, but somehow fate turns life around and gives back.

The first time the Ravens had released their feathers as a sign, a reward for the "good." This second time their feathers were evidence of their presence, in addition pearls on black ribbons, signifying the regret of losing a soul to the demons. Justified verdict, a sentence executed for the "evil" deeds.

As for Kosta, known by the Ravens as Brother of Light knew someday that chapter of life with his brother will close, but how it would end remained unknown, until this day, the silver thread, which held them as brothers and family, is no more. For Thomas, that chapter of his book of life has closed forever.

Years ago as Kosta was growing up alone his heart felt hollow. He missed his brother. These brothers lived a distance a bit far, yet not that far. Their visits were few.

As Fate has it, Kosta met Kathryn; they as one bound by love, their children and suffering known to many. His heart filled to capacity with their love never to be hollow again.

Kosta lived for Kathryn and his children, worked and sacrificed his own self for them, and willing to die for them. As of this day, his life will go on and his brother remain but a memory.

At the Estate, Cybilia her son and daughter sat stupefied, neither drank or ate anything the cook prepared. The three were in complete shock. Few of the field men and from the winery walked away, knowing deep down they would never be able to work here, because of what occurred this day. The cooks and servants on the other hand decided it had nothing to do with them, all stayed, after all the Lady of the house needed them. Flora made all decisions regarding Lady Cybilias welfare; she loved Cybilia since she was a little girl, watched her grow and become a beautiful woman, Flora respected by Sir Paulo and Lady Marianna had a good home with them, after their demise Flora feared for her life. Flora knew who took the mushroom and poisoned Cybilia's both parents. Now that the monster master is dead, she one day will tell Cybilia everything.

Eighty-One:

The Beginning and the End

In an instant, transformation took place from life to death, from earth to a void. The soul of Lord Thomas, Brother of Darkness, stood and blinked, nothing around him, silence, darkness, yet aware he stood on something solid. He glanced down to his horror, before him a display of reality scene on the ground. Shocked, stared at the scattered remains of a body. He recoiled, a scene of a scattered human he turned away, but a skull with a bloody face, whose face is it? Thomas stared and shrieked recognizing his own face. "*But how could this be*?" He felt his arms, legs, and chest and head, he felt alive, but for one thing which was different, he felt significantly lighter, seemed as if he had no solidity to himself, no weight, no body. This is a distorted dream, pure travesty. No, that head, those eyes there on the ground were the only part of his earthly body recognizable, it was *his* face. This was not a dream, but reality, from which he could not turn away, turn back or wake. "This is all wrong! This was not his plan! It all went awry!" he screamed but no one heard, he is in a void and, he is alone. Abruptly without any warning, unexpectedly his life snuffed out in seconds between these graves.

He no longer existed in the living world or had a body, or family, or all the riches and his plans to acquire more. On the ground he is just food for the waiting insects and maggots, his blood seeps into the soil; it is part of mother earth. Therefore, he no longer carried his childhood title given to him by his mother "Lord" his souls name for eternity shall be Thomas. He shall be as lowly as all the other dammed souls in hell.

The moment of transformation, Thomas had not realized he was on the threshold of eternity. Now Thomas confused could not fathom his life's sudden ending, not in such a way as this, much before his time. Severed from reality, from life, he stood, staring devoid of emotion and had experienced no fear yet. His feelings strangely enough were not for those left behind in the living world.

Now, he was not concerned about his children or Cybilia, surely, by now, have seen what had happened to him. He stood alone staring down at the head with those lifeless glassy eyes. To him it mattered not what effect of his death in such a horrid way would have on Mark, had Cybilia gone mad and Sabrina throwing her tantrum screaming? He felt transparent and empty, emotionless, without anger or outbursts as displayed in his living world, control and fear interjected in everyone's daily life were no more; they were not his concern at all, as if they never existed for the moment, not in his soul. He stood staring at his body in shreds. He stood alone without any feelings, sorrow, regret, or longing for his loved ones. *Loved ones...where are they now. Do they know what happened to my body? Where, am I going now*? Thomas thought and seemed to recall something of this day.

When he heard the choir of angels in the distance, he turned but all around him was darkness. The angels' choir reverberated into the vast space. Complete space. He was transfixed, mesmerized, he waited for something to happen, someone to speak to him. Then invisible faces and voices his soul heard calling to him...

"Come, come we are here, come to us, come home."

Where were they? Where is home. Where is the light? Where is God! Darkness all around, I am in darkness! *I do not like darkness!* Thomas was talking aloud. Suddenly he felt something, an awakening of feelings and he shouted, "Where are you, where is home! Show me the way home! He turned full circle trying to see into the darkness, nothing to see, no one was there.

Thomas, Brother of Darkness, could not see those spirits.

Out of heaven's space came a stream of bright light, the choir of angels sang louder and coming closer. Thomas heard the spirits calling again, spirits surrounded him reached for him with hands outstretched; he was in the midst of these spirits and this bright light shining on them. A feeling of joy washed over him; the soul of Thomas, the Brother of Darkness, reached for those hands reaching for him. Unfortunately, he could not touch them. A strong feeling of longing surged through him, he reached out when he saw familiar faces of his Father and Mother, Aunt Olivia, Baron Patrick, Horacio Chappaniac, Cybilia's parents Lady Marianna and Sir Paulo, and Joseph and James and Marysa the ghost, and so many others all calling to him to..."Come...Come Thomas, come!"

The soul of Thomas, Brother of Darkness, tried to walk up what seemed to be a path of stepping stones, but could not. In the light many hands, these hands just inches away, unreachable. Then the light in the heavens became brighter, he saw an angel descending ever so gracefully, Thomas was sure now he will join his family, this angel will lead him to them. This angel now very close, the most beautiful face he only glimpsed at for a second, the blinding light emitting from this Angel forced his eyes to close, shield his face and turn away. Thomas, Brother of Darkness, fell to his knees and bowed his head, to look at this angel again he could not, he heard the Angel speak in a melodious tone of voice such he had never ever heard...

"Thomas! You have transgressed against God's Law! Therefore, you Thomas shall never see your Creators face. You have chosen of your free will the other, the outcast, the evil one, Satan, at whose face you shall look upon for eternity. You have chosen and sealed your own destiny and eternal doom."

The choir receded into space and their voices softly fading. The beautiful Angel and the light receded into the vast eternal space as well. Those familiar spirits also retreating with the light, their voices soft and far away, Thomas looked up to his dismay they were gone, nothing but darkness around him.

"Wait, wait! Do not leave me in this darkness!" he cried in sudden distressed panic.

Thomas heard words resounding over the entire eternal space, he saw an angel pointing a flaming sword at him... "*Be gone! Thomas, brother of darkness be gone! Be gone Brother of Darkness*!"

Suddenly, he stood in total silence and darkness. He blinked hoping to see through this dark space. Suspended in a void no longer standing on a path.

Thomas felt disillusioned, abandoned, longing washed over him, waiting for the bright light and his parents and the Angelic choir to come back. He stood bewildered dismayed, so very alone, not knowing where to go, how to get there if he knew where. As on cue, he felt a slight tug at his sleeve, someone spoke to him in a persuasive manner.

"Come I will direct you to your friends and your rightful place."

Thomas eagerly complied, "Yes yes, please take me to my rightful place. Who are you, I cannot see you*!*"

"Oh but you will see me in just a moment!" came the reply.

A sudden feeling of weightlessness came over him, and in a split moment a strong grip at his feet pulled him down, as if gravity pulled him down, he was freefalling, darkness nothing but blackness, faster, faster plummeting down into oblivion. Thomas's soul the Brother of Darkness screamed.

"No, this is against my will! I want to go to the light and my mother!" Unfortunately no one could hear him or save him.

Confused, disillusioned, Thomas found himself in a brightly lit room, which was in complete décor of red. He stood alone in this room, gaping at the basket standing by a three-legged chair, rakes and pitchforks, he walked up to a shimmering brick wall as he touched it strange powdery soot stuck to his fingers. Thomas heard voices, barely, as if behind the wall, but he could not put his ear to it because of the soot, he walked over to the other wall, listened he heard screaming as if far in the distance. Thomas wondered what was happening, this room had no windows, just doors. Thomas stood in the middle of this room waiting for that someone who brought him here. Abruptly the wide red door opened with a grind and white mist rolled into the room, he stood in it up to his knees, in the background red fog and far off blackness. Out of the fog, a tall dark figure came forward, faced Thomas as if only a shadow, without eyes, or ears, his head, clean-shaven, took a step forward, not speaking. The wide door closed behind him. Thomas startled turned his head to his left, the shimmering brick wall rumbled as it opened, in came several short demons. Then to the right, the opposite shimmering brick wall opened, several more dark figures walked towards him, they were shorter in size by a head, but looked the same as the tall one. All of them bowed and remained so before the tall one. Thomas recognized these were subservient demons only to serve and obey. Thomas apprehensive, not knowing what to expect, waited. The tall dark demon stood several feet before Thomas, in a baritone voice said, *"Ah Thomas, Brother of Darkness...* welcome to our underworld. I have waited a long time for your visit. Now here you belong to me."

"I belong to you? Who are you? Where am I?" Thomas trembled, confused, squeaked. "I will tell you who I am, but you will only remember my name for a moment, I am Dionys-Sian. You were mine, all of your life. I am the voice you heard whisper in your ear," Dionys-Sian replied.

Then Dionys-Sian the tall demon motioned to the subservient dark ones, "Take him." Six short demons jerked him off his feet, grabbed by his arms and legs, face down, before he could utter a word, quickly whisked through the wide doors to what seemed an infinite room where fires of hell burned all around.

"Where are you taking me? I demand you let go of me!" Thomas horrified screamed.

"First of all, here, no one demands from us, we demand from you. Second of all, we are taking you for your first initiation, then to be judged," the demon snarled.

"Judged? Who is going to judge me?" Thomas stuttered. The subservient demons snickered.

"It is not going to be the 'good' judge," he said.

"Where is this judge? How much longer must you carry me this way?" The subservient demons were silent.

After a while, out of nowhere appeared Dionys-Sian.

"Much, much further and longer trail than you expected. Now be quiet, you are disturbing the dammed," he said.

Thomas forced to hang face down, barely off the black hard surface, several times his body scraped that surface and he felt pain. Unable to see what was around him Thomas closed his eyes these demons sped so fast and shook and jerked him so much, made him queasy and dizzy, his legs and arms were numb.

Thomas yelled from terror now and then, realizing he was a prisoner and had no idea where they were taking him. The demon said, "shut-up!"

Suddenly they stopped and dropped Thomas onto a hard surface, black slate. He saw nothing around him but grey mist, the demons vanished. Thomas looked down, precipice; he jumped back away from the ledge. Feeling sudden heat, looked down at his feet, his boots were gone. He was barefooted and naked. Then he heard a rumble, he turned full circle. The ledge shook, it broke away with him on it. He was falling, falling like a boulder off a cliff. When at last, the boulder instantly splintered into small shards Thomas fell onto a ledge, behind him an empty cubicle, no bigger than a prison cell, darkness and fog drifted up all around him. "Hello is anyone there? Hello! Thomas yelled, is anyone there? He was alone. He realized that when he called out, there was no echo, no one would hear him scream, no one to talk to, and he was naked. Thomas's memory had been erased, he tried to recall but could not remember if he stood before the judge or not, or the name of the tall demon. Thomas sat down on the warm slate floor and listened intently a long time for voices, nothing, he heard nothing. Has he lost his hearing too? Does he have any feeling? He pinched his arm then belly, slapped his face and then his leg hard yet felt nothing, though he had his bodily functions taken away one thing he had; *realization.* What am I now...where...when...why? How did all this happen? Realizing his doom and all his mistakes trying to outwit Fate, he visualized his whole life and his moment of demise. Those Ravens were spirits, they talked...transformed, and as Ravens were, much wiser. He shivered. Why...it was not cold in this cubicle in fact it was a bit too warm, still he felt prickles run up and down his naked soul. No...that never happened I am dreaming, no... I will wake up...I am a rich man I bought whatever my heart desired, that was my life's goal to be rich. Thomas sat down hoping to awake but as he eyed his surroundings out of his empty cell, nothing out there but mist or smoke, isolation, nakedness.

"No bed or pillow, no food or drink, a glass of good wine would quench my thirst, this must be hell..., and I am in hell!" Thomas said aloud and screamed "NO...NO...NO!" He screamed but there was no echo and he did not hear his own voice. Isolated in darkness feeling only the warm slate he waited, what he was waiting for, someone to come and rescue him or wake him from this devilish dream. In life, he had done many things others would never dare. Here and now, he only had one faculty left, realization. Here he had eternity to realize why and for what he is a prisoner of eternal hell. He sat realizing what he could from his life. Strange thing happened he recalled, he had his memory back, first he tried to recall Cybilia, he could not visualize her face, or Marks or Sabrina's or his brothers. None of the family could he see in his mind. He then realized that which he did not expect. Only one speck of his brain functioned, only one, 'realization' not for the good things, but only the bad. Thomas had the whole eternity to dwell on transgressions he committed.

Once in his life Fate had given him a choice to make, the good or the bad, he chose the bad, easier to be on the bad road, or struggle to be good on the good road.

Now here in hell he realized he listened to the wrong voice.

Thomas sat, eyes closed searching his mind for a good deed, found but few. Suddenly a huge boulder came crashing splitting the ledge and the cubicle in half. Thomas jumped, tried to stand on the narrow ledge, unfortunately it gave way and Thomas slid into the gaping black void, this time much deeper into the gut of hell, this time the ledge he lay on was much, much hotter.

The chance to be with those in the light has been forever lost, he realized. His mother gave him a title, "Lord" when he was just a boy. Thomas, while alive chose early in life to become, conceded, proud, controlling others with an iron hand of cruelty, murder, gluttony selfishness, disrespect and hate. Too late, Brother of Darkness lost his chance to eternal light. The demon Dionys-Sian welcomed him, and now the demons have control over him.

Doomed he is, to spend eternity in suffering, in slavery, betrayal, excruciating pain, eternally regretting of losing his soul. Eternal agony of hell...the yearning to be with his parents, their faces shone with joy and love in that light. Those faces in his lifetime he chose to ignore. Those faces he thought he never loved or needed. He believed in himself; he was number one, he only thought of himself, never considered the feelings of others. Trampled on whoever got in his way to get what he desired.

Now, all those material riches remained on earth, and all the gold he had hidden could not serve him now, to redeem his *Freedom* from *Eternal Damnation.*

"Brother of Darkness, justice was done."

At the estate, his chaotic saga continues...

David Komarod

Liana Komarod

Their sons:

Thomas Komarod

Kosta Komarod

Paulo Prozatti

Mariana Prozatti

Their daughter:

Cybilia Prozatti

Thomas Kamarod

Cybilia Prozatti

Mark Kamarod

Sabrina Kamarod

Kosta Komarod

Kathryn Komarod

Matthew Komarod

Tessana Komarod

jasemin Komarod

jason Komarod

Kras Komarod

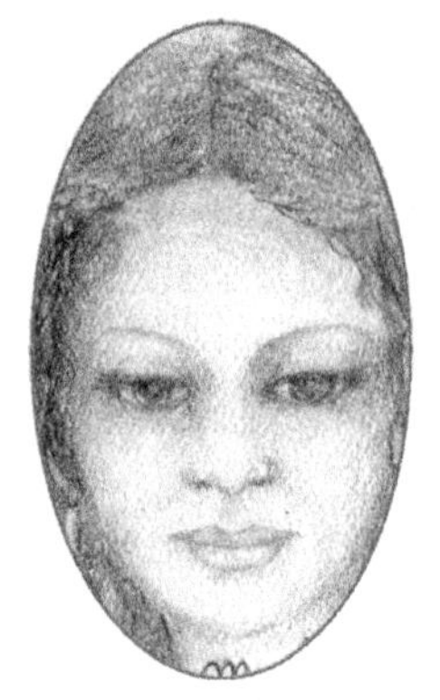

Marla Komarod

Rosie Komarod

Aunt Olivia

Baron Patrick

Michael Hartigard

Rabinna Hartigard

Rebecca Hartigard

Acknowledgments

I wish to thank all my family and friends for their support in my undertaking and completing such a great task.

I'd like to thank Susie and Eva for their hard labor and patience with the creation of my book.

About the Author

As a little Polish girl in a Nazi labor camp, H. W. Zadow dreamed of one day becoming an artist and writer. However, when she became an adult, her dreams were put on hold as she married, raised three children, and became a widow at an early age of forty-three.

The passion to create never left her, and this novel is a result of that enduring dream. In addition to her epic novel, H. W. Zadow has also written many poems in Polish and English, and regularly creates and sells her oil paintings.

All the renderings are the author's sketches of what she envisions the characters to resemble.

Made in the USA
Monee, IL
10 May 2022

96149960R00395